Elven Race Reborn

Book 1 of the Graves of Good and Evil

A.B.B. Olson

Elven Race Reborn

A.B.B.OLSON

COPYRIGHT 2016 A.B.B.OLSON

ISBN: Soft Cover 978-0997257205

For
Jennifer - The real Erdwyf

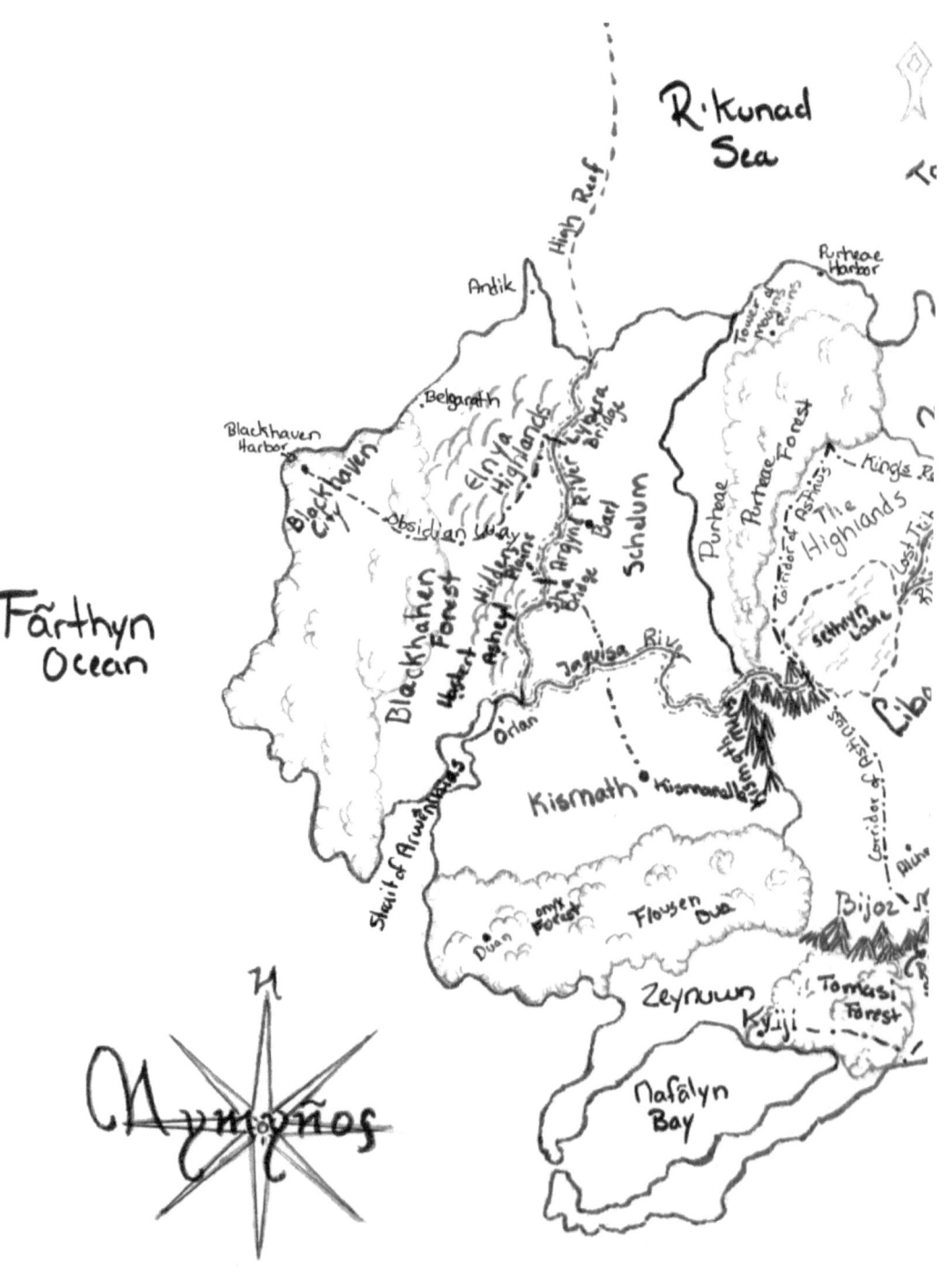

o Zaedio

Nestra

Althirim
Longman's Ford

aarnen

Himnale River

Norman's Reef

Dushvata

Seaduens

Amaden
White
Forest

Fãrthyn
Ocean

Stone River

Florwen
Hune

Fendir
Forest

then River

Kajgenja

Kajgen
Lake

Aedroi

Dirid

Forest of
Vilor
Lands

Kira's Deadlands

Klakhat

Avoro

Assassin's
Forest

crated

Trohasa
Forest

Plains
d Arado

Anuth

srintan-kvlara

rnian

Arseninis

Arseninis
City

Forest
d Closhmaa

Cyrea

Helum

Talenias

ntas.

mt
sterb

living of
Si-isandri

Kiys

Fãrthyn
Ocean

Legend
Forest   River   Border
mountain   Road   Hills

'LP Bull Clen

CONTENTS:

Darkness will mar the land of beauty and evil will wage war. One will hold the power to deliver life from death, but must bow to shadow's caressing touch to find this power. The guardian will fall, the lover will rule, the friend will perceive, and the moon heiress will free the slaves of death.

-Seer Astinus's Last Prophecy

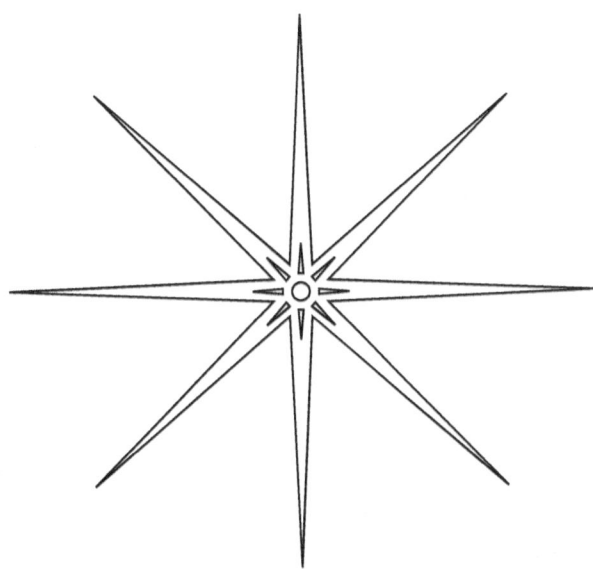

Prologue

Veries Gurgen sighed as she knelt by the large bed, shadows littering the ornate room, the single torch flickered unsettlingly in the sconce across the room. The old man turned his milky gaze on her and Veries had the uncomfortable feeling that he could see her despite the blindness.

"How are you this eve, Astinus?"

The man took a rasping breath and fumbled for her hand. She took it gingerly, the skin felt like too-thin parchment in hers. Thick veins protruded, grossly enhanced by the shadows.

"Veries!" Astinus croaked in a whisper. "Veries, long have you knelt by my side, listened to me. Now listen once more! You and I have had many discussions about the future, yes?"

"Yes, Astinus, but I do not underst-"

The seer cut her off with a grunt. "No time. I have written down my last vision. I have written it in my journal. You are to have the key, Veries. The only one I trust. My time has ended, I go now to the Summerland we all seek. Veries, beloved friend, the future is dark, too dark. Nymyños is failing as Serenyi did so long ago. Save what you can. The key," the old man reached beneath his shirt and drew out a glittering silver key threaded on a leather thong about his neck.

Veries had often wondered what was on that string he always wore. She swallowed hard as he handed the key to her.

"Astinus, are you sure?"

"If you do not know, then no one will, and my life will have been in vain. Read carefully, Veries, for shadows will descend upon you when you read, but you alone will know the truth of things. Share what you must, but I ask you to not reveal all. Promise me this."

"I swear on my soul, Astinus. I will not reveal anything but that of utmost importance," Veries said, bowing over his withered hand.

"Veries..." Astinus smiled serenely then, his milky eyes filled with what looked to be reverence.

Veries, scrunching up her face to stop the tears, leaned closer to his face when he beckoned. The smile was beautiful, despite the horrible jaundice that had taken over his face.

"Veries, the moon heiress shall free the slaves of death," Astinus whispered, and died.

Staring at the seer, Magin Veries Gurgen cried, clutching the silver key to her chest. Gently, she folded his arms across his chest and laid a hand on his forehead.

"Find peace in Summerland, my friend, your memory will linger forever," she whispered, and pulled the blanket over his face.

Once the Silencers had taken Astinus's body from his chamber, Veries closed the door, locked herself in, and took a deep breath. Striding determinedly toward the massive desk, she gestured to the torches on the wall and flame roared to life. Now properly illuminated, the Magin sat at the high-backed chair that rose above her head and took out the silver key. Her hands trembled as she placed the key into the lock and twisted it. The thick leather binding snapped open and she hastily put the key away.

Before she could stop herself, Veries flipped open the cover and stared. The first page was crammed with Astinus's precise writing, along with drawings, margin notes, and diagrams. Suddenly, Veries had a headache. Turning random pages, the Magin sighed, the entire book was filled to bursting. It would take weeks to read it all, and more to decipher it. Selecting a random paragraph somewhere in the middle of journal, she read.

The sling is laughing, the stone screaming. The plate cries, the spoon roars angrily. The sun and the moon fight.

Veries laid her head back against the chair and moaned. The man, spirits bless his soul, was trying to drive her mad. Slowly, she turned the phrase over in her mind. The sling and stone...yes. Obviously something, or someone is going to be used against their will, or perhaps fall *in* use, while the user is happy about the using. But who? Obviously enemies. When? The plate and spoon...? That could be a battle, a battle between things, perhaps cities that usually go together, work together. Perhaps the plate deceived the spoon?

"Gibberish," Veries muttered.

The sun and moon are blatantly at odds with one another, they never go together, but they need each other. That's obvious. Old enemies were going to clash, perhaps again, perhaps after a long time of tension.

Groaning loudly, the woman wiggled about angrily in the chair before flipping back to the first page. She pulled a sheaf of parchment from a stack on the desk, dipped a feather quill in ink, and began reading in earnest.

Alayen Hurtsen grabbed Tayrn Verla as he passed and shoved him against the wall.

"Alayen! What do you think-!"

The woman cut him off with another shove. "Veries, where is she?"

Magin Tayrn blinked at her. "Veries? Why would I know? The woman hates me and I feel no kindness toward her."

"Curse you, Tayrn! Have you no ears? Astinus is dead, and Veries has not been seen since the Silencers took his body. They were close, man, and she knows something. She has his journal, I would stake my life on it!"

Tayrn cut off his biting remark when her words sank in. "His journal?"

"Yes!" Alayen hissed.

"Why do you tell me this? We are not in a Triad together. We have nothing in common, Alayen. Why?"

"You are closest to Roluf, Tayrn. You are Second Magin, you have more power than I, being Tenth," Alayen sneered; the position galled her; even if she was only powerful enough to be the tenth, she deserved more for her talents.

"Gah, woman, why not ask Roluf himself? Wait, what do you seek that you need my position to get?" Tayrn asked, suddenly cold with alarm.

"To get the journal away from Veries!" Alayen shrieked. "She will think it only knowledge, perhaps to give us little tidbits now and then, but she will keep it to herself! Maybe share it with Feela, but they are the same, in my view."

Tayrn grimaced. "No. Ask Roluf, but I will not do it. Veries can rot forever, but I respected Astinus well enough to respect his choices. If he gave his key to Veries, then that is what he chose. I will not disrespect a dead man."

Alayen shook her head at him, face full of contempt. "I used to think you had some sort of backbone, but you have no more spine than a *stergi*."

Tayrn watched in disgruntlement as Alayen swayed away from

3

him and down the hall. *Comparing him to a serpent, really.* It was then that he felt the eyes on him. With a start, the Magin watched as Buftren Julyt stepped out of the shadows.

Only one rank below him, and in the same Triad, along with Roluf Gwemheoad himself, Buftren was very near to his strength in the Weaving.

"Cowed by a woman, and the Tenth, really Tayrn. Perhaps Alayen has the right of it. Stergi indeed."

"I am no serpent, Buf, and you know that as well as I. What do you want?"

Buftren shrugged languidly. He did everything languidly, as though he had no reason to move at the speed of others. He even spoke with a distinct slur. "Reatun has been asking around about you. Seems he is interested in that little experiment of yours. That pond idea. Come now, Tayrn. A pond to regenerate magic. Bah."

Tayrn gave the man a disgusted look. Even his derision came out slowly. "What right does that little rat have to be looking in on my things? He has a long neck for someone in the Fourteenth spot. Leave me, now. You may be of interest to Alayen."

Glaring at the dismissal, Buftren meandered away.

Luen stopped short in the entrance to Hylen's room. Cari glared at her over Hylen's sweaty shoulder. The man twisted to look at what had grabbed her attention. Luen glared at him, and then at Cari. With an amused look, Hylen resumed his lovemaking to Cari. The woman had the gall to let her head fall back against the pillow and even to reach her crest. Luen did not leave, but rather spread her feet and folded her arms, glaring at the pair even as they finished their coupling. Contempt filled her, but she had her dignity.

With deliberate arrogance, Hylen slid out of his bed and walked over to her, clad in nothing but his skin and sweaty for it. He reached for Luen but she slapped his hand away. Cari stood and slowly began to dress. Luen knew for a fact that she was far from beautiful, as far from it as Cari was from being ugly, but Hylen was too good looking for his own good, and had enough superciliousness to know it.

He licked his own teeth and swept his auburn locks from his brow as he did. It was not her body that he was attracted to, but her knowledge. She had an unfavorable habit of speaking her thoughts when in bed, but she could not help herself. Luen knew that any other man who looked like him would never glance at her once. Cari was thick-headed and weaker in the Weaving as well, but she was beautiful.

"Did you want something, Luen, or were you just here to watch us?" Hylen said finally.

Luen sneered at him. "Buftren claims Veries has Astinus's journal, and with it all that knowledge. Alayen has gone to petition Roluf to see if he will take the journal from Veries."

Cari snorted in the background. "Why should we care? We have your mind, Luen, and is that not enough?"

Luen noted the mocking in the other woman's voice. "You are as cow-brained as ever, Cari. Clearly sharing a man's bed is the only talent you have."

"One more thing you don't," the woman snapped.

Hylen laughed, then. "My ladies, come. We will see what Roluf has to say about the journal. It would be useful to have available."

Roluf Gwemheoad, founder of the Council of Magins, First Magin, and head of his Triad, sighed. Twelve of his council was now gathered in the council room. Veries was still missing, and Feela would not go against her friend even if she believed the journal of Astinus would save her life. Every one of the twelve before him had some notion of what the seer's journal held, though he figured only he, and now Veries, knew more than that it contained knowledge beyond imagining.

Finally, the angry mutters giving him a headache, Roluf spoke to his fellows. "Seer Astinus, may he be in Summerland, gave his key to Magin Veries," the titles made this a formal statement. "As such, only Magin Veries will be allowed to read it. Only Magin Veries will know what it contains in full. If I hear of Magin Veries being molested for her wisdom, I will personally see to the punishment."

That stilled the furious outbursts. He was well known for his severity, even among his peers. Tayrn then spoke up, the only one brave enough to. He stood only below Roluf himself, and by a small margin.

"Is that wise, Magin Roluf? Even a small portion of Astinus's visions could give us great insight into the future, into what we are going to become. Such knowledge... it has no price. Veries must be made to hand over the journal, or at least relay it to us."

That brought on consensual murmurs. Half the council was always at each other's throats, even now when they all agreed on a matter. Roluf noticed Shelan Turwen sending scalding glares at Quorn Jester. Those two never got along. But Vurn Seratinaine and Cerin Maorn were standing closer together than usual, which meant they were either plotting or had found some interest in each other. Roluf grimaced at that last. How one could be attracted to the same gender was beyond him, but some of his council did not seem to notice the sexual barriers. Hylen, he knew, lay with both Cari and Luen, and he had caught Alayen coming out of his bedchambers twice, as well, but they were women. He had even been with Cari and Alayen, though only they three knew, and the women only about themselves. The council, which had begun as the pride of Nymyños was now a bickering, licentious, seditious collection of overly powerful people. It dismayed the First Magin.

"I have laid my decision, Magin Tayrn. You will obey, or suffer the consequences."

Tayrn sighed, but he bowed his head slightly. "As you command, First Magin Roluf."

Roluf nearly started at that. Tayrn really must be in a fit, to give him full title. Tayrn was a nefarious man when it came to enemies. Enemies that would threaten peace and stability, at least, but otherwise, he was a kind enough fellow. Roluf knew he disliked Veries, but he would never harm her, or anyone on the council, except perhaps Buftren, which was a shame. Buftren simply creeped Tayrn out, and brought a fair amount of willies to Roluf, though he would never admit it. But Buf was brilliant, and slow to anger. Buf was slow to do anything, in fact. It was a shame because both men were in his Triad, and a strong trio they were.

Roluf rubbed a finger across his chin. He was no seer, but he knew what the histories would make of the people gathered before him. Most of them, himself included, would be seen as monsters, wicked and ruthless people. Few, Veries and Feela, perhaps even Teral, would be seen as decent.

It saddened him it would be so. They did what they must to survive. Some truly deserved that title, Reatun and Buf, certainly, but the others, no. Roluf wondered what the future people of Nymyños would make of Astinus. The First Magin grunted, bringing wondering looks from his peers. Quorn moved to open a discussion with him, but Roluf strode from the room before he could. The man would talk his ear off about flooding the elves and spirit-folk from the forest beyond the tower grounds.

Roluf grimaced to himself. Elves. He had not wanted a war, he just wanted to study them, but it had become war, and now he intended to end it as soon as possible. He would have no more massacres on his hands. He scowled now. This is what they would be remembered for, he thought sourly. The war. And they would be the dark side. Cursing quite vividly, Roluf nearly ran into a young man too pretty for his own good. Student Jair, yes, that was his name. A half-elf, not a man at all.

"First Magin! Please! Forgive my clumsiness, I will go straight to Magin Eron for penance," he said quickly, bowing till his nose nearly brushed his knees.

"No, no Student Jair. There is no need. Get on with your studies, boy," Roluf said absently, not noticing the shocked look of relief.

"Yes First Magin. Thank you."

As Jair fled the corridor, Roluf brooded. That boy would be trouble. By far too strong in the Weaving, as far as he was concerned. He wondered vaguely if Astinus had Seen something about the half-breed.

So absorbed in his thoughts, Roluf did not even notice Feela Oren until she called his name a third time. The man turned to look at her.

"Yes?"

"I said, have you seen Veries lately?"

"She's reading Astinus's journal, Feela. You were not at the meeting."

"Meeting?" Feela, a pretty woman, girl really, asked cautiously.

She was one he was interested in bedding more than once, though she easily evaded his approaches. From north Kismanelle, she had the pale complexion that her mountainous homeland demanded.

Roluf nearly smiled. "The meeting about what to do about Veries being the only one to read the journal. Do not worry; I will hold Astinus's choice as though it were my own. But if she tells you anything, would you be willing to share them with me?"

Feela shifted her stance without really moving. Her chin stiffened a little, too. "If Veries tells me anything, I will hold it my confidence, Rol."

"Ah," Roluf said, slightly put off. "Right."

The young woman made to leave, but he put his hand on her wrist as she passed. He was not about to let her out of his sight. He enjoyed her in it. "Feela, have you made any progress in your studies? With the, what was it again, a...?" he really could not remember. The woman had the strangest ideas sometimes.

Feela's chin went up a little higher. "A ship, Rol. A boat that goes to sea. I am calling it a ship."

"That's right. How does that go?"

"Fine. I have run into a few problems with actually keeping it adrift, but well enough, in the time I have worked on it. The Serenyi elves knew the way of them, but we lost that knowledge, and now I seek it again."

"You must have need to go to the sea, to do so, Fee," Roluf said, feeling like a fool. She really was inventive.

"Yes," Feela said slowly, sounding an awful lot like Buftren.

"I suppose that takes time?"

The woman made a face. "Of course not. I just Step there, Roluf, what is going on?"

The First Magin nearly blushed. Blushed! Of course she Stepped there. Any Magin worth their salt would. Stepping, a simple matter of standing on the map in the Stepping Chamber, and then walking to the place they needed to be, going through the Weave of the Chamber the whole time, and they would be at their destination in moments.

"Going on? Nothing. I'm just preoccupied," Roluf said, almost adding, 'with you', but he didn't.

She raised her brow at him, and then stepped, quite normally, away from him.

"What *will* the histories say about us?" Roluf mused out loud.

Veries closed the journal with a soft thud. It had taken nearly a month to get through the whole thing. And she did not understand most of it. Her son had come in a few times to visit. Her son, the result of a short affair with Teral she remembered fondly, but no more. Her son, a bemused young man with middling power. He had become friends with that unsettling Jair, but perhaps that was for the good. Veries thought about one of the prophecies Astinus had seen. Jair would bring about their downfall. And begin a massive chain of events that would echo through history for thousands of years. She shivered, Astinus had been right. Shadow had descended upon her.

Veries struggled with herself. She very much wanted to end her life, wanted to end that never ending warren of prophetic torture. Too much knowledge was deadly, she believed that whole-heartedly now. She wanted to run screaming off the top of the tower and fall to her death. She wanted to stab herself in the heart.

Instead, Veries drew tight the leather strap, inserted the silver key, and locked it. She also added a nasty tangle of Weaves that would stop anyone from getting close to it. Anyone but herself, that was. Very carefully, the woman stood, tucked the chair tight against the desk, deliberately centered the journal on the desk, and doused the torches. Taking a deep breath, Veries left Astinus's room for the last time wondering.

"What will history say about us?" she whispered, fearing she knew the answer all too well.

The Chronicles of Astinus was later found in the ruins of the Tower
of Magins:
What follows is the Aftermath

Chapter 1
Journey's Beginning

It was the rain soaking through her clothes that woke her. Groaning, Tlonna rolled around on her back a bit, attempting to gather the strength needed to sit up. When she finally did, she almost grinned with pride, but let out a howl of pain instead, gasping. Hooking her long, summer blonde hair behind pointed ears, Tlonna drew her knees up and rested her forehead on them. Shaking, the elf fought back the nausea that swarmed through her body. After a few agonizing moments, she frowned at her thighs.

Fear clouded her mind, settled in her gut like a ball of ice. Try as she might, Tlonna could not remember a single thing beyond the moment of waking, other than her name. Trying to recall anything, even the slightest moment, brought waves of torture that left her breathless from the screams.

As a ray of sun peeked through the clouds, Tlonna squinted as a flash from her wrist caught her in the eye. Looking down, the elf studied the delicate silver bangle carved in a cipher she could not read. Letting out a whimpering sigh, she turned her head and saw a small pack lying a few feet from her. Scowling now, Tlonna crawled to it and flipped open the cover. Inside were five thick books, a change of clothes, and a few odds and ends that confused her. One such item was a bar of pale blue wax and seal that bore a sun and star emblem.

After cinching the pack and hoisting it over one shoulder, Tlonna forced herself to her feet and stumbled a few steps in the mud. By the time she reached the sparse wood that began a few hundred yards away from where she had woken, night had fallen. Her knees were bruised and muddy from falling over and over again. Dried blood, partially cleaned off by the rain, caked her arms and face, though she had no idea where it had come from.

Days passed as Tlonna wandered through the wood, resting often and slowly regaining her strength. It was on the fourth day that she found the horse. It was grazing in a small clearing, a massive black stallion with feathered fetlocks and long mane and tail. Its head shot up at her approach, but it did not move. The horse snorted when Tlonna stepped up to him. He turned his great head to peer at her from one large dark eye.

"Hello," Tlonna whispered.

He whuffled.

He still wore both saddle and reins. They were fine, embossed silver over pale blue leather. On the strap across his forehead was the name Takîreaes. Tlonna scratched him behind the ears and he lipped her shoulder. After introducing herself thoroughly, Tlonna wearily pulled herself into the saddle and they set off.

Yet another day passed before horse and rider emerged from the wood. Putting a hand over her eyes to shield the sun, Tlonna sighed. Before her stretched an immense plain. To the far west was the faint outline of a vast mountain range, and to the south and directly ahead, was a plateau rising just before the horizon. Tlonna urged Takîreaes into a steady trot toward the plateau.

It was deep night by the time they reached the winding road that wound up and over a shallow canyon. At the top, a gate barred the way. A guard leaned out, shining a torch down to see her.

"What do you want?"

Tlonna squinted in the light. "I just need a place to rest for the night, and to replenish my supplies."

The guard disappeared and then reappeared with another. They leered down at her, obviously suspicious.

"Please, I can hardly stay up. I just need a place for the night, one night," Tlonna pleaded, her voice cracking under her weariness.

"Oh, all right," the original guard said and turned to the gate house.

After a few seconds, one of the doors opened wide enough to admit her and Takîreaes. As soon as they were through, it slammed closed. A small group of men approached her as she dismounted.

"Thank you, kind sir. Where is the inn?" Tlonna asked, and got a fist for an answer.

She reeled backward into Takîreaes, who reared up as one of the men grabbed his reins. Another fist cracked into her jaw as Tlonna fought to stay conscious. After a few more hits, she went down into the inky blackness of unconsciousness.

When Tlonna came to, she was in what appeared to be a hollowed out rock. The rough stone walls curled in above her with a tiny hole at the very top to allow for air. She shifted on the thin pallet she was stretched out on and sat up. Pallets were strewn about the rock floor haphazardly, a few personal belongings cluttering a few. Tlonna rubbed her aching head and winced when she touched a tender spot on her cheek.

Pulling her fingers away, the elf saw blood. She was wiping the blood on her pant leg when a section of the wall started to roll away and voices filtered in from outside just ahead of their owners. Filthy men and women straggled in, smelling of sweat and dirt. Tlonna stared at them, bloody hand forgotten. A few of them glanced in her direction, but most ignored her completely.

A guard strolled in after them with a sack over his shoulder. He tossed the sack down and left, closing the door behind him. The people opened the sack and started divvying out hunks of bread and what looked like raw potatoes. One of the women walked over to Tlonna and shoved the food at her.

The elf jerked back and stared at the food being held out to her. Slowly, she raised her eyes to stare at the woman. She rolled her eyes.

"Do you not know food, elf?"

When Tlonna continued to stare at her, the woman tossed the bread and potato onto the pallet and started to walk away.

"I am Tlonna."

She pivoted and cocked her head to the side. "Am I supposed to care? You are a slave now, which means your name is nothing."

"Slave? To whom?"

"King Darren. You made a grave mistake, elf, when you wandered up that winding road, because you wandered into hell," the woman replied menacingly, and returned to her fellows.

Tlonna sighed and picked up the hard bread. As she nibbled on it, the door slid open and then shut as a slender woman squeezed in. The slaves rushed her, babbling and taking the things she held out to them. Through the hum of voices, Tlonna heard the word 'elf' and the woman looked over at her.

When she started toward her, Tlonna rose to her feet and swiped the blood-matted strands of hair away from her face. The woman's skin was brown, her features exotic. Long, silky black hair hung in gentle waves to her lower back, caught up in elegant combs.

Her green eyes swept over Tlonna and she grimaced. Expecting another verbal attack, the elf started back when the human bowed her head a bit before speaking.

"My name is Miazie, the others say your name is Tlonna. Is that correct?"

Tlonna squinted. "Aye."

Miazie smiled sadly. Her head was lowered so Tlonna could see only the crown of her dark hair at her height. The woman stood nearly one and a half feet shorter than her, but Tlonna felt a great presence in her.

"You are the princess here, are you not?" Tlonna asked suddenly, making Miazie's head jerk up to meet her gaze.

"How do you know that?"

Tlonna blinked as she looked down at her. "The way you carry yourself, your manner of speech. Only a fool would miss it, Princess."

"Then I guess you're no fool then, aye?"

"I guess not. What is this place?" Tlonna asked, folding her arms.

Miazie gestured for her to sit, and then did so herself. When Tlonna situated herself on the pallet, the human swept out an arm.

"This is Anutch, home of the Ughtren family for eight generations. My father, King Darren, owns this plateau and the area just beyond the canyon. As I'm sure you know the Liberated Lands is riddled with smaller kingdoms and villages, Anutch being the largest. What's that look for?"

Tlonna shook her head. "Liberated Lands?"

Miazie's eyes widened and she smiled a little, as though not sure if she was the butt end of a joke she didn't understand. "Yes. You know, the massive free land in the middle of Nymyños?" she said, waving her arms around.

"What is Nymyños?" Tlonna asked, eyes wide.

Miazie scowled. "What is...what is Nymyños? Are you daft? Nymyños, the land we all live on, bordered by the twelve kingdoms with the Liberated Lands in the center. What are you playing at?"

Tlonna shrank inward. "I...I am not playing at anything. I do not remember where I came from. I do not know who I am, other than my name is Tlonna. Please, do not be mad at me."

Miazie's scowl deepened. Her nose wrinkled and she turned to look at the slaves gathered around the fire they had built. When she turned back to look at Tlonna, her eyes were grave.

"If you are not making this up, then something very odd is happening, something very..." her exotic face tightened suddenly, "portentous."

Tlonna's face went blank. "How can anything dealing with me be portentous? I am no one important."

Miazie's jaw tensed and she lowered her head. "Of course. I am probably wrong. I need to go, but I will see you in a few days. Goodnight."

As the human stood to leave, Tlonna nodded. "Goodnight."

A few days passed before anything happened. The slaves came and went, pulling Tlonna out to the fields with them. She worked from dawn to dusk, harvesting wheat and barley. Just after lunch on the fifth day, a guard took the scythe out of her weary hands and shoved her forward.

"King Darren will meet you," the guard said as he yanked her into the large manor house.

Tlonna self-consciously wiped at the dirt on her face and ragged clothing as the eyes of nobles turned on her. At a table sat Miazie and two other women, one holding a baby girl who gurgled in the silence.

"So!" A deep voice rumbled through the hall. "This is the new slave?"

Tlonna turned to look at the man who strode toward her. He had the same exotic features as his daughter, light brown skin, and green eyes. His shoulders were broad, his arms powerful. When he reached Tlonna, the top of his head came up to her collar bone. He grinned up at her, his hands reaching for her.

Tlonna slapped his hands away and stepped back, eyes glaring. The king sneered.

"Who do you think you are? You are mine, wench, mine. I will do what I please with you. Understand?"

Tlonna's lip curled up and she bent down to be eye to eye with him. "I belong to no one, human. I am no one's property."

There was a collective gasp from the humans in the hall as Tlonna straightened. Darren's face lost its cocky smirk and went hard.

"I will break you. Bring her."

The man spun on his heel and marched away. Tlonna started to turn around when a guard's cudgel slammed into the back of her knee. Sent off balance, the elf fell to one knee and kicked out. One guard went down while others raised their weapons. Tlonna shot forward, using her foot to propel her. The guards scrambled after her, grappling for her legs. Twisting, the female skidded a few feet on her back and then leapt up. She yanked a torch out of a wall sconce and swept it out like club. The men veered back as the flame roared inches from their faces.

"Stay away from me!" Tlonna yelled.

One of the guards stepped forward and caught her wrist before the torch could touch him. He crashed his gauntleted fist into her face and his knee into her gut. Tlonna's head slammed back into the stone wall as she dropped the torch in pain. The other guards descended on her and beat her into oblivion once more.

Tlonna woke up to oddest sensations. When she finally willed her eyes open and her mind started working, she screamed. Her ankles and wrists were bound to the four posts of a bed as Darren pounded himself into her. His naked body glistened with sweat in the red light of a massive fire. His face was a mask of pure ecstasy as he rode her.

His eyes popped open when she screamed, and then he grinned. "About time you woke up. It was getting a little boring without you moving beneath me. Yes, that's it."

Tlonna struggled against her bonds until the four posts creaked and Darren slapped her. The pain of his hand against her raw wounds made her scream all the louder. Tears leaked unbidden down her cheeks as the human released his seed within her. As his body shuddered, Tlonna pulled her arms and legs inward in a final effort to free herself. Darren reached over her head and picked up a wooden shaft.

"I was going to use this in a different way, but this works too." He tightened his grip on it and whacked it across her cheek.

Tlonna let out a rough gasp as the agony stole her breath. Darren, still encased in her, cracked it across her face again and again until she slid away.

Months passed as Tlonna worked as both pleasure and field slave. She moved stiffly, brokenly. The scars from her numerous beatings had faded. Miazie brought her ointments every few days to help her heal from the times she was with Darren. It was a never-ending nightmare.

Tlonna looked up from her pallet as the door slid back and Miazie slipped in. After exchanging pleasantries with the other slaves, the princess rushed to Tlonna.

"Tlonna, my father is furious with you."

Tlonna snorted. "And this is new because?"

"He wants a child from you. Are you stopping yourself from getting pregnant?"

"No. However, I would if I did quicken. Could be my loathing of him stops me, or his human seed is weak and inferior," the elf growled.

Miazie blew out a breath. "Tlonna, he means to kill you if you don't get with child. Please, please do what you can to do so. I don't want you to die."

"I would rather die than birth a monster from him, from anyone," Tlonna replied.

Miazie's face darkened and she looked down at her hands. "Am I such a monster?"

"What?" Tlonna snapped, and then sighed. "No, Princess Miazie. The only one that came from him that is not a monster. You and your brother Haldred."

The human nodded and sniffed. "Aye, Haldred is a good man, but he is shadowed by his duty as heir."

"Miazie!" One of the older slaves, Franklin, yelled from the firepit. "Princess Miazie! Someone is coming!"

Frowning, Miazie turned and watched as the door slid back. King Darren ducked into the stone barracks and pulled up short when he saw his daughter.

"Miazie...what are you doing in here?"

Miazie went white and her mouth merely opened and closed as she searched for the words. "I...I..."

The blood rushed into the king's face and he growled. "Have you been helping them? Have you befriended the *slaves*?"

"Father, please..." Miazie whispered as the man started to shake with rage.

"I was coming in here to announce Tlonna's execution tomorrow, you will be joining her. I will not have one of my blood cavorting with grubbing slaves!"

"No, please, Father, please, don't do this. I am sorry, I will behave, please, Father. Please change your mind. Oh, please...Father!" Miazie screamed as the king swept out of the barracks and slid the door shut behind him.

The woman collapsed into a sobbing puddle at Tlonna's feet, who stood very still. It took a moment for the slaves to shake themselves into moving. When they did, they covered Miazie in a supportive group, completely ignoring the elf towering over their shuddering backs.

Fear and anger rippled through Tlonna, warring with each other until she felt her body would explode. Slowly, she walked around the stone dome that made up the barracks, probing with her fingers. Closing her eyes, the elf focused her mind, focused on the stone beneath her fingers. As the voices came, Tlonna's lips pulled back with the effort. Miazie had often coached her on how to call upon the earth magic, the innate ability elves had that allowed them to communicate with the spirits of the earth. The voices, which had begun as indiscernible mumbles and whispers, strengthened and became a cohesive language. *Yest eshoun akod, hayn ekoch klamen yest eshoun akod.*

Tlonna jerked back from the wall as the spirits nearly screamed through her, and then felt the skin on her arms prickle as they breathed a last word before fading away.

Tlonna...

Tlonna gave the wall an experimental push. Over and over again she shoved her shoulder and her arms into the rough stone wall until they bled. The slaves watched her with empty eyes, looking like they thought her gone mental. She growled in frustration as the spirits whispered again through her mind in the language she couldn't understand.

"I am trying!" she howled, and slammed her hands into the wall, palms flat.

Sparks of blinding white light sizzled into the rock, speeding along the surface, leaving cracks in their wake. Tlonna screamed as she yanked her hands away from the wall. Her hands were covered in the crackling light though she felt nothing more than a rush of air. Shaking her hands frantically, the elf screamed louder as the light crawled up her arms. One of the slaves splashed some water on her, but it merely hissed as the light convulsed and spread up to Tlonna's neck. She watched in fear as a tentacle flashed in front of her face before latching on.

Panic seized the elf as her hair lifted off her neck and roiled in the air above her head. The sound of rushing air filled her ears. Tlonna had a brief glimpse of Miazie's tear-stained face telling her to ground and center herself before unbelievable terror blanked her mind, and she fainted.

"Tlonna, wake up. Come on dear, wake up. It's all right, everything is okay, come back."

Tlonna moaned and lifted a hand to her eyes as she opened them. Miazie's head wavered in her view, but the elf sat up.

"What happened?"

"You lost control. Come on, can you stand?"

"Yeah. Lost control of what?" Tlonna asked, standing on wobbly knees.

"Your magic. Look what you did," the princess said and turned around to gesture at the wall behind her.

The wall looked to have been bashed in by a massive hammer. Blackened cracks exploded out from a central point of impact in the shape of two hands.

"You almost saved us," Miazie said quietly.

"No, not almost," Tlonna whispered and swung her pack up over her shoulder. "I did. I will. Come on, get your things everyone."

As the slaves hastened to follow her order, Tlonna pulled Miazie over to the impacted wall. The elf flattened her palms in their imprint and pushed. Those behind her watched as her shoulder blades tightened as the muscles in her back rippled with immense strength. The wall made a grinding sound as chips and flakes of stone clattered to the floor. The muscles on Tlonna's arms stood out against her pale skin, quivering with exertion. Her booted feet slid a few inches back.

"Help her!" one of the slaves cried, joining Tlonna at the wall.

As the men and women joined the elf, the cracks in the wall increased twice as much. After a few minutes, most of them had dropped away, exhausted from the strain. Tlonna gasped as sweat ran down into her eyes. Finally, with a massive heave from Tlonna and the few men left at the wall, it crumbled outward. Slabs fell among the slaves, injuring a few. Dust and debris filtered up through the night as the wall landed with a resounding crash. Guards came running, swords drawn as the slaves leapt out. A few went immediately to their knees as the guards yelled for surrender.

Miazie, limping after being too slow to move out of a falling slab's way, fell into Tlonna. The elf, exhausted from pushing the wall, stumbled to the side. Darren flew out of the manor house, robes flapping.

"Tlonna, I'm too weak. Go, free yourself," Miazie gasped as she took a step and nearly fell.

"Quit," Tlonna growled and picked up the princess.

Draping her over her shoulders, the elf sprinted in the direction of the gate. The other slaves with her followed, ducking as arrows flew past them. Tlonna went down as a stone from a sling slammed into the back of her knee. The slaves skidded to a halt to help her up. She shook them off.

"Go! Do not worry about me! Go!" she screamed. The now unconscious Miazie lay sprawled a few feet from Tlonna's head.

Scrambling to her feet, the elf scooped up the human and started running again. The gate was nearly in sight when a few of the guards caught up with her. Tlonna stumbled in exhaustion and nearly dropped Miazie again.

"Stop! Elf, stop!" the guards bellowed as they labored to keep up.

A couple guards came in unexpectedly from the right and blocked Tlonna's path. She veered off to the left, headed south through the fields.

"Hey! Halt!"

Ignoring the commands, Tlonna leapt over a low stone wall that divided two fields and kept running. The other slaves had already reached the gate and the road beyond. An arrow zipped past Tlonna's head and she swerved a little to the right. The edge of the plateau loomed suddenly before her and she slid to a halt. Frantically, the elf looked for a way free of guards. Finding none, she turned in the direction of the gate and made a break for it.

She sped along the edge of the plateau, her feet causing little avalanches of pebbles to tumble off the edge and into the canyon below. She could see the gate; see some of the lagging slaves leaping off it to land hard on the road behind it. Some of them seemed to be looking for her and their beloved princess, but most just kept running.

Tlonna was so immersed in the sight of freedom that she didn't see the archer aiming at her. She turned just in time so that the arrow didn't hit her heart, but rather pierced her shoulder and exploded out the back. Screaming, Tlonna's feet stumbled on the edge as it crumbled beneath her and Miazie's weight.

She lost her grip on the princess who had startled into consciousness when the arrow had skimmed across her cheek to hit Tlonna's shoulder. The elf scrabbled for a hold on the cliff wall, her fingers being scraped to the bone. Finally, her hand caught, and Miazie caught her ankle. The added weight pulled Tlonna away from her handhold and into the air. Frantically, the elf flailed with her free limbs and snatched a thick root sticking out of the dirt. The two females slammed into the earthy wall as the root broke off, sending them careening once more into the air. Tlonna's arms cart wheeled desperately as she fell, screaming. Miazie clutched Tlonna's leg, hugging her ankle as though in hope that the elf might suddenly grow wings. The elf and human fell downward, just out of arm's reach of the wall.

The pressure on her eyelids woke Tlonna with a start. Groaning in pain, the elf turned her face away from the sun and stared at the arrow shaft sticking out of her shoulder. Reaching across her chest, the elf felt the back of her shoulder. The point had broken off with the impact when she had landed. Biting her bottom lip, Tlonna yanked the arrow out. Her gasps of pain woke Miazie, who was draped over the elf's stomach.

The human scrambled off Tlonna and frantically began feeling all over her body. "I'm alive? Not broken? How in the nine hells...Tlonna!"

"Shh! Not so loud, woman," Tlonna mumbled as she sat up.

"Oh, thank the gods we're alive. Praise the spirits," Miazie said hysterically.

"You should thank me. If you had not landed on me, you would be dead and broken, now quiet," Tlonna growled, ripping her sleeve to bandage her shoulder.

"Let me do that, Tlonna," Miazie said and slapped the elf's hands away.

After a few minutes of cleaning wounds, Miazie stood and

brushed off the seat of her pants. "We're on Hidden Ledge."

"What?"

The human turned to point up at the plateau high above them. "Hidden Ledge. It is only visible from the ground. They can't see us from up there. What luck."

Tlonna raised her eyebrows but said nothing. After a few minutes, she too willed herself to her feet. "All right, so how do we get back up there?"

"Get back...get back up there? Tlonna are you mad? We can't go back, we'll be killed for sure."

"Then we had best not be seen then, eh?" Tlonna replied waspishly. "No one enslaves me, rapes me, shoots me off a cliff, and leaves me to die without paying heavily. Besides, my horse is up there."

Miazie looked dumbstruck. "Your horse. Your damn bleeding horse is out of reach! Deal with it!"

"Shh! Not so loud! My head feels like, well like I landed on it after a hundred foot fall."

Miazie snapped her mouth shut with a sheepish look. "Sorry."

After a few days, both females' patience was wearing thin, as were their foodstuffs. They huddled around a small fire in the shadow of the cliff overhang, staring out at the starry sky. Miazie sighed.

"I'm so bored."

"Me too. I have some books," Tlonna replied.

"Books? What books?" Miazie asked, absurdly alert.

"I do not know. Books."

"Can I have one?" the woman asked eagerly.

"Yeah. Here," Tlonna tossed her pack over to the human.

Miazie pulled the five books out and stared at each of them in turn. She took one and shoved the other four back into the elf's pack.

"Here," she said and tossed Tlonna her belongings. "This one, this one is rare, *Chronicles of Astinus*. He is my favorite study. A seer of great power. I can't believe you have this, the others too, but this one in particular. Wow."

Tlonna shrugged and immediately regretted it when her shoulder screamed in agony. "It is a book."

Miazie fixed a death glare on her. "This is not just a book. It is Astinus's complete record of prophecy and visions. He foresaw

Aderiaen's War, *thousands* of years in advance, the birth of his son Midian, the Magins coming to life, everything. He is, was, brilliant."

"Okay," Tlonna said blankly, staring at the sky.

The next day, Tlonna woke to the sound of Miazie grunting. Jolting upright, the elf stared in disbelief at the human who was attempting to scale the wall.

"Miazie. Miazie! What in the nine hells do you think you are doing?" Tlonna yelled as she stood.

"I can't take it! I can't sit here another day!"

"Is this about that damn book? Miazie, stop it!" Tlonna shouted.

"No...yes! Something huge is about to happen, and I have to get...get somewhere! I can't stay here."

"Yes, something *is* about to happen. You are going to die! Get down here!" Tlonna roared in rage.

Seeing her book discarded by the cold fire, Tlonna cast a disgusted look in Miazie's direction and picked it up. She flipped it open to where Miazie had placed a leaf to mark where she was. Among a bunch of confusing symbols and charts, a short paragraph was circled many times, almost frantically. Licking her lips, the elf smoothed the old, crinkled page and read.

'*I have seen it, the possible end of days. I sat in my parlor and it came upon me like a heathenish voice coming from the deep ninth hell. Images of blackness, never-ending winter. Snow, which is so pure and white blanketed the land in waves of inky tainted midnight, like ash. The sun shone dark, and nothing but demons lived. It will come when those of great power are born, the descendants of my time. Their blood will run stronger and thicker than any others in their far time. There is no branching from this vision, I know. It will come, and only those with the truest and most honorable of hearts will be able to defeat this poison of evil. It will begin when the greatest of kingdoms fall, when the winter is bitterest, and the one many times prophesied is born.*'

Tlonna curled her lip and looked up at the still-climbing Miazie. "What is this rubbish? How do you know it is upon us, hmm? You are mad."

"Am not!" Miazie gasped.

"Are too, now come down here and we will work together,

come on Miazie, you are not going to make it!" Tlonna snapped, shading her eyes from the sun.

As the human looked down to reply, her foothold crumbled and she skidded back a few feet. She cursed in pain as blood seeped from her scraped torso and arms.

"See?" Tlonna shouted, and vaguely realized she could smell rain.

"I can do this, Tlonna!" Miazie said, no longer arguing, but attempting to convince herself.

She reached up to pull herself a few more inches, and lost her grip. Tlonna had only a few seconds to brace herself as Miazie careened into her.

When she came to, Miazie's body was stretched out on her legs. Tlonna shoved the human off of her and stood, groaning. The princess did not move.

"Damnation," Tlonna hissed, nudging her with the toe of her boot.

The sharp smell of rain touched her nose again and the elf felt the first brushes of wind against her skin as a storm reached the plateau. While sheeting rain fell, Tlonna dragged Miazie next to the overhang in the cliff wall that would offer some protection from the storm. Throughout the torrent, the elf nursed her wrecked shoulder. She lay in the rain with the wound bared for a time in an attempt to clean it. After a few minutes, the pain became unbearable and she crawled back to crouch in the shadow of the cliff.

The day passed miserably wet and chilly as Tlonna sat by the listless human, her hair and clothing sopping wet and clinging to her body. When night fell, the storm abated and Miazie stirred.

"About bloody time you woke up," Tlonna grumbled, glaring at the human.

"Why are we wet?"

"Because there was no place to hide from the storm that you so kindly slept through. I hope you catch something."

Miazie snorted, "Well that's not very considerate of you. I saved your life."

"And now I have saved yours, twice. If you had not conveniently landed on top of me this last time, again, you would have broken every bone of yours, and starved to death from your inadequacies as a human. I have every right, and every motive to break your neck right now," Tlonna shot back, retying her make-shift bandage.

"Look, it wasn't me that made this all happen. I try to fix the horrid things my father does. I at least gave you a chance to escape; it just turned out you saved both our lives, not just yours. Don't blame me for the things that go wrong in your life. I have only known you a short time, and I have no idea how the bloody nine hells you wound up way out here. That's your past, and not my bleeding problem," Miazie retorted, getting to her feet.

Tlonna sniffed derisively and stalked away as far as the ledge would allow. She spent the rest of the night staring out at the land that spread out hundreds of feet below her, her mind in a fog.

When morning dawned, the elf walked to where Miazie was sitting with her knees drawn up into her chest, staring out at the sunrise.

"There's nothing quite so beautiful as a fresh sunrise after a storm."

Tlonna followed her gaze and felt the rays of sunlight on her flesh. The sun rose, a pale orange against an indigo sky where the last stars still shone high in the horizon.

"No, nothing quite as beautiful indeed. May I sit?"

"Of course," the human said, resting her chin on her knees.

"Do you know what is wrong with me?"

"You have a wounded shoulder, and a few bruises."

The elf shook her head. "That is not what I mean. Why did I survive a fall that should have killed me, especially when you landed on top of me, and what was that... lightning... that came out of my hands in the compound?"

Miazie sighed and stretched out her long legs. "You're an elf, Tlonna. Elves are not immortal, but they live for thousands of years. You're not prone to illness like the race of Man, and your bodies can withstand almost five times the amount of injury or pain that any other race can. As for the lightning, it's magic. You're a Magin, obviously, which also gives you more strength and durability. Is this another thing you don't remember?"

Tlonna narrowed her eyes and shook her head. "Yes, what is a Magin?"

"Er," Miazie stared at the elf incredulously. "A Magin is a

magical being, one of great power. The power is stored within their body and is able to be called upon at any time, but it can take a great amount of energy, and oft times, the Magin has to rest for many hours. There are many Magins in Nymyños, but most are weak and use their powers for daily uses, like cleaning. Others, like Shadowsoul, are very powerful and use them to destroy, kill, fight, and to rule."

Tlonna nodded slowly, "Who is Shadowsoul?"

"Lord Midian, Aderiaen's son, a Magin of great evil. He has destroyed many great kingdoms just in recent times. Are you sure you don't know any of this?" she asked again.

Ignoring the question, Tlonna switched subjects. "Where does your father keep the horses?"

"Behind the manor, in the stable. Are you serious about getting your damn horse?" Miazie said, annoyed at the change.

"Aye, we cannot get far on foot, especially injured as we are. Are they guarded?" Tlonna said.

"Yes. Everything is guarded, probably more so now. There is no way we can get by them all," Miazie replied.

At Tlonna's stubborn look, the human sighed.

"Listen; since the Quad Kingdoms were destroyed every other kingdom has doubled its army, its guards, its everything. No one trusts anyone. The guards are ruthless in keeping the peace, as they call it. A person who scowls at a stone that stubs their toe can be put to death for being dangerously minded. Things are different, now. It is impossible, what you are planning."

"What Quad Kingdoms?" Tlonna asked.

"Some eighty years ago, the four Kingdoms; Blackhaven Forest, Kismath, Schelum, and Purheae all shared an alliance, the Alliance of Four Kingdoms. When Lord Midian attacked Kismath, Blackhaven Forest came to its aid but no one else. So when Schelum and Purheae were attacked, no one came, not even Blackhaven. The Alliance of Four Kingdoms had failed. They were all destroyed, even Blackhaven, which none thought possible. It was the greatest kingdom in all of Nymyños. They survived battle after battle, campaign after campaign, until the final battle. Most say they lasted so long because of the High Commander of the Blackhaven Militia, a she-elf of awesome ability. They say she is truly immortal, unable to die even if hacked to pieces. Some say she just comes back from the dead, whole. Anyway, the destruction caused all the free-land kingdoms, like

Anutch, to become separated and weak. Great cities in the province kingdoms have been decimated, left to rot. Now everyone is up on their toes, guards are rampant," the woman explained.

"I do not understand." Tlonna replied.

"What do you mean?" Miazie shot her companion an irritated glance.

"I..."the elf sighed, "these things you say, province kingdoms, free-lands, these great Quad Kingdoms, they do not seem real to me," she paused, "nothing makes sense to me."

Miazie pressed her lips together to wet them. She scratched her eyebrow, attempting to find the words. "You are telling me you really don't know a bleeding thing about who you are, where you come from? That basic knowledge that even the most witless of children are aware of, escapes you. Pretty much, that you lost your mind to...I don't know," she waved her hand in the air a couple of times, "amnesia."

"Yes, I suppose so."

"Tlonna, elves don't get human illnesses like that, like I said. It has never happened before, and I highly doubt it has happened to you," Miazie said, wrapping her arms around her knees.

"Then why do I not remember anything? How can I wake up in a place I do not remember going to, and have no memory of my life before that moment?"

"I don't know, but it sure isn't amnesia. There has never been a case of amnesia in an elf. Things like that just don't happen, even in these dark days."

The two females looked at each other, and then out at the brightening sky.

Conceding to Tlonna's insistence that she had no memory whatsoever, Miazie schooled Tlonna in the use of her magic. Using the book *The History of Magic and Its Uses*, they formed a cohesive link between Tlonna's inner control, and Miazie's knowledge. When not working with power, the two females schemed. Using a twig blackened in the fire, Miazie drew out a rough map of Anutch on the rock face. Tlonna placed marks where the human said the guards were posted. They were often prone to arguing heatedly over which route was most effective, which guards to attack first.

While Miazie slept, Tlonna played with her innate power,

sometimes tossing a ball of light around or moving small objects from afar. When she successfully started a fire with it, she panicked and waved her hand in an effort to stop the jets of flame pulsing from her fingers. When that only made the fire spread, the elf kicked Miazie awake.

"What?" the human shot to her feet when she saw the terrified expression on Tlonna's face. "Ground it Tlonna, release your hold on the power. Visualize yourself letting go of the magic. Calm down, Tlonna, breathe."

The elf stared at the human, sucking in air and exhaling it in gusts. Finally, the power ebbed and sank back into her fingers. Shaken, the female looked around at the damaged done by the fire and winced. Miazie patted her on the shoulder and rolled back into a ball on the ground, already asleep. Tlonna went back to tossing the ball.

The next morning dawned crisp and cold. Tlonna woke weary and aching, her fingers still tingling unpleasantly from the fire accident. Without warning, a dreamlike vision took her. A massive black castle loomed beyond an equally massive wall. A city spread between the two like a blanket, immersed in the trees as though the homes and shops had been built within a dense forest. Roads snaked through the trees and buildings, made of tightly woven grass. The black castle sparkled in the sunlight, veins of pearl, gold, and silver making it seem mystical.

Tlonna was suddenly thrown back into real time, along with a pounding headache. Squeezing her eyes shut and then opening them wide, the elf strolled over to Miazie.

"Have you ever heard of a city within a forest overlooked by a castle of black stone and veins of minerals?"

"Aye. Blackhaven. Why?" Miazie replied absently, fiddling with one of Tlonna's books.

Tlonna bit her lip, "I just saw it, sort of. It was so beautiful. It was like being in a dream, but I was awake and aware. Is it part of my power?"

"It is called scrying, the ability to see things not within eyesight. Most elves can do it, actually, though most have forgotten how. Elves all have a natural magic that gives them the ability to speak with plants and animals, not like you and I, but through feelings and emotions.

They have awesome hearing and eyesight and can feel the slightest changes in the earth. They are stronger and have amazing metabolism and unnatural resiliency to intoxication, so it is very difficult to get an elf drunk. Plus they don't get sick, and the whole longevity is a big hit. Not to mention that they have the quickest minds and longest retention span. You're an amazing race, really. A bit weird, but amazing."

Tlonna yawned as she watched the back of the human's head. "Oh...okay. Are you ready?"

Miazie stood and slung her make-shift pack over her shoulder. "Yes," she groaned animatedly. "So ready."

Tlonna smiled tightly and followed her companion's act. After her pack was settled, the elf focused her energy and pushed her hands up into the air. Wind whipped around the females for a few seconds before spiraling upward. Tlonna held the picture of a ladder in her mind as she pushed the air. Panting, she felt the Weave of power lock into place and dropped her hands.

"Come on, before it dissolves," the elf said and reached forward to grasp what wasn't there.

Miazie followed on her heels, rapidly placing one hand on the next rung of solid air. It took almost half an hour to reach the top of the plateau, and by that time the rungs had started dissipating as soon as Miazie's foot left them. Tlonna rolled onto the ground and reached down to help the woman up. They clasped hands just as the ladder dissolved completely, leaving Miazie suspended.

Tlonna hoisted her up and they clambered to their feet. The fields rattled in the wind, but no slave was in sight. Crouching low, the two moved north through the high wheat and were about to turn toward the stables when a man hailed them.

"Oi! Wait!" he ran the short distance to meet them and his face split into a genuine grin. "Princess Miazie, you're alive!"

"Shh, Tyre, we're not supposed to be, remember? What are you doing out here?" Miazie replied, pulling the man down into a crouch with them.

"After you all escaped, your father started a civilian watch. Anyone who sees anything out of ordinary from the slaves that surrendered is to immediately report them. Today was my watch. How are you alive?"

"I landed on Tlonna, on Hidden Ledge. How many

surrendered?"

Tyre scratched his thigh. "About a dozen, nearly a score made it out. A few were caught, and were immediately put to death. You need to leave, now. If anyone sees you, you'll both die, and not easily."

Tlonna poked Miazie to stop her from asking another question. "We need to get to the stables, and then we will leave. Can you get us there?"

The man nodded. "Follow me."

As the two females crouched low, Tyre strode upright, apparently scanning the empty fields. They reached the stables without any problems, and the guards had their backs to them. Tlonna stopped Tyre and slipped by him before either of the humans could stop her. She gently eased one of the guard's knives out of its sheath and rammed it up into his kidney.

Unable to scream, the guard went stone rigid. Tlonna twisted the knife and yanked it out. The guard started to crumple. The second man was just turning in confusion at his partner's action and Tlonna rammed the knife into his side. The guard opened his mouth to scream and the elf cracked her fist into his throat, crushing his windpipe.

Gasping futilely, the guard died. Tlonna pulled the dead humans into the stables and waved to Miazie and Tyre to get the horses. The two humans stared at her in shock, their faces pale, mouths gaping. She sent them a bland look, shaking her head a little, and then took the knife, the best sword, and the only bow from the dead men. Strapping the quiver on her belt, Tlonna undid the gate to Takîreaes' stall and soothed the jumpy stallion. While she found her tack, Tyre strode up to her.

"I would like to get a few of the good people from the city to come. At least my wife and daughter. It will only take a few minutes, I promise. I will bring them back here."

Tlonna sighed, and then saw Miazie staring at her in hope. "All right, but make it quick. We do not have time to fool around. I will get horses ready."

The man ducked his head and ran out of the stables. Miazie brought her mare over and Takîreaes eyed her.

"This is Kaia, bred her myself. Who is this proud young man?" Miazie asked, stroking Kaia's nose.

Tlonna looked back at the antsy stallion. "His name is Takîreaes."

Miazie's brow rose. "Warrior? What a name. I hope he lives up to it, there is going to be a lot of fighting soon, I feel it."

"Is that what it means? Good to know," Tlonna replied, ignoring the last statement.

The two females started pulling horses out of stalls and fitting them to tack. When the door opened a few minutes later, Tlonna flipped the knife she had ready to throw back down into her palm. Three men and two women, one with a baby, slipped inside and rushed to Miazie.

"Rebecca, Alisia, my friends. Are you sure you want to leave? This is your home, after all," Miazie replied to their heartfelt greetings.

The woman with the baby, Rebecca, nodded. "Aye, it is no home without you. You made it bearable. No offense intended, but your father is a bastard."

Miazie smiled while Tlonna grinned in the background. "Yes, he is. Do you know who else is coming?"

One of the men shook his head. "No Princess, Tyre only said that you and the elf were alive and in the stables waiting to leave."

Tlonna cleared her throat for attention. "Saddle yourselves a horse. These we will leave for stragglers."

The five humans nodded and went to the tack room. By the time they had saddled and secured their packs, three more people had arrived. Nearly a half hour passed, in which Tlonna was forced to kill two more guards when they came to switch with the dead ones, before Tyre returned. The people milling around in the stables numbered nearly to forty.

They were all mounted and waiting for orders within a few minutes. They looked to Miazie, and Miazie looked to Tlonna. The elf shifted in her saddle to look each of the two score people in the eye. A few stared back hard but most dropped their eyes.

"I do not know what we will face by the time we reach the gates, and I really do not know what we will face outside those gates. You came here because you want to be free, free of tyranny and fear. You are going to have to fight, because freedom is not free. You have to fight to live, work to be happy and prosperous. This is not going to be an easy journey, do not expect it to be. I can protect you, but you are going to have to be able to protect yourself, as well. Are you ready?"

With a roar of approval, Tlonna burst out of the stables, her stallion racing beneath her.

They were halfway across the plateau before the guards came after them. The men raced after the riders, shouting orders. Tlonna motioned for the others to keep going and then brought Takîreaes out in a long sweeping arc to head back toward the guards. Guiding with her knees, the elf lifted her hands and pushed forward, knocking the men back with a Weave of air and dirt. As they flattened out, Tlonna zeroed in on Darren, standing just outside the manor house, fury writ on his face.

She reined in just a few yards from him and drew a knife.

"You... you are dead! I watched you fall off the edge! You are not real!" the king shouted, shaking.

Tlonna grinned horribly. "Sorry to disappoint."

Arrows raced toward her only to shatter against the shield of air she held up around her and Takîreaes.

Darren drew his sword and took a few steps forward. "I'll kill you, you unnatural heathen!" He raised his sword and Tlonna took aim.

The knife buried itself to the hilt in his manhood. The king stopped, dropped his weapon, and stared at the blade in his crotch.

Tlonna's grin faded. "I would kill you, but I would rather you live in shame and humiliation until you die. Payback for all the girls you destroyed. Revenge, Darren, is the justification of my life," Tlonna said quietly as she watched the pain reach the man's face.

He started screaming when she turned away and rode to meet the mob of people waiting for her just beyond the gate.

Chapter 2
New Beginnings, Old Endings

Tlonna studied one of the books she had, running her fingers along the faded edge of the pages. *Legends of the Moons*, Miazie had said it was called, though all Tlonna saw on the cover was the strange cipher that matched her bracelet. The elf sat cross-legged on a small bump in the ground. Before her was a tidy camp where people meandered to and from places, doing things Tlonna couldn't imagine were important.

With a groan, she stood and tucked the book into the crook of her arm. Tlonna walked over to where Miazie was talking to Tyre and his wife, Rebecca.

"Greetings."

The man bowed slightly to her and then smiled. "My daughter, Zerah."

Tlonna studied the infant's face and received a giggling smile in return. Miazie cleared her throat. Tlonna looked up at her.

"What is this cipher?" the elf asked, pointing to the cover of the book.

Miazie shrugged as though it were the simplest question in the world. "Parlêthian. Your native language, the language of both Elf and Magin."

"Can you teach it to me?"

Miazie nodded and took the book. "Ah, *Legends of the Moons*, I'd like to read it, if you don't mind."

Tlonna was in the middle of saying she didn't when a loud 'Oi!' came from the forest. A group of Anutchian men emerged from the forest carrying between them a ragged, unconscious man. Tlonna rushed over to them and took their burden. She grunted. He wasn't heavy, but he seemed to be all leg and shoulder. When the elf stretched him out, the stranger's eyes snapped open and stared at the female holding him. His lips peeled back in a snarl, but Tlonna easily held him down. The elf looked up at the men who had brought him.

"Who is he?"

The closest man, a hunter, shrugged. "Don' know. He was layin' face down in the dir' when we foun' him, bloody like this. No horse within sight, no sign of a struggle, nothin'."

Tlonna frowned and turned back to the once again unconscious man. His face was angled and his dark blond hair fell to just below his collar bone. Something inside her felt odd as she studied him, something uncomfortably familiar.

That night, Tlonna ducked into the grove where the man had been taken and looked him over. The man standing guard cleared his throat and shuffled his feet. Tlonna ignored him. The stranger's clothes were dirty, but well made. He was very tall and slim, with a young face that had one long scar down the left side. It was thin and white, running from the corner of his eye to his chin. Although worn and tired looking, he was unnervingly attractive.

Turning to the guard, Tlonna said, "I am going to check him for any wounds. Go get some rest, and I will come get you later."

The guard bobbed his head and strode off.

Turning back to her senseless companion, the elf gently took his tunic off and grimaced when she saw the grime and bruises that covered his entire torso. She turned to the little pond that ran through the grove and soaked the dirty shirt in it. Hesitantly, Tlonna applied the wet garment to his upper body and wiped away the dirt that threatened to overwhelm him, and found a few splotches of dried blood. Carefully, the elf untied his trousers, pulled them off, staring at the fine, slim, muscular legs, and refused to remove the breechclout.

With a gasp, she discovered a long cut running from his hip to his knee. The wound was deep and padded hastily with filthy rags. Concentrating, the elf peeled away the ruined skin and flushed it with water. The man awoke with a cry and grabbed Tlonna by the neck.

His fingers were like stone as she pried at them, his eyes alight with danger and fury. With a shove, he sent her sprawling backward.

Gasping for breath, Tlonna rubbed at her sore neck and glared. "I am sorry if I hurt you, I was just trying to help. There was no need to do that."

The man scowled and Tlonna felt a chill go down her spine. He looked as though he could he snap her in half, even wounded, and would like to do so. His dark blue eyes penetrated her flesh and sank into her soul. His mouth twitched angrily. His body tensed and Tlonna looked away, her face burning. He was *beyond* handsome, every inch of him made her quiver. His skin was pale, though it looked healthy despite the blood. Shadows wavered along his chest and stomach as the dips of his muscles deepened when he moved.

"Who are you? What do you want with me?" he snapped finally in a voice that made her stomach flip.

It was husky, though not low, as if he would have a seductive singing voice. Tlonna had a hard time envisioning this man doing anything but killing. With a fluid motion, he grabbed his filthy trousers from her startled grasp and pulled them on, wincing as the wound reopened and began bleeding.

"You are injured. I need to clean your wounds so they will not become infected," Tlonna finally managed, irritated that she sounded so tongue-tied.

He scoffed, his upper lip twisting slightly. "It will not become flaming infected, woman. Give me my bleeding shirt." The man grabbed at his sopping shirt, but Tlonna tossed it into the pool behind her.

"You are right, it is bloody, and it needs to be washed. Leave it alone." Tlonna replied, watching in fear as fury mounted within the male.

"I do not give a blazing god's damn how flaming dirty it is. Give. Me. My. Shirt."

Tlonna pursed her lips and crossed her arms. "What is your name?"

He glowered at her. After a moment's hesitation, he huffed out a breath and said, "Losolin."

Tlonna forced a smile. She had to swallow a few times before she could speak again. "Merry meet, Losolin. I am Tlonna."

"Not so bleeding merry, *Tlonna*, what do you want with me?"

"I have already told you," the Magin replied hastily.

Losolin was becoming more and more irate by the second. His body fairly vibrated with tension. His hands clenched and unclenched twice as she watched, obviously itching for a weapon.

"You need to be tended to, Losolin, and your clothes need to be cleaned. They will do you no good to be wandering around like this, wounded as you are. I will have them washed. In the meantime, you may borrow one of the other men's clothes."

Losolin stared at her for a full ten seconds before folding his arms across his chest. "Fine. Get me some clothes, then. I will wait here. Do not bring anyone back, Tlonna, or everyone out there will die," he said as he leaned menacingly toward her, his pale blond hair fell forward and his ears poked through.

Tlonna shivered from the force in his glare before his words caught her. Her back went up, and then she saw his ears. "You are an elf!"

Losolin stopped mid-movement and looked at her. "Yes, I am. What about it?"

Tlonna shook her head, her mouth working uselessly. His body was making her even more uncomfortable now. Losolin straightened, watching her through narrowed eyes.

"The clothes?"

Tlonna fled the grove and found a tall, lean man sitting by a fire outside his tent. "Good sir, I have need of clothing. Could you supply me with them?"

The man stared at her incredulously. When she begged him, he sighed and retreated into the tent. A few moments later, he emerged holding a bundle of clothing. After finding some bandages, Tlonna sped back to the stranger. When she stepped between the high bushes, she found him standing waist high in the water.

"Here," the elf tossed the borrowed clothes to the ground, blushing deeply when she saw the breechclout lying next to the pool.

Losolin glanced at her once, then resumed his washing. He pulled the breechclout into the water and began scrubbing vigorously at the leather. The water began to lap against his fair skin with the motion, and she caught a glimpse of his hips. Blushing again, Tlonna looked at him in a new light, he was further away now, and she felt a mite bit safer. His hair was wheat colored, with streaks of chestnut brown that glinted even in the moonlight. She could remember his gaze, the dark blue of the ocean. Eyes that knew too much, had seen too much. Sad eyes. Angry eyes. His muscles glided under his skin smoothly. They were long muscles, not bulky and mannish, but lithe and attractive.

The Magin did not notice her breath coming faster than usual. She stared at the curve of his back, where shadows sat in pools between the spinal extensions of his lower back. His fingers were long too, and almost delicate looking. Deceptively so. Tlonna rubbed the spot where he had tried to strangle her. She did not notice that Losolin had stopped washing his items and was watching her stare at him.

His face tightened, and he dropped his hands into the water, making splashes that startled Tlonna.

"Do you want something?" Losolin asked quietly as Tlonna tried to control her rapid breathing.

Her knees almost buckled when he spoke. His voice... his *voice* drove her mad. Swallowing, the Magin shook her head. "I...uh...no."

Losolin's eyes narrowed again. He seemed amused. Slowly, his gaze left her face and traveled down her body and back up again. So slowly. His lips curled into a knowing grin. Tlonna cleared her throat unnecessarily. Her knees wobbled, and she sat down. Licking her lips, the elf stared at a spot just above his shoulder. She could see Losolin's grin out of the corner of her eye.

"S-so, what are you doing out here alone?" she finally asked.

The question seemed to rock the male out of sorts. His grin faded and he resumed his washing. "I am originally from Blackhaven, but I became a White Hand Warrior.... The others I was with are all dead, now. Our camp was raided a week or so ago by a squad of bandits we were chasing. Nearly everyone was murdered in their sleep, some of us woke and fought, but they were too many. Those of us who survived became their captives. Most of my brethren died soon after. When only three of us were left, the bastards were set upon by a few of their rivals. It was a massacre. My companions died in the fighting, and I got this," he gestured at the wound in his thigh. "Then I was hit on the head and left for dead. When everyone had gone, I tried to get to a village, but I must have passed out because the next thing I know, I am here," Losolin said, speaking to his hands.

"I took you for a fighter," Tlonna replied honestly, studying the elf's writhing arm muscles as he resumed scrubbing. "You have a strong grip."

Losolin sniffed in a laughing sort of way. "Yes, well, sorry about that."

Tlonna ducked her head to hide her blush. She felt foolish. "Where will you go now?"

He shrugged. "I do not know. Back to Seaduens to see if another company is there that will hire me, perhaps. Perhaps not."

"You could...you could stay with me. With us," she amended quickly.

Even though he was not looking at her, Tlonna saw Losolin's

brow rise in surprise. After a moment, he said, "Why not? It seems I have nowhere else to run and being with a company is by far safer than traveling by one's self. I do not particularly like Seaduens." Losolin paused. "Your men took my pack. I have more clothes in it, and my sword and bow."

Tlonna nodded, "I will get it back for you. There is not really any spare tent though, if you do not have your own."

"I can sleep in here well enough. I could use some company though," he replied, finally looking at her in earnest.

Tlonna's mouth went dry. Losolin tossed the breechclout onto the ground by the pool and waded out himself. He was completely naked, and his wound looked better having been submerged in water. Tlonna's mouth dropped and she found herself staring up at him. He was so beautiful. He did not seem abashed at all by his nudity, and Tlonna could not blame him. Every ounce of him was tamed muscle and smooth, hairless skin.

Tlonna shivered. He was standing in front of her, a little to the side, but close enough. She found a spot on the ground between his feet and stared at it. She saw his knees bend, watched his body loom closer.

"You are the first elf other than myself I have seen in ages. Even those in my company were human, and male." Losolin's head tilted a little to the side.

Tlonna was crimson, and she was positive he could see her heart beating through her shirt. He was so near, she could feel the heat from his body.

"Do I not meet your standards?" Losolin crooned, tilting his head to the other side.

The Magin raised her gaze to his and lost whatever willpower she had held in reserve. "Y-you...are s-so..." she couldn't finish.

Losolin's teeth gleamed whitely in the moonlight as he grinned. Suddenly, his fist was wrapped in her tunic, the other in her hair. Their lips met. Tlonna's body quivered uncontrollably. Losolin's hand left her shirt, trailed across her bosom, and settled on her waist. His fingertips brushed her flesh, sending goosebumps racing up and down her skin.

Suddenly, reality slammed back into Tlonna's head. Losolin's hand was now under her shirt, tight against her waist. Panicking, the elf shoved at Losolin, her hands connecting with hard muscle. The male grunted and pulled out of the kiss, frowning.

Tlonna pushed at him again, this time sending him reeling backward. He regained his balance almost immediately and now looked irritated.

"What in the bleeding blazes is wrong with you?" he growled.

Tlonna stared at him with wide eyes. "I cannot do this. I cannot!"

Losolin raised an eyebrow at her. His jaw was clenched. His fingers dug into his thighs, leaving white marks whenever he moved them. Tlonna unwillingly glanced down and then away. He was fully erect, which explained his tenseness.

"I am sorry, I should not have let it go that far," she whispered, and stood.

Losolin stood with her, grabbing up a cloak from the pile of clothes she had brought. It was deep purple, lined in silver. He tied it around his waist, though it did nothing to hide his desire.

He yanked a white shirt from under a pair of boots and clenched it in his hand. "No, you should not have. If you go one step, you need to finish the journey," he snapped.

Tlonna turned on him. "You started it!"

Losolin's mouth opened angrily. Tlonna slashed her hand at him to silence him, but a shock of white power burst from her fingers. It lanced into Losolin's abdomen, making him howl. He grabbed her shoulders and rolled her into the water.

Tlonna shrieked, but it came out a gurgle as water rushed over her head. Strong hands held her down as surely as an iron bar.

When he finally brought her up, Tlonna felt as though her lungs would burst and her eyes would pop out. Before she could catch her breath, Losolin's mouth descended on hers and demanded surrender. His tongue took over. Tlonna moaned in spite of herself. After quite some time, Losolin withdrew, his teeth scraping along her bottom lip. His head lowered and he kissed her neck where it joined the shoulder. Tight against her body, Tlonna felt him trembling as though it was all he could do to contain himself.

Suddenly, she realized he was not doing anything. He merely had his head buried in her shoulder; his hands loose on her hips. Tlonna moved slightly, but he did not tighten his grip, or raise his head. Confused, she took a step backward. His hands slid off her hips and he looked away, eyes closed.

Tlonna sloshed out of the pool and stumbled onto the bank. Her knees gave way and she pitched forward. The elf caught herself, and then rolled onto her back. Losolin was looking at her, a slight crease in his forehead. There was something very familiar about him. Sudden agony gripped her, and she clamped her teeth shut to stop the gasp of pain. Her eyes rolled up, and her lids slid closed.

An arm thrown across her belly woke Tlonna with a start. She stared at the arm, the strong wrist, the fingers loosely curled. Her eyes traveled down the arm to a strong shoulder, brushed by wheat blond, brown streaked hair. Losolin's face was turned away from her, the tendons in his neck standing out. She swallowed several times. Gently picking up his arm, Tlonna rolled away and onto her feet.

She was barefoot, but otherwise dressed. Her boots were upside down next to his, leaning against the lilac bush that covered half the grove. They looked so small compared to Losolin's. She quickly tied her boots and then took the opportunity of the male's vulnerability to study him fully. Her body was warm by the time she reached his abdomen. Her gaze moved lower and she blushed, noting how his hips stretched across the pelvis in an arrow that pointed to-

Checking herself, Tlonna turned and left the wild grove.

Stretching in the sunlight, the elf yawned and pushed her tousled hair out of her face. With a hesitant determination, she walked toward the fine woven tent that housed her friend.

"Where were you last night? I wanted to discuss some things with you, but I couldn't find you," Miazie snapped as soon as Tlonna entered her tent.

"I...um...was speaking with the young man the hunters brought back. He is an elf too," Tlonna muttered, trying to forget his attack.

"Yeah, everyone heard him howling last night like a beast. What'd you do to him?" the human replied waspishly.

"Nothing! I was only checking to make sure he did not have any wounds. He does, but nothing that is worrisome. He got angry and tried to drown me, after *and* before he kissed me like some lovesick rogue," Tlonna snapped, irritated at the presumption.

"You *undressed* him? You idiot! That alone would make a man angry enough to kill unless he warranted it. No wonder he tried to drown you! Where is he now?"

"I do not know! Probably ran off somewhere as soon as I left

him just now."

"You mean you slept with him? Oh for bloody...Tlonna! Did you fornicate with him as well?" Miazie shouted, throwing her arms up.

"No! I fainted, and then woke up next to him," Tlonna shot back, not thinking.

"So, you were unconscious, and woke up next to the devil, and you don't think he took advantage of you? Please tell me you were clothed when you woke up."

"Of course I was! What do you think I am? A *human?*"

"Well, if you were, you'd at least have sense to fall asleep *after* he did!" Miazie hissed, leaning forward.

"Am I interrupting?" a male voice asked, unwanted.

Tlonna looked back at the male standing at an askew position with a controlled look on his face and only his pants on and felt a sudden urge to touch him. The gray pants were rolled up to his knees, as they only reached his ankles when all the way down. Even so, they rode low on his hips, showing off his hip bones. They were far too small.

"Yes!" both women snapped, staring at him.

Miazie stalked forward, "You think you can just waltz in and take Tlonna as your mistress? I don't think so mister. I don't care who you are, and I want you gone this instant!"

"No!" Tlonna protested, surprising herself, and both her company.

"Why not? He probably ravaged you as you lay prostrate and vulnerable, Tlonna. Why in the nine bloody hells would you want him to stay?"

"I-I do not know."

"I did not just waltz in here, and I did NOT ravage her! How dare you accuse me of such atrocities!"

Miazie shook her head and stared at the two. Finally, she said, "What is your name then, oh perfect one?"

"Lord Losolin, White Hand Warriors," he said. "And you are?"

"Miazie Paron Ughtren of Anutch, Daughter of King Darren."

Losolin looked at Tlonna then back at Miazie and said, "What is a flaming princess doing out here in the middle of the wild? I do not believe you. Tlonna, you should be more wary of her than myself."

Tlonna gave him a sneering look.

"My father tried to kill me so I escaped with all these people," Miazie said dismissively.

Losolin nodded and looked down at Tlonna. For the first time, she noticed he was a few inches tall than her. The elf scowled at Miazie, his eyes narrowing dangerously.

"Why would your own father try to kill you? Are you a turncoat? I do not like traitors, especially not blood traitors."

Miazie took in a sharp breath and then exploded toward the male. Her nails were less than an inch from Losolin's face when his hand swept up and caught her wrist.

"Now that, I *really* do not like."

Tlonna pulled the struggling Miazie back a few steps and then placed her hands on her hips.

"Why would you suspect such a thing? Miazie was put up for execution because she was helping me, a slave, who was also going to die because I did not get pregnant with his brat."

"Ah. Well it does happen. Humans are not the most chivalrous people around," Losolin declared angrily.

Miazie shook her head and began to walk away from the two when Tlonna ran to meet her, with Losolin right behind.

"You said that you wanted to discuss some things?" Tlonna said when she caught up.

"Yes, they are about those books you have. Well, mainly it's basic history that you should know," the young woman replied.

"All right, where are we going?"

Miazie pointed to a small dip in the land near the campfire.

The trio situated themselves on the ground and Miazie held up the book, *Parlêthian Council of Magins.*

"This is not a book in the most usual sense. It is more a record, or journal, of Magins during the Sixth Age, some two thousand years ago, one of the few copies. By the look of it, it could be the original preserved by magic through the years. To start, I would like to explain the... well the theory of the coming of Magins." Miazie tapped the book significantly. "At the end of the Sixth Age of Nymyños, there were fifteen humans that sort of... popped into existence with the most amazing powers. Now, the people had been known, but their power was sudden. Scholars over the ages have questioned their existence, saying they were anomalies in the human race, or experiments of alchemy, some even say they were gods sent to earth as punishment. I like to believe the alchemy theory, as it makes the most sense.

"There were, as I said, fifteen of them, both men and women. They formed a council, the Parlêthian Council of the Magins. Parlêthian means, in essence, first, but it is defined as 'the eldest of many'. They were led by the most powerful of their number, a wicked and devious sort of man by the name of Roluf Gwemheoad," the woman explained. "Since then, every single one of their descendents have been Magins, some with vast amounts of power, some with very little, only able to lift small things from a few feet or cast a slight Weave, as it is called. They used to be a separate culture, a different religion, but non-magical people started to fear them and they were persecuted nearly to their extinction, about one thousand years ago. They were called pagans, heathens, worshipers of demons and Hel, the goddess of the underworld. These... pagans did not believe Hel to be evil, but rather a spirit guide who watched the dead, kept them safe from soul-stealing demons, until they passed into Summerland, the world beyond death."

"They do not seem evil to me, why were they persecuted?" Losolin asked.

"People fear things they don't understand. During the Sixth and Seventh Age, Nymyños went through a massive religious and economic dark age. People were slaughtered for having power, for having more money than others, for the most mundane things. A new religion popped up, one that preached submission to a single god, the forgiveness of hated enemies, and sacrifice for others less fortunate, even if those 'less fortunate' were lazy pickpockets who deserved nothing more than a hanging. This religion swept through the provinces and Liberated Lands like a plague for three hundred years or so until factions started to spring up, people who saw through these insane ideals.

"It was torn down piece by piece until it became a religion equal to all the others. These monotheists were now a minority as they once were, while polytheists took over again. Magins were accepted again. Religion once more took a back seat to everyday life, but for those fanatics that every group has. By the way, why are you here?" Miazie said.

Taken aback, Losolin's eye twitched angrily. "Because I bloody well want to be. Besides, I am here by Tlonna's invitation, and I am to be a guard, of sorts, for her people. I am not going anywhere."

Miazie gave a painful smile. "Lovely."

"So, these fifteen Magins started a council, and a thousand years later there was a religious revolt against them. What else?" Tlonna asked, trying to avoid confrontation.

Miazie turned back to her. "There is a lot that happens before and in between those years. I just wanted to give you a quick overview of Nymyñosian history first. Now," she picked up the book, "the title of this is *Parlêthian Council of Magins*. It is mainly the records of the fifteen first Magins. They recorded their studies, experiments, wars, and combinations of hand symbols and was added on by Magins that later came into being after the First Council. The Council was held in the Purheae Region, most of the Kingdoms had not yet been founded, though the provinces existed. Many were called different names, as well. Kismath was called Kismanelle, Arseninis, Arsenisisia, and so on, but it's not really important. The High Magin was Roluf Gwemheoad; as I said. He was the first to write in it. The first paragraph of the book is,

'I, Roluf Gwemheoad, have brought together, on this day, seventeenth of Xul, this seven hundred and forty-ninth year of the Sixth Age, a council. In this council sits myself, as well as fourteen of the most powerful people in the world. It has taken me a long time to track down each person, but as the power became strengthened within our bodies, it was easier for me to feel them, their presence. Through this council, I will teach them how to control their gift, the Weave, as I call it, and together, we shall rule with an iron fist, while wreathed in the flame of power.'

"The council, under the influence of Roluf, grew in power and ability. They went from being able to do menial tasks to creating flesh and bone from earth and stone. From the communal house, they built a great tower in which to work and live. In a few years, the villagers who had congregated around the tower grew fearful of the Magins' power and fled into the Forest of Purheae.

"The people, ignorant about the forest in whose shadow they had lived in, were easy prey to its magic. The magic of the forest twisted and deformed the people. A few became stunted and hairy; some their ears grew large and pointed, and others grew small and developed the ability to fly. So was the creation of creatures such as tree elves, gnomes, and sprytes. Elves, being the oldest of all races were living in the forest all along, but tree elves were very small and they, well...lived in the trees. The Magins observed this change and decided that they wanted that power for themselves. The council went into the forest and massacred a village. They were headed to the next village when they were attacked by creatures they could not see, what they recorded as invisible demons of evil intent. But they were just the tree elves and others who had taken the forest as their home.

"When the council went in again they were careless and destroyed the inner forest with power. The forest, however, was alive and the magic within it eventually began to commingle with those born in the forest. The children born had innate powers that tripled the natural magic within them.

"The forest began to heal itself. The Elves came from their realms of the wood and rallied the Little Folk, as they called them. Their strength began to grow and they populated into a large colony, the Little Folk, under command of the Elves, attacked the Magins. A great war waged between the Magins and Elves for fourteen years and all the while the Magins were trying to find a way for elongated life. They often did experiments on elf captives, trying to find out what allowed them their immortality. After a while, the Elves grew tired of the war, and decided to end it with a full out massacre. At midnight on Thursday, the twentieth day of Maen, year five hundred and sixty nine of the Sixth Age, they raided the Tower of Magins and burnt it to the ground. Most of the Magins survived, having protected themselves from the flames. They retaliated and slaughtered the Purheae forces. Of almost seven thousand, only about two hundred survived.

"The Little Folk fled back into the sanctuary of the forest and disappeared from knowledge for almost one and half thousand years. The Elves limped back to their woodland realms and remained hidden for a little under thirteen years. However, during the war a young Magin who was created as an experiment fell in love with a beautiful elf, Tonora. They would sneak out to see each other, and in the end their coupling brought to life what some considered an abomination. Half elf, half human Magin, but stronger than both. The Magins found out and killed the young man. The elf mother raised the child deep in the forest under the lie that she had been raped by one of the enemy soldiers. One day while he was playing, the boy saw a faery. He came back to his mother and told her how it had come to him and touched his face.

"It was well known that the faeries were reclusive creatures and never showed themselves to anyone, and especially never touched another being. The magic within the child had drawn the faery. The mother worried that she would be found out, and the child's heritage would be revealed. She took him away without a word to anyone in the colony. Soon after, the Elves realized she was missing and sent out a search. They found her and her child in a section of the forest that was thought to be tainted and forced her to come back to the village. The mother made the child leave and said that he had killed himself when he found out what his father had been.

"The young elf, Jair, wandered across the Magins' land and was taken capture by one of the Magins and brought back to the council. Soon he learned their trade and became the most powerful of the Magins. He went on a rampage against the other Magins and killed them all, except two that he had made as friends. The Elven Magin went into the forest, brought his people out of hiding, and raised a castle on top of the area where the Council had been stationed. He learned his mother had been killed in battle a few years earlier. The family had fled afterward. He decided he needed to keep the blood of the new race, only carried in him, alive. He also adopted the language Parlêthian as the Elven language because the original had been very complicated and hard to understand." Miazie licked her lips and glanced once at Losolin, then resumed her lecture.

"One night he went among the elves and after a long search, found the most beautiful elf he could and took her as his bride. A few months after the marriage, she became pregnant. The child was born one and a half years later, twice as long as the usual gestation period. The child was a boy named Amram who grew to become a king after his father had died some eighty years later, from an explosion. Amram wed a young Magin, who after trying to have a child many times over the course of two years, died from the strain. He married another Magin and got a girl from her just under two years later. The young couple was assassinated about a hundred years later, but before that, they built the kingdom up into a large prosperous city and named it the Purheae Kingdom. When they died, it left the heiress Sha to rule. She, for some unknown reason, left it to find a new place, leaving a knight in her place as king. Sha traveled across the lands and found a beautiful place with a forest of trees which were silver with black leaves, and large obsidian stones. She erected a small shelter and began to make her home. Later in the year an elf came to her doorstep and told her that he had come from the Purheae Forest in search of her.

"She let him in and after a while, they wed themselves. The male was named Laheeka. He and Sha had many children; so many, they had to build more homes. Other elves began to come to their little village and wed the children. Soon, there were so many people that they built a wall around the homes and erected a castle from the great, black obsidian stone that surrounded the place. Later, when the kingdom was thriving, a guild of masons decided that the castle was a foreboding presence, despite the benevolence of the people within it. The masons carved veins into the great walls and filled them with molten silver, gold, and pearl. Sha and Laheeka's eldest child took over rule when they died shortly after, and named it *Kairhotuss Buwai*, or Blackhaven Forest. The boy's name was Damian and he wed an elf by the name of Gredeil who gave him a child named Dietirin who gave himself the last name of Ewôsdírn or Great Wind. He married another young elf named Constancias." Miazie paused, fingering the edge of the book. "It is odd that the rule of elves was so short over the course of the Sixth and Seventh age. Most did not reach four hundred before dying, though both their ancestors and descendants outlive that by far. No one is quite sure why this is so, even I have argued with myself over it. But, it is not something you need worry about right now.

"As far as I know, Dietirin and Constancias continue to rule and they produced a single heir, a daughter, who died eight years ago in the siege of Blackhaven. It is said that their marriage was arranged by Gredeil, who was a wicked elf and thought only of building the power of her house. Constancias is the daughter of an extremely wealthy Grand Duchess who was killed, along with her father, and Dietirin's parents, by Aderiaen Rahlan in Aderiaen's War."

Tlonna squinted at the woman "It is a blood soaked history, Miazie, and a short one, it seems. Why do the dwarves and the humans not come into it? Where were they during this upheaval?"

Miazie gave a small laugh. "You don't understand. What I just gave you was an extremely dried up, corn-husk version. This history takes years to know it, and even then, you don't know it all. There is the formation of the provinces, the wars of kings, the *Zaynzura* era in Zeynuwn, on and on through the ages."

"*Zaynzura* era?" Tlonna asked, tilting her head to the side.

"Aye, it was a culture of warriors in Zeynuwn. These men were fighters of ability beyond reason, Tlonna, as good as any elf. Every day they practiced, meditated, and worked. Their sword, called a katan, was part of their soul. They were able to achieve a blankness or control of their mind that allowed them to focus solely on fighting. It is an art of warfare called Uyai-shin. Their greatest precept was honor. Anyway, that went on for about seven hundred years, and while the *Zaynzuras* are still around, they are a few in number after having been slaughtered by the imperial army of Zeynuwn, passing from the time of the warrior into the time of the soldier."

Tlonna smiled sheepishly. "I guess it is easy to forget that other things happen when you are involved in something else during the same time. What else is there?"

Miazie nodded, staring at the ground in front of her. "It is easy to forget. The book goes on with the notes of the other fourteen Magins, Weaves they had invented, important events that happened in the tower, which I am told is still there. Well, at least remnants of it and the castle Jair erected around it. One of these events was the creation of the Magin Stones, fifteen ordinary stones given extraordinary powers, singular to each stone. The stones are said to have been passed down through the years from Jair, and today still reside in Blackhaven, or they did, unless Midian got his hands on them," Miazie's face twisted with the thought.

"After the first fifteen died, other Magins followed their example, adding on to the book until it filled. Once that happened, they got another, and another. Some of them were destroyed, others lost or hidden. There are supposed to be seven or eight still in existence, including this one. At least of the originals. They have been copied down, as well, and available to almost anyone determined to read them.

"But rather than go into the tedium of Maginic records, I am going to tell you about Blackhaven."

"Why?" Tlonna asked, glancing at Losolin, who was plucking idly at a tuft of grass.

Miazie rubbed the bridge of her nose. "I have come to believe that is where you are from. By your accent, and the scrying you had, and your clothing. The other kingdoms have a bit more frill to their clothing, but Blackhaven is known for its decency and efficiency."

"I have an accent?"

Miazie smiled. "Yes, Tlonna, you do. You sound like Losolin."

"I do?"

"Yes," this time Miazie laughed.

Grinning, Tlonna rolled her hand in the air, "Okay okay, go on please."

"Blackhaven is the youngest kingdom, but by far the most powerful. The capital, Blackhaven City, more properly said *Kairhotuss Aela*, is the largest in Nymyños. Surrounded and filled with trees, it is very easy to miss, unless you know what you're looking for. It gets its name from the massive forest that covers half the province called Blackhaven Forest, *Kairhotuss Buwai.* The trunks are silver and the leaves so dark a green, they appear black. There are three of the trees within the castle itself and are said to be the oldest living. They rise above the castle's highest tower, the Tower of Winds, the royal suite, and are said to take a hundred people to surround, standing with hands outstretched. I have always wanted to see them," a wistful expression washed over Miazie's face.

"Anyway, after Sha and Laheeka raised the castle and founded the city itself, trade exploded. Merchants from all over Nymyños started setting up shops that they had agents run, forming a large market district in the center of the city. The city spread out from the wall and into the forest proper, so, another wall was erected. The wall went around trees and boulders so that not one thing was felled in order to accommodate bipod life. Eventually though, the trees in the shadow of the wall died, clearing about a nine foot space between the wall and the forest itself.

"While the elves didn't like it, they knew that if Blackhaven was ever attacked, having trees coming right up to the wall would destroy them. They conceded to clear the dead trees away and maintain that space. Within the wall, however, the forest thrived, nursed by the earth magic of the elves and other elementals in the city."

"What are elementals?" Tlonna interrupted.

"Creatures of the earth. Dryads and nymphs. There are five different types of nymph; fire, water, earth, wood, and stone. Dryads are spirit forms of the earth so they live inside trees, or waterfalls, things like that. Anyway, with the forest thriving, the city split into seven separate districts. The Civilian District is the largest, consisting of mostly homesteads of the common folk and takes up the entire northern half of the city. In the center of it is the Militia District, where the barracks and training compound is. Split in two by the main road is the Market District, which is where, obviously, the shops are. On the other side is the Inner Farm District, which is set aside for farmland within the wall, in case of a siege, there is little threat of starvation. On the western side of that is the Peerage District, where officers, dukes, barons, the rich, live. The High Commander and her husband, the Captain of the Guard live there as well, in a sandstone mansion that is said to rise out of the ground like a hill. The most magnificent building, other than the castle itself. On the backside of the city is the Harbor District. And then the Royal District that surrounds the castle.

"The army is called the Blackhaven Militia, and is commanded by High Commander Yayènia er'Tiena and Second Commander Ghealan Tomyvon. They are the fastest, strongest, deadliest, most dangerous fighters in all of Nymyños. They've never lost. Both of them have been to brink of death and survived. They've walked alone into enemy camps and walked right back out, untouched. Legend has it that three hundred and fifty years ago, before they took over charge of the military, they were going to be married, but then Ghealan disappeared for a few years and Yayènia went mental," Miazie leaned in close as though sharing a secret. "It's said when Ghealan left her, she lost her mind and went on a killing frenzy. Then Ghealan comes back, married, to some Narnenian viscountess, so Yayènia marries this Count Suneelo Tiena. Biggest scandal in years, people go on a rampage, saying Yayènia only married Suneelo because he has a status higher than this Viscountess Erdwyf. Then Yayènia, Ghealan, and Suneelo all join the militia and rise up through the ranks like wildfire, defeating every enemy thrown at them. Anyway, when they competed for office, Yayènia broke one of Ghealan's legs.

"The old High Commander, an elf named Hegan, promoted Yayènia and put Ghealan in as her second. The army was never defeated, until this last battle. No one survived. Men, women, children, Man, Elf, Dwarf, Spryte, slaughtered and left in the streets.

Their own princess was skinned alive."

"What was her name?" Tlonna asked, horrified.

"I don't know. Very few knew her name, for it was kept a secret."

"Why? She is the princess, how could it be a secret?" Tlonna said, taken in by the story.

"She was known as Princess of the Everwood, or Everwood alone," Losolin said quietly, more husky than usual.

Miazie nodded, "Aye, her name was kept secret for her protection. You see, Tlonna, Everwood is, was spoken about in many prophecies. She is the destroyer of great evil, and is more powerful than any other being alive...well she was. Midian sought her out specifically to destroy her. With her death, the shadow of evil became tangible."

Tlonna made a face. "So, the crown princess of the most powerful kingdom in Nymyños who is prophesied to destroy evil has no name to the greater population? Seems odd to me. And the fact that you have all this knowledge about things that do not concern you, like magic, it seems to me you should know her name."

"What are you saying?"

"I am saying do you not find it odd that even Losolin, who lives there, does not even know the dead princess's name? It does not fit. Something is wrong," Tlonna replied angrily.

Miazie scowled. "It does seem off, but that is the way it is, okay? You can't change the way the world is."

Tlonna huffed. "I just do not see how it is possible. What else?"

Miazie told her about the cultures of the separate kingdoms, about the major wars throughout history, and the monarchy of Blackhaven.

As night approached, the camp settled down, warmed by fires and companionship. Tlonna and Losolin donned their cloaks and set out on a walk into the forest. Their companions watched them go with wary eyes, uncertain of the unearthly glow that surrounded them, common to all elves. The darkness of the trees shrouded them from sight within just a few steps of the trees. Miazie looked to her friend Tyre and then back at the elves. The soldier nodded and stood, smiling at his wife and daughter. With a gesture, two hunters stood and joined him.

The three men followed the elves into the forest and found their faint tracks on the dew-dampened trail. Many yards away at a bend in the trail, Losolin and Tlonna smiled faintly at each other as their sensitive ears picked up the humans' sounds. They laced their fingers together and sped up, running through the forest like children at play. The humans were left behind, unaware of the elves' knowledge of them.

Once out of hearing, Tlonna and Losolin slowed and grinned at each other.

"I am afraid we have lost them, Tlonna," Losolin said.

"Oh yes, perhaps we should go back and save them from the evil forest."

"Evil, indeed," a dark voice said from behind them.

The elves whipped around and searched the darkness before them. A shadow emerged, an outline darker than the blackness behind it. Two silver rings shone out from the cowl, blinking every so often.

"Who are you?" Tlonna asked, feeling around her back for a weapon.

"I am your death,"

"That is a brave claim for one who has not seen his enemy's strength," Losolin growled, gripping his baldric.

"Even the sstrongesst one will fall before many. Do not make assumptionss before you know the play, boy."

At the shadow's words, the two elves looked around and saw more materializing out of the dark. Losolin pulled the strap across his chest that swung his bow around into his hand. He yanked an arrow out of the quiver and knocked it to the grip. The shadows suddenly and silently faded into the dark of the forest. As Tlonna and Losolin looked around in bafflement, the three men wandered into sight. As realization hit, the two elves held out their hands to stop the men.

"No! Go back! Stop!"

The men scrambled to a halt, frowning as they did. It was too late. The shades reappeared, surrounding the five. The hunters spun around in surprise, drawing their swords and bows. One of the shadows joined the leader and sniffed audibly.

"Lord Kelus, we have better things to do than play games with fools. Let us feast upon this man-flesh and depart."

The leader, Kelus, sniffed again and held up a hand. "No...

thesse two are not Men. They sstink of purity. Elvess..."

"*Elves?*" the demon said, sounding skeptical.

"Yess...what iss your name, sshe-elf?" Kelus demanded, pointing a clawed finger at Tlonna.

"Why?" Tlonna asked slowly.

"Becausse I demand it!" the shade hissed.

"Not good enough!" Tlonna chirped, and swung her arm outward.

White light sizzled through the air, burning through two of the demons. Kelus shot forward and grabbed her wrist as she prepared to swing again. The silver bracelet on her wrist caught his eye, and he stared at it. His silver eyes flashed down to Tlonna's face and then back to the bracelet. With a shove, Kelus released her.

Losolin cursed as one of the demons attacked him, its dark blade sliced through the wood of his bow as he lifted it to defend himself. He shook the string off the broken ends and shifted his grip. The elf spun the makeshift weapon and retaliated against the demon. It hissed as the wood whipped against its tainted flesh.

The other shadows drew their swords on the remaining four. Tlonna felt many pairs of claws grip her waist and shoulders. She writhed in their grasp, struggling to free her sword arm. Finally, with a strong jerk, she twisted partially away from them and was able to strike at one of them. It shrieked and she stabbed it until it fell silent. The others reached for her, but with freedom, her superior strength overpowered them when added to the strength of a Magin.

With a few more strokes, the five finished off the demons, other than the leader. Kelus leaned out of Losolin's reach and hissed in an odd, multi-tonal howl.

A great shadow covered the canopy and descended to the ground in the form of a massive black bird. The demon crawled atop the bird and took up the reins. The five watched him, staying well out of range of beak and claw.

Kelus pointed a gauntleted hand at Tlonna, "You may take thiss to be a victory, but do not hold to hope, for there are a great many more of uss than your dwindling race of flower-loving weaklingss. The power King Rahlan wieldss iss far greater than any meager magic trickss you may perform. Whatever you did to esscape him thiss time will not ssave you again."

He yanked on the reins and the massive bird leaped into the

air, disappearing into the night. The elves and humans let out a collective sigh of relief. Losolin was staring at Tlonna. She looked at him, worried. When they returned to the camp, they agreed not to alarm the others by relating what had happened to them. They washed the blood and grime away in the stream by the grotto and returned to their tents. The elves went to Miazie's tent and told her of the attack.

She sat quiet for a moment before taking a deep breath. "Darkwights. Creatures tortured by Midian, and his father Aderiaen for use as slaves and soldiers. Demons that were once Men, Dwarves, Elves, and all manner of races. They retain their old memories and feelings, but are consumed by the evil that has corrupted them for so long. There is a leader of them, hailed by both Rahlan kings as Lord of the Darkwights. Kelus, the first of that kind, an elf once, of great ranking and power, hailed by his followers as a leader of greatness. His is a legend among historians, thought by some to be the missing Furntil Eldrout, or a descendant of him. Some say it is like looking upon death itself when one looks into his eyes. Silver, I believe they are, with black where a normal eye is white."

"Yes, he was there tonight. He rode a great black bird like the legendary Rocs," Losolin said, rubbing his chin.

"Not a Roc, a Keylode, their evil cousins, but much larger than a Roc, and always black. They can fly great distances in just hours," Miazie replied. "Get some rest, my friends. It has been a trying night."

Tlonna shook her head. "But what about what he said to me? It does not make any sense."

Losolin turned from the tent entrance, eyes on Miazie. The woman's gaze unfocused for a moment, and then she shook her head. "I don't know," she sighed. "Perhaps that is how you lost your memory. Perhaps you angered Midian in some way, and he destroyed your past."

"Is that possible?" Tlonna whispered, horrorstruck.

Miazie frowned. "Midian Rahlan is the most powerful Magin since Roluf Gwemheoad. He can do anything."

Tlonna's eyes widened and she turned silently, unknowingly, into Losolin's arms. The male and Miazie locked gazes over Tlonna's bowed head. The human's jaw clenched and Losolin guided Tlonna back into the grove.

A few days later, across the continent of Nymyños, Midian Rahlan raised his head from his hand as Kelus shuffled in.

"You're back earlier than I expected," Midian crooned, as was his natural habit. "Did the Samiis not put up much of a fight?"

"We did not reach Ssamii, my lord. Masster, I have newss of the Magin and her followerss," the cloaked figure glided over to him and bowed slightly.

"The *Magin*? What Magin?"

"The elf princesss, my lord. Sshe iss alive," the demon said.

"Tlonna *Ewôsdírn?*" Midian roared.

"Yess my King, sshe wearss the bracelet, and lookss like her. Sshe iss alsso a Magin, very powerful. Her lover iss with her too, the elf boy, and a human woman who sseemss to be their guide."

"How? HOW?" Midian bellowed, shaking his fists at his slave.

"I don't know, Ssire," Kelus replied, "but it iss sso."

Midian's howl was not quite human, and it echoed through the halls of his conquered castle.

Losolin lay in the grove with Tlonna clinging to his body as though he were a pillow. He was not sure if she was awake or not. Her knees were clenched together on either side of his thigh, painfully tight, her feet flat against his calf. One arm was stretched across his chest, fingers digging into his right shoulder. The other was wrapped around his left arm, her head resting on his bicep. She had been so distraught after finding out about Midian's power she had not even noticed him lying her down in the grove. He had stretched out a few feet away from her, but she had scooted up close and arrayed herself as she was now. The male was thinking of Miazie in order to stop his body from responding to Tlonna pressed tight against him.

It was thoughts of the human that finally made him drift into a nightmare-filled sleep.

The night was cold and his fingers could barely hold onto the reins. Tlonna was shivering next to him on her horse. They were clothed in brown and gray clothes that did little to ward off the cold. He turned his head to the side; something was moving within the forest. Tlonna had heard it too. The trees next to him rustled unnaturally. He heard Tlonna draw her sword, and he copied her. Shadows detached from the trees and exploded toward the elves. Two of them slammed into Losolin, knocking him off his horse. Tlonna shrieked somewhere behind him. Losolin could not get his arm free to use his blade. A fist smashed into his face over and over again. The elf lurched around, trying to free himself.

Tlonna screamed, and then fell silent. Losolin's mind whirled. Blood covered his face and his nose felt broken, but he refused to give in. One of his attackers kicked him hard in the groin and he bellowed in pain. Lights danced before his eyes. The steel-toed boot slammed into his groin again, and Losolin lost consciousness.

When next he woke he was in a whitewashed room tied to a splintery old table. His hands and feet were stretched by chains so that he could not move. A door opened. Four men came into the room holding jars filled with blue liquid that hissed and bubbled with every move. They surrounded him and laughed. One of them forced his mouth open and shoved a glass tube down his throat. Losolin gagged, unable to breath. The man tipped his jar into the tube and Losolin gurgled a scream as he felt it burning down into this stomach. Bile rose, choking him further. Each man tipped his jar into the tube, forcing it into him. He felt fire in his brain, behind his eyes, in his gut.

Finally they stopped, the pain still raging in his body. When he was able to open his eyes, he saw a blurry vision of a man standing at his feet. Pain sliced across the arches of his feet and Losolin felt warm blood gush down over his heels. He jerked on the splintery table, trying to free himself. One of the men was holding a long needle attached to a glass bulb. A brown sludge filled the egg-sized bulb. The man jabbed the needle into Losolin's neck. He screamed.

"Losolin! Wake up!" Tlonna kneeled over him as he writhed and gasped for breath.

The male let out a cry and convulsed. Tlonna shook him and he opened his eyes.

"Are you all right? You were having a nightmare," she said.

Losolin sat up slowly, holding his head between his hands. His neck throbbed. When the male brushed his fingers against the pain, though, no blood glistened as he had expected. The pain receded.

"They tortured me..." he whispered.

"Who?" Tlonna asked, frowning slightly. She brushed a

strand of hair from his face. The intimacy of the motion shocked her, and she withdrew her hand.

Losolin shook his head, his eyes closed. "I do not know. It was no nightmare, though. It was a memory."

"A memory? Losolin, what are you talking about?"

"It bloody happened, Tlonna. I do not remember it, but I know it happened. It was too real. Why do I not remember it...?" the male said, his voice trailing away.

Tlonna stared at him. She had been pressed so tight against his body that when he had started thrashing around, she had nearly been hit. His presence comforted her more than it should. He was a stranger, and a dangerous one at that.

"...drugged with some... poison and then stabbed in the neck... we were bloody riding together..." Losolin was muttering, glaring at the lilac bush.

Tlonna waited. When he continued to mutter for another minute, she sighed. Gathering all her willpower and her determination, the Magin touched his face. He cut off instantly, looking at her with wide eyes. Tlonna pushed him down and then crawled onto him. With her cheek warm against his chest, she wrapped one hand in his hair and curled the other around his shoulder.

Losolin did not breathe, but she could feel his heart beating rapidly against her arm. When he finally took a breath, it was deep and long.

"Sleep, Losolin, and I will guard you from dreams," she whispered, half asleep herself.

Losolin grimaced at the top of her head. If she thought lying on top of him would stop dreams, she was badly mistaken. But he rested his hands against her hips, and fell asleep. His dreams were pleasant.

He woke a few hours later and did his best not to jump. Tlonna had half slid off his body in her sleep, but their legs were entangled and her shirt was twisted halfway up her back. His left arm was numb from the elbow down, where her head rested, though his fingers were wrapped in her belt just below the small of her back. One of her arms was tucked under her body, and the other was light atop his chest, her fingers curled loosely on his sternum.

She murmured in her sleep, and he did jump. Tlonna murmured again and burrowed her face into his armpit. Losolin frowned at her. She was making it very difficult not to take advantage. Her shirt was shoved up far enough to reveal the slightest curve of her breast. Muttering quietly, Losolin laid his head back and silently cursed the gods.

Tlonna woke slowly, opening first one eye, then the other, then closing them just as slowly. She was comfortable, and her head was cradled gently in something warm and pleasant. There was a pleasurable hint of harvest, not overpowering, but soothing and slightly arousing. Still in a sleepy haze, Tlonna moved her free arm and her hand brushed something solid, a leather belt. She trailed her fingers up and met a bump...a nipple.

Jerking away, Tlonna shook her head and stared at Losolin. He had his eyes closed, but his jaw was set and his hands were clenched. He opened his eyes and turned his head to glower at her.

"Do you do that on purpose?" he grumbled, his voice huskier than usual.

"Do what?" Tlonna squeaked.

"Arouse me until I can hardly stand it, then stop, leaving me about to burst?" the male grunted.

"I...I...*nooo*. No. Oh...Losolin I am so sorry," Tlonna breathed, pulling her shirt down.

"Yeah well..." Losolin mumbled, sitting up. There was a red spot on his bicep where her head had been.

"You smell good," Tlonna blurted, and then put her hands to her mouth in humiliation.

The male squinted at her, then smoothed his face until it was expressionless. He blinked once. Twice. Tlonna bit her lip.

"You did not stop me from dreaming," he said suddenly.

"What? You had another nightmare?" Tlonna replied too quickly.

Losolin's lips twitched into a smile. "No, a dream. Several, in fact. You were considerably less clothed and considerably more forthcoming with your teases."

Tlonna blushed, then opened her mouth in indignation. She launched herself at him, but her caught her wrists and pinned her to the ground. The Magin tried to glare at him. Her lips would not stay where she wanted them to, but rather curled upward until she found herself grinning. Losolin was succeeding in his glare however. Feeling mischievous, Tlonna moved her hips slightly. Losolin's eye twitched.

Tlonna grinned. A laugh bubbled out of her until she was giggling like a girl. Losolin's glare faded, and he too was laughing within seconds. The sound of it filled Tlonna with joy. Then he moved *his* hips. Tlonna's giggles turned into a moan. And another. Losolin still had her wrists pinned above her head. Her body was beginning to ache for him. She arched her back, and suddenly Losolin was standing.

She rolled her head to stare at him. He was smiling, though there was a playful malice to it that made her sigh.

"Now you know how it feels," he said, and left the grove.

Tlonna laughed once, then grimaced. Her body was too warm, her breasts tender, between her thighs...

It took her almost five minutes to gather herself and leave the grove.

Miazie strode over to Tlonna and dropped a blue silk bag in the elf's hands.

"What is this Miazie?" Tlonna asked, straining to keep her voice normal. Losolin was standing with some of the soldiers from Anutch. He ignored her.

"These are the talisman stones of the fifteen First Magins. They are very powerful and must be used very carefully. They may be used to heal, destroy, or transfer magic into another non-Magin and make them half Magin, any number of things. I found them in the binding of one of your books."

Tlonna bounced the bag in her hand. "Okay then, will you explain them to me on the ride?"

"Ride?"

"Aye, I want to leave here. Where is the closest town?"

The human rubbed her chin and stared at the horizon behind Tlonna. "Probably Kiys, Capital of Talenias. About a week's ride from here, I think."

"Then to Kiys it is," Tlonna said smiling.

Tlonna turned to the camp sprawled behind her and raised her voice so they could all hear her. "We leave today, now, for the city of Kiys. Can you all be ready within...a half hour?"

The humans murmured in assent and started striking camp. Sooner than expected, they were saddling their horses. One of the spares was brought forth and given to Losolin, a long-legged gelding.

The days went slowly by as the group trudged along an old path through the dense and silent forest. They hardly heard a bird or small animal around them, and Miazie spoke quietly while telling her the story of the fifteen stones, their god-derived names and their purposes. Tlonna put her hand on the hilt of her sword as they passed an outlet to the path they traveled. Her hand bumped against her hip and she felt the bag tied to her belt. She fingered the bag and felt the sharp edge of a rock.

She called a halt at the approach of nightfall as they came into a small clearing. As she stretched her cloak out on the ground, Tlonna watched Losolin help pitch the tent he now shared with one of the soldiers. So absorbed in watching the elf, she didn't hear Miazie approach.

"That boy wants you, Tlonna," the human whispered, jerking her head toward Losolin.

Tlonna grinned. "I know."

Miazie arched an eyebrow. "Is this a good thing, then?"

Tlonna laughed quietly. "I do not know. I like him, though. And he is just so wonderful to look at. We have already had some close encounters, though, and they are odd. Just so absolutely spectacularly wonderful to look at. Do you not think?"

Startled by the question, Miazie jerked a shoulder. "I...well...yeah."

Tlonna grinned again and slapped her friend heartily on the back, sending the woman sprawling. "Oh! Sorry!"

While Miazie got to her feet, guffawing, Losolin strode over. Smiling uncertainly at the chortling human, the male touched Tlonna on the arm. The female jumped, startled, and then blushed crimson.

"Losolin! Oh...we were just-" she caught herself. "Yes?"

Now completely bewildered, Losolin's smile sickened. Clearing his throat, he looked at the ground.

"I, well, I thought it might be a good idea to do some basic training with these people. I was talking to Christian and he said most of them were merchants or nobles with no fighting skills whatsoever. I have seen you fight and so I know you know more than I. Will you help me and then, in due time, them?"

Tlonna stared at him wide-eyed. "Uhm...yes. Yes I will."

The male nodded his thanks and strode away.

She called back to him. "When do you want to start?"

Losolin shrugged. "Whenever."

Tlonna bit her lip and nodded, thinking. "Tomorrow night?"

"Sounds good," Losolin called from his tent.

Grinning like a fool, Tlonna turned to the still chuckling Miazie. "I am going to train him."

Miazie nodded. "You must fight like a warrior, if he admits you are better than him," she said, admiringly.

Tlonna nodded and then bid her friend goodnight.

It felt as though she had just closed her eyes when frantic yelling awoke her. She wondered if she would ever just get to sleep in. "Tlonna! Tlonna, wake up! Get up!"

Miazie was shaking her, hard. The elf grimaced and caught the woman's flailing hands. "Stop it. What is wrong?"

"You are her! You are Everwood! Curse it Tlonna, you are the bleeding Princess of Blackhaven!"

These words hit Tlonna like a slap in the face. She sat up so fast she knocked Miazie over.

"What?"

Miazie looked half-crazed. Her hair was tangled as though she had constantly played with it, her eyes puffy with exhaustion. She shook a book in Tlonna's face, *Legends of the Moons.*

"This is your family history, Tlonna. It is all here! From Jair all the way down to you. It even describes you! Seven foot three, pale blue eyes, hair down to your mid-back, I mean, it is longer now, but it has been eight years. That's why you have the stones of the Magins! Tlonna Arune Ewôsdírn, that is your name! You are Everwood!"

Tlonna squinted, her head suddenly pounding. She glanced down at the silver bangle on her wrist. She held it out to Miazie.

"What does that say?"

Miazie grabbed her hand and yanked the bracelet off.

"It says your name, Tlonna. It says Tlonna Arune Ewôsdírn."

Suddenly pain beyond imagination gripped Tlonna. She couldn't scream, for her throat had tightened. Fire ripped through her body, slashing like a poisoned knife. Her body went rigid and she fell backward. Back arching extremely, Tlonna's eyes strained open, fingers clawed into the ground.

Miazie shrieked, stumbling away from the prostrate elf.

"Losolin! Reb... Rebecca! Losolin!"

Losolin launched himself across the camp half dressed, and looking thunderous. "What in the nine hells did you do?"

Miazie's mouth opened and closed uselessly before she whispered roughly, "Nothing!"

The woman, Rebecca, joined them a few seconds later, curly hair flying. Tlonna gasped again as her body loosened, allowing her to breathe. Before she could pull in another full breath, her body tensed again. Losolin crouched over her, his strong hands gripping her waist.

"Tlonna, come on love, listen to me. Tlonna, no... no, stop," he said the last when Tlonna's unblinking eyes started to tear.

Miazie gripped Losolin's broad shoulders, her thin fingers digging into them.

"What is wrong with her? What is happening?"

The elf shook his head, staring at the female by his feet. "I do not know."

Rebecca attempted to push Losolin away and then gave up when he didn't even tilt an inch. The human scooted around to the other side of the female and pressed her hands to Tlonna's throat.

"She's not breathing!"

Losolin snorted. "Obviously. There is nothing we can do. It is... magic."

The crowd that had grown around Tlonna went suddenly still. The only sound was the quiet, sporadic gasps that came from Tlonna every time her body relaxed for a second.

Tlonna could hear the voices of two women and a man, but they floated around like so many whispers. Her mind was encased in a fiery labyrinth of pain. Visions swirled around behind her eyes, pausing only to allow glimpses of scenes that, when vaguely recognized, brought only more agony. She'd have screamed if she could, convulsed and flung herself about, but she couldn't. The pain was too horrible. Her body relaxed and she felt Losolin's hands on her, cool and strong.

Terrified that if she went under again, she might not make it out, Tlonna clutched at his hand. "Please," she gasped, forcing her eyes to stare directly into Losolin's.

His dark blue irises were overwhelmed by the dilated pupils. Worried and frustrated lines were carved into his forehead and he looked impossibly beautiful. Tlonna wheezed in a breath as she stared at him, the many colored moons high in the dark sky illuminating his hair, wreathing it in golden light. She wheezed again as her body contorted, her muscles tightening.

The elf strained to hold on to the god-like image of Losolin watching her, but her vision darkened again and she was lost.

Miazie had tears in her eyes as she watched her friend suffer. Rebecca now held a wet rag to Tlonna's chest, trying to keep her cool. Losolin stared at the female clutching his wrist painfully hard. Torment raged through him. He wanted to help her, wanted to take the pain away, but he couldn't. Knowing this frustrated him beyond words. Somewhere in his mind lurked a need to heal, to ease the suffering of others. And somewhere along with that thought was another, a harder one to understand. He knew this elf, this beautiful, entrancing, annoyingly difficult female.

She was digging gouges deep into his flesh with her nails, short as they were. Bruises were already forming under her fingers. He welcomed the pain. It connected him to her, helped her.

"How can I help you?" Losolin whispered, imploring Tlonna to hear him. "What do you need?"

With his free hand he wiped away the blood now squeezing out of her eye like a vivid tear. Somewhere, a vein had burst. Rebecca removed the cloth and looked up at Losolin.

"She has to get through this herself. There is nothing we can do. I'm sorry. We should move her somewhere safe."

Losolin nodded. "Is there a tent we can borrow?"

The soldier he had been sharing with stepped forward. "I can bunk somewhere else, Lord Losolin. You can have my tent."

The male bowed his head. "My thanks, James."

He gently peeled Tlonna's fingers from his arm and picked her up. It was like picking up a log. She was stiff and tense, another bloody tear leaking from her eye. Losolin carried her to James's tent. He gently laid Tlonna down on his bedroll and wiped away the blood.

Every few minutes, Tlonna would relax and suck in breath, gasping out meaningless words.

He watched her all night, wiping the occasionally bloody tear away or letting her squeeze his wrists so tight his hands went numb. When the sky started to lighten, Miazie came in to check on her.

"Have you stayed up all night?" she asked him when she ducked into the tent.

"Aye, she has not gotten any better," Losolin replied, looking up at her. "What happened last night?"

Miazie frowned at him. "I don't catch your meaning."

"You were with her when this started, were you not? I want to know what happened just before," the male snapped wearily.

Miazie paled a little. "I... I know who she is. I told her."

"And who is she?"

The human fixed him with a dark look. "The Everwood Princess, Tlonna Arune Ewôsdírn, heir to the Wind Throne of Blackhaven."

Suddenly Losolin knew, as though something had clicked in his mind. "Yes, she is betrothed to Iyaner Lostug of Seaduens... but she had a lover, a consort who was... is... of low status. They both disappeared eight years ago, and Tlonna turned up having been skinned alive," he scowled. "But then how is she here?"

Miazie scowled with him. "I don't kn-" She cut off suddenly, paling further. "Midian, he's a Magin. He... he made an illusion of her, took her captive, and erased her memory. Along with..." she made a face and then hissed, "*you*!"

Losolin looked up sharply. "What?" he snapped.

"You grimy, worthless, lying son of a codger! I'll break your filthy little neck!" Miazie screamed and launched herself at Losolin.

The elf ducked out of the way and grabbed Miazie's shoulder before she could whip around. He slammed the human down onto her knees with one hand and kept the pressure on her shoulder so that she couldn't rise. His head suddenly pounded worse than ever before. His chest felt impossibly tight.

He pointed an accusing finger at her blazing eyes. "You have no right," he growled softly. "You have no right."

Miazie's face twisted venomously, but she stayed silent, glaring up at him. She was eye to eye with his naked stomach, which was tightened angrily.

Losolin's voice softened fractionally. "But...you may be right in saying I was taken with her," he screwed up his face, thinking. "I have a memory, but it seems awkward, as though parts were taken from it. I woke up one morning about a year ago, hazy minded and injured. I wandered around until I had the sudden urge to go to

Seaduens. I joined the White Hand Warriors and traveled around Nymyños tracking and destroying bandits and rogues. I have memories of growing up in Blackhaven City, of having family and friends, but I cannot remember their names. I know when I look at Tlonna, I feel all squirmy inside as though if she left, I might die from sadness. I want to be around her all the time. I want to touch her, know her, love her," he finished in a whisper, staring at the still torturously tense elf on his sleeping roll.

Miazie had felt his hand loosen its grip when he started talking about Tlonna, but she stayed on her knees, staring up at the gorgeous male before her. His face had lost its anger and was suffused instead with pained sadness. His head was turned so Miazie could see the pulse in his neck throbbing heartily.

Suddenly, Losolin moved away from her and knelt beside Tlonna. He placed his hands gingerly on each side of her face and stared down at her. He ran the fingers of one hand through her hair and then down her arm. He was kneeling beside Tlonna as though in prayer.

"Tlonna..." his voice came out hoarse and quiet. "Come back to me."

Tlonna didn't respond. Miazie still knelt on the ground, feeling immensely guilty. She watched the elves for a full minute before trying to stand. She couldn't. Losolin had slammed her so hard into the ground her knees had sunk into the soft earth beneath the tent. She had to crawl away and then stand, immediately regretting it. Pain lanced up and down her legs. Her back felt as though it was two inches too short.

Feeling horrible and awkward, the human limped out of the tent and went back to her own. There, she flopped down on her bedroll and wept.

Tlonna did not come out of her agonizing torment until late that night. She came out of it with a gasp and shudder. She blinked the blood out of her eyes and then moved gingerly to look at the male beside her. Losolin was next to her, asleep. He was flat on his back, knees up in the air as though he had merely fallen back from sitting with his knees drawn up to his chest. He looked so exhausted, even in sleep.

Tlonna moved to sit up and bit back a moan. She felt as though she had been rigorously training for a month without stop, she was so sore. The relief of being out of the pain-filled abyss was overwhelming though, and she almost smiled. Losolin stirred. She touched his arm.

The male shot upward and then rushed her. His hands covered her face, her arms, waist, legs, back to her face, finally digging into her hair. He stared at her. He stared and stared. Tlonna began to feel a blush creep up from her chest. He didn't seem to be breathing, or have a need to blink.

She opened her mouth to speak but he beat her to it.

"How... how are you feeling?"

"Like I have been beaten to the very last inch of my life. You?"

"I..." his eye twitched. It was a sign of strain. Tlonna recognized it now. He had a very odd look on his face, as though she were a species he had never seen before and he very much wanted to find out what she was.

Tlonna swallowed audibly. "Losolin...?"

"Do you," he began slowly, "remember me?"

Tlonna was about to reply with a snide, "I just bloody met you," but she didn't. Suddenly, painfully, a memory swam to the forefront of the others. It was of her and Losolin kissing. They were naked. He was *in* her. Tlonna blinked it away hurriedly, blushing crimson.

"Yes," she whispered. "Yes I do."

Losolin's face lit up with hope. "What do you remember?"

"I-" she tried to find the words, "we were...are...were...are?" She blinked at him.

Losolin waited.

The words came out in a rush. "We were together kissing we were *together.*"

A faint blush appeared in Losolin's taught cheeks. "We were making love," he said monotonously, "because we are *in* love."

Silence greeted his words, Tlonna had gone very still. Finally, she took a deep breath. "I know."

"You do?"

"Aye. Ever since the grove, I have wanted you. I have wanted to touch you, explore every inch of you," she blushed deeper, her voice dropping to a mortified whisper. "I thought, after Anutch, I would never want to be touched in that way again, but I do, by you.

And not just because," she gestured lamely at his attractively muscled abdomen, "but because you bring out in me... something. I do not know what, except that... I... I... want all of you. Mind, body, heart, I want it all," Tlonna finished, shaking with humiliation.

Losolin opened his mouth slightly and just sat there for a moment. Then he leaned forward, took her chin in his hand, and kissed her. It wasn't like the time he had ravished her mouth in the pool, but gentle, close-lipped, and slow. When Tlonna's fingers found his shoulders, he deepened the kiss, opening his mouth and taking hers hostage. Tlonna's body was still unbelievably sore, but she pressed herself against him when he drew her close.

She was trembling uncontrollably. Losolin smoothed his hands down her back and then gripped her waist. Memories were flooding their minds, filling in blank spots as they embraced. It seemed the longer they held each other, the more vivid and connected the memories became. Visions of grand balls and masquerades, soft kisses, laughing escapades with faceless friends, hot and sweaty nights of intense passion, and a terrified ride through the night.

When they finally parted, they were breathless from both the kiss and the memories. A fire burned in Tlonna's eyes, while it simmered, hot and restless, in Losolin. They were standing, now, in the middle of the tent. Still tightly embraced, they gazed into each other's eyes and felt years of love and companionship rush back to them.

Tlonna reached up and brushed away a strand of hair that had blown in front of Losolin's face. He smiled.

"Tlonna..." he said quietly, but there was a world of meaning behind it.

Tlonna smiled back, tears in her eyes. "Oh, Losolin, how could I have forgotten you? How? You are my everything, the half that makes me whole, the reason I am alive."

Losolin shook his head and shushed her. "Do not worry about it, love. I forgot, too. But now, now everything is right. We are together."

The Magin nodded and gazed up at him, memories still flooding in to deepen her love and affection for the male that held her. Losolin dipped his head to nuzzle her neck a bit before turning his mouth to her ear.

"I love you."

Those words sent Tlonna reeling. She grabbed his bare shoulders and pulled him down as she sat on his bedroll. Laughing, he undressed her and then himself. She reached up to him as he positioned himself over her. Their lips met, and then their bodies. Tlonna felt him slide inside and grinned as he fit like a key to a lock.

"I love you too," she whispered.

They made love until the sun rose.

Chapter 3
Learning

Days passed, and then a week, and another, as they moved slowly through the forest Miazie had called the Cleshnoe. Food and tempers ran short as the cold seeped through the land. They bundled up in layers of clothing, rubbing their hands together and breathing into them.

Miazie and Tlonna were often prone to arguing about supplies. Tlonna thought they should make rations a bit smaller, while Miazie blatantly refused.

"We are going to run out of food if everyone keeps eating the way they do!" Tlonna bellowed at Miazie at camp, for the fifth or sixth time.

She and Losolin now had a tent of their own, having badgered Miazie into making one out of the hide of deer they had killed a week earlier. Losolin was setting it up, plainly trying to ignore the argument. He still had the borrowed deep purple cloak lined with silver, and he had it draped over his shoulders like a stole. His blond head was bent away from the two females.

Miazie rounded on him. "Why don't you talk some sense into her? She wants us all to starve!"

Losolin straightened with a sigh. "Look, Miazie, I agree with Tlonna. We are not sure how far the closest village is, and it is almost winter."

Tlonna sent him a beaming smile while Miazie huffed, her breath frosting in the air before her.

The woman threw her arms up in the air. "Fine, whatever you say, you're elves which means you must be by far wiser than any of us regular humans! Have it your way, we'll starve sooner rather than later."

Losolin rubbed a hand over his face. "Miazie, you know that is not what we meant. Come on. I mean, obviously we are wiser than any human," he said with a grin, "but we starve just as surely as you do."

Tlonna couldn't help herself. She laughed as Miazie stomped away, cursing.

The snow fell thick after that. The company trudged through it. The horses nibbled at the sparse grass and tough pine needles as they passed. Takîreaes whuffled loudly every time he was forced to eat the needles, as though disgusted. Neñyos, Losolin's gelding, seemed perfectly happy however, and would tug stubbornly at the branches.

Later in the week, a few of the hunters found a herd of giant deer and were able to pick off three before they bolted out of range. Miazie and her women salted the meat and stored it in baskets woven from pine branches. The night after the successful hunt, Miazie strode over to where Tlonna and Losolin were huddled by their fire.

"We need to talk," she said softly, looking a bit frightened.

"Then talk," Tlonna replied cautiously.

The human sat down and stared into the fire. "You know who you are now, and we know who Losolin is. We are all on the same page, as far as that," she dropped her eyes to her folded legs.

"Yes..." Tlonna said, again cautiously.

"There is a prophecy, a major prophecy, you see. And it revolves around you. I don't usually put much store in prophecy as it usually turns out to be interpreted totally wrong, but this one is different. You know the one of which I speak," Miazie mumbled to her knees.

Tlonna squinted a bit. "The one that made you start to climb the cliff side, and then fall on me?"

"Aye, that's the one," the woman took a deep breath and recited, "*I have seen it, the possible end of days. I sat in my parlor and it came upon me like a heathenish voice coming from the deep ninth hell. Images of blackness, never-ending winter. Snow, which is so pure and white blanketed the land in waves of inky tainted midnight, like ash. The sun shone dark, and nothing but demons lived. It will come when those of great power are born, the descendants of my time. Their blood will run stronger and thicker than any others in their far time. There is no branching from this vision, I know. It will come, and only those with the truest and most honorable of hearts will be able to defeat this poison of evil. It will begin when the greatest of kingdoms fall, when the winter is bitterest, and the one many times prophesied is born.*

"You are the one many times prophesied, and the greatest of kingdoms has fallen, Blackhaven. This weather, right at the start of winter, is colder than it has been in these parts for hundreds of years, maybe even thousands. That seals the prophecy as valid, as these things have all happened in succession."

Tlonna shrugged. "So? What about it?"

Losolin glanced at her and then poked at the fire a little. Miazie watched him a moment before explaining. "It marks the beginning of war and devastation that will swallow Nymyños whole if we don't do something to stop it. There are others involved in the prophecy, but they are hidden as of now. There is another prophecy, a sort of branch from this one, that says an army must be massed to defeat the hoards of evil, and they must be led by the Everwood, who we know to be you."

Tlonna felt a slight pang in her head when the word Everwood was spoken. She rubbed her temple. "All right."

Miazie looked exasperated. "Tlonna, somehow, you need to get an army and march on...somewhere."

Tlonna looked bored. "Yes, I caught that part. What I want to know is how I am supposed to get this great invisible army so I can march on an unknown place. Really, I am not going to worry about something impossible."

"You are the princess of Blackhaven, nothing is impossible for you," Miazie said imploringly.

Tlonna snorted, "Blackhaven, a grand city which you tell me has been defeated and everyone slaughtered. Not much help there, Miazie."

The human raised her eyes to the heavens. "There are still people around who are willing to fight. I mean, out of little Anutch you've got forty."

"Oh yeah," Tlonna said heatedly. "A bunch of hunters and high born fruitcakes. The only reason most of them came is you. Sure, there are a few strong soldiers, like Tyre and James, and Christian, but most of them are more concerned about the fashion in the cities. Will they be up to date? Will they be invited to parties? Come on Miazie, you know as well as I that we cannot count on them for strong physical ability. They are good people," she said consolingly to Miazie's upset look, "but they are not fighters. So, until I have thought something up, there is no use worrying about cryptic prophecy."

Miazie reluctantly agreed. "Fine, fine. But I want to know your plan as soon as you have it, all right?"

"Yeah, all right," Tlonna conceded, absentmindedly lacing her fingers with Losolin's.

Miazie gave them a sour look. "And people are starting to wonder what it is exactly that you do in that tent of yours."

Losolin grinned. "That is none of their business, now is it?"

"No, but they still wonder what is going on when light flares brightly for a couple of hours at a time each night."

Tlonna shrugged, slightly embarrassed. "When I am happy, flames seem to be bolstered."

"For three and four hours a night? My gods, even the most fit of humans have a problem with that," Miazie said, a bit put off.

Losolin grinned even wider. "We are elves, Miazie. We can control it a lot longer, make it last, and we have many times the stamina humans have. We could go hours more than we do, but we need sleep."

"Hours?"

Losolin nodded. His eyes were gleaming in the firelight, making him look slightly roguish. Miazie looked stunned, and more than a little jealous. She stood up suddenly.

"Well, I think that is enough for tonight. I...I am going to bed."

Tlonna and Losolin stood after her, smiling broadly.

As they turned into their tent, the elves heard Miazie invite one of the soldiers into hers.

Tlonna jerked awake in the early hours of the morning. Losolin was sleeping a few inches from her on his side. His head was pillowed on his bicep, his breathing deep and even. For a full minute, Tlonna lay still, listening. *Something* had woken her. Her ears straining, she heard it. A rustle of velvet outside her tent, a quiet mutter. Losolin tensed next to her, and Tlonna put a finger to his lips.

His eyes glittered in the dark, watching the entrance to the tent. It moved marginally. Slowly, he leaned back and picked up his sword. The murmuring outside continued. The elves moved onto their feet, crouching. Tlonna reached for her magic and felt it swell inside until she was sure she must have been glowing. Losolin looked at her, then at the flaps. She nodded.

Silently, they burst out of their tent and rammed into a cluster of bodies. Grunts and curses filled the nights, but not loud enough to cause alarm. Losolin's blade flashed in the multicolored glow of the moons. White lightning sizzled out of Tlonna's fingers and down from the sky. One of the velvet clad figures shrieked as it sizzled. Lights appeared in the tents.

Losolin spun, grim faced, yanking his sword out of a falling body. Black blood squirted through the air. Anutchian men stopped dead in their tracks. Most of them were half dressed, some not at all. The last black-shrouded intruder fell with a thud as Tlonna casually stepped away from him, velvet robes smoking.

Seven bodies lay sprawled in a circle around the two elves. The fight had taken less than a minute. Lightning still crackled around Tlonna, but it seemed to be fading. The humans watched it warily. The rest of the night was still, and storm-less. Tlonna herself looked stunned.

"I did not know I could do that," she said quietly as Losolin bent down to clean his sword on black robes.

"You are new to your power, love. You still have a long way to go, yet," he replied.

Miazie appeared, wrapped in a blanket and nothing else. Christian, the soldier she had taken to bed, was naked. The woman did not look abashed, but a little worried.

"Darkwights, again. They know you, now," she said calmly, nudging one of the demons with a toe. "Midian knows you are alive, then. Let us hope he knows only that."

Losolin suddenly noticed the stares of the humans. He shoved the point of his sword into the ground. "What?"

James cleared his throat twice before speaking. "Can you teach us? To fight like that, I mean."

Tlonna frowned at him. "Yes. But you are soldiers. You should already know."

Tyre shook his head. "No. We could not take down seven Shadowspawn in less than a minute, not without taking wounds as well. But you are elves, and we have no magic either."

Losolin shrugged. "We will do what we can. But for now, we might as well get moving. None of us will sleep more tonight."

The humans murmured their assent and hurried off to their own tents. Miazie smiled at Christian as he turned back toward her tent, but she moved closer to the elves.

"This attack was aimed at you. None of the others were bothered. Tlonna, if Midian knows where you are, he knows by far more than we want him to. He must be watching us."

The Magin nodded absently. "Aye, I know. There are creatures in the forest under his will, I would say. And others too, I suspect. People, demons."

Miazie glanced at the trees. Her voice was steady, but the elves saw the tightness in her face, the fear. "The war has begun before we had a chance to see our enemy. We must get to Talenias."

"What is in Talenias?" Losolin asked.

The woman gave him a cool stare before answering. "People."

Chapter 4
Informative Mists

As night drew near the next day, Losolin emerged from the tent and stretched. Snow was falling from the deepening sky. His head still swam with pain, but it was a dull throbbing. Feeling the need to stretch his legs, the elf wandered around the camp until the stares made him hurry back to his tent. Ducking under the flaps, he saw Tlonna sitting on the ground before a pile of ordinary looking rocks.

"Those are the stones Miazie gave you, are they not?" he said.

"Yes. Miazie said that if they were all put in this pattern," she indicated the spiral of stones, "and I Wove a stream of power into them, they would show me something."

"Is that wise? Tlonna, you know only a fraction of the details of magic."

"Aye, and how am I supposed to learn more when I am the only Magin available?"

Losolin shrugged, a little irritated. "Do what you must then."

Tlonna sent him a smoldering look and he squinted back at her, resisting the urge to tumble her as a distraction. Then she smiled, and felt his knees go weak. It had been such a long time he had not known her, and she was so beautiful it was almost painful to look at her directly. Before he realized he had moved, Losolin was running his hands through her hair, caressing her mouth with his.

"Ah Losolin," she murmured, "being here with you, having lost eight years of our love, it seems unreal. I do not understand it, but I know that you are my heart."

"Shh..." Losolin replied, tugging at her laces. "Do not dwell on the past when the present is so sweet."

"Losolin." Tlonna's voice had changed, it was no longer soft and husky. "Losolin get off me."

"What? What is wrong?" the male said, complying immediately, and then he saw her fear.

The air swirled and flashed as though there was a tiny thunderstorm in the tent, above the fifteen Magin stones. Tlonna stared at it in rapture, her mussed appearance making her look like a creature given ecstasy by the gods, the initial fear fading, replaced by serene desire.

"What is it?" he asked her quietly.

"I do not know, but look, you can see shapes moving, fighting, I think. I wish it were clearer," Tlonna whispered back, her voice shaking. She did not move her eyes from the roiling air.

Losolin frowned, leaning closer to get a better look, but he could see only the swirling mist.

"I do not see anything. Tlonna..." he looked back at her and cursed.

Tlonna had stretched out her hand and touched the mist. It flashed and became clearer and the sounds of war flooded the tent. Tlonna gasped and yanked her hand back. Losolin slanted a look at her before studying the image within the mist. It was still murky to him, but he could see figures struggling back and forth, Men, Elves, Magins, and many other small folk as well. In the foreground, a lovely, ferocious elf wielded a bow with great skill, her face a more exotic, older image of Tlonna's.

By the time Losolin was able to draw his gaze away from the disturbing image, Tlonna was standing, her eyes riveted on it. She put her hand out again and touched it. Then her body was half emerged in the swirling mass. Losolin lunged forward and grabbed her foot before it entered and she was completely submerged. He pulled and she kicked her leg to shake him off. He pulled again, putting all his strength into it and she was flung out of the mist and tossed onto the rocks. The picture flashed and was gone. Tlonna gasped and blinked. She sat up and looked around.

She was breathing fast and her eyes were round with fear. He laid a hand on her arm and she jumped. There was a gash across her shirt, though the flesh was untouched.

"What the flaming nine hells were you thinking?" he yelled.

"She was calling me, that elf, she was my ancestor. I do not know what came over me, but I had to help them. The elves were being driven back."

Losolin sighed, giving up before even trying to reason with her. "I will go get Miazie, she will know, though I think that was the Council War when the elves and the Little Folk were forced out of the forest."

"Yes, get Miazie then," Tlonna said absently, fingering the stone created by Roluf Gwemheoad, *Harpadaimôn*.

When Losolin returned with Miazie, he glowered at his lover before sitting down, deliberately scattering the stones. Miazie sent him an odd look, but she settled herself. "Losolin says you called on the stones?"

Tlonna unexpectedly flushed, which startled both her companions. "I was going to ward the tent of sight and sound so that Losolin and I could... that no one would know what we were... well it got away from me and I guess I sent a Weave into the spiral."

Ignoring the blushing female and mildly annoyed Losolin, Miazie stared at the scattered stones. "You put them in the Triad Spiral? Were you planning on calling upon them without a guide on how to do so?"

"Yes." Tlonna said bluntly, daring the human to berate her for it.

"Tlonna, you are beyond powerful, you can't afford to make mistakes like this. The stones were created for a reason, do not underestimate their strength. As the rightful heir to them, you will have a different effect on what they do. Losolin said he could barely see what was happening. It was very clear to you, though, wasn't it?"

Tlonna nodded silently. Miazie shook her head despondently.

"Don't ever do that again. Don't ever call on them again. What you saw, if I understand Losolin's description, is the Council War, foremost, Tonora, Jair's mother, your ancestor." Miazie sighed. "Fifteen ordinary rocks turned into awesomely powerful tools of magic and war. The Magins who created them were no less dangerous and potent. What you saw in the mist was real. It is a portal, of sorts, that works only one way. Had you gone all the way in, you would never have come out. Understand?"

The blood had drained from Tlonna's face and she nodded again. The tent was silent and awkward as the three stared at the stones.

Losolin broke the quiet. "These stones are very valuable, and dangerous. Midian wants to have them for himself, understandably. They would make him truly invincible. It would also give him motive to attack Blackhaven, as the descendents of Magins are prominent in the Ewôsdírn bloodline. They would be the most likely candidates for having them. They should be destroyed. Here. Now."

The woman was staring at the pile, her face twisted in

concentration. "You may be right, but the stones can only be destroyed by the combined power of the Magins that created them, or by fifteen extremely strong Magins of this era. Midian does indeed want the stones and to be King of Nymyños. There has not been a King of Nymyños in thousands of years, before the First Magins even."

"I thought there were twelve kingdoms, with the Liberated Lands between them," Tlonna asked, frowning.

"I thought you had regained your memory," Miazie grumped.

Tlonna blushed. "Only about... certain things. Certain people." She pointedly looked at Losolin.

Miazie made a face. "Brandon Stynbek was the last King of Nymyños. He ruled after his father, only the third. In that time, the dwarves swore fealty to Brandon first, to stem the slaughter of their people, but the elves clung to their freedom, they were the first on Nymyños, and the oldest race as well. But they could not win against the amassed armies of both Man and Dwarf. They were all imprisoned, or killed. That is where they lost their true immortality. Elves cannot live in shadow and despair, their...your...hearts break."

Losolin and Tlonna scowled at Miazie in unison. It was the male who spoke. "Our people are not so weak as that. Die of a broken heart," he scoffed.

Miazie glared at him. "They were jailed underground with never a chance of sunlight. They were tormented and made to eat sewage. They were forced to watch their friends and family tortured to death. They had boiling water and other such things tossed on them, as they stood helpless in cells packed so tight they could not move. They lost the will to live, Losolin. It was no weakness."

Both the elves looked down in shame. Miazie continued as though she had not been interrupted. "Twenty-four years later, an elf named Furntil Eldrout, an assassin, escaped from his cell. He scaled the castle walls and broke into the king's chamber. Furntil stuck the king with a dozen arrows and then hung Brandon out his window by his robes. Furntil escaped and let the elves free. In the morning, man and dwarf awoke to a dead king with no heir, and the elves gone. On the king's bed, Furntil had left a single white arrow. That is why assassins are held in great esteem in elf communities, rather than feared and shunned like usual.

"The elves were not seen again by human or dwarf for nearly

seventy years, until the Magin's time. Furntil was considered a great hero and was made King of Elves, and remains one to this day. It is said he died, but no body or burial site has ever been found."

"How do you know all this history, Miazie? This cannot all be recorded," Losolin asked suddenly.

"No, not all of it, some of it through stories, some through family history that has been passed down since the beginning. But most of it, I just know. My grandmother told me before she died that we have elf blood in us, but it's so thin it does not show. This allows me access to knowledge that I otherwise would not have. Through this, I have learned much. I live for history, and the arcane people of it."

Tlonna shifted and studied Miazie before speaking. "What would happen if there was another King of Nymyños?"

Miazie stretched her legs out and yawned. "Well, I suppose that would depend on the king. If he were a benevolent leader, then the lands would continue to have their own government, but answer the sovereign when he called. If he were a *ma*levolent man, then all independent governments would be abolished and every kingdom would be turned into a province for real. Right now, the kingdoms are called provinces of Nymyños, but they are in all actuality independent countries. For instance if Nar-"

Tlonna held her hand up to silence her friend. "Get up, Miazie, tell everyone to pack up, we must leave."

"What? Tlonna it's the middle of the night," Miazie said, startled.

"I do not care, we must leave," she said, pinning her cloak on. "Hurry, I will explain later."

Losolin stood to put his cloak on as Miazie left. "Tlonna what is the matter?"

He stooped to pick up the books scattered on the ground. His head snapped up as he felt his skin prickle. He heard a movement in the forest behind them. He then understood the female's urgency.

The two stepped outside as Tlonna put the last stone in the blue pouch. The people were hastily taking their own tents down, packing up their belongings, and strapping it on their horses' backs. Tlonna tied the tent to Takîreaes's haunches and strapped the saddle on. The two elves leapt onto their horses lightly and waited until the others had mounted. Tlonna drew her bow and notched an arrow to it as Losolin drew his sword. Tlonna shouted back to the people gathered behind her.

"You must ride hard; we will not stop till night fall, if I find a suitable place. Keep any weapon you have drawn and be alert," she turned and urged her stallion on.

She was intent on riding and did not realize that Losolin and Miazie had caught up with her. Branches whipped at their faces and they had to keep their weapons low so they wouldn't get caught in the vegetation. Tlonna looked up and saw the sky through patches of branches. Her eyes swept the sky and she saw a large shape flying above them. It screamed and the horses shied away from path. Tlonna looked into the forest and saw shapes running with them. She did not know any two-footed being that could run as fast as a horse. Glancing at Losolin she noticed that he was looking into the forest as well. She looked at Miazie on her right and saw that she was still looking ahead, as was everyone behind her. Tlonna looked ahead of her and ducked before a low branch slapped her in the face.

The night wore on as the group rode through the forest. The horses started to slow and sweat lathered their backs. As the sun began to rise, Tlonna saw that the animals would not make it far without rest. She looked at the sky again and did not see the bird. The forest seemed empty enough to her. She signaled them to stop and brush the horses down and feed them.

Jumping down from Takîreaes, she took the saddle and blanket off. Losolin pulled Neñyos closer and whispered in her ear.

"We are being watched, though I cannot see anything. Did you see the bird, and the shapes in the forest?"

"Yes, but what are we going to do about it? We must keep moving, get out of this damnable forest," she replied.

Telling them to remount, she jumped onto Takîreaes again. Losolin's eyes flickered up to the sky, then into the forest. Neñyos danced nervously next to the rigid stallion. Tlonna, forgetting to dig her heels into the horse, whispered, "Go," quietly urging her friends to move faster. Takîreaes snorted and lunged forward. He touched ground and sped off, leaving behind the group. Tlonna shrieked in surprise and wrapped her arms around the stallion's thick neck. Losolin yelled after her and urged his nervous gelding forward. Miazie kicked her horse and followed the elf. The people followed her, looking into the forest nervously.

The rode for another half hour before Losolin caught up to Tlonna who was standing next to her horse and looking at the ground. Losolin jumped off his horse before it stopped and stood next to her. He found himself looking down into a large canyon that turned to shadow before it ended. Tlonna spoke without looking at him.

"It was a trap. They were hunting us. And I almost led us into it," she looked at him, straight into his deep blue eyes.

He saw a look in her eyes that he had not seen before, he couldn't tell if it was fear or anger or sadness or something else. Miazie reined up behind them with the band behind her. Losolin pushed Tlonna's hair away from her face and smiled, a small twist of his fair face.

"You cannot blame yourself. None of us knew it was here, and you and I were the only ones that know we are being followed. But we cannot stay here. We need to pick our way down into the canyon."

Tlonna's eyes flashed to the canyon then back to his. Her ice colored irises fixed into his deep, sea blue eyes. She nodded, an unspoken agreement made. Losolin told them all to dismount and tie their belongings on tighter. Miazie dismounted and walked over to where Losolin was tightening on his saddle.

"You are crazy; you're going to kill us all. There is no way that we will make it down the cliff!" she shouted at the elf.

"Miazie, I know what I am doing and I do not need you questioning me," Losolin said irritably.

"Then what are you going to do? Jump down?" Miazie retorted.

"I just might do that! You go first to see just how far it is." Losolin waited while the woman sputtered and cursed him. Finally he put a finger to her lips, causing her to go cross eyed looking at it. "Listen, this is a trapping cliff, which means that there must be some way to get down safely."

Miazie stared at him, then turned to find herself face to face with Tlonna.

"Tlonna, I ...uh." the woman stammered.

"Miazie, Losolin tells the right of it. Go back to your horse and tighten your belongings," Tlonna passed her and stood in front of Losolin.

"There is a narrow path leading down into the canyon, but it is guarded and locked. It is not far from here and they know we are here," the Magin whispered to him.

Her mouth was next to his ear. Heads turned their way and a girl giggled, her tiny pig tails bouncing as she laughed.

Tlonna backed away from Losolin who was smiling broadly. He grabbed her face and pressed his lips to hers. Tlonna gasped and grabbed his arms. The male pulled away from her and smiled again. Tlonna laughed and she saw his eyes twinkling boyishly as he did too. The little girl screamed with joy and her mother turned red. The father approached hesitantly.

"I am s-sorry for my daughter," he looked down and started to kneel.

Tlonna pulled him up and laughed again. "It is fine. A little laughter was needed."

Tlonna turned back to Losolin as the man walked away and he was still smiling. Tlonna pushed him lightly and walked back to Takîreaes. The group proceeded slowly to the trail and stopped as the guards looked up, their bows drawn back.

Chapter 5
Painful Remembrances

Miazie gripped Tlonna's shoulder hard, putting her lips near the elf's pointed ear.

"Goblins, Tlonna, they're goblins. Something is wrong here; they shouldn't be this far south."

"What do we do?" Losolin hissed out of the corner of his mouth.

The goblin that had tightened his bow let out a tittering shriek and the arrow thudded into Tlonna's thigh. The elf fell into Losolin, who caught her against him. Before any of the three could react, a dagger whipped between them and buried itself in the skull of the goblin. The other guard bellowed like an animal and drew a notched sword.

Before it could take two steps, another dagger was planted between its eyes where it stuck, quivering. As the goblin fell, the two elves and human turned their heads to stare at the man who stood a few feet from them.

"Tyre? How...?" Miazie stammered, her brows knitted.

"When you're in battle, one learns many tricks not taught at military camp, milady," the soldier replied, retrieving his daggers.

"Losolin?" Tlonna murmured, watching blood soak her trousers from the arrow wound.

Miazie turned her confused face as Losolin laid Tlonna out on the ground. The human studied the bolt for a second before cursing softly.

"It's been poisoned, Losolin, and goblin poisons are...treacherous."

"But I thought you said elves were immune to toxicities!" the male said, alarmed.

"Yes, but this, this is different. Goblin poisons are *meant* especially for elves. There is hardly a bitterer rivalry than that of elves and goblins. During the First War, King Brandon recruited goblins to his cause, and since then, it has been worse than the Elf/Dwarf hatred," Miazie replied.

"That does not help, Miazie! What are we going to do?"

Losolin shouted as Tlonna's head flopped to one side of his lap, her face white and listless.

"Let's set up camp, there's nothing I can do for her like this."

The camp was struck right at the gate after the carcasses of the goblins had been buried. Tlonna was placed on Miazie's pallet so that she was raised a few inches off the ground. Her forehead was slick with perspiration, the rest of her body cool, too cool. Losolin fretted as Miazie and the women from her home tended to the elf.

Her eyes flickered open; blue drapes covered the bed. Tapestries of landscapes and maps covered the wall. She sat up, rested. Her body was clothed in satin, and her hair woven into graceful plates and ringlets, slightly mussed from sleep.

A quiet thump whipped her head around and she smiled. Losolin stepped the rest of the way through the opening. Many openings dotted the wall. They stood a few feet off the floor, but rose to the ceiling. When bad weather hit Blackhaven City, glass would be set in them, snug between a ridge and hinged wooden slats.

Tlonna slid out of her bed and lounged against a bedpost as Losolin strode over to her. He looked irritated, but his mouth was gentle on hers, his hands soft. The princess wrapped her arms around his waist and leaned her head against his chest. There was dirt caked onto his shirt.

"What bothers you, heart of my heart?" she asked.

Losolin sighed, and then slid his hands down her back to cup her bottom. "Nothing you need worry yourself about, Loni."

Tlonna smiled slightly, though he could not see it. She began to undo his shirt ties. Losolin stood placidly as she undressed him, but grunted when she pushed him backward. The elf reached for his lover's silky nightgown, but she slapped his hand away.

"You are not touching me until you have had a bath," Tlonna growled, but smiling all the same.

Losolin sighed, but he moved to the large tub that seemed to grow from the floor. He pumped hot water into it while Tlonna summoned a maid. As Losolin emerged into the water, the maid arrived, curtsying deeply.

"Fetch me the finest white tunic, breeches, and cloak from the spare chest. Also I will want boots, and a silver belt, do it discreetly," Tlonna said.

The maid curtsied again, flashing a smile at the folding screen that hid the bath from view.

"Princess Tlonna, could you tell Sir Losolin that I think he looks lovely even with dirt in his hair?"

"Of course Lhia. Now go get those clothes."

Tlonna entered the bathing room again, as Losolin poured hot water over his head. "You know, your mother will do whatever is in her power to stop us from wedding," he said.

"I know, but I have a plan that I think will get Father on my side, he will help me at least," Tlonna said, "He does not like this betrothal any more than I do, I do not know why he agreed to it in the first place. Lhia says hello."

Losolin smiled knowingly. "I heard." The smile faded a bit. "I do not believe it will work, love. I am a peasant. I think that your mother has poisoned his thoughts with her constant bleating. But I suppose it is worth a try."

Tlonna bent over and kissed him, Losolin's wet hands closing around her face. She dunked one of her hands into the water to caress him. Losolin moaned. Letting him go, Tlonna trailed her fingers up his belly and chest to slide over his shoulder. She had little warning before Losolin's hand left her face and yanked her into the massive tub with him.

Gasping, Tlonna floundered in her skirts as they billowed up around her. Losolin yanked at the laces on her gown until they loosened and he was able to tear the material off his lover. The nightgown floated away as they embraced, fitting together.

The maid, Lhia, entered the room as they climaxed. She placed the garments quietly on the table and left, smiling.

Gasping, Tlonna laid her head on Losolin's shoulder. The male kissed her forehead and then leaned his cheek against it.

"Losolin?"

"Hmm?"

"What were you doing to get that dirty anyway?"

"Your mother's guards attacked me at the bridge and threw me in the canal. You know, Loni, I would think that being the consort of our great princess would do something for my status. It just seems to get worse every day."

"Well, my prince, your...status...gets raised every time I see you. Does not that count?" Tlonna teased coyly as she reached down *to prove it.*

"It counts," Losolin moaned, "but we have not the time now, my love."

Tlonna sighed and withdrew her advances. She stepped out of the tub and walked, dripping, across the tiled floor to grab a towel.

"Now you just torture me," Losolin said as he too vacated the tub.

The dress floated languidly in the water.

"It is my job, dearest love, to torture you," Tlonna replied.

Losolin laughed; a wondrously deep musical sound that filled Tlonna with warmth. He tied a towel around his slim waist and bent to kiss her.

Once dry, Tlonna took the pile of garments Lhia had brought in and laid it out. Losolin dressed himself in small clothes brought in by the maid. Tlonna gave him the breeches and helped him with the frogs on his tunic. She wrapped the white velvet cloak around his shoulders and clasped it with a black obsidian brooch cut into an oval. Losolin buckled the silver belt around his waist and then followed his still naked love to the dressing table.

"We must hurry, there is a dinner with Lord Conner this evening and I want you to be there. I was supposed to bring Iyaner Lostug, but Lord Conner will see you."

Tlonna talked while she straightened the long blond hair with the comb. She carefully pulled bits of his hair into braids, but left the rest loose around his shoulders. Losolin stood and watched Tlonna emerge into her huge wardrobe. He heard her moving things around then she stepped out again holding a finely wrought white leather scabbard outlined with metal silver vines that wove along the edges of the white leather. The sword hilt was wrapped in white leather as well, with a pale blue eight-point star pressed into it. There was a gray sun in the center of the star. As Tlonna drew the blade, it flashed and glinted in the sunlight coming from the windows. It was a thin blade with the star and sun symbol etched upon the metal. A blood runner ran down the side and off to the edge just before the hilt.

Losolin stared at the blade wondering what she was doing with one so fine. She pressed the hilt into his hands but kept the blade. Losolin stared at the elf before him and opened his mouth to speak. Tlonna put a finger to his lips and put the baldric around Losolin's back and chest. She handed him the blade and he sheathed it. Tlonna smiled at him and made little adjustments to his attire.

"Welcome, Prince Losolin of the White Sword." she whispered. "Play the part, my love. Mother and Father do not know of the sword, they will not know it is mine. I have one more thing."

Tlonna opened a chest on the floor and pulled out a roll of shredded leather. She unrolled it and picked up a silver pendant. It was slightly curved, engraved on both sides with his name. "Put this on."

Losolin took it and clasped the fine chain around his neck, "Then you did get them," he said quietly.

"Of course. Now help me dress," Tlonna said, turning back to her wardrobe.

She settled on a white and blue floor length dress that accentuated her small waist. It was made of satin and flowed with her every movement. Losolin could not help himself when she turned her back to him so that he could pull the laces tight. Reaching under the still loose bodice, the male slid his hand down between her legs. Tlonna gasped and leaned against him. It was all she could do, as his arm was snug between her body and dress. His fingers glided into her, and Tlonna shuddered with pleasure. Losolin wrapped his other hand around to cup her breast.

Tlonna's arms came up to encircle his neck, the back of her head pressed against his sternum. When she came, her entire body trembled. Losolin grinned against her neck then withdrew his hand.

"Oh," Tlonna moaned. "That was evil."

"But you liked it," Losolin whispered into her ear, then dipped his hand in the bathwater to clean his fingers.

Finally, he tightened the laces on her dress and then lounged on her bed as she did her hair.

Something flickered in Tlonna's mind.

Loud pounding woke Tlonna with a start. Losolin groaned in her ear. The princess looked over his shoulder to peer at her door. It was shaking as someone on the other side pounded it mercilessly. Nearly falling out of bed in her haste to dress, Tlonna shouted for patience. Finally, she dumped all the blankets she could find on top of Losolin, to hide him, and opened the door.

Constancias shoved the door hard so that it rebounded off the wall and came to smack against Tlonna's palm. The queen was red with fury.

"Tlonna! What is wrong with you? You have destroyed our alliance with Seaduens! You have forced my hand in this, and you will regret it. I will not have my rule and my name dragged through the dirt for you. I will not have it!"

"You have no power, Mother. Leave," Tlonna said coldly.

The blow from Constancias nearly knocked the princess off her feet. Her jaw felt as though it had come unhinged. Glowering at the queen, Tlonna tried to shut the door.

"You will regret your choices, daughter." Constancias snarled, and left Tlonna standing in the door. She slammed it closed and Losolin climbed out of the bed.

"She does not deserve life!" Tlonna shouted angrily.

Losolin sighed, wrapped the sheet around his waist, and took her hand in his. "She means to have me hanged, or you, possibly. Maybe both."

"I know," Tlonna said quietly, leaning against him.

After a full minute's silence, Losolin sighed. "My love, I will not linger in your life any longer. I am sorry I have brought this pain upon you," Losolin kissed her, putting in it all the passion and love they shared.

The elf donned his clothes and stepped out the window that sat directly above a turret. He swung one leg out and steadied his footing on the wooden tiles.

Sobbing, Tlonna called to him. He stopped and turned, waiting.

"My love, will you not fight?"

"Fight for what, Loni? No matter what I do, we will lose. I am but a beggar and heathen, and you suffer for it," Losolin said as he moved back to take her hands.

"No you are not! I love you, and...and I will go with you! We can leave here and find ourselves a new home. I have plenty of money, and we could start a new life. Perhaps have a child and never have to answer to anyone but us. Please Losolin, do not leave me!"

"No, Tlonna. The people need you here. You will fall in love with some other elf, and forget about me in time, you will have all the ages of the world to live and love. I have held you back already, I set you free, now."

"Losolin! Please, I could never love anyone but you. Please do not leave me, what am I going to do?"

"Tlonna, you will live the life you were born to live. And you will be many times the queen your mother could even dream to be."

Tlonna sniffed, holding back her tears. Losolin pulled her into a tight hug before returning to the window. He disappeared, climbing along the low sills and turrets.

The images flickered again.

She swung gracefully, her hand tight in Losolin's as he brought her back, feet moving to the music. Tlonna could not help a laugh as her lover grinned from beneath the hood pulled low over his face. Suddenly, someone screamed.

Iyaner was already in midair from leaping off the dais and rammed his entire body into Losolin's midriff. As he fell, the prince kneed Losolin in the groin. The younger male gasped in pain, hands blocking against Iyaner's. The noble leapt off the peasant, kicking him hard in the ribs as he did, and grabbed Tlonna by the waist. She hit him hard in the mouth, but he paid no mind. Iyaner yanked Tlonna through the crowd of people until they were in the wide corridor. Losolin ran after him. The people scattered, leaving a path for him. Iyaner disappeared into a hall and Losolin sprinted after him. He searched every room until he found them. The other male had Tlonna's skirts pushed up around her hips and was attempting to mount her.

His lover, however, fought back, pushing her skirts down and swiping at him with force. Losolin picked a fire stoke up and crept up behind Iyaner. The male was unaware that he was behind him until Tlonna looked up and noticed. Iyaner turned and caught the stoke just before it crashed into his skull. Losolin yanked his weapon out of the prince's grip and backed away. Iyaner jumped over the bed and made for the door.

Being faster, Losolin blocked the door and swung the poker at his foe. The other male dodged and jumped for the bed. Losolin propelled himself forward and caught the prince's ankle. The two males struggled against each other until Losolin's superior strength won out. The poker slammed into Iyaner's head and it cracked. Another swing sank in with a morbid thunk, and Iyaner went still, his head caved in on one side. Losolin dropped the stoke and gathered Tlonna up in his arms.

"Tlonna, Tlonna! Wake up!"

Tlonna jerked awake. Her breath came in gasps and she

forgot where she was for a moment. The forest was close to her right, the sky a dismal gray above her. Losolin's face was blurry as she tried to focus. Smears of blood marred his masculine beauty, coming into focus as she blinked a few times.

"What happened?" she said quietly.

"The arrow that was in your leg was laced with poison. Miazie saved your life, but we had to make camp for a few days while you healed. There was an attack. Few survived."

Tlonna felt her heart drop as she heard the news. Her thoughts turned morose. She heard footsteps coming toward her and looked around Losolin's shoulders.

Miazie was limping towards them, her face bandaged with her tunic sleeve. The woman's trousers were torn and blood stained. Tlonna tried to get up, but found she was too weak to support her weight. Losolin pushed her back down needlessly as she had fallen on her own. Miazie crouched next to them and laid a hand on Losolin's shoulder for support. His young face was contorted with worry for the both of them.

Tlonna finally took in the extent of Losolin's wounds. His forehead was torn and he had taken a blow to his left cheek. Miazie's teeth were red with blood when she grinned at Tlonna.

"Glad to see you're alive. The goblins are under the control of Midian. That tattoo on their hands is his mark. The black is for his evil, the red for blood, and the blue for domination. The yellow star is for power," Miazie shook her head. "The fact that he has guards out here means bad things for the Nymyñosian twelve lands."

Giving in to Losolin's tender administering, Tlonna turned her face to the human. "Miazie, what are the twelve lands?"

"They are the twelve kingdoms that dominate Nymyños. There's Kismath, Purheae, Blackhaven Forest, Schelum, Narnen, Florwen Hune, Seaduens, Kajgenia, Flousen Dua, Talenias, Zeynuwn, and Arseninis. Seaduens and Flousen Dua are Elven cities and Purheae is deserted, tainted by the forest and the ruins of the Tower of Magins. The kingdoms of Kismath and Schelum, as you know are almost gone. There was once an alliance, as I told you before, between Blackhaven, Schelum, Kismath, and Purheae. It was destroyed when Aderiaen Rahlan attacked them. Now, the populations have been destroyed and only a few still live in them. Most were killed in the War of Monotheism. But I will explain it all to you when we have time. We need to get out of here before the goblins come back," Miazie straightened herself and squeezed Losolin's shoulder.

The male elf sighed and began putting things back into bags. Tlonna saw that it was all healing supplies. He tied the bags onto Neñyos and stooped to pick Tlonna up. She tried to fight him but found all her strength gone. With a sigh, she let him pick her up and carry her over to Takîreaes. The stallion stamped and tossed its head as the two elves approached him. Tlonna pulled herself over on to his back and looked down. Losolin seemed to be much smaller from atop the horse's back. Neñyos plodded over to where Losolin stood and for the first time Tlonna realized how dwarfed the large stallion made the gelding look. Losolin leaped over onto his back and settled into the saddle.

Tlonna looked back at the people behind her, the eleven people left of two score. Her stomach lurched. Tyre and Rebecca, Zerah's parents, one of the hunters, Alice, the girl, Yaqquil, Tonyai, and Alisia, Miazie, she and Losolin made the count eleven. Every one of them moved lethargically, as though slogging through mud up to their shoulders.

"Hurry, or we will all be dead. Come on!" Tlonna growled, sawing at the reins.

Takîreaes snorted irritably, gnashing the bit. The Anutchians lifted their eyes to her in anger and disbelief. Their faces were dull, colorless, but their eyes blazed.

Tlonna shuddered and turned around. Losolin let out a sigh and nudged Neñyos in the ribs. Tlonna followed suit and did not look back, hoping that they were all following.

The small group covered many leagues through the day and did not stop for the night. Miazie handed out small rations of food to them as they rode and many times someone gasped as their nose hit the back of their horse's neck because they had fallen asleep. The girl murmured to herself constantly and Tlonna heard a sob every now and then from Rebecca.

As the gray morning dawned, Tlonna called a halt and the travelers slid off their horses wearily. The elf tensed when Tyre stalked over to stand before her.

"I don't know if you are well enough yet, but I would at least like to see if Losolin would like to take up the training again. Now that there's only me and Ryun who have any skill at fighting, it would be for the best if we at least knew something of the skill you and he have."

Tlonna blinked. It was perhaps the longest speech she had ever heard from the man. "Yes, of course. I am well enough. Let me get Losolin, and we shall begin. Yes?"

Tyre nodded and stalked off again.

A few minutes later, the elves joined the two men. Losolin stripped off his shirt and rolled his shoulders. Tlonna eyed him for a second and then dropped her belts on the ground so that, other than her clothes, she wore nothing but her sword. Tyre and the hunter, Ryun, copied Losolin. They stood shivering, casting annoyed glances at Losolin, who, unbeknownst to him, was steaming as his body adapted to the cold.

Without warning, Losolin attacked Tyre, blade flashing impossibly fast. The soldier cried out in shock, but his sword met Losolin's, if only just. Tlonna stood watching for a moment, then glided toward Ryun, who was staring avidly at the dueling pair. He shouted in alarm as Tlonna's blade whistled by his nose.

"Never let your guard down, Ryun," she said, and stepped again.

This time, the hunter got his blade up fast enough to block her thrust, but she was moving before he had finished his follow through. Within minutes, both humans were breathing harshly and sweating despite the cold.

"All right, all right," Tyre cried, gasping with hands on his knees. "Let's start with the basics. What is that first movement you did, Losolin, when you came at me?"

"It is called Moving the Wind, and it is an attack form," the elf said, and demonstrated it in increments to the humans.

The blank-faced Anutchians formed a small audience as the night progressed. As Tlonna explained the blocking position, Blushing Maiden, to Ryun, Rebecca stood and strode into the makeshift practice ring.

"I want to learn, Lady Tlonna," she announced, and planted herself firmly as though expecting to be denied.

Tyre slipped as his wife's words reached him and he stuck his finger in his mouth. Losolin cursed, yanking his sword back and reaching for Tyre's hand.

"It is fine. Rebecca, what do you mean by this?"

The woman lifted her chin, then turned to Tlonna again. "Will you teach me?"

Tlonna handed the human her sword wordlessly. Rebecca's eyes widened as the tip thunked into the snow. She licked her lips, and hoisted the gleaming blade up with both hands. The other women behind her watched with glittering eyes.

"Can you work with Losolin and Tyre?" Tlonna asked Ryun, and smiled when the hunter nodded.

"All right," the elf breathed, "we will start at the beginning. This is called a scabbard, or sheath."

Every night they camped, Tyre, Ryun, and Rebecca worked with the elves. Sometimes Tlonna worked with the men, sometimes with Rebecca, every so often they all worked together.

"Aaugh!" Rebecca growled for at least the twentieth time as the blade was twisted out of her grip to land in the snow yards away.

"It is fine, go get it," Losolin said, gesturing.

The woman stumped over to the blade and rejoined Losolin. "I don't understand what I am doing wrong! I hold it just like you told me!"

The elf smiled and stuck his sword point down in the ground. Standing behind Rebecca, he bent down, his arms on top of hers. "Are your hands sweaty?"

"When you stand this close to me, they are," she joked.

Losolin chuckled. "What about when I am coming after you with a naked blade?"

After a second, the woman sighed. "Yes, I'm terrified."

"Do not be scared of me. Or Tlonna. Neither of us will hurt you. Now, remember, this is a two-handed sword, for you. You have to have both hands on the hilt. You are not strong enough or big enough to hold a sword like this with one hand. And do not crowd your hands together, Rebecca, give them room to move."

"Yes, like this. See?"

"Perfect. Now, loosen your shoulders a bit. I can feel the tightness in them. You have to be languid for swordplay, not rigid. Rigid gets you a blade through the belly just as surely as not having a weapon. Ease up. I know it is hard work to hold that blade up the way you are supposed to, but if you want to be a blade...mistress...you need to work hard."

Rebecca giggled. "A blade mistress? Please. I just want to be able to defend myself."

"And well you should. I hope you will teach your daughter all this, one day."

"I hope I don't have to."

Losolin straightened. "Me too, but it is good exercise none the less. Now, back in formation. There you go."

"Your lover is touching my wife, Tlonna," Tyre grunted as he blocked a jab from Ryun.

"Yes, he is," Tlonna replied.

"I wish you would do something about it. She is all giggly at night when she gets back from these practices. Can't get a word or anything else in edgewise when she starts talking about 'sweet lord Losolin'," the human grumped.

"Ah, well, the price we must pay for our association with those more beautiful than ourselves," Tlonna said airily.

"I...don't think that's...possible, Tlonna," Ryun gasped as he parried Tyre's thrusts.

The hunter was having a hard time keeping up with the soldier, much less the elves. He barely turned Tyre's sweeping arc, but turn it he did. When he dropped his weapon in the snow and nearly fell over, Tlonna called them to stop.

The two men clasped wrists, grinning. When Ryun flopped onto his back, sending up billows of snow, Tyre joined him, watching Losolin and Rebecca. The male elf laughed as Rebecca abandoned the blade and launched herself at him instead. The woman took Losolin in the knees and sent them both sprawling. Tyre grimaced.

The two rolled about in the snow, laughing till they were breathless. Tlonna grinned at Tyre, who scowled back at her, though his eyes crinkled in a smile. She went back to watching Losolin and the woman.

"See, now, you are flailing. It is irritating for an attacker, but it does not do much. Think, Rebecca, slow your thoughts down and analyze your situation. Stop where you are, see your position?" Losolin said, grappling with her.

Rebecca stopped, one thigh pressed against Losolin's hips, both arms spread wide by his hands. Her other leg was twisted slightly, making her hop about to keep balanced. The air puffed out of her, visible to everyone in the cold.

"I...don't know. You have both my hands," she gasped.

"Where is the most sensitive spot on a male?"

"The...groin," Rebecca replied, looking at where her thigh was.

"That is correct. The easiest way to cripple a male is to hit him hard in the groin. It is brutish, but it works. So, how would you get me from your position?" the elf said patiently, still holding her arms wide.

Rebecca studied her stance, and then slid her leg down and rested her knee between Losolin's legs. She drew her leg back, but before she could do more than tense her grounded leg, Losolin twisted slightly, moved his hands up, and flipped her onto her back. She landed with a poof, snow flying up around her.

Tyre watched her with glittering eyes until she sat up sulkily, brushing snow from her face. Then he smiled. Losolin put his hands on his hips and grinned down at her.

"You should know better than to try that on me, Rebecca. Besides, Tlonna would not like it if you crippled me."

Tlonna laughed and stood, brushing snow off the seat of her pants. Tyre and Ryun followed her over to the others. "It is true, Rebecca. I like him whole."

The human got to her feet and giggled. "I would think so, my lady, I would think so." Turning to Losolin she said, "I did not see that coming. You seem to know what I am going to do before I do. How?"

"I know you, I know your ways, and I know your strengths. Females have more strength in their legs and they use them. It is something you learn over time. It is not something I can teach you. I am sure Tyre knows about it. He knows his enemies well enough to know how to defeat them, yes?"

Tyre nodded, chewing on his lip. "Yes. I wonder..." he tapped a finger on his stubbly chin. "I wonder if perhaps it has something to do with *how* you are trained, too. See, I've known men who, despite having been in numerous battles, still had to revert to brawler-like tactics. They would take wounds and seemed to survive only because of their wild flailing. But men I trained always developed the ability to see beforehand what their opponents were going to do."

Losolin shrugged. "Most likely, yes. I know elves have the ability in them, innately, though not all of us know it."

"It is a form of foresight, a bit like Seeing. All elves have it," Miazie said, coming to stand with them.

"Seeing?" Tlonna asked, noting the emphasis the woman had put on the word.

"Yes, what Seers do, looking into the future, prophecy. Though it is not Seeing, it allows an elf to 'see' what their opponent is going to do seconds before they do it. That's why they're so deadly in battle and challenges, too. Games, and such. They know what is happening."

The five stared at her. Rebecca seemed to shrink in a little. The women from Anutch made it a point to disdain her training. It is men's work to fight.

Miazie noticed. "Rebecca, I am not one who thinks you a fool. I would like to learn, as well."

Tlonna could not help her eyebrows from going up in shock. Losolin shut his mouth a second later. Miazie looked at her feet and shrugged.

"I know what it is like to be helpless. I...don't want to feel that way ever again. Will you take me on?"

"Yes," Tlonna said and pulled her away. "What do you know, exactly, about fighting, Miazie?"

The woman shrugged again, not looking at the elf. "I know some things, like...how to *hold* a sword."

"And?" Tlonna urged.

"That's about it, Tlonna. But I don't really want to learn swordplay, at least, not first. I want to know how to fight with my hands. I don't own a sword, and I'm not as strong as Rebecca. I can't swing one around much less take blows. She's getting to the point where she can actually hold up against you and Losolin for a few seconds. I wouldn't even last after the first touch."

"All right, but Miazie," Tlonna hesitated, "it is easy to get hurt, grappling. Broken bones being common."

"I know. But Tlonna, I meant it when I said I don't want to feel helpless again. I was helpless in Anutch, and I was helpless when the goblins came. I don't like it. Will you teach me?"

"Yes."

When Tlonna did not move, Miazie frowned. "Well? What's first?"

The elf sighed and put a fist close to Miazie's face. "This is the proper way to make a fist. Put your thumb here... this," she flattened her fingers against her palm rather than curling them under, "can break your hand. Okay, now hit me as hard as you can."

"What?"

"Hit me with as much strength as you can," Tlonna repeated.

"No!" Miazie said, appalled.

"Then you will learn nothing. Would you rather punch Losolin?"

Miazie shook her head, eyeing the shirtless Losolin a few yards away, showing Rebecca and the two men how to flip a person over their back.

Tlonna planted fists on hips and glared at her friend. "Hit me in the stomach, Miazie, or I will hit you. Your choice."

"Okay! Okay!" the human said, and balled up her fist.

Tlonna blinked when Miazie slammed her fist into her belly, but nothing more. She tried to hide a smirk by pushing her lips together, but her eyes crinkled in amusement. Miazie glared at her.

"Get on your hands and knees, Miazie, and do as many push-ups as you can. You need some muscle."

"I will not! You can't make me! It is *snowing!*" the human protested, but when Tlonna raised an eyebrow at her, she got down on her hands and knees, and started doing the exercise.

After ten, she was shaking with effort. Tlonna sighed resignedly. And so the training continued.

Tlonna let her head fall back against Losolin's pack with a groan. Her body trembled slightly as it healed from the after-effects of goblin poison. Losolin smoothed her hair back and kissed her lightly.

"Is it any better?"

"Ach," Tlonna grunted. "Feels like my head has a forge inside, and my body is on fire. The practice seems to help though. It lets me forget for a time."

Losolin nodded, reaching over her to tighten one of the door-flap laces. A puff of snow slipped inside before he could, and settled on Tlonna's hip. She brushed it off with a frown. When she let her head back down, it landed on something hard and round inside Losolin's pack.

"Ow," she muttered and sat up.

"What?" Losolin asked.

"What is in your pack? I just hit my head on something really hard," the Magin replied, yanking it open.

The white sword from her dream gleamed in the elf's magic little ball of light. Magin light, as she called it. A shiver ran through Tlonna as she drew the sword out from the pack and rested it across her knees. She'd hit her head on the pommel.

"It was real," she breathed, swallowing.

"What was real? Tlonna? What is wrong?" Losolin asked, eyeing his sword.

"Losolin, there is something I have to tell you. I do not know if you remember or not, but when I was out, I had a dream. Well, it was not a dream, but rather a memory, three memories." And she told him, fingering the dull point of a leaf on the scabbard's metal frame.

"I tried to leave you? And then killed Iyaner Lostug?" he asked finally, when she finished. "I like the part in the tub, but not the rest of it. Tlonna...I am a murderer. Not just a peasant, but a *murderer.*"

Tlonna snorted. "He bloody well deserved it, stab me thrice if he did not."

"We should ask Miazie what she knows of the Lostugs. They are the royal family of Seaduens, I believe. Terrible place, Seaduens," Losolin muttered, grabbing his cloak.

"I suppose," Tlonna said, and followed him out of their warm tent.

"The Lostugs?" Miazie said, wrapping a thick cloak about her person. "There's a lot to them. You might want to start a fire."

Tlonna sighed and Wove a strand of heat into the cold firepit outside the human's tent. The three huddled around it as Miazie began to talk.

"Stoffnias Lostug is the patriarch, King of Seaduens. His wife is Enyis Lostug, an elf so dim-witted she is barely accepted as elf-kind, but beautiful enough to appease Stoffnias. They had five sons, only two live, now. Herrich, the oldest, perished about two hundred years ago in a battle between Blackhaven and Seaduens. Oh yes," she said when Tlonna gasped. "The two kingdoms have hated each other since their foundation. Only once has a treaty been sought, destroyed when you refused to marry Iyaner. But to continue in chronological order, Jaichren, became the crown prince. He died fifty years later, in yet another battle between Blackhaven and Seaduens.

"Iyaner was next in line, and that is when Queen Constancias arranged the betrothal between you and Iyaner, to secure peace with the kingdom. Obviously, you refused adamantly, and Losolin bashed in Iyaner's head."

"You know that?" Losolin asked, astonished.

Miazie nodded. "A lot of things came to me when you regained some of your memories. It was as though a dam had been built in my mind, and then suddenly, it broke and all this knowledge came to me, as if I had merely forgotten it. Part of Midian's Weave, I am sure. Anyway, that completely destroyed any sort of hope of peace, and Stoffnias swore to raze Blackhaven to the ground. Midian reached it first. Now Isadorr is the heir, and his younger brother Gothier is being kept *very* safe. Stoffnias and Enyis rarely let him out of the castle. Isadorr is given a little freedom, but he seldom is allowed outside the borders of Seaduens."

Miazie adjusted her cloak and stretched out her legs. "Now, Stoffnias hates you with everything he has, Tlonna, and you even more, Losolin. Some say he and Constancias had an affair, and that is what caused the attempted treaty. He put a price on your head, some hundred thousand geld, I believe it was. I am actually surprised you survived being in the White Hand Band, Losolin, being that they are Seadueni. That's probably why you were attacked originally. Someone wanted their bounty."

Losolin squinted at her. "Everyone wants me dead," he grunted.

"A few, certainly not most, but a few, have a right to," Miazie said quietly.

Chapter 6
Dark Informants

Losolin sighed and poked at the fire. The embers were glowing red and the warmth was dwindling. As he stared at it, his mind went slightly blurry, as though he had fallen into semi consciousness. Lazily he looked over to Tlonna, who was staring into the fire dreamily, as though she too were about to doze off. There was an odd clicking noise and then suddenly a desire to move had him on his feet and striding toward the sparse wood off to the right.

Tlonna followed a strange urging through the wood, not noticing Losolin a few steps ahead of her. Behind her, Miazie stared ahead as though possessed, her feet moving of their own accord. Tlonna blinked slowly, when, after a few minutes, she and the others arrived at the edge of a large pond.

Miazie gazed at the still surface of the water and felt revulsion. There was something tainted, something unnatural about the water. It hardly moved, and when it did, there was no sound. On the opposite bank a waterfall plummeted but made only a soft sound like wind through tall grass. No fish swam in its depths, and though it was clear, there was no discernible bottom.

"Welcome," said a high, soft voice.

The three started and the shock made them come to themselves. Miazie stepped away from the water's edge and pulled a disgusted face. Tlonna hunched over as though expecting an attack, and Losolin stared out over the water to where a silvery blue figure was gliding toward them, arms folded across his chest.

Tlonna turned on her heel and grabbed Miazie by the elbow.

"Come on, let us go," the elf said roughly, dragging the human back a few steps.

"No, please stay," said the voice, which came from the figure now less than ten paces from the bank. "I very much wish to speak with you."

"About what?" Tlonna growled, still holding Miazie's elbow in a vice-like grip. The human started to whimper.

"You are the Everwood Princess, the Belau, and the Consort and I am the Cyree," the figure said, gliding to a stop at the edge of the still water.

"The Cyree?" Miazie blurted, turning awkwardly from Tlonna to stare at the glowing figure. "The Cyree, the woman who was sacrificed by the first Fifteen to ensure the continued existence of magic?"

"Yes, the Cyree," the figure said lightly.

Tlonna squinted at the glowing face. It was young, flawless, and innocent, but there was an edge to her features that bespoke of a great tragedy. Her body was slender and just blossoming into womanhood. She was draped in a single cloth so that one shoulder was left bare and gathered at the other.

"You were sacrificed? By Magins?"

"Yes, to ensure that there will always be a source of magic, this pond, my home."

Losolin stepped behind Tlonna and placed one big hand on her shoulder and the other on his hip. "What do you want to talk about? Why did you bring us here? It was you, was it not?"

The Cyree nodded serenely and smiled. "Yes, it was I who brought you here. I was trained to feel when great power came within my borders. I felt you, and brought you here, so that we may speak."

Miazie finally wrenched free of Tlonna's loosened grip. "You called me a Belau. Why? There is no way that I am a Belau."

"You have great knowledge of things you should not know. You have memories that are not yours; you have flashes of insight that are completely unavailable to you. You, Miazie Paron Ughtren, are a Belau. And you," the Cyree looked to Losolin, "are the Consort, Losolin Ullor Grisholm. And Tlonna Arune Ewôsdírn, the Everwood Princess and Magin of Prophecy, also known as Astinus's Magin."

"How do you know this?" Tlonna growled, stepping forward.

"I know many things, Everwood. Now we must move forward," the Cyree said in her high, innocent voice.

"Wait," Tlonna said sharply. "How were you sacrificed?"

The Cyree tilted her head a fraction. She blinked her empty, silvery blue eyes. "My innocence was taken with a knife, to ensure that the blood spilt was pure and untouched by human hand."

"They raped you with a *knife*?" Losolin whispered, horrified.

"If you must put it so uncouthly, yes, but that was a very long time ago. We must progress," the Cyree replied, this time her voice slightly lower than before.

Tlonna pushed back her horror and nodded slightly. "Please, go on then."

"You have been brought here so that I may give you the means that will be your success, or your downfall. Each of you has been brought here because you possess a singular gift. Belau Miazie, you have the knowledge to take your journey the length it need go. You will provide information otherwise unavailable. All wisdom and knowledge is worth possessing.

"Losolin the Consort, you hold within you an extraordinary gift of healing that when coupled with magic is nearly infallible, except when used on the original magic. Your steadfast love and devotion will be the rock and foundation on which Everwood will build her legacy.

"Everwood, you hold within you a great and untamable source of power. I warn you now that your power is too much. But not enough. At the end, you must have a weapon, a tool, with which you will lay the last brick of your legacy, place the keystone that will hold up the mighty arch of your life. At the end, when there is no further step to be taken, this tool will give you your greatest achievement, and you will be remembered beyond ages for it."

Tlonna did not like the Cyree's monotonous account of her destiny. "So, you say that I am going to die, but with this tool I will be remembered for dying? How cheerful."

"Death is not so bad, once the pain recedes. You are left with no feeling, floating in oblivion, peaceful and unable to be harmed. No one can reach you there, no one can bother you," the Cyree said, tilting her head again.

"But you are here, so obviously you can be bothered, and harmed, otherwise you would be able to move beyond the water's edge," Losolin countered.

The Cyree smiled. "I am not here. What stands before you is merely a projection, a thought left behind to deliver a message and a means. The girl I once was, Andramaky, has long since departed from this earth, forgotten by those who matter and unimportant to those who do not."

Tlonna felt immense sadness for the girl, Andramaky. "What will happen to you now that you have delivered the message?"

"When we are finished here, I will fade, and will no longer guard this place. My waters will continue to live, for I am not the only guardian of this sacred area."

"What is this place called?" Tlonna asked, not wanting the Cyree to suddenly start fading from sight.

"It is called the Cyree, as I am called, for we are one. We must proceed."

"Oh...right," Tlonna said, confused.

"I have given you the message, but not the means, Everwood." The Cyree lifted her arms and backed away from them a few feet. She began to chant. "From the shadows, from the night, I command the wild, its earthly might. From the shadows, from the night, I take from you, to aid the fight. From the shadows, from the night, cloth of darkness, hide them from sight. Make it three and as I will it, so Mote it be."

All three of the living people spun around as a keening sound came from the wood behind them. Out of the shadows flew three black shapes that swooped over them and draped over their backs. Tlonna grabbed a fistful at her shoulder and stared at it. Slippery cloth bunched in her fist. She looked at Losolin and yelped. Only his head was visible, the rest was shadows. Miazie looked the same. The Cyree spoke.

"They are cloaks meant to hide you in darkness, and blend in the day. They are lightweight and will alter with the weather. In heat they will cool, in the cold they will warm. They are not made of any civilized material; they are made from the earth and shadow. They will work for only its owner," Andramaky's image said.

"Cyree...you were a Magin, weren't you?" Miazie asked gently.
"Yes."

"You used a Pagan incantation, from the Ages of Religion."
"Yes."

"But you died long before that time."

"Yes. I have been worked on by Magins throughout the ages, altered and improved so that I may serve my purpose better. And now, for the rest."

The Cyree raised her arms again. "Inner strength, outer bone, light for only the one you own. Not made of bronze, or of steel, not this blade can anyone steal. Come to greet your destiny, as I will it, so Mote it be."

This time a bone white object rose from the ground to present itself at Tlonna's feet. A sword, pure white and shining in a scabbard of white wood.

"Made of ivory, only the one who is worthy can lift it," the Cyree intoned, watching Tlonna.

The elf picked up the shining blade and pulled it free of its sheath. The blade and hilt were one, made of pure white ivory. Nothing was etched on the blade nor was there any adornment on the hilt. Losolin was staring in awe at the blade so Tlonna passed it to him. Immediately, it sank to the ground. Try as he might, the male could not move it. Tlonna plucked it off the ground and sheathed it. She added it to her belt.

"And finally," the Cyree said, "that which is most important."

She did not chant another incantation, or even raise her arms. Instead, she looked at her feet and took a deep breath. The water of the Cyree pond began to shimmer and from its depths rose a stick. It was nearly as tall as Miazie, dark with age and cracked a bit down the length of it. At the top and bottom were two rows of ciphers, and the rest was covered in glyphs, runes, and celestial signs. The staff rose completely out of the water and sailed over to Tlonna. There it thunked into the ground and stood, quite on its own, in the earth.

"Take it, Everwood," the Cyree urged.

Tlonna hesitantly reached out and wrapped her fingers around the staff. It glowed white for a mere second and then went back to being normal wood.

"The Staff of Cyree, a most powerful object. Never let it out of your sight, Everwood. Never. And the final thing..." the Cyree slid over the water and beckoned to Tlonna.

The elf walked to her, waiting. Without warning, one glowing hand reached out and yanked Tlonna into the water. There were no shallows, only a sheer drop into the water. Tlonna sank, clutching the staff and trying to swim upward. It did no good.

The Magin sank and sank until all light faded and she landed with a quiet thump on the bottom of the pond. Tlonna, though panicked and confused, realized her lungs should have been burning, but they did not. She opened her mouth and felt no rush of water. She took a breath. Nothing happened. Even more confused, Tlonna lifted her free hand and pushed it out in front of her. Bubbles rushed by her fingers, but there was no resistance.

Her eyesight was changing. One second her vision was perfect, and then suddenly she could see things lurking in the dark far beyond her normal range of sight. Then all color was bleached from the world, and then it returned to normal. Panicking even more now, Tlonna jumped up and felt her body float slowly, almost languidly upward. She started swimming up. The staff in her hand glowed faintly.

After a few strokes upward, the non-water started to get wetter, colder, and heavier. Tlonna's lungs began to burn. She had to squint in order to see, though her eyesight kept changing. Finally, with one extra push, Tlonna's head broke the surface of the water and she gasped for air.

Losolin and Miazie were kneeling at the edge of the pool, yelling. Across the water, by the fall, stood the Cyree, her figure slowly fading. When the two noticed Tlonna struggling in the water, their yelling became louder and more pleading. Tlonna paddled in their direction. When she reached them and pulled herself onto the bank, Losolin fell over her in his desperation to check her for injuries. Miazie was still screaming at the now nearly invisible Cyree. Tlonna looked over just in time to see her wink out of existence.

After catching her breath, the Magin sat up and rubbed her forehead. "What the bleeding hells was that about? Why did she throw me in the water?"

Miazie slumped on the ground. "She wouldn't tell us. Just said she had to give the message and means. When we tried to go in after you, she said we couldn't alter the water, and we couldn't touch the water. Then she floated over there and watched us. Stupid dead shrew."

Tlonna let out a short laugh. "How long was I down there?"

Losolin looked at his knuckles. "A few minutes."

"Minutes? I thought it was only a few seconds. I could breathe on the bottom, though. And this thing was all happy to be down there," Tlonna shoved the staff away from her.

Suddenly, Losolin grabbed her chin. "Your eyes, what is wrong with your eyes?"

Tlonna wrenched away. "I do not know. They started changing down there. Sometimes I can see far better in the darkness than before, then everything becomes sort of bleached out, washed away. I do not know what happened. It does not hurt, though."

Miazie studied Tlonna before looking away.

Losolin looked back over the Cyree pond and watched the waterfall. "She was very sad, I think."

Tlonna studied the profile of his face. A few short hairs fell over his forehead like usual, but now they seemed to magnify his beauty. Love swelled in her belly as she watched Losolin. The rounded corners of his lips twitched slightly and he turned his head to look at Tlonna.

She looked away, to where he had been staring. "Yes, I believe so as well. But she was not angry. Even though they did those horrible things to her, she was not angry. I would have been angry."

Miazie sighed softly. "It has been a very long time, though. Maybe she forgave them."

"No," Tlonna shook her head. "She never forgave them. I could see it, in her eyes. She was not angry, just...sad."

Tlonna looked at her friend and the two females linked fingers.

"She should be remembered," Miazie said after a few seconds. "Her death may have been violent and painful; her body long gone to dust, but her memory survived the ages until she was able to fulfill her duty. She should be remembered."

"Aye," Losolin said, fidgeting with his boot lace.

Tlonna took her hand from Miazie and rubbed her face. "All right, when we get...wherever it is we end up, we will put up an effigy for Andramaky. How is that?"

"Perfect," Miazie said, standing.

The elves followed her example.

"We should probably get back to camp. Do you remember which way we took?"

Tlonna shook her head, looked at Losolin, and then sighed. He didn't either.

"We came out here, so we should be able to find Miazie's prints and follow them back," Losolin said after a moment.

The three walked back into the wood, and after searching for about a minute, Tlonna found Miazie's tracks. They followed them back to camp.

Miazie rubbed her forehead when they arrived at Tlonna and Losolin's tent. "I am tired, and so tomorrow we will talk about this. How does that sound?"

"Fine. How long until we reach Kiys?" Tlonna said.

The woman shrugged. "A day, maybe two. What do you plan on doing there?"

"Speak with the king, see if he knows anything more than we do. Maybe he will supply us with some men, or allow us to recruit in the city. You said I need an army...that is the best way I can think of getting one."

The human nodded, biting her bottom lip. "A good idea, Tlonna, but I worry. There are rumors of Athelias, the king. Some say he is mad."

Tlonna shrugged. "Right now, it is the best option we have."

The Magin nodded, bid her friend goodnight, and entered her tent with Losolin. When they were dressed for bed and snuggled under their cloaks, Tlonna turned to him.

"Have you ever heard of a Belau? I mean, I would say it is a person who is really smart, but there must be something more, something...extraordinary."

The male squinted at her. He could just see her eyes in the dark. The pupils elongated and then went back to normal, the icy blue faded to gray, then black, and then white, then back to blue.

"I do not know, my love. There is so much happening these days, and I know not what to make of any of it. I say sleep, and listen to what Miazie tells us tomorrow."

Tlonna rolled into him, cuddling against his side, her head resting on his shoulder. "You are so wise, my heart. I do not know what I would do without you."

Losolin stroked the back of her head. "I can say the same, Tlonna. Rest, now."

As the camp mounted and the traveling continued again, Miazie pulled out a roll of parchment. Tlonna and Losolin looked at her askance.

"You want to know what a Belau is, right?"

The elves nodded.

"Well this is the best explanation I've got. From the library at Anutch, it was one of my favorite readings. The story of Ezrel and Alaina. Ezrel was a bard, Alaina a scholar, and they were in love. Back around the Fifth Age, a scholar was almost as praised as a lord, and a bard, a beggar. But nonetheless, they found a way to make their love work. When they were together, it is said the sun shone brighter, the grass grew greener, so strong was their love. But they were discovered and punished. But they had had years together, and Alaina had birthed thirteen children and secreted them away to live in orphanages.

"Now, Ezrel and Alaina both loved their arts, knowledge and literature, so much that when they were together, it fused. Each child was born with a love for art, stories, music, and knowledge. Each of the thirteen married and had children of their own. Every child had this love of their grandparents. And so it passed through the ages, lost in family trees all over Nymyños. These people, gifted with extraordinary knowledge and insight were called Belaus, from the word *belas*, an ancient Hindarün word meaning wisdom.

"I had forever longed to be one of those once coveted people, and then I gave up hope when I realized none of my brothers or sisters had loads of intelligence, in fact they were all quite dim-witted. To be told that I am a Belau..." Miazie grinned at Tlonna, "is a dream come true."

"So," Losolin said, "you are really smart, have appreciation for the arts, and are descended from Ezrel and Alaina. Good to know."

Miazie glared at him, but she couldn't help her lips from smiling. "Now, remember what the Cyree said, she was to give you the message and means, but she called me and Losolin?"

Tlonna nodded, "Yes."

The Belau bit her lip. "I think *we* are part of the means. You are supposed to use us, somehow."

Losolin frowned at Miazie. "I thought you were supposed to know everything. She *said* how Tlonna is supposed to use us. You are to be her advisor, give her information and advice. I am supposed to be her support."

Tlonna lifted an eyebrow at him. Miazie scowled. "Yes, but there is something more, Losolin. Something hidden in her meaning. No creature from ages past ever says precisely what they mean."

"And how many such creatures have you met, Miazie?" Tlonna asked, amused.

The human glared at her. "I know what I'm about. Now let me think. A tool...with which to lay your keystone of a life...no, no...not a tangible tool. Magical, yet more than magic? Perhaps. A person, another Magin, someone more powerful? No, you're the most powerful, ever. So Astinus said," Miazie muttered, twirling a bit of dark hair around her finger as she rode. "Well there's something. Astinus, Astinus's Magin, is what Cyree called you, yes?"

Tlonna nodded, but the human paid her no heed.

"Yes, Astinus's Magin, obviously from the prophecy...but why Astinus's Magin? He never actually *said* Magin...did he?" Suddenly she was digging through Tlonna's saddlebags, bumping her mare Kaia against Takîreaes.

The stallion snapped at the smaller horse.

"What are you doing?" Tlonna shouted in surprise.

Miazie blinked up at her, "The book, Tlonna, The *Chronicles*?"

The Magin shrugged. "What about it?"

"They're Astinus's prophecies. His journal. His life. Ah..." she said, pulling out the thick tome.

Pulling Kaia away, Miazie flipped open the book and began thumbing through the old pages.

Distracted, she started talking. "Astinus's journal was fought over after his death. Because of what Veries Gurgen wrote in *her* journal we know it was left to her, but we don't know what happened after that. Some say the Tower murdered her for it, others that she read it and burned it, then passed on the knowledge to her son, who then wrote it all down again. Ridiculous, of course," she mumbled, her eyes still on the book.

Losolin nodded at Tlonna with a mocking look, making her giggle. Miazie did not notice.

"Everyone knows Temas Gurgen was an idiot," the Belau continued, waving her hand absently in the air. "A worthless Magin if he could even be called that. I mean, one would think being the son of Veries and Teral Shedaerd he would have great talent, but no! A bump on a log who somehow befriended Jair. Even Roluf once said he was surprised at the brainlessness of the boy. One time, he nearly killed Jair and their other friend, Randi, by thinking he had learned how to fly using a Weave of solid air. Convinced the other two to jump off with him. I tell you, if it hadn't been for Feela, all three of them would have died."

Tlonna and Losolin stared at Miazie. The human's voice had changed, becoming slightly higher, and she had affected a strange lilt.

"Miazie? Are you okay?" Losolin finally asked, cutting her off in the midst of another reminiscence.

"What?" the human said, blinking.

"Are you all right?" he repeated.

"Of course I am. Why?" she asked, sounding normal.

"Do you know what you just said," Tlonna replied, gazing at her friend in concern.

Miazie blinked again, and then went white. "Dear gods...how...it was as though I had that memory, as if I had been there. I remembered it as Yuern Luen...that was her memory. How?"

"Perhaps that is part of being a Belau," Losolin said gently.

"Yes, yes of course," the human replied, licking her lips. After a moment, she said, "What was I talking about before?"

"You were mumbling about Astinus's Magin, why the Cyree called me that, rather than something else, and you were going on about his journal when you started...well...remembering," Tlonna explained.

"Ah, right. As I was saying, Astinus's journal was very sought after. I wish I could remember what happened to *it*. That would be useful. Nonetheless, what I do know is this. A short while before Astinus died, he had that vision, you know the one, Tlonna. About a taint and you being the prophesied destroyer of evil?"

"Yes, and I prefer to ignore that when I can, Miazie, thank you," Tlonna said irritably.

"Sorry, but you can't run from your destiny."

"I make my destiny," the elf grumbled.

"Of course you do. Now, that is why, I presume, the Cyree called you Astinus's Magin. I've never heard that term, but it fits. I'm sure he called you his Magin."

Tlonna grimaced at the thought of a man, dead ages ago, claiming her as his, but she did not stop Miazie in her lecture.

"It would fit that the Cyree would call you that, having been formed by the first fifteen. But there's that part about you having too much power, and not enough. What does that mean? Is that where the tool comes in? *Is* there another Magin with whom you...combine? Or is the tool an idea? Is it a belief that gives you strength? She called it your keystone. A keystone is a very powerful symbol. It holds up great weight, keeps everything together."

"Does this prophecy say anything about a Belau, or the Consort?" Losolin asked, interrupting her again.

Instead of glaring at the male, Miazie blinked, her lips parted. "*Yes,*" she breathed excitedly. "Well, not directly, but close enough. And not that prophecy, but his last one. *The friend will perceive*, and *the lover will rule.* Obviously I am the friend who perceives, the friend who knows, and the lover will rule...Losolin, you are going to rule...something. Perhaps Tlonna?"

Tlonna snorted. "He is not going to rule me, Miazie. No one rules me."

"Maybe he rules you indirectly, you see, without you knowing? It would make sense. People who love each other habitually make their choices while taking in the consideration of the other person. It's a symbiotic part of a relationship."

"I have never heard you talk about a prophecy with those words in it, Miazie," Tlonna replied, surprised.

The Belau waved her hand in the air dismissively. "It's not a major one, I don't think. At least, not as important as the other. And being that it was Astinus's last, I am inclined to think he may have muddled it. Other scholars believe so, too. It's rather obscure and contradicts itself a few times."

Losolin made a face. Miazie stuck her tongue out at him. Tlonna laughed out loud, receiving odd looks from the humans behind her.

As evening approached, the small company crested a hill and stood staring down at a large city surrounded by a crenellated wall, guards patrolling stiffly, saluting every time they came face to face with one another. Tlonna urged her stallion forward, followed by the others.

Takîreaes bellowed as he galloped down the hill, feeling Tlonna's anxiety. The guards looked up in surprise and with seconds, crossbows were cranked and aimed at the advancing party.

"Halt, who travels on King Athelias's land? What business have you here in Kiys?"

"We are but travelers, good man, seeking an inn," the elf called back.

"Travelers? Who travels these days?" said the guard.

Miazie squeezed Kaia between Neñyos and Takîreaes and flipped her cowl back to glare up at the man. "I am Miazie Paron Ughtren, Daughter of Darren Ughtren, and Princess of Anutch. I seek admittance to the city of Kiys for myself and my entourage."

The guards shifted a little, and another one spoke loud enough for Tlonna and Losolin to hear, if not the humans with them.

"She looks the part, Sir. I seen her once before, from afar, when she came with her father a year back or so. An' I heard, Sir, that no few nobles have hired elf survivors to be their guards."

Tlonna and Losolin glanced at each other, feeling a deep sadness for their kin. Finally, the first man spoke to Miazie. "You may enter, Princess Miazie. I am sorry for the delay. We must be careful these days."

The Belau bowed her head graciously and smiled prettily. "I understand, my good captain. I shall report to your king how studious you and your men have been."

The men seemed to preen up on the wall before going to open the gate. Once inside, the Anutchians and the elves were met by the captain.

"My Lady, I am Captain Asem Bartholomew, and it is my shining honor to accept you into the glorious city of Kiys. May the sun embrace you," he intoned, bowing deeply.

Miazie gave a small shake of her head to Tlonna, who had opened her mouth, and replied, "I am warm with its rays, Captain Bartholomew. May the sun embrace you."

"I am illuminated by its radiance. May I escort you to the Sun Palace?"

"No, Captain, we are not here on official business. We seek an inn," Miazie said, ignoring the man's surprised start.

"An inn? Yes, of course, Princess Miazie. If you would follow me please?" Asem said after a moment's hesitation.

Miazie nodded serenely and lifted her reins. The man moved into the street, shoving people out of the way to clear a space for Miazie's mare. Tlonna moved Takîreaes close enough to rub thighs with the woman.

"Is it wise to announce who you are?" she whispered.

Miazie leaned in closer. "You cannot reveal that you are alive just yet, Tlonna. Too many people saw or heard of your fleshless corpse. Besides, Anutch is small enough to escape most rumor trains, but a princess is a princess wherever she is."

Tlonna had to concur, but she still felt uneasy, as though every other person was staring at their little parade. When she glanced back, only one or two people were watching, but the elf felt a trickle of uneasiness settle between her shoulders.

They turned down many winding streets and narrow alleys before coming to a square. A massive statue rose in the center, a muscled man holding a spear planted determinedly in the base. It gleamed in the sunlight, a behemoth of white marble laced with gold. Tlonna could not help staring at the face of the man, the fierce set of the jaw, the narrowed gaze.

"Whoever carved that wanted to let people know resolve," she murmured, glancing at Miazie.

The Belau nodded, also gazing up at the statue. "Yes, it is called The Courage of Men, carved about four hundred years ago by Arnelias Cormel. He carved one for the dwarves, and elves too. The Dwarven statue is in Florwen Hune's capital city, as well as it is here, called The Valiance of Dwarves."

"And the Elven?" Losolin prompted when the human fell silent.

The corners of her lips twitched into a small smile, but it was there and gone so fast the elves barely caught it. "The Passion of Elves stands in the center of Blackhaven Forest, rather than the city. Any traveler going to any city in Blackhaven will see it. The statue in the rear courtyard of Blackhaven Castle was carved by Cormel as well. A male with a bow drawn back, called The Archer. All the statues have striae of metal or marble. This one has gold, Valiance has black marble, and Passion has silver. The Archer has red marble."

"It must have taken him years to do all that. This statue is massive," Tlonna said, craning her neck to look up at it as her and her companions rode beneath its shadow.

"His entire adult life, actually. He retired at seventy-nine, died at eighty-two," Miazie said, also looking up.

"Which one was first?" Losolin asked.

"Courage, The Archer was last," she replied.

"Yes, ours is oldest, and grandest," Asem said suddenly, startling everyone. He had remained silent the entire time through the city.

"I am sure," Tlonna said dryly, then looked around sharply when a gong sounded.

Asem stopped, as did every other person in the crowded square, and dropped to his knees. The elves and the Anutchians stared around at the prostrating people as the gong sounded again. In the silence, Tlonna heard other gongs ringing further away in the city. Surprisingly, Miazie looked as startled as her companions.

Two or three other groups of people stood staring around as

well, clutching at skirts or belt knives. They noticed the companions on horses and seemed relieved not to be the only people out of sorts. Slowly, Tlonna became aware of a low singing, more a chant, floating through the air. Losolin looked at her and shrugged. A few seconds later, the humans noticed it too.

The low voices rose, unaccompanied by music. A men's choir, Tlonna thought. A few awkward minutes later, the gongs sounded again and the people stood, brushing knees to remove the dust from their clothes. Asem did not offer any explanation to his charges, but rather motioned for them to follow and set off through the square as though nothing had happened.

"*What* was *that?*" someone said at Miazie's shoulder, and they turned to stare at Rebecca.

Miazie shrugged. "Some sort of religious devotion, I'm sure. Talenians are noted for their religious devotion and love for ceremony. They worship mainly the sun, and it is about to go down, so maybe that's what they were...praying about."

No one had the chance to reply because Asem suddenly turned and bowed low. "I present you to the Tradesman's Hall, my lady, Kiys' finest inn. Please allow me to announce you and your people to the honorable innkeeper."

"Very well," Miazie sighed, doffing her riding gloves.

Asem ducked into the inn while they dismounted. When Tlonna and the others started for the door, the woman stopped them.

"No, protocol demands we wait out here until Asem tells the innkeeper how many of us there are, and who we are. That allows for them to be prepared, rather than having to feel put upon. Soon, Asem will come out to lead us in while grooms take the horses. It's all very important to keep the grandeur of Talenias legendary, even if it is only illusion."

The ten others exchanged glances, but they moved back to stand next to their horses, impatiently folding their arms.

"And what if rains, or is windy?" Alisia muttered, looking extremely irritated. She was a lady, after all.

"I'm sure they put out awnings, or something," Miazie said in a pacifying manner.

They had only a few more moments to wait before Asem reappeared, looking pleased with himself. "The Honorable Master Doyle is prepared for his honored guests, Princess Miazie. I leave you now in his capable hands, and bid you a good night. May you wake to the sun."

"And you, Captain Asem, I thank you for your aid, good sir. May you wake in radiance."

The man smiled in pleasure and bowed low before striding away back across the square. Miazie shook her head and guided her companions into the inn.

Upon entering, a thin man with a short beard to hide his non-existent chin bowed low to them. His hair line had receded to halfway across his scalp and the lamplight glanced off it. Tlonna heard someone cackle behind her. She had to fight a grin, too.

Miazie curtseyed very slightly, a bare bending of her neck and knees. "Master Doyle, I am honored in the light to meet you," she said loudly.

The chinless innkeeper bowed again. "The light is honored to have brought you here, Princess. Please allow me to show you to your rooms, and then speak with your accountant to settle the cost of your stay."

His eyes settled on Tlonna when he spoke of the debt, and widened when Tlonna scowled down at him. Brown eyes shifted to Losolin, who crossed his arms and spread his feet, bending his back a little so that he loomed, rather than merely stood head and shoulders, above the man.

The human's eyes seemed to bounce off the hilt of Losolin's sword and he began staring at each of the humans behind them. Finally, he spoke.

"Wh...who is your accountant, my lady?" he stammered, having been stabbed by piercing glares from each of the companions.

"I have none. You and I will settle the debt, good master," Miazie said calmly, idly slapping her gloves against the palm of her hand.

Doyle seemed to take that as a threat, as he bowed again, much lower than before and sweat popped out on his forehead. "As you say, my lady. My office is back this way, if you would please follow me?"

Miazie nodded gracefully and started after the man, who gestured at a serving girl who immediately smiled at the ten others. "I will take you to your rooms, if you please?" she said brightly, and the humans followed.

Tlonna and Losolin moved after Miazie and an older woman put a trembling hand out to stop them. "You are not allowed back here, ah...sir and miss."

Losolin rested a hand on the hilt of his sword and Tlonna cocked her head to one side. The male affected his looming stance again.

"We are Princess Miazie's guards, woman, and you will let us pass unhindered," he snapped.

The woman paled, her eyes skipping along Losolin's sword and up to where another hilt jutted up from his shoulder. She started to dismiss Tlonna but the elf shifted an inch to spotlight the two swords on either hip and the bow on her back.

"Yes, All right then, follow me," the woman said weakly and hurried away after Miazie and Doyle.

Losolin raised an eyebrow at Tlonna, who bit her lip to stop from grinning. They strode into a cramped room filled with boxes, a small desk, Miazie, and Doyle. The man's head jerked up when the woman bustled in, followed by the elves.

"What is the meaning of this, Cairon? You know only the money handler..." he glanced worriedly at Miazie to see if she was offended, "is allowed back here."

"I know, Doyle, but they insisted. They are her guards, see?" the woman, Cairon, muttered, wringing her hands.

Miazie had to hide a grin with her hand when the woman stopped talking. After a moment, she said, "Indeed, Master Doyle. I go nowhere without them. Andramaky, Aemon, let the poor woman out, will you? You must have frightened her half to death," she said admonishingly, giving a pointed look to both Tlonna and Losolin as she gave them fake names.

In a moment of perfect understanding, the elves bowed low together and moved out of the doorway to lean against the wall. Cairon fled the room. Miazie turned back in her seat and waited until Doyle had reclaimed his before speaking.

"You were saying the cost of thirteen horses was...?" she prompted.

"Ah...yes," Doyle stammered, staring at the elves. "Twelve coppers for each horse, plus an extra ten for special care of the dun mare, the stallion, and the gelding. A-and that takes care of the horses."

Miazie counted out the coins and then sat back again, waiting. Doyle's eyes wavered up to stare at Losolin a full five seconds before turning back to Miazie.

"For the p-people it depends on how m-many to a room. The regular rooms have two b-beds, and the suites have o-one."

"I will take a suite, and Andramaky and Aemon will have one as well. The rest can have rooms. I will need...four rooms. Two of the eleven are children. Four rooms and two suites. How much?"

Doyle tore his eyes from Losolin yet again and did a few calculations on a sheet of parchment. "Fifty coppers or ten silver or five gold, whatever you prefer, my lady."

Miazie counted out five gold coins and slid them across the desk to Doyle. He scooped them up and placed them in a lacquered box.

"That should cover all expenses, Princess Miazie, including meals. Would you like-"

He cut off as Miazie stood. As soon as her chair scooted back, Tlonna and Losolin straightened, glaring at the man as he dry-washed his hands.

"If you will, Master Doyle?" Miazie said and gestured to the door.

The innkeeper sidled nervously around the desk and between the elves. When they closed behind Miazie, the man jumped, paling further.

"Th-this way, my lady," he whimpered in a high voice and hastened away. Tlonna had to stifle a snort of laughter before following Miazie.

The other patrons of the inn stared as they swung around a corner to move up the stairs. The elves favored them with a glare suitable for royal guards. The humans hastily went back to their food and gambling.

Once inside Miazie's suite, all three burst out laughing so hard they cried. Losolin was the first to sober.

"He kept staring at me as if I were Sirna himself," the male grunted, sitting on the edge of the four-poster bed.

"I highly doubt he would stare so if the keeper of souls did show up. He's terrified of you both," Miazie chuckled.

Tlonna frowned. "I wonder why?"

The Belau scratched her chin. "Elves are not common in

Talenias. It is a human kingdom, more so than any other, and they fear what they do not know. But, what they do know is of the Seadueni elves that live just across a stretch of water. Seadueni are not known for their courtesy nor their love of the human race. They despise anyone not elf-kind, and despise even elves if not richly born."

Losolin rubbed his nose. "When I was there, they treated me very badly. The only reason they allowed me to join the Band was because I beat them all in the tryouts. Even so, they hated taking orders from me. They are stuck-up cow brains, the lot of them."

Tlonna chuckled, but Miazie nodded in agreement.

After a moment, the Magin said, "I am going to wash, then. I feel filthy."

Miazie grunted and stood, grabbing a bag from her pack. "I'll come with you."

Losolin yawned and followed the females out. When they reached his and Tlonna's room he flopped down on the bed. Tlonna retrieved her soap bag and walked back out to join with Miazie.

She stopped when they passed the common room entrance. A figure, sitting slouched in a chair in the shadows, hand gripping the hilt of a sword, had beckoned with one long, gloved finger. Miazie, stopping behind her, put a hand on her arm.

"What is it?"

Without answering, Tlonna strode to the man and stood before him. "Who are you?"

"I am Aladorn, and you are supposed to be dead, *Andramaky*," he replied in a surprisingly deep voice, though it was smooth as butter.

Tlonna heard Miazie suck in a breath in shock. "How do you know me?" she breathed, trying to look inside the cowl.

"Much of what was lost has come back to me. Memories I did not know I had lost, Andramaky. I have been to Blackhaven many times, and I know your face, and that of *Aemon*."

Tlonna swallowed and put on a coldly regal face, and tried to use her royal lineage. "Then, if you are who you say you are, you will lead me to Athelias so that I may speak with him."

Aladorn stood. He towered over Tlonna by a foot, and while he was slender he seemed to fill a great deal of space. "Lady, do not presume to think I am one of your dim-witted, star-struck followers who is here only to see if it is true you have come back from the dead.

I know why it is you are here, and I tell you now that to go to Athelias would be a *very bad idea*. Not only is it extremely foolish, it could end in death."

"Death?" Tlonna whispered, staring up at the hulking male.

"As one of your race, I feel it prudent to tell you that your true death would be a very large blow to Elf-kind. We have lost you once; we would not survive it another time. Athelias is mad, and has most likely gone corrupt. In the eight years of your absence our people have been slaughtered, chased to the brink of extinction. The only true place of safety is Seaduens, and it is run by a king more cruel and dangerous than any other."

"Sir Aladorn, I am sure you have suffered greatly, but I must speak with King Athelias. I need help."

"Help? You will not find help here. Leave with me tomorrow for Arseninis and you will meet King Tyular, who is a man of morals and intelligence."

Tlonna gave up trying to be his superior. He was obviously not impressed. "Aladorn, I have great need to speak to King Athelias. I cannot leave tomorrow."

There was a terrible silence as Aladorn all but trembled in frustration. "Fine. Go tonight and hope it does not end as I believe it will," Aladorn folded his arms and was gone.

Tlonna and Miazie stood looking at the spot where the cloaked figure had been. Sighing resignedly, Tlonna pulled Miazie into the bathing room. The humans in the large tubs looked up, quickly dried, and exited, leaving them alone. Tlonna sank into the warm water and began to wash herself. Within minutes, the door opened and a maid stepped in carrying a pile of blue silk.

"My lady, this was brought for you by the Lord Udu. He said to wear it when you visit the king, and also that you must go alone. He said to meet him in the commons tomorrow at dawn."

Tlonna sighed as the maid left. "Miazie, will I ever be free to live my life as I choose to?"

"I fear not. You are a princess, and will become queen someday. We never seem to live our lives the way we choose."

Tlonna laid her head back and then looked up again. "Who is Lord Udu?"

Miazie blinked, and then laughed quietly. "Aladorn, I would say. Udu means doom, in Parlêthian. He seems the type to use an alias like that."

Tlonna grunted. "How did he disappear? Is it an elf thing?"

Miazie laughed again. "No, it's probably a magical talent he has, or something. I've never heard of people just disappearing on the spot."

Tlonna accepted that silently. After a while, they hoisted themselves out of the tubs and dried.

"Losolin will not like you going alone to see a mad king," Miazie said as they dressed.

"No, he will not. That is why I should probably not tell him. Why do you think Alad...Udu said to go alone?" Tlonna replied.

The human pondered for a moment as they opened the door and strode into the hall. "Probably because Athelias will believe anyone else will mean an attack. Two against one, or something. You by yourself will throw him off kilter. He is a very unstable man."

"Why do they allow him to remain king? Why not overthrow him?"

"Talenians are very odd people, Andramaky. They will not overthrow a king unless he makes a very big mistake. So far, he has not done so. He is mad, yes, but that is not a crime. He knows military back and front, so the people still believe him to be a decent man."

"They are all insane," Tlonna muttered, glaring at a passing man, who started and nearly tripped.

"Stay behind me," Miazie whispered when Tlonna moved to join her side. "You're my guard, remember?"

Tlonna sighed and moved two steps back, trying to look dangerous even though she wore the form-fitting dress Aladorn had sent. She did not notice the people she passed stiffening in fear, or the young maidservant fainting.

Opening her door, Tlonna smiled with overwhelming love when she saw Losolin splayed on the bed. One long leg was off the bed, his foot resting on the floor. Miazie followed her in and smiled fondly. The male was sound asleep. Putting a finger to her lips, the Magin gathered her cloak, staff, and belt pouch with the Magin stones. With a last glance at Losolin, she herded Miazie out of the room and shut the door, sealing it with a Weave so that he or Miazie could come and go, but any other would find it hard to turn even the handle.

"When he wakes, tell him where I have gone. He will be angry, and try to leave, but remind him that someone has to stay near you, so as to keep the illusion of guarding you," Tlonna said quietly.

Miazie nodded. "I will, but...be careful Tlo...Andramaky. You have the courage of ten men, but sometimes courage can be as deadly as a blade. Announce yourself only if Athelias demands it, otherwise go along with this," she gestured in the air between her and the elf.

"I will be fine, my lady. I will," Tlonna replied quietly, smiling.

"I know," Miazie sighed.

The Magin grinned, threw her cloak about her shoulders, and strode off, swaggering. Slanting the staff from the Cyree across her neck, Tlonna glided into the common room. Conversation died as she swayed to the door. Wide eyes locked onto the staff and the sword and followed her until she stepped into the night.

Tlonna stepped into the dark streets, dressed in the foreign clothes and feeling exposed. The sleeves opened at the wrist and fell to a point near her knees. The back was left open and came together at the small of the back. The neckline showed much of her breasts and shoulders.

As the elf walked towards the castle visible in the distance, she clutched the wooden staff. A carriage rumbled up behind her and stopped.

"My lady, have you need of assistance? Lady Magin!"

Tlonna stopped, her eyes staring at the staff she held. Turning around she smiled and walked towards the carriage.

"Kind sir, would you take me to the castle?"

"Of course my lady, anywhere," the carriage driver jumped off his horse.

"Thank you," Tlonna moved towards him.

"May the sun embrace you," he intoned when she reached him

"Ah..." Tlonna stumbled, searching for the proper words. "And you...I am warm?"

"New to the city, yes?" the man chuckled.

"Indeed," Tlonna said, relived she had not met a mindless devotee.

"I am illumined in its radiance," he said, smiling. "My name is Mershius, who do I have the pleasure of meeting?"

"Andramaky, Master Mershius," Tlonna replied and took his help into the carriage.

As he climbed back onto his horse he asked, "Where, may I ask, do you hail from? Seaduens?"

Tlonna was surprised at the amount of venom kindly Mershius was able to pack into the kingdom's name. "No, no...Blackhaven."

"Blackhaven!" Mershius exclaimed. "A refugee, then?"

"Yes, from...Belgarath," Tlonna said hastily, dragging up a town she remembered Miazie naming.

"Ah, well, at least you weren't involved in that awful siege. I am sorry if this topic upsets you. By the sun, I mean no offense."

"No, not at all," Tlonna replied absently, watching the castle looming closer.

"Belgarath now...that's near the city, isn't it? On the coast?"

"Yes, halfway between Blackhaven City and Andik. Large town just off the western coast," she said, unmindful of the fact that Miazie had never told her that.

The back of Mershius' head bobbed as he nodded. "That's what I thought. Always wanted to see Blackhaven City. They say it is more beautiful than even the sun. Of course, only a fool would travel within twenty miles of the place now. Deadly foolish. Still...if that Rahlan fellow ever vacates it, I suppose we humans will move in, take it over like we did Zeynuwn ages ago. Terrible business, that, but I suppose necessary," the driver babbled.

Tlonna made a noncommittal noise. The castle was close, now.

"Of course, that is if Rahlan does leave. He seems settled, now. Wherever he and his kin came from, it must have been a terrible place to drive *them* out. Worse than a sunless hell. Ah."

Tlonna put a hand on her sword when a rap on the door made her jump. A guard opened the small door and peered in at her.

"What's your business here at the castle so late? I have received no notice about any visitors," he growled, dark eyes glittering in the night.

Tlonna drew herself up. "I am Andramaky...Arrden," she said, stumbling as she made up a last name. "I come with a message from Princess Miazie Paron Ughtren to King Athelias Embina. It is urgent."

The guard's eyes widened, but his mouth drew down in a frown, making a comical face. Tlonna fought the urge to smile.

"What is the message? I will take it to King Athelias myself. You may trust my word, my lady."

"No." Tlonna said curtly. "I was entrusted with Princess Miazie's missive. I will not pass her private words for King Athelias to any but the king himself. Let me through."

A twitch caused the guard's frown to break. Instead he drew back out of the carriage. "Fine, but I will accompany you," he said, and slammed the door shut.

The carriage lurched forward and Tlonna prayed that she would not have to reveal herself. Guards gossiped just as much as serving girls did. A minute later, the door was yanked open again and the guard held out a hand for her. She took it.

Apparently the carriage had hid her features somewhat, for when she straightened to her full height and the light coming from the castle doors illuminated her face, the guard let out a slow breath, staring at her. Tlonna stood head and shoulders above him.

"An elf..." he breathed.

"Yes," Tlonna said irritably, jerking her cloak about her, "I am an elf."

"I never knew you were so tall!"

Tlonna scowled down at the human. Mershius was fidgeting behind him, obviously uncomfortable. She gestured to him.

"Master Mershius, will you stay with your carriage to take me back to town?"

"Yes, good lady, I will. Yes. Right here. No matter how long it will be. By the sun, Lady Andramaky," he said, stumbling over his words as they rushed out. He plainly did not like the guard.

The guard though, was too busy staring at Tlonna. She turned her scowl into a glare, and he took a step back. "Ah...King Athelias...yes. Follow me."

With a glance back at Mershius, Tlonna strolled along with the guard toward the castle doors. "What is your name?"

"My name? Ah...Bryce. Bryce Kring."

"Nice to meet you, Bryce. How long have you been a guard?" Tlonna asked, trying to make him talk, rather than stare.

"Seven years. Why?"

Tlonna shrugged one shoulder. "Just curious. I like to get to know people. Everyone is different, everyone has a different story. It is what makes life interesting."

"Yes...yes indeed. What about you? How long have you been a...what are you?"

Tlonna smiled. "I am Princess Miazie's personal bodyguard. I have been one for nine years."

"A body guard? But you are so...well...you're a woman?" Bryce said, incredulous.

"No, I am an elf. Women are humans," she explained lightly as they reached the doors and were encased in warmth.

The man was about to reply when a gaggle of servants approached with smiles. Their smiles slid off their faces when they saw Tlonna. A woman in the front of the group fainted. Tlonna tensed, glowering.

"I am Guardsman Bryce Kring, where is King Athelias?" Bryce snapped at the eldest of the group.

"In his dining room, Guardsman. What is your business here?"

Tlonna spoke before the human. "I am Andramaky Arrden, and I am here on behalf of Princess Miazie Ughtren. I have a very important, *private*, message from her to King Athelias. Take us to him immediately."

Two more women fainted when she spoke. Weak people. The old man bowed deeply, smoothly for someone his age. "Right this way, Lady Andramaky."

Tlonna and her guardsman followed the man through massive hallways and up wide stairs. The Magin studied the corridors they passed. Each one was lit with a multitude of torch lamps that illuminated it to the point of brightness. Tall tapestries of dark green velvet and gold silk with a wavy rayed sun adorned every other polished oak panel that made up the walls. Between the tapestries, on the other panels, were portraits in massive gilded frames.

Most of the people in the paintings were unsmiling and in stiff poses. Few were smiling, or seemingly in a natural setting, such as a pillared garden. Nearly half wore a gold crown of roses and suns.

Beneath her shoes was a thick rug of deep green with gold fringe. Tlonna wondered if the castle at Blackhaven was so lavish. After another turn, the old servant stopped and bowed.

"The king's dining chamber, my lady. I shall announce you,"

he said, and opened the door.

"My Great Illuminated King Athelias, a messenger has called. A Lady Andramaky for the Princess Miazie. May she enter?"

Tlonna waited nervously for the reply. She could see only the servant's bent back and the far wall covered in gilded carvings. Bryce shifted uneasily, plainly regretting his decision to come along with her.

"You may enter," the servant said, opening the door wider.

Tlonna strode in, trying to look foreboding. Her eyes fell on the man lounging in a high backed chair, one leg tossed languidly over the arm. It was a shapely leg, ending in a booted foot. The boot was tooled with gold. Athelias was younger than she had expected, though not youthful. In his late thirties, she guessed. A gleaming crown of roses and suns sat on the table by a plate, the same crown as in the paintings. Athelias's face had an element to it that made her uneasy. Something lurked in his eyes, something unnatural. Light auburn hair lay flat to his shoulders, which were broad and hunched.

He looked hunted.

Slowly, Athelias straightened in his chair until he finally stood, gliding toward Tlonna in an almost feminine way. Hazel eyes peered up at her from beneath winging eyebrows. "Tell me, Andramaky, has Anutch come so much up in power that it now has elves in its service? No, I think not. I have a liar standing before me, don't I?"

Tlonna felt her heart skip a beat, but her face remained cold. She arched an eyebrow. "You are an observant man, King of Talenias. Who do you think stands before you?"

The man grinned up at her, though it had a crooked side to it that made it a sneer. "Why, The Magin Princess Tlonna Ewôsdírn, of course. No one else would carry a staff like that, or have a face like yours. Funny, but it seems for a while there I forgot what you looked like. But we've met before, yes. You don't remember though, do you? Something's missing in here, yes?" he tapped her forehead.

Tlonna's heart stopped beating all together. She heard Bryce gasp behind her. The Magin drew herself up as far as she could and looked down her nose at the mad king.

"Athelias, what do you know?" she said coldly.

"I know much, Magin, I know much. But I do not know why you are here under the pretense of being a guard to the princess of a minute and useless kingdom. Why?"

"Princess Miazie is my counselor. I do what I do so that I will not frighten the people at the inn I am staying at. I am here for advice."

The man's lips twitched. "Advice? I thought you had a counselor."

"Yes, but she advises peace, sitting back and waiting." A lie, but Tlonna felt the need to boost the man's own importance of himself. "I need the advice of someone who knows battle, and the necessities of war."

The king grimaced, but his shoulders straightened for a moment. "Indeed. War on who?"

"Midian Rahlan and his army of demons."

"Rahlan should not concern you. Your land and throne are gone. Give up, Magin. His army of Darkwights is more massive than any army of Men in Nymyños. Do not foolishly hope that you can win a war against evil. We all must give up, now. The shadow has consumed the heart of Nymyños. Accept defeat, and you may be allowed to live, if Rahlan feels merciful."

Tlonna glared at him. "You are not a king; you are a coward, and a lesser son of weaker men. Kings of Men are supposed to be proud, courageous, and strong. You suggest retreat? You? When that statue stands in your city? What of the courage of Men, Athelias? Have you no reason to fight back? What of your people? Have you no honor?"

"You are a fool, Princess. Were you a person of less influence I would strip you bare and hang you for all to see, as is protocol. You come before me, asking help when I know you are after things I cannot afford to give you. Men! You ask for men!"

Tlonna made a face. "Why would I ask for men?"

"You ask for my soldiers to defend your people! What of my people? Would you have them suffer and die? Would you leave them defenseless and weak? Why should I defend your people when there are none left? You are of a dying race, lady, and the world will be less than sorry for your extinction!" The king stepped forward and grabbed her by her elbows. Shaking her roughly he began yelling insanely.

"Midian has come for his price! Those who refuse will fall into a never-ending pit of torture and pain. You and your kind have done naught but cause more grief and hurt!" The human bellowed wordlessly and lashed out.

Tlonna grabbed his fist before it could connect with her face and pushed the king down onto his knees. Bryce swore, but he did not stop her. He knew it was useless.

Tlonna shoved Athelias back, releasing his fist. His head connected with corner of the table and he sat down hard, rubbing the tender spot. The elf spread her feet indignantly and pointed an accusing finger at Athelias. "This is your war, too! You will suffer as much as I, Athelias!"

The man stared at her in shock, then snarled. Madness roared in his eyes. "I have made my peace with that," he said calmly.

Rage replaced indignation and Tlonna leaned forward, looming over the man. "What of your people? What right have you to choose their deaths for them? You are mad, and weak! This war is for Nymyños, not Blackhaven, Athelias, and you would abandon it now? Now?!" she bellowed, making the humans, both of them, jump.

Athelias giggled. The elf stopped short, unsure what to do. The king's giggles increased until he had tears running down his face.

"Now? No, elfie, long ago," Athelias whispered gleefully.

Tlonna took a step back, then another. She nearly fled the chamber, Bryce on her heels. When the Magin reached the entrance hall, she was running full tilt. Mershius stared in surprise when they burst from the castle and came to a skidding halt before him.

Bryce leaned over and vomited, tears running down his face. Tlonna patted his back, looking to Mershius. The carriage driver watched the guardsman in concern, but his eyes flickered back to the elf now and again.

"What happened?"

"Athelias is mad," Tlonna said quietly. "He will bring you all down and give you to Midian Rahlan. You need to get out of Talenias while you can, Mershius. I am sorry."

"Mad? Leave? Why?" the man asked, shaking his head.

"Soon, I believe, Athelias will give Talenias to Midian in exchange for mercy. You, and anyone you care about, need to be long gone by the time that happens; else you will suffer as my people have."

"Your people? You mean the elves?"

"Her people, man!" Bryce grated suddenly. "*Her* people! She is the Princess of Blackhaven! Alive!"

Mershius's shoulder jerked, but his gazed locked onto Tlonna.

She nodded once, slightly. The carriage driver leaned to one side a bit, as though getting ready to bolt, but then he bowed low. So low his hat fell off.

"An honor in the sun to be of service to your highness. How may I serve?"

Tlonna scoffed. "Stop being ridiculous. I am the same person I was twenty minutes ago. I am the same as you, Master Mershius, and Guardsman Bryce here."

Both men stared at her as if she had just sprouted adders from her ears. She sighed. "Bryce, I give you the same advice as Mershius. Gather up your friends and family, and get out of Talenias before it is too late. Please."

The guard wiped his mouth the back of his hand and frowned. His glare took in Mershius and her in equal ferocity. "Can't I go with you?"

The comment stunned Tlonna. "W-with me? Why?"

The man shrugged. "Where else am I gonna go? I don't have anyone here. No wife or kid, or anything. What King Athelias said in there, you needed men? I know how to fight, Princess, and I don't shirk my duty."

The Magin gazed down at the man before her, twisting his fingers as though nervous. "Yes, you can come with me, Bryce. But I am on a dangerous journey, where we may be attacked at any time. My company has lost many already. You are bound by no contract, so you may leave at any time. I am a Magin, Bryce. I will do some things that may terrify you. We are at war whether Athelias wants to acknowledge it or not."

The man paled a little, but his back was straight. "I go with you, Princess Tlonna. I will defend you and your people with my life."

Tlonna nodded, and smiled. Mershius, behind her, was shuffling his feet. "Where will you go?" she asked.

The driver shrugged. "Arseninis, I suppose, or Kajgenia. I hear Kajgenia is really nice. My family will settle there, I think."

"Maybe you will come to Blackhaven some day, when things are over? I will welcome you with honor."

Mershius looked startled. "Yes, yes, I will. By the sun, I will. Shall I take you back to your inn?"

"Indeed," Tlonna replied and turned back to Bryce. "Gather whatever supplies you can and then meet me at the Tradesman's Hall.

You know of it?"

"Yes, across from the Courage. When do we leave?"

"Tomorrow morning, early. We are going to Arseninis."

Bryce nodded and bowed. After a furtive glance around, he trotted off into the darkness. To another guard, he would be abandoning his post. Tlonna turned back to Mershius and climbed into the carriage. Night had descended fully and there were few people in the streets, so the carriage rumbled along at a quick pace. Tlonna mulled over her latest experience in a dark mood.

After a while, the carriage rolled to a stop and she stepped out. Mershius closed the little door and bowed low.

"An honor, my lady, to have met you. I will never forget it, by the sun. May you ever be illuminated by its rays. You are a kind soul."

Tlonna smiled and took the man's hand. "An honor in truth, for me too, Master Mershius. I mean what I say when I will welcome you to Blackhaven. Now go in haste, gather your friends and get them out of Talenias. May you go in peace, my friend."

"Thank you. Travel in light," he replied and jumped back onto his carriage.

Tlonna watched it disappear around a corner before heading back into the inn. Losolin and Miazie were sitting at a table by the low fire playing a game that involved two pieces of carved wood, three dice, and a cloth board painted with curving lines perpendicular to straight lines. Other than them, the common room was empty.

"Athelias is insane," she said aloud, and they looked up at her. Neither looked surprised.

Losolin's eye twitched and he stood in a single fluid motion, pushing his chair back with his knees. "We had surmised that, Tlonna," he said stiffly.

"Losolin, please do not be mad. I had to go alone. But he is more mad than we thought. I mean, he has given up."

Miazie made an irritated sound in her throat, looking with significance to the kitchen door. Tlonna made a face.

"Athelias knows who I am, Miazie. Soon, everyone will."

"You told him!"

"No, he knew. He recognized me, just as Alado...Udu did. But he is mad. He was all for giving up, accepting defeat, then he would rage about defending his people. I do not think he will survive long."

Miazie nodded thoughtfully. "We must speak of this in more private areas. Come to my bedroom. I have something I want to talk to you about anyway."

"All right. Oh, there is a man, a guard, who is coming to join us. His name is Bryce, and he was in the room with me and Athelias. He will be leaving with us tomorrow."

Losolin nodded this time. "It will be good to have another man who can fight. Tyre and Ryun will not be enough to stop any attackers, even with Rebecca and Miazie."

Tlonna smiled at him as she passed by, following Miazie. She trailed her hand across his tight belly and kissed him quite thoroughly. When they separated, his dark eyes smoldered, a wicked grin pulling at one corner of his lips.

Swallowing her lust, Tlonna pulled away and met Miazie halfway up the steps. Losolin went back to the table to clear up the game pieces.

Miazie opened the door to her room and Tlonna followed her in. She picked up a book the elf recognized, one from her pack.

Miazie shook it at her. "I have been reading this, which has a lot to do about your family. There has been a lot of scandal and treachery in your ancestor's time. Like here-"

"Miazie, what is it I am supposed to be doing?"

The Belau tilted her head, frowning. "What do you mean?"

"King Athelias went on a rampage about how I am here to take men from his army to build my own. Why would he think that?" Tlonna asked, sitting on the edge of the bed.

"Do you not remember?"

Tlonna lowered her eyes to the bedspread. "I only remember some things, minute, unimportant things. I remember nothing of my family, my role as Everwood, Blackhaven itself. I have fragments of them, yes, but nothing cohesive. Nothing useful."

Miazie carefully closed the book, ran her finger along the edge of the rough pages, cleared her throat, and finally looked up at her friend.

"The reason you were taken, the reason Midian wanted to make the people think you were dead, is because you were, are, a threat. Eight years ago, you and Losolin left your home under cover of darkness and rain to seek out fresh recruits from the other provinces. Usually the High Commander or the Second Commander would do this, but Blackhaven City was under siege, and they could not leave its defenses. You left, and no one ever heard from you or Losolin for six months.

"Six months later, you showed up, dead. A wagon rolled in and behind it was your body, fleshless. You were still wearing your diadem and so the people had no choice but to believe."

Miazie took a deep breath and plunged onward. "A...an insight came to me while I was reading. Midian Wove your image, well your skinned alive image and used it to provoke those who had not fled into despair. The remaining few of Blackhaven City, the greatest city of them all, surrendered and died. Then, to finish the knot so to speak, he cast another Weave. One that would make anyone who knew your name and your face, forget them. Luckily he didn't know about the Everwood title and that is how your memory was rekindled. It was a sort of trigger, that when you heard it combined with your full name, you would remember. The flaw in Midian's otherwise brilliant plan."

"Oh, so you admire him now?"

Miazie sneered. "Of course not Tlonna, but think about it, he found a way to make your subjects, and anyone else who had even heard your name a single time, forget it. It's horribly evil, but brilliant."

Tlonna plucked at a stray thread. "So, how did he get me?"

Miazie leaned back against the wall. Her eyes went distant, her mouth slack. Tlonna watched her, startled. After nearly a full minute's time, the woman swayed forward and shook her head.

"He ambushed you and Losolin, just outside the Blackhaven border, in Schelum. He brought nearly an entire army upon the two of you. He knew if he brought anything less, you would be able to break away. He took some of your skin and hair, and that is what he used to make the image. That's all I can tell you. Anything more, we will have to seek out somewhere else. My sight is limited there."

"Miazie...how did...what did...what?" Tlonna stammered, a little scared.

The human smiled wearily. "You remember the Cyree, right?"

Tlonna nodded. "How could I not?"

"As a Belau, I can access knowledge otherwise inaccessible. It's almost like scrying, but with information. I don't see anything, but

I have sudden insights and if I concentrate hard enough, I can force them. Rather useful actually. But the sudden ones," Miazie snorted, "they can interrupt anything."

Tlonna grinned. "You are amazing. So," the grin faded to sick grimace, "should I start what I set out to do? Should I recruit men to follow me into battle?"

Miazie looked out her tiny window. "There must have been a desperate reason for sending their one and only heir out into the danger zone. To march into Blackhaven with an army at your back would bring unimaginable hope to your people. They have all but been butchered into extinction, Tlonna, and I don't believe it possible for anyone to escape now that Midian has his talons sunk into his treasure. I say yes, post announcements in the streets, speak with kings for permission to take their men, as this is a fight for Nymyños, not Blackhaven alone."

Tlonna watched the flame ignite in Miazie's emerald eyes. She almost smiled.

"All right, we will do it. But how? I cannot just walk up to the kings of the provinces and say, 'I need men for my army, supply me'. Athelias just went mad about it and he was the one who brought it up."

"Of course not," Miazie chuckled. "You ask their permission to post these notices, train the recruits in their yards, maybe even coerce them out of a few soldiers to help command. Use those big blue eyes to get some equipment, and that staff of yours if the eyes don't work."

Tlonna laughed. "You slithery woman!"

Miazie beamed, primping. "'Tis what we humans do best!"

The laughter faded as Tlonna remembered the other thing Athelias had said. "Miazie, Athelias said something extremely worrisome. I lost my temper, and said the same thing as you just did, that this was a fight for all of Nymyños, not just Blackhaven, and that he was abandoning it. He said..." the elf took a deep breath, "he said he abandoned it long ago. He is mad, Miazie, utterly insane."

The Belau's brow furrowed for a moment. "He *said* that he had abandoned Nymyños long ago?"

Tlonna nodded.

"I can only imagine that means he has gone to the blackness. He has either surrendered or allied himself with Midian."

"That is what I thought. But if he has allied himself, do you think he would let it slip, to me of all people?" Tlonna asked after a minute.

Miazie shrugged. "You said he was mad. Perhaps he did not even realize he had done so."

The two females puzzled over Tlonna's meeting with the king a while longer before moving on to the scandals of Tlonna's family.

Tlonna woke early and dressed. As the day lightened, those of her company finally trudged out of the inn and prepared to leave. Bryce rode up on a tall bay with bulging saddlebags, shocking the small group. Tlonna introduced him, and the men swarmed around each other. Even Losolin went to meet him, grinning from ear to ear. When they were just finishing, Aladorn appeared and took them out of the city, leading them on the winding trek to Arseninis.

Tlonna pushed off her stallion and rubbed her legs. They had ridden all week and not stopped but to sleep. Losolin came over to her and pulled the tent off the horses back. His eyes narrowed when he looked at Aladorn.

"He bothers me, for some reason. Why do you think he can disappear like he does?"

"I do not know, Losolin," Tlonna said irritably.

Losolin and Aladorn seemed to create sparks when they were near each other, and it was getting to her. Everyone walked gingerly around them, as though afraid to catch their notice.

"I wonder at his appearance too, he seems rougher than a normal elf, darker. He must have human in him. Or maybe goblin," Losolin smirked and began setting up the tent. "You should ask him, Tlonna. I am sure he would answer to you."

Tlonna pushed him, her annoyance getting the better of her. "Why do you not ask him? You and he have everyone walking on eggshells around here. I do not know what you two have against each other, but it is driving me crazy. You need to figure it out, and fix it, before I grab you by the ears and *make* you fix it. Understand?"

The shock on Losolin's face faded to stubbornness. "It is his problem, not mine, Tlonna. If you want something fixed, talk to him."

Throwing her hands in the air, Tlonna groaned. "You..." she pointed an accusing finger at Losolin. "You..." she snarled, unable to come up with an appropriate insult.

Losolin's eyes widened, but his jaw clenched, nostrils flaring as he stared at Tlonna. "You want him to create a rift? Do you want *him* to be the reason we, you and I, fail? When you are not watching, he looks you up and down as though he wants nothing more than to run his hands over you. He glares at me as if I am the reason his eyes are black. As if I am the only thing standing between you and him. You want me to reconcile with that, Tlonna?"

The venom in Losolin's voice stabbed Tlonna. He glare made her want to cry for his forgiveness. Instead, she stiffened her back, swallowing hard. "You do what you want, Losolin," she said quietly, and then pivoted away.

The crippling pain of walking away from him nearly sent her to her knees. Tightening her eyes, Tlonna stalked toward Aladorn, who was shimmering next to his fire as though considering disappearing before she reached him.

"Aladorn!" she snapped, pointing a finger at him. "Stay right where you are."

The elf hesitated, and then lowered himself onto his camp chair, a simple wooden box with canvas stretched tight over the top that collapsed for easy packing.

"Yes?" he asked cautiously, staring at her finger.

Tlonna planted fists on her hips and scowled down at the male. "What is your problem?"

"What problem?"

She considered smacking him, then reconsidered when she saw the glint in his dark eyes. Losolin was right, they were nearly black, albeit a very dark green.

"Your flaming problem with Losolin! He claims you want me, and hate him for that, but I do not think that is the reason. Why can you disappear?"

"I am a wiat, Tlonna. I can blend in with the background, seeming to disappear. There are very few of us left in the world now."

Tlonna started. It was not an answer she was expecting. "Is that why your eyes are so dark? And your skin? It is almost brown."

"No, that is because I am a Dark Elf. You, and Losolin, are High Elves. There are Tree Elves too, and Plains Elves. Just different breeds of elves, as there are humans. Dwarves are the only ones who all have the same physical traits."

Tlonna shifted her feet, feeling foolish. "Are there a lot of you?"

Aladorn frowned. "No. Just like wiats, there is a negative connotation that goes along with Dark Elves. We are darker, so we must be evil. There are some whose skin is nearly black as ash and their hair white as snow. Their eyes are yellow or green, which gives them a frightening appearance, but I am the usual stock. My brother was ash-toned. He was torn apart by a mob that feared him. I escaped, barely."

The Magin made a sound deep in her throat. She couldn't imagine losing a sibling, not that she had any. "I am sorry, Aladorn. I suppose I overstepped some boundaries."

"It is how we learn, Princess. If you do not ask questions, you do not learn. Now, as for my animosity toward Losolin...it is only male dominance. I am by far older, but he ranks higher than me, being Consort. It rubs me the wrong way."

"Well stop it, please. It is causing problems," Tlonna said irritably, folding her arms angrily.

Surprisingly, Aladorn smiled. He had a beautiful smile that softened his dark façade. His teeth gleamed in the firelight, straight and white. His canines were sharper than most, though. They gave Tlonna pause. "I will do my best, Tlonna, to rein in my temper. And do not fear to ask me questions, either. You once knew all about me, actually. We were not close friends, but we were good acquaintances once. After all, I am your subject."

The oddness of his words made Tlonna loosen. She smiled back. "Well then, how long until we reach Arseninis?"

"We are in it, but it is about twelve more leagues to Arseninis City, we should reach it before nightfall tomorrow if we ride hard."

"Really? What do you know of the king there, then?" she said, sitting on the ground next to him.

Aladorn sighed, stretching his legs. "King Tyular, as I said before, is a good man, but he is human. Arseninis is a human domain. Tyular is headstrong and likes women. You and he, to my knowledge, have never met. He was crowned king about three years ago when his father passed away from illness. He is thirty-two years old, and has no legitimate heir, or wife."

As the Dark Elf spoke, Tlonna stared into the fire, soaking in his words. Tyular seemed a decent man, at least. Aladorn also spoke of Arseninisian culture. Unlike Talenias, the kingdom was not weighed down by the worship of anything. They believed, mainly, in the freedom to choose, as it was in Kajgenia, and Blackhaven.

After a while, Miazie joined them, adding a comment here and there when Aladorn faltered. Tlonna was becoming overwhelmed with all the information. Suddenly she realized Aladorn and Miazie were arguing. The Magin turned her attention back to the two.

"He is not a descendant of Tayrn Verla!" Miazie insisted.

Aladorn scoffed. "Look at the details, Miazie. His mother's last name was Verl, which is widely known to be a derivation of Verla, obviously. And she was a Magin whose grandfather came from Purheae. He fled when Hadian Rahlan wiped the rest of the kingdom out. It is clear that Tyular is descended of Tayrn. The points are too perfect."

"I'm telling you, Aladorn, it is not possible. Tayrn did not have any children," Miazie said adamantly.

"How do you know that?" the wiat said, sounding as if it were impossible.

"I am a Belau!" Miazie replied loudly.

Aladorn sat up straight, looking embarrassed. "Well...then...I guess you are right, then."

Miazie looked smug, never considering that she could be wrong. "Of course I am."

Tlonna laughed out loud, bending over her crossed legs as she did so. It saved her life. An arrow thunked into the fire and immediately caught. Had she been sitting up, it would have pierced her skull. With a curse, Aladorn was up, drawing a long, curved blade. Tlonna rolled, kicking Miazie's side to knock her over as another arrow followed the first one. The Magin rolled onto her feet and drew her own sword. The other two were back in her tent, with Losolin.

Panic seized Tlonna when she thought of him, unaware. He could be dead. Rage replaced panic, and the elf roared. A dim shape moved off to her left, a shape with a bow. Without pausing, Tlonna stepped closer, pivoted, and took off the archer's head. A golden sun was embroidered on his wool cuirass. Athelias's man.

She saw Bryce moving ahead of her, but he was hesitant in killing men he had recently fought beside. Because of that, he took a hit to his thigh and he fell. Aladorn was slicing through the attackers as though they were air. His movements were smooth and deadly. He made Losolin seem almost coarse. Tlonna had never seen anyone move that way. The wiat's thin sword thunked into a man's midriff and, with a quick pull, sliced him in two.

Tlonna snarled wordlessly as she yanked her blade, the ivory sword from the Cyree, out of a man's chest and kicked him back. Her heart skipped a beat when she saw Rebecca fighting side by side with Tyre, grim faced and sweating, but she was unharmed as of yet. Suddenly, Losolin was there beside her. Their argument seemed a petty thing now, when she saw him. His eyes ran a quick search over her, then he moved ahead, slicing away at foes.

No, he was not coarse, he was more violent. His movements were as smooth as Aladorn's; he just put more wrath into them. Aladorn killed emotionlessly, Losolin killed because the people deserved to die. They were there to take his life, so he punished them for it. His life was his own. Tlonna realized she was standing still, transfixed by her consort as he mowed down the swarm of humans.

There were dozens of them, outnumbering their party by more than twenty people. Athelias wanted her dead. Tlonna forced her gaze from Losolin and sheathed her sword. She let energy fill her, raw and violent. Her power was meant to kill.

The Magin raised her hands to the dark sky and released her magic. Lightning crashed down among her, striking down her enemy. Where her hands pointed, it killed. Men writhed as their flesh melted. Strands of power lashed out from her fingers and it fell from the sky. Losolin launched himself at a man who had been missed by the lightning and was running full tilt at Tlonna, sword raised. Just as Losolin collided with him, the soldier flipped his sword at Tlonna.

It whistled through the air toward her, spinning faster than thought, straight as an arrow. Time slowed for the Magin. She watched Losolin's mouth open in a howl of fury as his eyes followed the sword. Aladorn appeared from the mess of bodies and his hand lifted inch by inch as though to reach out and pluck the sword out of the air. Tlonna felt her power raging through her body, sharp and primal. As the sword came within arm's length of her, the elf turned to the side a bit. As it sailed passed her, she reached out, wrapped her fingers around the hilt, and stopped it.

Her arm was pulled back by the momentum of the sword as time resumed its normal pace for her. Tlonna spun the blade around and stabbed it into the hard ground, lowering her body as she did so, howling with fury. What right had these men to kill her? To kill her friend and loved ones? What right?

Silence seemed to pulse as she straightened, leaving the quivering sword in the ground, sunk halfway to the hilt. Losolin and Aladorn stared at her. Miazie stared at her. The man under Losolin's foot stared at her. Everyone stared at her. Lightning crackled around the entire camp, though it didn't seem to be harming anyone.

Tlonna ran her eyes over the standing people, mentally counting her followers. Thirteen...no one had died, though a few sported wounds, like Bryce. Forcefully, she tamped her power down to a simmering anger just below the surface of her flesh. Her body tingled with the essence, and it made her skin glow.

She walked to Losolin, who still had his boot pressed hard between the man's shoulder blades. Her consort watched her with calm eyes, though he swallowed twice when she reached him.

"Let him up, please," Tlonna said quietly, and he lifted his foot.

The man scrambled up to his knees, then he caught sight of her and froze. His eyes went wide and his mouth gaped.

Tlonna glared down at him. "What is your name?"

"Erich."

"Why did Athelias send you to kill me?"

Erich hesitated, glancing at all the people gathered around him, glaring at him in hatred. His eyes fell to her boots. "He is afraid of you."

"Why?" Tlonna snapped.

He flinched. "He said you were a threat to peace. That you were going to throw us all into the nine hells in order to save your race."

"My race is gone, Erich. There is no one to save."

The human nodded his head once. "That's what we told him. He said he wanted Bryce back, too, so that he could strangle him for a traitor."

At Erich's words, Bryce folded his arms, scowling. "Athelias is mad, Erich. You know that as well as I. Why would you throw away your lives for a madman?"

"It's not like we had any choice, Bryce! He told us he would kill us if we didn't do as ordered."

"You had a choice! I told you to run, to get out of Talenias, but you stayed, knowing. You made the choice to bring these men out here to die. Look around you, man! You are the last survivor of a file, and you are not going to survive long! Forty-two people against eleven, and you were beaten in minutes. Athelias knows Princess Tlonna's power, and yet he sent you to your death. How can you have been so foolish?" Bryce roared, waving his arms about.

Erich hunched his shoulders. "The end of peace, Bryce. I want to live in a safe world. I want peace."

"Well you can have it," Losolin growled bending to slice the human's throat.

"No," Tlonna said quickly, stopping him. Turning to the kneeling man, she squatted to bring herself closer to his height. "Will you choose to join us? We fight for peace too, for life, for freedom. We want to live in a safe world too."

Erich looked sick as he stared at Tlonna, her skin still glowing with simmering magic. "You just butchered my entire file of men. How can I trust you?"

Tlonna let out a slow breath. "Know that, unless you kill anybody not an enemy, I will treat you as a friend. Despite what you saw here, I do need men to fight with steel for me. I cannot win this war alone. There are those out there more powerful than I."

"Midian Rahlan," Erich said quietly. "But he's the only one."

Tlonna nodded. "Yes, Midian. But he has Magins on his side, I believe, and I cannot defeat him and others by myself. Will you join us?"

After a moment, Erich nodded. Tlonna stood. "Then go get your sword."

The man looked over to where his weapon was standing half buried in the ground. He grimaced, but stood and limped over to it. After a few hearty tugs, it came loose with a shower of frozen dirt. He stared at it, twisting it this way and that to examine the blade for flaws. The human's eyes turned back to Tlonna, a shadow of doubt lurking beneath the surface.

"How did you do that?" he asked quietly.

The murmurs that had arisen among the people stilled, even Losolin and Aladorn watched Tlonna with wondering gazes. She licked her lips, trying to find a suitable answer. A line in the book of Veries Gurgen floated to the surface of her mind, an obscure title that chilled her bones.

Finally, she said, "I am the Magin Queen."

Behind her, Miazie drew in a sharp breath, but it was the only sound among the group. Wind whipped through the trees an acre away, creating a keening moan that fit the mood. Snapping her cloak tight about her body, Tlonna strode away from the camp, her mind racing.

Losolin and Aladorn shared a look, then grimaced when they realized it. Miazie was shivering, though not from the cold. Tlonna's hard words pounded in her skull, echoing loudly.

I am the Magin Queen.

The Belau wanted desperately to follow Tlonna, but she knew it would not be wise. Her friend was walking a thin line between sanity and madness. Coupled with her changing eyes, which happened only when she Wove, the glow from barely tamped power created a terrifying look on the elf. Miazie's eyes followed Tlonna's retreating figure with ease. Her flapping cloak did not hide the ethereal glow from under her skin, making the elf a beacon in the dark.

I am the Magin Queen.

Losolin cringed inwardly as Tlonna's voice whispered through his mind. He loved her without condition, but she terrified him. He had felt her rage lashing through the night sharp as any blade. Watching her snatch the spinning sword out of air as it whistled by her had been beyond shocking. It had happened in seconds, though Losolin had seen her blink calmly once, as though time had been standing still. He wondered if it had, for her, at least. The Lord Consort watched his lover wander away as though lost. He wondered if she was.

As soon as Tlonna knew she was out of sight, she slumped down and drew her knees to her chest. Breathing deep, she let her power flow out of her body. With a quiet detonation, it flowed down the rest of hill she sat on to coalesce at the bottom in a pool of light before dissipating. Great sadness welled up inside her as she stared out at the dark night. The seven colored moons sat in a deep arc, illuminating the sparsely forested flat before her, and as always when she was alone in silence, the earth's spirits whispered to her, meaningless.

The Magin drew her slippery black cloak around her and sat hunched in misery. Behind her she could faintly hear the noise of the small camp. They were probably cleaning up the bodies she had left behind. Tlonna put her head on her knees and cried, great shivering sobs wracking her body.

After a while, the elf's tears subsided and she looked up, blinking. A soft sound behind her announced a visitor. Tlonna twisted around and stared up at Miazie. The woman held out a steaming bowl and then sat down when Tlonna took it from her.

"Are you okay?" she asked softly.

The elf sniffed, blowing on the stew, sending tendrils of steam off into the night. "I will be. How is everyone else?"

Miazie sighed, wrapping stiff fingers around her own bowl. "Nervous, but they're settling. You have friends, Tlonna, and people who believe in you. You are not alone in this."

"Yes I am," the Magin replied quietly, swallowing. "Maybe not in a physical form, but mentally, I am alone. There is no one who can help me, in the end. You know that, too, do you not?"

After a moment's silence, Miazie nodded. "I do. But until that end, we are all here for you. We are here because what you do is right. You fight for the right to live, to be who we naturally are."

"Then why are so many people against me?" Tlonna cried, tears streaming anew.

"Because evil has so much more power. That is why we have to fight. Without that fight, how would we know what is right?" Miazie said. "There will always be people who want to blame everyone else for their problems, blame everyone for their failures. No one wants to admit that they are weak, that their unhappiness stems from themselves. Good people will always be outnumbered by the wicked, which is how it is, how it always has been. To be good, to be virtuous, is to work. To be evil is easy. One just...doesn't care. Let others take the blame, the weight of life, and give up on it yourself.

"To be good is to accept your faults as a part of who you are, and to work to correct them. To care, to love, to need, they are all components of being an upright person. The syllogism is quite simple, really. If you believe in the right to live as you will, and accept that right in others as well, you are a moral person."

"And of me, Miazie? I just butchered over two score men. Did I not just refuse to accept their right to live as they will?"

The Belau sighed. "That is where it gets complicated. As soon as a person makes the decision to sacrifice someone else's life, their life is forfeit. Those men made the choice to come here and attempt to kill you, and everyone with you, long before you killed them. They willingly followed the orders of a malicious man, knowing they were wrong to do so. You saved the lives of twelve innocent people, Tlonna, and allowed a man who tried to kill you to survive, because he repented.

"Now, not everyone who repents should be forgiven, but right now, we really need people on our side. If we go around killing everyone who comes after us, even if they surrender, it's only going to turn folk away."

Tlonna rubbed her face despondently. "It is too confusing, right now. All I can think of at the moment is mercilessly massacring forty odd men in less than thirty seconds. The rage, Miazie. It was driving me insane. All I could think of was that they deserved to die, and my power responded. All I had to do was point, and people would die. What if I had pointed to the wrong person. To Losolin, to you? What about what the Cyree said? That my power was too much, but not enough? What if that was what she meant?"

"What do you mean?" Miazie asked cautiously.

The elf lifted her face to the stars, letting a look of utter despair spasm across her face. "What if I go mad? What if my magic drives me insane? Maybe it is too powerful for one person to hold within them."

The thought horrified Miazie, but it could not be discounted. "I don't know, Tlonna. But whatever happens, you won't be alone. Remember that."

Feeling a bit lighter, Tlonna rested her head on Miazie's shoulder, scooting close to share her warmth. The human put an arm around her, accepting as well as giving comfort.

Losolin stood next to Aladorn on the top of the hill gazing down at the two females. Pain wrenched his heart when he saw Tlonna throw back her head in obvious emotional agony. The wiat next to him seemed to shimmer, bits of him disappearing, creating a very uncomfortable visual.

"Would you stop that?" he whispered irritably.

The Dark Elf glared at him. "It happens because I am not focusing wholly on staying visible. It is almost natural for me not to be seen. Deal with it."

Losolin scowled at him, but said nothing in return. The male was difficult at the best of times. After a while he said, "What do you think they are talking about?"

"Probably the lightning, or the display with the sword. I do not really know. Oh look, they are hugging. Must be better, now."

"Or cold," Losolin whispered, but he knew Aladorn was right.

The wiat sighed resignedly. Losolin looked at him askance. "What?"

"I have no interest in Tlonna as a lover, Losolin. You are her Lord Consort, and everyone knows that. Only a fool would try to step between you two."

His companion's words shocked Losolin. He stared at Aladorn for a moment before replying. "Then why do you dislike me so?"

"As I told Tlonna, it is dominance, not dislike. By rights, I am higher in rank than you. I am, by centuries, your elder...but as Lord Consort, you outrank me. It does not sit well with me, nor any elf your elder, except your close friends. We all accept it, but we do not have to like it to do so."

Again, Losolin found himself too startled for words. "Bloody dominance, Aladorn? That is the reason you have treated me worse than a dog? You want to lead, be my flaming guest. I gladly hand you that mantle."

"You are an idiot, Losolin."

"What?"

Aladorn turned to face him full on. "You are an idiot. No one, not even a king, could take your place, nor could they do a better job. You are the Lord Consort to the...to the Magin Queen," the wiat stumbled over the admittance of the title. "You are the anchor to that," he pointed to where Tlonna and Miazie sat huddled together. "Without you, she would fall apart, lose her mind, and destroy us all. You do not understand the necessity of your role in Nymyñosian future."

"Nymyñosian future...? What are you babbling about Aladorn?" Losolin breathed, not wanting to alert the females of their presence.

"Prophecy," Aladorn hissed. "She cannot survive without you, Losolin. Whether you or she knows it, neither of you can survive this war without the other. Do you understand that?"

Losolin blinked, turning his eyes to Tlonna. "Yes," he said quietly. "I am afraid I do."

The wiat sniffed. "That is a blessing."

Losolin sneered at him, but he grabbed the older elf's arm and pulled him back to the camp.

The sky was pitch black when Tlonna and Miazie walked back into the camp. The yawning Belau stumbled into her tent after bidding her friend a good night. Tlonna ducked into her own tent to find Losolin sitting up against his saddle, chin in the palm of his hand, staring at her bed. When she entered, he looked up at her, blinking.

She stared back at him, shivering. The Magin had to hunch her shoulders when standing, and Losolin had to actually bend over in the tent, but as he was sitting, he had to crane his neck. Silence stretched as they stared at each other. Slowly, Losolin lifted a hand, waiting. Tlonna took it and let him draw her to him. He cradled her in his lap, resting his cheek against the top of her head.

"You are everything, my heart," he whispered.

Tlonna buried her face in his shoulder and wept until she had no more tears left in her. Losolin's scent, slightly woody, calmed her at last. His strong hands held her tight against his body. Feeling at home, Tlonna kissed the slight hollow between his shoulder and neck. His arms tightened for a second before he pulled back to look at her.

"I love you, Tlonna."

"I love you too, Losolin."

With a kiss, the male conveyed all his yearning for her, all his love. Tlonna sank into his embrace, warmth spreading from her heart.

Her breath frosted as Tlonna wrapped her baldric across her chest and shoved the ivory sword into it. Losolin yawned as he shoved the tent into Takîreaes' saddlebags. They had not gotten much sleep, but neither regretted it, and the others seemed to feel their calmer mood, for they too moved lighter than they had previously. Even Erich moved with a sense of ease while saddling his horse that had been tethered in the woods along with rest of the file's, which had been set free.

Miazie moved groggily, but she smiled at Tlonna and Losolin every time they passed each other. The horrors of the night behind them, the small company faced a new day.

Within a couple of hours, they were passing farmsteads. Boys and young men worked in the chilly air bundled in furs as they fed cows, rubbing their large, pregnant bellies. Snow started to fall in fits, light and lazy. As the day wore on, more and more people appeared on the dirt road they now followed. Aladorn tugged his cowl until it hid his face in shadows. Tlonna and Losolin did the same, shading their distinguishable faces from the haggard humans that watched their mounted party with interest.

Arseninis City came into view as night descended, a walled city surrounded by pasture land dotted with huts. As they neared the gates, they could see guards watching the incomers with hard eyes, lances held at precise angles.

After entering the city, Aladorn led them to a sprawling, windowless building named Tamarisk's. Tlonna dismounted her horse as a man came and took them away. The elf and her companions followed the wiat into the building and gasped aloud as a torrent of women ran towards them. An older woman, obviously in charge, stopped them.

"Aladorn," she crooned, giving the Dark Elf a sweet smile. "Have you brought me customers, or guests?"

"Guests, with perhaps a few customers among them. Tamarisk, I bring to you Tlonna Ewôsdírn of Blackhaven, the Magin Queen, and her companions, the Lord Consort Losolin Grisholm, and Princess Miazie of Anutch. These are their people."

The brothel owner's eyes widened, settling on the three as Aladorn named them. All blood drained from her face. "Aladorn...they should not be here. They should be at the castle. I will not shame them," she gasped finally.

Tlonna, unnerved that Aladorn would announce them so, clicked her tongue in exasperation. "Good lady, your...building...will be good enough accommodations. We have slept under the stars many times. Your rooms will be fine, if you will have us."

"Have you?" the woman asked, her voice much higher in pitch, "An honor, my Queen, an honor. And your men are free to have my ladies at their leisure, free of charge. Please. Let me show you to your rooms."

Tlonna sent Aladorn a hooded look that he returned just as stonily. She turned back around to follow Tamarisk as she glided through the brightly lit, draped room. Beautiful girls blinked at them from open doors leading into lavish rooms lit by flickering candles. Here and there, a half dressed man would peer over the shoulder of one of the girls. They mounted the narrow stairs at the side of the room and proceeded upward to a more spacious, though no less populated upper floor.

Losolin growled as yet another prostitute tried to touch him. Tlonna sighed with relief when Tamarisk opened the door to an empty room at the end of the short hallway on the left side of the building. Losolin followed her in and thanked the woman before shutting and locking the door behind him.

The room was gaudy enough to make the elves flinch. Red walls covered in white and gold sashes that came together above the bed created the feeling of being in a palace room. The bed itself was a massive four-poster curtained with a sheer white veil. There was a porcelain tub set in the corner, shielded by a floor screen painted in erotic positions. Gilded mirrors, tables, and a wardrobe completed the flagrant room. Red and white candles sat cold in brass holders.

Tlonna dropped her saddlebags with a thump and knelt beside them to start unpacking. She had decided they would stay in Arseninis for a week or so, to rest and recruit, if not more. Everyone was happy about it.

Tlonna sank into the warm fragrant water and brought her head up out of the water. She poured soap over her hair and body, scrubbing the grime and dirt from her skin. As she soaked, relaxing, Losolin paced the room.

Tlonna watched his face, darkened by prolonged scowling.

"Losolin? What is wrong?"

"Tlonna, do you think it is possible for an entire race to just...disappear? Aladorn and I were talking and he said that, during Aderiaen Rahlan's campaign, thousands of elves just vanished. And then Midian wiped out most of the survivors. He said that there are probably less than a thousand of us left, of our entire race. Of course there is Seaduens, but they do not deal with anyone else, and they are so consumed with having perfect blood that they breed only with high born elves. Consequently, the number of births is getting smaller as more and more of them become related. Seaduens is failing, too."

"I know, love, but what can we do other than what we already are? Unless the rest of the elves are...hiding somewhere, what can I do? I cannot bring back the dead, Losolin, as much as I wish I could." Tlonna said, sighing.

Losolin stopped his pacing and knelt by the tub. "It is not your responsibility alone, Tlonna. You are doing nothing wrong, at all, but sometimes I feel as if I am not doing anything. I have no power, I have no great title to give me sway."

"You are the Lord Consort, Losolin."

"I know, but next to you, what is that? You are the Princess of Blackhaven, and the...the Magin Queen, and the prophesied destroyer of evil."

Tlonna laid her head back against the rim of the tub. "You think that makes it easier? Losolin, I do not want those titles. I just want to be your wife, live in a house somewhere in the woods, and not worry about anything. I am doing what I am because others say I must."

The sadness in Tlonna's face broke Losolin's heart. He smoothed back her wet hair, smiling slightly. "I know. But...to get back on track, I feel as if we are missing something. There is an element in the disappearance of the Elven Race that we are overlooking."

Tlonna shrugged. "We will figure it out in time. We do not have a choice."

Losolin sighed. "You are right. I am sorry, go back to relaxing. You need it. I am going to find some food."

"Losolin!" Tyre shouted down the hall as the elf stepped out of his room.

Turning to the human, Losolin waited. "What is it?"

"There's a courtyard out back. The men and I were going to go down and work out some forms. Do you want to come? We could use your help, and Aladorn's too, if he's interested."

"All right, let me get something to eat and I will join you later. I will see if Aladorn will come."

"Sounds good," Tyre said as he trotted back the way he came. Halfway back, Bryce and Erich stepped out of the room they were sharing and followed him.

Losolin strolled down the front stairs and saw Aladorn lounging in an overstuffed chair with a book on his lap and several women staring at him. He pointedly ignored them. Their attention turned to Losolin and they started toward him. The elf stopped them with a shake of his head and a look. They turned away looking dejected.

Losolin pushed open the door to the kitchen and took a deep breath. Several women in aprons turned to stare at him, mouths agape. Each of them had some sort of utensil in their hands, but they looked to be prostitutes themselves, scantily clad as they were, despite the aprons. He frowned at them. "Do you all cook, too?"

One of the girls nodded. "Aye, Mistress Tamarisk says if we don't want to be with a man for day, or a week, we can work in the kitchens or do laundry. That way she don't have to worry about hiring servants."

"Ah...then can I get something to eat?"

"Of course my lord. What would you like?"

A while later, Losolin wandered out of the kitchen with a fresh hunk of bread in one hand and a steaming meat pie in the other. Traversing the many tables, poufs, and lounge chairs in the center room, Losolin sat down near Aladorn, who was obviously not reading. His eyes were on the page, but they did not move.

"The four men with us are out back training. Tyre wondered if you were interested in working with them."

"Is that something you do?"

"Yes. Tlonna and I have been training Ryun, Tyre, Rebecca, and Miazie as well as we could. Rebecca is actually getting decent at swordplay," Losolin replied, blowing on the pie.

"You work with the women?" Aladorn said, shocked.

Losolin shrugged. "Only the two. The others have no desire to learn. But Rebecca and Tyre have a child, so I would expect them to want to protect her at all costs. Will you help me? I was going to go out in a few minutes."

The wiat nodded, and went back to staring at the page in front of him. Losolin ate in silence.

"Ha ha!" Bryce shouted as he flipped Erich over his shoulder with ease.

Losolin laughed, ducking under a swing from Tyre. Ryun cursed when Aladorn landed a swift kick to his side, but he grinned as he regained his balance.

"Switch!" Losolin yelled, and the men rotated. The elf found himself facing Aladorn.

"You and me, then?" the wiat asked quietly.

Losolin shrugged. "We will see how it comes out," he replied.

Aladorn smiled slightly, but he was moving a split second later. Losolin evaded the quick flurry of fists and then rolled to one side. He sent in his own right hook, followed by a left upper thrust. The wiat caught his fist as it sailed toward his face, and jerked back to avoid the thrust.

Unsurprised, Losolin twisted, freeing his fist and tossed himself in the air. His foot connected with Aladorn's upper arm as he lifted it to block. The Dark Elf's other hand wrapped around Losolin's ankle and yanked downward.

Losolin slammed into the ground, but rolled onto his feet and knocked aside Aladorn's own kick. The elves became aware that the men had stopped to stare at them. Losolin opened his hand and slammed it into Aladorn's chest, shoving him back a few steps. Before the wiat could recover, the other elf round-housed him in the face.

Aladorn grunted with the contact and he stumbled to the side, but before Losolin could mount another attack, he dropped to the ground and swept his leg out. Losolin barely caught himself from falling flat on his face. Aladorn's other leg slammed into his back, pinning him. With a groan, Losolin twisted, yanking on his opponent's leg. Aladorn cursed as he was pulled toward Losolin. With a heave, he freed his leg and sent the toe of his boot into the younger elf's face.

Blood sprayed from Losolin's mouth, but he was on his feet in an instant. Aladorn stood as well, wiping the blood from his own mouth. The two male's came together again, their fists flying faster than the humans could see. It looked to them like a blur.

Their feet moved in a slow circle as they grappled. Aladorn grabbed a fistful of Losolin's hair, yanked downward, and kicked the younger male in the back. Losolin grunted, but he spun around, wrapped his hands around Aladorn's elbow, and pulled down.

The wiat cried out as his arm was forced down at an unnatural angle. Losolin released it just before it would break. As Aladorn staggered back a step, Losolin again slammed his open-palmed hand into him, this time just below the diaphragm.

Aladorn sat down hard, dazed. There was a moment of utter

silence, and then the four humans burst into cheers. Losolin worked his jaw where Aladorn's boot had slammed into it. Suddenly, he realized Aladorn was laughing.

Confused, he sat down too, staring at the chuckling Dark Elf. "What is it?"

It took the elf another moment before he could speak. "I really thought you could not beat me. I have never been defeated. You earn your place over me, lad. Feel threatened by me no longer."

Aladorn's words shocked Losolin, but he grinned toothily. "I never did."

That only sent the other male into harder laughter.

Tlonna smiled as she watched Aladorn and Losolin spar. She would have worried for her lover, but she had seen them both fight, and she knew there was no danger. To her, they moved fluidly, as though dancing. Entranced by the spectacle in the courtyard, the Magin did not notice Miazie entering her room. The human joined her at the window, gazing down in wonder.

"They move so fast," she said after a minute.

Tlonna nodded. "I think we all appear to move fast, to humans. To me, they are moving at a normal rate, almost casually."

Miazie's brow rose, but she said nothing. She heard her friend's intake of breath when Aladorn spun Losolin around by his hair and kicked him hard in the back, but seconds later, Losolin was pulling out of a hard shove to the older elf's chest. It had happened in a blur. Tlonna was smiling slightly as though she had known what the outcome would be.

Losolin sat down too, and then both the males were laughing hard enough for the two females to hear them. The men in the courtyard were staring at the elves in confusion and awe. After a while, Miazie shifted, pulling Tlonna's focus to her.

"We need to find something for you to wear when you go see Tyular. You need to be dressed in your finest when you visit a king, and you have a few torn dresses and traveling clothes. There's a shop a few streets away that some of the women here recommended. The seamstress will be able to fit you easily enough."

The elf sighed. "Miazie, I do not have time to wait for a dress to be sewn. We can fix one of mine and then I can go see Tyular tomorrow. Yes?"

"No. Come along."

Before she could protest, Tlonna was being hauled out of her room by her friend. Some of the courtesans smiled at them, others glared quite maliciously. One actually looked at Tlonna and licked her lips as though staring at something she desperately wanted. Tlonna shuddered and thanked the spirits when she and Miazie were standing outside in the cold. Once safely inside a carriage, Tlonna addressed the issue.

The Belau waved away the elf's uneasiness. "Some humans are attracted to their own sex, Tlonna. It is the way of things. You are an exceptionally beautiful elf, which means you are above and beyond any human. If one of the women fancies other women, it would make sense she would desire you."

"But it is not natural! Not normal!" Tlonna insisted.

The human raised an eyebrow at her. "And are you the one to judge that?"

Shame automatically replaced disgust. The elf hung her head. "No, no I am not. Each person has a right to feel what they feel, to choose as they will. I am sorry."

Miazie shrugged. "What are you going to do about it?"

Tlonna looked up sharply. "I do not plan on doing anything about it, Miazie. Why should I?"

"Because we are going to be staying at Tamarisk's for a while, yes?"

"Yes."

"Then she is going to start hounding after you. It is not a normal thing for a prostitute to not get what she wants, sexually. Understand?"

Tlonna grimaced. "Yes. But...I do not feel that way, at all. In any way. Besides, I am with Losolin. That should warn her off."

"Should," Miazie shrugged again, "but won't."

"Why ever not?"

"Because she is human, Tlonna. We're a determined, stubborn, fast-paced race. You should know that by now. She is going to go after you, most likely. I'm not blind. I've seen the way she looks at you."

Tlonna swallowed to keep down the disgust in her throat. "That is an...unpleasant thought. I am not going to do anything, and if she does come...after...me, then she is in for a surprise. No," she said sharply when Miazie opened her mouth in protest. "She is entitled to desire as she will, but she will not push it on me. I have a right to my life, too."

Defeated, Miazie sat back in the seat and fingered her purse. After a while, she said, "We should probably get something for Losolin, too. Do you know his height, and width?"

Tlonna frowned in thought. "No, but I know how tall he is in relation to me. And how wide. Is that good enough?"

"We'll see," Miazie said as the carriage stopped.

The driver opened the door and handed them down in front of a large, slat-faced building crawling with jabbering women. When Tlonna and Miazie ducked into the low entrance, silence fell like a thunderclap. All women, of all sizes and ages, stared at them. The elf realized she was standing with her back rigid, which made her stand head and shoulders above the tallest person in the large shop. Immediately, she hunched her shoulders and lowered her head a bit to seem less imposing.

Suddenly, all the women were flowing toward her, hands outstretched. Most like claws ready to rip her open, a few as though to ward off a blow.

"Ladies!" a strong voice bellowed, stopping the charging women in mid-stride. "I will not have stampeding in my shop. Hold yourselves!"

Tlonna straightened again to see who had spoken and found a plump woman standing on an upper level with hands braced on her hips. She was not pleasant looking, but Tlonna felt grateful for her interference. The woman stared down at her with a fixed glower that made her look more aged than she probably was. Miazie, clutching Tlonna's forearm in a claw-like grip, stepped in front of the elf.

"Mistress Karin?"

It was then that Tlonna realized how small Miazie really was. The top of the Belau's head barely reached Tlonna's chest. Her raven hair glistened cleanly, and she stood with shoulders back, spine stiff. A proud woman, Tlonna thought. A strong woman. A queen facing an angry horde bent on murder. That's what she appeared to be at the moment.

"Yeah, and who are you to create such a ruckus in my shop?"

Tlonna put a hand on Miazie's shoulder. "We are only customers, Mistress Karin. We come only to shop."

Karin's gaze shifted to Tlonna and the elf realized she had been pointedly ignoring her. "Your kind is not welcome here, elf."

The words ripped through Tlonna like a blade. She winced.

Miazie cursed loudly, and avidly. "She is not from Seaduens. She is the Magin Queen of Blackhaven, the Everwood. I am Princess Miazie Ughtren of Anutch, Belau. Who are you to deny us?"

Shock rippled through the women and even Karin rocked back on her heels as though struck. Tlonna folded her arms in front her and waited, trying to seem nonchalant.

Finally, Karin spoke. "A queen and a princess should not be clothed as you are. Please allow me to outfit you."

Tlonna curled her lip at the dead tone of the woman, but Miazie bent her neck in a graceful concession. "We have need of two gowns, and a suit for the Lord Consort of the Everwood. We need them by tomorrow."

Karin did not show any emotion more than tapping one nailed finger on the rail. Without a word, she disappeared into a doorway. A few seconds later, she was making her way through the silent crowd of women toward them. When she reached Tlonna and Miazie, the human spun around, waving her arms.

"Get back to your activities, Ladies. Go on, now. Go!"

The women bustled away, chattering loudly. Karin turned back to the two royals before her. Up close, Tlonna could see liver spots folded into the fleshy, wrinkled skin. She had to concentrate on not making a face. Miazie actually topped Karin by a few inches. Tlonna felt like a behemoth.

"You will follow me into my studio?"

Tlonna and Miazie merely waited for the grouchy woman to start for her studio before following. Once they reached it, the Magin stared in awe. Bolts of cloth, from course wool to spun gold, sat wrapped around thick beams. Karin turned and studied them both head to toe.

"What do you need these gowns for?"

"A visit to King Tyular," Miazie replied coolly.

Karin nodded, still running her eyes over them. They were an unsettling deep green, the only beautiful part of her. They paused on Tlonna a bit longer the second time. When the silence started to turn awkward, she said, "A crème, for you, then, Everwood. With silver accents. And a copper for you, Princess. Yes, that will work. What coloring is this Lord?"

"Darker than I, though the same coloring," Tlonna supplied, wondering what Losolin would think when he received his new clothes.

"Then a gray, I think. Yes. Let's get your measurements, then. Elf, you first," Karin said after a moment of thought.

She dragged a chair over so that she could reach the top of Tlonna's head and stepped onto it with a groan. She held a tape up and grunted. "Seven foot three," she muttered, scratching on a pad of paper. After taking several different measurements, the woman moved onto Miazie.

After an hour of holding material up to her chin, Tlonna was irritated and bored. Miazie actually seemed excited as she held up different fabrics of the same color up to *her* chin.

"Isn't this fun, Tlonna? I mean, doesn't it just make you feel beautiful?"

"Sure," Tlonna mumbled, glancing longingly at the high window.

Miazie laughed. "I loved going to Rebecca's, picking out colors and fabrics, choosing different styles. Father always told me I was wasting money, but I never thought it was wasted. I just mourn the fact that I had to leave them behind when we..." she glanced at Karin, "when we left."

Tlonna listened with half an ear. "Mmhmm."

"I think you should go naked, Tlonna."

"Mmhmm. Yeah, sure."

"Naked as the day you were born. Well, maybe a sash?"

"Okay," Tlonna murmured before her friend's words reached her mind. She yelped. "Wait, what?"

Miazie burst out laughing, and even Karin managed a grimace that could have been a smile. "What were you daydreaming about?"

"Freedom," Tlonna said heartily.

"Are you bored? I thought this would be fun," Miazie said, sounding a little disappointed.

"No, no...just preoccupied," Tlonna lied.

Miazie smiled faintly. "Tlonna, if you could put aside all your worries for a little while, you would be a far more remarkable person than anyone ever born. You already are more than most could even dream of being. But..." she moved over in a rustle of cloth to lay a hand lightly on Tlonna's arm, "let your heart rest easy for an hour."

Tlonna shook her head. "How can I, when even going into a shop, I become a threat? Those women wanted to tear me apart just for being an elf. How can I put my troubles aside when they are thrown at me with every turn I make?"

Faced with the words, Karin looked away from Tlonna's piercing gaze and shifted her feet a little.

Miazie sighed. "You're right. I'm sorry, Tlonna. I guess I just wanted to give you a small time of ease."

"And you have, my friend. Do not doubt yourself."

Karin cleared her throat pointedly. "I have made my selections, and if I am to get them done by tomorrow evening, I need to start now. I also need payment."

Tlonna shifted irritably at the woman's tone, glowering, but Miazie smiled excitedly. "Of course. Your price?"

As the two humans bartered their way through monetary issues, Tlonna roamed around the room, running her fingers over bolts of cloth. Some slicked through her fingers liquidly, others were stiff, some scratchy.

"Tlonna?"

The elf turned at Miazie's voice. She was done with Karin and waiting patiently by the door. Tlonna strolled to her, and with a glance back at the seamstress who was counting her money, walked out. Women still seethed all over the place, but they pointedly ignored the two as they made their way to the door.

"Do you think it would be safe to walk?" Tlonna asked once outside.

Miazie shrugged. "It's a fair distance, why?"

"I do not feel like being confined. I need air in my lungs. Sometimes I feel as though I am drying up inside a building. My heart seems to weaken."

"It's part of being an elf. Buildings are not natural structures, so your earth magic suffers inside them. It's one of the things that interests me about Blackhaven City. It is a city, but an elfish one. The castle is supposed to be magnificent and huge, and yet elves live within it comfortably. I'm terribly confused about it."

Tlonna could not stop a chuckle at her friend's honest bafflement as they started down the crowded street. People bundled in thick cloaks hurried past, their faces wrapped in woolen scarves against the biting chill in the air. Most seemed intent on their destination, but one or two looked up in time to notice, and stare at, Tlonna.

"The feeling is so hostile here, Miazie. At least in Talenias they were kind enough and did not resort to automatic violence," Tlonna muttered as an old man hissed at her when they passed each other.

"They share a border with Seaduens, what do you expect?" Miazie replied softly. "Any elf they have had contact with has probably sneered down his nose at them, then done something drastically cruel."

"I am so proud of my race," Tlonna said bitterly.

Miazie grimaced at her. "It's just the Seadueni. I'm sure if one of them moved to Blackhaven, they would have a complete turnaround of behavior."

"Oh?" Tlonna asked, "and have you met a Blackhaven elf that has their memory intact?"

"Aladorn."

"Yeah, he is a great example," Tlonna said, though she smiled.

Miazie snorted. "He is. He is kind, quiet, smart, and viciously lethal."

"Ah...the perfect male. Viciously lethal is not a good quality, Miazie."

"It is when you're an elf, Tlonna. You know he would jump into the line of fire for you. As would Losolin, probably quicker too, and you know he's a good model of behavior."

Tlonna grunted. "He is hot-tempered, irritable, stubborn, and in a bad mood most of the time. If you call that model behavior, I do not want to meet misbehaved people."

Miazie just laughed as they strolled down the street. When they finally reached Tamarisk's, the males were sitting in a circle sharing a pitcher of ale and laughing uproariously. Tlonna was relieved to see both Aladorn and Losolin in their midst. Suddenly she felt a smooth hand glide up her arm and settle on her shoulder.

The elf looked down and scowled at the young whore who smiled sweetly at her. "You are tense, my lady. Let me ease your aches."

Tlonna shrugged her shoulder out of the woman's hands and stepped away, turning so she was face to face with her. Miazie sighed resignedly.

"Listen," Tlonna snapped quietly, shoving a finger in the woman's face. "I do not like that. I am betrothed, young lady, to a *male* and I will keep it that way. You stay away from me."

Rather than look upset, the woman wrapped dainty fingers around Tlonna's pointing hand and lowered it. "My name is Nicole, Lady. I have strong, smooth fingers and I can make the tension drip from your muscles. I can ease all your pains."

"Is that so," Tlonna muttered, yanking her hand away.

"Yes, and Lady? I think our skin needs to touch..." Nicole breathed pushing herself closer to the elf.

Fury lashed through Tlonna before she could even think. With a hard shove, she sent Nicole flying. The woman landed hard on a couch, flipped over the back, and rolled a few times before lying limp as a rag. Silence rang in the room, then shouts as everyone ran toward her. Losolin reached her first, eyes staring at the listless whore. A few of the girls ran to Nicole, shaking her shoulder.

"She's breathing! She's alive!" one of them cried, huddling over the still body.

Tlonna snorted. "Of course she is alive. I did not push her hard enough to do any damage."

Nicole groaned and Tlonna held out a hand. "See?"

Tamarisk hurried into the room, took a quick scan of the scene, and carefully put away the cloth she had been wiping her hands on. "Ladies, please take Nicole into her room where she can recover. I see nothing wrong with her other than a knocked head. She probably deserved it."

The women gingerly picked up their friend like a fallen comrade. Tamarisk casually strode over to the couch and leaned her forearms on the back of it, watching Tlonna. "Did she push herself on you?"

"Yes."

Tamarisk sighed. "Then I do not blame you. I have talked with her many times before. She cannot control her unnatural urges. I am sorry you had to deal with it. Know I hold no grudge."

Surprised, Tlonna nodded. "I am sorry, Mistress Tamarisk. I do not usually let my temper get the best of me, but I am wrung tight today. I will pay for any healing she needs."

"Were it any of my other girls, I would be upset, but Nicole has caused problems since she started here. This is not the first time she's been tossed away."

"Perhaps you should kick her out," Miazie said.

Tamarisk shook her head. "I promise my girls a place to stay, to earn money, to do as they please, as long as they give something back. People do not always come here to enjoy the lush pleasure of women, as you yourselves are evidence to that. Others come for food, too. My kitchen is well known around the city. Nicole is one of the best cooks I have."

Losolin grunted. "She made me a meat pie this morning. It was good."

Tamarisk beamed at the male, then, with a curtsy to Tlonna and Miazie, bustled off in the direction Nicole had been taken.

Tlonna sighed and scrubbed her hands over her face. "I cannot believe I just struck that girl. I could have killed her. Even so, I probably took her out of commission for a couple of days."

Losolin rubbed her shoulder. "Our temper gets the best of all of us, love. You heard Tamarisk, the woman gets shoved away all the time. I saw what she did to you. I have not seen any of the other ladies here do that, not even to men."

"I warned you Tlonna. I told you she would pull something," Miazie said angrily. "I told you to be easy with her."

"I was easy with her, but she persisted. She will be fine, Miazie. Just because she is a human does not mean every fall will break her," Tlonna snapped back.

The Belau merely glared at her before flouncing off. Tlonna sighed and laid her head on Losolin's shoulder. "Have you been chased by any of them?"

"No, well...not since the first couple of hours. I told them I was not interested, and they backed off. I did not know humans liked their own gender, too."

"They do not, usually," Tlonna said wearily. "I guess a few of them go that way, though."

Losolin made a noise that she heard through his neck. Tlonna looked around when she felt another hand on her arm. Aladorn gave her a small smile, more comforting than happy.

"You handled that better than most. I have seen people torn apart because of that sort of attraction."

"And what do you think of that sort of attraction?" Tlonna

asked quietly.

The wiat shrugged. "To each their own, I suppose."

The three elves stood silently for a while before the Magin sighed. "I am tired. I am going up to bed. Will you be there soon?" she asked Losolin.

He nodded. "I want to finish this hand up, first. Aladorn?"

"I have you boy, you are defeated. Accept it."

Losolin laughed, kissed Tlonna on the top of her head, and walked back to the table with Aladorn. Tlonna rolled her shoulders and headed up the stairs to her room. Exhausted, she merely stripped and stumbled into the bed.

Losolin slipped into bed an hour later, careful not to wake Tlonna. She looked peaceful as the soft moonlights glittered through the window to play across her face. His heart melted when she rubbed her cheek against the pillow in her sleep. It started racing when he realized she was completely naked. Cursing silently, the male resisted the urge to wake her up and turned his back to her.

Grumbling about the unfairness of life, Losolin blew out the candle on his side of the bed and lay in the darkness until sleep claimed him.

Tlonna sent a letter to Tyular the next morning, writing in the most formal script she could. Miazie stared at it for a second before adding her signature.

"What?"

"I have never seen such elegant writing in Hindarün, Tlonna. How'd you manage that?"

The elf shrugged. "It put a little effort into it. Is it all right? Not too demanding, not too weak?"

"Perfect. Do you have your seal?"

Tlonna handed the human her seal and bar of wax before getting up from the desk. "I am nervous. I know everyone says he is a good man; new to the throne, but a good leader nonetheless. I just cannot help worrying if he is in with Athelias. What if he, too, is mad?"

Miazie smiled as she dripped the silvery blue wax onto the seam of parchment. "Contrary to popular belief, Tlonna, not all humans are insane. We like to think elves are."

"Bite your tongue, you tosspot," Tlonna said, laughing.

Miazie snorted so hard she choked. "*Tosspot?*"

Tlonna grinned. "I heard one of the whores say it. I thought it fit."

"Did you now?" Miazie giggled, pressing the seal into the pool of wax.

"Indeed. How long do you think Karin is going to take with the clothes?" the elf asked.

Miazie shrugged. "Who knows. She had a whole team working on them, so not too long. Record time, I would guess. She knows what's on the line."

"Do you really think she does?" Tlonna asked, sobering.

The human nodded. "Yeah. She's a grouch, but a smart one. Seamstresses are not the wealthiest people in the trading business, they're far from the poorest too, but she has thousands of geld worth of material in that shop of hers. She knows what's at stake if she fails us."

Tlonna took the letter requesting an audience that evening, if possible, and nodded. "I suppose."

"Don't let Bryce or Erich take that, or Aladorn or Losolin. They're too edgy and recognizable. Anyone else should be fine," Miazie said, pointing at the letter.

"Bryce and Erich are too?"

"Aye, they only have their Talenias cuirasses, or they go in poor soldier clothes. Also with the Sun of Talenias on sleeves and whatnot."

"Ah," Tlonna said as she left the room searching for one of her companions.

She found them all in the rear courtyard again, sparring and watching. Striding up to Tyre, she shoved the letter at him. He gave her a blank stare.

"I need you to take that up to the castle, make sure it gets to Tyular. Do not come back without a reply, please."

Tyre groaned. "I'm going to have to change, aren't I?"

Tlonna shrugged. "If you want to deliver a message to the King of Talenias in your sweaty woolskins, be my guest."

The man grunted, but he waved a goodbye to his pals and trotted back up the narrow stairs that would lead him to the upper floor. It was used for discrete exiting for shy clientele of the bordello.

The clothes came before the reply. Miazie bubbled into Tlonna's room carrying the brown paper packages. She and Losolin were sorting through their meager possessions and tossing out clothes that were better fit for rags.

"Look! Look Tlonna! She got them done! Look!" Miazie cheered, shoving the packages at the Magin.

Laughing, Tlonna took the one with the name Everwood scrawled across it and opened it. A bundle of white slashed crème silk unraveled into a magnificent winter dress. Embroidered with a simple swirl design along the hem and square-cut neckline in silver, it was not the most decorated gown, but it shocked Tlonna. For the amount of time given, Karin and her team had pieced together a work of art.

It was satin lined with velvet, floor length and belled out at the bottom. The bodice was tight and laced up the back to leave the shoulder blades bare. Tlonna held it up to her skeptically.

"I am not this thin, Miazie. I think this is for you."

The human giggled. "Oh, yes you are. That would leave me wallowing in satin, anyway. This is mine." She held up a gossamer bronze gown that shimmered to a deep gold when the sun hit it at different angles. It too was simply decorated, but made up for it in sheer, bold color. The skirt was not as full as Tlonna's, but it moved with a mind of its own. The elf fingered it.

"What is this?"

Miazie beamed down at it. "Lustring. Isn't it beautiful?"

"Spectacular. Would you mind telling me what this is about?" Losolin cut in, shaking the package with his name at them.

Tlonna flushed. Miazie grinned wickedly. "It's your new clothes, Losi. To visit the king. Open it."

"Losi?" Tlonna and Losolin said at the same time.

Miazie grinned even wider. "Losi and Loni. Aww."

Tlonna made a lunging motion toward the human, but she merely folded her arms and cocked her hip. "I want to see Losolin's."

"Open it, Losolin," Tlonna commanded.

Sighing, the male undid the string and flicked open the paper. Black, fine-spun wool breeches sat folded upon a dark gray velvet tunic. Losolin plucked the tunic up and held it out with a grimace. Unlaced, it would fall open to his navel. Full sleeves ended in a loose cuff. At the bottom of the package was a wide black leather belt. Losolin sent the two females a burning look.

"I am not going to wear velvet."

"Yes you are. I paid good money for this, so yes you are. It's suitable to be received by the king in. At least she made it a belted tunic. Most men here wear theirs tucked in to show off their manly goods. You should be glad that's not what she made for you, not that you should be embarrassed by any stretch," Miazie said.

"Oh really?" Tlonna said with a raised eyebrow.

The human shrugged. "I'm a woman, Tlonna. I notice things. I'm not dead, which is what you would have to be not to notice his figure. He's got some decent qualities that will make any female take a second glance."

Losolin's mouth tightened, he tossed the shirt down and folded his arms. "As happy as I am to be discussed like chattel, I would really appreciate it if you two would tell me what is going on."

Tlonna frowned at him. "We are going to see Tyular tonight. If he responds."

"Yes, I know that. What is this mess about? We have perfectly decent clothes. We should not be spending our precious little money on new items that will be worn once."

This time Miazie frowned. "You do not have perfectly decent clothes. Look at this." She held up a pair of trousers with a rip all the way up the calf. "This is trash."

"I know that, too. That is why it is being tossed out. What about that blue thing you wore to see Athelias, Tlonna?"

"He ripped it," the female responded sullenly.

"Then sew it back up and wear it again. This is ridiculous," Losolin growled.

Tlonna hugged the new dress to her and looked down despondently.

Miazie snapped her fingers and stepped forward, the beautiful gossamer gown clutched in a fist. "You will regret those words when you see Tlonna in that dress, Losolin. She is the princess of Blackhaven, for spirit's sake! She shouldn't be parading around in bleeding rags. You wear what you are told to wear, and you better bloody well like it!"

Losolin's face turned from irritated to stubborn in the blink of an eye. Tlonna braced for the tongue lashing about to come and blinked when it didn't. Looking up, she stared at Losolin who was staring at her.

"All right," he sighed. "I will wear the flaming velvet thing, but I will *not* like it, and you can deal with that, Miazie. I am no princeling to frolic around in females' clothes."

The human sighed. "We are all well aware that you are very much a male, Losolin. All anybody has to do is look at you to know that, but wearing velvet is the fashion, right now. You don't want to spurn the fashion in the capital city you are trying to win over."

Losolin was about to reply when there was a knock at the door. Tlonna turned and opened it. Tyre thrust a piece of parchment at her. "Took all bloody day, but I got your reply."

Tlonna broke the yellow seal and opened it. In a slightly blockish hand, Tyular, King of Arseninis, greeted her. She read it out loud.

"'An honor, Princess Tlonna, to have been contacted by you. There have been rumors floating around my staff that a goddess had descended upon Arseninis City. I know now they are true. It would give me great pleasure to grant your request for an audience. If my friend Aladorn is with you, please bring him. Feel free to bring a few retainers as you wish, I will not take offense. I will be ready for you at seven this evening. In reverence, Tyular Ambrose, King of Arseninis.'"

Miazie snorted. "I heard he had a heady view of himself."

"He is a king, Miazie. What time is it now?"

The Belau looked out the window. "About five, I would say."

Tlonna sighed and yanked on her hair in frustration. "Why is there never enough time?"

Miazie shrugged. "Who knows. I'm going to get ready. We need to leave in an hour or so."

Tlonna shut the door after her and pulled off her tunic. Losolin resignedly began dressing in his new outfit as well.

"Losolin?"

"Yes?" he mumbled, yanking on his boot laces a few minutes later.

"Will you lace up my back?" Tlonna asked, moving toward him.

Losolin looked up and went still. He swallowed twice before nodding. His limbs felt numb as he moved close to his lover, fumbling with the delicate laces. "You look stunning, my heart," he murmured in her ear.

Tlonna smiled back at him over her shoulder. "So do you regret what you said?"

"A little. But I still think our geld should be spent elsewhere."

"Me too, but Miazie was persistent. I think she ordered another set of clothes anyway. I do not know for sure, but she seemed nervous whenever I moved close to the table where they were tallying up the costs," Tlonna replied honestly.

"Well, she will do as she pleases, I suppose," Losolin said as he gently tugged on the laces.

After a moment's silence, he kissed her shoulder. "All done. Now turn around so I can revel in the sight of you."

Tlonna obediently turned and smiled when fire leapt into his eyes. "Tonight, my love. Afterward. We do not want to show up for an audience with the king looking like a pair of fresh-out-of-bed lovers."

"Why not? It is what we elves are good for, yes?" Losolin muttered, but he simply reached out to tug on her hair.

Tlonna took his hand and pressed it to her cheek, swimming in the warmth of his skin. It was on that intimate moment that Miazie burst into the room, spinning in her glorious dress.

"It's spectacular!" she giggled, whirling in front of a mirror. She caught sight of the elves in the glass and gasped. "Wow...you two...wow."

Tlonna smiled. "You look beautiful, Miazie. Really."

The human turned around slowly, her mouth gaping. Her green eyes roamed over Tlonna and then jumped to Losolin. She swallowed hard before taking a deep breath. "You're the most beautiful people on this earth. Do you know that? There's no one in this world or any other that can compare."

Losolin grinned boyishly, irritation forgotten. "You are just realizing this now?"

Miazie blushed. "I guess I never thought about it because you're always in normal clothes, mostly ragged normal clothes, and travel worn. But..."

Tlonna laid her head on Losolin's shoulder, gripping his hand in both of hers. "I do not believe you, Miazie, but *he* makes me feel beautiful. He makes me feel worthy of him."

Losolin tangled his free hand in her hair and kissed her

forehead. "Same to you, Loni."

Miazie was beaming at them so contently Tlonna became uncomfortable. "How much time do we have left?"

The human started and then looked out the window. "About twenty minutes before we have to leave. Losolin, can you find Aladorn and make sure he's ready?"

Losolin grunted. "Does he have to wear velvet too?"

"No, but that's because he's not the Lord Consort. And he's from here, at least recently. And apparently he and Tyular know each other. Please go find him, I need to do Tlonna's hair and fill her in on Arseninisian customs."

While Tlonna surrendered to Miazie's primping, Losolin strode into the hallway and down to Aladorn's room, which he shared with Ryun. When he knocked, the hunter opened the door and blinked at him.

"Is Aladorn here?"

Ryun shook his head. "Nope. Velvet?"

"Bite your tongue. When you have two females telling you what to wear, you wear what they tell you to. Do you know where he is?"

The human shrugged. "Probably in the common room driving those women mad by ignoring them. He gets some sort of perverse pleasure from that, I think."

"Probably," Losolin muttered absently as he turned away. "Thanks."

"Yep."

As predicted, Aladorn was reading in the common room again. Women sat all around him, though far enough away so as not to be obvious about it. Instead of a book, however, the dark elf had a journal on his lap, a long feather quill quivering while he wrote. He was half faded, the burgundy of the chair visible through him.

Losolin navigated his way through the chairs and couches to sit down next to the wiat. Aladorn did not seem to notice his presence, so he stayed quiet until the older elf looked up.

"I see you are ready to meet Tyular," he said.

"Yes indeed. You are supposed to come, too," Losolin replied. "What is that?"

Aladorn glanced at the half-filled page under his hand and set the quill down. Suddenly his body was solid again, making the women titter quietly. "A record of my life, if you will. Not many wiats are left, and I have been swept up in the currents of history. I decided it would be a good idea to write down what happened in my life for future reference. There are few accounts of live wiats left, most were burned during the wiat persecution."

"Ah," Losolin said, feeling awkward. "Well, Tlonna and Miazie are nearly ready to go, so I would suggest you be ready when they are. They are in a right mood today."

"Clothes?"

Losolin could not help his grin. "Indeed."

"Well, you will fit in perfectly with the castle folk in that costume, then," Aladorn said gleefully.

Losolin glared at him. "I suppose so. It made Miazie stutter."

"Plenty of things make Miazie stutter. For instance, my alluring body in her bed, by her designs too. Little twig has a forceful tongue."

The wiat's words shocked Losolin into silence for nearly a full minute. Aladorn went back to writing.

"Y-you...and Miazie? What?" he finally managed.

Aladorn set the quill down again and glanced at Losolin with an amused smile. "Does it surprise you? I have no intentions at all. In fact, that was the first and last time, whether she wants it to be or not. But, she does have a taste for muscle, I hear. Went after soldiers in her own home. You cannot really blame her anyway. Apparently I hold some attractive qualities to human females." For evidence he waved the quill at the near dozen women staring at him.

"Is that a good thing?" Losolin asked, glancing at the whore sitting closest to him. She gave him a saucy smile and then went back to staring at Aladorn.

The dark elf shrugged unconcernedly. "It does nothing, good or ill. I take what I want when it is offered, and no more. They usually do not last long enough, though, women. We are too good, Losolin. It drives them crazy."

Losolin managed a sickly grin. His friend's words sounded too close to what he had said to Tlonna minutes ago. As though the thought had summoned her, Tlonna, with Miazie appeared at the base of the stairs and headed toward them. He nudged Aladorn and they stood together. When they all met in the middle, Losolin glanced from Aladorn to Miazie.

The human would move an inch closer to the elf, and he would move an inch away. Soon, he was pushing against Losolin's arm.

"Stop it," he snapped, and shoved Aladorn away.

Tlonna watched the go-around in confusion. "What is going on? Miazie? Leave the poor elf alone. Spirits."

Miazie jerked and then folded her arms sulkily. Aladorn looked relieved. Losolin sighed and then guided the other male toward the door. Tlonna and Miazie followed, the former badgering the latter about what had just happened.

After a minute, Losolin winced when Tlonna's voice reached him, razor sharp.

"You did *what* with him? For the good gods' sake, Miazie! Have you no control?"

The human flounced up to stand by Losolin. She looked thoroughly embarrassed. She leaned out so that she could glare at Aladorn, who blinked back at her, his dark eyes cool and emotionless.

"You *told* him, didn't you. Losolin? He told you, didn't he?"

Losolin rubbed a hand across his face, sent a reproachful glare in the direction of Aladorn, and then turned back to Miazie. "Yes."

"Gah!" Miazie shouted, throwing her hands in the air. "Can't be with anyone around here without the whole crew finding out. Stab me thrice and drown me."

Aladorn was chuckling quietly on the other side of Losolin until he shoved him hard enough to send him into the road. The wiat disappeared before he took two steps though. Within seconds, he was standing in the same spot next to Losolin, but with a self-satisfied smirk playing on his lips.

Tlonna wriggled between him and Miazie and sighed. "What are we waiting for?"

"Tyular will be sending a carriage," Miazie snapped, and then pointed. "That would be it."

A red carriage outlined in gold trundled to a stop in front of them and the driver gingerly stepped down, trying to look down his nose at the elves. He primly held out a hand to Tlonna and helped her into the cabin, followed by Miazie. Losolin and Aladorn crawled in after her. Miazie looked horrified that the carriage had tilted the most under her weight.

"Bloody, flaming, air-filled elves," she grumbled, shoved in next to Aladorn who seemed just as displeased about the arrangement.

"King Tyular has had me bring you here because he knows you were in Talenias. He does not know why you are in this region of Nymyños. He has his suspicions, as do I, but I think it best you tell me now. What are you going to say to him?" the wiat said after a moment of shifting about.

Tlonna linked fingers with Losolin. "I am going to ask him permission to recruit men from his city. I am going to ask him for a few seasoned soldiers to help command these men. I need an army to defend Nymyños."

Aladorn's eyebrow rose an inch. "Is this what you asked Athelias?"

"No. I asked him for help. He was the one who brought the army up."

"You are lucky Tyular is a fair, benevolent man. He may aid you, but do not be too broken up if he denies your request. It is a rather odd one, after all," Aladorn replied after a moment.

"What do you think he will say?" Tlonna asked.

The elf shrugged. "Hard to say. If war is coming, he will need all the men he can get to defend his own people. But he is honorable and will want to help all of Nymyños," he sighed. "I do not know, Tlonna. We will see."

Tlonna laid her head on Losolin's shoulders and closed her eyes. Seconds later she was asleep.

The cart rumbled to a stop, waking her. She blinked a few times as the door was opened and a torch thrust in. A guard's helmeted face looked up at them.

"Ah, right," he said, peering around. Without another word to them, he shut the door and was heard shouting, "All right open the gates, hurry up, this is important!"

Tlonna leaned back and tried to calm herself. After her last meeting with a king, she was anxious about meeting another. The elf gathered the crème dress about her and clenched her hands over Losolin's. He smiled down at her, though nerves flickered across his face every so often. As the carriage slowed to a stop, much smoother than the first, the door opened once again. The driver helped Tlonna and Miazie out, then climbed in after the males vacated the cabin.

They were led up to the great castle door by a guard and

ushered inside. Immediately a servant came to take their cloaks and bowed away. Another servant led them into a large hall with rows of tables lined with linen and silver dinnerware. A small group of men sat at the end of a table perpendicular to the others and on a dais.

One man stood out above the rest. This man had a golden crown, made to look like writhing fire, resting on his brow and a dark blue cloak draped around his shoulders. His tunic was the color of snow, and velvet, and his pants gray. As the four entered, the king rose to his feet and strode over to greet them. Tlonna regarded his handsome young face and broad shoulders with apprehension. Aladorn fell to one knee, beckoning them to do the same. As the young king reached them, he told them to rise.

"Aladorn, my friend, I have been waiting for your return," Tyular said, clapping the taller male on the shoulder. "Princess Tlonna, my deepest pleasure and greatest honor to receive you in my home. I hope you find it to your liking. Ah." He turned to Losolin with a short bow. "You must be the Lord Consort Losolin? Yes, I thought so. An honor, as well. And who are you?"

Miazie glowered at him a second before coming to her senses. "Uh...Miazie Paron, Advisor to Tlonna, and Princess of Anutch. My pleasure to meet you, King Tyular."

Tyular regarded her with a raised eyebrow before turning back to Tlonna. "Will you and your esteemed company follow me to the table?"

"All right," Tlonna said, and then cursed herself for being less versed in the smooth talk of nobles.

They trailed the king up to the dais table and sat at his behest. Tlonna was seated between a sour looking man and the king. Losolin and Aladorn were bidden to take seats next to each other, between two young, identical men. Miazie was shoved next to a fat man at the end of the table.

"Ah, Milady, I haf waited for thith moment for long yearth. I am Theneral Robuth Thut," the fat man said to Tlonna.

"Eh, forgive our general Princess Tlonna, he is quite drunk. His name is General Robus Shut. I am Captain Junta Flunt, I am the Captain Guard. My brother here is-

"I am Captain of the Third Rank, Felus Flunt. I have been very honored to be invited here to meet with the renowned Princess Tlonna Ewôsdírn," the men were twins, smiling and handsome.

Introductions went around the table. Finally, it was Tlonna's turn to speak. "Tlonna, please. Just Tlonna, and this is the Lord Consort, Losolin Ullor Grisholm, and my Lady Advisor, Miazie Paron. It is an honor to meet you all. I thank you for your warm welcome."

The men all tried to reply at the same time, resulting in a loud clamoring of nonsense.

"Silence, my friends, silence!" Tyular cut in and motioned his men to sit, for some had risen to their feet in their excitement.

"This, ladies and gentlemen is a council of great importance. Tlonna has come here at my request, brought by my good friend Aladorn. Now, there must be a reason you are in East Nymyños, and with everyone thinking you dead, I believe an interesting story is to come. Will you share it with us Tlonna?"

Tlonna took a deep breath and looked at Losolin. He offered her no help for he was staring at his hands in deep concentration. "Well, I..." she started. "It has been a strange journey, for sure."

The Magin plunged into her story, looking at the faces in front of her. The Flunt brothers no longer were smiling and General Robus appeared to have sobered.

Losolin listened intently to Tlonna's tale unfold. He stared at his hands, trying not to look up at the faces around him. They were all intent upon Tlonna, but every so often, eyes would flicker to him in jealousy or cold interest. When Tlonna had finished, the room was echoing with silence. The small council was silent for long moments before King Tyular spoke.

"Athelias actually attacked you?"

Tlonna nodded.

"The bastard. I shall write to the others and see about having him removed from his throne. No king is to attack any member of a royal family, no matter what race they come from."

"The others, my lord?"

Tyular nodded sharply. "Yes. Those of us in the East Nymyños Alliance. Talenias, Arseninis, Kajgenia, and Florwen Hune. Stoffnias of Seaduens refused, the old codger. Said he would be in 'no bleeding alliance with men and dwarves.' Athelias, Demetrius, Barukh, and myself have a treaty and a set of rules. Not attacking benign visitors being one. He may lose his crown for this. Of course," the king rubbed his chin, "his son, Athelan, is worse than he is."

"My king," a lieutenant named Aaron said, "what of the Princess's request?"

Tyular squinted. "Right. Princess Tlonna, I need men to defend my own people from this storm of battle you say is coming. Nevertheless, I understand that you are not fighting for your people alone. Nymyños is mother to us all, and as such, it is our duty to defend her. I regret to say that I cannot supply you with a great number of men, but those who are willing to come," he rubbed his chin again, "will go with you. I will also round up five of my officers to accompany you. How is that?"

Tlonna blinked, surprised. "I...thank you my lord. That is very gracious of you. It is more than I had hoped for."

"Good," Tyular laughed, reaching over to clap Aladorn on the shoulder.

The wiat stared warily at his king.

"Aladorn, you will be one of the five?"

"If my king commands," the elf said, with a reluctant glance at Miazie, who pursed her lips.

Oblivious, the human grinned at Tlonna and stood. There was a loud scraping of chairs on the dais as everyone at the table stood with him.

"Come, eat with me, you must be famished," the king said, directing Tlonna in front of him. "Lord Losolin, Aladorn, Lady Miazie, come along."

The king herded them into a smaller room off the side of the dining hall where a table was set with glinting dishes. Servants appeared out of nowhere to pull back chairs and set down steaming platters of food.

They conversed lightly, mainly matters of state between Tyular and Aladorn. As Tlonna finished her meal, and drank the last of her wine, a messenger bowed to the king and bent to whisper in his ear.

"Ah," the man said, looking irritated. "Please excuse me, it seems one of my sons has made unwelcome advances on a serving girl. Stay as long as you want, don't feel rushed because of my absence. We will speak on the morrow?"

"Yes," Tlonna replied.

"I bid you goodnight then," the king said, and stormed out of the room.

"He has sons?"

Aladorn chuckled. "Many, all illegitimate, but he claims them all and takes good care of the mothers. Usually serving girls or pretty girls off the street, always with their consent, of course. Though one time it was a baron's daughter who tried to make him marry her. Her father was given a second plot of land and the daughter a place at court. Tyular remains unmarried however."

"How old is he?" Losolin asked.

"Thirty-three. His father died a few years ago and he has been ruling since. His mother died giving birth to his sister, Arina. She is married to Felus Flunt. She is twenty-three."

"Which one was he? I know he was one of the twins, but I cannot remember who was who," Tlonna asked.

"Felus has a scar above his elbow. He was next to Losolin," Aladorn replied.

Miazie dropped her fork with a clang. They all looked at her. "Sorry. I'm just not used to being ignored. That old fat man kept hitting me with his elbow then blinking at me as if surprised to find me there."

Tlonna sent an unreadable look at her friend. "I am sorry for your misfortune."

Aladorn and Losolin snorted in unison. Miazie glowered at them, but stayed silent the rest of the time. After a while they finished talking and Aladorn led them back through the castle, retrieved their outerwear, and woke the carriage driver up.

Once back at the brothel, Tlonna stretched out on the bed. "Losolin, tell me, what are we looking for in army men? Strength, cunning intelligence, willpower, bravery, or loyalty?"

"I think, Tlonna, that you are looking for all of those things. We need men with courage and wisdom, loyalty and strength. I believe that whomever you choose will be right."

Morning came with a messenger.

"My Lord and Lady, the king requests your presence at the castle," the boy said, staring at them with wide eyes.

Losolin gave him a silver geld and sent him away. "I wonder if Aladorn will be joining us again. Or Miazie," he mused, pulling a shirt over his head.

Tlonna shrugged. They left the brothel and hired a carriage to take them to the castle. When they arrived, Tyular greeted them in the entrance hall.

"My friends, come with me," he said, and turned.

Tlonna and Losolin followed the king up a stairway, down a corridor, and into a large room decorated with shields and weapons.

"This is my war room. I thought it an appropriate place to discuss things. Please, sit," Tyular said, sitting himself in the largest chair.

The elves took seats on his right, waiting. The human ordered a carafe of wine and finger dishes to be brought, and then sent another servant to fetch a girl by the name of Leann.

"My head scribe," Tyular commented when the elves questioned him.

Tlonna nodded her understanding and then said, "Was the business with your son concluded?"

The man sighed. "Amon is my eldest at fifteen, and thinks that because he is the king's son, he can do what he chooses. It doesn't matter to him that he will never gain the throne. My last name seems to be all he cares about. He has already accosted five girls, touching them and kissing them even when they fought. I fear he may take it too far one day. I sent him to the city dungeon for a sentence of five days. Maybe he will learn."

"You sent your son to prison?" Tlonna asked.

Tyular shrugged. "He needed to be punished. I have seen what Athelan is like, and his father allowed him free reign. I do not want that for my own children, no matter how illegitimate they are. My own father sent me to prison for two weeks once, when I stole a horse. I learned my lesson. Justice should be served to all."

"You are a good man, Tyular," Losolin commented, amazed.

"Why thank you. And now-ah, there you are," Tyular said as a young woman curtseyed into the room. "Tlonna, Losolin, my Head Scribe, Leann. Leann, Princess Tlonna, Lord Consort Losolin."

Leann, a plain young woman with curly black hair, curtseyed again. "An honor, my Lord and Lady. My king sent for me?"

"Yeah, I will need you to record this meeting, and I also require you to help our friends in whatever they need."

"Of course, my lord," Leann said, taking a seat on the other side of the king.

She pulled a roll of parchment out of her satchel, along with a quill and ink bottle. She unscrewed the bottle, dipped her quill, and then looked up at Tyular who was beaming at her.

"All right, I commence this meeting between myself, King Tyular Philip Ambrose, and Princess Tlonna Arune Ewôsdírn of Blackhaven Forest and the Lord Consort Losolin Ullor Grisholm on this eighteenth day of Resen, year five forty-three of the eighth age of Nymyños."

Leann scribbled fast and she finished the paragraph quickly. Tyular smiled at her briefly and then turned his full attention of Tlonna.

"What are your plans while you are here? I know you want to recruit men, but how do you plan to do that?"

Tlonna laced her fingers on the table. "I thought I would put out flyers around the city, ask you to send an outrider to your other cities with the letter, if that is possible."

"Certainly, but what sort of men are you looking for? Do you want married men to come? Specialties? Are you looking for blacksmiths and healers, tanners and fletchers as well?"

"Why would I want them?" Tlonna asked, suddenly feeling overwhelmed.

Tyular smiled thinly. "An army on the move needs the same accommodations as one sitting behind a wall. A man with armor rarely knows how to fix it when a spear gets shoved through the back plate or a sword severs the leather straps holding it all together. You need those craftsmen to support your army. You will need servants as well, to run messages, entertain the soldiers, help carry and bury the dead."

"This is war, my lord, I doubt we will have time to watch performances," Tlonna said.

"Not entertainment like that, my dear. Entertainment at night, in the soldier's tents."

Tlonna pulled a face. "That is deplorable!"

"As you said, it's war. Lonely soldiers are angry soldiers, and angry soldiers don't fight well. A marching army is a marching city. Few things change except the scenery and quality of life," Tyular replied simply.

"All right," Tlonna breathed. "We will need craftsmen, servants," she looked up at Tyular, "wagons and drivers."

"You're catching on. I would also advise taking a few scribes. A war is history, and history is knowledge for future generations. It should be written down. I would suggest taking at least two."

Tlonna sighed again. "Two scribes, seamstresses, we will need men with horses, but it is not required."

The food arrived along with a blustered young man.

"My king," he said as he bowed low. "There is a woman in the entrance saying she is required here. She says she is advisor to the Princess Tlonna."

Tyular's eyebrows rose. He turned to the elves. "Do you have an advisor?"

Tlonna frowned. "Yes, you met her last night. Miazie?"

"Do you want her here?" Tyular asked, picking up his goblet and ignoring the fact that he had forgotten the woman.

"Might as well. Otherwise she will badger our ears off later," Losolin replied as Tlonna rolled her head back to rest it against the chair.

"All right, have her brought in," Tyular said to the man.

He bowed and rushed out of the room.

"I am sorry about this, my king. Miazie, though she still claims the title of princess, was actually exiled from Anutch. Do you not remember her from last night?" Tlonna said.

Tyular shrugged. "I have a habit of forgetting things that have no immediate reason for me to remember them. Especially people. Anutch, you say?"

Tlonna nodded.

"I heard there was a massive breakout and that the king was castrated by one of the slaves. An elf, of great beauty and strength. Perhaps Darren and I have a common acquaintance?"

Tlonna could not suppress a grin. "Aye, Darren will never destroy a woman that way again. Do you know him well?"

Tyular shook his head. "Only well enough to know he is a cowardly bastard, but cruel in his own demesne. As he rules the largest *kingdom*, if you can call them that, in the Liberated Lands, the East Nymyños Alliance sent an invitation to him to join us. He declined, obviously. Had the same kind of morals as Stoffnias Lostug. Now they have something else in common."

"And what would that be?" Losolin asked.

"A kinship of hatred. They both despise Tlonna because she denied them, and now they are both mockeries of men...well males in Stoffnias' case. Stoffnias lost his testicles in a battle the year after his son Gothier was born. He still has his member, but it's rather ineffective."

Tlonna was laughing so hard she didn't hear the door open once more.

"Tlonna!" Miazie's voice cut through her laughter. "What are you doing?"

Tyular stood to greet the woman, grinning. "She is enjoying my joke. Miazie, right?"

"Yes. I am sorry to have interrupted your meeting, but I should be here for Tlonna and Losolin," Miazie said, curtseying to the king.

"No problem, my lady. Please, have a seat."

Miazie sat on the other side of Leann, who was watching Tlonna in amazement. The elf had finally composed herself, but was taking deep breaths to control the bubbles of laughter in her throat.

"So," the Belau said finally. "What has transpired so far?"

Leann handed the parchment to her while pulling out another. "My Lord and Lady, shall we begin to draw up the letter?"

"That would be good," Tyular answered for the elves. "At the top, write it as a royal proclamation and I will sign it at the bottom. How about...Royal Proclamation, A Chance for Glory. Join the Nymyñosian Army under the command of Magin Princess Tlonna Arune Ewôsdírn and Lord Consort Losolin Ullor Grisholm. Any man willing to bear arms and march across the continent to face the darkest of evil must come to the capital within the week?"

Tlonna nodded, "That sounds fine. Should we add that the others are needed to? The craftsmen?"

Tyular waited for Lean to finish the last line before continuing. "Blacksmiths, Tanners, Fletchers, Healers, and any others wishing to join will be welcomed. 100 geld per year will be paid upon return, and families will be compensated for any loss."

Tlonna jerked slightly. "How am I to pay them?" she said, panicking. "I have no money."

Tyular leaned forward. "My lady, war is expensive business. Both you and I have full access to royal treasuries, and the taxes of the people. By the time this war is over, I have full faith that you will be once again seated on your throne."

"Then you have great faith, indeed, my lord," Tlonna said quietly.

Tyular smiled. "Lady, sometimes faith is all we have."

The proclamation was copied a dozen times and sent out with riders across Arseninis. The same day, people began trickling in from the nearby villages and towns. Tlonna and Losolin were sitting at a table in the common room of the brothel when four men strode in, smelling of horses.

"Glory, boys, can you imagine it? Our names could be plastered across the pages of history if we make ourselves known. We will be heroes among our people. To fight under the command of Everwood!"

The smallest of the men shrugged. "But it said we are to go against the darkest of evils, Rodger! We could die! What will happen to my shop? Who will dye the silks, weave the cotton? Who?"

"Evan, you worry too much. Your shop will run on through your wife and daughter. We're talking about glory, riches, and victory," Rodger said.

"Yeah," said a skinny man with a bulging left shoulder that marked him as a blacksmith. "One hundred geld for every year we are gone, that is more than I make in a year, usually. Even if we do die, our families will be well taken care of."

The fourth man said nothing, but stared at Tlonna with bugging eyes. Tlonna looked down and then over at Losolin, who was eating his soup a little too heartily. She heard the footprints and cursed under her breath. When she looked up, the four men were staring down at her in awe.

"My lady," Rodger said, "I mean no dishonor, but are you...Everwood?"

Tlonna stood so that she looked down on them instead of up. "I am."

The four men went to their knees in one movement, hands flat on their thighs, heads bowed. The others in the brothel were looking around in amusement, as they had grown accustomed to the elves' presence.

Losolin had stopped pretending to be oblivious and was now grinning lopsidedly. Tlonna rolled her eyes and made an involuntary cluck.

"Stand up will you," she growled, pulling the man Evan to his feet by the back of his coat.

The men stood, still staring at her.

"Are you here as recruits?"

"We are, my lady," Rodger replied quickly, bowing low.

"As soldiers or craftsmen?"

"Soldiers, though Jorun here is a blacksmith."

"Aye, I am, but I know how to fight ma'am, that's what I want to do. I will do as you command me to, however," the skinny man said.

Tlonna laid a hand on his shoulder. "We will see how many soldiers come, and if we need you as a smith, that is what you will be. But for now, you will sign on as a soldier."

"Thank you Lady Magin Princess...Commander...Everwood."

Tlonna hid a sneer by grinning fully. Behind her, Losolin choked. "My name is Tlonna, Jorun."

"Right," the man said, and then bowed again. "An honor, my lady."

He stumbled away behind his friends while they all started jabbering away at her. It wasn't until Miazie squeezed beside them to sit next to Losolin that they silenced. The Belau looked up from Losolin at the sudden quiet. Her green eyes widened, and then she smiled. Standing, Miazie held out a hand.

"Miazie Paron, Advisor to Princess Tlonna. Is there something you men need?"

The last man released her hand and shook his head. "No, Lady. We was just introducing a'selves to the Magin. We's solda's in her army."

"Good to know, now gentlemen, Princess Tlonna was in the middle of a meal, if you wouldn't mind," Miazie made a shooing motion with her hand.

"Of course, Lady," Rodger said, and pulled his friends back.

"You can't befriend them all, Tlonna. You have to learn that," Miazie said once she had seated herself again.

Tlonna plopped into her chair. "But I feel as though I should. I may be marching these men to their death. How is it right that I do not know them? They give their lives for me, it is the least I can do."

"They are not giving their lives for you, Tlonna," the human replied shortly, "they are giving it for Nymyños, for freedom, and for glory."

"What glory is there in death?" Losolin asked, lacing his

fingers with Tlonna's.

Miazie sighed. "I hope for my sanity's sake you recover your memories fully soon. The elves honor life above all else. Life in plants, animals, and people. But they honor death as well, for it is the only constant. Everyone dies, even elves with their near-immortality, for they weary of life after so long. To die in battle, especially one fought for the right reasons, justice, freedom, truth, honor, and glory, is called *Estsyp*, beautiful death. It is one of the highest senses of pride for a family if one of their own dies in such a way. *Lãn emyar nasior, lãn takireaes soyems, lãn sen bayno*. A memory preserved, a warrior remembered, a life lived. That is carved into the headstone of a mass grave from a war called The War of Monotheism, also called the war of the devil. It resides in Seaduens, where the final battle was fought.

"Thousands died, elves, humans, and dwarves. It was fought against idealist monotheists who tried to burn anything with so-called 'unnatural' power or belief in more than one god. Even some monotheists joined the defense in an attempt to stem the slaughter. Even they saw the evil in what their fellows did. At the end, the people did not understand the need for such a war, but they knew why it had been fought. For the preservation of culture, life, and freedom.

"Many looked back and were saddened that there had been such a needless loss of life, but the dead were honored as near martyrs. They gave their lives for the preservation of righteousness. The mass grave was dug and all the elves were buried there. Two others exist for the humans and dwarves.

"That is how warriors want to die, that is how elves want to die. That is how there is glory in death," Miazie said, a little breathlessly.

Losolin raised his eyebrows. "Ah."

Tlonna chuckled at Miazie's appalled expression.

"Remember, Miazie, you know by far more than we want to," she said, laughing.

The woman rolled her eyes, but laughed all the same.

Chapter 7
Recruitment

Tlonna and Losolin waited until the end of the week to organize the flock of people that had answered the proclamation. Over five hundred stood in the courtyard, blinking up at the elves and Tyular, who stood next to them on the balcony. Miazie was on his other side, hands folded within the sleeves of her dress.

The king lifted his hands from the rail and gestured out to his subjects. "My good people, you are here in answer to the proclamation that went out last week. Know that this campaign will not be short lived and easy. Many will die, some will suffer. But this is a battle of Nymyños, not just Arseninis, and all the people within her borders. From the R'Kunad to Nafâlen Bay, the shadow of evil has spread. You are the first to offer your services, and I, King Tyular, now pass you from my loyalties into Magin Princess Tlonna and Lord Consort Losolin's, until this war has passed."

Silence greeted the man's words, but Tyular smiled at the now worried elves. "Tell them what comes from your heart, from your mind. You are legendary, my lady, and they will be honored to follow you."

Tlonna nodded, swallowed, and stepped forward. The people below raised their heads to stare at her. "Good people, I thank you for coming. I know it will be a hard road, and we will suffer loss and pain, but we fight for life. For freedom and glory, my friends. What greater order is there but to fight for what is right, for what is true and good? The coming darkness that awaits us is massive and evil beyond comprehension. All will surely perish if we do nothing. Nymyños will burn, and her people made slaves or worse. Man, Dwarf, Elf, and all other manner of creatures in this land are in this fight together. We are of different races, but our hearts beat the same, our blood is the same crimson red, and it will flow in equal measure if we do not stand against this tyrant. Do you wish this for your home?"

The people gathered in the courtyard shook their fists in the air and roared.

"Will you fight? Will you follow me into battle?" Tlonna roared even louder.

"Yes!" the five hundred bellowed.

"Then prepare for glory!"

The courtyard rumbled with the resounding shouts of the recruits. Tyular grinned, and the four left the balcony.

"Well done, my lady," the king said as they walked the corridor to the main hall. "I believe you stirred their hearts beyond hope. Far better than I have ever done, as well. I applaud you."

"Thank you, Tyular. What now?"

The human groaned falsely. "Tlonna, your eloquence has shamed me. I must now throw a feast in your honor. I hope it will not be too much trouble?"

Tlonna laughed. "I suppose not."

"Good. Losolin, will you accompany me to the library? I remembered your question about roaming tribes. I found a book that might interest you," Tyular said.

Losolin raised his eyebrows, looking surprised. "Oh, yes, of course. Really? There is a book..."

The two males wandered off, leaving Tlonna and Miazie quite startled.

"I think Losolin has a friend, Tlonna," Miazie said, smiling.

"So it would seem," Tlonna replied, still shocked.

The Belau grabbed the elf's elbow. "Come, I have something to show you."

The two females made their way to the brothel and into Miazie's room.

"I was out on the city and picked up the rest of the order from Karin. Look at these," she exclaimed, pulling out sets of winter clothing. "And, this, Tlonna, I simply could not resist. It was too perfect," Miazie said as she picked up a package of brown paper.

She handed it to Tlonna. The elf frowned at her. "I thought I told you not to get anything other than the dress clothes for the first meeting."

"Open it," Miazie urged.

Tlonna untied the strings and opened the flaps of paper. A long dress of black velvet spilled out of her hands and onto the floor. The sleeves were dagged, falling from the elbows all the way to the knees. Slightly off to the side and in the curve of the waist was a silver leafless tree. The roots were thin and some of them stretched all the way to the bottom of the hem.

"Put it on," Miazie said, grinning.

"Oh, Miazie!" Tlonna said, awestruck at the beauty of the dress.

"You are too beautiful to wear the same dresses to each occasions, and you are royalty. You deserve this."

Tlonna tore her eyes from the dress to glare at Miazie. "You did not. This must be very expensive. No."

"Put it on, and if you don't like it, I will find someone who does," Miazie replied.

Tlonna sighed and went behind the wardrobe to change. The dress slithered over her arms and down her body. Adjusting the sleeves, Tlonna looked down. The top branches of the silver tree reached just over her bosom. The neckline was square cut and showed ample cleavage.

"Well?" Miazie's voice said excitedly.

"Oh...Miazie...it is so beautiful."

She walked into view and Miazie stopped in mid-stride. Her green eyes widened. "Tlonna, it's perfect. My gods, you shame the moons."

Tlonna blushed. "I will have to pay you back, of course."

Miazie snorted. "Nonsense. You saved my life twice. I owe you far more than this. You should wear it at the feast."

"I will," Tlonna said, twirling.

The feast was set for the next evening, the night before Tlonna and her company departed. Tlonna changed into the black dress and then succumbed to Miazie's pampering once more. Her hair was tied with ribbons of black and silver and a few strands curled with the use of a metal rod heated in the fire.

Tlonna stared at her image in the mirror. Miazie applied a subtle line of coal to her eyes and the elf blinked at the sudden change.

"You're lucky you're an elf, Tlonna. You don't have to worry about blemishes," Miazie grumped, rubbing at her own face.

"Blemishes?" Tlonna asked.

"Yeah, marks and pimples that the rest of us get. And your skin is all the same tone, not blotchy, like mine."

"I think your skin is very nice, Miazie. I do not see any of these blemishes or blotches you are talking about," Tlonna replied honestly, studying her friend.

The human rolled her eyes. "They're there. But let us see about jewelry."

"You did not buy jewelry, Miazie, did you?" Tlonna said threateningly.

"No, at least not for you. But you have a few things in your bag, I think, that will work," Miazie replied, grabbing Tlonna's saddlebags.

After rummaging through it, she pulled out a pendant of black diamond and silver.

"This is *perfect*. Simple and delicate, but still a statement. Wow," the Belau said, staring at the pendant. Miazie placed the necklace on Tlonna's neck and then stepped back. "You're an image, Tlonna. Losolin's going to lose his legs, among other things."

Tlonna frowned. "Why would he lose his *legs*? What other things?"

"It's an expression, my friend. He's going to be stunned, let's say. Now help me."

"Oh Miazie I know nothing about this sort of thing."

"Sure you do, it's all there, you just need to remember it. I'm sure it will come to you. What is my best color, do you think?" Miazie said dismissively.

"Uh..." Tlonna stammered, "brown, or green? A coppery brown, or emerald green, I think."

Miazie grinned excitedly. "Perfect, I purchased a dark green dress today, what do you think?"

She picked up a deep forest green dress with sheer bell sleeves and a satinet body. The skirt puffed out slightly from the bodice and fell in lustrous waves of emerald. The hem and collar was dotted with tiny diamonds.

"Miazie...it is gorgeous. You should wear that," Tlonna said, nodding.

Miazie dressed and combed out her long raven hair. She tied a part of it back, letting the rest fall in a sheet. After adding a necklace of jade and applying coal and rouge to her face, she finished.

"Let's go collect Losolin and get a carriage," Miazie said, linking arms with Tlonna.

The two females walked the short brothel hallway to Tlonna and Losolin's room and strode in. Losolin was tugging on his boot when he looked up, and went stock still. Miazie grinned, Tlonna flushed.

"Do you not like it?" She finally asked, releasing Miazie and hugging herself.

Losolin made an attempt to speak, but instead had to take a few seconds more. He finally cleared his throat and stood. He sat down promptly again.

"Tlonna...you look...amazing. Miazie you too, but Tlonna...my love...you are...I do not know...divine," he stammered.

Miazie had to hide her grin with her hand as Losolin stayed firmly on the bed. Tlonna's face went from humiliated to radiant in one second.

"Really?" She rushed to her consort and pulled him up from his seat.

Losolin stared at her, swallowing. "I love you."

Surprised, Tlonna laughed. "I love you too. Does not Miazie look beautiful as well? She did all of this, too," the elf said, gesturing at her own body.

"She looks wonderful. Very pretty," Losolin said, still staring at Tlonna.

"*Losolin!*" Tlonna giggled, but Miazie laughed outright.

"I told you! What did I say, Tlonna. Come on you too, Losolin are you ready?" the Belau said, grinning.

"Oh, yeah. I do not know if this is good enough next to you too, though," Losolin said, finally pulling his gaze away from Tlonna.

He wore black trousers, a black silk tunic, and black boots.

"Rather morbid, aren't we?" Miazie joked, taking in his dark appearance.

"That is not all, I have had this in the bottom of my pack, never knew why or how," Losolin said and picked up a cape.

It was spun completely from cloth-of-silver and reflected light every time it moved. Losolin pinned it to his shoulders and then flourished it a bit. "Better?"

Tlonna grinned. "I love it. We match!"

Miazie laughed and the three of them strode out of the room. The entire common room went silent at their arrival. Miazie ushered them forward and soon they were standing on the street as a carriage rolled up.

When they arrived at the castle, Tyular himself met them at

the entrance. He was garbed in his house colors. Black trousers with gold threading up the hems, a golden tunic, knee-high black boots, and a black half-cape. His crown gleamed in the torchlight, beams of light reflecting off the rubies that made up the third color of House Ambrose, set in the flames of gold.

The king grinned toothily at Losolin and then stopped when he turned to greet Tlonna and Miazie. His eyes glazed over when he saw Tlonna and burned when they landed on Miazie.

"My ladies...words escape me. Even the moon and stars must be jealous tonight, for their beauty pales before the two of you. Losolin, you are one lucky lad. Lady Miazie, I do hope you will accompany me to the table?"

Miazie's color went slightly white. "A-as your companion?"

"Indeed, if you would not mind. My original...companion has fallen ill, so I happen to have an empty seat next to mine. Would you care to fill it? I mean, you are a princess so it is quite appropriate," Tyular said.

Miazie went paler still. "Yes, I would be honored, King Tyular. Thank you."

"No, thank you. Think how daft I would look attending my own feast without a beautiful woman by my side."

Miazie grinned as Tyular took her hand in his and led them down the main hall to the great feast hall.

"Now," he turned and addressed Tlonna and Losolin. "The herald will announce me first, with Lady Miazie, and then you two. Enter right after he says Losolin's name and come straight for your seat. It is at the far end on the dais, where we first met. All right?"

"Okay," Tlonna said, taking a deep breath.

The young king leaned toward a castle official standing by the double doors and whispered to him. The man nodded, knocked softly on the door, and then waited for it to open a tiny crack. He whispered into it, and the door closed tight again.

"Ready?" the official asked them all, and when he received nods all around, pounded his staff on the floor.

On the other side of the door, a strong voice said, "Please stand for the arrival of your king, Tyular Ambrose, and the Lady Miazie Paron."

The double doors opened and Tyular and Miazie strode through. The doors closed again. After a few seconds, the herald called out again.

"Please greet the Princess Magin Tlonna Ewôsdírn and the Lord Consort Losolin Grisholm of Blackhaven Forest."

The doors opened and Tlonna and Losolin stepped into the feast hall. Long trestle tables were lined with people all clapping and stomping and staring. The elves caught sight of Tyular and Miazie standing at the dais with a few others and headed for them. When they arrived at their seats on the right hand side of the throne, Tyular raised his hands.

"Please be seated and enjoy," he said and sat down himself.

The people took their seats and the level of sound in the hall rose to a roar as people took up their conversations.

"Was that so bad?" Tyular asked them when the servers had finished placing platters of food on the table.

"No, I could do without all the staring, though," Tlonna replied, picking up a goblet of wine.

"Ah, Tlonna, it wouldn't be a problem if you were not so beautiful!" Tyular laughed.

As the feast progressed, Losolin and Tyular conversed unceasingly about the history of Arseninis.

Tlonna and Miazie talked about where they should go next.

"Well, Seaduens is closer, but I don't think you want to go there. The next border is Kajgenia. I would bet that the elves have been wiped out there as well. I know King Demetrius is an astonishingly good man. He fought hard against Aderiaen, and sent mass amounts of men to Blackhaven when it went under siege. I would definitely plan on going there. Kajgenia is a good province anyway. Moreover, with winter almost in full swing, we will need a place to stay for a while."

"Miazie, what do you think happened to the elves? They cannot have all been killed," Tlonna said, selecting a hunk of seasoned beef smothered in gravy and bits of potato.

"I don't know. It seems like they have been. But it is sickening to think that the elves could be wiped out like that. I don't know how it happened, but according to most of the stories I've heard, during Aderiaen's War, elves just started...disappearing. No bodies were found, the houses were all boarded up, and covers put on the furniture. It's very odd. I wouldn't believe such stories if only a few people were telling them, but everyone I have asked tells the same.

"Now that the main city of the elves has been taken, and none of that population seems to have escaped, we are the only hope for your kind. Well, humans and dwarves too, as Midian is trying to outdo his father and take over *all* of Nymyños," Miazie stopped to take a few bites of oiled lettuce.

"Why has he not hit Talenias and Arseninis yet I wonder," Tlonna mused.

"He has. Look around you, Tlonna. This city used to teem with elves. What happened to make every single one of them vanish? That's what I wonder. The cities cover it up well, but if you look, you see the scars. Eight years is not long when it comes to the devastation of a people. Houses in the middle of the populace with lawns overgrown, windows smashed in, burn marks on the walls. And on either side, perfectly maintained homesteads of humans. Shops abandoned while its neighbors carry on a bustling trade. It's all there, but the people are trying to forget."

Tlonna put her forkful of buttery noodles back on her plate. "Why would they try to forget? Do they not care what happened to my people?"

"Tlonna, humans and elves have never *really* gotten along. Your city is the closest anyone has ever come to true peace. Think about the things you have said to me. Things like, 'what do you think I am, human?' and such. It is nature, like cats and dogs. The elves look down on humans as lower forms of life, scummy and stupid. Humans think of elves as prissy and snobby. And while neither race is any of those things in majority, it is the biased opinion of both.

"Ergo, the humans are not going to be too mournful about the sudden disappearance of a race they considered irritating and diminished. They worry about what it means, maybe mourn their neighbors, but in general, they don't really care. The elves would be the same if the humans started disappearing. Albeit, they would pay more attention and try to find out what was happening, but they wouldn't really care about the humans, just the cause."

Tlonna nodded and went back to the debate. "Is it possible the elves are all just hiding, like they did after the Council War?"

"Possible, yes, improbable, too. People would have noticed a migration of the "first folk" as you lot are called. Humans find elves fascinating even if we hate to admit it; dwarves keep tabs on you like naughty children. There has been no such information pertaining to a migration. Something has happened to either kill off your brethren in great, immediate waves, or they've been taken."

Tlonna squinted at her noodles. "Taken? Where? By Whom? Midian is far too busy to deal with a couple thousand brassed off elves, and surely people would have noticed great herds of chained up elves being marched to some secret hideout."

Miazie shrugged, "They're all dead, then."

"They cannot be. I cannot be the last of my race, but for a few others. I will not believe it, Miazie, I will not."

"Then we will find the answer. But first, dessert."

Chapter 8
Truth of Sickness

Tlonna stared at Losolin. He was illuminated by moonlight coming in through the high windows in their chamber. The elf turned on his side so that his back was to her, the rigid muscles creating shadows on his skin as the moonlights cascaded over them. Tomorrow she would set out for Kajgenia with a small army. Tlonna smiled as she watched his shoulder rise with each slow breath. She could still feel his lips and hands on her. Still felt languid from his...administrations.

Tlonna tucked herself against his back, molding to his body, and fell asleep.

"Tlonna, wake up, it is time to go." Losolin shook her gently. He sighed and dropped the blanket from his body. Naked, he walked across the room to the wardrobe and pulled out his riding breeches. Putting them on, he tied the laces and tried unsuccessfully to wake up Tlonna once more. He pulled on a tunic and bent down over the elf.

"Tlonna," he whispered in her ear.

When she did not stir, he smacked his hands together just above her face.

Tlonna's eyes snapped open and she gasped. Losolin smiled at her.

"About bloody time. It is time to go," he threw her a pair of trousers and a tunic.

She dressed and after pulling on her riding boots, she packed all of her belongings in her bags. They strode into the brothel commons and saw Miazie sitting at a table, looking groggy and unkempt, while Aladorn lounged in his chair and stared at her with wry amusement.

"Morning," Losolin said to her as one of the girls sauntered over to take their order.

Miazie mumbled something akin to a response.

"Did you not sleep well?" Tlonna asked. "What happened to you last night? You never came back from the latrine."

"Tyular saw me heading back, and we got to talking. Then,

well, we went to his bedroom and I got back this morning around four," Miazie replied, looking the Magin in the eye.

"You slept with Tyular?" Tlonna asked blandly.

Losolin snickered. Aladorn, who had purposefully ignored the feast from the night before, looked a bit put off.

"Well...we did not *sleep*," Miazie said.

"Oh for...*Miazie*," Tlonna intoned, shaking her head.

"What? I'm human, I have to get all my joys in now, or else I will miss them."

Tlonna nodded, conceding, and then leaned back in her chair. Aladorn saw Losolin watching him and schooled his expression to a stony indifference.

Around them, the people from Anutch were saying their goodbyes to the ladies of Tamarisk's, who had grown to like the people staying in their brothel. Their food arrived and the four tucked into breakfast.

Afterward, they went to the stables and readied to leave. Takîreaes and Neñyos were irritable after their long stay in the stables. As noon approached and people were lining the streets waiting to see the procession of soldiers out of the city, Tyular rode to the brothel.

Tlonna, Losolin, and Miazie were waiting for him in the street, the escapees from Anutch behind them. Behind Tyular was the army. Hundreds of people cheered as they passed, throwing bouquets of flowers and herbs on the street. Tyular reined his horse in before the three. He grinned.

"Lovely day for a march, I almost envy you."

"You are welcome to join us, Tyular," Tlonna replied, watching Miazie out of the corner of her eye.

The human blanched. The king grinned even wider. "No, no. I must stay here. Give my word to Demetrius, will you?"

Losolin clasped hands with Tyular. "Of course, my friend. Anything specific?"

The man waved his hand in the air, "Oh...tell him to watch his back, and he can count on Arseninis to come to his aid. Also, make sure you mention Athelias. I sent him word, but it would be more useful for you to relay your story. But let me hold you here no longer. Tlonna, an honor and a joy to have finally met you," he kissed her hand.

"My friend, Losolin, take care of her, will you? And write any time. We may live in kingdoms far away, but messengers ride fast, as do pigeons fly. Miazie," Tyular turned to the Belau. "My dear, stay safe and write me as well. What we have shared is nothing exclusive, so feel no fear nor doubt. Find love, and I will be happy."

Miazie smiled sadly, her green eyes wide. "I will, thank you Tyular. I will if you will."

"An accord then, my lady," Tyular kissed her fingers and then turned his horse so that he could address Aladorn, who had been inspecting the front row of recruits.

"Aladorn, comrade in arms, I will pray for your safe return," he said affectionately.

The dark elf took his hand with a feral warrior's grin. "Aye, do not pray too hard, else I will have naught but a tedious journey, yes?"

Tyular laughed, though his eyes were saddened slightly by the departure of his friends. "As you wish, then, wiat. I will await word from Kajgenia! Fair expedition, and may the gods keep you in their favor!" the king shouted as he withdrew to the cheers of all congregated.

The army moved forward, staring at Tlonna and Losolin on their horses. Tyre, the man from Anutch, rode forward to join the elves. He had been given command of the army.

"Move out!" he shouted, holding his sword in the air for those in the back to see.

The men marched forward and the four at the front turned their horses to the gate. With a final look back at the king, Tlonna and her companions rode out of Arseninis City.

Tlonna sighed and drew her cloak closer around her. Snow was falling in fits while the wind constantly howled. They were halfway to the border of Arseninis and Kajgenia, in a wide meadow, and they were unprotected from the elements. As night approached, the small army stopped to make camp. Yellow tents marked with a silhouetted phoenix, Tyular's sign, were pitched, forming long rows down the meadow.

Tlonna stared into a fire; the wood cackling and spitting sparks.

A shadow passed over the encampment. Shivering, she looked and saw the tail of an enormously large bird pass into the trees.

Looking over at Losolin, he shook his head slowly and rubbed his hands together.

"Losolin, is something wrong with your hands? You have been rubbing them together for days now."

Losolin scowled. "Yeah, they have been tingling since the night before we left Arseninis. That night we...well...were up for a while?"

"I know what night you are talking about, Losolin," Tlonna replied shortly. "What happened?"

"I do not know," he said, shrugging. "It is like, I felt this extra something, other than what is normally felt right near the end," he blushed.

"An extra something? Like what?"

Losolin sighed. "I do not know. But it has been bothering me. It feels as though my hands are being constantly pricked by thousands of little needles, all over. I just...want...it...to...stop!" he shook his hands with each word.

With the last shake, green light flared out of his fingertips and sank into the ground. Where it landed, small flowers bloomed and then withered.

Tlonna and Losolin stared. Aladorn, whose tent was next to theirs, stuck his head out of the opening and stared at Losolin.

"What in the...?" Miazie said.

The elves looked up to see the human frozen in mid-stride, staring at Losolin too.

"Since when are you a Magin?" she asked, sitting down.

Aladorn joined them, sitting between the two females with a wary look on his face.

"I am not," Losolin replied shakily. "At least, I do not think I am."

Miazie turned an accusatory glare on Tlonna. "When was the last time you two copulated?"

"What? When we what? What are you talking abo--oh..." Tlonna said, blushing. "The night before we left Arseninis. The night you did with Tyular."

"Were you wearing anything?"

"Why would I be wearing anything? That would make it a bit difficult, do you not think?" the Magin replied.

Miazie ignored the jibe. "What about on the bed. Was there

anything on the bed? That might have rolled over and touched your skin?"

Tlonna's blush was crimson now, but Losolin was snickering.

"What?" Miazie snapped.

"The bag of stones was on the bed. The Magin stones. I remember. We were in such a hurry that we just tossed her belt on the bed. I remember waking up later because they were digging into my back. You do not think...no," Losolin explained, laughing fully now.

"Aye, I do. When you reached your...well the stone reacted, as it is supposed to and made your bodies one, for a moment. Was the, was it extraordinary?"

Tlonna could not respond for her mortification. Losolin, now cackling, nodded. Aladorn was trying to hold in his amusement, which resulted in him make an odd, unelfish grunt.

"It's because you felt each other's, as well as your own. For a second, you were one being, one entity. It took some of Tlonna's magic and made it yours. Tlonna does not have less power, it will have regenerated, and now you are a half-Magin. But your magic may be different. Certainly less powerful. Let's see," Miazie situated herself a bit more comfortably on the ground.

"Concentrate hard on the ground before you. Imagine energy pouring out of your hand and onto the ground."

After a few tries, Losolin succeeded in creating another flash of power, with the same results.

"Let's try something different," Miazie said and kicked a log out of the fire. It rolled into a patch of snow and went out.

"Concentrate on the log and see what happens."

He did, and after a couple more minutes, the green light suffused the log. When it faded, the log was normal, not charred or scarred in any way. The bark glistened wetly with sap and roots were extending slowly outward into the ground.

"You're a healer!" Miazie exclaimed, clapping her hands. "Oh, that's so wonderful! Here!" she picked up a sharp rock and sliced a shallow cut in her arm.

The woman held it out to Losolin, who stared at her in horror. Tlonna was staring at her friend in a mix of disbelief and irritation. Aladorn shook his head.

"Heal it!" Miazie urged, pushing her arm closer.

Losolin put his hands over the cut and closed his eyes. Miazie's arm was shaking with exertion from staying outstretched by the time the green light flared. When she pulled her arm back, the cut was gone, though a thin bead of blood was still on her arm. Losolin was panting.

"That is exhausting. Tlonna, how do you do it?"

Tlonna shrugged. "I was born with it. My body is used to it. You will get there, my love, it just takes time."

The next night, Tlonna read from *The History of Magic, and Its Uses*, as she did every night, while Losolin practiced basics with Miazie. Tlonna secretly listened in on their conversations, gleaning information while appearing to ignore them. Often, she would lose her concentration and her skin would glow with barely controlled power until she realized what was happening. Aladorn watched the proceedings with a mix of amusement and trepidation, for once Tlonna's wandering mind had resulted in him slamming face first into an invisible wall of air in front of their campfire.

"Damnation!" Losolin growled as his hands flared but nothing happened.

Somewhere in the camp, men were dueling. Laughter and curses rose on the night wind as there was a victory. Tlonna marked her place in the book and shut it.

"I am going to walk," she said, and left.

She strolled along the aisles between the tents, acknowledging the various greetings from the men. When the elf arrived at the ring of soldiers cheering on the next two duelers, they quieted. Tlonna walked to the empty space where the two men stood, panting, their chest and limbs shining with sweat. They wore only vambraces and the leather loin guards worn under the usual chain mail of soldiers. These men were warriors, not recruits from the countryside.

Tlonna smiled. "I will fight the winner," she said.

The men stared at her until she gestured for the combatants to continue. The two clashed together, wooden swords clacking. Tlonna watched them. They moved fast, grunting as dense wood smashed into their bare flesh. A blow from the larger opponent sent the other sprawling, but he leapt to his feet in one smooth movement and readied his sword.

The larger man lunged. The smaller one stepped to the side at the last second and slammed the wooden sword into his adversary's back. The warrior went down with a grunt. His victor raised his sword to the cheers of the men. The defeated man got to his feet, shook his opponent's hand, and then turned to Tlonna.

"My lady...are you sure?"

Tlonna grinned. "Do not doubt me because I am a female, sir."

"That is not why I doubt you," he replied, handing the wooden sword to her. "It is because you are an elf, and we have never seen one fight."

"Then tonight, I will put your fears to rest," Tlonna said, taking off her cloak.

When she had removed her real weapons and wore only her trousers and tunic, the elf stepped into the ring. The man looked nervous.

"Are you worried?" Tlonna asked him.

"I do not want to hurt you, my lady," he said.

"You will not. What is your name?"

"Aselios, princess, Knight of Aman, city of Arseninis."

"Good," Tlonna replied, and took her readying stance.

Aselios sighed resignedly and took his. When he did not move, Tlonna straightened.

"Duel me, Aselios, and if you impress me, I will make you a captain," she said, watching his eyes widen.

When she had taken her stance again, Aselios charged. Tlonna moved out of the way just in time. She spun, knocking his sword aside. The human whirled around, ducking low as her sword whistled above his head. He straightened out of his duck, wooden sword swinging, and found Tlonna's at his neck. The elf was leaning forward, back foot pointed into the ground, arm outstretched so that had Aselios taken another step, her sword would have hit him in the throat.

His heavy breathing echoed in the silence. Tlonna had beaten him in three moves, less than twenty seconds into the fight. Suddenly, roaring cheers rose from the onlookers. Tlonna dropped her stance and smiled. She tossed the wooden sword to a soldier in the front row.

"Good fight, Captain," she said, taking Aselios's hand in a shake.

Aselios sucked in a breath and expelled it. "You are not even winded."

"No, I am not. Perhaps next time you will not underestimate the strength of a female or an elf?"

"Never again, Lady," Aselios vowed, lowering his head.

"Good," Tlonna replied, and dropped his hand.

When Tlonna arrived back at her tent Losolin was alone, lounging by the fire.

"Miazie and Aladorn retire for the night?"

"Aye," Losolin grunted, watching her. "You look happy."

"I am. I just dueled with a man named Aselios. I made him a captain for his skill," Tlonna said, gazing down at her love.

"He beat you?" Losolin asked, looking surprised.

The Magin chuckled. "Of course not. But he was skilled. Beat a man nearly twice his size."

Losolin nodded his head slightly in appreciation. "Well...I am tired. Are you coming to bed?"

"In a bit," she said, turning her head to stare out over her camp.

Firelight was sparkling in the darkness as tiny flakes of snow drifted down onto the frozen ground. Silhouettes of men moved against them, laughing or dicing. Some were dueling and others staring blankly into the fire. In the glow of a tent, a man and woman undressed and joined.

"Love?" Losolin said after a minute, coming to stand behind her.

"It is almost peaceful, is it not?" Tlonna said, her gaze riveted on the camp.

"Almost," Losolin replied quietly, his own gaze on Tlonna's profile. "There will always be beauty in this world. Even in the darkest of times there is a spark of hope and beauty."

Tlonna finally turned to look at him. In silence, they stared at each other across the fire. Wordlessly, Losolin held out his hand and drew Tlonna into the tent.

The next morning as the camp was readying to march, a screech echoed out of the woods on the edge of the meadow.

Tlonna was strapping her saddlebags onto Takîreaes when a swarm of dark creatures burst out of cover. Losolin straightened from checking Neñyos's hooves. He looked at Tlonna. The recruits in the camp shouted and ran amok, shoving on armor and grabbing weapons.

"Miazie!" Tlonna shouted, watching the creatures as they rushed towards them, well over six hundred. They were desperately outnumbered and out skilled. But they had not counted on Tlonna's power, or the lethal skill of Aladorn and Losolin.

The Belau rode up, looking frantic. "What?"

"Get the non-soldiers on the march. We will meet up when we are finished here," Tlonna ordered, taking the sword that Losolin handed her.

Miazie nodded and rode off, Kaia's hooves tossing dirt into the air. Out of the milling men, Tyre and Aselios appeared, along with the other officers.

"Your armor, my lady, my lord?" Aselios asked.

"We have none, my friend," Tlonna replied, situating the ivory sword across from the thin bladed katan sword from Zeynuwn she had picked up in Arseninis. Aladorn stepped up to her side, solid and focused, his fine-boned features stone cold.

When the mass of attackers was close to the edge of the camp site, the soldiers formed a line behind the officers and elves. Tlonna drew her blades. Losolin drew the scimitar he had bought in Arseninis.

When the creatures were close enough for her to identify, Tlonna sneered. "Goblins and Darkwights," she said to Tyre who was on her left.

He nodded. "Good to know," he replied, and adjusted his heavy broadsword. "I've a score to settle."

The demons smashed into the line of soldiers and were hewn down. A few of the recruits went down as well, hindered by their lack of skill. Tlonna smashed a goblin's face in with the pommel of the ivory sword and then shoved it through its belly, her deadly lightning pulsing above, near the rear of the attacking company. Aladorn flickered into sight in her left peripheral, his blade taking out two of the enemy in one arcing blow.

The battle was short and violent. The frozen ground became slippery with the dead. Losolin slashed his scimitar across the throat of a Darkwight attempting to flee and then punched another in the face. Tlonna yanked her katan out of the belly of a goblin and then looked up at the remaining demons.

Behind her, the recruits gathered into a line again.

"Haah!" shouted one of the officers and the men repeated it in a bellow.

The demons fled. A few arrows pinned some of them to the ground, but nearly a score made it to the cover of trees.

The army had suffered losses, nearly two hundred had died, leaving a measly three hundred to clear the field of the dead. The carcasses of the demons were piled high and burned without ceremony. The humans were buried in a mass grave, dug primarily by Tlonna's magic. After a brief ceremony, the three hundred finished striking the camp, and followed the non-soldier recruits.

It was late in the evening when the army reached the camp. Miazie ran out in relief when they rode in. Tlonna and Losolin dismounted and let the officers handle the men.

"Dear gods, I was so worried. So few of you returned though. How many did we lose?"

"Around two hundred," Losolin said sadly, pulling the tent off Neñyos's saddle.

"And the attackers? Who were they? How many survived?"

"Goblins and Darkwights," Tlonna replied. "About twenty of them escaped into the forest. There is a rear guard behind us by about a half hour. They were going to make sure we had no followers. Did you run into any problems?"

Miazie shook her head. "Only the women not wanting to leave their men behind. Tonight will be rough."

Tlonna nodded silently. "Once we get to Kajgenia, things will change. I will make sure of it."

Aladorn appeared, dropping his tent onto the ground between Miazie's and Tlonna's, and wiped his forearm across his cheek, leaving a bloody smear. He gave the three a searching glance, and then wandered off, disappearing from sight after a few steps.

Miazie sighed, her eyes where Aladorn had been. "We're still very far away from Kajgenia. Almost four hundred leagues. And there are wounded now. They'll slow us down."

"No they will not," Losolin said as he unsaddled Neñyos. "The grievously wounded have been healed, and those lesser can still march or ride. I made sure of it."

Miazie scowled. "Losolin, you are not strong enough to do

such an undertaking. And you're not skilled enough yet."

"Necessity beats out talent every time, Miazie," Losolin growled.

"But you're-"

"Hold your tongue!" he shouted, yanked his saddlebags onto his shoulder, and stormed off.

Miazie's face fell. "I didn't mean anything!" she said to Tlonna, her voice shaking.

Tlonna watched Losolin's receding back. "He is very tired, Miazie. And a man he could not heal died in his arms. He gave Losolin his ring, and asked him to return it to his son in Arseninis."

Miazie sniffed, "Things are going to get much worse."

Tlonna nodded. "Aye, I know."

The elf picked up Neñyos and Takîreaes' halter leads and led the horses away from a downcast Miazie. By the time she had hobbled them and pitched the tent, Losolin arrived. His face was weary and his knuckles bloody.

"My love, did it help?" Tlonna asked quietly as she examined the torn flesh. Bits of bark were protruding from the wounds.

Losolin did not say anything, but drew his hands away to cup her face. He merely looked at her, his oceanic eyes red-rimmed and sorrowful.

Tlonna watched him, watched the single tear form in his eye and slip down his cheek. The only tear he had shed all day.

Finally, he said, "He did not tell me his son's name."

Tlonna wrapped her arms around his waist and laid her cheek against his shoulder.

"We will find him, love, we will find him."

When they finally lay down to sleep, it was to the sounds of sobbing women mourning the loss of their men.

The week wore on. The host reached the Trohasa forest and was forced to slow their pace.

Losolin, ashamed of his behavior, would not acknowledge Miazie who rode behind the elves and in front of the officers. Her horse Kaia whickered and tossed its head. She clicked and patted her neck. The mare was still young, but she was fast and strong. Miazie sighed to herself and hoped that the elves' sharp ears didn't pick it up. They did, and looked back at her with worried eyes. Aladorn handed her his flask and she took it reflexively. Downing a swallow of the burning ale the wiat had brought from his own house, Miazie thought about the short time she had known them. Tlonna had saved her life more than once, putting her own life in danger over and over again.

A wave of gilt and pity washed over her as she thought about the young Magin. Her whole life she had been controlled by people she didn't like and now that she was free from them, Miazie was doing it for them. As for Losolin, he was a mystery to her. At times he seemed so clueless, but at others more intelligent than she thought possible. He was always quiet and calm, and so caring.

Aladorn had ignored her, then brought her a night of unsurpassed passion, and then been coolly benign to her. He was aloof, she admitted, but in a kind way that made her yearn for a companion, though she did not think the wiat would be it.

Pushing a branch out of her way, Miazie felt something sticky spread across her palm. Making a face, she went to wipe it on her pant leg but stopped when she recognized it. Immediately she rode up next to the elves and touched Tlonna lightly on the arm.

"What is it?" she said.

"Tlonna, look, it is old blood. I don't think it is very old though. It was on a branch back there," Miazie gestured with her hand.

"Let me see it," Tlonna said, sucking on her bottom lip.

Miazie held out her hand and showed them the blood. Losolin squinted at it with a frown, dark eyes flashing from her hand to the trees around them. Aladorn took back his flask that was still in her other hand.

"Goblin blood," Tlonna stated blandly, leaning away from Miazie's hand.

Losolin averted his gaze from the human's when she looked at him. She sighed. Before the air had totally been expelled from Miazie's lungs, Tlonna cried out. A thick crossbow bolt buried itself in her thigh.

"Tlonna!" Losolin gasped, drawing his scimitar.

Tlonna shook her head and looked around wildly. Arrows were flying haphazardly through the air.

One struck Miazie, glancing off her arm and skimming by her temple. Aladorn was off his horse and nowhere to be seen in seconds.

A few soldiers dismounted and disappeared into the trees. A

few minutes later, the arrows stopped coming and the soldiers reappeared, along with Aladorn.

"It was those few who escaped!" one of them shouted to the officers. "They were left behind by their superiors and decided to rectify their mistake."

Tyre turned to Tlonna and Losolin and then cursed.

Tlonna keeled over and fell out of the saddle.

Tlonna woke up being smothered by soft, fragrant material. Momentarily spasing she panicked and tried to get away. Something underneath the cloth was hard and unmoving. Immediately, it backed away from her and let her breathe. Once she had caught her breath, she looked up.

Losolin held her close so she would not slip off the horse. Her body was pressed up against his, safe from the onslaught of wind. He felt her struggle and released his grip. She stared at him for a moment before recovering her wits. She smiled weakly and then rested once more against his body. His arm went around her waist and held her. Feeling, more than seeing her fall asleep again, he smiled grimly.

The bolt in her leg had been poisoned with the same as the other goblin arrow that had taken her out before. Losolin sighed quietly. It seemed repetitive, though Miazie said elves were immune to illness. And he could not heal her. That was the worst. He could not heal Tlonna without causing them both extreme agony. Losolin brooded.

Miazie coughed quietly, bringing him back to the present. Losolin looked at her and his heart sank. She was trying to hide a wound on her head, exposing her arm, which had another deep cut on it. He laid his hand on her arm and brought it down. He put his hand to her cheek where the cut was and healed her.

Her forehead was beaded with sweat and there were lines of worry, or fear, etched upon it. He pushed her hair away from the beautiful, but pale and ill face. He put his hand on her wet forehead and whispered soothing words to help his magic along. Tlonna, who had been sitting upright against him, slumped down with her head on his chest, bobbing in the saddle listlessly. Aladorn finally grabbed Miazie's reins and handed her his flask again.

"Drink it all, and go to sleep. I will guide your horse," he growled.

Miazie obliged, sputtering as the potent alcohol burned down her throat. Within minutes she was swaying and before too long was slumped over her saddle. Losolin sent Aladorn a measuring look, which was returned with a tense shake of the head. Giving up on trying to understand the dark elf's thoughts, Losolin situated Tlonna against him once more, and went back to brooding.

His thoughts strayed to where they were most, his past and his future. What would happen to him when he and Tlonna returned to Blackhaven Forest? Would they make it to the kingdom? What had happened to make them leave in the first place? How had he and Tlonna come together? Did Constancias really hate him that much that she would exile her own daughter to be rid of him? Did he have a mother and father? Where did he live? Would he survive long enough to find answers? A day passed.

An enigma, a total enigma. What is it about him that was...fascinating yet lustfully eerie about him? Miazie glanced at the elf riding beside her. She felt a strange twist in her stomach as she looked at Losolin. She loved him. The thought startled and frightened her. *No, I cannot love him. He loves Tlonna. Besides, I am just a human. Plus, he's now a Magin.* The Belau argued with herself. *He would never give up Tlonna for me anyway. I don't want him to either. If he did, it would change everything. He and Tlonna are meant to be together. I must leave. If I cannot control my feelings about him, I must leave. Two more days, if anything happens in two days, I will leave.* Sighing, Miazie scowled down at Kaia's neck.

"Miazie? Miazie! Are you all right? Miazie!" Losolin shook the woman gently. She had nearly fallen off her horse. They'd been riding all day but she had not shown weariness. The Belau opened her eyes slowly. Obviously feverish, she reached for Losolin. Taking this as a plea for help, the elf gathered her up in his arms and laid his hand across her forehead. Miazie pushed his hand away and put her arms around his waist. Losolin, thinking she was just too weak to hold herself up, let her. He called a halt as it was near dark anyway. Gently untangling himself from Tlonna, he pulled Miazie off her horse and dismounted himself. In her delirious state, Miazie pushed against him and stood up slowly, using him as a stabilizer.

"I love you. I need you," she whispered into his ear. "Don't leave me, please, don't leave me. I love you. Don't let me go," sobbing, she stroked his hair and hung her arms around his neck.

Putting her head down on his shoulder, she cried. Her body shook with the convulsive sobs. Lifting her head the Belau pulled his head down to hers and kissed him. Her tears ran down her face and his. Miazie pushed her lips against the elf's and tightened her grip on him. He was so much taller than her that his body had to bend away from hers to reach her height.

Losolin, taken by surprise stood rooted to the spot. His mind screamed at him to push her away, make her leave him. She loved him? He felt her fingers running through his hair, her soft body pressed against him. *No.* He felt her lips touch his, her tears wetting his face. *No.* Her arms tightened around his neck, her lips pushed harder. He pulled back his lips in a snarl and opened his mouth to yell at her. Her tongue entered his mouth. Finally his body reacted to his mind. With a growl, he pushed her away from him. She fell to the ground. Losolin stared at the woman crawling towards him, calling out his name. His eyes narrowed and blazing anger flashed through his mind.

"Miazie! Calm yourself!" he shouted, backing away from her. "What do you think you are doing?"

Aladorn stopped in mid-stride to stare at them, half fading with shock. When Losolin looked up, the wiat was gone.

Tlonna still lay slumped against Neñyos's neck. He could still feel Miazie's body against his, her lips, her tongue in his mouth. Gently he pulled Tlonna off the horse's back and held her up. Losolin studied her face. Small drops of wetness landed on the fair skin. Looking up he blinked as raindrops hit him in the eye.

Cursing, he laid Tlonna on the ground and pulled the tent off of Takîreaes' back. The stallion snorted and looked back at him. Ignoring the horse, Losolin pitched the tent and pulled Tlonna into it. After hobbling the horses, he brought in all the pack baskets and bags, lit a candle and pulled off Tlonna's now soaked clothes. Rummaging through her belongings he found dry clothes and dressed her. When he finished, he did the same for himself.

"Losolin! Come back to me!" Miazie shouted at him from outside.

"Gods' curse it," Losolin swore, pulling his cloak on once more.

He pulled the delirious Miazie up and dragged her through the mud into his tent. After clearing a spot on the ground he laid the shivering woman on the bare ground. Sinking onto the blankets next to Tlonna, he heard a faint moan. Looking over at Miazie, Losolin groaned in frustration as she writhed around, pulling at her clothes as though they pained her. Searching around he found one of the fur cloaks Tlonna had made and pulled it over the Belau. She thrashed around and the cloak slid down around her waist. Grimacing, Losolin picked her up and tucked the cloaked around her. She murmured to him and he dropped her. Miazie whimpered once then settled into the cloak. Sighing, Losolin dropped down next to Tlonna and succumbed to sleep.

The night was dark and his creatures had given him good news. Midian smiled to himself. Everything was going just as he had planned it to. He was a man that, if anyone had cared to notice or dared for that matter, would have been one hundred and sixty one years of age, though magic had slowed the aging process so that he looked no older than thirty. His face was handsome with dark blue eyes and framed by thick, raven black hair. He was slender and muscular with slightly honeyed skin. A shadow of movement caught his eye.

"What is it, Kelus?" his voice was a caress that many women had fallen for. With his island accent, it was smooth and quiet, just above a whisper unless he was irritated.

Midian's eyes locked onto the shadow within the cowl. Silver rings glinted back at him.

"The party wass attacked, ass you ordered, but they triumphed. Losst nearly half their number, but took out almosst all of company ssent againsst them. Thosse that were left after the original attack, other than the two that fled to uss, decided to attack the company. They were sslaughtered, obvioussly, but they managed to poisson both the elf Magin and the human woman. It wass jusst insside the Trohassa, and they are now weakened, disspirited by their losssess and the ssicknesss of the Magin. Now would be the time to attack, my lord king."

"No," Midian smiled faintly at the widening of the silver rings. "Don't attack them now. I want the Magin for myself. This time, I will get from her what I need, and then make sure she dies. I will not have another mishap," he said as he rose from his throne.

Kelus, the First Darkwight, stepped smoothly off the dais steps and to the side as Midian moved.

"Send my Cleicks, Kelus, make sure they kill the whelp, and the woman, but bring the Magin back to me. In fact, I want the boy's head brought at the same time. I find myself unable to trust the word of my subjects."

"Yess, King Rahlan," Kelus hissed.

Midian smiled to himself, never minding the female slaves that skittered out of his way. He grabbed one that was too slow and ripped her black dress off. Sinking his teeth into her flesh, he dug his fingers into her back and created long bleeding slashes with his power. She screamed and he flung her to the ground. He sneered and turned on Kelus. The Darkwight hissed in shock as the man grabbed his black robes and swung him into the wall. The cowl came off and the creature's hideous face was revealed. What used to be an elf's face was blackened and torn with blood still fresh from the day he had been tortured mercilessly, one hundred and twenty years ago.

His hair had been ripped away and his scalp had been sealed with boiling oil. His eyes were black with silver rings where there used to be a gray green color. Once he had been named Aleac. But those days were far gone. His clawed hands snatched the hood up over his head once more concealing everything except the silver eyes. Everything elfin about him had been scoured away, everything, except his soul.

"Kelus, why are you afraid to show your face? Do you not like it? Do you not like what I have given you?" Midian's eyes danced with insanity.

"No my king. I am not worthy of what you have given me. You have been generouss to me."

"Take this one," the dark man said, shoving the girl at him. "Share your bed with her. If she does not comply, bring her back to me and we will rectify the problem."

"Masster, I am not worthy of thiss. Do not give her to me," Kelus shied away from the girl.

Inside his head, Kelus screamed in mental agony as his demon's blood roiled with lust and his soul wept.

"No, I insist. Take her!" Midian shouted at him. The girl was skinny and dark skinned with black hair and large brown eyes. Where

Midian had touched her there was an oozing burn. Kelus grabbed the girl and hastened out of the throne room.

The girl lay sobbing on the floor. Kelus pulled on his robes, avoiding her naked figure lying on the floor. The pain in his mind was still excruciating while his body seemed to float with satisfaction. She had raw claw marks on her dark skin and her small breasts were red and bleeding. Kelus had not meant to bite her but he could not scream and let Midian have the pleasure of his pain.

The curse of the Darkwights, evil and cruel in everything but the soul. It was what Midian called their gift, what made their rage justified. As if to prove the mad king's point, Kelus heard the ragged cry of a Darkwight in his room, a desperate and insane howl that left the body weak with despair.

When he turned, the girl was pulling on the rags of her dress. It was only just above her breasts when Kelus looked at her. Her fear angered him and he grabbed the front of the rags and with his claws made five long rips down the front. She gasped and tried to pull together the shreds. It did no good. Her breasts were still visible and so was her rear. Kelus snarled at her and she screamed and ran out of the room. Kelus clawed at his face and neck. The memories of his wife screaming as Midian tortured her invaded his mind.

The demon fell to his knees, his claws digging into his ruined scalp as he writhed on the floor. Lesia had been young and innocent when they wed. Not a decade later Midian raided their town and found them hiding in the root cellar of their home. The present Kelus snarled into the stone floor of his room. Lesia was bound hand and foot like a calf for slaughter as Midian pulled off strips of flesh from her little body until there was nothing left but a quivering pink mass. The elf Aleac screamed at the madman murdering his wife, screamed and pleaded for him to stop. She was still alive. In an act of insane mercy, Midian slit her throat. Then he turned to her sobbing husband, trussed to the bed like a dog.

Kelus felt the raw pain of his nails being torn from his fingers as they dug into the stone. The Darkwight howled into his robes, shaking with the still-fresh memory. It was what happened every time he had a woman. It was his punishment for loving Lesia too much.

"Kelus!"

The call echoed through the halls of the black castle.

"Damn him to the nine hellss," Kelus sobbed, gathering himself before he ran through the halls towards his master's hall.

"Yess Masster."

"I see you enjoyed her more than usual Kelus," Midian sat with the girl on his lap, sobbing.

"Yess my King."

"Tell me, do you want her as your own?" he traced her back with his fingers. He had supplied her with a new dress.

"No my King."

"Are you quite sure Kelus? You can have her if you want her."

"Yess Masster. No Masster."

"What is your name sweetling? You are new here."

"Arianna my king."

"Arianna hmm? Come with me. I will show you real pleasure. Do you want me to, hmm?"

"Y-yes my Lord King."

"What do you say to get things that you want?"

"Please Master. Show me pleasure."

"All right come closer," Arianna pushed closer to the king and straddled him with her legs.

A flash of steel appeared in Midian's hand and he shoved the knife into the girl's side. She screamed and it ended in a gurgle. Midian laughed and dropped her on the ground. Her eyes stared upwards in pain.

"You never ask anything of me, wench," Midian kicked her away from his feet and settled his eyes on Kelus.

The Darkwight stared back, equally unconcerned about the dead girl.

"You are my oldest and most valued Darkwight. Don't fool with me Kelus or I will end your life, and it will not be a quick nor pleasant death."

"I know Lord Rahlan," Kelus bowed slightly and his eyes narrowed with the effort of maintaining his demonic cruelness. "I have been waiting for you to do that for a long time Masster. It sseemed you had grown ssoft towardss the girlss ever ssince we conquered thiss bleeding kingdom."

"Soft eh? No not soft, bored. Restless. I need some action Kelus. Give me something to act with. Start a war or something. What about the Liberated Lands? We could create havoc on those fools.

They haven't had a good fight for a while," Midian paced. "Alas no, I need the Magin in my hands. I should have done this when I had her eight years ago. I should have thought of this eight years ago. Why did I not?"

Kelus stood silent as his king raged.

"Why did I think wiping the memory of her from the minds of every benighted soul in this blasted land would solve the problem of prophecy? How did I miss a trigger? I felt it, you know. I felt the moment her memory returned though I didn't know what it was. It was like being hit in the temple with a brick. Do you remember? I was in a girl and I accidentally crushed her windpipe with my teeth. Do you remember that night, Kelus?"

"I do."

"What was the trigger?" Midian roared, tugging at his hair.

Cords of black power lashed around the room as the Magin lost control in his wrathful frustration. Kelus stood calmly in the middle, a few feet from the human in what he considered the safe zone. Even in the clutches of insanity, Midian would not let himself come into harm, so the demon stood in the circle of protection the man had around him constantly.

The women were not so lucky. Most of them died within a few seconds of being lashed by the magic, others writhed on the ground in torment as they clenched on ruined limbs or pressed lurid burns to the cold stone floor. One girl crouched next to the throne, hugging her knees and sobbing in terror. She was untouched, as was the throne, but she was only other survivor besides Kelus and Midian. The ruined girls would die soon enough.

Midian brought his hands down from his hair and looked around at the devastation he had caused with cold, half-surprised eyes. "Get someone in here to clean this mess up."

Kelus turned, about to follow the man's order, but he found himself staring through the window. He thought he saw a flash of blonde hair, the light-catching hues of elf hair, but that was impossible, they were all dead or in the dungeons. The demon cocked his head slightly, frowning. Then took a step forward. He could have sworn there had been fingers on the ledge just a second ago. He crossed to the window.

"King Rahlan!" Kelus beckoned to Midian who was glaring at him from around his throne. "An elf!"

Midian strode to the window and stared down to where Kelus gestured.

"Where? Show me where!"

"There!" Kelus pointed downwards.

"I don't see it."

Kelus growled and grabbed his king's head. "There!"

Lord Midian ignored his Darkwight's breach of conduct and stared down at the small retreating figure. "Bleeding hells! You told me they were all dead or captive! Get him! Kill him!" the king roared in his rage. "Get him!

Kelus ran down the staircase shouting at his horde. He burst through the doors and set his demons off in different directions to scour the grounds. He ran around to where he had seen the elf and stopped dead when he saw him...or more correctly, her. Crouching behind a tree, the Darkwight watched the elf disappear. Kelus grunted in surprise and ran to the spot where she had just been. Swinging his sword around, the Darkwight didn't notice his men surrounding him and watching him in bewildered amusement. Suddenly, the elf reappeared beside him and put an arrow to his throat.

"Do not shoot, or your master dies," the elf's musical voice addressed the crowd whose bows were pointed at her.

Kelus growled and glared at her. "How did you get out elf? Are you alone?" his silver eyes flashed.

"In your present position, I would not be asking the questions, slum. I know what you are, just men, foolish men tortured and beaten. Used for the Shadowsoul's purpose, and when he is finished with you, he will rid himself of you like trash. You believe you have completely conquered *Kairhotuss Buwai* do you not? Ha!..."

Kelus flinched when she laughed, the arrow point digging into his neck.

"...Oh no, you have not conquered it in the least. We are free, demon, even the Dwarves, Men, and independent creatures are free. Go tell your master. Our leaders are still alive, and his little coup eight years ago did not fool us. Go!" she shouted, laughing. "Tell them High Commander Yayènia, friend of Tlonna, spits in his eye!"

Kelus was pushed to the ground amid the crazy elf's laughter and screams of pain from his fellow Darkwights as she sent them on her way with well aimed shots from her bow. Kelus lurched to his feet and grabbed the elf's ankle and tried to pull her down. Still laughing, she shot him in hand. He looked up and found himself looking into bright blue eyes set into a beautiful pale face, so much like his own Lesia. He snarled and stumbled away from her, trying not to trip over his own robes. Her harmonious laughter followed him until he slammed the great door shut.

Yayènia looked around at the once beautiful greenery that was now dead and bleak. Grimacing, the elf strapped her bow onto her back and ran to a statue in the center of the courtyard, flitting from one cover to the next to avoid detection. For a moment she merely stared up at the white marble visage. His face was calm, though fierce pride and strength was reflected in the eyes. Braids of marble hair coiled over his shoulders and onto his chest and back. Every detail of him was perfect, the weight of the bow reflected in the bulging arm muscles, the arrowhead just as deadly as one that would fly.

Yayènia drew a shaky breath as she looked around once more at the devastating sight of the courtyard. Finally, she yanked open the hidden door in the statue's base. Climbing down the ladder, she lit a torch and followed the dark winding passageway. The darkness crowded around her, making her wish that the light from the torch was brighter. As she passed the dormitories that the dwarves had made, her husband opened their door and beckoned her in.

"No, Suneelo, I must go to King Dietirin," she pulled away from his grasp.

"Yayènia, come here. I found something that might help us get out of the gate. Once we are out of the first wall, the city is nearly empty, and we can leave," the elf pulled at his wife again.

"All right, but make it quick," Yayènia followed Suneelo into the room and sat down on the blanket that was their bed.

"Here, I found it in the gatehouse," he handed her a yellowed piece of parchment with lines scrawled on it.

Opening it, she gasped. It was a map of the forbidden underground tunnels that lead to the gates in the wall surrounding the castle.

"Excellent, my love. I knew there was a reason I married you," Yayènia said after a minute, beaming at Suneelo.

The Captain of the Guard made a face. "You burn me, wife."

"Aye, I know. That is why you moan so loudly when we-"

"Nia, do you not have some place else to be?" Suneelo cut her short, laughing.

The High Commander rolled her eyes. "All right, but come with me. Together we are stronger."

Suneelo nodded, tracing her face with his finger. "I love you."

Yayènia stopped moving. She wrapped her fingers around his hand and kissed his palm.

"You fear for me," she said quietly.

Suneelo replied with a kiss, gentle and soft. Finally, he said, "Every time you strap on those swords of yours, I do."

"You have never before spoken to me like this, Suneelo. Why now?"

Suneelo placed her hand on his chest, above his heart. "Because, this day we move forward in our lives. This day may be our last day of peace, such as this is," he gestured at the earthen walls, "and I know that if my heart stops beating, it is because you are gone. And I cannot fathom such a thought without knowing that you know I love you. Every inch of you, every moment we are together, I treasure. I know that you do not need me, that if I passed, you would move on as the warrior that you are, but I have always and will always love you."

Yayènia blinked, a line forming between her brows as she stared at her husband. "You are wrong, Suneelo. If you passed from this world, my life would be dust. And I do need you. You are...everything to me. The one person in this entire world that I trust completely. The one elf in my life that I can lean on without shame or fear. As Eliam and Iyabel were one in story, we are one in life. Never doubt my love or need for you, my husband," Yayènia replied quietly, removing her hand from his chest and wrapping it in his hair. "I love you, as well."

Suneelo wrapped his fingers around the leather strap that held her makeshift bow in it, and pulled it over her head. Yayènia watched him as he tugged the leather thong at the end of her knee-length braid off and undo it. Her hair, wavy from being braided, cascaded over her body, full and heavy. Forcing himself to breathe slowly, Suneelo undressed his wife, and then himself.

The muscles that glided under her skin put any male to shame, her form any female. Suneelo bent over her, taking her mouth captive.

Yayènia was startled. Never before had Suneelo been this gentle, this loving. Usually it was passionate, almost violent, which suited her just fine, but this...this was wonderful. Erdwyf always told her that Ghealan made love to her in ways no other male had. Yayènia, who long ago, had once been with Ghealan, was confused. With him too, it had been rough. Love between warriors could not be soft. There was no room for softness. Suneelo knew it as well, being a warrior himself.

But this new tenderness, she understood finally what Erdwyf spoke so quietly about. Her Suneelo, the epitome of masculinity, capable of this romance. Yayènia almost laughed. He was a beautiful male, she thought as she watched him bend over her. His face was fine boned and youthful, as elves were, but there was a hardness to him that made him the adult he was, his eyes had seen death and war. His mouth twitched in a small smile as she looked up at him.

His honey blond shoulder length hair curtained over her as he kissed her. Her hands dug into his naked back, feeling the muscles roll beneath them. Then his hands touched her, and she lost the ability to think.

A little while later, the elves strolled through the crude hallways to the center of the underground city.

"My King!" Yayènia said when they arrived.

People crowding the room turned to look at Suneelo and Yayènia, and then bowed out of the way so they could walk to the front of the line.

"High Commander, do not forget yourself," the king said to the excited elf, not unkindly. "Do you have information?"

"Right...does *she* have to be here?"

"High Commander! I am your queen and as such I demand respect from all of my subjects, especially you to whom some, foolishly, defer," Constancias, queen of Blackhaven snapped.

"*Pff.* You will never be my queen. King Dietirin, please..." Yayènia said, turning away to ignore the fuming queen.

Dietirin rested his head in the palm of his hand. At one thousand and thirty one years old, he had aged eyes in an otherwise ageless face. "Yayènia...you should show your deference to royalty. You will tell us what you discovered above, and then I will speak to you and Suneelo privately at a later time. Is that agreeable?"

Yayènia grinned her acquiescence. "Of course my lord." With a purposeful look at Constancias, she told the king what had transpired.

When she finished, Dietirin rubbed his chin. "Did they believe you that we had escaped?"

"The demons looked positively alarmed. Their leader, Kelus, I heard him called, went running to his master as soon as I let him go. I do not think many of them will survive the shots I gave them."

"You did well, of course. Constancias?"

The queen sneered. "You should have killed them all. You are a fool."

As Yayènia moved to reply, Suneelo grabbed her arm and yanked her back. "My Lieges...excuse us, but we must eat. Yayènia has been out all day. Are we excused?"

Dietirin gave them a knowing half smile. "Of course, go, eat. I will come to you later."

The two elves strolled out of the room accompanied by Constancias' outraged words to her husband.

"You know she blames you for Tlonna and Losolin's disappearance," Dietirin replied to his wife's threats.

"But I am her *queen*, Dietirin! She may be High Commander, but I can strip her of that rank at any time. If it were not for her heathenish talent to kill, I would have already!"

"You must have my signature to do such a thing, Constancias...and I would never remove Yayènia from her position, or Suneelo from his. They are the best at what they do, and even you cannot dispute that."

"But they must learn some sort of deference to me! They give you all the credit as king, but treat me as someone beneath their notice. I will not have it any longer. I will not deal with it! I have been queen for over five hundred years, and yet they still treat me as scum!"

"I do not think they are going to stop. Tlonna and Losolin were their best friends, and Ghealan and Erdwyf's as well. They see you as the one who sent them away; ergo they will not forgive you, nor defer to you as queen. Anyhow, I have had enough of this today. I am going to retire. Good evening," Dietirin stood and walked out of the room, followed by a score of guardsmen and his personal servants.

The queen of Blackhaven watched her husband leave the small cavern in the ground through narrowed eyes. Thoughts of her daughter flashed through her mind. Fury erupted in her, and she stood, not knowing what else to do. The commoners looked up at her expectantly, waiting to be heard.

"Does my queen require something?" Feorien, her personal guard, asked.

"No," Constancias sniffed and followed the king out of the room.

Dietirin found Yayènia and Suneelo in their small room, huddled over a piece of aged parchment. "What have we here?" he asked, shutting the door in the faces of his constant entourage.

"Routes," Suneelo said absently, moving over on the bed to allow the king to join them.

"Routes? Routes to where?"

"Outside, Dietirin. Do you not wish to be free of this?" Yayènia asked, waving her hand at the dirt ceiling above.

"Of course I do, but that does not mean it is going to happen because we find a way out. We have too many weak and elderly to do such a thing. This is a city, no matter how decrepit, and all things must be considered."

"We are not talking about moving the city, Dietirin. We are talking about moving us, outside, to find help," the High Commander explained patiently.

"Right. And who would safe guard my people?"

"You would, you are the king."

"And you are the legendary Yayènia er"Tiena, protector of masses. The people would panic."

"And if we found your daughter?"

The king of Blackhaven felt his heart skip a few beats. "You know where she is?"

"Have no idea, but we know where she and Losolin were headed. They are bound to have been seen somewhere, yes?"

"I suppose you are right, but how can she be found. You saw her corpse, along with half the city. Do you, like some, believe it was a hoax?"

"Yes. Midian is severely unstable, he would do anything to prove his superiority, including fake the death of someone he was unable to kill," Yayènia stated bluntly. "You must have felt it, a short time ago, a certainty that Tlonna was alive, that she was real. You know as well as I the horrible feeling that perhaps her memory was a false one, that the Tlonna we know and cherish was but a dream dashed by Midian. Then, suddenly, it came back to me, and to everyone I have spoken to, that Tlonna was indeed real, and that she was very much alive."

"Yes, of course I did, but that does not change the fact that we have no idea where she is. You could be gone months, years!"

"And? It would be worth it, Dietirin."

Chapter 9

Foreshadow of Fate

Tlonna rolled over and opened her eyes. Losolin lay next to her, his face darkened with worry even in sleep. Hearing a moan, Tlonna looked over his chest and saw Miazie shiver and pull her legs up to her chest. Her eyelids were red and puffy, as though she had been crying. The human whimpered in her sleep and murmured Losolin's name. Scowling, the Magin rolled to her other side and stood. Steadying herself from the wave of nausea that swept through her, she stepped outside. Blinking in the sunlight, she looked down the rows of tents. Men were huddled by fires, cooking traveling food on spits. As her eyes roamed over the soldiers, Tlonna spied four men near the end of the far row involved in a rowdy game of dice. Walking over to them, she sat down to watch. The soldiers leaped to their feet and bowed, murmuring her name.

"Sit down," Tlonna looked up at them and smiled.

Hesitantly, the four men sat down. One caught her attention as he lowered himself with fluid motion unnatural for men. He had long black hair and smooth pale skin. Reaching over, Tlonna pushed his hair back behind his ears and smiled as they were revealed. Long, pointed ears, belonging to an elf. The man stared at her uncertainly and glanced around at his fellows. They stared back at him silently.

"Why do you fear to reveal yourself? I am an elf. Do you fear that being an elf will bring Midian's forces down on you? Hmm?"

"I-I was afraid they might make me an outcast. Men and Elves have not been friends for years," he looked down at his hands, clamped in his lap.

"Arseninis was an Elfish city. The humans took it over when Aderiaen destroyed it long ago. Times change, man, elf, and dwarf will fight together once again. Remember this. What is your name?"

The young elf lifted his eyes and stared at her. His mouth worked silently before he answered. "Locton. You know my father, Aladorn."

Tlonna stared back at him. "Aladorn's son? Aladorn has a son? Where is your mother?"

"She was killed by elf-haters. They could not get to me or my father, being that we are both..."

"You are both what, Locton?" Tlonna knew the answer, but she wanted him to say it.

"We are both...wiats," the elf shied away as his fellow soldiers gasped and backed away from him.

"Stop! Stop this madness now!" Tlonna glared at the retreating men. "There is nothing wrong about being a wiat. Tell me, what is wrong with them?"

"My lady, wiats are spawns of evil. They were used during Aderiaen's War to ravage kingdoms. Aderiaen used them to kill."

"Used. Used is the key word, fool. I know the history of wiats. They resisted as long as they could against the evil of Aderiaen. They were overrun and taken as slaves. Do not hold that against them. Locton is no different now than he was before I came. Apparently, you do not like elves either. Why?" Tlonna turned to another man, the closest to Locton.

"No, we don't hate elves, it's just, well. Huh, I don't know why. That's just the way we were trained. We have never fought elves before," he looked at the man next to him.

He shook his head and they both looked at the soldier Tlonna had questioned first. His eyes narrowed and shook his head too. Tlonna nodded and beckoned to Locton. He edged forward slowly, his dark eyes searching her. The Magin studied his face.

"How old are you?" she said when he finally reached her.

"Seventy-three."

"Seventy-three! What are you doing in an army? You should still be at home. I will not have a boy fighting in my army. Where is your father? I have not seen him since the fight," Tlonna stood up, dragging Locton with her.

"I do not know, please my lady. No my lady. No. I will not go back. It is my duty to go, besides, I would be hanged for a deserter. And, I am sorry to be blunt, but you yourself are still a child."

Tlonna looked at him coldly. "How do you know that?"

He took a deep breath and began talking as though reciting something he had been forced to memorize. "Princess Tlonna Arune Ewôsdírn was born on the fifteenth day of Maen in the year four hundred of the Eighth Age, twenty-nine years after the birth of Shadow King Midian Rahlan." His eyes focused on hers and he said quietly, "This is the month of Resen of year five hundred and forty-three. My lady, you are one hundred and forty-three years old. Lord Losolin was born six years after Midian, on the twenty-fifth day of Tala. He is one hundred and fifty-five."

Tlonna continued to stare at him.

"It is part of the history of Nymyños. Your life and everyone's around you was tracked until your death...well, what everyone thought was your death. It is part of the curriculum in Talenias to know the ages and dates of important figures."

Tlonna stared at him and then hugged him hard. Locton slowly put his arms around her and patted her awkwardly on the shoulder. Tlonna felt his body tense as she hugged him harder but did not care. Whatever thoughts the elf had running through his head were his. The Magin was hard pressed to stop the tears from reaching her eyelashes. Then came the memories, with their now customary twinges of pain. Memories of fetes, glorious and filled with laughter, people coming up to her with indiscernible faces to press gifts into her hands.

"Thank you Locton. You do not know what you have given me. I will not take you back, but I will not let you fight until you have laid me on the ground a few times with your sword," Locton started to protest then he sighed and nodded. "Why are you not with your father?"

Locton shrugged. "He passes me by every night to say hello, but other than that, he stays away from me so others do not know that I am his son."

"What? Why?" Tlonna asked, aghast.

"He does not want me to be shunned because I am his son, a wiat's son."

Tlonna's anger faded, replaced with sorrow. "I am sorry, Locton. Do not fear what you are, for then you are always living in fear, and that is not right."

Locton nodded grudgingly. Tlonna patted him on the shoulder and turned to walk back to her tent.

"I am glad you are better, Princess," Locton's voice said behind her.

Nodding silently, Tlonna sat by her tent, enjoying the warmth of the fire and the quiet sounds of Losolin and Miazie, who seemed to be having a debate. She had only read a few lines from *History of Magic and its Uses* when she began to overhear their conversation, one she did not like.

"I am sorry Losolin, I didn't know what I was doing. Remember I was sick. That kiss was truly nothing, and when I said I loved you and needed you, well, that was probably just delirious rambling."

Losolin sighed heavily, "You cannot think to let this merely pass by, Miazie. What you did, it speaks of thoughts you hide in your head, and you cannot let them fester and rot, as they are bound to do. They will drive a wedge between us, and Tlonna as well, if you do not confront them, and solve them in turn."

"You would have me say things that I have kept hidden for a long while, Losolin. Thoughts even I did not know I had until recently. You ask too much, and as for this wedge...do you not think that when Tlonna finds out, she will retaliate. Losolin, she is the Magin Queen, she has said so herself, and therefore not only named herself the one many times prophesied, but set in motion those that were not already. She can destroy us all."

Tlonna found it hard to maintain her seat, but she wanted to know more before she betrayed her presence. Then Losolin spoke, and the anger in his voice made her glad she was not in Miazie's position.

"If you think Tlonna would *ever* do such a thing, you can leave. Just because there a myriad prophesies about her does not mean she is bound to follow them. Miazie, you should know better than that."

"But when she finds out we kissed, we may unleash something within in her."

"*We* did *not* kiss, Miazie. You threw yourself upon me like one of those whores at Tamarisks'."

Fury erupted inside Tlonna and she shot to her feet, ripping open then the tent flaps in the process. Her magic seethed within her, vying for an outlet and finding none. Losolin and Miazie stared at her from their positions on the ground, fear and alarm etched in their every angle.

"Tlonna!" Losolin said belatedly, swallowing.

"What is going on?" she said coldly, folding her arms and digging her nails into her own flesh.

"Listen Tlonna, Losolin did nothing wrong, it was me. I-I got sick and tried to seduce him. Please don't be mad at me Tlonna, please. I was sick. Losolin tried to get away but he couldn't oh, Tl-."

"He could have easily gotten away if he wanted to. He can hold me down, you would be nothing more than a twig," Tlonna growled.

She cornered them until they were forced to stand or be trod on. "Did you want to Losolin? Did you want her to touch you?"

Losolin's dark blue eyes widened and did not blink when he answered. "N-no! Tlonna, of course not! She is *human*, and she is not you! I would rather die than be touched by another being that way. I left her out in the rain until she started yelling my name and bawling like a child. I would have left her it is just that...I could not," he finished lamely.

Tlonna could smell his scent. A hint of autumn with that musky underlay that filled her nostrils and almost made her want to embrace him, but it was the scent of fear that hurt her. She clenched her jaw, keeping a tight rein on her emotions. "Get out. Now," she whispered to them both.

"Tlonna..." Losolin pleaded.

"No! Get out of my sight. Do not come back tonight," she said, louder.

Miazie fled, but Losolin did not move.

"I. Said. Get. Out!" Tlonna shouted, shoving him.

Losolin took a step back, but did not fall. His face was furious. "No."

"What?" Tlonna hissed.

"No. I did nothing wrong. I will not leave until you give me a good reason to," he snapped, folding his arms.

"Good reason? How about...I will rip your cock off and make you eat it?"

Losolin's eyes widened further and paled. "Tlonna, nothing happened. She was ill, fell off her horse, I grabbed her, she kissed me, I dropped her. She started screaming my name, once I had the tent up and you dried off, I brought her in here and threw a cloak over her. That is all."

"Then why are you afraid?" Tlonna growled, shaking.

"Well usually when someone threatens to rip my jollies off, I get a little worried!"

Tlonna snorted. "That is not why. I can smell it on you. It is like a taint, Losolin, your fear of me."

Losolin sneered. "If you think I fear you, you are sadly mistaken. The only thing I fear is hurting you! I fear losing you! I fear angering you because it means you are not happy!"

Tlonna had to clamp her teeth shut to stop her retort. His words shocked her. Losolin's anger was rising, the level of temperature in the tent getting warmer. Where Tlonna stood, the freezing cold from her fury was ebbing.

"You could have told me. You do not have to fear what I am, Losolin. And do not deny it, I can sense it," she whispered.

She could hear Losolin's heavy breathing behind her. Tlonna turned. There were tears swimming in his eyes. When he blinked, they rushed onto his cheeks.

"How could I fear the one I love most in this world?" he asked roughly, shoulders slumping.

Tlonna's face crumpled. She began to cry.

Losolin walked toward her, and stepped by her, and out of the tent.

Alone, Tlonna fell to her knees and wept.

Losolin returned to the tent hours later, soaking wet and looking marginally happier. Tlonna looked up from where she was sitting, miserable in her solitude.

"Is it raining?" she asked quietly.

Losolin shook his head. "There is a pond about a mile west of us."

They stared at each other for an awkward minute until Losolin finally sighed.

"Look, why do we not put this behind us and move on? Neither of us was right in the way we acted. I am willing to get over this if you are," he said.

"It is hard," Tlonna said, turning her gaze to the ground. "I am sorry."

"I know, love, I know. You have too much to worry about to add another thing to the list. I love you, and no one else, and I never wish to be with anyone other than you. Never doubt my faithfulness, because there will never be cause for you to."

Tlonna nodded, still unable to look at him. Losolin sat before her and lifted her chin up with his fingers. Drawing her close, he kissed her and she could taste the water on him. Wrapping her fingers in his sodden hair, Tlonna drew him down with her, pushed his tunic over his head, and tossed it onto the corner where it lay in a soaking heap. The night passed thusly as they forgave each other not in words, but in the feel of flesh, the meeting of tongues, and the leaping of blood.

Morning came swiftly, with no rest. Tlonna lay wrapped around Losolin, drawing warmth from his body, her head pillowed on his chest. A few minutes of silence passed before Tlonna spoke.

"Will you marry me?"

Losolin went ramrod straight and then slowly relaxed.

Searching for the right words, he finally came up with, "Now?"

"No, not right now, but when this is over. When we are home and the world is safe to live in again? Will you be my husband and prince?"

Losolin, his heart beating far too fast, sighed. "My love, I would give anything and everything in this world and the next to be your husband, but it would not be allowed. Remember our last attempt? A person *died*! I cannot have that happen again. I will not."

"Then you will never marry me? All this means nothing?" Tlonna's voice went slightly shrill.

Feeling trapped, Losolin rubbed his temples. "Tlonna, my heart, do not think I do not love you. Do not think I believe this an innocent little fling. Know that I want to spend the rest of my life with you, but the cost of life is a high price to pay. I would not want something regrettable to happen on the happiest day of my life."

Her eyes narrowed slightly and she sat up to lean over him. "Are you afraid?"

Losolin opened his mouth to protest, and closed it again. He could not think of anything else to say.

While Losolin took down the tent a while later, Tlonna strode over to Miazie's and stood watching the human until she noticed her presence.

"Tlonna! Morning!" Miazie said too heartily, terror written on her face.

The elf stared at the human blandly. "Morning."

Miazie took a few shallow breaths and a step back.

Tlonna flicked her hand at her, "Come here. Now, can you tell me where we are? How far away from Kajgenia are we?"

Miazie picked a map up from a tree stump to her right and unrolled it, approaching her friend cautiously.

"We are here in the Trohasa Forest, right on the southwestern border. We have not even passed the border yet. If we ride hard for about...oh three more days, we will pass it. This given if we aren't attacked by Midian's troops again."

Tlonna thanked her and returned to help Losolin tie the tent to Takîreaes's rump. "We really need to find a way to either put everything in one bag or basket or put the tent somewhere else. Neñyos has your saddlebags and the food basket, Takîreaes has my saddlebags, the tent, and supplies. Maybe Miazie can make something. I will go ask her," Tlonna said and walked off again.

The Belau agreed to make a set of saddlebags to accommodate the elf's needs. Within the hour, the army was ready to march.

The army moved onto the grassland on the border of the Trohasa Forest. Miazie and Rebecca, a woman from Anutch, rode side by side sewing bags. Each night when most of the moons were at their peak, Tlonna called a halt and they set up camp. And she, Losolin, and Aladorn resumed working with Tyre and the others. As promised, during twilight on the third day scouts came back and reported seeing posts that marked the borderline. As midnight approached, the halt was called and they set up camp. As Tlonna and Losolin were tethering the horses, Miazie and Rebecca walked up to their tent.

"Tlonna, we have the carrier bags for you. It took us a little longer because we were riding."

"Thank you. How do I tie them on?" Tlonna took them and handed one to Losolin. The male looked at it and picked at the strings that closed the bags. Miazie led Tlonna over to her black horse and began taking the baskets and bags off.

They were instructed in the use of the new saddle bags. Tlonna looked over at Losolin and saw Rebecca folding his clothes into a bag while he stood passively to the side, hands in his pockets. She walked to her tent and suddenly felt how heavy the swords were on her and took them off. Sighing, she stretched the fur cloaks out on the ground and lay on her own. Losolin entered and smiled faintly.

"We now have room for more food if we get any," he said absently.

The tent flap moved and they heard scratching. "Yes?" Tlonna looked at the man who entered.

"My Lady and Lord. Please excuse me for this intrusion but I have a message for you," he handed her a rolled parchment sealed with a badger's head in silver wax.

"Thank you..." Tlonna looked at the soldier.

"Oh, uh Keith. My lady," he bowed and exited the tent.

Tlonna looked at Losolin and broke the seal, one of dark blue wax with the head, and one forward paw, of a badger. Wispy ciphers were written across the page, elegant and seamless.

"We need Miazie for this, it is in Parlêthian," Tlonna said.

The elves stepped out of the tent and backed against it as a creature bounded toward them. It resembled a dog with scales instead of fur and no ears.

"What the bleeding blazes is that?" Losolin whispered in Tlonna's ear.

"It must be a messenger animal of some sort...it must have brought this," she waved the letter.

"Go away," Losolin said to it. The animal whined and then set off at run further into the camp.

"Miazie, we need your help again," Tlonna called when they neared her tent. The Belau stepped out of her tent and looked through the dark at the pair.

"What do you need?" she yawned and stretched her arms.

"We got a message but we cannot read it. It is in Parlêthian," Tlonna said and walked in after her friend. Miazie lit a candle and took the letter.

After smoothing it out on her lap, she read it through to herself. After a brief pause, she began, "It says:

'Dear Tlonna and Losolin,

My friends, how long it has been since I have seen your faces? Though such a time is usually a flicker in our lifespan, this seems to drag on as nothing has before. Our home is utterly destroyed, every vestige of life obliterated. The grounds have all died and the city is nothing but dust and ash and blood. Few dare to hope anymore. Suneelo and I have fled the underground in an attempt to follow in your steps, though the trail has long gone cold. We deeply wish to hear from you both. Please send word back with Allien. We do not know how much longer we have before Midian finds our hideout but we will be all right for a while. Your father desperately needs those pendants too, and that army. We all need the army. We are dying, Tlonna, all of us.

I sincerely wish to see you again, alive and well as my heart tells me you are. Suneelo wishes to see his brother again and I wish to see my closest friends. Your people need you, Tlonna. Come back before it is too late.

Yayènia'"

Miazie looked up and said, "Apparently Losolin, you have a brother named Suneelo who is married to Tlonna's friend Yayènia. You two have a letter to write, and who is this Allien?"

"That must be the creature, it is kind of like a dog with no fur or hair but scales. I hope he is still close," Tlonna said quietly and ran out of the tent.

"A Teelot? Really? To call back a Teelot, you have to use a special whistle. I'll do it," Miazie stepped out after her and whistled. It started out low and rose to a pitch so high that even the elves could not hear it. Not long after, Allien bounded into view and sat before the three standing there.

"All right, Tlonna, do you have a wax bar and your seal? I think I saw it when I was packing your jewelry. Go get it."

Tlonna ran to her horse and dug through the bag until she found a stick of pale blue wax and a silver bar with an eight-point star and sun on it. Running to Miazie's tent she handed them to the Belau and watched her prepare to write the letter.

"Miazie, how did the Teelot find us?" Tlonna asked after a moment.

Miazie shrugged. "They are Maginic creatures. They are shown a representation, a piece of clothing or a picture, of the person they are to deliver a message to, and then roam around until they find them. Not particularly the most efficient way to send word, but if one does not know where the recipient is, they are perfect. Now let me write this letter."

When she finished, she read it out loud.

"'Dear Yayènia and Suneelo,

It grieves me to tell you that Tlonna and Losolin were taken and their memories washed away. They do not know who you are. They do not even know the language of the elves. They were in an unconscious state for nearly eight years. I who am writing this letter am a Belau by the name of Miazie Paron. They do not know of any pendants and only have an army of three hundred. We are on our way right now to Kajgenia to ask for more men. We know of Midian's treachery and have been personally affected by it. We are coming to Blackhaven as soon as we can but we must have a very large army before we can even enter the land. Tlonna and Losolin are both Magins, Losolin is now a half-Magin. Tlonna's power has erupted, but as of yet she cannot contain it. Please be careful, we are moving as fast as we can. Tell your people to hold on. Do not put yourself at risk.

Miazie, Tlonna, and Losolin.'"

Miazie melted the wax onto the rolled parchment and stamped it with star and sun. She gave it to the Teelot and told it to go home.

When the animal had disappeared, she turned to the elves and said, "He will not let any but the true recipients read that letter. If unfriendly hands attempt to do so, he will eat it."

Losolin, who had been sitting quite still on Miazie's cot dropped his head into his hands with deep breath.

"What's wrong?" Miazie asked.

"I have a brother," he mumbled, shaking his head.

Tlonna knelt before him and stroked his hair. "One more thing to look forward to, yes?"

Losolin shrugged, closing his eyes. "If we ever get there, yes. If they survive. Tlonna, they said they are coming after us. What if Midian catches them? He would kill them on sight."

"Perhaps not," Miazie said quietly. When the elves looked at her, she smiled. "Yayènia is an old name, means 'deserving of love', and only one elf in recent history, with influence in both politics and war, has ever been named that. The High Commander Yayènia er'Tiena of the Blackhaven Militia. She is considered the best warrior ever born. Does the name not sound familiar at all?"

Tlonna frowned in concentration. "There is something...a face that is in many of my memories, but always hazy. It seems more focused now, more defined. A female, certainly, and she gives off the feeling of being lethal."

Miazie nodded. "That would probably be Yayènia. Do you remember me telling you of her?"

Tlonna nodded, "You said she went mad when her lover came back married, so she married a count...Suneelo."

Losolin's head snapped up. "My brother is Count of Blackhaven? And married to a crazy warrior?"

Miazie nodded. "Bravest elf in the world, if the stories are true. Now that we know they are close friends to the both of you...I doubt many of them. Losolin, if you are brother to the Count of Blackhaven, you are not a peasant. You are nobility."

Losolin shook his head. "I do not think so. We will find out, I suppose."

Later, Tlonna lay on her back staring at the top of her tent. The sky was beginning to turn grayish blue through the hide. She sighed wearily and shook Losolin who shivered in his leather riding clothes that he had worn to bed. Her clothing was fur lined and was barely just enough to keep her warm. Losolin rolled over and looked at her, his eyes still hazy from sleep.

"Come on, it is time to go." Tlonna said and pushed herself up.

Walking outside to wake up the camp, she shivered and rubbed her arms. Looking into the sky, she saw white flurries of snow falling silently to the ground. The bare earth had acquired a thin layer of white that crusted it like a too thin blanket. Walking along the rows of tents Tlonna scratched on the tent flaps. Soon after she heard the awarding sounds of life within the golden tents. Flinging back the tent flap of her own, she pulled her cloaks around her shoulders and pinned them together. Losolin stood huddled in his own cloaks as he pulled out the pole at the back of the tent.

"Winter is upon us, my love, we must get to Kajgenia soon, or we will not make it. I hope that the Teelot is All right," the breath before Tlonna frosted as she spoke.

Losolin guided her out of the tent before it collapsed. Taking the wooden props to Takîreaes he laid them by the horse. Tlonna rolled the tent, placed it into the bag, and closed it, securing the poles so they stuck up like a standard.

Reaching Miazie, Tlonna waited until her friend noticed her. "Miazie, how long until we reach a city?"

"Well..." the Belau scratched her back and screwed up her face, "about two and a half days to the kingdom itself, but only about..." she reached her arm up to the sky, with her hand open and standing up. Tracing the sky from the pale sun to about half way past her shoulder and stopped it. Studying her hand, she frowned slightly and then dropped it.

"Near about seven hours to the city of Klatchet. There we can stop for a bit, but they do not like large groups of soldiers," she frowned again.

"Something wrong Miazie?" Tlonna put a hand on Miazie's shoulder and stared at the frightened look on her face.

"They don't like Belaus either. They think them evil. There have been many Belaus hung in that city."

"Well, how will they know if you are a Belau? You did not even know," the elf frowned with her friend.

"They have...people there that can feel it. They feel a vibration when a Belau is near them. They are called Feelers. If one is anywhere near me I will be hung. I must skirt the city and join you at the kingdom. Don't worry, they like Magins. I don't know why they don't like us and like you. I think it's because they live for the search of knowledge. I don't really know."

"Well, if they like Magins, then you will be safe with me and Losolin. If they come near you, I will stop them," Tlonna said it without hesitation.

"I'm not sure Tlonna, they really hate Belaus. Not once has one ever entered the city and come out again."

"You will come, Miazie. I will protect you, I promise," Tlonna smiled and patted her friend's shoulder.

As the army proceeded to the city, Miazie fretted uncontrollably and thought about sneaking away. Knowing this was impossible; she breathed into her hands and hunched her shoulders. As promised, when the sun was near where Miazie had pointed, they saw a small city rise up before them. Guards patrolled the walls and two common village people stood by the gates, flanked by a score of armored men.

"Halt! Who tramples the grounds of Klatchet, an army? What treachery is this? Who is in charge here?" the guard in front of the gates eyed them suspiciously through the slits in his metal helmet. He walked towards them with his sword in hand.

"I am Princess Tlonna Arune Ewôsdírn of Blackhaven Forest, Magin Queen, and Daughter of Dietirin and Constancias. I come here in peace, I ask for a place to rest in the city with my army," Tlonna held the Staff of Cyree forward and adjusted her three swords to where they could see them clearly. The man hesitated and stared at the staff and swords. As he started to bow, one of the villagers shouted.

"A Belau! She has a Belau with her! Get it, capture it now! It's the dark haired one!" the man leaped forward pointing.

The man who had addressed them first looked up in surprise and drew his sword. Tlonna drew the ivory blade and balanced herself on Takîreaes. She could hear metal scraping leather behind her as the men drew with her.

"Stop!" she pointed her blade at the officer. "You will let us through the gates and allow us safe passage through the city. I command this. If any one of my people is hurt, it will be on you and your men's heads. Do you hear me?"

"But, my lady, she is not a human! She's one of the accursed! We must kill her," he stared at the steady point in front of his nose.

"I am not a human either. Does this mean I should be killed too?" Tlonna pushed her hair behind her ears and watched the faces in front of her tighten. "She is my Belau and I will not let any harm befall her. Let us through," she said, her voice dangerously calm.

"I will lead you, but your army must make it on their own. This I draw the line," He narrowed his eyes threateningly. The guards on the wall were now looking down on them, some with their bows drawn.

"No, you will lead us all. This I draw the line, man," the elf arched her eyebrows and stared down at him, scraping the flat of her blade along his jaw. "Now."

"N-no m-my lady. I c-cannot do that. I am s-sorry, but it is law," he stammered.

"What is your name? And your rank," the Magin curled her lip as she spoke.

"Oel Tabern. Captain of the Guards of Klatchet, my lady," he shifted his feet but stopped stuttering.

"Oel, lead us through, or I will make an example of all the men I see in front of me," Tlonna ignored the gasps of terror from the wall.

"Yes my lady, right through here my lady. Come come. Make way you fools!" he pushed his way through the crowd in front of the gates.

The two villagers grabbed at Miazie and succeeded in pulling her down out of her saddle. Tlonna whipped around in her seat as one of them drew a knife from his belt and was trying to get it to her wrist. Weaving, she burned the knife to ashes and slammed the men onto their backs. Immediately shouts arose from the walls and the guards surrounding them, weapons bristling.

"Get us into the city, NOW!" Tlonna shouted at the captain over the din.

The gates swung open and they charged through. Moments later, men were swarming around them trying to pull them down. Miazie had clambered back into her seat and was now fending herself off from reaching hands.

"Oel!" Tlonna grabbed the man and held him up for all to see. "Leave us be or your captain will be mounted on your own walls!" The fighting stopped almost immediately. "Good, now take us to an inn."

They reluctantly formed a wall around them and marched them to a massive inn that was quite empty. Oel still hung suspended by Tlonna's hand, shaking and weeping like an infant.

An hour later, Tlonna and her army were eating in the common room and sharing the fire. The elf had bullied the guards into paying the price of staying at the inn, and then dropped Oel outside without ceremony.

The inn was well kept. The building had over one hundred rooms, though they were small. The innkeeper was a man who was tall and lanky with a short-cropped hair and a clean shaven face. The apron he wore was white but for three bands of color striping the chest. They were green, gray, and blue. The man lounged behind his desk waiting for a command, staring at Tlonna with his eyes wide open and his mouth opening and closing uselessly. The elf tried to ignore him but found herself shifting in her chair. The common room floor was hard wood, though expensive woven rugs covering most of it. Chandeliers hung from the ceiling with flickering candles casting wavering light over the diners. The tables were what seemed to be polished oak as were the chairs. Once up in her room, Tlonna looked at the four post bed, oaken wardrobe, and the red wood furniture. Losolin stared as if struck dumb at the furnishings.

"The innkeeper must be some sort of lord. I have never seen an inn like this before. What is it called? I cannot remember."

Tlonna recalled the wooden sign hanging outside the door. "I think it is called the Iron Thorn," she laid her saddlebags on a chest and started pulling out clean clothes. "I am going down to take a bath. If you want to come I will warn you Miazie is coming with me, that is if there is more than one bath."

Losolin shook his head and opened the curtains to the window. Outside snow was falling and the trees were bare and frosted. "No, I think I will stay here until you are done."

"Do not brood too deeply, my heart," Tlonna said quietly, and met Miazie out in the hall and they proceeded down to the baths.

"I wanted to thank you Tlonna, for what you did out there. That was dangerous. You could have been taken, you know."

"Miazie, it is my job to protect you, you are my friend as well. I promised I would, did I not? Even if I had not I would have done what I did. I will do it again if I must. If we are attacked in this city two hundred times, I will help you if I can. Do you not understand that? It is...a privilege to me," she smiled and opened the door to the bathing room.

White tubs covered the floor with stools standing next to them laden with towels, a bucket, soap, and a robe. A large basin stood in the center of the room filled with steaming water. The females took two buckets and began transferring water into two baths. Once they had settled into two baths that were next to each other they began talking again.

"How can it be a privilege to save me? It must be nuisance to have to save others time after time. You could overuse your magic one of these times and kill yourself and others. I don't want that on my shoulders. Losolin would kill me if you didn't. The elf loves you more than life itself you know."

"I know, but sometimes I think he loves me too much, there is no room for deterrents. He is so afraid of losing me that he does anything and everything in his power to keep me safe from harm, even if it means the doom of creation, though he is scared of marrying me. I hope one day he understands that my role in life, no matter how preordained it is, is a dangerous one. Rulers do not live forever, they are assassinated, killed in battle, usurped, and maimed, among other things," Tlonna said. "If I know anything, it is that. People in places of power die, and very seldom by nature's way."

Miazie pondered her friend's words for a moment. "We will find a way, Tlonna, to make this work. We will make it to Blackhaven and wipe out Midian and his hordes. The key is to take it one day at a time, sometimes one hour at a time," she replied finally.

"I dearly hope so," the elf murmured, and laid her head back on the rim of the tub.

Losolin stared out of the window at the bare trees. The gray sky filtered through the branches and into the room. Clouds that barred its way to the world below blurred the pale sun. Few people walked on the muddy street that ran next to the inn. Even fewer looked around, but walked by quickly with their heads down.

'Gray sky makes for gray hearts, my son...' A female voice drifted through his head.

Losolin scowled at his pale reflection in the glass. He watched an elderly couple shuffle their way across the street, arms linked. The elf's eye twitched slightly. Irritation simmered in him, deep and uncontrollable. Dark thoughts battered at his mind, though he tried to clear it of all things. He did not understand the irritation. He did not understand his brooding mood at all.

The trip to the inn had put him in a bad mood, but he was far beyond that now. Perhaps it was just weariness. Losolin started towards the bed, but found himself still staring out of the window a few moments later. He studied his reflection. Frustration and temper lined his face, arms crossed, shoulders hunched, hip cocked.

Sighing, Losolin leaned his forehead against the window, and let the dark mood take him. Within seconds the old questioned plagued him. Who and where were his parents? Were they even alive? This...Suneelo the letter had spoken of claimed to be his brother. What did that mean? Was he really nobility like Miazie suggested? Did he have any other family?

After he had gotten himself thoroughly upset, Losolin turned from the window. "Well, there is not much that I can do about them here," he muttered to himself.

Rubbing his throat absentmindedly, the elf finally lay down on the bed.

Returning to the room, Tlonna saw Losolin stretched out on the bed, fast asleep. He had one arm thrown over his face as though shading his eyes. The other was resting on his stomach, rising slightly with each breath. She smiled and dressed as quietly as she could.

Carefully, so as not wake him, Tlonna lay down next to Losolin and, resting her head against his shoulder, fell asleep.

Later, Tlonna woke with a start to find Losolin sprawled, one leg and arm tossed over her. Slowly she scooted out from under his limbs and adjusted her rumpled self. Gazing once more at her consort, Tlonna left the room and ordered dinner in the common room.

The Anutchian hunter Ryun smiled at her and motioned for her to join him. Tlonna happily obliged.

"How goes it?" Tlonna asked him when she took her seat.

He sighed. "It goes. You?"

The elf smiled. "Same. Why are you sitting alone? Where is Tyre and Aladorn? Bryce and Erich?"

Ryun shrugged. "Most of them are too busy with the recruits for me, now. I'm no true fighter, Tlonna, though I do better now, with the training. Do you remember my friend Sarue?"

A passing soldier whipped his head around in shock hearing the man say her name casually. Tlonna grinned up at him and he moved on, shaking his head.

Tlonna nodded. "He died in one of the first goblin attacks," she said somberly. "A brave man."

"One of the bravest," Ryun replied. "He was my best friend, since we were boys and I watched him die. I cannot bear that kind of pain again. These men are all trained in warfare, trained to know death, and come from a great city. I am a simple hunter from a small kingdom. We have few ties anyhow."

"Do not let death separate you from men who fight for the same cause as you and I. There are more ties here than you see. And I know even Aladorn enjoyed your company. We are all soldiers in the fight against evil and doom. I watched you spar with the best warriors, I myself sparred with you, and you never flagged or gave up. You march under my command, and someday, my friend, I will make you an officer."

"My lady?" Ryun said, shocked.

Tlonna smiled. "Ryun, I have seen you fight. I have seen you bear great pain. I have seen you lead the men of Anutch to victory. And I have seen the way Miazie and Tyre, who is already a captain, include you in their decisions. I would be a fool not to put you in charge of something."

Ryun gave her a small grin. "Do you really think so?"

"Aye, I do," Tlonna replied. "Now go, get acquainted with your fellow soldiers."

The man got to his feet and walked to a table full of laughing men tossing dice. Ryun stood quietly behind one of them until they noticed him. Soon, he too was laughing and throwing the dice to the amicable dismay of the soldiers.

Tlonna was so engrossed in watching the men that she did not notice the young woman standing timidly off to the side of her table. When the elf noticed her, the human flushed crimson and curtseyed so low her hair brushed the floor.

"Queen Magin, I humbly ask for an audience," she said quietly.

Tlonna scowled, which made the woman turn sheet white. "Why would you ask me that?" Tlonna said. "I am no better than you, girl, and you can talk to me without my permission."

"Oh!" she wheezed, color flooding back into her face.

"Sit, before you lose your head, and tell me what you will," Tlonna said, gesturing to the seat Ryun had vacated. "Well, go on then."

"I...I wanted t-to ask you, my lady, how you became free."

"Free?" Tlonna asked, bewildered. "I was born free. All people are born free, it is their decisions that take that freedom away."

The young woman shook her head. "Pardon my words, Lady, but no. The infants of slaves are born slaves. Women are born slaves. My mother told me that. She says that we were put on land to serve men. She told me stories about you when I was a child; I have always been fascinated by your life. I know that you are not very old, for an elf, but you are still my hero," the girl took a deep breath and looked down again.

Disgust fought a battle to show on Tlonna's face, but she defeated it to replace it with careful blankness. "No one is born a slave. True, the children of slaves live a slave's life, but it is their choice to stay slaves. I have led a revolt, and people who were once slaves now live free, as they were born to do. And *females* are no less free than males. I do not know who fed your mother such lies, but she is deceived. The greatest thing we are given is life, and the least we can do with it is live. The best thing is to live life. Does that make sense?"

The human nodded slightly. "It does...But, Princess-"

"Tlonna, please."

"Oh...Shireen, my la-Tlonna. I do not mean to argue-"

Tlonna grinned crookedly. "Yes you do."

Shireen's eyes bugged a little. "I..."

"It is a good thing, Shireen. It shows that you are not as meek and spineless as your mother seems to think you need to be. Everyone has a right to their own life, and that includes the right to speak the words of their heart. Now...continue."

Shireen sat a bit higher in the seat. "How is it that no other woman has ever told me this before? I have asked many times, but they all say that we women were meant to be the man's tool. There when he needs us, in our place when he doesn't."

All humor drained out of Tlonna. "Is this Kajgenian law?"

"No, my lady Tlonna, it's just proper. No one has ever done anything different here in Klatchet. You're the first person, ever, to disregard our ways, talking down to the guards like you did, and bringing that Belau woman into the city. I was there, and I saw what you did. The way those men follow you without question, and that...man elf, the handsome one. He fought like a demon to stay by your side. I have never seen such devotion given to a woman. It gave me hope," Shireen said quickly, but quietly, looking at her hands all the while.

"Losolin is my consort, Shireen, and we love each other very much. We fight equally to be able to have our love. You see, people do not want us to live our lives the way we are, so they try to tear us apart. They try to hurt us through torture, mental and emotional trauma, even murder. What we fight for, what these men follow me for, is freedom. And love, and all that is good in this world. You see," Tlonna leaned forward, "there are people in this world that believe whole heartedly that what you are telling me is the honest to the gods' truth. But they are wrong.

"I have seen people in the worst of conditions, the worst of places, and the worst of times, who respected each other the same. Male and female, honoring one another as equals, because they are. Shireen, never let anyone tell you that you are less of a person because of your gender, or your race. Only you can make that distinction."

Shireen's eyes were massive. "My lady, I never thought of such things. You have given me much to think about. I must speak about this to my husband, and see what he thinks."

"You are married?" Tlonna asked sharply.

"Yes, for two years."

Tlonna could not help the disgust showing on her face this time. "How old are you?"

"Seventeen, my lady."

"Seventeen! What in the bleeding blazes are you doing married? You were married at fifteen? Why?" Tlonna said angrily.

"My mother sold me, as is customary. Please, my lady, do not get upset," Shireen said quickly.

The elf went still. "You were sold? By your *mother*? Are you happy?"

"That is not a requirement, Lady Tlonna. Happiness does not bring wealth."

"Answer the question," Tlonna snapped.

The young woman, frightened again, looked down at her lap. "No," she said finally.

"Does he hurt you?"

"When we are in bed, sometimes he does things that hurt, yes, but he is kinder than some of the others I have heard about. And he keeps me in good health," Shireen confided in a horrified whisper.

"Do you wish to be free of him?" Tlonna asked gently.

Now trembling, Shireen nodded once.

"Come," Tlonna said, and stood.

They left the inn and Shireen led the way through the dark streets. Tlonna wore her hood up to hide her face, though she still stood head and shoulders above most of the people that they passed. Within minutes, the two females were hurrying up a tree lined lane leading to a small manor house.

When they reached the front steps, Tlonna grabbed Shireen by the elbow.

"If something happens, I want you to run back to the inn and ask for either Miazie or Losolin. Tell them...tell them Arune sent you for safe keeping. Understand?"

Shireen nodded, though her face was milk white. "Do you think something will happen?"

Tlonna shrugged. "Anything is possible."

They strode into the house and Shireen led the way to an upstairs room. Knocking, they waited until a man's voice granted entrance.

"Ah, wife you are home ear-" he stopped speaking when Tlonna entered the room, a study.

The man was young, but fat and hairy. A wiry beard shook as he snapped his sagging mouth shut. "Wife, what have you brought me?"

Shireen, still trembling, turned to face her husband full on. "My honored husband, I present to you the Princess Tlonna of Blackhaven, Magin Queen."

He grinned. "Lord Benjamin Hurdler, Lady. A pleasure to meet you face to face," he said, wriggling his way out of the chair.

Tlonna pushed her hood down and glowered at the man, who stood at the same height as her chest. Benjamin was staring at the slight bit of cleavage that showed through the laces on her tunic. Tlonna bent down so that she was eye to eye with the human.

"I am afraid I cannot return the pleasure, Lord Hurdler."

Benjamin grinned again, "Oh, you have lady, you have."

He reached out and wrapped his fingers around one breast, squeezing slightly. Tlonna straightened, his hand still gripping her. When his other hand started to move, Tlonna struck him. He slammed into the wall, spitting out a broken tooth from the impact of her fist. Shireen shrieked and hid behind the chair. Tlonna, sneering, walked over to Benjamin and placed one leg on either side of his. He looked up, shocked.

"The last man to touch me without my permission lost his cock. Do you wish the same fate?"

Hurdler wheezed, but he glared up at her all the same. "You...are a woman! You are not worthy! I will have you drawn and quartered for this, slut!"

Tlonna stared down at him. "You forget two things, man, I am an elf, and I am royalty. You will never touch another woman against her will. I will make sure of it."

She reached down and picked up his hand, on which he wore a gold band to signify his marriage to Shireen. Tlonna closed her fist tight around his, and felt bones snap. When he stopped screaming, the elf yanked off the ring and crushed it as well. The elf grabbed Shireen's hand and pulled the ring off her finger.

"No longer is she bound to you," Tlonna said, and added it to the list of crumpled things.

Dropping it in the man's lap, she took Shireen and gave her time to collect her things.

By the time she was ready, Tlonna could hear Benjamin howling for his servants and guards.

"We are out of time, Shireen. Go!" Tlonna said, and shoved the woman out of the door.

They sprinted down the lane and skidded to a halt as armed guards blocked the gate. One man approached her and bowed slightly. Terror was etched upon his face as plain as if the word were written there. He took Shireen's hand and tried to pull her away from the Magin. Tlonna raised an eyebrow at him and he let go.

"Let us pass through these gates," Tlonna said quietly.

"I'm sorry my lady. I cannot do that. We have strict orders from the lord himself not to let you out," his voice stayed steady but his knees shook as well as his hands.

"All right, have it your way," Tlonna had barely finished the sentence before she was moving.

Shoving Shireen back, Tlonna launched herself at the crowd of armored men and twisted, sending her fist into the open spot of a guard's neck. He gasped for breath and then fell to the ground. Grabbing his spear, she hit another in the temple then swung around to crunch it into the throat of a third. The seven remaining guards launched themselves onto her. The spear point dug through two abdomens before it snapped under impact. The elf felt a booted foot kick her in the throat. Stars danced before her eyes for a moment before fading. She lay there as the men tried to get to her. Grasping the spear shaft tightly, Tlonna shoved the broken end through a man's eye and pushed him off her as he screamed his last. A cloak whipped in her face and she punched the man in his gut. Forcing herself to her feet, she faced the guards with a broken and bloody spear shaft. She was vaguely aware of Shireen screaming and yelling behind her. Swinging the shaft, she let it fly toward a man's head. There was a sickening crunch but Tlonna paid it no heed. A flash of steel was all her warning before a spearhead struck home.

Pain exploded in Tlonna's side as the point dug into her flesh. Screaming, she summoned her power and smashed the guards, gate and anything else that was in her path. Grabbing Shireen, she ran out into the street clutching her side. The spear dragged behind her as she ran. Pain continued to burst, causing convulsive lurches in her body.

One last time it wracked her body before everything went black.

The elf opened her eyes and blinked in the bright light.

"Tlonna? Are you awake? Healer! She is awake!" Losolin shouted from his chair by her bed.

"Losolin?" Tlonna said softly then squeezed her eyes closed when pain flashed through her.

"Ah, my lady, you are up. Here drink this," a woman handed her a flask filled with vile smelling liquid. Tlonna opened her eyes again and backed into the pillow.

"No," her voice was barely a whisper, cracked and harsh in the quiet room. "Let me be."

"Ha, never have I seen such strength after a wound like that one. Drink child," the woman lifted Tlonna's head and poured the liquid down her throat.

Coughing, the elf spat and rubbed a hand across her mouth. "What is that?" she asked incredulously. "Get it away from me," her voice became stronger.

"It is warmed goat's milk and bitterroot. Even asleep you fought it. Let me look at your wound." Without waiting for permission, the nurse pulled Tlonna's blanket down and pulled the white cloth off of her side. The loose fitting shirt she wore hindered the elf's sight of the wound but she saw enough. The cut was deep, blood and puss leaked out of it in bubbles. Tlonna frowned. Losolin did not look at her or the wound but stood at the end of the small room studying the wall.

"What happened to me? Losolin..." Tlonna reached out her hand and touched his lightly. He started.

"You went to the manor house of Benjamin Hurdler who is the lord of Klatchet. You took his wife and attacked the guards. One of them stabbed you with this," the elf lifted a bloodstained spear and showed it to her. "Shireen had to drag you to the closest house and they took you to a Healer's house and she fixed you up so that you could travel. In the morning, Miazie, Shireen, the Healer, and I brought you here to Derid, the capital of Kajgenia where the largest Healer House in the east is. The king is coming to see you today. Good thing you woke up," he put the spear down and looked at her. "You should have told me what you were going to do."

"Losolin, I am so sorry. I had not planned on leaving the inn, really. Please do not be mad at me."

The Healer straightened her back and spoke, "Well, whatever you did, you proved yourself a fighter worthy of mention. Not many can hold their own against one of the Gray Guard, much less ten. Oh yes, you'll go down in the books my dear. Now lay back while I get you dressed for a visit from the king," the woman left the room muttering.

Losolin approached Tlonna's bed in two steps and kneeled before her. "I was so scared. That spear went right through you, and one of your kidneys. The Healer said you would have died were you not an elf. Do not ever do that again. Tell me you will never do that again. I love you and I cannot stand to see you like this. You have been like this for days. Take me with you if you leave, anywhere," the Healer entered again and Losolin stood up and backed away from the bed.

"This I suppose will work. Your friend gave it to me from your saddle bags," she held up the black dress. "Come on, man, get her on her feet will you. The king will be here any minute."

Losolin pulled the blankets back again and put his arms beneath Tlonna. He lifted her gently to her feet and held her steady. Tlonna grunted with pain, but refused to lean against him. The Healer pulled off the loose shirt and pushed the dress over her head. Once the two got Tlonna's arms through the dagged sleeves and tugged it down to its full length; they moved Tlonna to a different room. The room was a visiting room, full of large upholstered chairs and small tables.

They sat her in one of the chairs and arranged her so that she could lounge carefully, but not look indulgent before the king. After a few minutes, there was a bustle in the hallway and a man entered the room. He was clad in brown trousers, a dark blue tunic, and a white cloak. On his graying head was perched a crown of finely wrought gold. Losolin and the healer stood and bowed while Tlonna tilted her head slightly. The King of Kajgenia smiled at Tlonna, and then at the two beside her.

"You are strong, Princess Tlonna of Blackhaven. Only a strong Magin and elf could survive what you have. I would have that fool exiled, but I hear you punished him well enough. I like your style. No one, *no one*, attacks a princess, a Magin princess at that. And I have word from Tyular that you received the same treatment from Athelias? I am truly ashamed of my cohorts. I feel I must apologize," the king pulled a chair up beside her own and took her hand.

"I do not ask for your apology, good king. Rather, I have a more serious request," Tlonna said.

"Ah..." the king said, raising his eyebrows. "The army?"

"I would also like to ask your name," Tlonna took her hand from the king and placed it on her lap.

"King Demetrius Plaukler, at your service, my lady"

Tlonna inclined her head to indicate respect. "Princess Tlonna Arune Ewôsdírn, at yours, good king, and this is my consort, Lord Losolin Ullor Grisholm."

"And Miazie Paron, Advisor," Miazie said loudly, entering the room.

The healer, standing quietly all the while, clucked exasperatedly. "My Lady, I know not how you know of this meeting, but it is for those who only *need* to be here. Please leave."

"She may stay, Healer," Demetrius said when Miazie's shoulders went back.

Everyone looked around at the king, who was watching Miazie with a kind of inspecting fatherly way. "But you may go. I don't see why Princess Tlonna will need your assistance during our audience."

The healer looked as shocked as Miazie, though by far more injured. When she huffed out of the room, Miazie curtseyed gracefully to the king.

"My thanks, your majesty," she said coolly, and then glided over to sit in the chair next to Tlonna's.

Demetrius nodded. "Tyular sent me word of you, Belau Miazie. He said to expect you to barge in unexpectedly to voice your opinion. He also said that your opinion is one he regards highly. My young comrade seems to respect you very much, Lady Paron."

Miazie blushed. "I would hope so, your highness."

Demetrius grinned slightly. "Now that we are here, we may start. I know you come seeking recruits," he said, turning to Tlonna. "And I am willing to do what Tyular did. But I will go one step further, as I have the means to do what he cannot. I will grant you one thousand men from my own ranks to join with the recruits. Tyular would have done the same, but he does not have the numbers I do. The soldiers will, of course, expect to be returned to my services as soon as you are done with them," he smiled a grandfatherly smile.

Tlonna heard the underlying threat beneath the words. "I will take all you offer, and do my best to make the soldiers proud to serve under me for a time, King Demetrius. I must say I had heard about your generosity and kindness, but I never expected this."

"I have found it in my good interest to throw the might of Kajgenia behind the fate of Nymyños. Besides, elves, men, and dwarves are not all that different, and we once fought side by side against other evils. How is this any different? We all love this land, and it is our duty to defend her," Demetrius said softly.

Tlonna swallowed audibly. "It is nice to know that I am not the only one who thinks that."

"It always is," the king replied, slapping Tlonna on the knee.

The elf smiled broadly. "Now, about these men, will I be choosing them or you?"

"I think that in your present position, I or your consort will have to choose. How long will you be staying here?"

"I think it would be best if I, and my companions, stayed here until the end of winter...if that does not pose a problem."

"No problem at all. In that case, when you are healthy once more, you can choose the thousand men from my army. I will give you information on all of them that I can spare. From that, you can choose. Unless you have something else you do to choose."

"I do not know. We will figure something out, I suppose." Tlonna replied.

"I would like to look at your records, King Demetrius, if I may," Miazie said quickly.

"That would be fine, my dear," he said, and turning to Tlonna, "come to the castle when you are ready."

Tlonna bowed her head as the human stood.

"It was an honor to meet the three of you. I hope that we become good friends in the times to come."

Losolin shook his hand heartily. "I cannot thank you enough for your generosity, your highness. It is a nice reprieve."

Demetrius sighed. "Well, yes. And I'm sorry about that. I do wish we could afford a dethroning of Athelias, but his son is far worse. As for my countryman, he will be punished severely for his actions. I don't condone the laws in Klatchet, but there are times it seems too insignificant to start what would become a revolt. It is my fault this happened, and I am truly sorry."

Tlonna, Miazie, and Losolin all burst into denying his statement. After being thoroughly lectured, the king left the Healing House.

Once he and Miazie had helped Tlonna back into her bed, Losolin took to wandering the sprawling building. It had only a single floor, lined with rooms on either side of the numerous halls. Robed healers bustled about carrying trays or walking with sickly humans. Losolin veered around most of them, the illness making him uncomfortable. Every now and then he would pass a young healer who would go pale and flee his presence.

Irritated, the elf stopped paying attention to where he was going. He passed open doors occupied by miserable looking people, and closed doors muffling the sounds of coughing or sobbing. When he reached the end of a corridor, Losolin was about to turn around when he heard to healers talking quietly in the very last room.

Leaning against the wall, the elf turned his head slightly so that one of his ears was pointed at the closed door.

"She was brought in late last night," a woman was saying, "from Aedrid. The young man who brought her said their farm had been attacked, along with some of the outlying homes, just outside town. Said they were men, not demons, like usual. Maybe even elves."

"Nonsense!" said a shrill voice, "Elves? What codswallop. Elves don't attack people."

"Shh!" said the other woman. "That's what he said. Says they killed her parents and ravaged her afterwards. That's why she so delirious. Lost her mind, he says. Thinks she's a little girl again. Poor thing."

"Yes, poor child," the shrill healer responded. "I still just don't believe elves would do such a thing. Have you seen the two around here? That woman elf who took out those Gray Guards, got a spear through the side, and lived? Such a nice creature when she's sleeping. Felicity says she has a bite to her when she's awake, but I suppose you can't help it when you live for such a long time. But that mate o' hers. Have you seen him?"

"Yeh, gorgeous, ain't he?"

"Gorgeous? That's an understatement! I would like to see him out of those clothes he wears, tight though they are, I just want to run my hand all over him. I almost wish he were the one injured. And those ears. I just love them. All pointy and delicate. I helped to dress the she-elf, and ain't she a beauty. Not a flaw on her, unless you count the scars. I bet he's mere perfection."

"Oh!" the cooler voiced healer giggled. "I don't think there's anything *mere* about him!"

The two women behind the door lapsed into giggles and Losolin left, feeling hot about the ears, which he now felt obligated to cover with his hair.

The next day, Losolin went back to the room where he had heard the two healers, and, making sure they were not there, opened the door. The room was dark, and musty. The smell of fear and medicine made him wrinkle his nose.

On the small bed was an even smaller lump. It was shaking. The girl was curled into a ball, the blanket over her head. Losolin sat down on the bed and watched ball stiffen, the shaking stop. Slowly, three fingers appeared at the edge of the blanket and peeled it away until a tangle of thick brown hair and dark hazel eyes peeked out from the top.

When she saw Losolin, the girl squeaked and covered herself again.

"I am not going to hurt you, please. My name is Losolin, and I may be able to help you. Can you tell me your name?" he said softly.

Quiet gasps were now emitting from the blanket.

"Please?" Losolin said again.

One eye appeared, red-rimmed and terrified.

"Y-you l-look j-just l-l-like th-them. P-plea-ease g-go aw-ay."

"I will not. I want to help you. What is your name?" Losolin persisted, still softly.

"N-no."

Sighing, Losolin scratched his nose, which was still tingling from the unpleasant smell of fear. "I know not who hurt you, or why, but believe me, if I did, I would make them pay. You see, the female I love was hurt by people who had no right to attack her. She was only trying to help another young woman like yourself. Her name is Tlonna, and the woman she rescued is Shireen. There is another young woman with us named Miazie, who is a princess from Anutch, but she left in order to save others. That is what we are doing here.

We are trying to help those who have been hurt by evil people, and prevent others from being harmed.

"You may have heard of Tlonna, she is the Princess of Blackhaven Forest, also known as Everwood, and the Magin Queen, and I love her very much. She is trying to save all of Nymyños from the type of people who hurt you," Losolin said, staring at the wall opposite him.

When he looked over at the bed, his audience was now staring at him over the edge of her blanket, both hands clutching it.

"K-Kayra," she whispered.

"What? Is that your name?"

She nodded.

Losolin smiled. "It is very nice to meet you Kayra."

She swallowed loudly. "Do you have sex with Everwood?"

Taken aback, Losolin stared at her for a moment before answering. "Well...yes."

"Do you have sex with other women too?"

Losolin frowned. "No. Why would I do that?"

Kayra's eyes filled with tears. "That's what they said. They said they lived too long for one partner, so they had to get joy from others too," her voice rose to a keen.

"The one who hurt you? He was an elf?"

Kayra nodded, still keening. Finally she sobbed out, "They all were!"

Losolin stood abruptly. "More than one? How many Kayra? From where did they come? Do you know?"

The human shook her head, still crying. "Too many! Too many! They did this to me!"

Kayra threw her blanket off and stared at Losolin. Losolin stared at her. She was naked. Her thighs were covered in wounds and bruises; her stomach was black as well. One breast was still raw with teeth and nail marks. Losolin forced his eyes away from the ghastly sight and pulled the blanket up to Kayra's chin.

"I am so sorry, Kayra. Will you let me help you?"

"What. Are. You. Doing. In. Here?" said a very angry voice from the doorway.

Spinning around, Losolin found himself looking down at a seething healer. It was Felicity, the Supreme Healer.

"I was about to see if Kayra wanted me to help her, Healer,"

Losolin replied coldly, infuriated at the way the human was glaring at him.

"And how were you going to do that? Add to those cuts and bruises? Just because your lover is down doesn't mean you can go around raping other women!" Felicity screamed.

Rage flooded into Losolin. "RAPE?" he roared. "I AM A HEALER!"

Behind him, Kayra was keening again. Felicity was glowering. Other healers were watching out of doorways, duties forgotten. Someone dropped a tray and something liquid sprayed along the wall. Looking around, Losolin spotted a young man with a bruise under his eye.

Pointing, the elf said. "What happened to your face?"

The healer touched the bruise. "A-angry patient, m-my lord."

"Come here," Losolin growled, cocking his finger.

The young man moved forward haltingly until he stood before the elf. Losolin put his hand over his cheek. Green light swelled out of his hand and into the human's cheek. when Losolin took his hand away, the bruise was gone. Everyone in the hall gasped and the man touched his face in shock.

"It doesn't hurt anymore! How did you do that?"

Losolin glared at Felicity. "I am an elf...and a healer."

Felicity paled. "I am sorry, my lord," she said, staring straight ahead at his chest.

Losolin pivoted and strolled back into Kayra's room. She was watching him, no longer crying.

"You can do that to me? You can take away the pain?"

"I can take away the physical pain, but the emotions you must deal with. It will not be as easy as that young man's, for his bruise was very mild, and there was only one. You may get a little uncomfortable, and you can tell me to stop at any time. Do I have your word on that?"

Kayra nodded, looking a little frightened.

"What do you want me to heal first?" Losolin said, kneeling by the bed.

Kayra looked over at the door where the healers were all still gathered before pulling down the blanket to expose her bosom.

"I am going to have to touch you," Losolin said, watching her face. "Is that acceptable?"

She nodded. Losolin laid his hand on her breast as gently as he could and Wove. Kayra sucked in a breath and then let it out in a whoosh when the green light flared and Losolin pulled his hand away. The skin was whole and unscarred, though still a little red.

"Was that okay? Does it hurt anymore?"

Kayra looked at Losolin with wide eyes. "No, no it doesn't. It stung a bit, but it was okay."

Losolin nodded. "What next?"

A half hour later, Losolin finished her leg and stood, muscles aching with fatigue. Kayra pulled the blanket up to her shoulders and wriggled a bit. "I don't hurt anymore. Everything feels right."

The healers outside in the hall let out a collective cheer. Losolin rolled his shoulders.

"As I said, the physical pain is healed, but what is inside your heart and your mind will be much harder. The lady Tlonna and I are always willing to listen, Kayra, and if you need anyone to talk to, we will be around."

Kayra nodded. "Lord Losolin...is there any way I can repay you? Anything?"

Losolin smiled slightly. "Nothing. It is a gift, and a gift never requires payment," he responded, and left.

Slipping into Tlonna's room, Losolin sighed as he stretched out in the only chair. The room was dark and smelled of healing, but no fear permeated his senses. No rancid stench of terror and helplessness made him want to gag. Tlonna shifted on the bed and groaned a little.

"Losolin?"

"Tlonna, did I wake you?"

Tlonna yawned. "No. Where have you been?"

The male rubbed his eyes and leaned forward to take Tlonna's outstretched hand. "I just healed a young woman named Kayra. Tlonna, she was forced to watch the murder of her parents, and then was raped by a group of elves. Our kind, my love. They destroyed her life. She was so scared of me. I could smell the fear coming from her. Her body was mangled and her youth ripped away. I think Seaduens has joined ranks with Midian." The hand in his tightened a bit before letting go.

Tlonna sighed. "From what Miazie has told me, Seaduens has never been known for its pleasantries. If you are not a high born elf, you are slave class. They have public auctions and someone who is bought becomes less than property. They can be replaced, beaten, raped, starved, or killed, without a thought. Many have tried to revolt, but it always fails. The army of Seaduens is vicious. Miazie told me that the soldiers are given power equal to lords and they have no boundaries. They can do anything they choose.

"Seaduens would be ripe for Midian. Cruelty and tyranny already have their claws deep in the fabric of society. King Stoffnias is embittered towards the other provinces, especially Blackhaven. He would, I am sure, do anything to harm us," Tlonna said.

"Do you really think someone would be foolish enough to ally themselves with Midian, though?" Losolin asked.

Tlonna shrugged slightly. "It is hard to say no when the chances of winning are on your side."

"True," Losolin grunted, and leaned back in the chair again.

"It is hard to fathom, though," Tlonna said after a moment. "You and I value life so much, as does everyone around us. I do not like to think that others would willingly give it up."

"How do you mean?"

"Stoffnias must know that at some point, even if Midian wins this war, others will rise to the occasion and defeat him, defeat evil. He must know that," Tlonna explained, sitting up against her pillows.

"Maybe not," Losolin responded. "Maybe his so blinded by his ambition and foulness that he cannot comprehend the idea of defeat."

Tlonna gazed at Losolin for a moment, pondering. "Perhaps," she breathed finally.

Another two days passed before Tlonna could move around on her own. Kayra, now a bit more comfortable, took to wandering the halls with Losolin. When the elf stopped next to Tlonna's door, he looked back at Kayra standing behind him.

"This is Tlonna's room, Kayra."

She beamed. "Can I meet her?"

"Ah...no. Not for a while more, I think."

"Why not?" Kayra asked huffily.

"Because she had a spear go through her," Losolin snapped.

"Why don't you heal her like you did me?"

"Because I cannot. It hurts us both too much. Something

about our magic conflicting because it came from the same source," Losolin explained wearily, his hand on the doorknob.

"Losolin?" Tlonna asked from behind the door. "Who are you talking to?"

"Uh...Kayra."

"Well let her in!" Tlonna laughed.

Rolling his eyes, Losolin opened the door and stepped aside as Kayra rushed by him. The human went into a deep curtsy, her hair brushing the floor.

"My Lady, an honor it is to meet you face to face after hearing all the stories. Truly am I graced to be in your presence."

Losolin snorted and turned away at the two glares he got. He pivoted on his foot and left the room.

"An honor for me, it is as well, Kayra. Losolin has told me all about you."

"Really?" Kayra asked, shocked. After a moment she said, "My lady...why don't you let Lord Losolin heal you? He gave me some half hearted excuse about conflicting magics, but it just seems absurd."

Tlonna sighed and situated herself more comfortably on the edge of the bed. "Absurd is what it is. What he told you is the truth. I made Losolin a Magin. For some reason his powers developed a healing base whereas mine are limited to more devastating and forceful areas. For him to use his powers on me...it causes us both extreme pain because it is like me trying to heal myself," the elf sighed when Kayra frowned. "Losolin's magic is the child of *my* magic. It is the same power, just in different bodies so it has different capacities. When Losolin uses his magic on me, my body recognizes it as my power and turns it back into my skill...destruction. I can use my power on him because his body did not originally create magic."

The girl made an understanding face. "Ooh...I get it. It must drive him crazy not to be able to help you. All he's been able to do is follow Healer Felicity around and avoid the advances of the other healers."

Tlonna sighed again and patted her blankets absently. "Losolin will always be chased by women, though he does not see it. It hurts him when he cannot help someone in need. He has too kind a heart, if you ask me."

Kayra twisted her face around. "Not with me. He was so nice

when he healed me, but now he's just cranky."

Tlonna could not stop the chuckling snort that escaped her. "I have heard Losolin described in many different ways, but cranky is a first. He is very agitated these days, and bored. You would think being in a Healing House would give him plenty to do, but he does not want to take the work from the healers. I suppose cranky would fit him."

"Fit him it does," Miazie said as she walked into the room, glaring behind her. Kayra shot to her feet and curtseyed again. Miazie frowned at her. "Who are you?"

"Kayra, my lady. Please take my seat."

Miazie's frown turned into a scowl. "No, keep it," she said, sitting next to Tlonna on the bed. "Your beau is like to drive me insane. He keeps pestering me about training. I'll tell you, Tlonna, if I have to sit through another hour with him blowing magic at me, I will hit him."

"Be my guest, Miazie. It would give him an excuse to hit you back, therefore expelling some of his pent up energy," Tlonna said blandly.

Miazie snorted.

The three females burst into laughter but stopped short when the door shuddered and Losolin cursed. Baffled, Tlonna stood and opened the door. Losolin stumbled backward into the room, followed by two healers.

Oblivious to their audience, the two young women continued to grasp at Losolin's clothes.

"Oh please my lord, you do not wear the ring on your hand and neither does she. That means you aren't pledged to her. We have heard of the legendary stamina of elves, and you would never be bored with two of us."

"Yes, my lord, Tyra speaks true. And we are both Healers so you would never take sick."

"Elves do not get sick! Get off!" the male backed further into the room and wrapped his hand around Tyra's wrist. Pushing the human away, Losolin tried to twist away from the other healer, Uana.

"What is the meaning of this?" Tlonna asked, amusedly.

"M-m-my lady. I-I uh..." Tyra snatched her free hand away from Losolin.

Uana turned, but did not let go.

"Let him go."

Uana released her grip on Losolin's belt and sleeve. He scrambled away from them and over to Tlonna.

"We are betrothed, ladies, and our rings were just finished. I would ask you not to touch him again."

"Yes my lady," the two healers said in unison and then fled the room.

When Kayra shut the door behind them, Losolin turned to stare at Tlonna. "We ordered rings?"

"Not exactly, but we have them now, nonetheless. Here," she said and pulled a silver ring from the pouch she was carrying and slipped it over Losolin's finger.

"Tlonna, were did you-?"

"Look at it closely, and I think you will know, my love," Tlonna said, and sat back down on the bed.

Losolin studied the ring on his finger. It looked as though a twig had been turned into solid silver.

"You turned twigs into silver, did you not? Tlonna, you should not have done that. It must have drained you."

"Yes, but as my strength returns, it gets easier. Do you not like it?"

Losolin glanced up at her, ignoring the other two females gazing at him. "I will wear it always. Even when we return home will I wear it."

Tlonna studied him for a long moment. "That is good to know."

Later in the evening, Miazie sat in her room reading the *Chronicles of Astinus*. She turned the page and read the passage dated a few months before his death. Fear seized her gut as she re-read the text.

A dark dream took me last night as I lay prone to the eyes of the future. I saw in shadow a man of great evil and in blazing light an elf of unbelievable virtue. They stood apart while the lives of thousands swarmed between them screaming and crying. When the last life fled the abyss between the two, they came together with terrible ferocity. When they clashed there was no light and no darkness, just a presence that consumed all. When they separated, neither lived. A great power swarmed the abyss and life felt renewed, though sadness was great, as was pain. I clung to this dream as long as possible, but as it faded, I saw with lucidity two graves. One was barren and dry, the other flourishing. I woke crying knowing I had just seen the end of an age, and at that end, they lay heavy with importance, those graves of good and evil.

Miazie dropped the book heavily onto her lap and stared at it. With utter certainty, she knew the two subjects of the prophecy were Midian and Tlonna. Shaking herself, Miazie stood from her bed where she had been sitting and walked over to the window.

Thoughts pounded her, mysteries she could not solve. The pendants the elves Yayènia and Suneelo had mentioned in their letter were one of those mysteries. Miazie leaned against the sill of the window. Legend said that there were two pendants forged by Magin Gwemheoad and passed down to Jair and his line to what was now the house of Ewôsdírn. One took life, the other gave it.

The mystery, though, was where they were. Who had taken them and why? Midian seemed a good candidate, but what would he do with something that gave life? Midian's sole purpose consisted of murder and torture.

Groaning to herself, Miazie turned back to her bed. Stacks of books were leaning perilously against the footboard. Sitting back down, the Belau grabbed one at random and flicked it open.

A warrior must prepare himself to die at all times. Death is a constant, no one escapes, and when one is hired to do such deeds, he too must accept that his fate is as doomed as his enemies.

Frowning, Miazie looked at the cover of the book. *The Zaynzura and their Divine Duty.* Groaning again, Miazie dropped the book on the floor to be taken back to the library.

"I have spent seven years exploring Zeynuwn and its peculiarities, I need no book to tell me about them," she complained to herself.

It took her another two hours to find a book that mentioned the first Magins and their descendants. *The Darkness of Power* was a skeptic's guidebook to Maginic powers. Miazie, disgusted, forced herself to find the passages about the latest descendants.

As for the Magin King Dietirin, he married an elf of no particular attractions save her status. Constancias, a highly disliked elf-maiden, was soon given the power of a half-Magin. Her husband said he did it for her protection, clearly not thinking of his people as he did so. In the years to follow, the citizens of Blackhaven were forced to acknowledge what Constancias labeled her natural gift, given her by the gods themselves. She used this power to terrify her subjects into submission, beating them until they admitted that she was greatest in all the land.

Their terror and persecution doubled when Constancias unearthed the two great pendants of her husband's ancestor, Magin Jair himself. It is said when Magin Jair burned the tower and murdered his cohorts, he stole the pendants from Roluf Gwemheoad and called them his own. Such is the tainted stain of power. These pendants, the epitome of evil and unnaturalness, became the doom of House Ewôsdírn, for it is said that when the daughter of the king and queen is born, her life will be connected to these pendants as surely as though they were her own beating heart.

As the foretold daughter has not yet been born, we cannot call this prophecy false or true. But we can certainly call it dangerous and unreliable.

"Her life is connected to them?" Miazie whispered, staring at the book without seeing it. "We don't even know what they look like!"

Growling in frustration, Miazie threw the book at the wall. A few moments later, Tlonna and Losolin rushed into the room.

"Miazie! Are you all right?" Losolin asked, glancing at the book splayed on the floor.

"No! There is so much we have to do, and we don't know where to even start!" Miazie shouted, burying her head in her hands.

"Miazie, shh...we will find a way," Tlonna said soothingly, rubbing her friend on the back.

"Oh? And what of these pendants you're supposed to find? Do you know what they look like? Or where they might be? Who has them?"

"Midian, I would guess," Tlonna shrugged.

"Every passage I have read about them says your fate is tied to theirs. We have to find them, Tlonna. I don't know why, I have tried to figure it out, but I can't. I've tried so much, but it just won't come to me."

"That is okay, Miazie, you have given us so much already. I would never expect you to know everything," Tlonna said, chuckling. "Besides, everything is tied to my fate, it seems. One more thing does not change anything."

Miazie nodded and sighed. "I know, sometimes it just seems

completely hopeless."

Tlonna grunted. "Try getting a spear through the side and then talk to me about hopeless."

"I'll pass," Miazie laughed.

"Come," Tlonna held out her hand. "We are going to walk about the city, try to get a feel for it."

"Are you well enough?" Miazie asked, noting Losolin's irritated look.

"Healer Felicity says I should be fine, so yes," Tlonna replied, ignoring Losolin.

"Then let's go," Miazie said, standing.

"Shireen is coming with us, and Kayra," Losolin said, opening the door.

"Okay," Miazie responded, sharing a look with Tlonna.

A few minutes later, the five left the Healer House and stepped into the city. A few people wandered about, as always. The air before them misted as they breathed.

"What in the?" Kayra said, staring at Tlonna and Losolin.

"What?" the elves asked in unison.

"You're steaming!"

"Well thank you...?" Tlonna said, unsure what the human was talking about.

"No, you are steaming. Look!" the human pointed at Losolin's shoulder where a fine steam was rising.

"Their bodies are adapting to the cold, Kayra," Miazie explained, waving her hand in the steam above Tlonna's shoulder.

"So they steam?" Kayra asked, looking skeptical.

"Yes, and in the heat their skin is cool to the touch. They will stop in a bit, but their bodies will remain warmer than ours. Not comfortably warm exactly, just warmer."

Tlonna and Losolin looked at each other with raised eyebrows. Kayra and Shireen stared at them in awe. Miazie rolled her eyes.

"Read a book, people," she said exasperatedly.

The city was a decent place, clean and well maintained through the ministrations of King Demetrius. The castle itself sat on a hillside overlooking the city proper. It was a smaller castle, but made up for it with a myriad of towers, walls, and courtyards. Over it all snapped the forest green and teal pennants of House Plaukler. Tlonna's group passed through the streets without any major ruckus. Many of the women stared at Losolin as if they had never seen a male before. The elf bore it all with a new found stoic resolve that Tlonna very much appreciated. She herself noticed that whenever she looked around, men were whispering to each other, looking in her direction, and smiling.

Merchants hailed them, parading rolls of cloth or bits of jewelry before them. Food sellers wafted the scents of their goods towards them, shouting. Lamp lighters wobbled around on stilts, illuminating the darkening streets. Losolin bought them all wreathes of flowers for their hair, bringing beaming smiles from Shireen and Kayra, and smirking grins from Tlonna and Miazie.

It was nearing midnight when they started back toward the Healer House. They were still a good five blocks from their destination when Miazie doubled over, her knees hitting the cobblestone street.

"Miazie!" Tlonna cried, following her friend to the ground.

Losolin knelt beside her, one hand on Miazie's back. "Miazie?"

The Belau gagged, convulsing violently. She drew in a choking breath. "It's here, I can see it," she gasped. "The pendant, death," she drew another shallow breath.

"Miazie?" Tlonna asked, worried.

Miazie's lips peeled back in a snarl. "I can see it, Tlonna, the blackness," she wheezed.

"Where?"

"A manor, red and yellow flag. Wellenton Manor," she said, breathing rapidly.

"Can you stand?" Losolin asked.

Miazie shook her head, and collapsed onto her side, shuddering. Tlonna, ignoring her own pain, grabbed her shoulders in panic. "Miazie!"

Losolin's hands swelled with power and he unleashed a Weave into the human's body. Immediately, Miazie stopped seizing and lay limp and panting in Tlonna's lap.

After a few more deep breaths, Miazie nodded. "I cannot see it anymore. It passed. Dear gods," she said, putting a hand to her forehead.

Losolin helped Tlonna up, Shireen and Kayra helped Miazie up.

"What was that?" Shireen asked, her voice high with fright.

Tlonna discreetly pressed a hand to her throbbing wound, earning a warning look from Losolin. "She is a Belau, and that means she can scry things, information. Scrying is an elfish trait, and the human body is not meant to handle the power of it. It is the price a Belau pays for her knowledge."

Miazie gasped and stared at Tlonna with wide eyes. "How do you know that?"

Tlonna frowned slightly. "I just do," she replied flatly.

The Belau nodded her acceptance and continued to lean on Kayra.

"Do any of you know where Wellenton Manor is?" Tlonna asked, looking around.

Miazie, still breathing deeply, shook her head. Shireen nodded. "It is Lord Deric's house, he lives there alone, his wife and daughter were killed some years ago. It is about a mile away, back where we came from."

"Can you walk, Miazie?" Tlonna asked.

The Belau nodded, but moved over to lean on Losolin's arm.

The five turned around and followed Shireen back up the street, Miazie leaning heavily on Losolin. They arrived at a wrought iron gate a while later. Tlonna leaned forward and pushed against the metal. The gate creaked inward, frost falling to the ground as it shook away from the iron.

They squeezed through the small opening and then shut it behind them. Tlonna and Losolin took a step forward and then stopped. Both of them went pale.

"Evil is thick here," Losolin said, clutching at his chest.

Tlonna nodded, grimacing.

The three humans with them looked at each other concernedly, Miazie still short of breath and shaken, stepped away from the sudden cold around Losolin. Steeling herself, Tlonna started forward again, fingers linked with Losolin's. They progressed forward through the garden-lined walkway until they reached the door. Nothing moved in the darkness.

Kayra started to shake, but stopped when Losolin put his free hand on her shoulder. Tlonna put her hand on the doorknob and twisted. Her muscles bunched against her skin as she twisted. Finally, with a crack, the wood around the knob splintered and the door swung inward.

They entered the manor. Silence greeted them. Shireen shut the door as best she could and then hurried to catch up with the others. When they reached the next room, a yawning servant spun around to stare at them. His mouth stayed open, eyes bugging out. Losolin leapt forward and wrapped his hand around the man's face. He punched his elbow into the soft spot between shoulder and neck. The man went down. Tlonna grabbed a towel from a shelf and gagged him.

They moved on. They encountered another servant who received the same treatment. They finally reached the second floor and found the bedroom. Deric Wellenton snored loudly in his large bed, another form curled beside him.

Pushing the three humans against the wall, Tlonna silently threatened them to stay put. Losolin was bending over the bed as Tlonna joined him. He drew a dagger from his boot and put it to the sleeping human's throat. Tlonna did the same to the other sleeper, too shadowed to determine who it was.

With a jerk, Losolin yanked Deric out of bed. The human woke with a shout, and then went silent when the dagger pushed into his flesh. The other human woke and Tlonna yanked it out of bed as well. It was a young woman, bound hand and foot, and naked, Deric wore only his undergarments. The two humans froze in terror as they stared at the elves holding them.

Tlonna pulled the blanket off the bed and covered the woman. "Who are you?" she asked, ignoring Deric.

The young woman shook, but she answered quaveringly, "Lela, my lady."

"Why are you here, bound as you are?"

"I am Lord Wellenton's whore, my lady," Lela replied.

Tlonna glared at Deric, and cut the bonds on the woman. She scrambled to her feet and backed against the wall, the blanket trailing after her.

"You," Tlonna pointed her own dagger at Deric, "are about to die."

Deric was sweating profusely, his beady eyes staring at her. Losolin had his dagger-free hand fisted in his thin hair.

"Where is the pendant?" Tlonna asked coldly, moving around the bed to stand before the kneeling man, who now came up only to her waist.

"I don't know vhat you are talking about. Vhat pendant?" he squeaked in his peculiar accent.

"Do not lie to me, human," Tlonna growled, backhanding him.

Spitting out blood and a tooth, Deric tried to back away, but received Losolin's knee in the back instead.

"I know of no pendant!" he squealed again, shaking now.

"Liar!" Tlonna snapped, and raised her fist again.

"Okay! Okay! I know of zee pendant! Vhat do you vant?"

Tlonna sneered. "I want *it*, you moron. Where is it?"

"Not here!"

Tlonna smashed her fist into his face fully this time, knocking out three more teeth and breaking his nose. Losolin had to yank him back upright by his hair, twisting his fist so that he forced the man's chin up.

"Where are you from?" Tlonna asked, shaking the blood from her knuckles.

"Novhere you know!" Deric screamed.

Rolling her eyes, Tlonna flipped her dagger around and prepared to throw it. Deric winced and fell forward, leaving a fistful of fine hair in Losolin's hand. The elf dropped it in disgust.

"Eet ees there! Eet ees there!" he wailed, pointing at his dresser.

Losolin moved over to it and yanked open drawer after drawer, tossing the clothes on the ground. Finally he reached in and pulled out a rotted tweed bag. He tossed it to Tlonna. She caught it and dumped it into her palm. The pendant gleamed even in the dark. Kneeling, the Magin held the pendant before Deric's pale and bloody face.

"How did you come by this Lord Wellenton?"

"Eet vas given to me! I svear!"

"By whom?"

"A man! A man!"

"Midian?"

"Yes! Yes! King Rahlan! Please!"

"What?" Tlonna asked sweetly.

"I cannot fail him! He vill torture me!"

Tlonna raised her brows. "Well, we cannot have that."

With a quick jerk, she slit his throat. Blood welled forth onto the expensive rug.

The whore, standing against the wall, screamed. Losolin leapt over the bed and put his hand over her mouth. She flailed, the blanket falling to the ground. Losolin looked to Tlonna pleadingly, and she walked over and picked up the blanket.

"You can have this if you be quiet. We are not going to hurt you."

Lela stopped screaming, and snatched at the blanket. Losolin let go of her and she dived for it. Once she had covered herself up again, the whore turned frightened eyes on the elves.

"Why did you kill him?"

"Because he is evil," Tlonna said simply, shrugging.

"He did nothing to you!" Lela cried.

"Why do you defend him?" Losolin demanded. "He kept you bound!"

"Yes, but he did nothing to *you!*" she replied loudly.

"How do you know?" Tlonna asked, holding the pendant tightly.

Lela made to reply and then gave up.

"Listen," Tlonna said, "we gave him a quick death, which is a mercy compared to what Midian would have done to him once he found out he had failed. His death would have lasted for days."

"Others will come for you now, his followers."

"Followers?" Losolin asked sharply.

"Yes, his Purgers. People who rid the land of unnaturals," Lela replied.

Miazie stepped forward. "Do you mean Cleick, girl?"

"Cleick?" Tlonna asked as Lela nodded.

Miazie snorted. "A legion of assassins and rapists formed by Aderiaen to slaughter Magins and any other form of powerful life form in the land. Including elves."

"Interesting. What I would really like to know is why he left an authentic pendant here in the hands of such a fool."

Miazie shrugged. "You should silence her, too. She will talk."

Lela turned sheet white and started shaking her head. Losolin looked contemplative. Kayra and Shireen watched him. Tlonna cleaned her dagger off on the bed.

"If you think it wise. I do not want to anger Demetrius," she said after a bit.

"Demetrius will not know it was us," Miazie said.

"The other servants saw us, though," Losolin countered.

"In the dark, and only for a second, they will not remember," Miazie explained.

"Fine," he sighed.

Lela started trembling, "Please! I don't want to die! I won't talk, I promise!"

Losolin squinted at her. "Do you know how to write?"

Lela shook her head.

"Good," the elf said and then put his hand to her chest, between her breasts.

Green light expanded out of his palm and sank into Lela's flesh. She squeaked, and then shivered. Losolin withdrew his hand and shook it.

"Say something," he demanded.

Lela opened her mouth, and silence came out. She tried again and again, until she screamed in silence.

"Excellent," Tlonna said. "How did you do that?"

Losolin turned to face her. "Just like sealing a burst vein, or artery. I just closed her larynx."

"Let's go," Miazie said, pulling Kayra toward the door.

The five left Wellenton Manor in a hurry, the pendant in Tlonna's pocket. They arrived at the Healer House around three in the morning, to the fury of Felicity.

"Where *have* you been?" she whispered angrily.

"Busy," Tlonna snapped.

"*Busy?* I will not have my patients running about the town!"

"Fine, we will leave," Tlonna shot back.

"You will not!" Felicity shouted, forgetting her sleeping patients.

"Will!" Tlonna said, and strode by the angry healer.

When she reached her room, Tlonna began packing her things. The others, seeing what she was doing, hastened to their own rooms to do the same. They left the Healer House chased by

Felicity's admonitions.

The five found an inn and bought two rooms. When they returned to the common room, they ordered spiced wine and settled down. The group sat quietly, brooding. Tlonna lifted the pendant out of her pocket and held it up for the others to see. The black circle twirled slowly, the light from the inn glinting off the shiny black obsidian. Everyone leaned in closer to stare at it, transfixed by the dark talisman.

"Is it really real? Can you actually feel it?" Shireen asked, her eyes never leaving the pendant.

"Oh yes it is real. It feels like touching death itself. Slimy, painful, cold, tainted," the elf replied quietly, setting it on the table.

Losolin tore his eyes away from it. "Put it away Tlonna, people are watching us."

The talisman was swept off the table and back into her pocket.

"Where are the others, Losolin? Aladorn and Bryce, Tyre and Ryun?" Tlonna asked suddenly.

"Bringing the recruits up from the border. They will be here tomorrow, I should think. I had them flee the town after the incident," Losolin glanced at Shireen, " so that there would be no repercussions on that side."

A woman sidled over to them with their drinks.

"Can I get anything else for you, my lord and ladies?"

Her large hazel eyes settled on Losolin and slid down his form. She moved her slim hips closer to him and blatantly dropped a mug on purpose. As the glass shattered, she bent down, her white tunic opening to display her bosom. The male looked at her calmly, blinking slowly.

"You dropped a glass."

"Oh dear, I guess I did. I suppose I will have to clean that up now, won't I," the serving girl got on all fours and scooped up the glass. When she stood up, her brown hair was mussed and her face flushed.

"My name is Anna, by the way."

Losolin gave her a bored look. "Okay."

Anna pouted and turned away with the mugs and glass shards. As soon as she was out of hearing range, the females at the table burst into laughter. Kayra laid a hand on Losolin's arm.

"My name is Kayra, by the way. Want to romp?"

The females erupted further, clutching their sides. Losolin blushed and tossed Kayra's hand away.

"I am good, thanks."

Anna returned and they settled into silence, struggling to hold in their amusement. "I need payment my Lord...?"

Losolin dumped a few silvers and coppers into her hand, more than enough for the single round they had, and waited for her to count it.

"This isn't enough for seven. If you don't have enough money to cover it...I know a way you could pay..." she twirled a lock of hair around her finger.

Losolin stood, towering above her by two feet. Her eyes roamed up his body, settling at last on his face. The elf's head tilted slightly, bringing his hand up to cup her chin. Anna melted. Losolin brought his lips within kissing distance and stopped. "I think, that that is plenty enough to cover us all. Perhaps you should recount it, *Anna.*"

The servant stared at him, her body trembling. As she stood on tiptoes to close the distance between them, Losolin let go of her and backed a step away. Anna stood still, breathing hard. "Of course, my lord. I must have miscounted. Please forgive me."

Losolin sat down and she left, gliding across the inn floor. Tlonna exploded, tears running down her face. The women followed her example, their laughter ringing in the common room.

They did not stop laughing until an elf entered the inn in a flurry and swept up to their table. He wore a bow strapped across his back along with a full quiver. His black cloak settled against his body, bulging where more weapons were hidden. The male's black shirt and gray trousers were travel stained and worn.

Bowing slightly, he said, "Tlonna, Losolin! I cannot believe I found you at last! Thank the gods!"

"Who are you?" Tlonna asked, bewildered, slowly getting to her feet.

The elf looked up sharply. His dark eyes saddened. "I see the letter was not a false one. I am Aidyn Sestuns, trained assassin for the throne of Blackhaven. I come with tidings from your people."

Tlonna eyed him warily and motioned for him to sit, then followed suit. The elf unhitched his bow and quiver and sat down at the table. Shireen ogled him. Tlonna admitted to herself that he was quite attractive. His black hair hung to his middle back, tied back from his face with braids, and his skin was the color of honey. Dark green eyes lined with thick lashes searched the inn for a server. Anna was nowhere to be seen.

"What is this message, Aidyn?" Tlonna leaned back into her chair and looked at him calmly.

"Yayènia and Suneelo were caught a few weeks back, and are being held captive by Midian's demons. The people are losing what little hope they had. Food is running short, tunnels are collapsing faster than the dwarves can repair them, and disease is dropping humans, dwarves, and others like cattle. Blackhaven is finally succumbing to defeat."

Tlonna still lay back in her chair, but her jaw was clenched and she let a breath of air out in a long whoosh.

Aidyn gave up trying to find a server and instead took Losolin's cup. When he saw the other male's face, he set it down again. "Sorry, old habit."

Losolin shook his head slightly and pushed the cup towards the assassin. "No problem," he said awkwardly.

After a few uncomfortable seconds, Aidyn perked up again. "Dissent toward your mother is growing! Nobody expects King Dietirin to keep her around much longer. Apparently she lost control of her temper in front of Erdwyf and the entire court and Erd just shot her down. Reduced the wench to hysterics with a few well-aimed words."

Tlonna frowned. Aidyn wilted.

"You...you hate your mother."

Tlonna made a face. Aidyn gave her a sickly grin. Anna appeared out of the back. The assassin looked at the people staring at him.

"I...uh...I am going to retire. See you all in the morning," he said, and left the table.

Once in his room, Aidyn flung his pack onto the bed and kicked the post. It cracked. Cursing, the elf flopped down next to his pack and sighed when the bed shifted and fell off the cracked post onto the floor so that it sat at an awkward angle.

"Flaming human made junk," he muttered.

Aidyn looked up when his door opened and Anna slunk in.

She carried a tray of food and drink.

"The group downstairs said to bring this up to you," she simpered.

"My thanks," Aidyn grumped, taking the tray.

When Anna did not leave, he looked up at her. "What?"

"The other elf downstairs would not have me, will you?"

Aidyn sneered. "No."

Anna stomped her foot. "I am the most desired maid in this part of the city! You would be privileged to have me!"

The elf stared at her, tray forgotten. The human slammed the door shut and locked it. Aidyn sat up straighter, still watching her as she undressed.

"I will have you, whether you want it or not!" she growled.

Aidyn set the tray on the floor and stood. Anna barely reached his chest.

"What are you doing? Do you think you can force me, an elf, to lay with you?" he asked incredulously.

The human looked up from pulling her skirt down. "Yes."

"Okay then," Aidyn said. "You know, once you have had a good romp in the bed with an elf, you will always compare your human lovers, and you will always be disappointed."

"So what! At least I will have had the experience!"

Resigned, Aidyn undressed himself slowly, ignoring the now completely naked human. The elf stretched and motioned for her to get in the bed. He followed her, and immediately began caressing her soft skin masterfully.

Anna moaned and writhed next to him, begging for him to enter her. Ignoring her pleas, Aidyn moved his fingers between her thighs and worked her until she began crying. The human's body convulsed, her skin flushed with excitement and pleasure. Aidyn, knowing that the tension was about to drive her mad, finally entered her.

The assassin moved slowly, drawing it out, making the human beg and cry for her release. He did not give it. The elf pulled away and once more began caressing her body, using his hands and lips as only an elf with over half a century's experience can. Anna screamed for him to finish, her voice husky and full of need. Her gasps and moans fueled Aidyn's lust, and his hatred of the human race. He pulled away from her grasping hands and held her wrists above her head.

He stretched out on top of Anna and licked her collarbone. In a howl, Anna pushed her hips up to him, pleading. The assassin once again entered her and led the writhing woman to her climax, releasing her. The elf rolled away from her and off the bed. Within moments, he was dressed and watching her lay in the bed, her eyes closed, still in the throes of pleasure.

When it did not stop, Anna began to cry as her body pulled more and more energy from her. Finally, when she was completely drained, it stopped. She lay still, tears leaking from the corners of her eyes.

Aidyn stood over her as she slowly opened them.

"Was it worth it, slut? Do you wish you had never asked me? Or Losolin?" he growled.

Anna whimpered, shaking her head.

Aidyn grunted. "That is the difference between us, human. Elves and Men are not supposed to go together. We have unending stamina, you have none. Now get out."

Anna slithered off the bed and dressed with shaking hands. She stumbled out of the room while Aidyn ripped the blankets off the crooked bed and piled them in the corner. Opening the window, the elf leaned out and breathed in the clear air.

Tlonna looked up from her glass of cider as she heard light footsteps on the wooden stairs the next evening. Aidyn approached the table and took the empty seat between Kayra and Miazie. When he looked at them, Kayra blushed, Miazie scowled.

"Ah, you must be Miazie, the Belau?"

Looking surprised, Miazie took his offered hand. "Yes."

"Pleasure," Aidyn said. "And who are you two?"

"K-Kayra, my lord," Kayra stammered.

"Shireen, Lord Aidyn."

Aidyn grinned at them as a maid approached the table. Losolin looked up at her.

"Where is Anna this evening?"

The older woman grimaced. "The poor girl couldn't walk this morning."

Aidyn choked and then started laughing. "That ought to teach her, eh Losolin?"

"Teach her what?" Losolin asked, looking worried.

"To try to bed elves. I am surprised she did not die."

"You...you lay with her?" Tlonna spluttered.

Losolin grinned at Aidyn, "Aye, that should teach her."

Aidyn glanced at Tlonna. "Well, she forced the issue. I gave her what she wanted and she could not handle it. She probably will not be able to walk for the rest of the day, perhaps tomorrow as well."

"Does sleeping with elves always do that?" Shireen asked.

"Yes, it does," Kayra responded quietly.

Aidyn glared at her. "You are the same as Anna."

"No," Tlonna, Losolin, Miazie, and Kayra said at the same time.

"I was raped by elves. I could not move for three days after," Kayra explained, even more quietly.

"Raped? By *elves*?" Aidyn repeated, shocked.

"Seaduens, we believe," Tlonna said, nodding.

Immense hatred flooded into Aidyn's face, making Miazie and Kayra scoot away from him. "Seaduens," he spat. "I hate those bastards. I am sorry, Miss Kayra. And no, Miss Shireen, it does not always happen. If love and emotion is there, it is extremely pleasurable, for both parties. More so than between humans, but that is natural. And it does not harm anyone. What happened to you, and with Anna last night, though the situations were entirely different, the outcome is the same. There is no emotion other than hatred, or disgust. The power of the elves takes the human body over and gives both extreme pleasure and pain. I purposefully did not hurt Anna, but I did not stop the pleasure, which is too much for a human to endure if it is not controlled by the giver. Her orgasm lasted over a minute, very unhealthy and very unsafe. Elves, that is normal, actually quite short, but human climaxes last what...a few seconds usually?"

When Aidyn stopped speaking, the three humans were staring at Tlonna and Losolin. Tlonna was crimson, Losolin leaning back with his hands behind his head, grinning at Miazie.

"Wow," Shireen exclaimed, turning her gaze from Losolin to Aidyn. "That must be incredible. Is it? Tlonna?"

Tlonna left.

A while later, Aidyn followed her up, asking permission from Losolin. He knocked on her door and smiled uncertainly when she opened it.

"Oh, Aidyn, what can I do for you?"

"I wanted to apologize. I did not think about what my words would mean for you."

Tlonna sighed. "It is all right. I suppose that kind of topic does not faze most elves."

Aidyn shrugged, "Not really. You should hear Yayènia and Erdwyf go at it. You used to, as well."

"I wish I could remember, I do," Tlonna said sadly and opened the door further. Aidyn stepped in and sat on a stool by the wardrobe.

"Tlonna, there are things I must tell you that I could not say in front of the others."

Tlonna locked the door and sat across from Aidyn, on the bed. "What is it?" she asked.

"Everything I said is true, but much worse. Even elves are starting to die. Eight years without sight of cloud or star, no fresh air, just what comes in through the shafts, can do things to our kind that illness cannot. People are beyond despair. Before I left, two nymphs were murdered by a dwarf that had gone mad. Your people are dying, and they believe you already dead. Your letter was shown to the masses, and they think it a lie. They need your help, Tlonna, more than ever."

"What is it you think I am doing?" Tlonna shouted. "I woke up a very short time ago with no knowledge other than my name, and nothing but a pack. Now I am here recruiting men to lead in battle against Midian. What more can I do, Aidyn? Tell me!"

Aidyn watched her pace around her room. "I cannot."

"Well then how do you expect me to know?" Tlonna asked.

Aidyn sighed, "I do not know, Tlonna, I wish I did."

The Magin stopped pacing and glanced at Aidyn. "How good of friends were we?" she asked.

Aidyn looked puzzled, "Well, Losolin, Suneelo, Ghealan, and I were best friends, and you, Yayènia, and Erdwyf were as well. We were nigh inseparable. Why do you ask?"

"You call me Tlonna without hesitation. I am not used to hearing that from anyone other than Losolin and Miazie."

Aidyn nodded. "You have always hated it."

Tlonna finally turned to face him full on. "Tell me, friend, what would do now, if you were me?"

Aidyn picked up his bow and plucked the string. After pulling out a bar of wax, he sighed and began waxing the string as he talked.

"I suppose...I suppose I would do what you are doing. I would try to destroy the source of the problem. But me being what I am, I would go it alone. I would go after Midian myself. I know where he is, and I would probably die trying to get to him, but I would certainly try my best to slaughter anything or anyone in my path. And I would fail, I know that. Even so, knowing that, I would still do it. But this is not my mission, Tlonna, it is yours, and Losolin's.

"So much depends on you, I am sure it must weigh heavily on your heart and mind. Tlonna, my friend, I know it all must seem hopeless, but remember you have friends here, and at home. Losolin is your rock, he loves you more than life itself, and I know that sentiment is returned wholeheartedly from you. You cannot ask me, or the Belau, or any of the others at home to do this for you," Aidyn said, standing. "You are in this as Tlonna Arune Ewôsdírn, Princess Magin of Blackhaven Forest, the Everwood, the Magin Queen, as I hear you are called, now, but if you add Tlonna the friend, the lover, the leader, and the warrior, you will not be defeated.

"There is a saying among our people, '*kresno günna yayena, behkt jerwlyn ushna akod.*' Do you know what it means?"

Tlonna, tears in her eyes, shook her head.

"It means as long as we love, nothing can defeat us. Cling to that, and it shall remain true."

Tlonna looked up into Aidyn's green eyes. They stood less than a foot apart. He matched her gaze, long dark lashes creating sweeping shadows on his cheek.

"Will you remain with me? Will you swear to me that you will not leave? Will you stand at my side and be the friend you claim you are?" Tlonna whispered.

Aidyn's face did not change. He barely breathed. "Do you know what you ask? Do you know what swearing an oath between elves...a Magin, and an assassin means? Tlonna, do you understand what you ask of me?"

The princess took a deep breath. "I am asking you to swear your life to me."

Aidyn blinked slowly, considered telling her the complete truth, and said instead, "Then I swear it," and held out his hand.

Tlonna took it. As their flesh touched, silent thunder shook the inn and light raced up Aidyn's arm and into his body. The assassin fell to one knee, dark head bowed as he clutched his arm. Tlonna, shaken and horrified, went to her knees with him.

"Did you know that was going to happen?" she yelled. "Did you know it would hurt you?"

Aidyn looked up. "Yes. It is an Elven oath, and if I break it, it will take my life, unless you release me by either death or will."

"Aidyn! No, gods, why did you not tell me?" Tlonna sobbed, shaking him.

The door behind her slammed open and the others rushed in. Miazie stopped Losolin from lunging at Aidyn by leaping on him instead. Tlonna pulled Aidyn up as she stood, ignoring the newcomers.

"Would you have let me swear it?" Aidyn asked, rubbing his shoulder.

"No," Tlonna replied after a second. "No I would not have. Does it hurt terribly?"

The assassin chuckled and shook his head. "I have had worse, much worse. And this will fade in a bit. I regret it not."

Tlonna finally turned to face her other friends and started when she saw Miazie clinging to Losolin's neck, perched on his back.

"What are you doing?" the Magin asked Miazie as she slid off Losolin.

"Keeping him from attacking Aidyn," the Belau replied, straightening her shirt.

Losolin shrugged when Tlonna rounded on him. Instead of admonishing him, the Magin pivoted and walked to the window where the moons glimmered in the crisp winter night.

"What is happening? What causes this?" she asked shakily.

The others crowded around the window to stare outwards in dread. Snow was falling, but it was tainted, black. It covered the ground like black powder. The few people strolling through the streets stopped, staring about them in fear.

"It has begun," Miazie whispered in dismay. "That which Astinus predicted so long ago. 'When snow blankets the land in waves of inky tainted midnight, as ash.' Midian's taint. The rivers will soon turn, and even rain will bring chaos. His evil is spreading, despair is settling over the land and people like shadow. Even the sun will not offer hope, if this continues it too will turn. Winter will be constant, darkness will be endless, and we will all perish."

Silence greeted her words.

Chapter 10
Theory of Moons

Tlonna shook with rage, her slender body shuddering as she stared at the falling stain. Blood dripped between her fingers as her nails cut into her flesh. The only sound in the room was the slow plop of the drops on the hard floor. Aidyn moved closer to Tlonna. Losolin made to stop him, but a look from the assassin froze him. Miazie pulled the worried elf back a few steps by his elbow.

When Aidyn put a large hand on Tlonna's shoulder, the Magin took a deep breath. "Tell me about the moons."

"What?"

"I want to know about the moons. Tell me about the moons. Please," the last word was a whispered plea.

Aidyn sighed heavily. He pointed to the seven moons that hung in a large arc across the midnight sky, attempting to ignore the black snow.

"The seven moons are a representation of the seven major race groups. A small group of magically-inclined-non-Magins called the Alchemian race is represented by the red moon, Loniare, which is the highest at its zenith. Gyntesa, the green moon was claimed by the humans. It is the youngest moon, and also the largest. Sonora is often called the Elf Moon, being that it is purely white and the oldest moon. The golden moon, Yunat, is the Spryte Moon. Nosarel is the faerys' moon, which works being small and silver like the faeries. The ugly brown one is Kaatesny, obviously named by the Dwarves," Aidyn pointed to the lowest moon, a sliver of pale blue a fingers' width from the horizon. "That one, is Tonora. It appeared in the sky about two thousand years ago, right before the end of the Council War. The elf queen Tonora died the same night it appeared. She was Magin Jair's mother...your ancestor. You were named after her."

Tlonna's eyes focused and she turned to the male standing next to her. "I...Tonora? She turned into a moon?"

Aidyn shifted, "They uh...it is said that your family, directly, is descended from the moons. So, from Jair to Amram down to Sha, Damian, and Dietirin...to you."

Silence ensued until she felt Losolin's hand on her back.

"Tlonna? Come on love, away from this..." Losolin said, gesturing broadly at the ashen snow and distant moons.

Tlonna glanced briefly at Aidyn, and with a small nod, left with Losolin.

Aidyn, Miazie, Shireen, and Kayra stood around in the room, glancing awkwardly between each other and the snow. Miazie cleared her throat and left the room hurriedly. The others filed out slowly, shuffling their feet.

Aidyn watched them leave and then turned back to the window. His green eyes followed the path of the moons until they came to rest on the sliver of Tonora.

"*And they shall be descended from the moons, and hold all the powers of the heavens,*" Aidyn whispered before leaving for his own room.

After a while, Tlonna and Losolin returned to their room, having had a good dousing of ale. Tlonna looked pointedly away from the window and slid beneath the bedcovers. Losolin joined her, desperately trying to follow her example. The black snow kept drawing his gaze, however, until he yanked shut the curtain.

The next morning, Miazie and Shireen sat in the Belau's room pouring over the books Tlonna had in her possession. The window curtain was drawn there, too. Shireen gasped and dropped the book she was looking at and pointed animatedly towards a paragraph written in Parlêthian.

The Belau looked at the woman next to her and said, "You can read Parlêthian?"

"Well, a little. My nursemaid was an elf and she taught me a few words. My father killed her when she brought a man into the house. I really liked Ahlana. She was really pretty and reminded me somewhat of Tlonna. Free spirit, brave, and caring. Oh, Miazie, you should've met her. She was really smart, Ahlana. I miss her," the woman paused for a moment and then continued. "That elf had a thirst for knowledge like you, that's why she decided to love a human man. She brought him home after they had wed, his name was Jotham. He was quite handsome actually. Red hair, green eyes, and tan skin like Aidyn's. I really liked him too until he was beheaded by my father. I hate him, he needs to meet Tlonna."

Miazie snorted, remembering her father's meeting with Tlonna and started reading the paragraph.

" '*The Sixth Age, year five sixty-six. The Triad Magins: Roluf Gwemheoad, Tayrn Verla, and Buftren Julyt, have forged two great pendants. A black encased in gold and pearl vines with a tree forged of obsidian, pearl, gold, and silver. Engraved upon the back, a star of eight points centered with a sun. The chain is silver linked by magic so that it never breaks. The black has only the power to kill, sucking away the soul and mind and life until only a dry corpse remains. The second, a white, encased with silver and gold vines with the star and sun forged in all four metals. The pearl pendant will never break unless by a powerful Magin. The star and sun is etched upon the back once more. Seer Astinus has told me personally that this sign predicts a light-wreathed elf maiden of terrible beauty. She herself will defeat the shadow. I trust the old seer, but can it be true? Only the far future can tell says Astinus. I must go now to a feast in honor of the Triad Magins. The gods only know what sort of evil will come of their creations.*'

> *Records of Magin Veries Gurgen*
> *Fifth Magin of Parlêthian Council'.* "

Miazie looked up and drew a shuddering breath. "This is what we have been looking for. There is more here.

"'*A few days ago, Feela and Cerin came to me whispering about advancements they had made in the study of immortality. I do not believe it right that they must perform tests on the elves that live in the neighboring forest, but they do as they will. I spoke once more with Astinus about his visions of darkness and light but he merely smiled and said 'the moon heiress will free the slaves of death.' Here, the seer lay back and began sleeping, never to wake again. He has given me the key to his journal of visions, a thing no one but he has ever seen. He warns me of it, but yet I must read. I mourn this day, so I leave this book, maybe someday my son will fill its pages.*'

"Here is where it ends with the small spidery writing to start with darker, fresher, thicker writing. I must think on this, Shireen..." Miazie leaned back on her pillow and closed her eyes. "It just doesn't fit."

Tlonna stared out of the window at the freshly fallen taint. No people walked the streets. A dog, skinny with malnutrition, huddled under a porch, as far from the ground as possible. The elf could see its hair standing on end. Losolin dinked around in the room behind her.

"Loni, do not bother yourself with something you cannot change right now. Please?" Losolin said finally, coming to stand behind her.

"But that is just it, is it not? It is my burden to carry, my enigma to solve. All the dead men say so, do they not?" Tlonna said, turning to face him.

"And they are dead," Losolin replied, smiling slightly, "while you live. No matter how many prophecies and omens there are, your life is *yours*, and if you so chose, you can turn away right now and leave Nymyños to fight for itself. No one is forcing you to make these decisions. Influencing and trying to force you, yes, but in the end it is only you who chooses to stand up and say, 'I will do this'.

"Salvation will come from somewhere else. Perhaps not in time to save our race, but it would come, and evil would be defeated. It is your choice to fight it now, your choice to stand in the face of annihilation and refuse to yield. Tlonna, my dearest love, heart of my heart, and all that is good in me, it is because you are kind, and brave, and loved, that you choose to do so. Deep in your heart you know, *you know*, that it is not the prophecies that cause you to do this, it is the person you are. Is that not so?"

Tlonna reached out, grabbed a fistful of Losolin's shirt, and yanked him into a passionate kiss.

When they parted, breathless, she whispered, "That is why I love you. And aye, it is so."

Losolin leaned his forehead against Tlonna's, grinning.

"I knew there was a reason you loved me. Now I know. Are you hungry?"

Tlonna grinned back, "What did you have in mind?"

The male stretched, putting his most arrogant look on. "Ah, well, I figure we can try and best Aidyn's description of-"

"Get out," Tlonna laughed, and pushed him out of the door.

The couple giggled their way to the common room.

"There is Aidyn and Kayra," Losolin said, steering Tlonna toward the far table.

They ordered breakfast and leaned in to listen to Aidyn's

quiet voice.

"...trains them each herself for months at a time until they can put her on the ground a few times, though no one can actually beat her."

Kayra stared wide-eyed at the elf. "I can't believe she's really real! I mean, everyone's heard the stories, but I don't think anyone actually believes them."

Aidyn snorted into his wine.

Losolin frowned slightly at the assassin. "Who is really real?"

"Your sister-in-law."

"She's the greatest warrior ever!" Kayra cried. "High Commander Yayènia er'Tiena of the Blackhaven Militia. She's never lost a fight, they say. Is she really your sister-in-law Losolin? Princess Tlonna, everyone says she's your best friend. Is she funny? What does she look like? What does she wear?" the human's eyes were wide as saucers as she stared at the elves in anticipation.

When Tlonna and Losolin looked at Aidyn, the assassin jumped in. "Yes, she is married to Losolin's brother, Suneelo, who is Captain of the Guard. Yayènia's humor is...lacking in appropriateness and decency, but those who know her well laugh at her jokes anyway because, when looking at them from her perspective, they are funny. She is very short, under seven feet. Hair down to her ankles, but she keeps it in a braid most of the time. Gray-blue eyes, pale, beautiful. Most female elves are though. Nia is a bit more so than the rest of them, but that is her most deadly tool. Men think she is an easy target because she is small and pretty. Usually they are dead within a second of touching her.

"She wears pants and a shirt most of the time, to the wrath of Queen Constancias, of course," Aidyn winked at Tlonna. "I think I have actually seen her in a dress twice since I have known her. Once at her wedding, and once at Erdwyf's High Advisor ceremony. She wore an overdress with trousers once, to a ball and Constancias just about had her hanged. Personally I think she looked rather nice, but that is your mother for you."

Tlonna sniffed disdainfully and glanced at the awe-struck Kayra, "I think you broke her."

Aidyn laughed and leaned back in his chair, "My dear, I can tell you tales about Nia, Suneelo, Ghealan, and Erdwyf that even the bawdiest of bards and tellers will not say. Like the time the four of them, these two, and I found all the pictures and busts of Constancias around the city, piled them in the square and burned them at midnight. Then, when people started to realize something was going on, we seven just happened to show up and be entertained with the rest of the people as the queen stormed around like an angry child demanding the cretins to come forward. It was wonderful to see her screaming and jumping about in her nightgown, on the verge of tears because someone had ruined all of her lovely paintings."

Losolin and Tlonna stared as dumbstruck as Kayra at Aidyn.

Finally, the Magin said, "Aidyn, we did not really do that, did we? I mean, I am her *daughter*! I would not do that to my own mother...would I?"

"You have done far worse, Tlonna, by yourself. Smearing ink on the arms of her throne so that when she touched her face she slowly painted herself green. Greasing the seat of her dinner chair so that she could not stay seated all throughout the meal."

"No! That is terrible!" Tlonna gasped, trying to hide her laughter.

"Tlonna, your mother once had a dwarf build his own gallows because the one he had built a hundred years before had snapped when a criminal was hanged. She is vile and cruel, and no one likes her. King Dietirin puts up with her for some blasted reason, but the things we do to her are nothing to what she does to innocent people. Your mother is a pox on the name elf and queen."

"Oh," Tlonna looked down at the table and swirled her wine around.

Their quiet conversation about the political structure in Blackhaven was interrupted when Shireen joined them, looking worried.

"Miazie has been sitting on her bed staring out the window for an hour almost. She read a passage in a book and then just stopped talking. She said something didn't fit and that's it."

Losolin frowned. "What book was she reading?"

"I don't know the title, but I think it was the journal of Veries Gurgen, the Magin," the young woman said, accepting a glass of wine from Aidyn.

"Ahh...that would explain it," the assassin murmured as he sat back.

"Explain what?" Tlonna asked.

"Your mother went on a frantic search for the ancient family volumes before the people fled underground. She found most of them in the library, but five were missing. The journals of the Fifteen were all there but for Veries'. Also *Chronicles of Astinus, Legends of the Moons*, the family history, *The History of Magic and Its Uses*, and *Parlêthian Council of Magins*. It would make sense that you would take those ones. Veries Gurgen was your idol for a while, and you were always asking about the history of magic, who wielded it, how, when, where. You did not even know you were a Magin until a few months before you left."

Tlonna grunted. "No wonder I have such a hard time controlling it."

"Yes, well, you have not had the chance to be trained like every other Magin. I mean, your father trained your mother, your father was trained by his father, and so on. You have been training with a Belau who is not at all powerful," Aidyn replied.

"I suppose you are right. I do not know about the rest of you, but I want to hear more of Aidyn's stories," Tlonna said, pushing back her chair and linking her ankles on the table.

The others followed her example and waited for Aidyn to finish his drink. When he did, they all settled in to listen.

A few hours later, when Miazie still hadn't shown, Tlonna left to find her. She knocked on the Belau's door and, when the allowance came, the elf walked into the room. Miazie was scribbling on a piece of parchment, her long raven hair spilling over her shoulders and onto the bedspread.

"Tlonna! Sit, sit. I would love some company."

Tlonna sat at the desk chair and studied the parchment her friend was writing on. At the very top were the words "moon heiress" circled many times with lines sprouting from them at every angle.

"What...what are you doing?"

The human sighed and sat back. "In Veries Gurgen's journal there's a passage that says Seer Astinus's last words were 'the moon heiress will free the slaves of death'. Now, I have heard of the moon heiress, I just can't remember when, or where. It could allude to the long dead Faery Queen Alinistorin who called herself the Moon Queen, or the ancient Plains Elf Chieftess Atrey Moon or any number of other women with connections to moons."

Tlonna squinted as she thought, "What about me?"

"What? You? Tlonna, I don't remember hearing about any family member named Moon, ever."

"Last night, what Aidyn said? Tonora is my ancestor, and she became a moon when she died. Maybe the moon heiress is not from a family Moon, but an actual heir *of* the moons."

The Belau stared at the elf for a full minute, running through possibilities in her mind, before her face lit up.

"*Yes*, Tlonna. Of course!" she scribbled out a few of the markings and then wrote in a couple more. "The moon heiress will free the slaves of death...slaves of death. *Slaves* of *death*. That could be, well, everyone. No one is truly immortal. But the slaves...I've never heard of that term."

Miazie's dark eyes glazed over again, her face slackening as she became lost in thought.

Tlonna laid a hand on her friend's arm and smiled. "Miazie, please, can you tell me about Tonora?"

The woman jumped and then turned to face Tlonna, eyes wide. "Tonora? The...Jair's mother? Well, she was queen of the elf clan in Purheae, the oldest elves, from the original discoverers of Nymyños, the Serenyi High Elves, which is a whole other story. Supposedly, all elves are descended from that clan. She was claimed to be the most beautiful of all elves, fair as a moon, powerful beyond measure, tall."

"If she was so powerful, how did she die? I mean, could she not beat back the Magins?"

Miazie swung her legs over the bed's edge and braced her arms behind her. "Tonora wasn't a Magin, Tlonna. In ancient times, elves had tremendous natural power, whether they were Magins or not. They could command the earth. They could sing trees to life and they would grow within days. They could command water to move where they wanted, even uphill."

"Why did we lose that power?"

"I don't know. Perhaps, as time progressed and more technologies came to life, elves didn't need to use their magic as much, so it slowly dimmed to the stage it's at now."

Tlonna looked sadly at her hands. "I wonder if we could bring it back..."

"I don't know, Tlonna. I wish I did, but I don't," Miazie replied, shaking her head.

After a few moments of contemplative silence, the two friends started musing about the slaves of death.

Miazie closed her book with a thud. She sneezed as dust floated up from the frail yellow pages. Sliding off her bed to retrieve her coin purse, the Belau left the inn in search of supplies. She found a quill-maker's hut within minutes and ducked inside. Quills, inks, tablets, parchment rolls, and all sorts of writing materials lay about in small wooden crates. The owner, a spindly old man with two tufts of white hair above his ears, squinted at her.

"Do you have bound parchment?" Miazie asked, peering at him through the dim light.

"Bound? Like a book? What size?" he shouted at her.

Startled, Miazie moved closer and held out her hands. "Something I can write in while I'm riding, or wherever I happen to be. A journal."

"Journal? Yes, I have journals!" the proprietor beckoned for her to follow and she found herself crammed into the back corner of the shop having dusty, leather-bound journals pushed under her nose.

"I'll take a moment to look, thank you," she said finally, waving away the onslaught.

"All right!" the man shouted, trying to hear himself over his apparent hearing loss.

Miazie selected a red leather journal, some new quills and ink, and a bar of green wax. Spotting a crate of seal stamps, the Belau bit her lip.

"I'm no longer the princess of Anutch," she muttered to herself. "I should have a new seal."

With her reasoning in hand, Miazie started digging through the silver and wood stamps. After a while, she found one with an open book under three stars and smiled.

"I'll take these, please," she said as she laid her purchases out on the table.

The man tallied up her cost and she paid him. Supplied and partially redefined, Miazie made her way back to the inn and settled herself at her desk. Opening the first page of the dusty red journal, she inked her quill and began to write.

12. Ealieaes. Eighth Age of Nymyños
My name is Miazie Paron Ughtren, and I live now in a time of

turmoil. Nymyñosian prophecy is coming to fulfillment and I feel it my duty as a citizen of Nymyños and as a Belau to record the happenings of this time. I hope I am not the only one taking notes, but I deeply regret that scholarly habits are lacking in these days. I can only hope that one day my words and memories will serve the purpose of unveiling history, as those legends of my time have done for me. I start now saying I am in close company of Tlonna Arune Ewôsdírn and her Lord Consort, Losolin Ullor Grisholm. Their lives will be forever entwined in the history, and the future of this era. May the pages of this journal not be shrouded in darkness.

Miazie set down her quill and studied her words with satisfaction. Slowly, she began forming her tale from the time Tlonna had wandered into her father's realm.

Kayra settled herself on her bed with the book Miazie had lent her, the *Chronicles of Astinus.* Academia was not her passion, but the young woman found the possible future fascinating, and the fact that someone long ago had predicted events that were unraveling around her now. Carefully opening the old book, Kayra squinted at the writing. It was faded, but she could tell whoever had copied it had been frantic, almost panicked as they scribed.

As she came to the end of a passage a few hours later, Kayra placed a leather strap in the brittle pages and lovingly closed the book. The cover was of worn red leather engraved with silver writing. The young woman ran her hand across the surface and started. A fine, barely discernible black line had appeared a finger joints length from the binding. Kayra brought it closer to her face and discovered the crack. Running her finger along it, she traced it all the way around the book. Taking out a thin dagger, she put the point carefully into the crack. Pushing the hilt down, a thin piece of leather came up with the blade. Pulling it carefully away, she gasped as a yellowed piece of parchment floated away from the book. Picking it up, Kayra smoothed her thumb over the edge and began to read.

"Miazie!"

The pounding on her door startled the Belau enough that she made a nasty blot on her page. "What?" she snapped.

Kayra burst into her room, waving a book at her in a panic. "Oh gods, Miazie! Look!"

Miazie took the *Chronicles* from the younger woman and flipped it over. "What about it? Did you spill something on it?"

"No! Gods, Miazie, look inside. I found it sealed within the front cover. My gods, what will we tell her?"

"Who? Tell who what? What are you on about Kayra?"

The brown-haired woman flounced onto the bed and flicked open the cover to reveal the yellowed parchment. "*Read.*"

Frowning, Miazie gingerly picked up the paper and read it, blood rushing from her face as she did so. "No, *no*," she breathed, shaking her head. "No, I don't believe it. It is a joke. It's...it's not real."

"You know Astinus was not a joker, Miazie. You know it's true. You have to tell Tlonna. That's who it's about, isn't it?"

Swallowing to dislodge the lump of grief and terror in her throat, Miazie nodded, intuition flashing through her mind. "We have to be sure. There are people who know far more of prophecy, particularly Astinus's prophecy, than I. I...I have to go."

"What? Miazie, go where? Who knows more?" Kayra asked in sudden alarm.

"Alchemian. Most of their studies are based off of Astinus's and the Third Triad's work. Veries, Feela, and Teral, Kayra. They were the Third Triad of the Council of Magins, and the founders of alchemy. I must speak with them about this."

Kayra jumped of the bed to block the door as Miazie headed toward it. "What are you talking about? It's one of the plainest prophecies I have ever read, Miazie."

"Which makes it doubly dangerous, Kayra. Prophecy is never clear, never plain. We cannot stake everything on this one because it has a supposed clear meaning, and then find out we were wrong when it's too late to do anything."

"But it says slaves of death, it coincides perfectly with Veries Gurgen's journal!"

"That doesn't change a flaming thing!" Miazie shouted, "If this is true, it means Tlonna dies!"

"No it doesn't!" Kayra shouted back. "It says she has to 'bow to shadow's caressing touch'. Nothing about death!"

"Tlonna is an elf, evil destroys elves! True evil will kill her as sure as any blade will!"

Kayra threw her hands in the air and was shoved aside as

Miazie bolted from the room. Tlonna and Losolin were sitting in their room repairing their torn clothes and cleaning their belongings when Miazie exploded into their room.

"I have to go to Alchemian."

Tlonna rose to her feet. "What are you talking about? You have to go where?"

"Alchemian, they are known for their devotion to Astinus, and they know his prophecy upside down and backwards. Please, I need to go."

Frowning, Losolin plucked the parchment the human held in her hand out and read it. His brow drew down and he looked up at her with a malevolent glare. "What is this?"

"Astinus's last prophecy," Miazie whispered.

"The one about the slaves of death? The one Veries Gurgen wrote about?" Tlonna asked, trying to take the paper from her consort's hands.

"The very same. The original, by the look of it, too. Alchemian is the best hope we have of deciphering it correctly," Miazie said, slightly calmer.

"It seems clear to me," Losolin snarled, moving to toss the prophecy into the fire.

"No!" Miazie shrieked, bowling into him, shifting him a few feet to the side.

"Miazie! Losolin!" Tlonna barked, grabbing the parchment from Losolin's startled fingers. Her brow rose, blood draining from her face. "Yes...it does seem clear. I am the Moon Heiress, Losolin is the lover, and you are the friend. I don't know who the guardian is, or the slaves of death, but it seems pretty basic for prophecy."

"No, it's not. I told you once Astinus was my favorite study. None of his prophecy was ever clear. They were always by far complex than the words hinted at. Like when he predicted the War of Monotheism, his whole prophecy was 'the savior of thousands will be slain, and the hammered gods will be victorious over them'. It seems pretty simple, until you look at what happened. The savior of thousands was slain, along with the entire ideal of monotheism, also called the saved religion. The hammered gods, the old gods, the gods of polytheism, were the gods of the victorious pagans, but they never truly won. After the war, religion was very nearly scorned as superfluous. It has never truly come back.

"Everything he Saw, comes true, and nothing he wrote is as it seems. You must believe me. I have to seek the council of the alchemists."

"And how would we go about doing this?"

Miazie looked relieved that Tlonna was no longer denying the paper. "I should go, but you two must stay here and continue on your purpose. I know the Alchemian route, I can find them. I will get their answers and come back as soon as I can."

"Miazie, you cannot be serious!" Tlonna cried.

"Alchemists?" Losolin asked, sounding skeptical.

Miazie frowned. "Yes, alchemists. The race of Alchemian, sort of a refuge for magically-inclined-non-Magins."

"Aidyn said something about Alchemian, said basically the same description too. They named the moon...Loniare, right?" Losolin said.

"Yes."

"If they have magic, how are they non-Magins?" Tlonna asked, trying to veer away from the thought of her friend leaving.

"There are a few different types of magical people. There are Magins, who are the most powerful. They can use their magic externally and internally. In other words, they can control magic in most forms. For example, it can be seen by others coming out of their bodies, or used to enhance their physicality. It is an actual physical and mental control of power. Then there are Maigs. They are very rare and can only use their magic internally, usually in a healing capacity. There are Illusioners, who can control light and shadow to form pictures and sounds. They are also pretty rare, but not as much as Maigs, and are usually used for entertainment with storytellers and bards. There are alchemists, who use chemicals and other natural elements along with a slight bit of magic to create objects, mainly things of wealth or usefulness. The last are Dabblers. They are basically Maginic scholars. They don't have much power, usually because of age, their bodies can't support two different forms of energy, but they know vast amounts about magic. Of course, in each race there are different forms and abilities as well. Like the elves and their earth magic, or the dwarves and their stone magic. Then there are the Sprytes, gnomes, goblins, Darkwights, dryads, nymphs, faeries, Tree elves, wiats, demons..." Miazie said, rushed, waving her hand about dismissively.

"And the Alchemists can help?" Tlonna asked, refusing to be overwhelmed by the amount of magical people.

"Yes. They are among the most brilliant people in Nymyños, and they will help a Belau. But I need to leave now."

Tlonna shook her head emphatically. "No. I do not want you to leave. Winter is set in and tainted as well, it is too dangerous."

Miazie's face tightened. "Tlonna, I've lived in the Lands my entire life. I know the terrain, I know the weather, and I know the people. Ryun and I could leave tomorrow morning and reach Alchemian within a few weeks at most. War is upon us. We can't risk losing any possible advantage because of a few paltry excuses. Let me go. Ryun will go with me and we'll be perfectly safe."

Tlonna hesitated. Losolin waited for her to speak. The Magin dry washed her hands as she turned to look out the window. *Too much.* Fear sat like a stone in her gut at the thought of sending Miazie away. Turning back to face the human and Losolin, Tlonna saw the resolve etched on Miazie's face.

"How long would you be gone?"

"I am not sure."

"All right...go. But...be careful. I know you know the land and the people, but times are changing. You are right, war is upon us, and that means no place is safe. Miazie...please do not make me regret this decision."

"I won't. We'll be fine. Now, the next kingdom you should head to is Florwen Hune. The cities are well kept and the people are kind enough and respect Magins. That is all I know. If it has changed, I cannot say anything about it."

Tlonna nodded. "All right...I do not like this, but I suppose we must do what is necessary."

Miazie smiled grimly and turned to leave. Losolin put a hand on her shoulder for a moment and smiled encouragingly, his oceanic eyes troubled. Tlonna stood with her arms folded, pain etched across her face as plain as if she'd been run through, the damning prophecy in her fist. When the Belau left, she glanced down at it again.

Darkness will mar the land of beauty and evil will wage war. One will hold the power to deliver life from death, but must bow to shadow's caressing touch to find this power. The guardian will fall, the lover will rule, the friend will perceive, and the moon heiress will free the slaves of death.

Sighing, the Magin smoothed the aged vellum. "I do not like this, Losolin."

"Nor I. It bespeaks of things that make my blood run cold. But come away, my heart, and let us inform Ryun about his new job."

Tlonna nodded and followed him out of the door to find the hunter. As usual, he was outside practicing in the courtyard with Tyre. Pulling aside the lanky human, the elves informed him of his task.

"She knows where to go, but Miazie is not physically strong enough to protect herself. I want you to be her muscle, Ryun. This will be your test for captaining my army. Please do not let us down."

"I won't, but why is this happening? Why now?"

Tlonna shrugged. "Things are coming to fruition that were predicted thousands of years ago. There is nothing for it but to follow the paths set before us, yes?"

"I suppose," Ryun said grudgingly, but he took her hands in a tight grip. "Thank you Princess Tlonna. I will take care of her, I promise. She is in good hands."

"I know, Ryun, I know," Tlonna said quietly.

The next day, the small company hugged Miazie and Ryun goodbye as the couple headed out to the stables. Miazie had braided her long hair and curled it around her head like a wreath. Her clothes were soft leather lined with wool. She looked like a warrior queen of legend with her darkly beautiful features and a figure that spoke of distant Elvish lineage. She and Tlonna embraced tightly.

"I'll return, Tlonna. Don't fear. Focus on your task and don't steal trouble from shadows you can't see. I'll see you in a few weeks' time."

Tlonna sniffed and waved Miazie and Ryun out of the inn. She spent the rest of the day morosely reading the book the woman had left her, the Magin Veries' journal.

Losolin yawned and lay on the bed, his arms acting as pillow for his head. "Tomorrow, we should go to the castle. The blunt of winter will be here soon and I do not want to be testing in bad weather."

"I know," Tlonna sighed. "We will go see King Demetrius tomorrow after we break our fast. I do not really know how to go about choosing the men Demetrius is giving us."

"We could put them through a series of tests, or something," Losolin closed his eyes and yawned again.

"No...maybe there is another way we can do it. We are going to be here throughout winter, so we have a couple of months. But there are some things that are starting to worry me," Tlonna sat down beside Losolin. "We need gold, and lots of it."

"We still have most of the coin Tyular gave as tribute to the campaign, and Miazie left us some as well," the elf sat up.

"Yes, but how long will that last? We have probably two or three years before we are able to go home. And we do not know what evil we are going to find there. We must find a way to get more gold."

"What about trading? We could trade some of our things," Losolin looked at Tlonna.

"What will we trade? We have nothing already," shaking her head, the elf stood and looked out at the moons hanging in the sky.

"Tlonna, remember the rings?" Losolin approached her.

"What rings?"

"These rings," he waggled the band on his finger at her. "I know it drains you, but what if you made more jewelry and sold it. Merchants would pay high price for goods such as these."

"You are right, it does drain me. I can only make a few at a time and I need materials. I was able to make these rings out of a few twigs I found under the bed. With this taint, nothing is going to be growing. No flowers, budding leaves, nothing."

Losolin studied the silver ring on his finger. "What do you need?"

"Natural things. Leaves, branches, rocks, pebbles, twigs, vines, bark, things like that."

Losolin kissed her forehead and headed out the door despite her contradictions that nothing was growing. While he was out, Tlonna catnapped, letting her muscles relax against the cool bed quilt.

"Got some!" Losolin said cheerfully from the doorway.

Tlonna's eyes snapped open and she took in her lover. He held a sack full of items from outside. He brought it over to her and opened it.

"Where did you find all this?" Tlonna asked in amazement.

"I can make things grow, Tlonna. It is one of my powers," Losolin said, smiling.

Digging through the random objects Tlonna selected a leaf and long section of a vine. She arranged them on her lap, the vine just touching the stem on the leaf and closed her eyes. The air before her hands, which lay limp beside them, began to glow and swirl. Sweat beaded the elf's forehead and her breathing became quickened. Soon, the leaf and vine started to shimmer and writhe slightly. Light flared briefly and a silver necklace sat where the flora had been. The vine was now a delicate silver chain with exquisite vine detail. The leaf dangled by its stem, a shiny silver pendant. Tlonna took a deep breath and lifted the necklace.

"I think that is about what...fifty geld? Sixty?" she asked, looking up at Losolin.

"I do not know, love. It is beautiful, though. Maybe I can do it too, if you explain it to me."

Tlonna patted the space next to her and went through the instructions on how to turn natural elements into fine jewelry. By the end of the day they had a score each of adornments. Tlonna wrapped them in a tunic and stored them away in the bottom of her saddle bags.

Miazie yawned and tugged her thick cloak around her tighter. Ryun began to nod off and shook himself.

"Do you see a place to make camp?" Miazie asked, squinting at him through the cold fog.

"No, it's all barren, miserable, tainted flat-lands, princess. Trust me, I've kept an eye out."

Smiling, the Belau pulled her most recent map out and studied it in the moonlight. The last sighting of the camp Alchemian was about thirty leagues from their present position. From her last account of the race, Miazie had discovered that they moved in an octagonal path. This would make them only about twenty-five leagues away. Tucking the map away in her wide sleeves, she looked over as Ryun tugged at her.

"Look over there. We could camp in that small grove," the man said eagerly.

"Excellent."

The two rode over to the clump of trees and set up their tents. They did not even light a fire before they fell, exhausted, into their sleeping furs.

Black snow fell silently around them.

Tlonna woke with a start. Shadows played across her and Losolin's face from the window. The male next to her was nearly off the bed edge and was starting to fall before Tlonna gently pulled him back on. Smiling, she pushed his hair away from his face and fell asleep once again.

The day dawned gray and the taint was still falling from the sky. Losolin sighed peacefully and drank from his mug. Tlonna smiled at him and sat back in her chair. They spent part of the day in shops, haggling with merchants for the best price possible to sell their natural jewelry. As afternoon approached, the elves headed toward the castle. The king greeted them warmly, though he looked irritated.

"Have we come at a bad time, your highness?" Losolin asked as a servant took his cloak.

"No, no. And Demetrius, please. Just call me Demetrius. I have just been dealing with one of my dukes. One of my city guards caught him sneaking around your inn last night. When questioned, he admitted he was trying to capture you and your friend, Miazie. Where is she?"

"She left for Alchemian yesterday. Why was he trying to capture us?" Tlonna replied, sharing a look with Losolin.

"I don't know. Probably afraid of you. Afraid of losing his power and rank to those better and more qualified of the position. It doesn't matter that you rule another kingdom, he just sees the power, and worries. He's an idiot." King Demetrius shook his head angrily. "Alchemian, you said? Are they supposed to know what this godforsaken catastrophe about?"

"Catastrophe?" Losolin asked, frowning.

"This damn black snow. It's unnatural and putting my people into riot mode," Demetrius said, opening a door and gesturing the elves into the room.

Tlonna looked sidelong at Losolin and shrugged. "It is the taint."

"The taint?" Demetrius asked, frowning as he took his seat.

"Aye," Tlonna replied, following suit. "Seer Astinus prophesied that snow turning black and winter being long and bitter marked the beginning of the doom of Nymyños unless an elf

Magin...me...destroyed Midian. It is called the taint."

Demetrius stared at her, expressionless. Finally he expelled a breath with force. "Soo...Miazie went to Alchemian to find a way to help you destroy Midian and thus stop this damnable taint?"

"No, Miazie went to Alchemian to understand a prophecy," Losolin said.

"Prophecy," Demetrius replied blankly.

"Aye," Tlonna said.

After an uncomfortable silence, the human slapped his hand on the table. "All right. We've got prophecy, black snow, sneaking dukes, and doom. My kind of day. I take it you're here about the men I promised?"

Uncertain, Tlonna nodded.

"Great," Demetrius said, "that is something I understand. Come, let's get started."

"Today?" Tlonna asked, incredulous.

"Today, right now. I've nothing better to do today anyway. Besides it'll keep those generals on their toes for a while," the king gestured aimlessly. "I do have one more question for you though. A rumor I heard, and I'm curious."

"All right," Tlonna said slowly.

"I heard elves are so light they can walk on snow. Is that true?"

Tlonna glanced at Losolin. "Yes..."

"Wonderful. Even tainted snow?"

Tlonna could not hold her tongue. "Yes, King Demetrius...how is that you have such a free schedule?"

The man laughed. "Well, once I dealt with Duke Byron, I wasn't really in the mood to do much else. And as this *taint* is stopping most people from working, there's not much else I can do right now, until they snap and start rioting."

"Oh." Tlonna chewed her lip. "How do you want to choose the men?"

Demetrius leaned back in his chair and said, "This is my records room. In here I have the records of every man in my army, written down by my own personal scribe. A very fine hand she has, very fine. Aletta! Come here my dear!"

A plump young girl rushed into the room holding a quill in her ink stained hands. "Yes, my king?"

"Aletta, these are the elves I told you about. They need to see the records of the army. Can you get the key?"

"Yes my king. Right away."

The girl rushed out of the room and was heard pounding down the hall. Soon she came back with a ladder and key in hand. Aletta situated the ladder against a large cabinet and gingerly climbed upward. She inserted the key into a lock and shoved one of the tall doors open. After climbing back down, the girl handed the key to the king, curtseyed awkwardly, and left.

"She is not fit for much, but she is faithful and knows her letters well. My advisor says I should get a pretty dame to replace her, but finding one with Aletta's talent is not easy. Besides, since my wife died, I find myself not wanting women as I once did. My son says I am mad," Demetrius pulled out a stack of stiff parchment from the cabinet. "Here we are."

Tlonna took the first piece and scanned it. 'Brady Marshals: position: cavalry lancer; age: twenty seven; status: unmarried, one son; years: eleven' It is very detailed, it will help a lot. Thank you Demetrius, may we beg a few hours alone with the records?"

"Of course. Call me if you need anything and Aletta is in the next room," the king departed.

As the hours passed, Tlonna and Losolin poured over the records and tried to determine those best fit.

"Maybe we should have a different test. One where we met the soldier face to face," Losolin suggested after reading his one hundred and thirteenth page.

"Maybe, but remember there is about four thousand men. That would be two thousand for each of us."

"Well, we could take the rest of our stay to choose and train them all at once." Losolin said.

"What are you thinking?" Tlonna put down her page and looked at him.

"What if we had each man fight us, personally? Whoever does best is recruited until we have one thousand men. We could use training weapons, and no magic of course, I do not think any of them have Maginic powers."

"That is a lot of work," Tlonna said, skeptical.

"Aye, but it would be good for us to keep active, and we would know what sort of training the men have," Losolin countered.

Tlonna glanced down at the paper she held in her hands.

After mulling over Losolin's idea for a while, she smiled. "That is what we will do. I like it. We need to find Demetrius, and have Aletta put away the records," Tlonna said.

Losolin grinned and shook his mess of papers into a semi decent stack. The elves alerted the scribe that they were leaving. She told them where to find the king.

"I don't see why that wouldn't work. It will take a while. Each round could be oh...say...thirty seconds. You could both go through a platoon a day with breaks and the preparation," King Demetrius stretched his arms.

"When can we start?" Tlonna yawned and scooted down in the hard oak chair.

"Tomorrow, I will call in the first regiment. They are the highest rank I have. They fight with swords and lances," Demetrius stood.

"All right, Losolin and I will put the practice weapons together unless you have some we could use."

"Uh...yeah, in the practice yard. Find the servant boy, his name is...Pok or something odd like that," the king shook his head "Tomorrow morning?"

The elves nodded.

"See you tomorrow morning," Demetrius said, and left the room.

Tlonna and Losolin found the servant Pok the next morning and followed him to practice yard.

"Here ye go. How many do ye need?" the red-headed boy asked them.

"As many as you have," Losolin inspected the thin bundle of hollow reeds in his hand. "These will leave some nasty welts and bruises, Tlonna. Are you sure you are up to this?"

Tlonna nodded as Pok bowed before her, a nerve in his cheek betraying his fear. "Here is all of 'em. Do ye need anything else?"

"No, thank you," Tlonna picked up the pile of wasters and headed out into the yard.

Already, men were filing into the yard and standing apprehensively. Tlonna and Losolin put the weapons on the ground then selected two for themselves.

"A woman? An elf woman is our challenger, and her little elfie lover? Come on!"

The man who had spoken stepped forward haughtily and grabbed up a practice blade. With an almost lazy gesture, he swept it toward Tlonna's face. She leaned backward and then rammed her entire body into his midriff. The human slammed into the grand, the waster bouncing away from his surprised fingers. He groaned as he rolled to his feet, rubbing a big hand across his belly.

Tlonna folded her arms and glared down at him. "I suggest that the next time you go up against an elf and or woman, you be prepared," she growled, handing him his wooden blade.

"Well, an elf, maybe, but a woman? No. No human woman is going to best me. Trust me."

Irritated, Tlonna smacked her weapon against his and then lunged to the left. Caught off guard, the man whirled around as fast as his muscled bulk would allow and swiped out. The Magin ducked, danced back a step, went into a crouch, and launched herself at the man. With a cry of triumph, she smashed the wood into his shoulder and landed in a puff of snow. Silence seemed to pulse in the practice yard as she turned to face the human, who was just regaining his feet again.

"What is your name?"

"Hyden Gath. Captain of the First Regiment," the man said through gritted teeth.

"Hyden, my name is Tlonna Ewôsdírn, Magin Queen and commander of the army you might join."

"So I hear," the human grumbled, rubbing his neck where a fiery welt was rising.

Tlonna merely raised an eyebrow at him and then turned to address the whole group that was assembled.

"You have been informed as to what you are here for, yes?"

There was a mumbled assurance from the men.

Fighting back her annoyance, Tlonna pointed at Losolin and then herself. "You will fight either Losolin or me. Two of you come forward, grab a waster and come to one of us. We will fight until one of us is down with a 'killing blow', or thirty seconds has passed. Come forward."

Two men stepped forward hesitantly as Hyden shuffled out of the way, following Tlonna's pointing finger to a corner of the yard.

Losolin moved his head away from a swing and 'stabbed' the man in the stomach. The soldier went down and was instructed to a corner. It was near evening and only five men were left to fight. Tlonna clasped hands with her opponent and sent him to a different corner. The elves accepted a cup of water from King Demetrius who had come earlier to watch. Now the entire group of the elf's companions, the occupants of the castle and a few curious nobles were gathered in the practice yard. The soldiers were placed in two corners, those who were going to be accepted, and those rejected.

Tlonna put her cup on the ground and swung her practice sword. "Who is next?"

The elf met a bearishly large man and dodged a thrust wearily. Pain shot up her arm as it connected with reeds. Sweat poured down her face making trails through the dust. With a half-hearted swing, the Magin slashed the man across the thigh and sent him sprawling. She shook hands with him and sent him to the right corner.

The man joined his comrades and was given back patting and hand shaking. Tlonna drank from her cup and watched Losolin for a while. He was contending with a bald man. The soldier gave the elf a welt on the shoulder and received one in return on the face. Sucking in her breath, Tlonna saw blood trickle down Losolin's arm. That shoulder had been a favorite spot for the soldiers. Numerous welts were piled on top of each other and had finally split the skin. The man received another blow to the head and went down on his knees. Losolin sent him to the left corner and gestured to Tlonna to choose an opponent.

A man with a long scar on his arm picked up a wooden sword and hefted it in the air. Compared to him, it looked like kindling. His grin was arrogant and he and Tlonna circled for many moments. Then he slashed left and right with such quickness that it caught the elf by surprise. She grunted as the welts rose on her arm and attacked him with renewed fury. Tlonna's waster whistled through the air, making the large man back away quickly. The female blocked a thrust from the soldier and then sent him sprawling with a punch to the gut and a slice across the belly.

He was sent to the left corner.

The elves faced the remaining three and sent two to the right, one to the left. Coughing from the dust, Tlonna and Losolin approached the right corner and addressed them.

"You all fought bravely and well, but you are needed here. I am sorry, or happy whichever the case may be, you will not be in my army," some faces fell; others rose with the news. The elves shook hands with all the men and dismissed them. Hyden glared at her, though he smiled to his comrades and sauntered off. As they walked to the other group, the looks they saw were excited and happy. None of the soldiers looked downcast at the news they were about to receive.

"I am glad to accept you into my ranks. I hope you are pleased. Congratulations men."

With her words, hooting and hollering men surrounded the two elves. Losolin was nearly knocked to the ground when they all decided to clap him on the back. Music drifted across the now dark sky as the new recruits met the old and celebrated.

Miazie hurriedly dried and dressed in fur lined leather breaches and a tunic made of thick wool. The Belau looked around to make sure Ryun wasn't in sight and breathed a sigh of relief. The night had been freezing; leaving the tents crusted with frost and made their breath appear before them. Miazie thanked the gods and the spirits for the clothes she had bought. The woman shivered and trudged back to the camp area. Ryun looked up from his position before the fire and smiled.

"A bit chilly this morning," the hunter rubbed his hands together and motioned for the Belau to sit.

"To say the least. The water is freezing. I am thankful I have winter clothes. The weather will be treacherous out here especially. I hope we find Alchemian soon. My maps say they should be just twenty-five leagues from here. I think we can make it there in less than a week," Miazie accepted a piece of venison from the hunter.

"Aye, the deep winter should be here in about a week too. I suggest we push on," the hunter doused the fire and pulled his fur cloak over his thin shoulders.

Miazie nodded and pushed her frozen tent further into its bag on Kaia's saddle. A sharp gust of freezing wind blew icicles off the trees and pelted the pair. Gritting her teeth, the Belau mounted her mare and huddled within her cloak the Cyree had given her. Even with the special abilities the cloak had, it did not ward off this biting chill.

"Look at that Lady," Ryun said a few hours later, pointing north. "What can you see up above?"

"It looks like a camp, maybe it's Alchemian! I wonder if they moved out of their ring," Miazie pondered.

"Let's take a look," Ryun kicked his steed into a slow gallop while Miazie followed.

Firelight revealed a well-ordered camp with guards posted outside of the makeshift gate. "Halt! Who are you?" a voice boomed down at the pair.

"We are travelers looking for the city Alchemian. Is this it?" Ryun raised his hands in a gesture of peace.

"No, this is not Alchemian. Stay where you are," the man disappeared and then reappeared at the gate. Three other guards followed him out armed with Zeynuwnian katans.

"Go! Princess, go!" Ryun shouted, and grabbed her reins.

Surprised, Miazie let him pull Kaia into a full-tilt gallop. Glancing behind her, she saw the four men pulling horses out from behind the wall, shouting to others. "Ryun!"

"Ride!" the hunter yelled, releasing her reins to mind his own.

Miazie ducked low to Kaia's back and urged the mare to fly. Together, she and Ryun veered around a large boulder and prayed for speed. Black snow spiraled up like miniature storms beneath the horses' hooves, betraying their passage. Terrified, Miazie looked back again and saw several riders advancing on them. Their horses had not been working all day, as Kaia and Ryun's horse had been.

"Faster!" Miazie cried to both Kaia and Ryun.

The hunter bared his teeth and, with a freezing hand, reached up grab his bow. Thankful he had strung it before going near the camp, he nocked it, and twisted around in his saddle. With a hunter's skill, he loosed, and reloaded before his first target hit the ground. Miazie cursed as their antagonists drew bows as well.

Ryun picked off two more before the dark-clad enemies loosed a volley. Miazie cried out as Kaia screamed, and fell. She heard Ryun's bellow of denial before she slammed into the ground, her horse landing beside her.

Robed men looked out from their dark cowls, their shadowed eyes glittering as Miazie opened her eyes. Groaning, she tried to sit up but found her arms bound behind her back and her ankles tied together. A cold hand gripped her chin and turned her head.

"She is fine, a little bruised, but otherwise unharmed," the hand's owner said loudly, and released her face.

Stunned and confused, the Belau tried again to rise and this time was shoved back. "Stop squirming."

Glaring at the man who had spoken, she spat at his face. The men around her laughed, and someone hauled her up.

"Untie her ankles so that she can walk. I'm not going to carry the wench to meet the general."

Once her ankles were freed, Miazie tried to lunge away, but strong hands gripped her arms and she was being half pulled, half carried out of the dark tent. The sky was dark as she was dragged through muddy streets lined with more dark tents. Midnight-clad men moved everywhere with the unhurried grace of warriors, black leather armor shining dully in the moonlights. Seconds later, Miazie was shoved into an enormous tent and someone kicked her in the back of the knees so that she fell forward ungracefully.

Getting to her knees, Miazie blinked at Ryun, whose bloody countenance beseeched her from a few feet away. Giving him an encouraging smile, she was suddenly grappled from behind, as was Ryun.

The man holding Miazie grabbed a fistful of her hair and yanked her head up, putting cold steel to her neck. By Ryun's grunt, the Belau knew his handler had done the same.

"General, these two came to our gate, ran, and killed four of our men. What would you like done with them?"

Miazie rolled her eyes down to get a glimpse of the man sitting on the dais before her. She could see only the top of a midnight blue cowl, and above, two slim sword hilts wrapped in alternating sky blue and black material. Above the hilts and the back of a carved high back chair, was a two-poled standard. On a field of black, two curved swords with the slim hilts of katans crossed. A jolt of fear ran up Miazie's spine as she recognized the standard.

"Take the woman to my chambers. The man...take him to Captain Hirshono," the man on the dais said after a slight pause.

His voice was soft thunder which rolled through the tent and its occupants like a wave of power. He did not speak loudly, but Miazie cringed nonetheless. Before she could react further, the man holding her hair yanked her to her feet and started dragging away. She was shoved back out into the cold night. This time, she studied the strolling warriors as they passed, giving her cursory glances. Each of them wore at least two of katans, some more. The man grabbed Miazie by the elbow and herded her through the makeshift streets to the back of the village where a massive dark blue tent was pitched, guarded by at least a dozen of the silent soldiers.

"Get in there," the man said, shoving Miazie into the tent.

He followed her in, pushing her to the very back. Sections were hidden by softly swaying layers of inner tent. The Belau stumbled down the little hallway to where the soldier forced her. He pushed her into a smaller section that was nearly filled with a massive wardrobe. Two young men knelt on each side of the doorway, their heads bowed, curtains of black hair hiding their faces.

"Colin, Darius, get this woman ready for General Damon. Now!"

The men leapt to their feet to reveal identical faces, which were full of fear. "Yes Captain Haiwe."

The soldier, Haiwe, tossed Miazie to the floor and left the little room. The young men helped her to her feet and introduced themselves.

"I am Colin, and this is my brother, Darius. We are General Damon's personal servants. We are proud to serve a man as brave and honorable as he. You will find great pleasure in serving General Damon, for he is both wise and strong."

Miazie stared at the twins, her fear warring with her worry for Ryun.

"This is a camp of assassins! How can you serve such a monster as the leader of murderous villains with pride?" she hissed.

Darius looked stunned. "We do not serve willingly. We were taken by force and made into slaves by General Damon and his men."

Colin shushed his brother and opened the wardrobe doors. Inside were a number of midnight blue garments, black leather armor, and a few sleeping robes. The man opened a drawer at the bottom and lifted out a folded robe the color of the summer sky. Miazie watched him shut the drawer and then the wardrobe until she felt Darius's fingers tugging her tunic out of her belt.

"What are you doing?" she growled, slapping at his hand.

"We must get you ready for General Damon."

The realization of her purpose hit Miazie like a physical blow.

She was too scared to stop the brothers from undressing her completely. Colin guided her down the hallway into another littler section and motioned for her to get into the tub that filled it. As Darius poured hot water over her, Colin washed her hair and combed it. After the bath, she was given the silk robe and walked to yet another room, this one larger than the others and shielded better. It was Damon's bedroom.

Darius gave her a small smile, "You must now wait for General Damon. He should be here soon."

With that, the twins left and Miazie sat on the edge of the bed to await her doom.

Tlonna sighed and lay back in her chair. Firelight danced before her eyes as the entertainers bounded and leapt across the courtyard. Wistfully, the elf wondered if celebrations at Blackhaven were anything similar. She could imagine elves dancing and twirling in beautiful dresses that were so precious to her race, so Miazie had told her. Thoughts of her friend darkened Tlonna's mood for a moment. Soon the shadow removed itself when a soldier came up and asked to dance with her. Smiling, the Magin was led out into the middle of the courtyard.

The man, who introduced himself as Jeremiah Took, led her in a traditional dance. Tlonna was swung around on her toes and then lifted into the air. Her feet touched bare ground and she was twirled around again. Jeremiah said the dance spoke of wind that danced and flitted through an ancient castle. Tlonna nodded and concentrated on not stepping on his toes. She was lifted into the air once more and she laughed. The soldier stared at her, his eyes glazed over slightly.

"Your laugh, it sounds like sweet twinkling bells. I have not heard that in years," he said as he caught her from a swing.

"When did you ever hear it?" Tlonna asked as she swung out again.

"I used to live in Arseninis, then Shadowsoul came through and destroyed all the elves. I moved here and the same thing happened. That's why I wanted to be part of your army so bad. My wife was an elf. She was murdered. My daughter is a half-elf, so she was able to slip away."

"I am so sorry Jeremiah. Where is your daughter now?" Tlonna grabbed his hand as he brought her back in.

"Syakblae is home. She lives with me. We found each other about a year afterward," Jeremiah caught her as the song ended and bowed.

"I am glad you have her, are you sure you want to leave?" Tlonna asked.

"As I said, Princess, I want to avenge my beloved Pertu. Syakblae is twenty-five now, old enough to be on her own for a while, and she has a beau who is not in the army to keep her company."

Tlonna stepped away from the dancers and turned to meet Jeremiah eye to eye. "I hate to ask you this, Jeremiah, but can you tell me how...how your wife was killed?"

The human blinked, looked at the sky beyond Tlonna's shoulder, and then back at the elf. "You want to know how he kills so that you can begin to know your enemy."

Tlonna nodded.

After another moment, Jeremiah spoke. "He grabbed her, turned her around so that he could see her eyes, and stabbed her in the back. He watched as she died. I could do nothing. He was holding me down somehow, with his magic. He stared at her, almost reverently, as she died. When she had, he carved out her entrails and threw them out the door. He looked at me, then left.

"His bonds did not release me until the next day," Jeremiah said quietly, staring up at the sky. "When the black snow began falling, I knew something was about to happen. Something pivotal. It marked the beginning of the end, whether for us or for him, I want to be there."

Tlonna felt a twisting knife of grief for the human before her. "I am so sorry, Jeremiah. I cannot imagine your pain."

He looked at her, his eyes tear-bright. "My lady, I would never ask you to. It was eleven years ago, and still I can see as though it were happening right now. Please, may I be excused?"

"Of course, Jeremiah. Of course."

Tlonna found Losolin lounging in a chair and related Jeremiah's story to him.

"How horrible," Losolin said when she finished. "I could not move on if I saw that happen to you. I would die, right then and there."

"Now we know one thing more than we did." Tlonna said,

grabbing Losolin's hand.

"What?"

"Midian needs to see the death happen. He cannot handle just knowing that the death happened, he needs to see it. He needs to feel that power over his victims, to let them know *he* was the one who ended their life. If he does not get that satisfaction, he will not be happy."

"So?"

Tlonna grabbed her consort and swung him around to face her.

"Midian is insane. He killed his own parents for spirit's sake! If we can somehow make him think that he has not slaughtered the race of elves, he will make a mistake. He will do something rash and then we will get him. He needs to know that he can commit genocide successfully or he will not be able to feel safe in his own power. We need to trick him into thinking he failed. That is his weakness."

Losolin's hand pushed her away lightly as the new song demanded, and then brought her back in, their hands linking automatically. "Yes, but that does not help us in raising an army, Tlonna, which is our main goal. We cannot defeat Midian with trickery. He knows how many elves, and innocent people, he has murdered. A few elves popping up here and there may concern him, but we will still lose if we do not have the manpower to overcome his armies. We still have thousands of men to train and recruit," Losolin replied.

"We still need information Losolin, things we can use against him. We do not know how many soldiers Midian commands. We do not know his range of weapons, or his soldier's skill with them. We need to have tricks up our sleeves that will give us the edge," Tlonna said.

She sighed and stepped out of the dance, pulling him with her. "I am too tired to do any more celebrating. I am going to bed. You?"

"No. I like watching happy people. It is a nice change."

Tlonna released him and bussed him lightly on the lips. "I will see you later, then," she said, and went back to the inn.

Losolin had barely taken his seat again when a young woman rushed up to him and begged him for a dance.

By the end of the night, he was thanking the spirits he had the heightened endurance of a Magin and elf.

Tlonna straightened her nightgown and sat down at the desk. Opening Veries Gurgen's journal, she lost herself in the words. So consumed was she that Tlonna did not hear the chamber door open.

Aidyn stood quietly in the doorway and watched Tlonna work. When the elf looked up and saw him, he smiled faintly and approached her.

"I did not want to disturb you my lady. I just wanted to speak with you in private," the assassin elf moved silently to the window and looked out on the empty, tainted street.

"What do you need to speak with me about?" Tlonna closed her book and swiveled in her chair to face Aidyn's back.

After a minute, the assassin's shoulders slumped.

"There is something I did not tell you yesterday. Something that weighs heavily on my mind, and my heart. I feared telling you at all, but I think with your present memory issues, it might not be so hard to bear."

Frowning, Tlonna waited silently.

"One of the main reasons I left Blackhaven was to tell you of the condition the city is in. The other cities and villages in Blackhaven Forest were not attacked as the capital was, but Midian has freed his demons on them. The people have fled or remain under the savage claws of our enemy. Many have died; more are injured and cannot receive help because the healers have been detained, killed or otherwise. Yayènia and Suneelo left out a part in the letter they sent to you, fearing your hasty return unprepared.

"They had planned on traveling to the other cities to aid the people in revolts. They feared you would return in order to stop them, as only you could, so they did not inform you. It is not as crazy as it sounds, even alone they could do it. But on their way to a village less than two days' ride from Blackhaven City, they were taken. An entire company came upon them and succeeded in capturing them.

"They took out almost half the company, but there was just too many. When I left, they were hanging by their wrists from a balcony on the castle. They are strong, but no one can endure that for long."

Aidyn finished talking, still facing the window. Tlonna stared at his back.

"Suneelo is Losolin's half brother, is he not?"

"*Aiya*," Aidyn whispered.

"Why do the people living underground not do something? Why do they sit idle while above them their city is overrun and their fellow citizens are persecuted and forced into slavery? Is there not an entire city population sitting beneath the castle?" Tlonna asked angrily.

Aidyn finally turned. "Aye, there is, but they are scared, leaderless, surviving on quarter rations, and without an army. They are civilians, elderly, and sick as well. Most of their children have died from disease. Depression weighs heavily on every heart. They would not survive, Tlonna. It would be a massacre."

"Is not my father and mother there with them? Are they not Magins? Are they not leaders? Can they not begin to train every able-bodied person down there in the art of combat? Why do they sit idly by, waiting for their salvation to come from a person they believe dead, when they could do so much to help themselves? Midian does not have all of his forces in the city. They are roaming Nymyños, looking for me."

"Do not presume to think I have not asked these questions, Tlonna. Nor that Yayènia, Erdwyf, Ghealan, and Suneelo have not. Even your father, the king, argues with the people about these same questions. Your mother and the citizens protest, saying they are not strong enough, they are not soldiers, they are innocents that must wait for those willing to risk their lives for their sake."

"When Blackhaven City fell, where was the army?" Tlonna asked.

"Defending her. They were outnumbered ten to one with one Magin to every five of Midian's. Thousands died defending the city, Tlonna, do not think we allowed Midian's forces to walk in unhindered. I was at the wall with Yayènia and Ghealan when it fell. I watched as the man I had stood next to for several days was blasted by magic. When I tried to pick him up to take him to a healer, his flesh fell off into my hands, clean off the bone. He was still alive. I was there, watching hundreds of soldiers die, trying to defend their city.

"I remember having to call in reinforcements to pull Yayènia and Ghealan from the wall. They would not leave it. I remember watching the Magin run up to the wall where we stood, stick his hands out, and take seven arrows in the chest. The archers were too late. The only reason I was able to get the commanders away was that a boulder-sized chunk of wall had rolled over Ghealan's legs and broken them. Only then would Yayènia and he vacate the area.

"I remember that night as clearly as if it had happened yesterday. We fought until almost every single one of our soldiers was dead or dying. Thousands, Tlonna, *thousands* died defending Blackhaven City. Nearly every weapon-bearing person was killed as they fled. The only fortunate thing was that Midian's forces did not see the evacuation of the civilians into the underground tunnels. I believe only five hundred or so soldiers made it back, and of those, only two hundred and forty-six survived their wounds.

"Perhaps our men would have fought better had they not been shown the skinless corpse of their beloved princess the evening before."

Tlonna stood and took the other elf's hands. "I cannot even begin to fathom the horrors of that time, Aidyn. I do not pretend to want to. I am sorry you had to experience that, but what do you expect me to do about it? I am already doing as much as I can."

"I do not expect you to do anything, I just wanted to inform you," Aidyn replied.

Tlonna nodded once and then said, "What do you think will happen to Yayènia and Suneelo?"

The assassin sighed. "I do not know. Knowing those two, I want to believe they can escape somehow, but they were very badly beaten. Midian had their arms broken so that they could not pull themselves up."

Tlonna gasped. "They are hanging by their wrists, and their arms are broken?"

Aidyn nodded wordlessly.

"Dear gods," Tlonna said, closing her eyes.

"*Aiya,*" Aidyn said again, huskily.

After a long silence, Tlonna joined Aidyn at the window. The Magin and assassin looked out at the taint, at the sparkling moons casting deceptively colorful shadows on the empty street. After a moment, Aidyn glanced down at Tlonna and watched as a tear fell from her chin.

"Ah, love," he said and wrapped his arms around her.

Tlonna put her head on the taller elf's shoulder and let silent sobs take her. A minute later, she withdrew wiping her eyes with the back of her hand.

"You seem to do very well with that, have we done that before?" she asked with a shaky laugh.

Aidyn smiled. "Sometimes even a great leader must lean on her friends, Tlonna. No one, not even an elf, can bear the lives of thousands upon their shoulders, and do it alone."

Tlonna nodded.

"We will find a way to win, Tlonna, do not fear that," Aidyn said quietly. "And never hesitate to come to me, or any of the people that follow you, if you need to unload. Now, I will depart for my room, and I bid you good night."

"Good night, Aidyn," Tlonna said as the assassin left.

Aidyn shut his door and locked it behind him. Sighing, the elf picked up his beloved recurve longbow and maintenance kit. Running his hands along its smooth, gray shaft, he inspected it. The willow vine wrapped around the center for grip was starting to fray. Cutting it carefully, he peeled it away from the wood. Taking a new vine out, he wrapped it around and tucked the ends in tightly. Removing a bottle from his kit, he pulled out the stopper. Rubbing the liquid sealing wax along the vine, he watched it dry. One of the silver caps on the end of the bow was slightly tarnished. He frowned at it. After polishing it, Aidyn waxed the string and tested it.

In one smooth action, he let loose a practice arrow. With a thud, the arrow buried itself into a tiny hole on the wall the size of a gold piece. Nodding again, the elf put his bow back and retrieved his dark cloak from a peg on the wall. Walking briskly out of his room, Aidyn slipped out of the inn.

The streets were empty, as they had been for days. The taint was knee-deep on humans. Aidyn stepped off the inn's porch and onto the snow. His feet made faint imprints as he turned down the street and set off at a jog.

Midian paced the throne room anxiously; Kelus had not yet returned.

It was another half hour before his demon's shuffling steps could be heard in the hall outside the throne room. When he entered, Midian pivoted to glare at his minion.

"It is about time, Kelus, where have you been?"

"I have been ssearching the groundss like you ordered my

lord. There iss no ssign of the elvess anywhere except the two you captured, and they barely cling to life."

"I told you to be quick about it! I know there are more of them out there, sneaking about my kingdom like the rats. They do not know when to accept defeat," Midian growled, striding by Kelus and out of the room.

The Darkwight hastened after his king, wary of the rage that wafted from the human. When they reached what used to be the formal reception hall, Midian yanked open the set of balcony doors and glared down at the two elves hanging below.

Yayènia glared up at him from between her mangled arms. Though blood caked her face and black snow littered her golden hair, she still looked regal. Her ice blue eyes narrowed as she stared up at the human and demon above her. "Do you think you have won, Midian?" she said coldly.

"Have I not?" Midian replied sarcastically. "Perhaps I had mistaken your situation as one that benefited you."

"You may have defeated us, human, but you have not defeated our people. They lie in wait, waiting for the opportune moment to strike at you, and they will bring you down."

Midian slammed his booted foot through the spaces in the balcony railing and into Yayènia's face. The elf howled in pain as her body jerked down, pulling on her broken arms.

"You will learn before the end, bitch, that even immortals can die," Midian whispered.

"Then perhaps you should not seek it, Midian," Yayènia shot back, spitting blood as she spoke.

Midian grabbed Suneelo's hand and Wove. Black magic writhed from his fingers and into the elf. Suneelo, previously unconscious, woke screaming. The male jerked on his chains, screaming, blood dripping from his mouth and nose as he flailed. Midian turned his gaze on Yayènia who screamed with her husband, though in wrath and helplessness. Finally Midian withdrew his hand from Suneelo's and the elf stopped writhing, though he continued to twitch.

"Remember, High Commander, you are not the only one in danger," Midian crooned.

Once the human and Kelus had left, Yayènia turned her tear-stained face away from Suneelo's pain-wracked body.

"Nia," he croaked.

"I am so sorry, my love, so sorry!" Yayènia sobbed, still looking away.

"Do not...be..." Suneelo coughed, spraying blood. "I have an...idea."

Yayènia waited.

"Would you...survive the fall?"

The High Commander stared at her husband. She slowly turned her gaze downward to the dead courtyard over one hundred feet below.

"I...I do not know," she finally said. "But you would not, and I will not leave you."

Suneelo laughed horribly, "What can you...do for me, my heart...other than live?"

"No! No, I will not leave you! I do not give a thousand gods' damnation what you say, I will not leave you!" Yayènia cried.

The male looked at his wife. She stared at him, her eyes brimming with tears.

"I love you, Yayènia, more than life itself," he said, and swung.

"NO!" Yayènia screamed as he careened into her.

Suneelo latched onto her with his legs and slammed his forehead into her hand until he nearly lost consciousness again. Yayènia continued to scream, fighting him. Blood dripped from his torn head as he smashed her hand between the obsidian balcony and his forehead. Her hand finally broke. The female shrieked as she swung downward, still held tightly between his knees. They locked gazes for a mere second.

"SUNEELO!" Yayènia screamed as he wrenched his body down.

Flesh ripped from bone as her other hand was torn from the iron cuff that held her. She fell, grasping for his leg, but missed.

Yayènia hit the ground hard, her legs snapping as they collided with the winter ground, black snow billowing up around her. The elf curled into a ball of agony, trembling. Tears and blood coursed down her face as she buried it in the snow, weeping.

It took almost an hour for her to uncurl and force herself to look up. Suneelo hung listlessly, though he watched her. Yayènia flopped onto her back, crying out in grief and torment.

"I will come back for you," she said, though she could only

muster a whisper.

Suneelo continued to watch her.

Finally, using her shoulders, Yayènia burrowed into the snow. It took her almost three hours to move fifty yards. When she reached the marble statue, she leaned against the hidden door, panting. It took the rest of her strength to push her entire body against it to open the door a crack before it was yanked open behind her. The warrior tumbled into the dark entrance.

A dwarf cursed and shoved the door shut. "High Commander!" he shouted, dropping his torch to kneel beside Yayènia.

The elf coughed out a glob of blood. "Suneelo..." she said, and lost consciousness.

She woke a few hours later in the infirmary, to the worried faces of a dozen people. Erdwyf, Ghealan, Dietirin, and eight of her closest warriors and officers.

"Yayènia!" Erdwyf gasped.

"Suneelo!" Yayènia shouted, reaching out.

Both her arms and legs were splinted, her hands wrapped into useless mitts. Her nose had also been reset, from when Midian had broken it with his foot. It seemed every inch of her body was wrapped, stitched, or splinted.

"I am sorry, Nia, he has not yet come," Dietirin said sadly, his crown resting on the table by her bed.

He was there as a friend, not as a king.

"Of course he has not yet come!" she screamed, writhing against her body's incapacitation. "He sacrificed himself to save me! He is still up there! We have to save him!"

Ghealan placed a hand on either side of her face. "Yayènia, we will get him back, but right now you have to heal. You are no use to us broken, we will need you," he said hoarsely.

The High Commander glared at her second before bursting into furious tears. "He is dying, Ghealan," she whispered, "he will not live the night. Dietirin, can you heal my bones?"

The Magin King's face tightened. "I am no Healer, Yayènia. You know that."

"May the gods damn you!" Yayènia bellowed, attempting to stand.

The twelve surrounded her, holding her back. The warrior roared as she flung herself back and forth on the bed. Pain lanced up and down her body, but something else as well. Suddenly, her left leg jerked up, the splint breaking, then the right. Use returned to her arms as well and she shoved the restraining people aside. Leaping out of the bed, she landed hard on her knees.

"Yayènia!" Erdwyf screamed, trying to hold her best friend back.

"You would do the same for Ghealan!" she yelled at Erdwyf, wrenching away.

Erdwyf let her go. Yayènia crawled halfway across the dirt floor of the infirmary before collapsing. The others rushed to help her up.

"How is this possible?" one of her officers, Sargotarh asked.

"I do not know," Dietirin replied, staring at Yayènia.

"Gah!" Yayènia cried as she stood shakily. "My weapons," she growled, holding out her bloody mitts.

As one of the soldiers unwrapped her hands, another ran to her room to fetch her weapons. He returned with her twin katans, her bow and full quiver, and her belt of daggers.

"How do you have these? They were left in Tiena Manor, when we were captured," Yayènia gasped as she placed her weapons in their various spots.

"We retrieved them," the soldier said simply.

Yayènia turned around carefully and took a hesitant step, and then another. When she was almost out of the infirmary, Dietirin called to her. He wore his crown.

"You are brave, Yayènia, but you will not go alone."

Ghealan moved to stand with the king, as did the others. Erdwyf folded her arms across her chest as she turned to look at Yayènia.

The High Commander stared at the dozen people arrayed before her. Finally, she said, "Erd, you had better trade pants for skirts."

Nodding, Erdwyf rushed from the room as the others helped Yayènia limp out. They met at the door, bristling with weapons. They crawled through the tunnel of tainted snow Yayènia had carved with her shoulders. Though still in tremendous pain, the female forced herself to move toward the one person she loved most in all the world. Blood still dripped from numerous places, and her limbs still felt broken, but they worked, and she used them.

They reached the castle and burst through the door. Weapons whistling through the air, the thirteen warriors slaughtered the demons posted in the once grand ballroom. They sprinted through the hall, killing anyone and anything in their way. They did not look around, nor could they as the hall was pitch dark. Reaching the stairs, Ghealan hoisted Yayènia into his arms and took the steps four at a time.

The thirteen battled their way to the third floor before Midian appeared. Shock and fear registered on his face before he spun his hands in the air. Dietirin stepped forward in front of the other dozen and met black with red power. Darkwights and goblins, traitorous men and enslaved soldiers attacked the others.

With a howl, Dietirin shoved his hands forward, drew his sword, and rushed Midian. As the human recoiled from the explosive Weave the king had thrown at him, Dietirin's sword sliced through his forearm. Midian roared in pain as the elf yanked the blade out of his flesh and kicked him. He was about to finish the evil Magin when Midian slashed his hands out. A wall of black power threw Dietirin back against the wall, shredding clothes and flesh. The elf king moaned as he stood. Midian had fled.

The other twelve finished off their attackers and Yayènia ran toward the reception room. The others followed. It was empty as they burst inside. Yayènia slid out onto the balcony and began hoisting up the chains that her husband hung from.

The others helped her pull Suneelo over the balcony and Dietirin severed the iron with magic. Suneelo's limp body was more broken and bloody than it had been. Midian had gotten to him. Yayènia slapped him over and over again, trying to wake her beloved.

"Yayènia! Leave him be!" Ghealan shouted, wrestling with her.

"He is alive! Suneelo! Wake up! Wake up! I came back for you! Wake up!" Yayènia screamed.

"Yes, he is alive, now leave him be!" Ghealan roared and lifted the flailing Yayènia into his arms. "Sargotarh, get him."

The elf captain gingerly picked Suneelo up and clutched him tightly against his chest.

"We cannot make it back through the castle, my king, what do we do?" Erdwyf asked.

"I can make a slide of air, but it will only last for a few

seconds," Dietirin replied, eyeing the ground below.

"If High Commander Yayènia can survive a free fall in her condition, we can survive it as well," the dwarf captain Orthak said.

"All right," the King Magin said, and stuck his hand out.

Wind whipped around the thirteen, suctioning into the center of the elf's hands. With a quiet *boom*, the air exploded outward.

"Down!" Dietirin yelled, and shoved Sargotarh over the balcony.

The elf, clutching Suneelo, flew downward on the invisible slide. The others followed him. Yayènia and Ghealan, then Erdwyf and Orthak.

"Go, my king, go!" one of the soldiers, Tarounen, shouted.

Dietirin leapt onto his slide and fell. The rest of the warriors followed him. When Sargotarh reached the bottom, the slide started to disappear. By the time Yayènia and Ghealan tumbled into Sargotarh, the slide was gone. The other ten freefell, landing hard on the ground. They dove under the snow as Midian's demons appeared on the balcony.

One of them picked up Suneelo's discarded chains and cursed loudly. Yayènia, her original adrenaline drained, crawled onto her husband's body, and lost consciousness.

The others dragged them through the tunneled snow, careful not to bump them too hard over the frozen ground.

Chapter 11
The Shitan-Kulata

Miazie started shaking as soon as the tall man entered the room. He wore midnight blue robes under black leather armor made from thick straps. His mere presence made the room seem terrifyingly small. He lowered his hood and studied her with dark brown eyes shaded by shaggy brown hair that curled about his ears and neck. His lips were thin, and twitched as his eyes roamed over her body.

"Stand up."

At the sound of his thunderous voice, Miazie leapt to obey, her limbs shaking uncontrollably.

"Take off my armor," he commanded, turning his back to her.

The Belau, with trembling fingers, undid the leather bands that were knotted down his spine. She slipped the armor off his shoulders and held it, not sure what she was to do with it. Just as she was about to ask, Darius bowed his way in and took the armor from her, his eyes averted.

General Damon turned and stared at her. He held out his arms to the side and Miazie hurried to obey the silent command. She undid the tie that was tightened around his slim waist and took off his robes, which were thickly layered and very heavy. Colin rushed in to take them from her. Miazie eyed the baggy pants that were now the only thing between the man and her. Instead of having her finish, Damon stepped up to her and ran a hand through her slick black hair. He yanked her robe open and fondled her breast, his eyes never leaving hers.

Miazie trembled, goosebumps prickling her skin. Her robe was pushed off her shoulders and onto the floor. The assassin leader shoved her onto the bed and pinned her down with a glare. Her hair was bunched beneath her shoulders, forcing her chin up awkwardly. Damon undid his trouser belt and his pants fell to the floor, pooling around his ankles. Miazie squeezed her eyes shut at the sight of his erect phallus.

The assassin joined her on the bed and trapped her wrists in a hand, holding them above her head. Without any warning, he forced himself into her until his body shuddered with pleasure, releasing his seed inside her. He pumped a few times more to release his remaining energy and then withdrew.

As he rolled onto his back, the man let go of her wrists and Miazie tried to scramble out of bed, reaching for her robe. Damon yanked her back by her hair and tossed her onto the bed next to him.

"You will stay with me until I release you. Understand?"

Miazie swallowed hard and nodded. "Y-yes."

"Good. If you try to leave, I will know, and if I don't catch you, my guards will. Now get some sleep," Damon released her hair and rolled back onto his side.

Miazie trembled shamelessly as she pulled the covers up to her chin, scooting as far away from the man as she could get.

In the middle of the night, Damon awoke Miazie and rode her again, slightly gentler, using his mouth to arouse her. When she woke in the morning, she found herself curled up next to him, their legs entwined, his organ tight against her rump. When she tried to move away, the strong arm around her waist pulled her tighter up next to him.

When Damon woke, he let her go. He had Colin pour a bath while Darius made breakfast. Miazie sat in the bedroom while the man bathed. After she had bathed in turn, Darius escorted her to yet another room and they broke their fast with eggs, bacon, and rolls. It was the first time she had seen the three men in a semi-equal appearance. It was also the first time Damon instigated a conversation.

"What is your name?"

Miazie nearly dropped her fork. "Miazie Ughtren."

"Ah...your father is Darren Ughtren, King of Anutch?"

"Yes."

"I heard a rumor that an elf cut off his balls when he ordered your execution. Did I hear right?" the man showed no pity for her father's demise at the hands of a severely brassed Tlonna.

"He had ordered both mine and hers. He deserved it. He was fond of raping women, but I am finding that that is a custom held by most leaders in the Liberated Lands," she replied acidly.

Damon set down the cup he was about to drink from. "I did not rape you. Had you said no, or stop, I would have. You said neither, nor did you try to fight back until after that fact, and even that was puny attempt."

The shock of his words rang through Miazie's mind. Before

she could think up a reply, Damon spoke again. "Your companion is safe and well. He has been told of your wellbeing also. You are both free to roam the village, but if you try to leave, you will be killed. The men will not bother you, and if they do, tell me and I will deal with them. Understand?"

"Yes."

"Do you have any questions?"

Miazie had to stop herself from snorting. Questions indeed. "You are the Shitan-Kulata? The mysterious guild of assassins?"

"Yes. I am their general. Below me are my captains, Haiwe and Hirshono, brothers from Zeynuwn. It is from that region that we adapt our skills in warfare and assassination. According to our physician, your friend, Ryun, is in good physical health and I have high hopes of training him to our art. He says he was a hunter for your father?"

"That's right. One of the best."

"Mmm...good. It is well that he is being honest with Captain Hirshono. He is not a patient man."

He was about to add something when three massive men entered the tent and Colin leapt up from the table to bow them in. Damon stood, not at all diminished by the presence of the brutes.

"General Damon," the three men bowed low and then stood straight.

"Aran, Inyias, Rayna, what news?"

The largest of the three, Aran, flicked a glance at Miazie before speaking.

"The tribe has been eliminated, General. We had three for questioning, but two of them broke their own necks and the third gave us nothing worth a cupful of spit."

"Did you bring it here?" Damon asked calmly, though Miazie thought she detected an undercurrent of temper.

"Yes, General. Shall we bring it in?"

"Immediately."

The three men exited and then reappeared moments later holding a writhing goblin between them. Damon scowled down at it as Miazie scrambled away from her chair, which was closest to the creature. Damon snatched her before she fled too far and draped a heavy arm over her shoulders.

"Goblin, what was your tribe doing east of Purheae?"

The captive squealed when Rayna cuffed it upside the head when it didn't respond.

Damon stepped a bit closer, pulling Miazie with him. "What was your tribe doing east of Purheae? Tell me, or I will remove each of your extremities, starting with your fingers, with a table knife," to add strength to the threat, Damon picked up Colin's knife.

The goblin whuffled a bit before answering in a gravely, thick, hissing voice. "King Rahlan sends us to spy. Sent Darkwight in to finds us, orders us out of our homes to watch the humanses of the middle lands. We's just doing our jobses."

"I don't give a damn what you think you were doing, you left your land to spy on the free people and send feedback to Midian so that he can have his war," Damon looked up from the goblin. "Get it out of here. Do what you will with it."

The three men manhandled the goblin out of the tent and Damon released Miazie. The man walked back to his chair and resumed eating as though nothing had happened. Colin and Darius followed his example, but Miazie had lost her appetite.

After the meal, Damon left his tent without a word. Colin gave her one his brown woolen robes. Being that he was slighter than his twin was, his robes fit her better, though they were still uncomfortably lose. After thanking the man, the Belau left the tent as well, in hopes of finding Ryun.

She wandered without direction for almost an hour, circling the camp city twice and then heading down the slushy path that was considered the main street. Assassins in their indigo garb and black pleated leather armor flitted hither and thither, their shaded eyes glancing in her direction before beginning their constant roaming.

On one of her circuits, Miazie wandered close to the gate. She stopped, surveying the guards and defenses about the place. Before she had been there half a minute, however, a man whipped a dagger into her face, his own visage hidden behind a mask of black silk that went up to his eyes.

"You are not to be here, woman."

"I-I'm sorry. I was just exploring. I am sorry," she stuttered, staring at the dagger a hair's breadth from her eye.

"Then I would suggest you explore away from here. Next time I see you within fifty feet of this gate, I will take an eye for punishment. Git," the assassin shoved her away from him, sending her sprawling in the partially frozen mud.

The other guards laughed as she scrambled to her feet and fled into a side path. Fear scraped at her, sending her into a fit of trembling. She leaned against a cart filled with casks of ale in order to catch her breath.

"Miazie?"

Miazie's head whipped around at the voice. She stared at Ryun before rushing into his arms.

"Oh, Ryun! I am so scared! We have to get out of here, please!" she whispered into his shoulder.

The wiry man patted her back and shushed her. It was then that she felt the cloth under her cheek. Stepping away from her friend, Miazie took in the gray muslin tunic and matching wide-bottomed pants. Across his chest were thick strips of plain leather sewn down the center and tied beneath his arms. His chin length brown hair was tied back to reveal the extremely angular face and hawk nose. Miazie took another step away from, and then another, shaking her head.

"Ryun...no. Please good gods no."

The hunter spread his hands. "Miazie, I didn't have a choice. They said if I didn't cooperate, we would both die. Besides, if they train me, it will be easier for me to fight our way out, and I will be better suited to captain in Princess Tlonna's army."

"But Ryun, they are *monsters*! Don't you know what they are? They're assassins! Half the murders in the Liberated Lands are on their hands. I would rather die than have you be one of them!" she hissed.

The hunter shushed her again and grabbed her shoulders before she could back away more. "Listen to me, Miazie," the Belau jerked when he used no title, "I did this for both our lives. Besides, I don't plan on killing *anyone* I don't have to. If we play by their rules, maybe, after a while, they'll let us go. What use are we to Princess Tlonna if we're dead?"

"About the same use as we are now," Miazie replied, snarling. "What is this?" She fingered the shoulder of his robe.

"It's a novice's garb. They said I have the potential to be a Weapon."

"A weapon of murder, perhaps. Ryun, I strictly forbid you from joining this band of...of...brutes and nefarious wretches. I forbid it!" Miazie growled, straining not to shout.

Ryun leaned away from her, an odd gleam in his eye. After a long moment he said, "You gave up your right to order me around when you decided to follow Princess Tlonna. I am sworn to her now, not you, and I don't have to do a bleeding thing you tell me to. Because I care deeply for you, I will protect you as best as I am able, and I will do what *I* see fit to keep us both from getting run through. Understand?"

Miazie gaped at him, unable to think up a response. Finally, she wrenched away from his grasp and gave him cold glare. "As you wish."

Ryun watched her turn on her heel and stride away before pivoting and heading to the practice yard.

Nearly a week passed before Miazie left the tent again. Damon took full advantage of her presence in his bed. Often he would return during the day and take her where she was, whether in the tub or reading in the tiny lounge. Later in the week Colin and Darius were taking her measurements for a few robes when the general strode in. He did not glance once at his slaves before he pushed off the strips of emerald taffeta and entered her. Miazie, horrified, tried to run but the man held her tight as his slaves cowered in the corner, their eyes averted, unable to leave unless ordered.

After that, Miazie tried to give him her all at night in order to appease his severe lust. The midday humiliations dwindled to a day here and there. Two weeks after her argument with Ryun, she and Damon were resting from a particular intense bout when the assassin general wrapped his hands in her hair and pulled her close.

"Miazie...I have been thinking these last few days. You are the most sensuous and brilliant woman I have ever met. My men think I need an heir, for none of them desire a position of power, and I am more their lord than general. Tomorrow, we will wed. You will wear that green gown that was just finished. You will have your hair down, all the way, and you will not fight against this. Understand?"

Miazie closed her eyes, giving in to the dashing of her dreams of falling in love. "Yes, my lord."

"Damon...call me Damon, woman," with that, he rolled over and fell asleep.

The next morning, Miazie woke to find herself alone in the bed, something unusual. She wandered into the bathing room and soaked until the water turned cold. Darius combed her hair out while

Colin pressed the emerald green taffeta gown. Within an hour she was being led out the door by a stolid Rayna. The whole Shitan-Kulata guild was standing in the center of the camp. Damon stood on a small dais along with two other men. The general was not in his usual assassin garb, but rather in full-body ornate leather armor. Miazie was led up the dais steps and positioned in front of her groom.

The ceremony was quick and to the point, a dagger point digging into Miazie's back the whole time to ensure she agreed to the questions asked. The priest handed Damon a sharp little knife with which the man sliced his palm. Grabbing Miazie's opposite hand, he slid the blade across her palm until blood welled. He placed his lacerated hand on hers and pressed until their blood dripped as one onto the wooden platform. The assassin's cheered as Damon led his bride off the dais and into his tent.

A few days later Miazie left the tent and followed Damon's instructions to where Ryun was housed. She ducked into the small gray tent and blinked in the dimness. A very luscious young woman stared at her, her hands poised to set down a wooden tray on a little table.

"Can I help you?"

Miazie squinted at her. "Yes...I was told that this was Ryun Kapatulet's tent?"

"Oh yes, I am Jacinth, Ryun's wife. You must be Miazie?"

The Belau stiffened, frozen by the woman's words. "Ryun's...? Ryun doesn't have a wife."

Jacinth smiled patiently. "Nor did you have a husband a few days ago, Lady Miazie. Things change here with the Shitan-Kulata. I used to be a daughter of a rich sea merchant, but I have been held captive here since they murdered my father three years ago. Now I am Jacinth Kapatulet. You are Miazie Suutson. Things change here."

Before Miazie could reply, Ryun walked in and straightened until his head brushed the top of the canvas. "Miazie..."

"Congratulations Ryun. Glad to see you've fit in well," she stood, her words of apology forgotten, and strode from the tent.

Ryun caught up with her, grabbed her arm, and swung her around. "Miazie, I didn't have a choice any more than you did! For the gods' sake, woman, quit laying faults on me that I don't have! I was forced to marry Jacinth just as much as you were General Damon."

"To what point, and purpose, Ryun?"

"To create a new generation of Shitan-Kulata. A civilization needs children to thrive, Miazie, you know this."

"This is not a civilization, this is a guild of murderers and assassins. How can you justify joining them so willingly? How?"

The initiate assassin snarled at her. "We've already been over this. I will get us out soon, Miazie, I promise."

"Perhaps I should come up with an alternate plan, then, eh? You might become too befuddled with your new plaything."

As the Belau pivoted away, Ryun's voice trailed after her. "I made a promise, Miazie, and I don't intend to break it."

"Ah, my wife, you look troubled," Damon said to Miazie when she rampaged into the tent.

Miazie backed away from him and said, "What do you care? Am I not just your captive?"

Damon looked hurt and sat down in a chair across from her. "You are not a captive, you are my wife."

"In my land, wives were treated as more than pleasure slaves, and were allowed to go where they would."

"Have I not given you materials for gowns? Jewels to wear? All of your possessions back? How else can I show my appreciation for you?"

Miazie sneered, the man actually looked confused. "My belongings were mine to begin with, and not usually are they taken away. I was a princess, once, and fabric and jewels came when I wished them. When I held visions of my husband, he was kind, loving, compassionate, strong, humorous, and decent. You are cruel, sadistic, and I loathe your touch. You try to buy my affection with baubles as though I were some favored pet."

Damon stared at her, his forehead creased in a frown. After a while he said, "I did not know women desired such things. Most only crave power and a willing man to share their bed. I believed you the same as those women."

"Well, I am not. If I am to be your...wife...I would suggest you start treating me as such, or you will wake up with a knife in your gut."

Against her expectations, Damon began to laugh, a deep belly laugh that ended with him gasping for breath. "Ah, Miazie, I made a good choice in you. Come, I have something to show you."

The two walked through the camp village and ended up at the

far corner where the blacksmith's shop squatted against the wall. Damon held the door open for Miazie and then followed her in.

The brawny blacksmith bowed low to Damon and smiled at her, his teeth blackened by ash.

"Is it ready Garet?"

"Yes, General Damon. I finished it last night. Shall I bring it out?"

Damon nodded and then turned to Miazie. "The wife of the Shitan-Kulata General should not be unprotected at anytime, no matter how noble and high-bred she is. I commissioned this for you, specifically, and I will personally train you to use it."

As he spoke, Garet reappeared holding a metal box. He laid it on a table and pulled the top off. Miazie gasped. Damon smiled. Sheathed in tooled black leather with a green cord threaded along the top, was a sword identical to the ones the assassins carried, though smaller. The hilt was diamonded white and green, the guard a wooden knob that surrounded the hilt. When Damon pulled it out, the blade of folded steel reflected the forge fire like a wavy mirror.

"I present you Luminor, Light of the Shitan-Kulata. May it protect you in shadowed times," he handed the sword to her, hilt first, and she took it with trembling fingers.

Miazie sheathed it after a while and held it, feeling awkward. Smiling, Damon lifted the baldric over her head and settled it against her back.

"You will get used to the weight. It will become a pleasure and a comfort. Come, let us see what you can do."

After thanking the blacksmith, Miazie followed her husband to the practice yard where she was thoroughly beaten to a pulp, though Damon obviously was using only a fraction of his skill. Though she was thankful of the training Tlonna and Losolin had started to give her, Miazie knew she was nowhere near any of their skill.

Weeks passed, and the Belau became familiar with her blade under the masterful eye of her husband and teacher. Every morning they sparred and assassins from around the village camp would watch in various degrees of humor.

On the day she actually touched Damon, Miazie looked up and saw Ryun standing among the crowd. He did not look amused, or happy in any way. As soon as he noticed her watching him, he turned away and disappeared. Damon roared with laughter as he inspected his bleeding arm.

"Miazie, my wife, you have done well. Come, to breakfast!"

The crowd dispersed to their usual routine and Miazie and Damon strolled back to their tent. To her great pride, the weight of the sword on her back *was* becoming comforting, and she often found herself reaching back to make sure it was still there. A few days later, she and Damon were lounging in the recreation room of their tent when Damon shut his book with a thud, startling Miazie.

"Miazie, you have been sad and distant this past week. What troubles you?"

The Belau marked her page with a thumb and shut her book as well. She stared at her husband's handsome face, at the vague concern in his eyes.

"It is just that I feel as though I have betrayed Tlonna. I have stopped my mission. I must get to Alchemian. I need to find the alchemists." Miazie sniffed and wiped her eyes. "If you would just let me and Sir Ryun go, I would promise to return at a later date, but I could not stay."

"Miazie, I cannot just let you go. I see that this journey is very important to you and the success of this Tlonna. She is an elf, yes?" Damon asked her.

"Yes, she's an elf and yes I must complete my mission to find Alchemian. If I do not, the fate of the twelve lands will be doomed. I cannot tell you why, but my need is greater than your need. I am sorry, but I must go," Miazie touched her husband's hand. "Please."

"I-I cannot let you leave. Not now, you are my wife and you belong here. You can't leave," Damon said curtly.

"Then you leave me no choice," Miazie stood and began to depart from the room when she felt a wall slam into existence inches from her nose.

"No, you cannot go Miazie," Damon said coldly.

"Y-you are a Magin! Damon, how? Why didn't you tell me? Damon?"

Damon shifted uneasily. After a moment of hesitation, the man let his hands fall to his sides and Miazie felt the wall disappear. His green eyes stared at the ground hard, sweat coming out in beads.

"I-you must not tell anyone. If the Shitan-Kulata knew that I was a Magin, they would murder me. I have not used my magic in over ten years. I cannot let you go," the Magin looked up and Miazie saw something in his eyes, though she was not sure what it was.

"Damon, come with me, please. The more Magins we have in this war, the greater the chance we have of surviving it," Miazie cringed at her next words. "Else I will have to let out your secret."

"No! You must not do-!"

"I will do what I must. This task is more important than your life. Don't you understand that you are stopping a great prophecy in its tracks? Do you want to be solely responsible for the doom of the land?" Miazie spit each word.

Damon fell to his knees, his dark robes spreading around him. "My wife, I thought that you would understand, but apparently I was mistaken. I will go with you if you just tell me that my secret will not be revealed."

"We leave tonight when Loniare is at its peak. I will tell Ryun and Jacinth," Miazie began to step away from the man before turning back.

Damon stood uncertainly and Miazie looked at his green eyes. In a sudden rush, the Belau kissed the Magin passionately, then departed hurriedly.

"Ryun, it is Miazie. I must speak to you," Miazie stepped into the tent and let her eyes adjust to the light.

Shadows were starting to lengthen outside.

"Miazie, what can I do for you?" the hunter appeared from another room.

"We are leaving, get your stuff ready to go, Jacinth's too, if she is to come."

"What?" Ryun stared at the woman in disbelief. "We cannot just leave Miazie, we are captives...in a way."

"I know this, Damon is coming with us," Miazie smiled.

Ryun shook his head but said nothing.

The Belau sighed and said, "Ryun, get ready to leave."

The hunter nodded and began putting his things into a pack bag. "Jacinth, pack your things. We are going on a trip."

The young woman entered the room with a bewildered look on her face. "What do you mean we are going on a...trip?"

Sighing patiently, Ryun explained, "We are leaving the camp for a while. I don't know when we will return, but General Damon is coming with us."

Tlonna shifted in her bed uneasily. Losolin sighed and lit a candle. "What is your problem tonight my love? You have not been still for hours."

"I am sorry. I am going to go for a walk," she said while standing.

Dressing in a warm pair of pants and a long belted tunic, and grabbing one of her swords, Tlonna gave her consort a small smile before slipping out of the room. She hurried through the inn and found the entrance to the private courtyard. Breathing deep the cool midnight air, the elf lifted her face to feel cold drops of snow against her warm flesh. It felt pure, despite its horrid appearance. Opening her eyes, she wandered down a stone path between stands of aged weeping willows. The leaves brushed against her shoulders like gentle caresses, no sound coming from her steps.

The Magin slowed when she heard a shifting noise ahead of her. Something was moving, quickly and deliberately, in the path before her. The elf crept around the corner and straightened with a smile. Aidyn, stripped to the waist, was moving through sword formations. He was graceful as a swan on smooth water, the sword in his hand flickering as the colored patches of moonlights, shining through the canopy of trees, danced on the folded steel. His feet were bare as well, covered in tainted snow.

Tlonna watched him from the shadows, mesmerized by the fluidity of his movements. Something about him seemed ethereal, even god-like.

"Are we all like that?" she asked finally.

Aidyn merely looked at her, as though he had known she was there. "Humans call us earth angels, lesser-deity creatures from the Age of Monotheism, human forms, though flawless and glowing."

Tlonna did not reply as Aidyn had continued to move through the formations. After a few more minutes, she walked into the small opening where he was and drew her own sword. Together they went through the formations, Tlonna a step behind as she learned the movements. After nearly an hour, Aidyn sheathed his sword and turned to Tlonna.

"I do this every night. Start with a run, usually about three or four miles, just to warm up, then go through every single weapon I use, starting with the bow, and ending with the sword. Resistance and endurance training, strength and patience. It all adds up, Tlonna, to make us what we are."

"And what are we?"

"Perfect."

Tlonna stared at Aidyn a full five seconds before a laugh of disbelief escaped her.

"Perfect? What do you think makes us perfect?" she asked amusedly.

Aidyn did not laugh, or even smile when he said, "One must think it, before they become it. To be an elf means to be perfect, flawless, in everything. The way we look, the way we act and speak, the way we fight. Otherwise, we would not have survived as long as we have. Even immortal, were we weak, or dumb, we would have been wiped out by the humans, or even the dwarves.

"The humans are courageous, and though we taunt them, they have a certain amount of determination and passion in them that allows their race to thrive. That alone could destroy our race, were they to put their minds to it. And the dwarves are strong and hearty. Our qualms with them are about land, and belief, mainly. That is what separates us Tlonna. Humans are courageous, dwarves are strong, and elves are perfection."

"You speak wisdom, Aidyn, but do you know what I see? We all bleed red, we all wear skin, and we all are of same basic build. We are all the same."

Aidyn laughed fully, so at odds with his usual stolidity. The elf finally managed to reduce his laughter to snickering when Tlonna looked affronted.

"What?"

The assassin grinned. "You always did try to make the differences between the races seem less than it really is. You should know that it is a useless attempt. There will always be a line between the three. The others...the elementals, they are a category all their own and seem perfectly fine to be left out of the loop."

Tlonna made a noncommittal noise as she bent down to pick up her discarded cloak. As she stood, something whistled through the air and knocked her flat.

Shouting, Aidyn grabbed his bow, knocked an arrow, and pivoted, looking for a target. Suddenly, the calm inn courtyard was a blizzard of tainted snow. Wind whipped at their hair and clothes, making it nearly impossible for Aidyn to aim true. Cursing, he tossed his bow aside and drew his sword.

Tlonna groaned as she stood, rubbing her shoulder where she had been hit. She too drew her sword. Shadows flitted around them through the whipping taint.

"Aidyn! What is going on?" she shouted.

"I do not know!" his reply came through the dark.

Gradually, a more distinguishable shape appeared at the entrance to the little clearing. Black light, blacker than the taint and the darkest of shadows, flickered in a pulsating aura around the shape as it approached. Aidyn roared as he lunged at it, sword held high above his head. The elf, already in mid-air, flew backward as Midian's hand lifted and pushed outward, fingers clawed.

The assassin landed on his back and slid a few feet. He rolled to the side, groaning as he stood.

"Midian!" Tlonna yelled, dropping her sword and filling her body with power.

The evil Magin did not turn to look at her, but rather stalked toward Aidyn. The elf, teeth bared, charged him. His blade flickered through the thrashing snow. Midian slid to the side gracefully and slammed his Weave-covered fist into the assassin's face. Aidyn stumbled back, spitting the blood from his mouth. Tlonna lashed out. Midian jerked, fell to one knee, and then retaliated with a Weave of his own.

Tlonna slammed against a tree, narrowly missing a branch that would have skewered her. Having taken advantage of Midian's distraction, Aidyn swung his blade at the king's head. The human swept up an arm and turned the blade so that only the flat of it smashed into his head. Slightly stunned, Midian staggered away shaking his head. Tlonna and Aidyn attacked at the same time. With a powerful blow, Aidyn swept Midian's legs out from under him, but the Magin caught the male elf as he went down. Tlonna tried to kick him in the face, but her leg was caught in a Weave.

With a grimace, Midian shoved Aidyn away and released his hold on her with a heave so that Tlonna staggered to her knees. Cursing, the elf tried to rise, but found her legs too weak to do so. She looked over her shoulder at the two battling males, trying to will her legs to move. Aidyn was a phenomenal blademaster, but even though he moved faster than Midian he could not deflect magic with steel.

Blood ran down his body to mingle with the snow, turning it to black sludge.

Finally, Tlonna was able to get to her feet, and she launched herself at the human. Aidyn's blade sank into Midian's thigh as Tlonna's Weave hit him with such concentrated force blood sprayed out in a fine mist. Midian howled as he stumbled against a stone bench and fell backward over it. Before either elf could take a step further, however, the bench was torn from its place and launched at Aidyn.

It careened into the assassin's midriff, slamming him into a granite pillar. The bench and pillar cracked. Aidyn barely raised his arms in time to shield his head from the crown of the pillar as it fell. The elf did not move.

Tlonna screamed as she watched blood seep into the ground, the taint whipping around them like a great hollow column. Midian, now standing, sent a Weave at the screaming Magin. Tlonna barely reflected it, sweeping her arm down to block the magic as it flew at her. White clashed with black, sending both Magins to their backs.

Midian was the first to his feet and he sprinted over to Tlonna. His magic-covered fist slammed into her face over and over again. The elf tried to turn her head, but Midian only grabbed her by the neck and swung her around. Her back cracked against a tree and she flopped onto the ground.

Shaking, Tlonna tried to stand, but Midian's boot pressed into her middle back. His hand slithered up her spine and then stopped at the base of her skull. Panicking, Tlonna writhed on the frozen ground. Burning cold sparked in her spine and she went still.

Midian stood and took his boot from her back. Tlonna scrambled to her feet, hands outstretched. Nothing happened. Shaking her hands, the elf tried to Weave again, futilely.

"No!" she screamed, "No!"

Midian grimaced at her, wiping the back of his hand across his bleeding mouth. Suddenly, the snow stopped whirling and fell to the ground. Aidyn's legs, the only part of him visible, were now covered in the taint.

Tlonna, magically useless, lunged at Midian, her hands fisted. Two powerful blows sent the human to his knees, holding his head. The elf's foot slammed into his face and he jerked backward. Grabbing a branch off the ground, Tlonna whacked it into the side of

Midian's head several times until the human stilled, blood flowing from his scalp and face.

Desperate, Tlonna shot across the clearing to start digging frantically at the tainted mound. She had uncovered half a leg when she was pulled back roughly. Swiping behind her, the elf kept attempting to pull Aidyn out from under the crumbled granite.

"Curse it, elf!" Midian growled, and kicked her in the back of the head.

Tlonna went limp.

Losolin leapt down the stairs, dodging screaming occupants, and flew out the door to the courtyard. He held an arm up to shield his eyes from the screaming wall of taint. The elf plunged into the whirlwind and was thrown back out. Cursing, he tried again and again, each time being forced away by the sheer strength of the contained storm.

When it suddenly stopped, Losolin shot into the courtyard, yanking out his sword. When he reached the small clearing, he slid to a halt, staring at the limp form of Tlonna in Midian's hands.

"No!" he screamed, and launched himself at the human.

Midian swept out an arm and Losolin ran face first into a bar of power while the rest of his body continued forward. He slammed head first into the ground. By the time he was able to breathe again, Midian was gone...along with Tlonna.

Losolin shot to his feet and started searching frantically around the small clearing, knowing all the while it was hopeless. When he stumbled over the mound of broken granite, he cursed, and then saw the wet sludge of tainted snow and blood. Digging, he unearthed Aidyn.

The assassin was slouched against the remains of the stone pillar, the bench atop his lap like a blanket, sprayed with blood. His arms were shredded from the crown that had smashed into them. Cuts all around his face and scalp seeped blood, though it congealed quickly in the cold.

"Aidyn!" Losolin shouted, shaking him.

The assassin did not stir. Grabbing chunks of granite, Losolin hoisted them behind him, freeing the other elf. Both legs were broken at the knee, and from the unnatural slant he sat at, so was his back.

"Gods, no!" Losolin cried, and pulled Aidyn out straight.

Shoving him onto his face, Losolin ran his hands up and down the unnatural angle of Aidyn's spine, green light throbbing out of his hands. Aidyn moaned. After a few minutes, the assassin's back jerked as the last bone healed. Losolin healed his legs, and then his arms and face.

Exhausted, the half-Magin slumped back into the snow. Aidyn twitched beside him. After a few moments rest, Losolin straightened and shook him.

"Aidyn, come one. Please. He has Tlonna. Come on," he sniffed; trying to hold back the wave of wrath and despair that was threatening to choke him.

Aidyn moaned again, and then opened his eyes. He put his hands to his face and took a deep breath. Sitting up slowly, the assassin grimaced painfully.

"Ahh..." he groaned.

Losolin staggered to his feet and held out his hand to help him up. Aidyn took it, and stumbled into the other elf. A gasp burst out of him as he leaned against Losolin.

"Dear gods," he shuddered, "what did that bastard do to me?"

"He broke your legs, and your back, and then that pillar fell on top of you. But he has Tlonna, Aidyn. He took her!" Losolin shouted the last, shaking him.

"Nine hells, stop it! You are going to kill me!" Aidyn said between gritted teeth. "We have to get to the stables. I cannot run, and if he has a Keylode around here, we will not make it in time if we go on foot."

Losolin nodded and picked up Tlonna's discarded sword and trotted out of the courtyard. Aidyn gathered his scattered weapons and set off after Losolin. They saddled their horses and rode out of the city.

"Which way?" Losolin cried, scanning the road and sky.

Aidyn slid off his horse, a long-legged, ash gray and black dappled mare named Whäd. He crouched on the ground and inspected it, moving hither and thither across until he reached a few feet off the road, heading north-west.

"Here, a horse, moving fast, definitely with a rider too. Recent. It is our best bet," he finally said, and remounted painfully.

The two males set off at a gallop, cloaks flying through the taint-riddled night air. They found the horse a few miles further on, lathered and wheezing. They passed it, setting their far-seeing eyes against the moving night.

"There!" Aidyn shouted, pointing.

Far ahead in the sky, an ink-black dot moved fast toward Florwen Hune. They urged their horses onward. It did not move closer to the ground until false dawn was threatening, the sky turning a deep blue. By then, both horses were wheezing and foaming, gnashing the bit as their riders urged them on.

Without warning, the Keylode dropped from the sky. Losolin and Aidyn sped onward. When dawn was fully upon them, the elves reined their horses in. A few yards away, in a forest clearing, camped a small contingent of Darkwights and Keylodes. In the center stood Midian.

Tlonna woke up with a throbbing head and a sick feeling in the pit of her stomach. Opening her eyes slowly, she groaned and rolled onto her side. Looking about she felt rock walls on all sides of her, less than an arm's length away. When she tried to Weave, pain lanced her body with such force that she cried out, doubling over. The Magin stood slowly and checked her person. All of her weapons were gone as were her boots and cloak. Wrapping her hair around her fists for warmth, Tlonna curled against the far wall, resting her head against the chill stone.

Some time later, she squinted as a widening crack of light filtered into her stone prison. The light was replaced by Midian's silhouette.

He stood, feet apart, hands on hips, watching her. Tlonna stood slowly, reaching her full height, which towered over Midian by nearly two feet. He sneered up at her.

"Why do you look at me so?" Midian snapped, stepping closer to her.

Tlonna rolled her shoulders back, lip curling. "It just surprises me that someone so short and completely unremarkable looking can frighten so many people. Even your little minions are taller than you, are they not?" she replied coolly.

Midian glared up at her. "Listen, elf. I own you. You are mine until I decide to do away with you. My power makes yours look like child's play. I will get what I want from you and whether you will it or not, *I* will take your power and make it mine," turning to look outside

Midian said, "Get her."

A dozen Darkwights shuffled in behind Midian and cornered Tlonna. They grabbed her ankles and wrists, pulling and yanking until she could do no more than writhe uselessly. She was pushed bodily onto a Keylode and tied tightly in the harness with her wrists shackled to a loop in the saddle. Sitting upright, the elf could see the whole camp. Nearly a hundred black clad demons and their massive birds were spread out across the small clearing.

Losolin smacked Aidyn's shoulder and pointed. The elves stared out at Tlonna sitting atop the Keylode.

The assassin sighed, "We can do nothing with Midian around. We have to get rid of him, somehow."

"How?" Losolin asked despairingly.

"Stab me thrice and drown me, I know not," Aidyn whispered.

"Wait," Losolin said, grabbing his companion's arm. "They are mounting."

Aidyn looked out from their leafy coverage and watched as Darkwights mounted the Keylodes. With a cry, the great black birds launched into the sky. The two elves exploded from their hiding place, bows drawn, arrows knocked. Two demons fell screaming before they had even taken honest flight. Seconds later, two more fell.

Midian's howl of anger was heard even above the screaming of demon and bird. Black magic lashed out of the sky, but the males dived well out of the way. Four more demons fell. A dozen or so Darkwights landed, leaping off the backs of the giant birds and sprinted over to the elves.

Abandoning bow for sword, Aidyn and Losolin slaughtered the demons, spinning through sword formations quicker than the Darkwights could react. As more and more landed, the two elves progressed across the field in the direction Tlonna and the rest had flown.

Tlonna's mount followed its brethren, flapping its massive wings to stay in the center of the two dozen others. Fearing for Aidyn and Losolin's lives, she twisted in her bonds, attempting to free herself. Of a sudden, two arrows thudded into Tlonna's bird, one narrowly missing her foot. She yelped as the Keylode jerked in the air.

As the beast shrieked and floundered, another came and

grasped Tlonna by the back of her tunic and tried to lift her off. Twisting away, the elf felt a lurch as her mount was attacked by another. The two entangled Keylodes were slowly moving away from the formation. Finally wrenching herself out of the harness tied about her waist, Tlonna clenched her teeth around the reins and pushed her body closer to the black-feathered beast.

Crying out in pain, Tlonna felt the talons of the second Keylode pierce her calf. Kicking frantically with her free leg, the elf heard the scaly legs snap in half. With a scream, the Keylode lifted away and clasped her bloody leg in its beak. Wrenching away roughly, Tlonna heard again the sickening crunch of bones as they snapped in two. Biting back a scream, the Magin kicked the bird in its eye. The beast twitched and Tlonna watched as two more arrows sped into the back of the bird. The Keylode on which she was mounted began to fall rapidly from the sky, its great black head lifted into the air at an unnatural angle. The female watched in terror as the trees below rapidly came up to meet her.

Tlonna roared in anguish as she and the bird slammed into the canopy. The harness caught on a thick branch and swung the Keylode around. They slammed into the trunk hard, Tlonna's head whacking against the rough bark. They hung for a short moment and then the heavy bird started to come loose from its saddle. Tlonna bit her lip and closed her eyes in misery.

Frantically she started jerking her wrists in an attempt to free them from the harness. With one leg still securely lashed to one side of the Keylode, the elf knew she would be torn apart when the bird finally fell. One arm came loose just as the creature rolled. With a scream, Tlonna was yanked downward, the harness still entangled with the branch. Her arm was jerked up while the rest of her fell with the Keylode.

Blood sprayed her face as her hand was ripped from the cuff. She fell.

Pain flooded into her mind and drowned out everything else. The Keylode hit the ground and she landed on top of it with a thud. Rolling off the feathered body, Tlonna lay limply on the ground, waiting, wanting to die. Blood seeped from her ruined arm and she could feel the bottom of her shirt sticking to her skin as the blood gummed to it. Tears slid unbidden from her eyes into the slightly damp ground beneath her. Looking around at her arm, Tlonna held back the rancid taste of bile as it rose in her throat. Her arm was bent at an odd angle from her elbow and the skin around her wrist was torn and laying open to the bone. Blood gushed out in large amounts from the wound. Forcing her head away from the sickening sight, she buried her face in the dirt.

After what seemed an hour, Tlonna heard frantic footsteps coming towards her.

"Where?"

"Over here, Masster, I think."

Booted feet crashed into view and a second later, the hem of black robes. Midian's knees appeared inches from her face, and she squeezed shut her eyes.

"Doess sshe live?" Kelus hissed.

"Yes, get her up," Midian snapped. "I can hear the others coming."

Tlonna heard them too, Aidyn and Losolin tearing through the forest from the other direction.

"I think they went down near here. The branches are broken and I can see black feathers," Aidyn said.

Midian jerked Tlonna upright and shoved her into Kelus's arms.

"Take her ahead, and make camp where we agreed. Tell the others to go on to Zaedic. I will take care of these two."

"No!" Tlonna moaned, feebly wrestling with Kelus.

Kelus ignored her and yanked her into the foliage. Fighting back the urge to start weeping uncontrollably, Tlonna cried out in a harsh, pained voice.

"I hear her! Come on," Losolin broke into the ravaged area where the Keylode lay, and Midian stood leaning nonchalantly against a tree.

"My my, what tough young boys you are. I say, I admire your determination."

"Where is she?" Losolin demanded, stepping forward.

"Gone, to be my whore in a few days, and give me heirs to my throne. She is mine, pretty one, not yours. You do not deserve such power," Midian crooned.

Wrath filled Losolin until he could not contain it. Green light burst out of him and shot into Midian. The human stumbled back a few steps before regaining his balance. Shock flashed across his face before he schooled it into mild annoyance.

With a sweep of his arms, black light engulfed green. Losolin was shoved backward into Aidyn.

"Do not play with me, elf!" Midian laughed, drawing his sword, a black steel single-edged blade that rang loudly as it escaped the scabbard.

Aidyn and Losolin copied him. Aidyn's elfish blade seemed to glow in the presence of Midian's evil weapon. Losolin roared as Midian came at him. His scimitar sliced through air and jarred with the black steel. The swords hissed as they slid down each other to rest at the hilts. Aidyn's blade went through Midian's hand. The Magin bellowed as the elfish steel sizzled against his flesh. Aidyn yanked it out.

Losolin shoved Midian back and kicked him hard in the chest. The human stumbled and fell. The elves advanced. Before either of them could deliver the killing stroke, however, a wall of magic blasted them backward. When they regained their feet, Midian was gone.

"Coward!" Aidyn bellowed, shaking his fist in the direction the human had fled.

They rampaged through the forest, searching for signs of Midian or Tlonna, screaming her name. When night fell, they knew it was futile. Losolin collapsed with a sob. Aidyn sucked in a deep breath and hoisted the younger elf up.

"Come on, lad, we need to get back to the city. King Demetrius will help us."

"No!" Losolin screamed, fighting his friend.

"Losolin, she is gone. We can do nothing for her now."

"No! Tlonna! No!" Losolin howled, his body shaking with grief and terror.

Aidyn squeezed his eyes shut against the sight as Losolin fell to his knees, face buried in his hands. The younger elf's soul-wrenching sobs broke his heart and he felt the tears run hot against his skin. Dropping his bloodied sword, the assassin, too, wept.

A few minutes later, he and Losolin jogged back through the woods to the clearing where the dead Darkwights littered the ground. Neñyos and Whäd snorted at them. The elves mounted the horses and sped back to Derid.

Though it was still very early, the two arrived at the castle and demanded an audience with the king. The castle seneschal seemed bent on refusing them until Losolin drew his sword and put it to the man's throat.

A few minutes later, they were sitting in Demetrius' informal reception room. The king arrived wearing loose cotton pants and a silk tunic. He looked mildly annoyed. The elves stood and bowed, and then both opened their mouths to speak.

"King Deme-" Losolin began.

Demetrius cut him off with a wave of his hand. "I am not used to being woken up at the crack of dawn by two elves who are not the queen of a province, and I am not very happy about it. What is this about?" he demanded.

"He took her!" Losolin shouted.

Demetrius stared at him. "Who took who?"

Losolin was overcome, so Aidyn answered. "Midian Rahlan took Princess Tlonna, my king. We ask for aid."

The human stared at the elf for a second before realization dawned on his face. "I will do what I can, starting with healers for you two."

Before either elf could protest, they were swept off to the infirmary.

Chapter 12
Turning Point

Yayènia lay on the bed within the infirmary. Fatigue lay over her as she stared at the dirt ceiling, too much in pain to sleep. Her arms and legs were swollen and bruised and back in splints, her body wrapped until she looked much larger than reality. Despite her pain, she worried more about Suneelo. He still had not regained consciousness.

She looked over at him, in the bed next to her, and reached out a stiff arm. Just able to brush his shoulder, she wrapped her fingers in material and hung onto him.

The healer that watched over Yayènia was a stout human with silver falling down her red hair in streaks. Green eyes looked the elf over as she handed her a bowl of stew.

"Try to eat this time child. It would not do if you get sick from not eating. And let go of Captain Suneelo. He is not going anywhere."

Yayènia snorted in effort to hide a snivel. "I know that, I still like to touch him. He *is* my husband."

Haly smiled as though a mother looking at a fond daughter. "Of course, Yayènia. Now, eat up and I think today I will be able to rid you of that swelling."

Yayènia glared at the human.

She put her hands on her hips. "Do not think I am going to call you High Commander, missy. This is my infirmary, and I am High Commander here, and until you can walk the length and breadth of it, you will stay just Yayènia. Now eat."

Still glaring, Yayènia spooned the stew into her mouth. Putting the bowl on the table, the elf lay back and closed her eyes. Despite the pain, she fell into a light sleep of nightmares and dreams.

The night was black, black as any she could remember. Yayènia shook with sobs as she held the limp body of the male she loved. His vibrant red hair looked akin to blood in the slashing rain. Hatred of the man who had killed him swelled in her until her heart threatened to burst.

The young elf shook Chris's body desperately, trying to wake him though she knew it to be useless. His large red eyes were closed forever.

"Please...oh gods...please come back to me. Do not leave me here. Chris...please..." she keened, her voice cut off by the rain and wind.

She knelt in the muddy garden for hours, her thin shift sodden and filthy with mud.

Yayènia sat up gasping and shaking, her shift sticky with cold sweat. She had never wanted to relive that night. Four hundred years and more had passed since that day, and she thought the memory had faded along with so many others. The fire nymph, Chris, had been her first love when she was barely eighteen. She had had only two after him, for love did not come easy to her. Rubbing her temples against the tightness in her head, Yayènia swung her legs over the edge of the bed and started to stand.

Haly clucked as she entered the infirmary.

"Now, Yayènia, what did I say? You only walk when I am around. Come on," the healer pushed her down gently and pulled the blankets up the elf's chin.

Haly took the bowl from the table and left with a warning glance at Yayènia.

Looking behind her, another female came in and smiled warmly at Yayènia. Erdwyf was High Advisor to the crown, and married to Second Commander Ghealan. "That human is going to drive us all insane with her constant *tsk*ing and sighing. How are you doing my friend?"

Yayènia attempted to smile back. "Ah, Erd, a sane face. You are High Advisor, get me out of here."

"Why, all you would do is sit a few more feet to the right, would you not?"

Yayènia looked over to where Erdwyf indicated and reached out to grab at Suneelo's shoulder again.

Erdwyf sighed. "I do not understand why she insists on putting these beds so far apart. Hold on."

Yayènia nearly yelped as her bed shifted beneath her, bringing her a few inches closer to Suneelo. She could now stroke his hair, or pull his arm close enough to hold his hand.

"Thank you," she said quietly as Erdwyf sat on the corner of her bed.

"If it were Lan, I would want the same. Does he ever wake?"

Yayènia turned her head to look at her friend. "Yesterday he moaned, which is more life than we had seen out of him yet. I just want him to wake up so I can kill him."

"Yayènia..." Erdwyf giggled.

"I am serious. He risked his own life to save mine. We would have figured something out, but he had to go and get himself pummeled to within an inch of his life."

"He did figure something out, and he got you away sooner. He did it because he loves you, and it was hurting him to see you hurt," Erdwyf said softly, playing with the warrior's golden hair.

"And it did not hurt me?" Yayènia replied.

Erdwyf sighed. "Of course it did, but it is the way of things. Females stand by their males; males try to save the females. Is it not?"

"*Aiya*," Yayènia conceded.

Beside her, Suneelo moved his head.

"Suneelo! Suneelo my love, are you awake?" Yayènia asked urgently, shaking his hand.

The male did not respond, but murmured and turned his face away.

Yayènia stopped shaking his hand and stared at him, tears in her eyes. "Never," she whispered, "have I seen him like this. In two hundred and sixty-eight years of marriage, never have I seen him like this. Not after horrendous battle wounds, or anything. I do not like it, Erdwyf. It scares me."

"It is good to know you can be scared, actually," Erdwyf commented lightly.

"Bloody nine hells Erdwyf," Yayènia chuckled wetly.

"But I know what you mean. When Ghealan had both his legs broken in the siege, and the arrow pinned his wrist to his shoulder, I could not sleep for weeks until he was better. I was so worried. But that is the life we chose, when I married him, and you and Suneelo married each other. Warriors, I have often heard you say, cannot love gently, or be gently loved."

Yayènia turned again to face Erdwyf. "Passionately violent, and violently passionate. But what is that?" She pointed at a rolled letter in her friend's hand.

Erdwyf raised her eyebrows. "This? Oh, this is just a letter for our good friend Aidyn."

"Aidyn?"

"Aye, and he has some interesting news. I have not yet shared this with Dietirin or his wife. I thought you should hear it.

'King Dietirin, Queen Constancias, the Council of Advisors, and friends of Princess Magin Tlonna.

I have found the Princess Tlonna and the Lord Consort Losolin. We reside here in Derid, capital of Kajgenia in the good company of King Demetrius and the Belau Miazie. Her letter was honest. Both Tlonna and Losolin have lost their memory, but seem to regain it slowly as the days go by. It seems they were separated, and found each other through sheer luck, and have regained their love for one another. I write also to inform you that Losolin is a Healing Magin of great success. I have also told them of the situation there, and they were distraught. They both weep for Yayènia and Suneelo, as I do. We hope they are well. An army follows Tlonna, though a small one, I believe it will grow. We will come back for you. I do not know when I will return, for Tlonna has asked me to remain with her. Be safe.

Aidyn Sestuns.'

He is a brave elf, Aidyn. Lord Consort Losolin? That is enough to make Constancias apoplexy. Although, that would be kind of entertaining," Erdwyf hid a smile behind her hand. "And this Healing Magin? What in the nine hells does that mean?"

"I would expect better language from my High Advisor, Erdwyf."

Erdwyf and Yayènia jumped and peered around at Constancias. The queen glided towards them, her black hair framing a beautiful face that almost did justice to Tlonna herself.

"Now, what is this?" the queen plucked the letter from Erdwyf's hand and read it, her eyebrows rising with each line. "LORD Consort Losolin? What is the meaning of this? Keeping letters from your queen to share with your friends first? How dare you! I should have you booted from your position, Advisor," white teeth showed in a snarl.

"Yes my queen. I am sure the king will agree," Erdwyf replied coolly, rocking back on her heels.

Constancias glared at her.

"Stab me thrice and drown me, Constancias, the letter was given to her, she is the High Advisor, therefore she had as much right to it as you. This...nonsense about you being all-powerful is all foolish quibble. Nine hells, the only reason you are on the throne is because you married into the right family. Honor and intelligence is not granted from a wedding band," Yayènia snapped.

Constancias' eyes were as wide as plates and her face was crimson with rage. The elf's hands quivered with the rest of her body as she spoke. "You..." she breathed. "*You* will pay for that, I am your queen and you will treat me as such. Do you understand, girl? Do not think that I will forgive you because you are in the sickbed."

Yayènia cocked an eyebrow and snorted. "I will treat you like a queen when you act like one."

Constancias' eyes widened further with fury and she grabbed hold of the front of Yayènia's loose tunic. "Do not think I will ever forget that you endangered the lives of twelve people, including my husband, your *king*, to save the life of *him*," she spat, gesturing at Suneelo.

Yayènia's splint snapped as she reached up to yank Constancias down closer to her face. "You do not *ever* speak of my husband in that sneering tone, you worthless cow."

Constancias ripped away from Yayènia's grasp and stood trembling with rage and fear. A sliver of purple light lashed out at Yayènia and blood blossomed on the younger elf's chest. Erdwyf screamed for Haly, shoving at the queen.

The healer came running in, red hair flying. "No, my Queen! Stop! Please!" the human screamed, grabbing a towel and pressing it to Yayènia's chest.

The High Commander thrashed about on her bed, shouting profanities at the half-Magin queen. Erdwyf finally succeeded in shoving Constancias out of the infirmary and locking the door securely as she could.

"What was that about?" Haly cried, ripping open Yayènia's shirt to inspect the damage.

Yayènia snarled and Erdwyf coughed irritably.

"Oh, thank the gods it's only a cut. Why did she attack you?"

"Because she is evil," Yayènia snapped.

Smiling a tight smile, Erdwyf sniffed. "She makes a better human, or dwarf than elf. No grace, dignity, or love in that one. I could see her wallowing in muck, smelling like a pig, and doing chores."

"Well, I don't see how being a human makes me more like her," Haly said stiffly.

"It does not, and you know that, Healer. Now please, work your magic so I can leave this bed," Yayènia replied.

Haly sighed and shooed Erdwyf off the corner of the bed again. "I will see what I can do, missy."

Yayènia settled against the bed and winced as the healer poked and prodded at her. "Your cuts are healing fine, and the bruises are fading, but your bones, dear. I don't know what you did that day when you made a mess of yourself and my infirmary. Saving Captain Suneelo was a brave choice, but it did something, lass, and I don't know what. Your bones reattached, as if they had been set and rested in a splint, but the muscles and flesh were still torn. Now, your body is healing at two different speeds."

"How is that possible?" Erdwyf asked, leaning over to look at Yayènia's legs.

"I don't know," Haly responded. "It's as if her bones have some sort of boost to them, and they are strengthening faster than muscle and flesh."

Yayènia tried to flatten down her chest so that she could look over and see her legs. "I can walk though."

"Yes," the human said, "but you are using your bones and the few tendons left to do so. I will see what I can do."

Yayènia stopped attempting to see what they were doing and laid her head back, looking over at Suneelo. He had turned his head again, still not awake. She gripped his hand, wincing, as Haly did something painful to her leg.

A few days later, Yayènia regained her strength enough to leave her bed. It was on the same day that Suneelo regained consciousness.

His violet eyes squinted open and he raised his arm to shield them from the torchlight. Yayènia rushed to his side.

"My love, you are awake!" she gasped, cupping his face with her hands.

"Nia..." he whispered, a ghost of a smile playing on his lips. "I dreamt of you."

Yayènia returned the smile. "And I of you, Neelo. How are you feeling? Where do you hurt?"

Suneelo managed a half-grin. "I hurt all over, but I am sure I slept through most of the pain. I take it you did not?"

The High Commander frowned. "Why do you say that?"

He put a hand to her face, stroking her cheek with his thumb. "I can see it in your eyes. Every hurt, every minute of it, is there. And you still hurt, though you try to hide it. My wife, do not be strong when you do not have to be."

Tears slid down Yayènia's face as she knelt by her husband's bed, leaning her head against his shoulder. "How can I not be when I am so afraid for you?" she whispered.

Their tender moment was broken when Ghealan strode in with Erdwyf, one heavy arm slung over his wife's shoulder.

The Second Commander went to the other side of Suneelo's bed and gently punched him in the shoulder. "Good to see you are alive. I was getting worried."

Suneelo laughed. "It would take a good deal more to take me out. I married Yayènia, remember."

They all laughed, Yayènia the hardest, more from relief than the joke. When the laughter subsided, Ghealan placed a hand gingerly on Suneelo's shoulder, where he had punched him. "It is good to see you in decent health, my friend."

"It is," Erdwyf said, holding Suneelo's left hand, as Yayènia had his right.

Suneelo smiled, genuinely touched. "Ah, well, it is good to be in decent heath, and to see all your shining faces. What happened after Yayènia arrived here? I do not remember."

As the three filled him in, Suneelo's mood grew darker and darker. "You should not have put so many, including yourselves, in danger for me. Although appreciated, any number of people could have been hurt, or killed."

Yayènia grunted. "As if any other's life is more important than yours, my love."

Suneelo squinted at her.

The next week was slow as Suneelo regained his strength and his body healed. The four friends were prone to huddling in the infirmary discussing plans of their impending departure from the underground city.

Erdwyf nicked maps from the makeshift archives while

Yayènia checked on guard routines, temporarily put under Captain Sargotarh's command. Ghealan snuck their armor from the armory where they were maintained by paid servants, for the rooms were too small to keep the sets themselves. Yayènia was mending her pack by Suneelo's bed when Ghealan walked in, frowning.

"What is it?" Suneelo asked, sitting up against his pillows.

"Constancias."

Yayènia rolled her eyes. Suneelo sneered.

Ghealan continued. "I think she is getting suspicious. She cornered Erd this morning to ask her why she was spending so much time in the archives. Erd told her as High Advisor, she could be wherever she pleased for however long, but Constancias would not take it. She said as queen, she had a right to know what her subjects were doing."

"And?" Yayènia prompted when Ghealan fell silent.

"My dear...loving...wife called our queen an over-involved hag."

Yayènia and Suneelo burst out laughing, but Ghealan grimaced more. "She struck her."

The laughter ended abruptly. Yayènia turned slowly in her chair.

"Constancias used her magic on Erdwyf," Ghealan said tightly, fists clenched.

Yayènia stood, half-mended pack falling to the floor. Suneelo pushed himself further against the pillows.

"That bitch," Yayènia growled. "First she hits me with it when I am in the sick bed, and now this? Where is Dietirin?"

"Yayènia, I have already told-"

"Where is Dietirin!" Yayènia shouted.

"In the throne room," Ghealan replied sullenly as Yayènia stomped by him.

Muttering, Yayènia shoved her way through the crowded tunnels. People scrambled out of the way as they recognized her, squeezing against the earthen walls. When she reached the throne room, the elf marched to the front of the line, drew her sword as she walked up the dais, and shoved the point at Constancias' face. People screamed, rushing to stand against the sides of the room, fearing to leave, fearing to stay.

Dietirin stood, robes whipping about him as he stared at

Yayènia. Constancias whimpered in her throne, pushing against the padding.

"High Commander! I demand to know what you are doing!" Dietirin said loudly, though he did not shout.

Without moving a hair, Yayènia answered the king. "Your wife attacked me while I was in the infirmary, insulted my husband, and then attacked High Advisor Erdwyf er'Tomyvon while in the archives, with magic, my king, while we have none."

The room fell silent but for Constancias' harsh breathing. Dietirin turned his blond head to face his wife. The queen stared at the thin point hovering inches from her throat.

"Is this true, Constancias?" Dietirin asked quietly.

The female shook her head, inky black hair flying. "No. She lies."

The king turned his gaze back to Yayènia. The warrior finally turned her face to give him a derisive look.

Dietirin sighed. "Constancias, I know Yayènia better than that. She is hot headed and stubborn, but she does not make false accusations. You on the other hand, seem hard put to tell the truth, and as queen, you get away with it. But I am king through blood, and even you must bend to my will. You will spend a week in the cells for your atrocities."

Constancias leapt forward in shock. Yayènia jerked her sword out of the way so that it skimmed the queen's neck, rather than impale it. The older elf howled in pain, slapping a hand to the cut. Yayènia stared at the queen in disgust, shaking the droplets of blood off her sword.

Dietirin cursed and pulled the High Commander back as purple light sizzled out of the queen.

"You barbarian!" Constancias shrieked, swiping at Yayènia with her free hand. "You heathen!"

Yayènia sneered at her from behind Dietirin's shoulder. The king shoved her back another step. When Constancias' light flashed again, it hit Dietirin in the thigh. The queen's hands flew to her mouth in horror. Yayènia, roaring in fury, launched by the king and drew her other blade so that the twin swords were crossed at Constancias' neck.

"Yayènia, no!" Dietirin yelled. "Stop!"

Yayènia's lip curled, but she stayed still. The king limped to stand next to her, one hand pressed to the bleeding wound.

Constancias quivered in terror between the two razor sharp blades.

"Put them away, High Commander," Dietirin said softly.

Yayènia did not move. The king sighed. "I know it is your life's duty to protect the royal family, but is not Constancias my wife? Is she not your queen?"

Yayènia's eyes were cold, her voice hard, as she answered. "Your wife sent my queen to her death, my lord. Tlonna is my queen."

Silence echoed in the earthen hall, the breath of hundreds held in suspense. Dietirin laid his free hand on Yayènia's shoulder. "Let her go, Yayènia, so that you may live to see them crowned. I ask it of you, but I do not command it."

Constancias stared up at her husband in disbelief and horror. Dietirin watched Yayènia. Yayènia glared at Constancias. Finally she put her swords up, freeing the queen. Immediately, the older female scrambled away toward the exit. Dietirin's voice stopped her.

"Constancias er'Ewôsdírn, you are hereby charged with assault against innocents, abuse of magic, attempted murder of the High Commander Yayènia er'Tiena, Countess of Blackhaven, Mother of the Silver Damnation elite, and for lying to the crown. You will spend the entirety of one month in the cells for your charges. Other than such a short term, you will receive no accommodations because of your status. Guards, take her."

Constancias spun around to stare at her husband, hatred roaring in amber eyes. The royal guards, usually under Suneelo's control, grabbed their queen and dragged her from the chamber.

Yayènia turned slightly as she sheathed her swords. "My lord, your leg is worth far more than one month alone."

Dietirin leaned heavily on the slighter elf as he pulled his bloodied hand away from the gash in his thigh. "Aye, but she is the queen, and her wrath will be terrible when she gets out. It would be worse if her punishment were longer."

"You should have her flogged," Yayènia growled as she helped him to his throne.

Dietirin chuckled dryly. "I should have let you cut off her head."

"Yes, you should have," the warrior replied, crouching to inspect the wound. "It is deep, but not irreparable. I will get Haly."

"No, send someone for her. You sit."

"Where, my king?" Yayènia asked, looking around the two thrones for another chair.

Dietirin patted the throne next to him. "It is only a chair, my child, after all."

Yayènia slowly moved to sit in the padded chair, her brows rising as she sank into the velvet. "Indeed. Now what?"

"We finish petitions. You have stood beside my throne for a hundred years, Yayènia, as have your friends. You know what is required," Dietirin replied simply.

Nodding, Yayènia sent a messenger to the infirmary, all the while pretending that her body did not pain her to near oblivion.

Beside her, Dietirin was ordering his people back into lines to continue petitions. The first up was a skinny old human covered in liver spots.

"My king...H-High C-Commander..." he stammered, staring at Yayènia with large eyes. "My room caved in last night. Not all the way, just a few chunks off the walls and ceiling."

"Was anyone hurt?" Dietirin asked.

"No Sire."

"Good, where is your room?"

As the man described the location of his room, the Royal Scribe, Ayona, wrote out the petition.

When the elderly man finished, Dietirin said, "We will send a dwarf to your room as soon as possible."

"Thank you my king," the human said, and tottered away.

The next petitioner was a stone nymph with gray hair, skin, and eyes. She fiddled with her leather skirt as Ayona readied another parchment.

"What is your petition, Lady Nymph?" Dietirin asked.

"My good king, High Commander, I have no petition, but a message. I work in the armory, and bits of armor have gone missing."

Yayènia shifted. Dietirin frowned. "What do you mean, bits of armor? Whose?"

The nymph's gray eyes looked to the ground. "High Commander's, Second Commander Ghealan's, High Advisor Erdwyf's, and Lord Captain Suneelo's, my king."

Dietirin's brow rose and he looked at Yayènia. "High Commander? Do you know anything of this?"

Yayènia looked at her lap, and then at the nymph. "What is

your name?"

"Granischolal, my lady High Commander."

"Granischolal, you have done your job well, but I am aware of those sets of armor. They are being inspected by their owners, including mine. But please, keep an eye on any other oddities you find in the armory, and you are welcome to bring your concerns to myself, or any of the elves you just mentioned."

Dietirin rubbed his mouth to hide a smile.

Granischolal curtseyed and went on her way.

"Will I soon be missing my four most valued advisors and protectors, Nia?" the king said quietly to Yayènia.

"We have our duties, Dietirin, the topmost being the protection of our true queen and future king. We received a letter, saying they are alive and in Kajgenia. We leave as soon as Suneelo is able."

Dietirin took a deep breath. "It is good to know that. I had feared the worst. Were you planning on telling me any time soon?"

"Aye, but we did not want Constancias to know. She knew about the letter. A wonder she did not tell you."

The male closed his eyes for a moment. "I curse my mother every day for putting me in this marriage. No wonder Tlonna felt the same." After a pause he said, "Is our friend Aidyn with them?"

"Yes," Yayènia replied simply, as another petitioner was ready.

The night came swiftly, and Suneelo was stretching in the infirmary when Yayènia arrived. Ghealan and Erdwyf were there as well. They all looked up when she took her seat.

"We heard what you did, Yayènia," Erdwyf said accusingly. "Haly rushed out of here faster than a blink when the messenger came and told us what happened. We thought we would stay here and let you tell us the whole story, rather than deal with the petition crowd."

Yayènia sighed and told them of her day.

Two weeks later, Suneelo could make it through a light training sequence with Ghealan. They readied to leave.

Dietirin clenched his jaw when he saw the four elves moving toward him with swift, purposeful strides. As one, they bowed in the military fashion, right hand on the hilt of the left sword, the left hand across their chest to grip either sword hilt or shoulder on the right, legs half bent as though in the middle of getting to one knee. It was Yayènia's idea that no one should be put on their knees when facing a friend, so she had devised the simple yet astoundingly aggressive bow.

Dietirin watched them rise in unison with knowing eyes, the muscles in his face straining to keep himself from demanding they stay. Slowly he stood, looking worriedly over the crowded, fearing their reaction. Yayènia, as highest ranking member of the city, besides himself and Constancias, who still resided in prison, drew a deep breath.

"King Dietirin, as High Commander of the Blackhaven Militia, I lay before you a petition."

Many of the nearest people stilled in surprise. It was not a petition day, and to lay out one was against the rules unless it was an emergency.

"Do as you must, High Commander," Dietirin said morosely.

Glancing at her husband, who nodded slightly, Yayènia moved a step closer. "Though it pains me," she began quietly so that only the king could clearly hear, "you knew this day would come, Dietirin."

"Yes, and what of it, Yayènia? Will my words yea or nay affect your decision? Will you stay because I fear for the four of you? No, you will not; so say what you will and get on with it."

"We leave tonight, while most of the people are asleep, so that we will not alarm them. We will travel through Purheae to reach Kajgenia, the last known place of Tlonna and Losolin. We will send word by Teelot if the need arise."

Dietirin swallowed to get the lump of sorrow from his throat. "As I said, my child, do as you must. All four of you," he said, beckoning to the three others. "Find her, my friends, and bring my daughter back to me. There are things at work in the world that bespeak of great things coming to fruition. I have scryed as much as I can, and I see a taint, I see pain and terror throughout Nymyños, and terrible grief. The land is crying, Nymyños is dying, and when it goes, all of us will die with her. I do not wish for you to go, but I see the need. You have the hope of all Blackhaven behind you."

Erdwyf briefly touched the king's hand, her pale blue eyes swimming with emotion. "Dietirin, we will not fail in this. I promise to you, we will bring back Tlonna and Losolin. And Aidyn as well. Watch for us, my lord, for we will come like a blaze of hope and victory."

Dietirin smiled at his High Advisor, great affection rumbling through his soul. Turning to Ghealan and Suneelo, he appraised them. "My boys." The two males smiled faintly at the honorary title Dietirin had taken to calling them a hundred years ago. "Are you well enough for such a journey?"

Suneelo nodded, the smile disappearing in a blink. "I am fit enough for this, Dietirin. I have been horizontal for too long."

The Magin King nodded at that, knowing the younger elf's strength and courage stopped him from showing how much pain he must truly be in. Clasping hands with Suneelo and Ghealan, Dietirin blinked back tears and held on tightly to the strong hands for what would be considered inappropriately long for a king. Releasing the males, he pulled Erdwyf into a hug. She returned it fiercely, not caring about the curious and worried eyes that bored into her back.

When Dietirin turned to Yayènia, she stepped into his arms willingly, but it was like hugging a bar of steel. Unlike Erdwyf, the warrior was stiff and unaccustomed to such gentleness. Releasing her, the king raised his head a slight margin.

"Go on then, and be safe. I will indeed watch for your return," he said huskily.

The four repeated their bow and strode from the hall without looking back. Dietirin sat heavily in his throne, watching the gossiping crowd move back into routine.

Yayènia blinked once to rid herself of betraying emotions and followed her husband into their tiny room. "It is good we are leaving before Constancias is released."

"Aye," agreed Suneelo as he routinely checked his gear.

"Neelo, are you positive you are ready for this? You still move stiffly."

The proud, bent back straightened as the Captain of the Guard stood to gaze down at his wife. "So do you, but nothing would hold you back, now would it?"

Yayènia shrugged, feeling the distant ache of recently healed limbs. "*Noya*, but you were far worse than I. I would stay for you."

Suneelo's brow rose in surprise. "Have I finally passed Tlonna in your book of importance?"

Hurt and stunned by her husband's venomous reply, Yayènia

gaped at him before jumping to her feet. "How can you make such an accusation? You are my husband, Suneelo! You have always and will continue to be the most important thing in my life. Tlonna is a beloved and cherished friend, but you are my heart. How can you be so cruel?"

"Cruel?" Suneelo snorted, flinging his hand out. "You ask how *I* can be so cruel? Yayènia, you have always put yourself in the line of fire for others. I understand that it is your job, but you have a family, and have had one for two hundred years! Can you finally accept that I love you just for you? I do not need for you to be the invincible warrior! I want you to be my wife! I want you to love me as you did Ghealan!"

Yayènia jerked back as though struck, her heart bleeding with pain. "I can never love you as I did Ghealan, because you are two different people, Suneelo. I love you only as I can love you. With all of my heart and soul, it will never change. My love for Ghealan has faded into an unbreakable friendship, but you, my husband, will always have my heart." She stepped to the door, looking back at him with cold eyes. "If you choose to step on it, then do so, but do not procrastinate any longer."

As she left the room, the warrior heard something smash against the earthen wall and her soul tried to rip itself to pieces. She strode down the corridor, ignoring the alarmed inquiries at her ashen face until she came to one of the nearly unused training rooms. A small domed cavern, it had been built in hopes of enticing the able-bodied people to become the new army. Yanking one of the sparring staffs from the dusty racks, Yayènia flowed into position, blanking her mind.

Ghealan knocked on the rough door of his friend's room and started slightly when it was yanked open a second later to reveal a distraught Suneelo. The other male's eyes tightened, but he stepped aside to allow Ghealan inside.

"What is wrong?" the Second Commander asked as soon as the door was shut.

"Nia and I fought, and now she is probably off working herself to death," Suneelo muttered, pacing the tiny room.

"Fought? About what?" Ghealan asked, though he feared he knew.

Suneelo sent him a look that told him he was right. "What do you expect, Lan?"

Ghealan shrugged one shoulder. "You can bloody well get over it, Suneelo. It was over two hundred years ago, and I love Erdwyf. Besides, you did not see the way Yayènia acted when you were both bedridden. She held onto whatever tiny bit of you she could, even in her sleep. The first thing she did when she woke after the first time was scream your name. Do you not believe that she loves you?"

Suneelo jerked his head in denial. Ghealan ploughed on. "What love there was between us is gone, Suneelo. Now we are friends, and that is all either of us wish. We were never meant to be together. You and her are, as Erd and I are. Understand that, please. Do you think there is anyone else better suited for Yayènia than you? Have you not stood side by side for two centuries? Well?"

The blond male sighed, stopped his pacing. "I know all that, Lan, but...there are times I think, given a chance, she would run to you before me, if she ran at all. The female shows no emotion! She might as well be carved out of stone! She said I could stomp on her heart if I wished, as long as I did not draw it out any longer. Do you know what that feels like when it is said with cold, dry eyes?"

Ghealan huffed out a breath. "That is Yayènia's way. She was taught at a young age to show indifference to her life, that she was just property. That is a hard thing to unlearn, especially when it is pounded into you for one and half hundred years. She loves you, more than she ever did me. Never doubt that."

Suneelo thumped onto the bed and dropped his head into his hands. "I know. It just gets to me sometimes and then I say things I regret seconds later."

"We all do," Ghealan snorted, thinking of his own wife.

"Do you have these fights with Erdwyf?" Suneelo asked.

After a pause, the brown-haired warrior nodded. "Yes. Not as often as we used to, though. About twice a year."

Suneelo drew a deep breath. "Thank you. You can always put it into perspective for me. Ah...is there a reason you came, or did you see Nia?"

Ghealan joined his friend on the bed. "No, there was a reason. Do you have a spare repair hammer? Mine seems to have gone missing."

"Oh, yeah. Here," Suneelo replied, reaching into his pack and handing the small hammer to his friend.

"Thank you. Erdwyf found a dent in her vambrace and about murdered someone."

"I do not blame her," Suneelo said, feeling slightly more cheery.

Ghealan slapped his friend on the knee. "Were I you, I would find my errant wife and seduce her until she forgets what she is angry about."

Suneelo nodded and stood. "If I am not at the door tonight, you will know what happened."

The Second Commander smiled. "Aye, I will, and I will be sure to upbraid my superior for murdering a decent Captain of the Guard."

Chuckling, the two males stepped out of the room and went separate ways, Ghealan back to his room, Suneelo to find his wife. It took him little less than ten minutes to find her, the sound of a bowstring twanging betraying her presence. Leaning against the open door, the male watched Yayènia bury yet another arrow into the bull's eye of a straw target.

"I wonder if it is my face you see in the center of those rings," he said after a while.

The warrior's head turned slightly, acknowledging his presence as little more than an irritant. Another arrow thudded into place, forcing two arrows to split.

"What do you want?" Yayènia asked finally.

Suneelo moved into the room and shut the door behind him. "I want you to talk to me. For the gods' sake, Nia, I know you feel, so let me in. You do not have to hide your emotions behind a steel wall. Please, let me be your foundation!" the last came out a plea as his wife continued to stare at the bristling target, the long bow in her hands held parallel to the ground in a white-knuckled fist.

Finally, when Suneelo thought she might just stand there all day, Yayènia's proud shoulders slumped. The bow clattered to the floor and the elf fell to her knees. Rushing to his wife's side Suneelo knelt before her, his hands cupping her face.

Yayènia looked up at him with wide, watery eyes. Her beautiful face contorted with emotions Suneelo had never seen her show. Grief, pain, confusion, and the one that shocked him the most, fear. Unable to speak, the male merely stared at his wife. Slowly, her hands came up to wrap around his wrists, not to draw them away, but to anchor herself.

"Suneelo...I...it is too much," and her face began to stone up again.

Suneelo shook her. "No! Yayènia, for once, please, now while we have the chance, *please.*"

And his wife crumpled into his arms, her strong shoulders heaving with heart-wrenching sobs that he knew contained four hundred years and more of pain and regret. He'd seen her cry, seen raw emotion flicker across her face to be contained in an instant, but Suneelo had never held Yayènia while she cried in unabated emotion. They sat in the middle of the room for over an hour while the High Commander of the decimated Blackhaven Militia sobbed in anguish. Every now and then gasping words would explode from her, breaking Suneelo's heart, even though he knew this was a step in the direction of mental stability. Words that told him she was reliving the most painful parts of her history, the most horrible and soul tearing things that should never happen to a person.

Finally, when Yayènia's sobs subsided into a weak sniffs, Suneelo held up her face and pressed a kiss gently on her mouth. He could taste her tears. "I love you."

Yayènia closed her eyes and laid her head on his lap, fiddling with the laces of his pants. "And I you."

Stroking her long braid, the male pulled it toward him until he could reach the end. Smiling a little, he brushed the tickly end across her face until, surprisingly, she giggled. Suneelo gaped down at her in shock, he'd never heard her giggle except when he could entice it from her in bed, and that was not the innocent sound she had just emitted.

Yayènia did not seem to notice that she had giggled, but she did sit up, wiping her eyes on the back of her sleeve. Looking at her husband with tear-stained eyes, the warrior took his hand.

"You were wrong, my heart," she said in a husky voice.

"Was I?" Suneelo asked in surprise.

"Mmm...it was not your face in the center of the target. It was Ghealan's."

"Ghealan's?"

"Aye, I was so mad at him for existing. I feared that maybe this would be the breaking point for us, and I blamed it on him. Suneelo, you know that I never regret marrying you. You *are* my foundation. Please understand that. There is no one in this world more perfect for me, but you know that, do you not?"

"I know it," Suneelo said quietly.

"That is good, then," Yayènia replied just as quietly, scooting closer to him. "Because I do not plan on ever letting you go."

Relief, sudden and unexpected, flooded through Suneelo as the female snuggled against his chest.

It was another hour before they stood and strolled back to their room, hand in hand. Passersby stared in open shock at seeing two of their greatest warriors meandering along the corridor, apparently at ease and deeply in love.

Night came swiftly afterward and soon Yayènia and Suneelo, Erdwyf and Ghealan stood in full armor in the dimly lit hall that led to the door in the statue. The two males shared a look over their wives' heads. Yayènia checked her various weapons and then needlessly inspected her three companions.

"Nia," Ghealan muttered, "this is not our first time going outside."

"Shut up," Yayènia said lightly and resumed pulling on his pack to ensure that it was secure.

With a final jerk, Yayènia left her second alone and then strode to the front of them. "Are we ready?"

Suneelo and the other couple nodded, taking deep breaths. With a slight grimace, Yayènia pulled the thick door open and stepped into the star-strewn winter night. Burrowing into the black snow, she beckoned to the others and they followed her into the cold tunnel. Ghealan pushed the door closed, making sure to cover up the disturbance in the snow, and then caught up with the other three. They tunneled through the thick snow as more of the taint fell softly, sounding a light rain to the elves' perceptive ears.

Disturbed by the lack of activity from the castle, the four moved cautiously once they ran out of snow thick enough to hide them. Yayènia padded forward, her bow knocked and ready in case she saw someone, her ornate armor glinting in the moonlights. Suneelo could see the bare skin where her short cuirass ended just above her ribs to allow for easy maneuvering on foot and on horseback. There was a good eight inches of vulnerable flesh all the way around, but the male knew she had never maintained a wound in the area. She moved so smoothly it was as if she were part of the shadows, silent even to Suneelo.

Behind him, Erdwyf moved with perhaps a sliver less refinement than Yayènia, her steps just audible to him. Ghealan, farther back, brought up the rear with the dangerous, wolf-like grace that made him distinct in any crowd. Vaguely, Suneelo wondered how he moved and looked in his armor. Yayènia was a shadow, Erdwyf a cat, and Ghealan a wolf.

When they reached the inner gate without happenstance, Erdwyf moved close to Yayènia. "Something is wrong. There should be demons crawling all over the place, even at night. It looks abandoned."

"It is not, there are lights in the windows," Ghealan said quietly.

"Aye, but still," the advisor said, looking up at the twinkling lights.

"I do not care where they are, so long as they leave us alone," Yayènia hissed, and slid into the deeper darkness of the gate arch, keeping her back to the wall.

Suneelo followed her, then Erdwyf and Ghealan, as usual, bringing up the rear. They sprinted across the open road into the shadow of a burned shop, looking about to see if they were spotted.

"The Black Door is across from here, is it not? North from here?" Yayènia asked Erdwyf in a hushed whisper.

The advisor looked out at the street and then nodded. "Yes, though it might be a bit west as well. I cannot be sure in this darkness."

Yayènia nodded her understanding and they crept in line to the next building. Suddenly, the High Commander's twin katans came free of their sheathes with a scrape and the female dived to the left. Confused and startled, the three behind her slowed to a halt and waited in the dark. A second passed and then two men came into view, lean humans with a mean look about them.

"I heard it, Goro, I know I did. Swords, I swear."

"Yer drunk, Drake, like always. I didn't hear nothin'."

Suddenly Yayènia moved into view and slammed her blade into Drake's kidney. The human stiffened in silent agony while Goro looked around in surprise. Suneelo bowled into him and they landed in a puff of tainted snow. With one powerful blow to the chin, the male simultaneously shattered the human's jaw and snapped his neck.

Yayènia straightened from cleaning her blade and they dragged the bodies into a building.

"There will be no hiding the blood or the tracks," Erdwyf muttered as she searched the stiffening body of Drake. "Ah...pretty," she said, holding up an emerald-hilted dagger.

"With this damnable snow, there is no need to hide the blood, and hopefully it will continue to snow enough to conceal the tracks," Yayènia said as she watched her friend turn the dagger.

Ghealan and Suneelo were stripping Goro of all his weapons too, which turned out to be quite disappointing. Two daggers, both of them wood, and a crude mace was all the human carried.

"Pretty pitiful for patrolling guards, I would say," Suneelo said.

"Aye," Yayènia agreed.

They left the building with its two corpses and continued onward. They met with no other guards when they reached the massive black wall. Creeping along in its shadow, the four elves moved west until they found the little side door named the Black Door.

Suneelo turned to Erdwyf. "Do you have your key?"

"My key? What-ooh, yes, I do," the High Advisor whispered back. She fussed with the small pouch at her side and then held aloft an ornate iron key.

Yayènia scowled. "You carry your key to the city around with you?"

Erdwyf scowled back. "No, but I was not about to leave it there for anyone to pick up when they discover us gone. A skeleton key is a very dangerous tool when it is in the wrong hands."

"Of course it is, now give it to me," Suneelo said, pulling it out of her fingers.

Ghealan smirked at his friend and then put a hand on his wife's back. "Erd, do not look so put off. Suneelo knows what he is doing."

"I bloody well know that, Ghealan."

The elf ran his fingers along the door feeling for the keyhole while the others stood guard. Yayènia moved away when she heard a pair of steps behind her. Glancing at Erdwyf's back as her companions looked out into the night, Yayènia pivoted. A short Darkwight stopped suddenly. His black eyes glinted in the starlight, staring at her.

"Aren't you the elf King Rahlan had hanging from the wall? Come here."

Yayènia stepped closer to him so that he was forced to crane his neck to look her in the eye. "What, exactly, are you planning to do?" the female asked calmly, releasing one of the hidden daggers on her wrist.

Before the Darkwight could reply, the blade was up to the hilt in its neck. Black blood oozed out onto the carved badger's head. Backing away the Darkwight stumbled on its robes and fell, its dark eyes widening in surprise and pain. Yayènia yanked her dagger out and cleaned it on his robes before running to join her comrades. They were watching her return from the door, Erdwyf's key protruding from the lock.

Her husband looked from the blood on her hand to her face, inquiring.

Yayènia sniffed. "Darkwight."

"Of course..." Suneelo replied, squinting.

Without another word, he turned the key and they watched as the stone lock twisted to form the shape of the Kairhotuss tree that was the insignia of Blackhaven. Suneelo pulled the key out and handed it to Erdwyf who stowed it in her pouch. The elf put his shoulder to the stone and pushed. The door moved ponderously outward, grating loudly. Yayènia drew her twin blades and stood guard in case anything heard the noise.

Three demons came running, their black robes billowing like inky wings. Ghealan smashed one of their heads in with the mace from Goro as Yayènia dispatched another with a scissor form of her two blades. The third ran directly at Erdwyf who was helping Suneelo push the door open. She was grappling for her axe when the demon fell against her, two daggers jutting from its back. She pushed it off as both Yayènia and Ghealan retrieved their daggers.

With a nod to her husband and friend, Erdwyf picked up her axe off the ground. Suneelo grunted as the door finally swung open enough to admit them through. The four slid through and then pushed the door closed.

Kairhotuss trees surrounded them, far more than they did in the city. The world became full of sound. Birds and animals moved within the huge forest, making it seem as though the trees themselves were alive. Above all, was the sound of leaves falling and a nonexistent wind moving through them, making the black shimmer above them. The pearly trunks made the wood look as though it was silver, shining and smooth, especially in the moonlights.

Yayènia shifted her pack on her back and sighed. "Once we reach Schelum, we need to get horses."

Ghealan nodded and then started walking through the midnight forest.

It took them three days to get through the dense forest and onto the rolling hills of the Elnya Highlands. They moved over the rising mounds slowly, fearing the openness of their position. No attack came, however, and they settled into the night with a small camp fire.

"Do you think they will still be in Kajgenia by the time we get there?" Erdwyf asked as she turned the spit over the fire, roasting three skinny rabbits.

"No," Suneelo said, leaning back to gaze at the stars. "But their passage will be known from there. Aidyn said they have an army behind them, so they will be noticed by everyone."

Yayènia nodded, oiling one of her swords. "Aye, and Tlonna would not go to Seaduens, so the only place that would make sense to go to would be Florwen Hune."

"Tlonna and Losolin may not remember that Seaduens is enemy territory, though," Ghealan countered.

Yayènia shot him a look through the dark. "I do not think they will go there. They will have heard the stories, I am sure. This Miazie sounds intelligent enough to inform them of Seadueni politics."

"We cannot make our plans on the written word of a human, Nia. I do not care how intelligent she may seem, she may not see Tlonna's necessary education to be the same as us," the eldest elf said.

Yayènia glared at her second over the crackling fire. "You forget that Aidyn is with them. He will not let them go there, either."

Ghealan conceded and followed Suneelo's example and lay back to study the stars and moons. For the first time in days it had stopped snowing and the sky was dark and clear.

On the sixth day from their departure from Blackhaven City, the elves reached the bridge that crossed the river border between Blackhaven and Schelum. The Argynd River stretched a quarter mile wide, and ran from the R'Kunad Sea to the Strait of Arwênlhias, the body of water that separated Kismath from Blackhaven. High Reef also stemmed from the northern mouth of the Argynd River, splitting the border of the Fãrthyn Ocean and the R'Kunad. The Jaquisa River flowed from Sethryn Lake in the middle of the Liberated Lands and met the Argynd at Silarnim Fork to flow in short but massive rapids to the Strait of Arwênlhias. Two bridges crossed the Argynd, though the southern Sha Bridge was rarely used as it opened on the harsh Hidden Plains. The northern Lybera Bridge was a behemoth of black-veined white marble.

It had no sides and sloped steeply across the river. The roadbed was carved in a relief of Furntil Eldrout's assassination of Brandon Stynbek, though it had been worn smooth by a thousand years of use, and from the edges hung finely wrought marble that looked as though it were lace draping toward the raging torrent of the Argynd.

Yayènia glared at the water as they approached the bridge, never one to like the wet. At the foot of Lybera Bridge, all four stared at the massive visage of Furntil as he drew back his famous white bow.

"I wonder, were Furntil to be alive today, what he would do against Midian?" Erdwyf murmured as they stepped onto the smooth marble.

"He would fight back," Yayènia snarled fiercely, clutching her elfin blade's hilt as she tried to ignore the roar of the water.

"Yes, he would," Suneelo said, knowing that he was the only person in the world Yayènia had told about her fear of water.

The four stepped off the bridge onto Schelumite soil and nearly gagged on the poisoned feel of the air.

It was a tangible difference between the two kingdoms. Behind them, though tainted, there was a feeling of restiveness and purity that cleared the senses and left one feeling refreshed.

"I was not prepared for this," gasped Erdwyf, a hand to her throat as though she really were choking.

Yayènia sent her a sympathizing look, though her hands clenched at her sides. Ghealan closed his eyes and shook himself, grimacing with disgust. Suneelo squinted against the unpleasant feeling of filth, crossing his arms to stop himself from wiping his skin.

"We must continue," Yayènia said in a thick voice and grabbed Erdwyf by the elbow.

The four set off across the snow-covered field that stretched for miles in all directions. By the time night was upon them, they had found the once grand city of Barl. Approaching the closed gate, they hailed a guard.

"State your name and business," he shouted down.

Yayènia smiled faintly and said, "I am Yayènia, this Suneelo, Erdwyf, and Ghealan. We are traveling to Kajgenia to find an old friend. We are from Blackhaven City."

The guard disappeared for a second and then reappeared with two of his cohorts. "Yayènia er'Tiena? Ghealan Tomyvon?"

"Yes..." Yayènia replied, frowning.

"The High Commander and the Second Commander of the Blackhaven Militia? The ones who led the assault against Aderiaen Rahlan a hundred some odd years ago? Really?"

"Yes, now will you open the bleeding gate and let us through?" Yayènia shouted.

"Of course. Just one second High Commander!"

The guards moved away from the wall and the gate began to open slowly. Suneelo grunted at his wife.

"What?"

"People know the commanders of the militia, but do not know the captain of the guard, or the high advisor to the strongest monarchs in all of Nymyños. I just find it odd."

Ghealan punched his friend in the shoulder. "Just because you have never done anything spectacularly courageous and stupid does not mean you should be jealous of those who do it as a career, my friend. We need wet rags like you to make us look better. You do your part."

"Watch it, Ghealan. I am not afraid to send Nia on you," Suneelo replied, grinning.

"Mmm...indeed," Yayènia said as the gate opened enough for them to walk through side by side.

A stocky man in a Schelum cuirass, which sported the city's boar, bowed deeply to the four. "I am Captain Byron. Welcome to the city of Barl," he waved his gnarled hand towards the devastated city behind him.

"I am Suneelo Tiena, Count of Blackhaven, and husband of Yayènia," the male tilted his head toward Yayènia. "Is there an inn we can stay at, and the market?"

"Yes, the Black Book and the market are both on the street

after this one. Anything else I can help you with?" the five started moving towards a street behind the buildings facing them on the left side.

"No."

"Very well then. Just follow me." the man moved through the small crowd and emerged onto the street on the left. "The inn is over there, Mistress Sary can speak Parlêthian, if that would be easier for you, and the market is over there. See you 'round," the man turned and walked away.

"Well, lets see what we can do about this market," Erdwyf said.

They moved towards a drab square where drab people looked at wares. A while later, the four elves walked out burdened with food and pots. Humans stared at them, their dirty faces full of suspicion and wonder. Erdwyf snarled at a young man who reached out to pinch her thigh. He backed away so fast he fell. Yayènia walked hand on sword and glared at anybody that looked at her twice.

A girl ran screaming to the elves and tried to hide behind Yayènia. Three grimy boys stopped dead in their tracks and looked up, terror written on their faces. The largest gathered himself and puffed out his skinny chest.

"The wench is ours. Can we have her back?" his voice faltered slightly, but he spoke Elvish perfectly.

"What do you mean she is yours, boy?" Yayènia said threateningly.

"My father said that if we catch her, we could have her to please us. We caught her but she got away. Come now pretty elf, give her back."

"You will not speak to my wife that way you little rat. Nor to anybody else of your superior," Suneelo growled, receiving startled looks from passersby.

The boy laughed and soon the other two started in. "What are you going to do? Throw flowers and leaves at us? Aren't you afraid of getting dirty?" he said as he pranced about on his toes and daintily holding up his grimy tunic.

With a snarl, Ghealan hurled forward, spinning the quarterstaff in his hands. Within seconds, the elf had the three boys on their backs, the weapon pressed lengthwise to their necks.

"Some flowers are poisonous."

The boys flinched away and nodded. Ghealan straightened and kicked dirt at them.

"Git."

The trio scrambled to their feet and ran, looking back over their shoulders.

The girl edged away from Yayènia and stood very rigid. Erdwyf gave a warning glance to her friend and reached out to the girl.

"How old are you, girl, and what is your name?" the Advisor asked gently.

"I am fifteen. My name is Carlima. Thank you for stopping Tyriol and his friends. They hurt me and-and do other stuff to me," the human said, speaking hesitant Elvish.

"Well, now, they will want you even more because they were stopped. Come to the inn with us and Lady Yayènia and I will help you," Erdwyf said cheerfully in Hindarün, the human language.

As the five made their progression to the inn, the inhabitants stared. Dust rose around the streets and old piles of ash lay soaked into the ground. The Black Book was a small wooden building situated on the corner of the dirt street. The wooden sign hanging above the door was of an old tome with a black cover. Yayènia pushed open the door and looked around. After seeing the common room was empty except for a man sitting by the fire, she sheathed her sword. The others followed, their weapons cased in the holders. Carlima walked in clutching her skirts and Ghealan's arm.

Erdwyf raised her eyebrows but stayed silent. A very robust woman came rushing toward them in a huff.

"I heard about four elves in the city. I take it you want to stay at the Black Book?" the woman spoke perfect Elvish, startling the elves.

"Yes that is cor-" Suneelo began but the large woman cut him off, speaking Hindarün.

"What are you doing with them, Carlima? Do not bother them," Mistress Sari said loudly. the girl next to Ghealan shook.

Moving in front of the human, Yayènia attempted to hold back a snarl. "We brought her with us, Mistress. She is going to stay with us tonight. Now, may we go to our rooms please?"

The large woman studied the elf for a long moment, then waving a thick hand said, "Follow me."

Ghealan placed his saddlebags on the bed and sighed. "You know, for such a tiny little human, that girl has a tight grip," he rubbed his arm where Carlima had held him.

Erdwyf chuckled and kissed her husband on the cheek. "Yes, but you handled it so very well, all tough and brooding like," she teased. "It is good that you have such fatherly tendencies, love. You will need to be, in a bit..." the female smiled slyly.

"What do you mean, I need to be? Are you...?" Ghealan stared at his wife and then laughed joyously.

Erdwyf laughed with him, "I wanted to tell you earlier but you were so busy and worried about Yayènia and Suneelo," the elf unconsciously put a hand to her stomach.

"When will it be born Erd? Soon?" the elf stood and put his arms around the female he loved.

"No, not soon. I just realized it about a month ago, so we still have the two years. I was hoping we would be back in control of Blackhaven by the time it was born. Now...I do not know," Erdwyf snuggled into the strong chest. "I have thought of some names, but I want you to have your say of course. If it is a girl: then Leliea, Jaryikin, or Fwoeur. If it is a boy: Ghealas, Wilaoq, Steanis, or Anuas. Which do you prefer, or do you have any ideas?"

"I am not one with names, but I like Jaryikin. I do hope it is a girl. But for now, I think, we should exercise," Ghealan smiled roguishly and pushed Erdwyf gently onto the bed.

Chapter 13
The Alchemists

Damon shifted in the small camp tent and snarled when he ran into Miazie's back. The woman sniffed and shifted away from him. The general of the assassin's guild was not use to being in a small two-man tent made of thick canvas. Muttering quietly, he slipped out of the tent and pulled his dark cloak about his person. Shivering in the winter cold, Damon knelt by the cold fire and poked it. Sparks stirred and then faded. A wind blew the remaining live embers away. Cursing, he looked around, though he knew no one was there watching him. Staring at the ashes, Damon focused on a flame in his mind and the fire sprang back to life. Sighing, he placed a piece of wood in the pit and sat back on his haunches. Staring into the flames, the man waited for the dawn to arrive.

A while later, Miazie stepped out of the tent and stretched. She walked over to Damon and sat by him.

Smiling, she rested her wrists on her knees and took a deep breath. "Why did you leave?"

"Hm? Oh, I couldn't sleep, too crowded in that small tent. I'm not used to it." He looked at her. Miazie stared back into the dark green eyes and suppressed a sigh. Dark circles shadowed them, a growth of stubble on his face making him look twice as scruffy.

"Damon, I know this has been hard for you, but you must get past it. If we are to help Tlonna, then we must be strong. Many more sacrifices will be made in order to preserve the world as we know it. Tlonna has lost her family, her home, her friends, and her previous life. Losolin as well. I have left my home and family as well as my title of princess. I lost my freedom because of you. Now you must sacrifice your comforts. Give up with this pitiful attitude," Miazie snapped.

"I'm sorry for that, Miazie, I really am."

"If you were sorry you wouldn't have done it in the first place. Now get going. I need to wake Ryun, and his little present you made for him, so we can leave."

"How was I to know you were a princess?" Damon said defensively.

"It doesn't matter what I am, it matters that you forced me into your bed, forced me into a marriage, and I will never forgive you for that. It is akin to rape, as far as I am concerned. Now move," Miazie snarled and then stood.

An hour passed and then they were on their way. Snow began to fall and soon the four were lost in a flurry of black. Miazie and Damon tied their horses together and tried to find Ryun and his wife. Shouting, the pair turned in circles until two figures rode up and tied themselves to the others. Nodding to Ryun, Miazie set to staring into the blizzard.

It was nightfall before the group found shelter behind a large boulder that curved into a sort of tiny cave. The horses were brought in and tethered to a log in the back. The humans huddled together until they fell into a fitful sleep. During the night, darkly clad figures surrounded the cave and peered inside. A woman's voice shouted orders in the howling wind and flying snow. The figures pulled the four people and their horses out and after mounting the comatose humans on the horses, navigated the dark, freezing landscape back to a large encampment.

Miazie stirred and opened her eyes just in time to see a huge shiny, black wall that moved with the wind before succumbing to the cold and falling asleep.

"Wake up woman. You must meet with the Lady Elwyn. Wake!" a hand slapped Miazie's face and the Belau sat up angrily. A gray clad man stood above her, his young face annoyed.

"I'm up, but who are you and where am I? Who is Lady Elwyn?" the woman rubbed her hands across her eyes and then snatched the blanket up to her neck when she realized she was naked.

"Here, I am Alchemist Wherman. You are in Alchemian, Lady Elwyn is our leader," he handed her a brown robe and she took it carefully. "Hurry, the Lady is not as patient as she used to be. I will wait outside."

The man left and Miazie slipped the robe on. After pulling her long hair into a braid, she walked outside and shied away from the bright sun.

"What happened to the blizzard? Where's all the snow?" Miazie said as she followed the man down dirt roads, staring at the perfectly lined up gray, white, and black tents. Small plants stood outside the flaps and children played among the little yards. Robed men and women hurried along the roads, some empty handed, others holding odd objects or jars.

"Alchemian always has sun and warmth. The snow is outside our walls, but we will stay warm and comfortable inside." The man turned and then stopped next to the largest striped tent she had ever seen. "Lady Elwyn is waiting inside. Curtsy and show respect to her. I leave you now," Wherman left and Miazie stepped inside the dark tent.

To her surprise, the interior was brightly lit and no shadows were visible. Stand torches and braziers were placed strategically throughout the tent. A large black oak desk was in the corner, and behind it sat a shadowy, misty black figure.

Miazie curtsied and averted her eyes. "Lady Elwyn. I am Mia-"

"I know who you are, Miazie Paron, exiled daughter of Lord Darren Ughtren, King of Anutch, wife of Lord Damon Suutson, General of the Shitan-Kulata. Sit, I must ask you some questions." The figure motioned to a stool and Miazie sat on it, her back rigid.

The shadow shifted and a woman sat in its place. "I am the Lady Elwyn, High Alchemist of Alchemian. I have heard some disturbing news. News of an Elven princess who is seeking our help in the defeat of the Lord Midian. What is it that brought you here from your place beside her?"

Miazie peered into the dark cowl trying to see the face of the woman who spoke. "I have a document, a prophecy, that I need your help understanding. It seems clear at first, but the more I ponder it, the more befuddled I become. Tlonna sent me here so that we may better understand it. She is recruiting armies to fight Midian, but as of my departure, had very few men. Her Consort is a half-Magin, but is still more powerful than most of the original Magins. His name is Lord Losolin."

The High Alchemist didn't move. Miazie could hear her breathing and licked her lips nervously. "Fetch the parchment. Alchemist Sodo will take you to your quarters."

Acknowledging the dismissal, Miazie stepped outside and found another man, clad in white, waiting for her. He was tall and fair, green eyed and blond haired. He declined his head to her and Miazie saw pointed ears peeking out of the pale hair. He moved with a fluid, powerful grace that reminded her uncomfortably of Losolin.

"You're an elf," she said nervously. "I did not know elves were also involved in alchemy."

"Yes. After the devastation in Arseninis, I had no place left to go. Hard times can bring about life altering changes in one's life. I wound up here with the gift of alchemy in my hands." Miazie nodded and followed the elf in silence until he stopped next to a gray tent. "This is your tent. Hurry up and get what the lady told you to get."

Miazie ducked into the tent and searched for her clothes. They were in a neat pile on a stool. She found the small leather bag in which the folded parchment was. She pulled the instructions out and took a moment to look around the tent. The tent had no bottom so the soft springy grass was the floor. It was bare except for a small rug that covered the area of grass next to a cot. A brazier sat next to the entrance as well as the stool with her clothes. A small dark entrance opened into the back of the tent. Miazie would have gone into it but Sodo called to her. The woman went outside and followed him back to Elwyn's tent.

The lady stood in the center of the large entrance room arguing with another black robed woman. The newcomer was skinny as a bamboo shoot and her movements were large and animated. She turned around and Miazie almost gaped in shock. Her face was very sharp, her eyes were huge dark green orbs. She snarled at Miazie and Sodo, showing very white, very sharp teeth. Miazie backed into the elf behind her and felt him tense.

"Kryll! Stop this nonsense! We will find you a new apprentice if Tymyn is not working out. Now, I have business to do with our visitor. Go back to your lab," Elwyn pointed to the opening and the odd woman turned, glaring at Miazie. As she exited, the tent flap brushed her cowl back to reveal dark green hair in a multitude of braids.

Miazie stared after her in shock until Sodo backed away from her and she felt his body leave contact with hers.

"She is a spryte, Miazie. A very irritable spryte as you can see. Her apprentice does not like working with her and so he ignores her most of the time. We just inducted a new boy, a spryte like Kryll. Handsome thing he is, but I think he and she will get along just fine. Now, back to our previous matter. This prophecy?" Elwyn sat down on the corner of her desk and Miazie sat on the stool. She unfolded the sheet and gasped in surprise when it floated out of her hands to hang suspended in front of the still shadowy cowl. Elwyn jerked while she read and then leaned forward to read it again, intently. When she finished, the alchemist folded it back up and took it out of the air.

"May I keep this?" Elwyn looked at Miazie.

"Yes, it is just a copy. The original is back with Tlonna. It was in the binding of a book called *Chronicles of Astinus*. Do you know it?"

"Yes, I believe so. Astinus was a seer, but he was also an alchemist you know. We are devout followers of his, and Veries Gurgen, his most treasured and trusted friend."

"Aye, of the Third Triad of the original fifteen Magins," Miazie added, receiving a startled look from the High Alchemist.

"Why does this prophecy befuddle you so much? It is one of his more transparent Seeings."

Miazie shrugged uncomfortably. "I don't know. It seems odd that it is so transparent. It is the prophecy that has made the most impact on the world, whether or not Nymyñosians have noticed it. There is something hidden within the simple words that I cannot understand. Something, that when tied with other information I have, is very sinister."

"Other information? What information?" Elwyn asked sharply.

Miazie hesitated. "We...Tlonna, Losolin, and I...were visited by the Cyree."

"The Cyree?" Elwyn nearly scoffed.

"Yes, the Cyree, and she told us many things. One of the more memorable lines was that Tlonna had too much power, but not enough. The thing that confounds me is the titles given in this prophecy. Tlonna believes the lover to be Losolin, the friend to be me, herself to the moon heiress, and perhaps an assassin named Aidyn to be the guardian. I, however, have come to wonder if Tlonna is all four? Different aspects of her nature that will in turn govern the near future."

Elwyn's eyebrows rose slightly. "An interesting insight. I shall ponder it."

"Is that it? Have you no thoughts of your own?" Miazie asked, incredulous.

Behind her, Sodo hissed in a breath. Elwyn gave him a look and he crossed his arms in a meek way. Miazie glared at the High Alchemist.

After a while, the robed woman spoke. "I have many thoughts, Miazie Paron, and it is not up to you to scorn my silence. I will tell you what I wish to tell you, and I will not what I wish to keep to myself. You are not exclusive to my thoughts."

Miazie felt her lip curl in defiance. "I brought you this prophecy, and it is mine to take away, *High Alchemist.* I am the advisor to Tlonna Arune Ewôsdírn, the Magin Queen of Nymyños, and I am also a Belau. I will have *all* your thoughts on this prophecy, or you will suffer mine and all of Blackhaven's wrath."

"Leave us, Sodo," Elwyn said sharply, casting a gloved hand toward the tent entrance.

Sodo bowed and then left the tent. Elwyn stood and walked to where Miazie was sitting. "Now we may speak freely." She dropped cowl to reveal her face. It was young and pretty. Her hair was shoulder length cinnamon brown, and was in tight springy curls. Her eyes were bright green and her skin was the color of honey.

"My name is Elwyn Arkayn. I came from Zeynuwn. I was of the Black sect of Alchemy, that which deals in the more violent of chemicals, living liquids and such, before I took my place as High Alchemist," the woman said, sitting on her desk.

Miazie did not let her guard down at the sudden change in topic. Instead, she crossed her legs at the knee and kicked her skirt in irritation. "You know who and what I am. Where are my three companions?"

Elwyn smiled. "They are in a separate tent, still unconscious. I knew you to be important so I woke you."

"How did you know I was important?"

"You had more items on you than any of the others, yet you did not dress as a servant. You were either nobility or a scholar. It appears you are both. A Belau has not walked Nymyños in over a hundred years. One of my alchemists recognized you from a trip to Anutch some years ago."

"Indeed. The prophecy?"

"Ah, not one to be taken of track, then," Elwyn said, smiling faintly this time.

"No. I have traveled far and hard to bring this to you. Do not make me regret it."

"You had a run in with the Shitan-Kulata. Is that not their general you were cuddled up next to?"

Now pushed past endurance, Miazie growled. "He is my husband, and yes. I was taken captive by them and forced into a marriage to Damon. I have lost both my honor and my freedom on this journey. Now, the prophecy!"

Finally, Elwyn looked down at the vellum she held and sighed. "I will have to study it for a while longer, but I have some theories. Will you allow me time to augment them?"

Miazie stood. "Fine. Do not take too long. I have a desperate schedule to hold to."

Elwyn stood as well, tucking the parchment into her robes. "Can you find your way back to your tent, or do you require assistance?"

"I'll be fine," the Belau snapped, ducking out of the large tent.

"Miazie, do not regret your choice in coming to us for aid," Elwyn said, following her out. "Give us a few days to review it, and then we shall come to a conclusion about it."

The woman had pulled her cowl back up and reformed her misty countenance. Miazie squinted at her. "Why do you do that?"

"It is the sign of the High Alchemist, a show of power, really."

"I was under the impression that alchemists were magically-inclined non-Magins. I'm starting to doubt that."

Elwyn chuckled. "No, we are not Magins. There may be a few seeking refuge within our flock, but none strong enough to be of any consequence. This shroud is about as far as my power extends. Nothing Maginic about it."

The Belau snorted, but she accepted the explanation. "Damon is a Magin. He hid his power for years."

"I've of no doubt that he did. The Shitan-Kulata are not known for their acceptance of magical people, of beings that can overpower them without using muscle. It is not their way of life. I'm quite surprised to find that their leader is one."

"Was. I forced him to desert, so he will be hunted until they kill him," Miazie said automatically.

"Do you not worry about that?"

"No. He forced me into his bed, married me at sword-point, and continued to debase my importance. If he dies, I shall be free once more."

"A cold heart you have, Miazie Paron," Elwyn said quietly. "I mourn any loss of life."

"Aye, that you might, but I have had too many encounters with vile, manipulative bastards who are bent on killing people that deserve to live to care much about preserving the formers' lives. You have no idea how many people have tried to kill me, Tlonna, Losolin, and those traveling with us. We are trying to rid the world of evil, and yet we are hunted as though we were the wicked ones," Miazie responded harshly.

"That is the way things are in this world," the High Alchemist replied.

"But it is wrong, and we are trying to end it. You can sit in your little camp and play with chemicals, but we are fighting a war."

"A war?" Elwyn asked. "I have not heard of a war."

Miazie could not hold back her sniff. "It has been going on for years, one hundred and seventy four years, actually. Called Aderiaen's War, which went into a cold war eighty two years ago when Aderiaen was murdered by his son Midian. Have you not heard of the disappearance of the elves? The sacking of Arseninis and Talenias? The razing of Blackhaven? How about the murder of the Everwood Princess? Any of it?"

"Of course I've heard of it all, but as you said, it's been dragged out over the course of a century. That does not constitute a war."

Miazie had to clench her fists in order not to hit the other woman. "Trust me, it is a plan to seize all of Nymyños for Midian Rahlan and whatever monstrous children he begets. It is the beginning of that prophecy, and yet another, which I am sure you are quite familiar with. The one where Astinus Saw the taint, Tlonna's birth, Blackhaven's fall. Tell me you don't know that, and I will know you for a liar."

Elwyn sighed. "Yes, I know it, as well as it can be known, but there are many branches from it, some-"

"Tlonna has begun massing an army to take against Midian's hordes. She is wielding her power with more strength and control every day. She has named herself the Magin Queen."

"Then she has condemned Nymyños to years of war."

Fury snapped within Miazie and she shoved the other woman back into the tent. Elwyn gasped with surprise, so startled that she dropped the mist Weave and stared at her assailant with wide eyes. The Belau wrapped her fingers around Elwyn's throat and bent her backward over her desk.

"Condemned? *Condemned?*" Miazie shouted. "Tlonna has taken us down the only path that will allow for victory, for freedom! She has chosen to give us a chance at redemption! She marches toward her death so that we may all have our lives! Do not bastardize her sacrifice because you are too cowardly to accept the truth of things. You cower behind your alchemical wall and pretend the world is fine while the rest of Nymyños rages around you, caught up in a bid for justice. *Zuskadi naht xellt! Duty above all!*"

Elwyn's eyes rolled to the tent's entrance as someone ripped it open. Miazie deliberately kept her hand tight on the alchemists' throat. Hands seized her from behind and the Belau was yanked away from her antagonist. Elwyn straightened slowly, rubbing her bruised neck.

"You are quite passionate in your arguments, Belau Miazie. Please, retire to your tent so that I may think."

Miazie jerked her arms out of Sodo's grasp and stalked from the tent, the elf following her closely.

"You should not treat the High Alchemist so, Belau Miazie," he said after a while.

"She should not provoke me so, Alchemist Sodo," Miazie shot back.

The elf sighed, discreetly pointing down a path when Miazie started to take another one. The human sniffed derisively and continued down the wrong one.

"High Alchemist Elwyn told you to go to your tent."

"Elwyn is not my mother, Sodo. I am a grown woman and will do as I please. You do not have to chaperone me around."

"No, I do not, but I choose to. I find you interesting. I have never seen anyone act like that around the High Alchemist and get away with it as you did, even Kryll, and she is the most short-tempered creature I have ever run across."

Miazie made a disgusted noise in her throat. "Elwyn is just another person, no better than you or I. What are we if not equal?"

"Anarchists," Sodo replied simply to the rhetoric.

Surprised, and a little put off, Miazie gave a small smile. "Indeed. Is it just my temper that interests you Sodo, or is there something else?"

The elf grinned suddenly, his hands linked behind his back as they strolled through the little streets. "I have never met a Belau, or a human who spoke with such intelligence as you. It is a rare treat to have a conversation that I know will not dull me."

"Were you listening to me and your leader while you were supposed to be away?" Miazie asked suspiciously.

"Precisely. Else how would I know you are so fascinating?"

The human laughed for what felt like the first time in months. "So, do you agree with me or your esteemed dictator?"

"High Alchemist Elwyn is not a dictator, but I agree with you. There are things at work now that even the smallest tribes cannot ignore. I hear even the Samiis to the north are becoming more active in their exploits."

"The Samiis?"

"*Aiya.* A small tribe of humans that pierce their flesh with bones and speak in a very primal language. Cannibals, if the rumors are to be believed. Personally, I do not know what to think. But it is hard to ignore the fact that they have been sighted in some of our hunting expeditions. Even the northern most point of our circuit is usually too far south for them. They do not come past the eastern border of the Plains of Arada. The last sighting of them was just south of the border of the Forest of Cleshnoe, five months back. Very odd."

Miazie nodded silently. After a moment she said, "Nymyños is changing Sodo, and we all need to be prepared for it. Despite what Elwyn thinks, there will be a climax of the war soon. You are elf-kind. Can you not feel it in the earth?"

Sodo nodded. "I can feel it. The land is bleeding, this taint is like an open sore that it cannot cleanse. My friend Ardenay also speaks of troublesome dreams, things that leave her ill at ease for days. There is a fear that is driving Nymyñosians to do terrible things to one another. Peaceful villages are erupting in sudden chaos, anarchical massacres that leave nothing alive. We have told Elwyn of these things, but she fears an upheaval."

"The upheaval is here. Why is she so determined not to see it?" Miazie asked.

The elf shrugged. "She is a regular human, she cannot see things as we do. She knows something is wrong but does not think it will touch our community despite Ardenay's and my warnings," his voice was quiet and smooth and Miazie felt herself wanting to touch him, hold him.

On impulse she asked, "Is Ardenay your lover?"

"No," Sodo replied, not unkindly.

The elf sighed and then said something that wracked Miazie's mind with shock and pain. "That man, he is your husband is he not? He wanted to touch you until we put him to sleep. I am right, yes?" his light green eyes sought hers.

"Yes. I was married to him at sword point. Did you not hear me tell Elwyn that?"

Sodo's lips twitched. "I tuned out of the personal bits. A habit of mine, I suppose."

"A good one, then."

"*Aiya.* So...you do not love him?"

Once again shocked by the question, Miazie did not answer for a moment. "No, I do not. I am beginning to like him as a person, but no, I do not love him."

The elf nodded once as though confirming something and then stopped. "This is your tent."

"I thought we went the wrong way," Miazie said, looking around.

"We did, but it is not a large place," Sodo replied, waving his hand around vaguely.

"Well, All right then. It was nice to talk with you, Sodo. I will see you later, then," Miazie said abruptly, feeling uncomfortable.

"Yes you will. Goodbye for now, Belau Miazie," the elf said elegantly and strode off, hands in his pockets.

Days passed, and Miazie's three companions did not wake, having been put to sleep by the alchemists. She strolled with Sodo through the little movable city, conversing about politics and philosophy, prophecy and rumor. She argued with Elwyn, wrote out long charts of possible prophetic meanings. She practiced swordplay with the resident arms master, a Gray Alchemist, called Seuq.

A week passed.

"Elwyn!" Miazie shouted as she entered the large tent.

The three figures within stood up stiffly, staring at her in shock. Elwyn, Kryll, and the spryte's human lover, Darmian, shifted around as she stalked toward them.

"You said a couple of days. It has now been a week! Why are

you delaying?"

The High Alchemist huffed out a breath and pointed toward the tent flaps, gesturing Kryll and Darmian to leave. The human obeyed, but the spryte bared her sharp teeth in a snarl.

"You are High Alchemist, why do you let this little tramp speak to you in such a way?"

Elwyn shook her head. "She is of an equal status to me, Kryll. And stubborn to a fault. Please go. Belau Miazie and I have things to discuss."

With a small bow, Kryll started for the opening. As she passed Miazie, she snapped her teeth in an obvious threat. The human glared back at her, unmoved, until she disappeared from sight.

"You undermine my authority in the presence of my people, Miazie," Elwyn said shortly, sitting back down on her desk.

The darker woman snorted. "Your ego is not my problem, Elwyn. Your obvious procrastination is, however. What have you discerned?"

The High Alchemist shook her head, cinnamon curls bouncing. "Not much. Though why I should reveal anything to you is beyond me. You treat me with little or no respect in my own demesne. And rumor has it you are carrying on a tryst with one of my alchemists while your husband slumbers in a cloud of chemicals."

Dumbfounded, Miazie could only gape at the other woman. After a while she spluttered. "A *tryst*? With whom? Who said that? What?"

Elwyn frowned slightly. "You mean it is not true? You have not been with Sodo?"

"Sodo?" Miazie shrieked. "No! We talk often, as he is the only one of your lot that I can stand for more than five minutes. He and Ardenay, really. But that is as far as it has gone. Ever. Who has spread such lies?"

"Well...Kryll."

"Aha! *That* creature!" Miazie barked, folding her arms.

"I did not take you to be racist, Belau," Elwyn said coldly.

Miazie scowled. "It is not her race that makes her a creature, it is her personality. I think the other spryte, Caydy, is quite congenial, thank you. You would do well to not to insult my acceptances, *alchemist*."

A tense silence filled the tent to the point of extreme until

Elwyn sighed and pulled out the sheaf of parchment that held the prophecy.

"We might as well get on with this, then. I have had a few of my more devout alchemists look at this, and though there are several points on which we agree, there is one we are all positive on."

Miazie waited silently.

"The first line, 'darkness will mar the land of beauty', obviously points to Nymyños, as it means beautiful in Serenyi speech. It means, we suspect, this taint. It darkens the earth, darkens spirits, and tells of evil spreading through Nymyños."

Impatient, the Belau waited for something she had not thought through herself.

Elwyn continued. "The second part of the second line also seems clear to us. Tlonna is going to have to succumb to evil in order to win. What she will have to do remains vague. Whether she will have to do something malevolent, or surrender, or kill an innocent, we do not know. That, I believe, will be unknown until it happens."

"That's it?" Miazie asked when the alchemist did not elaborate. "That's taken you all week to deduce? I figured that much out the first time I read it!"

"As did I, but not so others. Some had different views, different perspectives. That is what takes time, Miazie. Pooling all our thoughts together, comparing them to other prophecies that have either been deciphered or come to pass, and picking out the few similarities that are illuminated. You, of all people, should know that knowledge cannot be taken for granted until proven infallible."

Miazie groaned in exasperation. "I should never have left Tlonna. This is worthless. Try to pick up the pace, will you? And why are my companions not awake yet? What did you do to them?"

"Our serums keep them in a working, semi-conscious state so that their bodies will not atrophy, but they do not awaken to learn our secrets. You are different. Now I regret my choice to bring you out. You are an irritating twit."

"A twit? Me? What about you? You are a big-headed pedantic sitting at the head of a bizarre world!"

"Pedantic! *Bizarre* world!" Elwyn screeched, leaping up from her desk. "Get out of my tent! Now!"

Miazie turned on her heel and strode from the large tent feeling seditious. She later found herself stalking along the row of work tents where Sodo's and Ardenay's labs were. Dusk was falling when the elves appeared from their conjoined work tents. Ardenay, a heart-faced, brown haired elf with sparkling blue eyes, spotted her first and smiled.

Sodo turned when he heard his friend's call and then strolled back to the two females. Miazie eyed him discreetly, recalling the rumor of their friendship. Like his entire race, he was well built and ridiculously attractive. Though his skin was tanner than most elves, his eyes were a light green, his hair a pale yellow.

Ardenay was chatting about her latest experiment, an infusion of ground herbs and flowers with some sort of acid that helped to clear human blemishes. Miazie listened with half an ear, staring at Sodo.

"I would really like to try it on you, Miazie, if you would like me to."

"What? Oh...do I need it?" Miazie asked, her attention returned to Ardenay in a flash of humiliation.

"Not really, but I need to see if it burns. You have a spot on your forehead, and I want to see if it works."

Miazie's hand went to her forehead in embarrassment, flushing beneath Sodo's amused grin. "I...I...All right," she finished lamely and followed the female back into her lab.

"It is right here, let me see..." Ardenay murmured, grabbing a ball of cotton and soaking it in a horrible brown liquid sitting inside a beaker.

She bent down to peer at Miazie's face and then pressed the wet ball to her forehead. The Belau winced at the sharp sting, but then it faded slightly, leaving an almost pleasing twinge.

"Well?" she asked when Ardenay continued to stare at the offending spot.

"I do not know. Did you feel anything?"

"Yes. It stings, but...it feels good, sort of. Clean like, I guess."

"Clean like?" Ardenay asked in an amused voice, though it was laced with fondness.

"Mm..." Miazie grunted as the elf drew away. "As though it is burning away the dirt."

"That is good," Ardenay murmured, gazing at her concoction. "Maybe I will add more nytryn. Just a few drops..."

The three barely had any warning to dive out of the way. The beaker exploded, raining shattered glass and the flaming liquid down on them. Miazie shrieked as something heavy landed on top of her, but then lost consciousness as the fumes over powered her.

Miazie woke a few hours later in her tent with a throbbing head and reeking clothes. There was a fire burning in her brazier, though there was definite chill in the air. There was a movement in the shadows of the tent and she squeaked, grabbing around for a weapon.

"Miazie! Calm down, it is just me," Sodo said, leaning forward into the light. "Ardenay left a few hours ago to get some rest. She did not know what the vapors would do to you. How do you feel?"

The woman sat up with a groan. "Like I have been trampled by a few hundred horses. What happened?"

The elf dragged his chair further into the light so that he could lean back and not be in shadows. "We are not sure, but I think Ardenay may have created a serious weapon when she added the extra nytryn. It exploded, and the fumes acted like sleeping gas. It knocked you out within seconds. If I had not jumped onto you, I fear you would have burned to death. Ardenay and I suffered some minor burns, but I think you would have gone up like a torch. Even so, you have a second degree burn on your leg."

At the mention of her injury, Miazie could feel the pain in her right calf. "You saved my life."

Sodo shrugged. "My kind is more resilient than humans. I could not let you die."

Upset by the impersonal account of his heroic action, Miazie slid her legs carefully off the small bed and sat facing the elf. Looking down, she saw a bluish cream slathered on her calf.

"Did you know there is a rumor about us?" she said loudly, and then blushed when the male smiled slowly, so like Losolin it disturbed her.

"*Aiya.* Depending on who tells it, there are varying degrees of details. Most seem to think you are my wife from Arseninis and came to tell me you are carrying my child," Sodo said in a highly amused voice.

Miazie could not look him in the eye. She knew she was crimson from her shoulders up. Even her arms were showing patches of blotchy red.

"Is it so terrible a thought?"

"What?" Miazie asked, too startled by the hint of sadness in the elf's voice to forget her embarrassment.

"Is the idea of being with me so horrible that you cannot even look me in the eye?"

"Sodo...I...we've known each other for a week!"

"And, you tell me, the world is about to end."

So stunned by the sudden turn of conversation, Miazie forgot her injured leg and stood. With a cry she buckled forward only to have Sodo's arms come around her just in time. With her arms tucked between their chests, Miazie could only stare up at him.

"You move really fast," she said dumbly.

Sodo smiled, perfect teeth just visible between his lips. Before she could stop herself, Miazie pressed her mouth to his. The elf's smile widened beneath hers and his arms pressed her close.

The human's legs dangled uselessly as Sodo lifted her up to his height so that he did not have to bend over. The kiss deepened until Miazie's entire body seemed to be on fire, but one that warmed rather than burnt. Slowly, the male lowered her to the bed and then lay gently on top of her.

Surprised at how light he was, Miazie wrapped her arms around his waist to ensure that he was indeed atop her. His light green eyes shone brightly from lust and firelight. The human felt the desire wafting off the elf, heat pulsating from his body. Miazie felt his fingers slide under her shirt and she lost the ability to think. Sodo's control brought Miazie a night of passion of which she had never known, not even with the recalcitrant Aladorn.

The next morning, Miazie opened her eyes and jerked away from Sodo's body. His strong fair body moved in the deep rhythm of his breathing and his face was calm and relaxed. She took the advantage of his slumber to examine him fully. Even now, even after having traveled with Tlonna and Losolin for months, she was stunned by the perfection of the elfish body. The only hair on his body was on his head, which made her have to stifle a ridiculous giggle. There was an odd scar running from his shoulder down his spine to the small of his back, as though someone had tried to carve out his spine. That thought made her shudder because it might be true.

After another moment of feasting her eyes, Miazie ran her lips across the top of his clavicle where the white scar ended. Sodo stirred into a slow awakening, his lips pulling into a broad smile that made Miazie shiver with desire.

"Good morning," she said huskily, her voice unused yet.

"Blessed be this one that I may look upon you first," Sodo replied, his voice smooth as always.

Charmed by his words, Miazie fitted her body tight against his, resting her chin on his shoulder. "You are amazing."

The shoulder she was resting on bounced as the elf laughed quietly. "And you. But why do you say that?"

"You are perfect in every way. Do you know that? Your body, your speech, your personality, your...abilities," she finished with a coy smile.

"Mm...now what will the gossips say when they find out the rumor is true?"

Miazie blushed. "I don't know. Elwyn was furious when she thought it was."

Sodo frowned. "That is because High Alchemist Elwyn has been trying to get me into her bed for years. I have told her that I do not hold any desires toward her, but she persists. This will make things more difficult for you."

Miazie shrugged. "We already don't get along. What is one more thing to argue about?"

The elf laughed as he slid out of the bed and walked over to poke at the brazier. Miazie watched him with hungry eyes, running her fingers absentmindedly through the snarls in her hair.

"This was your first time with an elf, yes?"

The question was so blunt that Miazie stammered a few seconds before pulling her thoughts back together. "No. Why would you think that?"

"Your body responded faster than I am used to, which means inexperience in the art, at least with an elf, or it was your first time with one. Either way, I am honored."

A little miffed, the human could only think of the preceding night. They'd been at it for *hours.* She had responded fast? Crawling out of the warm covers to hide her astonishment, Miazie felt the burn on the back of her leg. Hissing in a breath, she peered at the raw injury. Sodo looked up from the brazier, sea green eyes scanning her body before settling on the burn.

The human stood and limped over to her pack to wrap a thick brown robe, lent from the alchemists, about her person.

"Lay down again, and I will see what I can do," Sodo said as he helped her back to the bed.

Curious, Miazie settled against the blankets and pulled the robe up to free her leg. She winced once when Sodo put his fingers on the inflamed flesh, but then there was a sense of cooling. With a start, Miazie realized Sodo was singing softly in Parlêthian, the words low and calming. In awe, the Belau watched the elf half-close his eyes, massaging his long fingers on her calf, singing. She started to feel her lids droop but she forced them open, afraid to lose the vision of Sodo in ethereal rapture.

There was a cool peace within the tent that ebbed with the male's baritone words. When Miazie thought she could no longer stay awake in such a relaxed state, Sodo stopped singing and gently laid her leg down. As his words faded, so did the peace. The world came rushing back, the slight wind buffeting the tent walls, the feel of the taint. Frowning, Miazie could not remember actually feeling the taint before, but now she did; an oily, seething presence that seemed to saturate the air, like a dirty steam.

Finding her voice, the woman said, "What did you do?"

Sodo paused in the act of lacing his breeches. "I sang to your body. It is an ancient practice among elves, that is until it faded from knowledge some two thousand years ago. I have always been able to do it, though. Just a natural talent that was lost to my people."

Miazie examined her leg with interest. The burn did seem to be smaller, and the pain was definitely less. "Thank you," she murmured.

For a reply, Sodo bent down to kiss her, burying his hands in her hair. When he pulled away, Miazie felt like she may just melt into a puddle of feminine delight.

"Can you stand without coming to harm?" the male asked her, holding out his hand.

She took it and stood, testing her weight on her leg. "Yes, I should be fine. What do you have to do today?"

Sodo shrugged as he laced his belt through the loops on his pants. "Ardenay said she wanted me to look at something that she is working on. Not that exploding liquid, something else. I am not sure what, though."

"Are you working on anything?" Miazie asked, studying him. It was odd to see him in something other than his caste robes or his skin. He dressed an awful lot like Losolin. The constant similarities were starting to unnerve her.

"I have a few projects I am working on, though none of it extensive. Namely a serum for cracked lips, a few iron statues I am trying to turn into something valuable, and other small things like that. I do not like to get into a big project unless I know I am going to have a lot of time to work on it, and I just have not had it."

"What keeps you so busy?"

"I go out a lot on the hunting expeditions, plant gatherings, healing missions. I am usually gone half of every month," the male replied as he pulled his white robes over his head.

"Sodo...can you explain the castes to me?"

The elf's head appeared from the inside of the robes and he nodded. "The whites, what Ardenay and I are, deals in earth-based chemicals, plants, and other items, usually in a healing capacity or something that will help advance civilization. The blacks use the more corporeal liquids: blood, sweat, saliva. They also use elements, but normally as conduits of energy. The grays sit on the fence, dabbling in both but not devoted to one or the other."

"Ah...so you never handle blood or anything like that for your experiments?"

Sodo shrugged. "Every now and again I do. There will always be a need to use an agent not of your caste's usual preference."

Miazie, intrigued, could not help herself. "So why did you choose the white?"

The elf chuckled and held out a hand to guide her out of the tent. "Would you want to handle blood and saliva all the time?"

Laughing, Miazie shook her head as they exited her tent.

"Aha!"

Both Sodo and Miazie jerked to a stop at the sharp exclamation. Kryll the spryte stood before them, a wicked grin on her pointed face. Miazie bowed respectively and tried her best to smile at the tall, green eyed, green haired creature.

"You must have forgotten that sprytes have the power at night to see heat. Your tent was indeed very hot last night and while your husband is sleeping," the skinny female turned on Sodo. "You should know better, Alchemist Sodo. You know the repercussions should

Elwyn find out about your dalliance."

Beside her, Miazie felt Sodo stiffen. "It is not your place to decide how I live my life, Kryll. You and Darmian are no different from Miazie and me. Back off."

"No, we are not the same. Neither of us is wed to another," Kryll hissed.

Miazie reddened, though more from anger than embarrassment. "You should know I was forced into that marriage, and it is as loveless as one can be. I am a free woman, Sodo a free elf. We will, as he said, live as we choose."

The spryte stared at her with her large green eyes in surprise. "The High Alchemist will not be pleased to hear about this."

"So you said."

Once again Sodo stiffened. Miazie wondered how anyone could be that tense and not strain something.

"Elwyn's interests should stay in the realm of the possible, Kryll. I have made my disinterest known to her, and that is how it will stay," Sodo said coldly.

"You are a fool," Kryll snapped and then flounced away, green hair flying.

Expelling a great breath, Miazie looked up at Sodo to find him watching the spryte recede. "That was...interesting."

"She is right. There will be consequences."

Irritated, Miazie crossed her arms in front of her. "Why? We are grown people, and we have done nothing wrong."

"You *are* married, Miazie."

"So what? As I said, it is loveless. I was forced into it. Damon is the leader of a band of murderers, and he raped me the first time. Why should I care about any vows I was forced into?"

"He raped you?" the anger in Sodo's voice made Miazie jump.

"Y-yes. He didn't consider it rape, but I did."

The elf immediately struck off toward where Damon, Ryun, and Jacinth were kept in their unaware state.

"Sodo?" Miazie called, hurrying to keep up. "Sodo? What are you doing? You have to meet Ardenay. Sodo!"

The elf yanked open the flap of the mending tent, strode to the back where Damon lay, and punched him in the face.

"Sodo! Oh my gods! Stop!"

The elf grabbed the human's shirt and shook him like a doll, howling for a healer to come. When the young man appeared, he shied away from the vicious elf.

"Y-yes Alchemist?"

"Wake this man!"

"Why s-sir?"

"So I can kill him!"

Both Miazie and the healer stood frozen at the vehemence in Sodo's voice. The elf glared at them, Damon dangling from his grip like an awkward manikin. Miazie found her voice first.

"Sodo, put Damon down. Please."

"Why?"

"Because you can't kill a man when he's asleep!"

"Then get the boy to wake him up!"

Miazie shook her head. "No. I will not allow you to mar your soul by taking a life that has done you no harm. I will not allow you to be labeled a murderer for my sake. You will put him down now."

Sodo unceremoniously dropped the general of the Shitan-Kulata back onto his bed. With another glare at the two humans, the elf strode out of the tent, white robes billowing behind him.

"Why did Alchemist Sodo wish to kill the man, my lady?" the mender asked, shaken.

"Because he is a chivalrous idiot, I'm afraid. I'm sorry about this," Miazie replied and she too left the tent without a backward glance at her crumpled husband.

Sodo stomped to the stables, tacked his horse, and rode out of Alchemian in hopes to cool his temper. His mare reveled in the fast pace, tainted snow wafting up around her fetlocks as she galloped with her head stretched forward. The elf guided her onto one of the hunting paths and let her go as she will. Feeling his anger and frustration drain away, Sodo smiled as he felt the horse move beneath him.

There was something wonderful in the freedom of riding, the cold air rushing against flesh. Sodo's thoughts drifted to the previous night and he grinned. Miazie's beauty was a rare find among humans, her intelligent an even rarer commodity. How anyone could hurt her was beyond him. His heart swelled with emotion when he summoned up the image of her face, her body arching beneath his. She was certainly the most magnificent specimen he had ever-

Sodo landed hard on the frozen ground, clutching his face where the club had smashed into it. Blood smeared his fingers, steaming against the cold air. He heard a grunt and rolled onto his side just in time to avoid another blow. He jumped to his feet, blinking blood and snow out of his eyes to see.

Blurry figures clad in black moved toward him, wielding weapons of various design. For one mad moment, he thought the Black Alchemists were attacking him, then he caught the sight of a clawed, mangled hand. Panic seized him before he quashed it down, analyzing the situation.

"What do you want?" he asked loudly, trying to buy time.

One of the Darkwights hissed at him, but it was the only answer he got. Before Sodo could back away any further, they were on him. He lashed out, striking one of the demons across the face hard enough to send it sprawling, but there were more than he could fight off. His mare was fighting too, lashing out with hooves and teeth.

Sodo was carried to the ground by the sheer weight of numbers. One of the Darkwights grabbed his wrist and yanked it behind his back so that he couldn't move for fear of breaking his shoulder. The most horrible pain the elf had ever felt ripped through his body while he thrashed on the ground, screaming into the bloody snow. Blackness hazed around the edges of his vision, sparking as it grew.

Suddenly the shadow of the Darkwight at his head was gone and there was the terrible sound of bone breaking. Booted feet ran past him, three pairs, four. Sodo felt the pain recede and he dropped his throbbing face into the cold snow. He could feel his body twitching with the remaining tendrils of agony dancing along his nerves. With a deep exhalation, the elf slipped into oblivion.

Miazie dropped to her knees beside the prostrate Sodo, ignoring the blood and snow that seeped into her pants. Behind her, Seuq, the arms master, and his group of hunters finished off the last demon and started toward her.

"Is he alive?" the elf asked, kneeling beside her to check Sodo's pulse for himself.

Miazie waited for his nod before succumbing to her fear. He was alive, but severely wounded, perhaps mortally. "What were they doing to him?" she asked in a harsh voice.

Seuq shrugged, turning Sodo onto his back. Both his eyes were black and swollen, his mouth and nose caked with blood. "Could be anything. The demons seem to abhor elves though. Perhaps they were just trying to kill him in the most painful way possible. Come on, help me get him up."

Miazie gently lifted Sodo's head so that the other elf could swing him over his shoulder. Seuq mounted his tall gelding and set off back toward Alchemian. The other hunters waited for her to get back on Kaia before riding after their leader. Silently thanking the gods Seuq and the others had gone out on a hunting trip when they did, Miazie watched Sodo's limp body the entire way back.

Elwyn stared down at Sodo while the menders cleaned him off, her heart thudding against her chest in a heavy cadence. Miazie stood next to her, tears leaking silently from her eyes. A few others stood around as well, twisting worried fingers or pacing a short distance. Ardenay had one arm clutched to her chest as if her own heart was trying to escape, and the other around Miazie's shoulders.

Sodo stirred feebly, and then settled again.

"Will he survive?" Miazie asked in a strained voice when the silence became unbearable.

Elwyn was taken aback by the fear and pain in the Belau's voice, and her heart softened toward the other woman.

The First Mender nodded as he bathed the elf's forehead. "Yes. He is in a lot of pain, though. I don't think he will wake for many days."

Ardenay emitted a strangled sound and left the tent, her shoulders shaking with sobs. The rest left too, leaving Elwyn alone with Miazie. They gazed down at the male in silence until Miazie lowered herself to her knees. She pressed her forehead to Sodo's arm and wept. Elwyn shifted, wanting to scorn the other woman's actions, but also wanting to take her place. Her eyes strayed to the back of the menders' tent to where the three companions of Miazie still slumbered. Where Miazie's husband slumbered.

"How can you do this when your husband lies not twenty feet away?" Elwyn hissed, pulling on Miazie's shoulder.

The Belau shot to her feet with surprising quickness, anger drying her tears so fast Elwyn took a step back.

"Damon is my husband by force only, Sodo holds my heart," she snapped.

"You're an adulterer, a tramp," Elwyn retorted.

Miazie's blow caught her right on the chin, hard enough to make the High Alchemist see stars for a second. Too stunned by the attack to retaliate, Elwyn stared at the raven-haired beauty. "You have known him for a week!"

"By far longer than I knew Damon, Elwyn, before he raped me."

Elwyn caught herself just in time to stop the scathing remark she had prepared. "I did not know he raped you," she said quietly.

"Yes, well, perhaps you should have all the facts before making an assumption," Miazie spat, and then resumed her place at Sodo's side.

Another week passed before Sodo was lucid enough to talk, though he said very little. Miazie was summoned to the menders' tent and ushered inside. When she saw Sodo awake, she let out a cry and rushed to his side.

"Sodo!" she breathed, pressing his hand to her face. "Oh my gods, I'm so relieved!"

The elf turned his head and smiled at her and she gasped in horror. His left eye was black where it should have been white, though the iris remained the same pale green as before, if a little darker. The right eye was unchanged as well, but it created a terrifying effect. Looking harder, Miazie detected strands of black mingling with the eggshell yellow of his hair. Trembling, she linked her fingers with his and tried to look him in the eye. His smile was gone.

"What is it?" he asked.

"Sodo...Sodo your eye...and your hair. Has your vision changed?"

Frowning now, the elf searched her face for a moment before replying. "Not really. Perhaps it seems a hair less sharp than it was, but nothing drastic. Why? What about my eye and my hair?"

Miazie fished in her purse for the tiny mirror she always carried and gave it to the elf's outstretched hand. When he looked into it, Sodo's face paled. His gaze traveled upward with the mirror to examine his hair. His jaw clenched and he pressed the mirror back into Miazie's hand.

"Please...go," he whispered, shaking.

"No," Miazie said tearfully. "I don't care. It has not changed you, and that's what I care about. Please don't send me away."

Sodo's hands shook as he drew her closer and pressed his lips to hers. "*Inkan yayena dü,*" he said when he pulled away, brushing a hand down her face.

Tears splashed down Miazie's face as she gazed upon him, his perfect face marked by evil but still warming to her heart. "I love you too," she said in a faint whisper, crawling onto the bed with him.

The elf shifted so that she could lie comfortably next to him atop the blankets. "I am relieved I do not have to make you love me, then. I was prepared for a fight."

Miazie chuckled wetly, her face pressed into his shoulder. "How I was not expecting this. Certainly not this fast. Can you love a human, Sodo? There are things that separate us greater than Elwyn's animosity."

Sodo's good eye was visible to her, and it closed for a moment before he answered. "As long as we love, nothing can defeat us. Yes?"

"Yes," Miazie said, finally understanding the old elfish proverb.

Chapter 19
Pity

Losolin and Aidyn fought endlessly to get out of the infirmary. Weeks passed. Losolin began to go mad. Aidyn killed a Healer in a fit. Demetrius kept the recruits in training, readying them for the march. Shireen and Kayra were brought from the inn to stay at the castle to help look after the elves. New armor was issued by Demetrius.

Gray cowhide boots, gray stockings, pale blue breeches, a gray tunic with Tlonna's sun and star sign on the right breast and lapels, gray gloves, and a white woolen cloak with the sun and star in the same pale blue. A coat for the soldiers when they weren't in armor was also supplied. It was dark blue with the insignia embroidered on the cuffs and down the front. The last things added were a gray belt, a sun and star brooch, and a side-pinned hat with a light blue feather.

The taint continued to fall from the sky. The rivers turned to poisonous sludge, choking the land with its rancid discharge. The sun began to fade into something malignant, something wholly wrong. It no longer warmed or cast shadows, for it too was becoming a shadow.

Tlonna rolled her head to the side and then back again as she tried to regain her senses. Her body trembled with pain, blood oozed down her arms and legs. She finally opened her eyes. Clumps of hair blocked her vision, but she could see a stone wall with a small wooden door in front of her. As she became more and more perspicuous, Tlonna felt the stab of panic rising in her breast. It was not a new sensation, but the sharp edge of it brought her closer to the devouring abyss of insanity.

She was curled up on the floor of a round cell. Straw stained crimson from her blood littered the floor. Against the wall, next to the door was a crude tray with a piece of moldy bread and a cup of brown water. Tlonna sniffed it, and then sank back against the wall. Hunger plagued her, but she did not have an appetite. She descended back into oblivion.

Every time she gained consciousness, Tlonna lost herself in

endless suffering as Midian either beat her or mounted her. A month passed.

The next time she woke, Tlonna stifled a scream. Midian stood just inside the doorway watching her. Seeing she was awake, he crouched down and lifted her chin up with his fingers. Blue eyes locked on blue eyes, a hatred strong enough to create war waged between them.

Midian's lips curled into a sneer. He shoved her hair back to reveal her ear and stared at it. One finger touched the delicate point, almost a caress, dark eyes half-closed. His jawbone clenched and he dropped Tlonna's head so that it smacked hard against the stone.

"Why?" Tlonna whispered as she sat up, no longer able to feel minute pain.

Midian scowled at her. "Why what?"

"Why do you hate so? What makes you hate me?"

The human's sapphire eyes narrowed further. "I have no need to explain to you my actions."

Tlonna studied his face. It was angular, but not thin. His lips were long and curved at the corners and when he sneered she could see white teeth. A lock of sable hair hung between his eyes and others curled around his ears and neck.

"What are you staring at?" he demanded after a moment's silence.

"My enemy," Tlonna said quietly.

Midian's face slackened for a moment in surprise, revealing a handsome visage, then tightened back up with the ever-present sneer. With a grunt, he stood and left the cell.

A while later, fresh bread and clean water arrived along with the Darkwight Kelus. Tlonna pushed against the wall with her good arm. The arm she had torn and broken had not healed from the fall of the Keylode and it festered. Her elfin body would not mend the broken bone while it remained unset, but the flesh had tried to heal over it in a horrible scab that cracked with every movement.

The demon shut the door behind him and grabbed her hand. Yanking on it, he forced Tlonna to let him have it. The excruciating pain nearly sent the elf into a fit. Kelus pulled out a bottle and dumped it over the wound. Tlonna screamed, her body writhing in agony. Debris and straw bubbled out of it to fall on the floor, along with a fresh dose of blood. After a few agonizing minutes, it subsided a little, and she was able to look down. The skin was still torn, but he was wrapping it up in gauze, and he set the bone.

Kelus's cowl had fallen down against his back and Tlonna saw for the first time the horribly tortured head of the Darkwight. He was bent over her arm, so she had a full view of his scalp and one ear. That ear, though blackened and missing a chunk, was pointed.

"You were an elf, once," she whispered.

Kelus stilled, then went back to wrapping her arm. "A long time ago."

"But yet you remember," Tlonna pressed.

Finishing with her arm, the demon sat back on his heels. "It iss my punishment, for being what I wass. Nothing will ever heal, the pains will never ceasse, and the memoriess will never fade." Kelus took a deep breath and shuddered. "I pity you for what he will do to you. You are to bear hiss child, you know. A boy child, for he can alter it to hiss will while it iss sstill in your womb. I pity you becausse of what hass been done to you and your kith and kin. Ssuch thingss sshould not be laid on one persson alone to bear."

"I am not the only one who has suffered, there are others who have had far worse done to them. I have not yet seen the destruction he wreaked on my home and family that I do not even remember. You yourself have suffered more than I, and you are his right hand. I do not understand your pity," Tlonna replied quietly.

"I pity you becausse you do not know. You do not ssee the hell he hass brought upon you and yourss. You have not yet sseen the ssuffering of thosse you know perssonally. I ssee in your eyess the pain and ssuffering of thosse you jusst met, and I fear the rage that will explode when you ssee that pain and torture reflected in thosse you care about."

Tlonna gingerly put her wrapped arm in her lap. "Why do you serve him if you believe the way you do?"

Kelus laughed dryly. "I have been thiss way for yearss, elf, I am no longer the persson I wass. I sstill have a ssoul, but I am ass dark hearted ass you originally thought, that night in the foresst. That iss all. I have a ssoul. And do you think I have a choice?"

"And Midian does not? How can one live without a soul? It is not possible," Tlonna countered.

"King Rahlan'ss ssoul is rotten. For one hundred and ssixty yearss, he hass been taught the way of evil. He hass never known goodnesss."

Tlonna plucked at the strings of gauze wrap on her arm. Kelus stood and left, locking the door behind him.

Another week passed before Tlonna saw another living creature. An old woman, fat and unpleasant, opened the door and yanked Tlonna out of her cell. The elf tumbled through the small opening and into the dark corridor. Staring about, Tlonna shivered, though not from the cold breeze that flitted through the castle.

There were no tapestries on the walls or rugs on the floor. Sconces placed every few yards throughout the corridor were the only decoration. The granite blocks glistened wetly in the torchlight. The castle may well have been abandoned.

"Move," the woman growled, and pushed at Tlonna's lower back.

Tlonna walked forward, not sure what was happening. The woman thumped along behind her. When they reached an intersection, she shoved Tlonna into the left corridor. The elf bit back a growl.

Instead she asked, "Where are we going?"

"Shut it," her escort snapped.

Tlonna glared at the long dark hallway before her, jaw clenched. Finally, after a few more shoves into the correct corridors, servants appeared. Just a few, but they hurried by without a glance at Tlonna or the fat woman.

"In there," she growled, and pushed Tlonna into a room.

It was a little more decorated than the halls. Two tapestries hung from bare rafters. One held a fire-wreathed sword, and the other, the red, blue, and black triple rings with the yellow four point star, Midian's symbol.

A large hearth blazed warmth into the room, and a single black rug with gold fringe covered the floor. Midian and Kelus stood next to each other in the center, haloed by the orange glow of fire.

"Leave Alys," Midian ordered, and the fat woman left.

Tlonna straightened her back so that she stood at full height. Midian and Kelus watched her, seeming to wait for something.

"If you think I am going to bow, you are sorely wrong, Midian," Tlonna drawled, folding her hands in front of her.

Midian scoffed. "Why would I expect such a thing? You

believe yourself higher than I, yes?"

Tlonna said nothing.

After the silence became awkward, Midian turned on his heel to walk away from her. "I have brought you here, to my home, for a single purpose. I will have heirs, Tlonna, and they will be the most powerful in all the world. They will have the combined strength and agility of Elf and Magin, the lifespan of both as well. I am the most powerful male Magin, and where was I to find my bride?"

Tlonna remained silent, though her insides churned.

"I thought long and hard on my decision. I could have the most beautiful human wife, perhaps she would even be a Magin, but where to find bloodline that was untainted, descended from the first Magins, as I was? Yes, I see your shock. I am the descendant of Roluf Gwemheoad himself, the greatest of Magins. It is the Rahlan's great legacy, from Gwemheoad to his son Athur, who had a daughter that married Sithian Rahlan, king of Zaedic, and so on down to me.

"To keep my bloodline pure, free from lesser and unworthy offspring, I needed someone just as pure, someone descended from Magin Jair, destroyer of the Tower of Magins, beginning our decline into darkness. And now, we stand here, lost in the midst of prophecy, you and I, to bring our kind into glory once more."

"Does not my being an elf make me unworthy?" Tlonna said coldly. "Despite the fact that you have pumped yourself into me more times than I can count, you have yet to plant your seed. Perhaps your human essence is too weak for my elfin body."

Midian made a face as though she had wounded him. "We must all make sacrifices to be the best, don't we? The reason you have not quickened is because I have not wished it to be so. I have powers you can scarce dream of, but that is not of consequence right now. I will sacrifice my pure human blood to gain your elfin powers, and you will sacrifice...everything...to me to keep your life. But now, I am thirsty. Bring that kettle over here so I may have my tea."

Tlonna did not move. After a moment, Midian gestured to Kelus. The Darkwight grabbed hold of the elf and shoved her close to the fire where the kettle hung. Taking a deep breath, Tlonna picked the kettle off its hoop and turned.

As Midian turned to watch her, she tossed the scalding water into his face. The man screamed as it sizzled onto his skin and then lashed out at her. Black magic struck her arm, but it only tingled for a moment. Midian stared at her in surprise when she did not scream. Tlonna leaped toward the human, her arms stretched for his throat. The impact took both Magins to the ground.

Tlonna, magic-less, pummeled him with her fists. Midian retaliated with his black Weaves. The air around the Magins sizzled and lightning struck the air as purity met corruption. Blood trickled out of many places on both bodies as they writhed in uncontained, unadulterated loathing. They tumbled into Kelus, nearly knocking the demon over. Midian screamed as he was pushed into the fire, and Tlonna bellowed in rage, embers floating up to meet her.

Kelus stood watching the fight with horrible fascination. He was brought out of his trance when the Magins rolled into him. Jerking away, the demon lurched towards the fighting enemies and grabbed Tlonna by the back of her shirt as she was pushing Midian into the fire. Without warning, the seal on her power snapped as Midian writhed in the flames. The elf flailed furiously, her magic lashing out everywhere. A strand hit Kelus across the arm and the rotted skin fell away, revealing pale, unscarred flesh. The Darkwight dropped the female in shock and fell back away from the Magins. Tlonna saw the renewed skin and stared, motionless.

Midian crawled out of the fire, skin sloughing off in places. Seeing her standing still, the male careened into her. He replaced the seal on her power, twice as strong. Tlonna struggled beneath him, trapped between his knees. For a moment, Midian leaned back, his hands on his shoulders. Where his hands touched the ruined skin, the flesh stirred and reformed once more. The shirt rewound itself, and the Magin ceased his Weaving.

Tlonna jerked one way and then another, trying to free herself, but Midian seemed far more heavy than usual. He seemed carved from stone, and attached to the floor for all the good kicking around did her. She could not free herself. When the human returned his attention to her, he grinned nefariously.

"Is this what you want?" he laughed, unlacing his pants.

Tlonna struggled harder. Midian ripped open her shirt. His hands grabbed her breasts greedily, squeezing them painfully. The elf arched her back in pain as magic sizzled from his fingertips. Midian began rocking his hips back and forth on her, his phallus tight between her legs. When he tore her pants off and shoved inside,

Tlonna wept.

Chapter 15
Maps and Plans

Tlonna leaned against a wall, her arms and legs bound with heavy chains that dragged at her thin body. Her beautiful face was sunken and bruised, her eyes hollow with listlessness. Damp stone walls encircled her and only one high window let the gray sky filter through. A ragged black dress hung on her starved and beaten body like a thin blanket. Blood had stained her lips deep red, her jaw hung slack like a skull's. Her long pale hair lay against her body in clumps of blood and grime. A door opened, and the Magin stirred enough to look up. A figure came in, shoved a torch into a bracket.

"Mother."

A beautiful boy stood framed in the doorway, the torchlight glistening off his black hair. "I thought you would like some company. This cell is a rather depressing place, isn't it?" He smiled a cruel smile that could chill ice.

"Why do you torment me, Sithian? I have done nothing but birth you, and not of my own accord."

"You hate me, Mother, and that is why. You hate both Father and me, and you resent my life."

Tlonna straightened, then fell back against the wall. "I do not hate you, Sithian, but I do hate your father. Had you been born to a male I loved, maybe things would have been different, but you are the child of a sadist and a murderer. You inherited his cruelty and his will to dominate. For that, I cannot forgive you, but I am your mother, and so I love you nonetheless. Remember that, Sithian, when you kill a young mother in front of her children and husband." Tlonna's voice gave way to a sob of weariness and despair. Another shadow filled the doorway.

"Sithian, leave us." Midian walked into the dungeon and smiled. He lifted the ragged dress and undid his own breeches. Tlonna screamed as his manhood entered her.

"TLONNA!" Losolin sat bolt upright and lunged out of bed.

Aidyn followed him up, grabbing him by the arm. "What is it?"

"Tlonna!" Losolin shouted.

"Yes, what about her?"

The younger elf struggled against the assassin until he fell against him, sobbing. "I cannot handle this, Aidyn," he choked. "I have to go after her!"

Aidyn smoothed the other elf's head, shushing him. "I know. We will, tomorrow, I promise."

The two elves stayed awake the rest of the night, packing their things and readying their weapons. The gray morning came fast, and Losolin strode into Demetrius' study while the human was just starting breakfast. The king stopped with a spoonful of porridge halfway to his mouth. It slopped over his chest.

"Losolin...how are you feeling this morning?"

Ignoring the question, he asked, "Do you have a map of all of Nymyños?"

"Yes, go to the library and I am sure one of the librarians can help you," Demetrius said quietly, despairing for the young elf.

Losolin found the library and walked inside. Huge bookshelves of oak and cedar lined the walls of the 'T' shaped room. A middle-aged woman stood bent over a podium near the center of the room. She looked up at Losolin's quiet entrance and smiled vaguely.

"May I help you, young sir?" she said, blinking at him.

"I need a map of Nymyños. Is there one here?" he replied.

"I should say so, young man. Come, come. Follow me if you will. I may have need of your height," the owlish woman scuttled to the back of the library and retrieved a tall ladder. She climbed to the top and began reaching for a large box at the very top. She gave a little hop and wobbled precariously on the ladder. Losolin darted up after her and stood on the step below her.

"Is it this box, madam?"

"Yes, I can't seem to reach it."

Losolin reached around her and took the box off the shelf. He climbed back down and placed the box on the table. He wiped the thick dust off the dark wood and opened the lid. Yellowed parchment lay inside, stacked in tight rolls and tied with various colors of ribbon. The elf pulled a heavy chair up to the table and sat, pulling the parchment out carefully. He took one with a black ribbon and unrolled it gently. The parchment cracked and little pieces of it fell away but the rest remained intact. The ink had faded with time, but Losolin could still see the faint lines of a map. In slightly darker ink, he could read the name Purheae. Looking closer, he could decipher a forest, and on the edge, a castle. With a jolt, he realized how old the map must be to still have the Tower of Magins detailed on it. He laid the parchment aside and took out another. This one was of Talenias, and another of Narnen. He unrolled each map to reveal another kingdom.

Finally, he pulled out a parchment tied with gray ribbon and unrolled it. With a sigh of relief, he looked down at the faded red lines of the continent of Nymyños. Carefully, he placed heavy books on each corner of the map. Losolin looked around and spotted another woman placing tomes on a shelf, tutting irritatingly. The elf walked over to her and glowered slightly.

"I am in need of some parchment, ink, and a quill. Would you happen to have some? I am rather in a hurry and I do not want to walk all the way back to my rooms to receive some."

The woman stared at him for a moment through tiny spectacles and then huffed. "Young Lord Losolin, I presume? Yes, I have some supplies in the study. Follow me," she bustled into a small office filled with parchment and books. "Here, take these. Return them when you are done," she handed him stiff white parchment and writing supplies.

He hurried back to the maps on the table. He had been copying the map down painstakingly when a voice made him jump, making a large blotch in the middle of Florwen Hune.

"Rather amazing is it not, to see how the land can change in just a few thousand years. And to know that people long dead sat here doing just what you are, only they had nothing but the land to go by. May I ask as to the reason of this chore?"

Losolin looked around to see the man who had spoken to him, and saw nothing. He shook his head, turned back to the map, and saw a darkly shrouded figure sitting in the chair next to him. The cowl fell back and revealed an irritated scowl, and deep, unsettling dark eyes.

"Aladorn! Where the bloody nine hells have you been?" Losolin yelped, gulping back his surprise.

"Running your damnable army. Aidyn found me in the training yard and told me of your plans to leave. Now I find you pouring over maps instead of out in the wild tracking her down. What is going on?" the wiat asked, glaring.

"You know Aidyn?"

"Now I do. Answer my question."

"I am trying to decide where to go. To Blackhaven, or search for Midian's home. Either way, it seems Tlonna is doomed. I had a dream that she bore that bastard a son. I know it was just a dream, but I cannot help but believe it is true."

"You are in a rough spot, son. I would not suggest going to Blackhaven. He would not take her there, not if he had an ounce of sense in him. He will have taken her to his home. No one knows where that is, but I have a pretty good idea. When I followed him to get my revenge for my wife, I reached the end of the land where there is water that stretches as far as one can see. There, I believe, is where you will find Midian's realm, and there Tlonna shall be. A little of a late start though, is it not? She was taken more than a month ago."

Losolin resisted the urge to strike his friend. "Aidyn and I were restrained here until we *healed sufficiently*. The healers paid for it though."

"Ah yes, the murder of the young healer. I did hear of that."

"It was not murder, it was an accident, but a well deserved accident. He should not have grabbed Aidyn the way he did."

Aladorn studied his young companion before sighing heartily. "I have an idea where you can start your search."

Losolin pushed the map he had copied down in front of the dark elf. "Show me where." He handed Aladorn the quill and ink.

"I followed Midian through the Liberated Lands, into Florwen Hune, then Narnen. That was where I ran into the R'Kunad Sea. I believe that there is an island or even another land out there, and that is where the bastard lives, and rules. If the king of Narnen will grant you ships, then you might be able to find it, but otherwise, you will have to barter passage with others," the wiat placed an X on the spot where he had reached the sea.

"March your army north and settle them in Florwen Hune. Make your captains continue the recruitment. Have Demetri send to Barukh for permission and it will be granted to you. You and I, Aidyn, and a few others should travel ahead; we are faster when in a small group, and head toward Narnen. The king and queen there are weak, but there is a couple, a count and his wife, who I am sure will help," Aladorn said.

"From there, we travel by boat, using what we can to determine a heading. There has to be some sort of trail we can follow, whether it be floating corpses or burning ships."

Losolin nodded and sprinkled sand over his map to dry the ink. He rolled it up and put away the others. After returning the supplies to the library study, the elves left to find Aidyn.

They found him in Losolin's and his room, talking with King Demetrius. When they entered, the human turned and spread his hands.

"My friend," he said to Losolin. "I don't know if you are aware, but I supplied the recruits with new armor."

Losolin nodded once. "I thank you, but I do not know when or how I can repay you."

"I did not ask for payment, Losolin, now did I?"

The elf frowned, but he shook his head.

"Well, being an old king with a son too interested in scouring the lands for women and enemies to kill, I find myself rich and unfulfilled. So I commissioned one of the last remaining elven blacksmiths in my city to do me a favor." The king moved aside and revealed his gift.

Losolin stared. Aladorn stared. Aidyn moved away from the bed to slap Losolin on the back. "Now you will look like the Lord Consort of Princess Tlonna, my friend."

On his bed was a set of greaves, vambraces, a shield, a blue, silver, and green plumed helmet, a green cloak lined in pale blue, and a cuirass. It was all steel, but was so masterfully made that it looked like bands of silver woven together. The Tree of Blackhaven Forest was embossed on each piece in blue enamel. Losolin picked up the shield. It too was steel, but he lifted it easily. It was long and half again the width of his body, though it curved in on the sides. The bottom of the shield came to a point and the Tree covered almost the entire surface.

Carefully, he set it down and turned to the king. "Demetri...how can I ever repay you?"

"By delivering Tlonna's to her," the human said, and gestured toward a long wooden box.

Losolin moved to it and pulled the lid off. Inside on a bed of straw lay another set of armor. Though made in the same style, it was decidedly feminine. The cuirass was made to fit a female of Tlonna's build, and the pieces were more slender and delicate looking, though they were made for battle. Her helm and cloak had no green as his did, but rather silver, and above the tree on each piece was her symbol, the sun and star.

Losolin shook as he closed the lid. "I...I do not know what to say."

He turned and leaned back as Demetrius held out another box to him, this one long and thin. He took it with trembling hands. The elf opened it and slumped onto the bed. Inside lay a sword, slightly curved back, made of folded steel and singled edged. The hilt guard folded upward to touch the blade, and then actually looked to have been melted in so that it merged with the blade itself. The hilt was wrapped in a braided vine, sealed with wax, and then hardened by some sort of elfin technique for a sure grip. The pommel was merely an extension of the hilt, though the vine wrap ended to reveal the dark wood it was made from.

"Ash, to lend strength to the blade," Demetrius said suddenly as Losolin examined it.

"Demetri..." Losolin breathed, staring at the sword. "I..."

"I was told that when you wielded magic, it was a light green. I took the liberty in making it one of your colors. I hope I did right."

Losolin swallowed. "It is beautiful. It all is. Perfect."

"Good," the human said simply, smiling.

Aladorn and Aidyn moved aside as the king turned to leave. "Losolin, my friend, make haste, and go with the blessings of Kajgenia, and myself. May you reach her in time."

Tears glistened in the elf's eyes as he nodded, still holding the elfin sword. "Thank you."

Demetrius nodded, and left.

After a moment, Losolin looked at the two older elves standing side by side, watching him. He was struck by how similar they looked. Black haired and dark eyed, honey brown skin and taller than he. Suddenly he smiled.

"Can you help me put it on? I do not think I have ever worn armor."

Aidyn grinned back, and Aladorn nodded.

Each piece fit perfectly. When he finally donned his helmet

and sheathed the sword in the leather scabbard, Losolin looked at himself in the mirror. He was shocked to see how easy he looked in it. His scimitar was on his right hip, the new blade on the left, and the bow he had bought to replace his old one, was on his back next to his quiver.

In the mirror, he saw Aidyn pulling off his tunic and tossing it into one of his saddlebags. Muscles rippled beneath the skin along his back, his shoulders wider than they looked normally. The assassin then took out a package wrapped in brown paper. From it, he took out an inky black bundle that turned out to be a different shirt, one that fell open to his sternum, exposing the hairless, muscled chest. He pulled on a new pair of britches as well, the same inky black that seemed to suck all light from around him. Losolin raised his eyebrows at how tight they were, feeling uncomfortably male.

Next the assassin yanked on his black leather boots and draped his black cloak around his shoulders. When he noticed the stares of the other two elves, he smiled grimly.

"Assassin's clothes. I thought I would go out in style too, rather than look like a dirty human next to Losolin."

Losolin smiled and Aladorn laughed. "Indeed. We should not let him have all the glory."

Aidyn strapped on his sword belt, which Losolin noticed for the first time was also black. His bow and quiver went onto his back, and he slid two daggers into his sleeves, and two into his boots, and another set into the black harnesses tightened onto his thighs that Losolin had not noticed before.

The half-Magin turned to comment about it to Aladorn to find the wiat gone. Shaking his head, Losolin hefted his pack over his shoulder, picked up his shield, and waited for Aidyn to sling his saddlebags onto his back like a sack.

"I left a note for Miazie, when she returns, telling her what has happened," Losolin said as they left the room. "And Shireen is staying here as well, just in case."

Aidyn nodded. "Do not forget to send someone to get Tlonna's armor into a wagon before we leave."

Losolin grabbed a passing servant and asked that he get some help to do the task Aidyn had said. The man nodded and trotted off to find help.

They were in the stables when Aladorn appeared, along with

Kayra. The young woman was dressed in breeches and a long belted tunic. She beamed at the elves and hefted her pack onto the back of the horse she had bought. Aladorn turned to his gray stallion and did the same. Rather than the drab brown clothes he usually wore, the wiat was now dressed in a black silk tunic and gray breeches. He too was covered in weapons.

A shuffling noise made the four turn to the stable door as a group of men carried in the box that held Tlonna's armor. They hefted it into the back of a wagon and pushed it to the front. They swiped the sweat from their brows and turned to look at the elves and the woman.

"Can't believe you can wear that and not get your back bent, Lord Losolin," one of them said, gesturing to his armor.

Losolin shrugged. "Thank you for bringing it down."

"No problem, sir," another man said, and they left.

The four mounted and rode their horses out of the stable, Losolin first, then Aidyn, followed by Aladorn and Kayra. Wagons were being loaded with trunks of food and supplies, and extra weapons. Two other wagons stood already loaded with more food and supplies.

Tyre was coming down the steps into the yard when he spotted the four. He strode over to them, looking daunting in his own new armor.

"You look good, like a king," he said as he got close.

"Thank you, yourself as well," Losolin replied.

"I am leading the army north, and riders have already been dispatched to King Barukh of the Dwarves. The soldiers that are riding with you will find you shortly, I assume, so you can be on your way. Don't worry, Losolin, I'll take good care of your men."

"My thanks, Tyre. I trust you to do as you say. May the gods favor you," Losolin said.

"And you, my lord," Tyre returned, and marched off to find his horse.

Losolin trotted Neñyos to the front of the milling mass of soldiers, servants, squires, and captains. He raised his hand and utter silence fell. He looked at Aidyn and Aladorn, surprised, and received encouraging smiles.

Looking back at the troops, he watched them watching him.

After a few moments he spoke. "Soldiers, friends, I stand here before you in the place of another. Princess Magin Tlonna has been taken from us wrongfully. She has been hurt and broken. A small company of us will be traveling ahead of you in hopes of trying to retrieve her from the grips of evil. Midian is our enemy, and this will not be an easy road. March in good faith, you have the support of kings, and the hope of nations moving with you. Follow your captains into Florwen Hune. Travel swiftly, and do not stop for long periods of time. Good luck and I shall see you when I return victorious."

The crowd before him raised their various weapons and cheered. The ground shook as they stomped. Losolin turned Neñyos around to find himself facing a much smaller group.

He studied their faces. Aladorn, Aidyn, Kayra, two scouts named Dawson and Nayn, three swordsmen named Randi, Merrill, and Augustine. Two pike men, Shawn and Felton, plus two archers, Jairus and Demus. Takîreaes, Tlonna's big black stallion, looked at him from one liquid eye.

"From here on out, I do not know what is to happen, but it is not going to be easy. We must all bond together as a family if this is going to work. You were chosen because of your skills as warriors. Are we all ready to go?" he received nods from everyone. "Then let us go."

They turned and watched the army lining up into formation, and then trotted through the city, past the gates, and into the farmland. People hailed them as they went, calling out blessings and luck. The small troop rode out of the capital lands and went northwest into the dappled, sparse forest of the Fendis.

Yayènia sighed and rolled out of the inn bed. The sun had not yet risen, but the elf could see a small sliver of predawn light reaching over the horizon. She pulled on a plain shirt of black wool and breeches much the same, and went into the common room. Only one other person sat at a table near the wall, his hands hidden in the folds of his cloak. He turned as the female walked across the floor to the door.

"Morning," his voice was plain and unobtrusive.

"Good morning."

"Tad bit early to be going about outside is it not?" he asked, still plain.

"Um...well, I suppose so, but I would like to get what I need before my husband and friends wake. Tell me, do you happen to know where I could get some horses, and a map?" Yayènia replied, turning toward him.

"Yeah, there is a seller just down the street, take a left when you pass the fountain, and you will see a pretty large pasture. He will sell you a few horses for a fair price, as for the map, there is a town library on the next street. Mistress Madeline should probably be able to help you," the man said, turning back to the table.

Yayènia smiled and bowed her head. "Thank you, sir. You have saved me a couple of hours," the female turned and left the inn, clutching her cloak about her.

She walked down the deserted streets until she came to a crossroads. There, she turned right and went up the next street. A tall, domed building sat in the center of the main buildings. Yayènia walked up the steps and opened the door. A tall, skinny woman sat behind a desk to the left. She looked up and smiled serenely at the elf.

"May I help you, Miss?"

Yayènia sighed and walked up to the desk. "I need a map of the easiest and quickest way to Kajgenia."

"Oh? To Kajgenia? This way," Madeline stood and beckoned to the female to follow her.

Yayènia obeyed and followed the human to the back of the library. "Here," she said handing the elf a roll of parchment. "From here to Kajgenia. It's a long way no matter what, but this should be the fastest route. In order to avoid any problems with the Liberated Land's villages and kingdoms, you should travel wide of the center, through the handle of Purheae and into the Lands, around the Wandering Tributary. There's a bridge, King's Bridge, that crosses it near here," she pointed to the map.

"From there, it's about two day's ride to Kajgenia's border."

"How long does this take?" Yayènia asked, gesturing widely to the route Madeline had pointed out.

"Oh...two weeks, usually," she said unconcernedly.

Yayènia drew in a breath. "Then I guess I had better be on my way. Do you have a copy of this?"

"Yes, I do. Three coppers, I think, is the price."

The elf paid the human and left the library with her map.

She went back to the street where the inn was, found the fountain, and saw the pasture with a few horses frolicking about. The elf hurried up the steps of the house behind the pasture and knocked. A thick man opened the door and stared at her.

"Yes? Do you speak Hindarün or Parlêthian?" he asked gruffly, squinting up at her.

"Both, good sir," Yayènia replied, bowing her head slightly.

"What can I do for you?" the man said lightly, his Elvish thick with Hindarün accent.

"I need four good horses, four that can help me get to Kajgenia through the Liberated Lands as quickly as possible. Do you have such horses?"

"Of course, madam. Come this way," they went back outside, past the pasture, and into a large barn. Horses lined the aisle, whickering and stamping their feet. "I raise the finest horses in all Schelum. Are you looking for stallions, mares, studs, what?"

"It does not matter. Fast horses," Yayènia replied, patting a bay's nose.

"Ah well, here's one, named Smithy. Good strong stallion. Come 'ere, pet him." He led Yayènia to the stall and placed her hand on the horse's nose. It whickered gently, and then nodded its gray head. "Quarter horse. And here's a thoroughbred named Selwyn, a Palomino, Odilia, and another thoroughbred, Verity. You can have all of 'em for oh...three hundred gold spikes. Best deal around, Miss. What say you?"

Yayènia looked at the horses the man had pointed out and studied them. "Bring them into the pasture; I want to see them in action."

"What's your name?" the man asked after they had been watching the horses for a few silent minutes.

"Yayènia er'Tiena, High Commander of Blackhaven," Yayènia replied absently, her eyes on the pasture.

"No..." the man breathed in disbelief. "An honor, High Commander, truly. An honor. I can't believe you're here! What brings you to poor old Barl?"

Yayènia finally turned to the man. "Disaster, murder, treachery, and a missing princess. What is your name?"

The man blinked in astonishment. "My name? You want to know *my* name?"

"I asked, did I not?"

"Oh, yes, yes you did. Apologies High Commander. Aaron Eckhart, High Commander."

"An honor, Master Eckhart. You have fine horses. I will take them," Yayènia said, turning back to the animals.

"High Commander, yes of course!" Aaron yelped. "Half price, High Commander, for you."

"Yayènia, please, and no. I will pay full price for them, otherwise you will not make profit, will you?"

Aaron stared at her. "I...no, High Co-Yayènia. No I would not."

After sorting out tack as well, Yayènia paid the man and returned to the inn. Her three companions were up and ready to leave, waiting for her outside.

"So that is where you have been. Are they good animals?" Suneelo said, stroking Smithy's back.

"They seem to be. I watched them in action and paid a good price for them. Where is the girl?"

Erdwyf turned away from Odilia and nodded. "Ghealan and Suneelo taught Carlima a few moves with a quarterstaff, and I taught her the basics of hand to hand so she should be fine. Who is this?" she asked, patting Odilia's neck.

Yayènia smiled and introduced the horses to the elves. "I want Verity though. She is my favorite."

Suneelo took Smithy, and Ghealan took Selwyn. By midmorning, the elves were headed out of the town and into a wide span of rolling hills and short, brown grass.

Chapter 16
Child of Shadow and Light

The nights passed bitterly cold, but the camp of Alchemian stayed dry while outside the walls snow piled up high, and blizzards wracked the land. Miazie wriggled closer to Sodo in the bed and tried to catch some sleep. She failed. The morning came and the Belau got up, tired and cold. She pulled on robes of brown wool and flipped the hood up. Stepping outside, she was startled by a hand grabbing her wrist and yanking her down the dirt street. Pulling back, Miazie stared at Ardenay in surprise.

"What is going on?" she pulled her hood back up from where it had fallen and crossed her arms stubbornly.

"So, you really are sleeping with him. I thought it was a mad rumor, but now this!" the elf cried, flinging her hand at the entrance to Miazie's tent.

Miazie stared at her friend in shock. "Ardenay...I...I thought you knew. I didn't...it's not some fling, you know."

"Then what is it?"

Hurt, the human sniffed. "It is two people who have fallen in love sharing the nights. Is that so wrong?"

Ardenay stilled, her eyes trained on Miazie's. "Love? You have been here just over three weeks!"

"We humans move fast, something about not having all of the ages to perfect our advances," the Belau retorted, feeling angry.

"Sodo is not human!"

"No, he isn't, but I love him in spite of it."

The comeback stopped Ardenay's anger. "Do you really love him?"

"Of course I do. I would not say it if I didn't."

"And...and Sodo really loves you?"

"So he says," Miazie snapped.

Ardenay sucked in a breath and then expelled it with force. She rubbed her fingers across her lips, gazing back the short distance to Miazie's tent. Finally, she looked back at Miazie, standing resolutely still, her green eyes tight with anger.

"I suppose...if it is mutual..."

"Which it is."

"Yes...well, congratulations then. Miazie...I thought maybe it was just a way to get back at Elwyn. She wants him."

Miazie could not maintain her anger at her new friend. "No, it is not revenge. Elwyn wants him, I love him. She will have to come to the conclusion all on her own if she has not already. Does she know?"

Ardenay shrugged. "I believe she suspects. If she knew, I think we would all know it."

"That is true," Miazie replied, unfolding her arms. "Now, I think I will go back to bed, now that I suddenly feel the need to."

"Yes, All right. I am sorry," the elf said as she turned away.

"I know," Miazie said.

When she reentered her tent, Sodo was awake, his black eye hidden in shadows. "Are you okay?"

"Yeah, just a little cold," she said, sliding between the covers to cuddle up against him.

"Mm...I am glad Ardenay accepts this. I would be upset if she did not."

Miazie stared up at him. "Were you standing in the entrance of the tent?"

"No, I was right here. My heart, I am an elf, I can hear better than you," Sodo replied with a smile. "I am glad you accept me in spite of me being an elf."

The Belau giggled, pressing her palm against his naked chest to balance herself. In that position, she fell asleep.

She and Sodo strode to a communal meeting a few hours later, called by Elwyn. The High Alchemist stood upon a platform and waited until silence fell.

"I received a message from our shadowy neighbors to the east, the Shitan-Kulata."

Miazie jolted, her hand going to the katan sword at her back. Elwyn squinted at her.

"It seems three of their captives escaped, pilfering their esteemed General Damon in the process. The descriptions of these four people were sent to us as well, but I take it we all know who they are. There is a prophecy that needs decoding, and I need everyone on it. Everyone. It can be viewed in my quarters and you may leave your ideas on my desk. The sooner we can decode it, the sooner we can send our four...acquaintances on the way. Dismissed."

Miazie lowered her head and swallowed, clutching Sodo's hand in fear. The male squeezed back, but kept their hands well hidden from Elwyn's glaring eyes. When the High Alchemist descended her platform, she made for them, her cinnamon hair bouncing.

Sodo released Miazie's hand, but not in time. Elwyn stalked up to them and visibly shook. "So I see you have decided to make rumor truth, then."

"High Alchemist, you know my thoughts on your...desires," Sodo snapped, his usual deference gone.

"Yes, well, more the pity for you. You," the older woman snapped a finger in Miazie's face. "You have brought me irritation beyond imagination, a lifetime's worth of bad feelings, but you make him happy. That, I suppose, is worth it all. I will tell you when I have made a final conclusion on your damned prophecy. Now git."

Stunned, but not trusting enough to second-guess Elwyn's words, Miazie pulled a thunderstruck Sodo away and back to their tent. There, she pushed him onto the bed and reveled in their newfound acceptance.

Tlonna lay on the pile of straw, her eyes half closed in pain. The days passed in a blur. Nearly two months had passed since she had been captured from Kajgenia. Her stomach grew with an unwanted child, and sickness and pain took her. Midian seldom visited her, and when he did, it was to torture her and change the child within her womb. The knowledge of the infant made her despair, for she knew she would not love it as her own. The door to her cell opened and Tlonna tried to scoot further against the wall, but could not find the strength. A servant woman knelt beside her and placed a pitcher of cool water to her lips.

"Come, it is time. The master is ready for you to give birth," the servant helped Tlonna to her feet and half-carried her to a clean room down the hall.

Midian, Kelus, and three other women stood around a large bed. Tlonna snarled half-heartedly at Midian and received a smug grin. The child in her swollen belly kicked her painfully hard, making the elf wince. She lay down on the bed and sighed, relaxing in the soft downy. A basin of steaming water sat at her left, a bundle of swaddling clothes in a pile on the bedside table, and rags lay strewn about a chair. Minutes passed as Midian chanted incantations at her side, his hands on her belly, shaking. Tlonna tried to push his hands away, but Kelus grabbed them and held them above her head. The scaly ruin of his hands held her gently, but firmly, keeping her from batting Midian away.

Suddenly, a terrible pain racked Tlonna. The elf screamed as the infant inside her kicked and fought. Midian stood back, breathing hard and sweating, his blue eyes bright and wide. Contractions tore at Tlonna's body, making her arch and twist in Kelus's grip. A servant bathed her forehead with a steaming cloth, another bent down between her legs, waiting for the child.

An hour passed as Tlonna strove to give birth to her unwanted child, conceived and grown in unheard of speed. Finally, the servant held the bloody, squalling infant in her hands, cleaning him gently. Tlonna lay back, exhausted and listless. A moment later, the baby boy, cleaned and wrapped in swaddling clothes was placed in her arms. Huge blue eyes stared at her, the face round and pudgy. Wisps of black hair stuck to his head and tiny, faintly pointed ears stuck out from the pink head. It gurgled and then began to cry.

Tlonna jumped, startled by the tiny hands that reached toward her. She placed her finger in its little palm and watched the fingers curl around it. Another hand, much larger, grasped the child's clothes and pulled it away from Tlonna.

Midian held the boy in his arms, smiling, bouncing lightly. Tlonna stared at the abnormal sight, her gorge rising. The servant who had delivered the infant brought the child a rattler toy made from wood and placed it in the crying baby's hands. The squalling stopped almost immediately and began shaking the toy vigorously.

"Already he shows great signs of advancing in life much faster than any other child, my lord, as you wished him to. But, King Rahlan, what is his name?"

"Sithian. It means deadly warrior, and is my great ancestor. What do you think elf? How do you like our child?" Midian said as he stared down at the infant.

"It is not my child. I will have naught to do with it. I cannot love it as my own, and so I will not let it think so. I have done my part, so why not kill me and get it over with?" Tlonna spat.

"Oh no, Tlonna. You will raise this child, nurse it, and nurture it, as it is your own flesh and blood. See, you left your mark," Midian pointed at the elfish ears, grimacing.

"No!" Tlonna flung herself out of the bed and attempted to crawl away. Pain erupted in her body, pinning her to the floor.

"Bitch! You will not die, and you will not leave! You will have your own room, which you will share with the child. He will feed on your milk and thrive on your presence. I will not let you abandon him!" Midian screamed at her, dragging her back to his feet. "Kelus, take her to the room that was prepared for her and Sithian. Lock her in there, and stay with her to make sure she does not starve my son. Go!"

Kelus pulled Tlonna up and took the child in his arms. The demon shoved the elf out of the room and down the hall to a small room elegantly furnished. He closed the door and locked it. He placed Sithian in a bassinette near the bed and then turned to Tlonna.

"I am ssorry, elf."

"It is not your fault, Kelus, but if you are sorry, why will you not let me die?" Tlonna hissed as she sat on the bed.

"Becausse if you die, then there will be no more hope of redemption from him. And I will die then too, and it will not be a mercy. Otherss will ssuffer far more than you or I, and they will never forgive you."

"Then why will you not let me kill the child?" Tlonna yelled, walking over to the bassinette. She looked down at the sleeping infant, sucking its thumb.

"Becausse you love him yet. I can ssee it in your eyess. You know what he will become, and you sstill love him asss your son. You would not be able to kill him. He iss innocent now, and you cannot, will not, kill an innocent person. I know thiss. You will not kill me becausse you have pity for me, even though I am evil. It iss becausse you are good, the esssence of purity. Can you not ssee it? Even now I threaten the life of the world becausse of my dessire to live, and you will not kill me becausse you pity me."

"I do not kill you because you are not evil. Evil made you what you are, but there is still good in you. You are not consumed by it. You can still love. You can still become what you once were. I would not have been able to burn away the ruined flesh on your arm and let your real skin come through if there was not some measure of virtue within you still. That is why I do not kill you. While the child, he will grow up not knowing morality or righteousness. He will be evil defined."

"But if you help raisse him, then he will know. He may believe asss hiss father doess, but in his mind, he will ssee the cruelty of his actions. Midian hass arranged for Ssithian to grow a year every week until he reachess ssixteen. Then he will grow asss a normal human, with the prolonged life of the elvess. Thiss meanss you do not have time to try to jusstify his exisstence, you musst teach him now," the demon said urgently, coming to stand behind her.

"But he is already evil! There is nothing I can do to help him. He is doomed. His heart is already blackened, and his mind corrupted. He may yet be innocent, but soon that will change. Sithian is not my son," Tlonna growled.

"He came from your womb, did he not? He iss of your flessh and blood, ergo he iss your sson. Look, he wakess," the demon pointed at the child who was slowly opening its eyes.

Sithian opened his mouth and began squalling. Kelus picked the boy up and held him out to his mother. Tlonna shuddered and turned away. It was almost humorous to see the demon holding the tiny child. Its blackened claws held the boy firmly by the belly, while Sithian yowled. "I will not feed him. He is not my son."

Damn you elf! Take him and feed him, otherwisse Midian will make it worsse for all of uss," the Darkwight shoved the infant into the elf's arms and waited.

Slowly, Tlonna pulled her sleeve down and bared her breast for the child. It began to suckle, feeding on her milk. When Sithian finished, he lay in her arms, staring at her with his dark blue eyes. The Magin set him down on the floor and arranged herself across from him, folding her legs to the side.

"Kelus."

"Yess?"

"Can you get me some parchment, a few books about the history of Nymyños, and some quills and ink?"

"Of coursse. I sshall return sshortly." The demon turned to leave, and then turned back. "Elf, do not leave thiss room."

"I know Kelus. Hurry."

While Kelus searched for the items she had listed, Tlonna began to teach the infant her little Parlêthian vocabulary. By the time the Darkwight returned, the visually growing child was gurgling odd noises back to her.

"Here, teach him well, elf," the demon sat down on the bed and watched Tlonna read to Sithian the history of Nymyños.

The days passed quickly. On the third week, Sithian was repeating Elvish phrases back to her, and Tlonna was able to learn the language by reading the one and only book in Elvish, translated into Hindarün in the margins, that Midian owned. It was on the fourth week that Midian invaded the room. In a flurry of black silk, Tlonna shoved all of the materials under the bed and wrapped her arms around the four-year-old boy. Midian sent a hand across Tlonna's face and snatched the boy away from her.

Sithian reached for his mother, but found the arms around him were like steel. He turned and faced Midian.

"Who are you?"

"I, Sithian, am your father. I am your king, and your master. Tlonna bore you, but she is just a tool. She will not have told you that, but then again, she is an elf."

"Father, I am an elf too, see? I have pointed ears," Sithian hooked his black hair behind his ears and showed them to Midian.

The king set the boy on the bed and stalked toward Tlonna. "Whore! You taught him to believe he was an elf? Kelus! How could you allow her to do that? Get out of my sight! Go to my throne room and await my displeasure!" the demon fled the room, and Midian turned back to Tlonna. "You were to feed and nourish him, not feed his mind with your blithering damning Elvish notions. Come here!" Midian grabbed Tlonna's ankle and pulled her back to him. He yanked her dress off and dropped his breeches. The human pinned the elf to the floor and ravished her in front of their son.

When he finished, he beat Tlonna mercilessly. Blood pooled on the floor beneath her as she lay weeping. A group of servants pinned her dress back onto her body and dragged her out of the room. She was thrown back into her cell and chained to the floor. Her body shook with fatigue and helplessness. Blood ran in streams across the floor to mingle in the straw.

Tears tracked through the blood and sweat on her face as Tlonna began to sob. No food and only a small pitcher of water came to her for days. Food began to appear every three or four days. Too weak to heal, Tlonna lay on the freezing stone floor, emaciated and broken. Many weeks later, the door opened and a young man walked in. His dark blue eyes and pitch-black hair terrified her. Sithian stared at her in shock, his slim body tense as he studied her.

"Mother?"

"Sithian. Help me, please," Tlonna's voice was quiet and weak.

For a moment, Sithian looked as though he was going to unlock the cuffs holding her. Then the young man jerked away and began to laugh. "You tried to teach me your ways, Tlonna, but then Father opened my eyes. I see now the insolent bliss you live in. Father taught me to enjoy life. Have you ever looked a person in the eyes as you're killing them? It makes you see that you have complete and utter control of their life. They scream and beg for mercy, and if you give it to them, they turn around and try to kill you, but if you don't, then they die in respect for you. They know they are worthless in comparison. Father taught me that, and then he let me experience it. Oh, Tlonna, you shouldn't have resisted Father's orders. You could have been right by our side as we take over Nymyños, but you had to go all-virtuous and try to teach me the ways of your kind. You left on me your mark and for that, I can never forgive you, but perhaps I can persuade you to join the dark side. No one could resist our power and strength, Tlonna, no one!"

"No Sithian! You know this is wrong! I made sure you had a conscience. Do not follow Midian's footsteps. He is evil, Sithian, evil!" Tlonna screamed, watching her son recoil from her.

"I know, Mother, and so am I. It really is the best way to live. No regrets, restrictions, or consequences to worry about, just plain freedom. I hold people under my little finger, and I can do with them as I wish. You will come to see, Tlonna, that your goodness and morality is futile against the strength of the Shadow. Your time has come to an end, Mother, and evil will reign."

Sithian left, slamming the door behind him, laughing. Tlonna heard Midian congratulating him and the two men left, leaving her to despair. Her world turned to pain, blood, and a pitcher of water. Slowly, the elf collapsed into herself, folding into nothingness.

The four elves traveled swiftly across the hilly landscape of Schelum and into the Liberated Lands. While Erdwyf's child grew within her, winter clogged the air. The taint whipped around them, obscuring even their vision.

By the time they had reached King's Bridge, they had heard of Tlonna's capture and Losolin's departure.

Yayènia yanked off her riding gloves in frustration when an innkeeper finished telling them about the events. Ghealan pushed Yayènia to the side and tipped the hat he had acquired in a small village.

"Good sir, do you know where Lord Losolin went?" he inquired amicably.

"To the Shadowsoul's home, wherever that is, my Lord. None know where that is, but there is a rumor that it is on an island far in the R'Kunad Sea. No one's ever found it, but who says t'aint there, hmm?" the man chuckled and beamed up at the elf that stood two feet above his head.

"Thank you sir."

The elves remounted and rode on, pushing their tired mounts hard. When midnight arrived, they stopped to make camp. They had only lain down for an hour when Ghealan felt the cold of steel pressed against his neck.

"I would expect better from the warriors of Blackhaven," a shadowed voice said.

The other three woke and drew weapons. The shrouded figure came further in the light, grinning.

Aidyn!"

"My friends," he said, and was crowded by them all.

Finally, when they broke apart, Yayènia asked the question they all were afraid to ask. "Losolin?"

"About an hour behind me. I rode ahead to give the scouts a break. We ride with a small group, an army following us, though they are days behind. We head toward Narnen, to the coast and beyond."

"Narnen?" Erdwyf asked.

"Aye, to visit a kindly count and his wife..." Aidyn said with a glint in his eye.

"Oh!" the High Advisor clapped her hands. "It will be good to see my parents!"

"Indeed," Ghealan muttered, and flopped onto his sleeping roll.

The rest followed his example. Suneelo poked the fire back to life. Aidyn watched him for a moment.

"It is a relief to see you two still alive," he said to Yayènia.

She nodded. "It is a relief to be alive."

Suneelo grunted. "What has happened since you left?"

Aidyn sighed. "A lot." He told them of his travels from Blackhaven to Kajgenia, and finally got to the present. "Tlonna is, we think, on an island somewhere deep in the R'Kunad. We believe it to be Midian's home. According to Losolin's recent dreams, she has given Midian as son named Sithian. He is to be a tool of evil with both Tlonna's and Midian's power."

"Abomination," Suneelo growled.

"Aye, and worse," Yayènia agreed.

Everyone fell into a gloomy silence.

Finally Aidyn spoke, disheartened. "I must warn you. Tlonna and Losolin are not the same elves that left home years ago. They are hardened, desperate, lonely, powerful, deadly beings. They do not remember you or any of their life before a few months ago."

Suneelo sighed shakily. "Time has changed all of us, my friend. Even you, hardened though you have always been, are more threatening than before."

"Yes, but we will make it through this time and into the next, no doubt about it."

A silence ensued once more, tense and awkward.

After a while Erdwyf sighed. "Well, we should set a watch and get some sleep before Losolin and the rest catch us."

"Agreed," Aidyn said. "I will take it. He will not recognize any of you."

With that heartbreaking notion, the four elves rolled into their blankets and slept.

Losolin sighed as he pulled himself onto Neñyos's back. Behind him, Takîreaes stamped impatiently. The small troop launched forward, their horses' nostrils spouting clouds as they ran. Weariness plagued the company as they moved forward through the plains of Kajgenia. Rarely had they stopped to rest or eat, and tainted wind whipped at them constantly. The horses struggled to move their fatigued bodies, and the riders fought to stay astride.

An hour later, Aidyn hailed them. The company halted and stared at the four new elves standing beside the assassin. Losolin dismounted wearily.

Suneelo rushed forward. "Brother."

Losolin backed away a step, and then squinted at the fair elf. "You are Suneelo?"

The older elf grinned, nodding. "Do you remember me?"

"Vaguely," Losolin shrugged. "And this must be Ghealan, Erdwyf, and Yayènia?" he said, looking at each of them in turn.

"Losolin, it has been so long," Yayènia cried, flinging her arms around his neck.

The half-Magin stumbled with her weight, light as she was. The High Commander pushed away from him immediately.

"Sorry," she mumbled.

Losolin shook his head. "No worries. What are you all doing out here? Is Blackhaven free?"

Ghealan shook his head. "*Noya*, we just escaped. Thought we would catch up with you, and help. Our place is by your side, as it always has been. Yours and Tlonna's."

"Ah well, Tlonna awaits us then," Losolin said grimly. "We ride on, are you ready?"

The four elves nodded. Aidyn leapt atop Whäd and watched the other elves mount. Losolin practically dragged himself onto Neñyos. The others behind him were little better, not having the stamina of the elves, but having had more rest.

Aladorn rode up to meet the newcomers, but when he took Ghealan's hand in greeting, they both froze.

"*Takireaese shä klamen xetian lauk rakna, nó kinë lada, Erion* Ghealan," the wiat said after a moment, and yanked his hand from Ghealan's.

The warrior had to pull his mount around to prevent him from staring at Aladorn. Beside him, in the light of the moons, Yayènia's eyes shone icily as Ghealan turned to look at her. She deliberately turned away, slamming her helm onto her head to hide the fury in her eyes.

Suneelo and Erdwyf shared a look. Losolin and Aidyn watched in confusion as Aladorn rode to the back of the party. Ghealan shook his head. Losolin rode closer to Aidyn and asked him to translate the wiat's words, and he did so with a dark voice. *Warriors of the shadow ride together, and never forget.*

The group rode on throughout the night, the tainted snow whirling around them, the moonlights flickering through the clouds to illumine the way. Stories were told about that journey, how a troop of fearsome and beautiful elves rode demon horses through the howling winds, never stopping, never slowing. Many said they were chased by the gods themselves toward some unknown destiny, others that they chased something else, forever bound to hunt and kill it. Whatever was said about it as people pressed against their doors and windows to watch the desperate procession, it was remembered as a fearful and awestricken sight.

Chapter 17
Mistake of Magic

Miazie jerked awake and stared at the elfin face across from her. A smiled crept across her face as Sodo woke as well, his eyes, now familiar, cracking open.

"I love mornings now," he murmured, reaching up to brush a lock of hair out of her face.

Miazie felt pleasant chills run down her spine and kissed his wrist. "I do too."

Sodo grinned suddenly and he twisted, pulling her underneath him in one smooth movement. Miazie let out a shriek that turned into laugher as the elf ran his fingers up and down her belly, tickling her. She wrestled with him futilely, laughing so hard tears leaked from her eyes. Sodo was laughing too as he playfully tormented her, getting their blankets tangled in their legs.

Then playfulness changed to desire, and his fingers became caressing rather than tickling. Miazie moaned as the elf pulled her into sublime oblivion, forgetting the fears the world presented.

Losolin watched Yayènia pull the saddle off her mare and pet her nose. Suneelo walked by her, putting his hand on her back as he did, almost unconsciously. Yayènia smiled at her husband and he smiled back and walked on. A pang of loneliness shot through Losolin. Off to the side, Ghealan was laughing, his head bent toward Erdwyf as she spoke. Aidyn strolled up to him.

"Is this your happy face?"

Losolin sniffed, shoving his hands into his pockets. "They are so happy together."

"Aye, and you will be soon, once we get Tlonna back. We were all the best of friends, and one day, it too will be so again. We all loved each other as friends, family, more like. We were inseparable."

Losolin looked at Aidyn. "You speak as if we are all dead and gone."

The assassin looked away. "It is hard, when you show no recognition to the people who helped shape you into who you are, Losolin. It seems like we are starting over, though we have known each other for over a hundred years."

Losolin lowered his head to stare at the ground. "I am trying."

"I know, they know it too, but that does not make it any easier. Is there any way I can help you remember?"

The half-Magin looked up at the dark sky. "Tell me about them."

Aidyn breathed out quietly and then gestured to a small dip in the land, a few yards from camp. They walked to it and sat down, facing the sky.

"Where to begin," Aidyn mused. "Yayènia er'Tiena, High Commander of the Blackhaven Militia, Mother of Silver Damnation, and Duchess of Blackhaven City."

"Silver Damnation?"

"The elite guard Yayènia personally trains from her army. They are nigh undefeatable. The silver part comes from their cloaks, which are silver, obviously. Yayènia is a tightly wound spring at all times, ready to explode at any moment. Threaten anything she does, or loves, and her sword will have pinned you to the ground through the belly faster than you can utter nine hells. I would never want to get in a fight with her. I can match neither her wits nor her skill, and I know you cannot either, because no one can. She lives through things that even normal elves would die from. Her skill in fighting is legendary, and she has never been bested.

"Suneelo, your brother, is her husband, plainly. Brave sort, he is. Born into nobility, Suneelo was raised to be Duke of Blackhaven, but then he met Yayènia and all his parents' plans for him flew out the window. He now is Captain of the Guard, second only to Ghealan and Yayènia.

"As for Erdwyf, she is a bit calmer, a little quieter, and not so violent as Yayènia, but still someone to keep on our side. She was born in Althirim, Narnen, as a viscountess, but left when she met Ghealan. She is Queen Constancias' High Advisor, extremely wealthy and one of Tlonna's devoted friends. She and Yayènia are almost connected at the hip as well. Brains to vex even Miazie too, I am sure. She can also best most males in a fight." Aidyn took a breath, swiping tainted snow from his chest.

"Then there is Ghealan, Erd's wife, and Second Commander of the Blackhaven Militia, just under Yayènia, and things get complicated. When he was younger, oh...three hundred years ago or so, he and Yayènia were together. He was in the group Warriors of the Shadow, as you know, and but before that, when he and Nia first met, he was just a common knight in a band of rogue elves called the Blackhands. Then they were disbanded, and he joined the Warriors of the Shadow, leaving Yayènia in Blackhaven, alone. Remember what I told you Aladorn said to Ghealan when they were introduced?"

Losolin nodded.

"That was their motto, Ghealan told me. Aladorn and he must have ridden together. It must have been a shock for him, and Ghealan, and Yayènia, to have that time shoved back into their faces. It is what broke their engagement."

"Yayènia and Ghealan were engaged? Why did he leave her?" Losolin asked.

Aidyn shrugged. "That I do not know. It is something they keep to themselves. I am not sure if Suneelo or Erdwyf even know. But one thing is for certain, while Ghealan was away, Yayènia married and had a son."

"What?" Losolin yelped.

"Aye. Raistlyn is his name. You see, her life has been hell ever since she was born. Her father, Baron Yinji Yedoc, sold her into the care of Governor Arakis when she was fourteen years old. He was seven hundred years old at least. He released her when she killed one of his senior wives, and at that time, I believe she was about ninety-three or four. That was when she met Ghealan. Then he left, and she fell back into poverty, having had only Ghealan's income to support her.

"It is said, as Yayènia nor Ghealan ever talk about this part of their life, that Yayènia got a job as a maid for High Archdeacon Raith, a human. Apparently, he either raped her, or they had an affair, because he got her with child, a middle-aged half-elf now named Raistlyn. Raith never allowed Raistlyn or Yayènia to come in contact with each other. She would not be able to pick him out of a line, nor he her. I have met him, and when asked, he said he never wanted to meet his mother. He is now Archdeacon. Anyway, she was with Raith for about eighty years, until he died.

"That was also when Ghealan reappeared with a new wife, a pretty viscountess from Narnen. Yayènia joined the militia, and though it was not common for females to be in it, she was accepted because of her skill. She rose through the ranks so fast that even when

Ghealan joined, he could not keep up with her. Hegan, the old High Commander, abdicated, passing his title onto Yayènia. That is when she married Suneelo, and moved Ghealan to the position of Second Commander. For two hundred years, it has remained so. Since then, they owe each other their lives. Yayènia has saved Ghealan's life, and he hers."

"How did Ghealan save *her* life?" Losolin asked, intrigued.

The assassin rubbed his face. "They rode into battle against Midian's father, Aderiaen Rahlan together. It was about four months into the war and everyone was exhausted and downhearted, even Rahlan's people, and they were winning. Yayènia led a raiding party into Aderiaen's camp, and they were almost out when a guard rolled under her horse's feet. The horse stumbled and fell, nearly crushing Yayènia. Aderiaen found her and was about to plunge his blade into her neck when Ghealan and his party rode up and attacked.

"Ghealan found Yayènia lying in the mud and was able to get his blade deep enough into Aderiaen's thigh that the man fled and he took her and got her back home. She had seven broken ribs, and her collarbone, right arm and shoulder, knee, and nose were all crushed, plus one of her lungs had collapsed. Luckily, she heals faster than anyone I have ever heard of. She barely survived, and would not have had Ghealan not done what he did."

"Wow," Losolin breathed. "They really are tied up in knots around each other. It is strange to think I once knew them, and loved them. They all are so...dangerous."

The assassin laughed. "Indeed...but you do not look so friendly anymore, either."

Losolin frowned. "What do you mean?"

"You used to be a warm, cheerful peasant elf who made the rest of us look like heartless bastards. Now...well...you look like the wrathful warrior whose love has been taken by the enemy. The armor and weapons do not help much, either. But your face, Losolin, your face makes *me* want to turn tail and run."

Losolin looked away and tightened his fist on the hilt of his sword. "I am scared, is all. I do not know what I will do if Tlonna dies. She is my life."

"I know. I know, Losolin, and these four will be the help needed to tip the balance in our favor. Their skill in fighting is unmatched anywhere in Nymyños. Even Erdwyf can best most in all types of war craft. Yayènia is the most feared and admired warrior in history, and Ghealan a close second. Suneelo once took down an entire company by himself using just two hand daggers *and* he is happily married to Yayènia. I have never heard of anyone doing either of those but for Ghealan and Yayènia themselves, and even Ghealan did not marry Nia."

Losolin found himself chuckling and stopped abruptly. Sighing, he sat up. Aidyn followed him.

"I suppose I should get to know them, then?"

The assassin nodded. "It would be a good idea, yes."

The two stood and walked back to the camp where Erdwyf was telling a story that had all the men, and Kayra, riveted. Ghealan, Yayènia, and Suneelo were cleaning their weapons, though they too listened.

"...and as we rode over the hill, the camp spread out before us like a sea, vast and dark. In the center, our goal. Aderiaen Rahlan's tent billowed like sail on a ship, inside, the man himself, Weaving his magic. We charged downward, into the gully, vastly outnumbered, but every one of our soldiers ready to die to give our home a chance."

Aidyn took a seat next to Yayènia, who smiled at him. She dumped a belt of daggers into his lap, and handed him a cloth. Silently, the assassin glared at her, though when she turned away, he smiled and began polishing her weapons.

Losolin sat next to Ghealan. The elf grinned at him, and then stood, patting his wife on the thigh. Gesturing to Losolin, he walked away.

Frowning, the youngest elf present looked at Aidyn, who shrugged. With a sigh, Losolin followed Ghealan.

When he reached him, he asked, "Do you ever use all of those weapons?"

The other elf laughed. "Evil lies like hungry wolves in this land. One must be armed to survive, and if one weapon breaks or is lost, what good are if you do not have another and another?"

Losolin nodded. "What do you want?"

Ghealan looked uncomfortable for a moment. "You...ah...you look well."

Losolin scowled.

"I mean...the armor, it does you justice," Ghealan fumbled, reddening.

"Thank you," the half-Magin said slowly, wondering at the other elf's awkwardness.

"Look, I just want to make sure you remember your skills, Losolin," Ghealan finally said.

"What skills?"

"Fighting and whatnot. I know have lost your memory, but have you lost your ability as well?"

"No," Losolin said, more sharply than he intended.

Ghealan put his hands up. "I do not mean to offend, but if you have, please, let me help you. I know you carry the weapons, but do you retain your knowledge of them?"

Taking a deep breath, Losolin replied, "I do not know. I have not found myself wanting in battle, and no recruit has been able to put me on the ground yet."

"Good, good," the warrior said, nodding. "I would like to set up a practice every night, though. For myself, as well, and the others. It is a common tool we use, Yayènia and I, I mean, with the soldiers. It just helps to maintain skill and endurance. I know Aidyn does his routine every night."

Losolin looked out across the gently rolling hills, the Fendis Forest miles behind them now. The moons peeked out from behind thick clouds moving slowly with the night wind. He nodded. "It is a good idea, I would appreciate it, as would the others, I am sure," he finally said.

When they returned to the campfire, Erdwyf had finished her tale and the others were begging her for another. She declined, smiling. Instead, Kayra started one. She had a smooth voice that soon captured the audience's full attention. She spoke of Aedrid, the half-mythical hero from ages long past that had given her home city its name.

"He rode a stallion that turned to fire when the sun was going down, and his sword was bigger than most men," she began.

Losolin studied Yayènia across the fire, her head resting on Suneelo's shoulder, his arm draped over her shoulders. Her features were similar to Tlonna's, but a little more rounded and wide-eyed. Wheat blonde hair was pulled back in one thick braid that curled around her feet, curled up as she was. High cheekbones and attractive lips made her look innocent and vulnerable, as did her grayish-blue eyes.

Her slim body was covered in leather straps over her black tunic that held daggers and throwing knives, a twin set of blades on her back along with a bow and quiver, a thick one held a battleaxe, and another around her waist supported a long sword.

Though she was not wearing her armor, Losolin remembered it clearly. It was similar to Tlonna's, though the cuirass barely reached her midriff. Her helmet was grandly plumed, as his was, though hers was black, blue, and silver. But it was her cloak, which she wore now as well, that he marveled at. It was completely silver, though black velvet lined the edges and the hood. When she made the slightest movement, it seemed to go into a slow fit, flowing and billowing of its own accord.

Losolin was so entranced by the part of the cloak he could see that he did not feel Yayènia's eyes on him. When he looked up, he started, blushing. Yayènia smiled slightly, then went back to listening to Kayra. Even though the taint swirled around them in gentle whirls, Losolin felt a sense of peace for the first time in weeks.

They struck camp at dawn. As no one had bothered to pitch their tents in order to move faster, they were on their way in minutes. Losolin looked back through the tiny ranks and saw that there had been an unspoken establishment. The two archers, Jairus and Demus rode off to opposite flanks, guarding the sides, while Randi, Augustine, Merrill, Shawn, and Felton had rotated themselves to guard the rear. Up ahead, Kayra rode next to Aidyn and Aladorn, though a little behind. The four warrior elves had taken up head guard, forcing everyone back to the rear. Losolin realized he was in the center, guarded on all sides. The scouts, Dawson and Nayn had ridden ahead and were disappearing over the crest of a hill. The party began to pick up speed until the horses were galloping down across the hilly landscape. It was that way when they passed the wooden marker into Florwen Hune.

Nayn rode into view as the sun was falling behind the horizon, galloping at full speed toward them. "Lord Losolin! Lord Losolin! There is a band of dwarves up ahead and they are looking for you. Dawson is waiting with them, and not of his own accord. Hurry my lord!" the scout joined their party and they launched forward, pushing their tiring horses.

They crested yet another hill and saw a group of short, bearded men holding the tall and lanky scout by his arms. Another tall figure with dark blond hair stood at the front. Losolin pushed between Erdwyf and Ghealan to the front of his company and reined Neñyos in just inches away from the tall fellow.

"Good evening, is there something wrong?" Losolin asked cordially, staring down at the man.

"Yeah, there is something, elfie. You're on King Barukh's land without leave. You are under arrest for trespassing, and will be taken to the king for questioning," the huge man growled, not at all abashed by Losolin's superior height.

"King Demetrius of Kajgenia sent word of our arrival. Besides, how were we to get leave, if no one is there to give it?" he asked, backing away from the man as he reached for Neñyos' reins.

"There're ways, elfie. Now you and you're friends are under arrest. Come 'ere." the fellow lunged for Neñyos and stumbled past as the gelding sidestepped him.

"Tell me, sir, who are you and what are you to be in the company of dwarves and stand as tall as an elf?" Yayènia asked, sneering.

"I am Anadin, dwarf-elf, commander of King Barukh's border patrol guard. And who are ye to be so fair and carry such manly weapons?"

Yayènia leaped off Verity and drew her longsword at the same time. The blade point scraped in Anadin's blond beard. The dwarf-elf grunted and stared down the blade at the female.

"I am High Commander Yayènia er'Tiena of the Elven Militia. I have killed my fair share of dwarves in my life time, and one more abomination would not hurt my record. Tell me, how would any dwarf get any elf to bed him?"

"Well, *High Commander*, my father captured an elf, 'bout as pretty as yourself, and raped her. That's how. Now remove your blade or my men will have to destroy that face and body of yours," Anadin sneered, unmoved by the dangerous glint in Yayènia's eyes.

Another blade joined Yayènia's, and Suneelo's was not nearly so kind. He shoved it into the dwarf-elf's cheek, ripping open the skin. The fellow did not even blink.

"Touch her, and you will taste steel at the back of your throat."

It was so unexpected that everyone jumped when Anadin laughed. "Ye are all good warriors I take it. So, what is your purpose here, hmm?"

"We are headed to Narnen to speak with the king. An army follows us, they mean your land no harm, but seek, as we do, the province of Narnen." Losolin said, sliding off Neñyos.

"Why are ye wanting to speak with King Emar? What business do ye and your army have in Narnen?"

"Our business is our own, but we travel for an island called Zaedic in the far R'Kunad Sea," Erdwyf said coolly, still on horseback.

"Only fools search for Zaedic, and none return, but it is not my business what elves do to end their own lives. I will escort you to our western border." Anadin brushed the swords away and turned to his men. He spoke in a gruff, guttural language. "*Takrin ud kumak urder oche sed thurak.*"

"What did he say?" Losolin asked Ghealan who had come to stand next to him.

"He told them to return to their posts and be on the lookout for an army. He told them to not hinder their passage, but to escort them to King Barukh," the elf whispered quietly.

"Is that good?"

"I do not know...look, the creature approaches," Ghealan glared at the dwarf-elf so violently that Losolin stepped away from him.

"Come, mount your beasts and let's move on," Anadin said gruffly.

The elves mounted and the party moved, guided by the swift strides of the dwarf-elf. Losolin realized with a jolt that a huge sword was strapped to his back and looked well worn. Suneelo, who had moved Smithy next to Neñyos, grunted.

The warrior leaned over to put his face next to Losolin. "Brother, do you trust this...creature?"

"No, but I would rather have some idea as to where to go than none. We have maps, but a living, breathing person if more reassuring to me. He is taking us to the other side of Florwen Hune, and that means Narnen."

"Loni would not like this. She was never a trusting person. I highly doubt she would approve of us giving ourselves freely into the care of a *dwarf-elf*," Suneelo growled.

"That is what you call Tlonna?" Losolin asked, smiling slightly.

"Aye, and so do you," Suneelo replied.

"Yes, I do."

The elder brother grinned. "Good."

After a moment, Losolin asked, "Suneelo, I have heard we are half brothers. Which parent do we share?"

Suneelo's jaw tightened and he scanned the heavens before answering. "We share a father, Loseen Grisholm. My mother changed my name to Tiena after my step-father Kranoma, so that the people would not know of her association with Loseen. You must understand that my mother loved Loseen very much, but the social rings would not let it stand. Their love affair was broken when I was born, forcing the city to see the proof of my mother's *fetish*." The male snarled the world so angrily Losolin jumped. "That is what they called it, anyway. Well, needless to say Loseen met your mother Mylea a century later, and then you were born two centuries after that. You and I knew of each other when you turned twenty, when we were introduced at a party held by Yayènia. After that, we became friends, and found our sibling love."

Losolin smiled faintly as he thought about that. After a moment he looked at his brother. "And where are Loseen and Mylea now?"

Suneelo's face tightened before he looked away. "They are...they did not survive the siege.

Losolin fell silent, brooding. Neñyos flicked his head and stepped sideways as he trotted. Suneelo glanced at the horse seemingly unconcerned; though he reached down to make sure his sword was clear in its scabbard, turning his head slightly to look at Anadin. Losolin eyed his half-brother, watched the bicep visible between vambrace and short sleeve tighten and bunch as it gripped the hilt of the sword.

The days passed swiftly as the small company was escorted across the stony ground of Florwen Hune. Stone obelisks and monuments decorated the land like trees, replacing the actual living wood. When Losolin mentioned the trees, or lack thereof Anadin only smiled at him eerily, a greasy, mocking smile.

"Trees? What use are trees when ye can have stone? Trees

wither and die with the seasons, while stone stands for ages, weathered, yes, but still standing. Stone will never die. It is the bone of the earth, and the books of the ages."

"Even bones break, and books rot, Lord Anadin. The earth has survived all these lifetimes, and even the stone of it has changed and shifted. There will always be stone, yes, but there will always be trees as well."

"Oh aye, and that would be the mistake ye full blooded elves make. Ye depend on the earth for yer station, while everyone else depends on themselves. That is why the other races, other than the faery folk of course, thrive, while ye and the rest of the tree huggers filter away until nothing of ye remain. Ye can't depend on the earth, for the earth changes, stone will always be stone, elf-prince, and nothing can change that," Anadin growled, slicing his hands through the air.

"We have not filtered out, you filth. We were persecuted until the humans and their...cohorts, thought us dead. There are hundreds, thousands, of elves out there, waiting until the opportune moment to reap our revenge," Yayènia spat, drawing her sword.

"Put it away, miss. There is law here that no blood will be spilled in the sacred places of Florwen Hune. This is an old battlefield, used in the First War of King Brandon. Thousands died here, and now, it is law that no other soul shall perish on this plain."

"Take it back, filth." Yayènia growled, sheathing her sword reluctantly. "I will not abuse your laws, but I will not hesitate to abuse you."

"Yayènia! Be quiet!" Erdwyf snapped, fully aware of her friend's fiery temper. "Anadin is being kind and helpful to us. Do not antagonize him."

"Yer an intelligent little dame aren't ye? That's the smartest thing I think I've ever heard come from an elven mouth. The sun's sinken low, let's get camp up," the dwarf-elf said humorously as he swung his pack off his shoulders onto the ground.

Losolin slid off Neñyos and yanked the bedroll out of Takîreaes' saddlebags. Yawning, he laid out his roll, missing the familiarity of Tlonna's roll next to his. He moved away to unsaddle the horses just as the sun disappeared behind the mountainous horizon. Yayènia was coaxing a fire out of damp wood while Suneelo stuck a black pot in the middle.

After a while, the rich smells of hearty stew wafted around the camp, making everyone hungry. Losolin finished hobbling Neñyos and Takîreaes and he sighed as he stretched out on the ground. Snow still fell, but here it melted into the ground, leaving only a fine dusting on the earth.

"Boy, ye are too young to be sighing like an old maid. What ails ye, young prince?" Anadin asked loudly, his eyes glittering.

"Just worry and exhaustion sir, that is all. And I am no prince," Losolin replied wearily.

Everyone around the fire snorted, even the guards. Losolin looked up, startled. "What is it?"

"My lord, if you are not a prince, then I am a woman," Felton said, grinning.

"Indeed," Yayènia muttered, resting her head on Suneelo's shoulder.

Ghealan handed him a bowl filled with thick stew and the younger male accepted it gratefully. Aladorn stood and bowed his head slightly to Losolin and the rest.

"I am going to take first watch tonight. Someone come relieve me at midnight." the wiat disappeared and they watched uneasily as the warrior's empty footsteps slew the innocent grass beneath.

The pike men also took a perimeter watch with the archers. Ghealan and Erdwyf cuddled together for warmth, the male's hand patting his wife's belly. Losolin wondered. Aidyn grunted as he sat down carefully to avoid spilling his stew. Anadin rolled into his blankets and began snoring just as Suneelo and Yayènia moved to do the same. Losolin stood and caught Yayènia's arm.

"May I speak with you in private?" Losolin asked politely, trying not to be intimidated by the iron muscle beneath his hand.

"Of course, Losolin. Go on," Yayènia replied cheerfully, making her brother-in-law suspicious.

They moved away from the camp and sat down in silence. The warrior sat with her knees up, arms looped around them loosely, clasping two of her fingers in her other hand. Losolin sighed, and watched Yayènia out of the corner of his eye. He looked back at the camp for a second and saw Kayra standing next to the fire, looking in their direction.

"She cannot hear us," Yayènia said quietly.

Losolin sighed again, wondering what he had been thinking,

asking her to talk with him. "I would ask one of the others, but there is something about you that reminds me of Tlonna."

"Ask me what?" Yayènia responded.

"I have been told fragments of our people, our lives, our city, lots of it, but still just fragments. And I have been told that I do some things that an elf would usually not do. Things I must not have done before."

Yayènia finally looked at him fully, big blue eyes expressionless. "Come, walk with me," she said, and stood.

Losolin followed her as she meandered farther away from the camp, taking slow, big steps. After a minute or two, she spoke, her voice quiet and smooth, completely at odds with the weapons that covered her.

"Our race, our people, has been alive for thousands of years, since the beginning of time. Long ago, before even Nymyños was discovered, a great civilization of elves lived in a place called Serenyi. It was the honored and most ancient civilization of the Serenyi High Elves that brought the destruction of it. Between the five nations there were fourteen wars. You see, the oldest nation, Jaquisa, was passive, harried on three sides by the younger nations. Political and wealthy, Bolarnia suffered mainly because of its persecutions of 'heathens'. Elnoris was the seat of intellectual power, the High Council's demesne. Silarnim was the weakest and most savage, always raiding and manipulating its neighbors. And then there was Amdaen, the true power. Through pure militant strength it became the largest nation, and led most of the wars on Elnoris, and also the revolt against the High Council. We are descended from the Serenyins, all the Nymyñosian High Elves.

"Because of the wars, the people, their power, and their greed, Serenyi began to fail. Civil war ravaged every nation, tragedies struck entire villages, plagues and floods and whatnot. Bits of Serenyi itself began to break off and disappear into the depths of the ocean. For a time, everyone ignored it, thinking it a minor irritation, until larger bits started breaking.

"The land was failing, the magic of the elves weakening as they fought one another in pointless battles that lasted for years. Hatred and corruption bred like humans, spreading its poison on villages and cities alike. Only when an entire city sank did the High Elves begin to despair," Yayènia lifted a hand to brush the side of a stone pillar.

"By the time they had evacuated the main populous and pushed everyone into the center of Serenyi, nearly half of it had been lost. Unfortunately, they moved too slow. Only a handful made it off what had become an island. Seven ships launched into the unknown. Four made it here and it is said they looked upon this untouched land and wept from the beauty of it."

"Where did they land?" Losolin asked, entranced.

"Zeynuwn, they sailed between the arms of Nafâlen Bay in a fog, and believed they had landed on a small island. They crested a hill, and before them was spread a vast rolling plain, and miles away, the base of a great mountain range, their tops hidden in the clouds."

Yayènia smiled softly as she spoke, walking slowly, lost in her story. "They traveled the length and breadth of Nymyños, finding no one. It was years until more people followed them. They built a home in the great mountain range, a sprawling building that blended into the wilderness. They named it *Shisandr*, ancient Elvish meaning hidden victor. Time passed, people came, Dwarves, Men, all sorts. Wars were won and lost. Our kin flourished, as they once had on Serenyi.

"Seaduens was founded, Arseninis and Kajgenia, settlers in Kairhotuss Buwai and Narnen, we spread all over Nymyños, friendly with the Dwarves and other creatures, though Men continued to bother us. We became known as the Fair Folk, Earth Angels, all manner of things, some much more unpleasant, pale demons, for one. Then the Stynbeks came to dictate, and Nymyños got a timeline. That is what most historians call the beginning of time, belying true history." Yayènia sighed, stopping to turn to Losolin.

He searched her face for some emotion, but she looked as stony as ever. "We believe the earth is alive, feeling the bite of every plow, the kiss of rain, the pang of war. Animals are the gods' messengers and aides, just as intelligent as us, if not more. They use the land, and give back to it, truer than any bipod creature. We believe in love, in hate, in grief, and fear. Honor is the greatest precept one can have. Chivalry, honesty, integrity, patriotism, and more such things, a close second. Strength, if not in body than in character is expected, weakness and cowardice frowned upon.

"We are as brash, aggressive, passionate, earthly, spiritual though not religious, and we accept death when we must. My house's motto, and that of the Blackhaven Militia is *Zuskadi Naht Xellt,* Duty Above All. *That* is Elf-kind, Losolin, at least from my stand point.

Erdwyf could explain it better, she has words where I have swords."

Losolin smiled at her, feeling at ease in her presence at last. "You did wonderfully. A better tutor there is not. It is no wonder you are so praised."

Yayènia laughed then, a clear, musical sound that drifted through the air like soft rain. "You, my friend, have always had a way with words, but you should know, they never worked on me. There was a time, when you were in your fifties, that you tried to get me to leave Suneelo, jokingly, of course. You told me I had eyes the color of crystalline ice and hair the color of summer wheat. Then you gave me a bracelet of said wheat, woven together."

Losolin blushed, though he grinned all the same. "I expect you tossed it the moment I left the room," he laughed.

In answer, Yayènia lifted her arm and showed him her wrist. "Never. I had Dietirin preserve it for me, and I wear it always."

Losolin stared. On the thin wrist was a bracelet of three wheat strands, heads intact, braided together. They seemed fresh as if they had just been harvested.

"Then you met Tlonna, and all thoughts of me faded from your mind."

Shock turned to shame when her words reached him. "I...I am sorry."

Yayènia laughed again. "Do not be! It was merely an attraction, and I was married to your brother. It happens to us all. Once, there was a young princeling from Narnen come to Blackhaven, and I, along with many, could not get enough of him. His name was Alendor," Yayènia's eyes glazed as she looked back into her past four hundred years gone.

Losolin watched her, amazed at her beauty. She was short, too, he noticed. The top of her head reached his nose. It made him smile.

"What are you grinning at?" she asked him suddenly.

"You."

Yayènia laughed again, pulling her long braid over her shoulder. It reached her lower knee. "Come, we should be getting back. My husband will be wondering what his little brother is doing. Perhaps making me another bracelet."

Laughing, they turned back the way they came.

The next morning, Losolin was shaken awake. Yayènia was

kneeling over him, shaking his shoulder roughly.

"Come on my pretty, get up. It is after dawn."

Losolin yawned, stretching. He stood, patting down his mussed hair, and then began rolling up his bed. When he pulled on his armor, he shivered. The steel had frozen in the night. Steam began rising from his body after a few minutes. Looking around, he saw the four other elves steaming in their armor. Aidyn and Aladorn did not wear armor. Losolin studied Erdwyf as she curried her horse. Her armor was more like Tlonna's, covering more flesh than Yayènia's, though her lower back and belly were still visible. Her helmet had only a two-colored plume as well, red and white. Ghealan's red and white had a third color of silver added to his, like Yayènia's blue, silver, and black. Suneelo's plume was only black and blue.

Losolin self-consciously ran a hand over his green, blue, and silver plume, wondering. When Erdwyf passed him, arms full of saddle, he stopped her.

"Erdwyf?"

She looked at him, smiling.

"What do the colors of your plumes mean?"

The advisor glanced at his, then at Yayènia's. "The colors represent our houses. House Tomyvon, mine and Ghealan's, are red and white, our standard a quartered field of red and white, with a shadowed arrow. House Tiena, Suneelo's and Nia's, is blue and black, their standard a slanted blue and black with the bloody-clawed badger. House Sestuns, Aidyn, a black field and a white dot. Yayènia and Ghealan have silver in their plumes because they command the Militia, and the colors of Blackhaven are black and silver." She glanced up at his again. "The new and most honored house of Grisholm, Losolin, has two thin crescents, black and white, opposite each other on a field of green."

Losolin's brow rose. "I have a standard?"

Erdwyf chuckled. "You are the Lord Consort, of course you do."

He smiled, and Erdwyf moved on. Yayènia strolled up to him, helm under her arm. She nodded at his shield. "I like that."

"I do too," he replied, grinning.

She beamed back. "Your armor fits you, it is very daunting. I like it, too. But your hair..." the half-Magin went cold at the crease in the fair forehead. She set her helmet down on the ground and shoved him down next to it on his knees.

"Your hair looks like it belongs on a woman, Losolin, and a human one just out of a romp in bed at that." The female yanked the tangled plait out and combed his fair hair out with her fingers. A few minutes later, he was handed a small looking glass and was told to learn it. The plaits were intricate and smaller, but they hung in only three places, above his ears and at the back. The rest of his hair was free and hung about his shoulders.

"Better?" Yayènia asked, taking back her mirror.

"Yeah," Losolin mumbled.

"Get used to it, Losolin," Suneelo called from across the camp. "I deal with it every morning, noon, and night."

Losolin gave a weak smile at his half-brother. Their attention was all turned to Anadin as he stomped up.

"If ye are done primpin', we need to move."

In a flurry of movement, everyone was mounted and awaiting the dwarf-elf. He eyed them all sourly, then strode away. They followed.

Anadin's strides matched the horses' easily as he loped along at a ground eating pace. Even Yayènia looked slightly alarmed at the half-breed's endurance and speed. Aladorn broke rank and rode to Losolin's side, ignoring Ghealan in passing.

The younger elf smiled at him. The wiat gave him a small one in return, though it faded from his face as quickly as it came.

"How are you holding up?"

Losolin shrugged. "It is easier if I think only of the next step. Sometimes, it is nearly impossible, but Tlonna needs me sane and fit, not raving mad and travel worn."

"You are wise in your youth, my friend. Wise, cautious, and courageous. None of those things can be said about the present elf-queen."

"Are you calling me a queen, Aladorn?"

"No, but you would make a damn fine one. I am telling you, you and Tlonna will make Nymyños a better place."

Losolin's ghost of a grin slipped away and he looked down at the shaking horn on his saddle. "What if she is already dead? What if this is all for naught? What will I do Aladorn?"

"Tell me my boy, in your heart, do you truly believe she is

dead? Do not you think you would know the instant her spirit leaves her body? Do not fret about things that have not happened yet, there are enough troubles on your shoulders without added imagined ones. Come now, watch where you are putting your horse. You almost ran him into a pillar."

Losolin ducked his head shamefully and stared resolutely ahead.

Winter clung to the lands harshly. While it should have been spring, the grass remained dry and brown, trees withered sickeningly. Tainted snow whipped through the kingdoms and across the Liberated Lands, killing fields, ruining the hopeful seeds that had just been planted. Rivers had all but stopped flowing, choked with debris, bodies, and sludge. The sun was a depressing orb of gray sitting high in the brown sky, casting a dead light over all.

Erdwyf yawned as the group passed yet another stone pillar. Losolin turned and stared at her, his tired, worried eyes red rimmed. Erdwyf stared back, her own bleary eyes watering with the effort of keeping them open. The taint on the land was sucking the very energy from the elves, as illness would a human.

The group trudged across the empty land, their horses weary, encountering the occasional dwarf or odd creature. Aladorn shifted uncomfortably, waiting for the tense mood to snap. For the third time in only a few minutes he checked his sword in the scabbard. Anadin glared at the wiat, his bushy blond eyebrows coming together.

"Nothing is going to happen, shadow elf. These lands are safe."

"Then why do you keep checking that big blade of yours, if this land is safe?" Aladorn chided, his temper flaring.

"They are, it is the company in which I travel that I do not trust," Anadin growled, sneering at the elves.

With a flash of steel, Yayènia leapt off her horse and had her sword at the dwarf-elf's neck. "Pull that bloody sword on us and you are dead, half-blood."

Anadin laughed and attempted to push the steady blade out of his face. It scarcely moved. The dwarf-elf gave an uncertain grin and backed away. "All right Elfie. Put the sword away and let us get on. We are but a day from the border. Ye don't want yer queen to be dead, do ye?" he turned and started walking away. With a growl,

Yayènia stalked after him, her blade raised angrily.

"No!" Losolin and Suneelo shouted as one, leaping off their mounts.

Losolin pulled the sword out of her startled hands while Suneelo wrapped his arms around her waist. Anadin turned and stared at the struggling female in anger and shock. Yayènia subsided and hung limp against her husband. "You should have let me kill the bastard," she muttered sulkily.

Suneelo stroked her hair gently. "I know love, I know, but we need him, and he has not pulled a blade on us yet. Remember Tlonna, remember her need. Okay?"

Losolin placed her sword back in her hands and shared a knowing look with his half-brother. The group resettled themselves and continued their tiring trek through the Dwarven land.

By nightfall the next day, a stone bridge rose against the sky, spanning the length of a wide river. Anadin turned to his followers. They stared back at him blearily.

"Welcome to Longman's Ford."

"Ford?" Kayra asked from behind Aidyn. "But there is a bridge."

"Oh aye, yer a smart one. It was a ford, we built a bridge, didn't change the name," Anadin snapped, glaring at the human. "Yonder is Narnen, the closest city, Althirim."

From a stone building a little way off, stocky guards stomped toward the tall half-breed.

"*Oy kronis!*" Anadin settled into a flow of Dwarven, his deep voice rumbling through the dark.

The Dwarven guards clapped hands with Anadin, staring at the crowd behind him. One of them studied Yayènia and Ghealan for a moment before turning back to his fellows.

"*Shur ku idina fur Sroma torak. Somta ec edren?* [1]"

Anadin sneered. "*Efica, sot iwudna oda gro emar. Sromis be ec Yayènia gro Ghealan. Yasfrac, eryn. Haftre ay id Kajgen akira derwa Narnis. Etana ka minray, gro Losolin eptima.* [2]"

---

[1] You travel with elf-legends, friend. How came you by this crew?

[2] A dangerous bunch, yes, and not friendly. You know the stories of Yayènia and Ghealan. Beastly savages the lot of them. They travel from Kajgenia to Narnen. I like only one of them, Losolin.

Losolin leaned to Ghealan, who was closest to him. "What do they say."

Ghealan was glaring at the dwarves. "He called us beastly savages. But he likes you."

"That is it? That is all they say?"

"Dwarven is a very complicated language. Some words are entire phrases, others single words and some are worthless, used to make the transition between words easier. Takes years to learn."

Losolin made a face.

Finally, the dwarves stopped talking and Anadin beckoned to the party. "Ride on, and get out of my land. Git."

Without a moment's hesitation, the party rode to the bridge. Losolin slowed when he reached Anadin. "My thanks, Anadin. I shall never forget your help, or your patience. I would call you friend."

The dwarf-elf grunted. "Oh, aye, yerself as well, Losolin. Now git, yer lady awaits."

Losolin rode back to his companions, and they crossed the long bridge together. Once they reached the other side, everyone drew a collective breath of relief. Erdwyf nearly danced in her saddle with excitement. As with Blackhaven, the air seemed cleaner than in other provinces.

"Althirim is a few hours ride away, and my parents will welcome us."

Losolin nodded to her and then nudged Neñyos into a trot, Takîreaes following close behind. They were about an hour's ride into Narnen when Kayra yelped. Everyone turned to stare at her. Jairus, who was riding next to her, grabbed her hand.

"I told you to be careful. Now look," he showed her hand to the group.

Blood glistened in the moonlight. Kayra looked shamefaced, tucking away a knife. Losolin rode back to see her hand. A gash about three inches wide had opened up on her palm where she had tried to catch the hilt, but missed. He took her hand, and closed his eyes.

Erdwyf frowned, and then leapt forward, nearly coming off Verity in her haste. "Losolin, no!"

But it was too late. Green light emitted from his hands and sank into Kayra's. Losolin felt a sickening wave of pain roll up into his arms from his belly, causing him to lose concentration. The magic snapped out of Kayra's hand and back into Losolin. The pain of it sent the elf backward, his body convulsing as he tumbled off Neñyos. Kayra shrieked, dismounting in a hurry. Aladorn, Suneelo, Erdwyf, and Ghealan leapt to action. The males held Losolin's arms and legs down while Erdwyf and Kayra stabilized his head and shoulders.

The humans began ripping through all the bags, looking for a sedative. Losolin's seizures grew more and more urgent, ripping through his wiry body like wild fire.

"Hold his head still Kayra! Do not let him bite his tongue!" Suneelo tossed a stray piece of wood to her. She pried open his mouth and placed it between his teeth. Aladorn rolled the young elf onto his side when the pike man Shawn reached them with a mixture of blood moss and warm water from his pack.

Shawn handed a cup to Kayra who pulled out the wood and placed it at Losolin's lips. Just as she began pouring it down his throat, Aladorn bellowed. The hand he held was surrounded by green light, pulsating and sparking out. The wiat screamed again as the magic shot into his body, ripping away flesh and muscle, leaving bone and organ bare. Three of the humans, Dawson, Randi, and Demus pulled the dark elf away. Augustine and Felton grabbed the arm, pinning it to the ground by the elf's wrist. Ghealan moved away from the hand he held, holding it too by the wrist. Jairus and Nayn went to help hold Losolin still.

Inside, Losolin felt red-hot blades digging into his body, peeling away everything to expose his soul. Through red hazed vision he saw Tlonna huddled helplessly, chained by her wrists to the floor, pain and terror cleaving through her body, her destroyed flesh seeping blood and puss. Her scream ripped through him, echoing in his own.

Suneelo moved from his brother's legs and crawled to his head. The warrior pushed Kayra out of the way and placed his hands at Losolin's temples. "Losolin! Listen to me! Damn you Losolin! Look at me! Whatever is happening is not real, it is *not* real! Look at me! Brother! Do not leave me! Ignore whatever is happening, it is not true. Listen to me brother! Please, little brother! Listen to me! Listen. To. Me!"

Losolin heard a faint plea coming from outside the wall of pain and rage holding him caged. "No! I cannot leave her to die! Whoever you are, please leave me alone. I cannot, will not let her die!"

"Losolin, it is not true!"

"I cannot let her die!"

"Brother!"

"Nooo!"

Losolin let out a last soul-tearing roar as the vision of Tlonna faded, along with the seizures. Exhausted, everyone around him fell back, giving the elf room to breathe. He sat up gingerly, tears running down his cheeks. With the threat of the half-Magin gone, the companions moved to help Aladorn who lay still, clutching Dawson's hand in one fist, and his torn belly in the other, half-faded as he sought to hold onto life.

"Dear spirits, he did this, and he is only a half-Magin," Erdwyf whispered as she and the others approached the dark elf. Losolin, who had followed them at a distance, saw his friend lying on the ground.

"No! Aladorn! Gods! What did I do?" He fell to his knees beside the older elf and gently took away the hand holding the wiat's guts. The sight of the innards of the elf forced Losolin to his feet. He stumbled away a few feet and retched. He made himself move back to the male's side. "I am so sorry, Aladorn. I-I did not know. I am so sorry."

"Boy...you...cannot...use ma...gic...let me...go." Aladorn's tanned face was pale, all the blood drawn to his stomach. His dark eyes closed in pain.

"Oh...Aladorn. I cannot, I will not let you die."

Losolin looked back at Suneelo who stood behind him, jaw clenched.

"Hold me by the shoulders," he said to his brother, who swiftly obeyed.

The half-Magin placed his hands over the still body of his comrade and went through the motions of getting ready to Weave his magic.

Erdwyf fell to her knees beside him. "No, Losolin, do not use your magic. *Please* do not use your magic."

Losolin ignored her.

Suneelo tightened his grip on his younger brother's shoulders, fearing the worst. He watched as Aladorn's body remade itself through the magic pulsating within him. Losolin screamed, but held still over his friend's body. Long moments passed as the companions watched Aladorn's muscle knit together, and finally his flesh. Losolin roared in agony as Tlonna's tortured body assaulted his mind's eye.

No scar marred the ribbed skin stretched tight across the wiat's abdomen. A collective sigh of relief passed through the comrades as Aladorn opened his eyes, once more bright with life. He touched his stomach gingerly, feeling the mended skin with trepidation. He sat up slowly, staring at Losolin. Suneelo let go of him, and the young elf toppled over, his arm across his face, hiding it from the view of everyone else.

Aladorn shook his shoulder gently, sharing a look with Suneelo. "Losolin? Losolin are you All right? Come on young prince. You did it. Come on."

Losolin slowly took his arm from his face, and opened his eyes. "Are...are you all better? I did not hurt anyone else, did I?"

"No my boy, no you did not." Aladorn pulled his shredded tunic off and tossed it away. "Come on Losolin. Get up," he bent down and helped the young elf to his feet.

Suneelo and Aladorn hauled Losolin to his feet, where he stumbled into his brother.

"What happened? Why did that happen?"

Erdwyf, standing next to Ghealan a few feet away, bowed her head in shame, and walked away. She yanked her dagger out of her belt and dragged it across the inside of her upper arm. Blood welled from the deep wound, flowing over the female's arm to fall on the ground. Losolin stared at Erdwyf, and then rushed to her side, reaching for her arm. She yanked it away, wiping her blade on the grass beside her.

"No, it is my debt. I now feel the pain you did, physically. It is the *El shä Rók*, Oath of Debt. It forgives a terrible deed, unless the debt is not worthy. I have never had to pay one." Erdwyf explained softly, cradling her arm. "I cannot clean, bandage, or help it in anyway. It must heal on its own."

Losolin shook his head. "What debt? What are you talking about? Is this something that you four dreamt up, or is it an Elven thing?"

"Neither, it is a promise one makes when they are sworn into the army back home. Very few uphold it, but there are still some of us who find it rightful. Yayènia has many scars on her arms and legs where she has had to take the oath. One time she almost killed herself because she slew a child. She had forty-six cuts, each an inch deep before she stopped."

"Why would she slay a child? What debt Erdwyf?" the male asked, worried.

"I was born and raised in Narnen. It is part of my duty as protector of the crown to keep harm from the royal family. I failed to do so by not warning you of the Narnenian law against magic. There is a boundary that follows the border of Narnen that stops magic, and punishes those who use it. I had forgotten that you were half-Magin now. That is my debt."

Losolin made a face at her, reaching for her arm again. "That is ridiculous, give me your arm."

"No," Erdwyf snapped, and stalked a few feet away.

"Wait, why did Yayènia kill a child?" Losolin asked, forgetting the presence of the others.

"It was...an accident."

Both Erdwyf and Losolin jumped at Yayènia's words.

She had walked over to check on Erdwyf, but now turned to Losolin, her eyes cold. "My soldiers were attacking a camp of Aderiaen Rahlan's men. I went into the captain's tent and killed everyone inside. He was the last one I slew; I did not know it was a child, for he was in the bed used by the captain. I did not pull the covers back before I stabbed my blade into him, forty-five times. When I pulled the blanket back, the boy was there, still alive. I can still see his green eyes staring at me, no tears, no whimper, nothing. He just stared at me. He asked me why, and I could not answer him. I knelt beside the bed and held his hand, not knowing what else to do. He told me his name was Ethan Rahlan, Aderiaen's first-born son. I slit his throat after that. Forty-six. I brought him to the feet of Aderiaen the next morning. I walked through his main camp, unarmed, carrying Ethan in my cloak. That was the first day I met Aderiaen, in his tent, holding his dead son in my arms."

Yayènia stared at the ground, lost in her memory.

"What have you brought me, elf?"

"I bring you a plea for forgiveness and passage back through your camp," Yayènia knelt before the tall powerful figure of Aderiaen.

"What is in the cloak?"

Yayènia placed the blood soaked cloak on the ground and

backed away. Aderiaen stood and arrogantly flicked the cloak away with his boot. Ethan's small, dark head rolled to the side, freed from the cloak. With an agonized cry, the king fell to his knees and cradled the dead boy in his arms. He looked up at Yayènia in fury.

"Who did this? Damn you, who did this?" he shouted, standing, still holding Ethan.

Yayènia stared at the child. "I did. I did not know it was he."

"Why did you bring him back here? Were it your child, I would have tossed him in a ditch after carving out his eyes and tongue. That way he would walk the nine hells blind and dumb."

"I guess that is the difference between Elves and Men. We mourn the deaths of children, no matter who their father is." Yayènia replied angrily. "I have lost my child and now you have lost yours. I mourn for Ethan, even though I have sworn to kill his father, and I would have sworn to kill him when he was a man."

"You know his name? How?" Aderiaen demanded, clutching his son.

"He told me, after I stabbed him. He told me his name and that he was your son, your first son. Then I slit his throat to ease his passing. I stabbed him forty-six times, and I have stabbed myself forty-six times." Yayènia pulled her cloak away to reveal her own blood soaked trousers and tunic sleeves. "It is my Oath of Debt. You owe me free passage back through your camp."

Aderiaen stared at the elf, his midnight eyes wide and sorrowful. "Go. My men will escort you to the edge of my camp, but that is the end of our truce. Tomorrow, I will find you and kill you."

Yayènia was taken to the entrance of the tent, and just when she was about to leave, Aderiaen choked on a sob.

"He was seven years old..."

"And so I left. The next day, my troops received a summons home, and I did not see Aderiaen for thirty years."

Erdwyf placed a hand on her friend's shoulder and squeezed gently. "We know it was not your fault."

Yayènia growled. "I should have killed him when I had the chance. I was right there in front of him. I should have grabbed something and killed the bastard."

"You would have died had you done that," Losolin said. "You were under a temporary truce, it would have been wrong to kill him."

"Yes, but then he would not have had Midian, and none of

this would have happened," Yayènia replied fiercely. "This is all my fault. I held pity for his father when I should not have. I know Aderiaen would have done just what he said he would have, had it been my child."

"Like you said, that is the difference between Elves and Men. They have no hearts. They have no honor or pride. They are weak and unreliable forms of life," Erdwyf countered. When the humans behind her growled, she turned around sheepishly and smiled. "Well...most of them are."

Losolin gave a little smile. "No matter. We have other pressing matters to attend to. That was all in the past, Erdwyf..."

"No," she said warningly.

Losolin looked at Ghealan, who shrugged, defeated before he even tried to reason with his wife.

The half-Magin sighed and turned to Aladorn, who was pale and still half-faded, but standing. "Are you sure you are All right?"

The wiat nodded as he pulled on a new shirt. "A little sore, but thanks to you, I am fine."

It was as the sun was rising that the company caught view of a sprawling manor sitting atop a hill, looking as though it had merely risen from the ground. Erdwyf pushed Odilia ahead of everyone else and sped up the cobblestone walkway. She reined her mare in before the large green door and leapt off.

Before the others reached the door, the advisor had disappeared into the large entranceway lit by a chandelier and the door was again shut.

"*A'da? E'na? Lault feaen valõn[1]?*" Erdwyf called as she stood at the base of the stairs of her childhood home.

Her father, an imposingly muscled elf that had made his fortunes in the War of Monotheism some two thousand odd years ago, appeared at the top and stared down at her in disbelief.

"Erdwyf? Is that you?"

"Father!" Erdwyf cried and ran up the stairs to launch herself at her parent.

They embraced warmly and the male beamed down at his daughter. "What are you doing here? Where is your husband? Let

---

[1] Father? Mother? Where are you?

me fetch your mother," Anuan Rhaeetigan said and drew away.

"I will explain it all in a moment, but I do have a number of companions. I hope they will be welcome," Erdwyf replied.

"A number of companions? Well, I surmise I will find out about them in a bit, yes?"

"Yes, of course."

Outside, Ghealan led the horses around the manor to the stables while everyone else approached the doorway. It opened and a massive male stared out at them, his straight brown hair tied back in a single braid. Amber eyes regarded them with cautious curiosity until they lit on Ghealan.

"My son, merry meet," Anuan said and clasped hands with the younger elf.

"And you, sir. I hope our intrusion on your land is not bothersome," Ghealan replied humbly, always nervous in the presence of his wife's father.

"Never bothersome, Ghealan, always a pleasure," said a tall female who appeared with an arm around Erdwyf's waist. Her blonde hair was pale and fine, floating with her every move. She seemed to be nearly insubstantial, as if the lightest breeze would carry her away.

"Lhia," Ghealan said and smiled broadly.

"You have quite the array of traveling companions, my children. Please, come in and be welcome," Lhia said.

As everyone jostled around to fit through the door, Losolin found himself next to Ghealan near the back. "They give off a feeling of the archaic, am I wrong?"

"*Noya*," Ghealan replied quietly. "They are both at least four thousand years old. They are among the oldest surviving elves left."

When everyone was assembled in the large foyer, Erdwyf introduced them. When she got to the elves among the group, they all found themselves blushing with the formality of their titles.

"You have met Baroness Yayènia er'Tiena, High Commander of the Blackhaven Militia, the Black Armada, and Mother of *Zephyr Leifen*, of course, and her husband, Baron Suneelo Tiena, Captain of the Guard and Third Commander of the Blackhaven Militia. Lord Aidyn Sestuns, personal assassin to the throne of Blackhaven. Lord Aladorn, Wiat. And..." Erdwyf hesitated, as if making sure she had her word correct. "And the Lord Consort Magin Losolin Ullor Grisholm, Male Heir to the Throne of Blackhaven."

Losolin jerked slightly in shock, but he contained it instantly when Anuan and Lhia's eyes trained on him with force. The Countess of Narnen bowed her head slightly to him.

"An honor, Lord Losolin, to host you and your companions in our home." Her pale blue eyes flickered to her daughter's injured arm, but she said nothing about it. "Anuan will you call Milan?"

The huge male turned and pulled a tasseled rope hanging by the door. Off in the distance a bell rang, accompanied by a loud thump. Anuan, too, noticed the crusty blood marring the pale skin on his daughter's arm. His mouth tightened, and he swept an accusing glare at the gathered crowd. Erdwyf frowned and looked askance at her mother.

Smiling, Lhia explained. "Milan is getting old. He often falls off of his bed when we call him."

"Milan is still alive?" Erdwyf asked.

Anuan laughed a clear bass. "He drinks a toxin every morning. Says it keeps him up and running. He is over a century now."

Just as the count finished his sentence, an old bent man came out from a large corridor, dressed in fine yellow and red livery.

"Milan, take these bags upstairs. These are paired, as are these. Everyone else gets their own room. Hurry now, our guests are weary."

"Yes Count Anuan," the old man looked up and stared at Erdwyf. "Dear Spirits...is that little Erdywyf? Certainly not. I haven't seen you in so many years. I almost forgot your pretty little face," Milan stepped closer to the elf and kissed her hand.

Erdwyf smiled and bent down to hug the old man, laughing. "Yes, it has been a long time, Mil."

"Wait! What's this? I sense another presence within you. You are with child, are you not?"

Erdwyf pulled away hastily and wiped her palms on her pants. She gave a hesitant laugh and then nodded. "You always were good at noticing things about me."

Lhia put a hand on her daughter's shoulder. "Is it true? How long has it been?"

"Ah...about three and half months," Erdwyf said, and was bombarded by everyone asking questions.

Yayènia looked at her best friend, hurt and betrayed. "Why did you not tell us? How could you keep something like this a secret?

You and the child could have been hurt during those rides and the issues we ran into. What possessed you to do this?"

"Yayènia, I did not want you to worry," she replied sadly, and then held up her hand for silence. "We can talk about this in the morning."

"Indeed," Ghealan broke in when the others seemed about to launch into another barrage of questions.

Anuan nodded. "Yes...I am sure we all have some catching up to do. You must be weary. Please follow Milan, here, to your rooms. There are private bathing rooms in each chamber as well as basic commodities."

Milan began placing their bags on a cart with an edge on one end and a flat surface for sliding up the stairs. The companions followed the old human up the staircase as Lhia went into the kitchens to order breakfast, but Anuan grabbed Erdwyf by the shoulder, sending a blazing glare at Ghealan, who had stopped as well. He hurried up the stairs after the others.

"Why do you sport *El shä Rók,* daughter? What happened? Why are you here?"

Erdwyf scrunched up her face. "Are you not happy to see me, Father?"

Anuan's face tightened. "I am happy to see you, Erdwyf, but your companions bother me. I would know the reason you have come so unexpectedly, with such a motley assortment of friends. Are they friends?"

"Yes, they are. It is not my place to tell you of our duty, Father. That is Losolin's alone, you must speak with him if you have need to know. I brought them here to shelter and rest, but we will stay only a night, I believe. Our task is urgent."

"Why should I speak with this Losolin, when mine own daughter will not tell me? Have you no trust for your father?" the count snapped.

Erdwyf winced. "You have it, but not Losolin's. Please, do not ask me to betray him. It is for him I bear the *El shä Rók*. He is a Healer Magin, and he used his magic within the border. I did not warn him. Both he and Aladorn nearly died because of my failure."

"Who does not know of the Border, Erdwyf? What fool is this Losolin?"

"Father! He has no memory, which takes his knowledge. It

was taken from him by Midian Rahlan. He is no fool. Please do not ask me to illustrate further," Erdwyf breathed.

"Then I shall ask *him*," Anuan growled, releasing his daughter. "I love you, but you do not know what trouble you bring. Evil stalks this land, and you bring strangers to my house. *Humans*, Erdwyf, you bring them here? And you with child. Do you have no wisdom, Ghealan either? You are young, but I thought you wiser. How can you do such a thing?"

"Father," Erdwyf wailed, teary-eyed. "I could not leave this task to others. It is Tlonna, Father. She needs our help," the female whispered.

"The princess is dead, Erdwyf."

"No! She lives, I promise!"

Anuan wiped the tears from her face with his fingers and studied her face for a long while. "I have brought you pain, Erdwyf. I will speak with Losolin, then. Come into the house."

Erdwyf sniffed, but she followed her father back into the manor. After a few minutes gathering herself, she went up the stairs. She ran into her old apartments and flopped down on her bed. Ghealan was pulling out their dirty clothes and laying them in a basket for washing. He walked into the bedroom and chuckled at his wife who was wallowing in pillows. "Love, do you want to take a bath before breakfast?"

Erdwyf's voice was muffled by her plush adornments. "You go ahead; I want to rest a bit beforehand."

"All right." Ghealan said, and went into the gigantic bathroom.

Using the water pump, he filled the bath with warm water from the hot springs that lay less than a quarter mile away from the manor. As he submerged himself in the tub, the elf felt all the wounds and tension he carried sting and then fade away. With a sigh, Ghealan set to scrubbing the grime and filth away. A while later he walked back into where Erdwyf lay on her bed with a towel wrapped around his waist.

Water from his dark wavy hair dripped tiny rivers down his back and front. The water droplets raced to his chiseled middle, over the muscles, and into the towel. Ghealan smiled as he looked at his wife, her hair flung over her face. Her injured arm was lying across her stomach. He was sure that was what his father-in-law had taken Erdwyf aside for. Debating whether he should wake her, the commander walked onto the wide balcony that overlooked the hilly landscape behind the manor. The horses grazed and frolicked on the tainted grass. With a sigh he turned around and went back to wake his slumbering wife.

Erdwyf opened her eyes one at a time and glared at him, the corners of her mouth twitching. She took his hand and hoisted herself off the soft bed onto the plush carpets that covered her floor.

"I suppose you are telling me I stink?" Erdwyf growled playfully, teasing her husband.

"Like a human, love. I already drew your bath," Ghealan pulled her into the bathroom and helped her undress.

As the elf climbed into the tub, Ghealan left and closed the door to give her some privacy. A little while later a knock sounded at the door. The male elf pulled on a pair of clean pants and tightened his belt. When he opened the door, Yayènia stared at him, her eyes failing to stay at his face.

"Yes Nia?" Ghealan asked huskily, standing aside to let the female through.

"Is Erdwyf washing?" she replied, walking past him into the front room.

"Yeah...she just got in. Do you need something?" the male said, shutting the door and following Yayènia.

"I just wanted to know if you had any more secrets to reveal."

"Nia..." Ghealan warned pleadingly.

"No! How could you keep this from me Lan? I do not understand. After all we have been through, you do not see it fit to tell me that Erdwyf is pregnant? The child could have been killed at any time during this entire journey! How could you deceive me? What if it had been Erdwyf instead of Aladorn holding Losolin's hand?"

The idea nearly buckled Ghealan's knees. After a moment, he said, "Yayènia, you know I would have told you, and everyone else, but Erdwyf did not want anyone to know. She worried that you would all get mad and make her go back home."

"She should have known that we would all understand and just kept her a little safer. We no longer have a home Ghealan, and we would not have sent her back there. But stab me thrice and drown me, she could have been hurt!" Yayènia yelled, frustrated.

"I know, but then again, all of us could have been hurt. And, except for the incident last night, nothing happened. I mean...you could have been hurt too, Nia," Ghealan said, drawing the female closer to him.

"Yes, but I am not with child," she replied, burying her face in Ghealan's shoulder. "I am not pregnant. That is the difference. And I have sworn my life to the battlefield. I plan to die in battle. I know I will, and I have made my peace with that. But Erdwyf has a lot going for her. She has a high position in the hierarchy of the kingdom, a wonderful husband, and a child. I have Suneelo, and he knows I will die fighting. He does not expect anything more from me. He knows that the chances of me having a child, and being able to raise it are slim. But you and Erd have so much to live for."

Ghealan put his chin atop Yayènia's head and closed his eyes against the painful, old urgings that took hold of him. The slim muscular body that shook with barely contained grief and rage molded into his arms, feeding the lust that threatened to overtake him. It was but a few precious, painful seconds that Yayènia let him hold her. With a gasp, she pulled away, wiping her eyes.

"Yayènia do not say that. So many would have lost their lives were it not for you. You are not a caregiver, you are a protector. Not all can be a lover all the time," he held Yayènia at arm's length. "And if I remember correctly, though it has been three hundred years, you *are* quite the lover."

Tears ran down her face from saddened, red-rimmed eyes. "Oh Lan, do you ever think about what...what might have happened? What could have been?"

Ghealan pulled his gaze into hers, the dark green pained and full of loss. "I...I do...not wish to speak of this. Please. Go now."

The spell broken, Yayènia jerked away, wiping her face. "Uh...well, tell Erdwyf I need to talk to her. I am in a room with a lot of green furniture," the warrior avoided her comrade's eyes as she turned and left the room.

Erdwyf leaned against the bathroom wall, clutching her towel. Ghealan stood rooted to the spot where he had held Yayènia. It was a long time before he moved slowly and shut the door. His strong back was tense and his shoulders pulled forward as though to protect himself from a blow. He reached up and ran his hands through his thick, long brown hair. Every inch of him bespoke of an internal battle, one that had been raging for three centuries. Finally, he turned and saw Erdwyf watching him from the bathroom. Shock and anger registered on his fine face, quickly replaced by shame and worry.

"Do you regret your choice?" Erdwyf asked coldly, not moving.

His voice thick with hurt, Ghealan said "No."

"I am loathe to agree, Ghealan. I thought you happy with me. I thought you joyous to learn of our child. Now I see old passions flaming in your eyes."

"How can you say that?" the male roared. "Yayènia is a friend, and only that! We loved once, but never again. We are both married, and in commitments that are good and loving. I was merely giving a friend comfort in a time of need. Were I to see you in the arms of Suneelo, crying, I would not worry, except about what saddened you!"

Still rigid, Erdwyf moved across the room and pulled on a pair of gray trousers and a white shirt. "You know that is not true as well as I do. You and Nia have always been close, too close for my comfort. I know not how Suneelo feels, but I doubt it is much different. I love her as my sister, but I love you as my husband. I will not forgive her if she still loves you. If you wish to be with her as was planned so many years ago, I will not stop you. But know this, if you do, I will remain here and take my place as Countess when my mother decides to leave the place. Never again would I set foot in Blackhaven."

Ghealan's face contorted. "What in the nine levels of *hell* would posses you to say such things? I would never leave you! Not if you turned into a human and became large and heavy. Nothing in this world or any other can compare to my love for you. Yes, Yayènia and I were going to be wed, but years passed as I was gone, and things changed. She married Suneelo, and she, nor I, could be happier. That was over three hundred years ago damn it! Is your brain muddled or what?" his voice shook the room, raised as it was.

Tears began to drip down Erdwyf's face; the feral look diminished with hurt. "I am sorry! It is just that she has known you so much longer and you both have those terrible debts to one another. I cannot help but think that you belong to each other!"

"Debts of war are not debts of love, Erd," Ghealan said, his voice softening. "I belong to you, and she to Suneelo. You and that child are my life and soul. I love you," the warrior moved to his wife and encompassed her in his arms. "I love you more than anything I have ever known. More than the moons in the sky or the earth I walk on. I would give it all up for you. I would give my life and soul for you, Erdwyf."

Erdwyf sniffed. "You would give up your life for Yayènia too, though, would you not?"

Ghealan sighed. "I would die for her, yes, but I would die for Suneelo as well. But Erd, I love them as *family*, as my brother and sister. You are my heart, and my life."

Erdwyf drew a shuddering breath and pulled away. "I know, Ghealan...sometimes it is just hard. You and Yayènia have so much in common. You are both always together and people know you as a couple, if not in love than in profession. I know you love me, and I love you," she snuggled against him again, resting her head on his shoulder.

It was in that position that Milan walked in on, his crooked frame filling the doorway. "Viscount Ghealan, Viscountess Erdwyf, breakfast is ready in the morning room."

Erdwyf broke away from her husband's embrace and smiled at the servant. "Of course Milan. We will be down shortly. Thank you."

The human sidled away and Ghealan pulled a black tunic over his head, leaving the ties open in laziness.

"Shall we go, heart of my heart?" the male held his arm out for Erdwyf who linked elbows with him and they progressed down the stairs.

Yayènia and Suneelo were both lying on the bed when Milan knocked at their door. Suneelo rolled off the edge of the bed and stood to answer the door. He smiled genially at the old man, who was forced to look up at the tall elf.

"Breakfast is ready sir, if you would kindly follow me."

"Milan, is it?" Suneelo asked curiously.

"Yes sir."

"If you would tell us where we are to go, my wife and I would like to go down ourselves, if that is not a problem."

"Of course not sir. Just go down the stairs, turn to your left, and follow that hallway down to the end door. The room is called the morning room, you will not mistake it, it is very purple."

"Thank you." Suneelo smiled again and shut the door as the human left.

He turned and saw Yayènia still lying on the bed like a crumpled sheet. She had come back from Erdwyf's room shaken and tearstained. He figured it had something to do with Ghealan. Yayènia always came back to him and made it very clear that she still loved her husband. Smiling sadly, Suneelo tied his hair back and went to the bed. Picking up his sheet-like wife, the elf stood her up and looked into her icy eyes.

"All better?" he asked, smoothing her wrinkled tunic and rubbing her arms.

Yayènia smiled up at him, her tear bright eyes trapping him. "Now I am. Thank you," she hugged and kissed him fiercely. "I do not know how or why you continue to handle these...confrontations, Neelo. You are too much of a hero, I think."

Suneelo laughed, cupping her chin. "And you are too much of a worrier. Let it go, sweetheart. It is time, I believe."

Yayènia felt a ball of panic settle in her throat, but she scorned it. To give up the memory of Ghealan was to fail. She had failed to keep his love, and he left her. But...she trapped her husband's face in her hands stared deep into his eyes which were no longer smiling. He had saved her. Suneelo was her hero. Over and over again he was there to pull her back from the edge of oblivion.

"Yes..." she breathed. "It is long past time. I have you, and that is more than enough. I have clung to memory, when I should have embraced you. I love you Suneelo. Do you believe me?"

"I do," he replied quietly, and for the first time, he really did.

They left the room and followed Milan's instructions until they found themselves in a very purple room, much like their very green room. As they entered, half of their company looked up in greeting; the other half not yet arrived. Erdwyf and Ghealan sat near the head of the table next to the count and countess. In a moment of hesitation, Suneelo was glad to see Ghealan motioning them to sit across from them. Yayènia looked straight into Erdwyf's eyes and nodded. The female on the opposite side copied her, and the two friends launched into a frenzied argument about which was the better way to use a sword from atop a horse. A rather old and never ending argument. Soon everyone else arrived and the purple room was abuzz with a dozen different conversations.

Chapter 18
Blood and Prophecy

Tlonna drifted in a haze, her body and mind ravaged by a torment of agony. Blood dripped in a constant rhythm down her body to the floor. The stone was now stained crimson from weeks of not being cleaned. She crouched like a feral animal, chained to the floor with only inches of freedom. Emaciated, she huddled in the center of the cell, shivering. As an elf, her body could store energy and nutrients, releasing it in tiny doses without being replenished for a month. But with little food for three months, Tlonna was dying, her flesh caving in around her bones. Her hair hung in limp, blood-red strands. Shadows tainted her hollowed cheeks and eyes, making the icy blue irises stand out like beacons of death.

The door opened to her chamber just as it had every day since she'd been put in chains. Midian and Sithian strode in, contempt in their identical eyes. Midian sat in the only chair and bowed his head mockingly.

"Hello, *dear.*"

Tlonna twitched as Sithian put his hand to her side. Pain lanced through her like the coldest ice. Then fire joined in, twining down her legs and through her chest. New lines of blood appeared on her flesh, adding to the flow. This continued for a long while until Midian stood.

"That's enough, Sithian. I think your mother needs a bath," the Shadowsoul opened the door and beckoned to someone outside. Two scantily dressed servants walked in, holding a large black cauldron between them.

The girls giggled at Sithian who ignored them. Midian glared at the servants who stilled instantly and with a heave, tossed boiling hot salt water onto Tlonna. The Magin screamed and thrashed about until a terrible pain seized control of her body. The elf froze, still screaming, blood bubbling up her throat. The maids left and the men turned to go but Sithian stopped and faced Tlonna.

"Mother, do you like the pain?" he asked in a sneering, laughing voice.

Tlonna forced herself to look into her son's eyes. Fear

crowded the dark blue orbs before disgust replaced it.

Her voice, unused except to scream came out frighteningly clear and low. "Yes."

Both Midian and Sithian stared and her in shock before fleeing the cell, chased by her insane laughter.

The next day, no one came to visit Tlonna except the maid who gave her water. Nor did they come the day after that, or the day after that. Almost a week passed and no one came. It was on the sixth day that the door opened to admit a shrouded figure. Kelus shut and locked the door behind him before he turned to face the elf.

"I come here against my own will, but fear that I too, am victim of having a conscience."

"Yes, and a whole thrice damned load of good it did Sithian," Tlonna spat.

Ignoring the jibe, Kelus half-opened his robes and drew out a large phial and some rags.

"If Midian catches you, he will kill you."

The demon grunted. "And you think that would be a punishment? Death would be a mercy. Already King Rahlan plans my execution, and it will be an extravagant one."

Tlonna laughed. "Then I guess you and I are both on the way to death, hmm?"

"You have months left before you are granted that gift, elf."

"Your voice...it is not sibilant anymore..." Tlonna said, staring at him with wide eyes.

"Yes, and I have you to thank for that."

"Oh?" Tlonna crooned.

Kelus wordless pulled back his right sleeve to reveal a flawless forearm, ending in fingers rather than claws. "Your magic is creeping through my body like a poison. I am becoming what I once was."

"That is why Midian plans to kill you," she stated.

"That is one reason. There are many more. King Rahlan plans to get more children out of you yet, and I will not be present to allow you to ruin his children," he dabbed some of the liquid on a rag and began wiping Tlonna's face.

"No!" the elf cried as her cuts began to heal under the rough administration.

"Ah yes. He wants another son, and a daughter. Haydyn and Rhiannan. They will be raised as Sithian was, in sixteen weeks they will age sixteen years. You will be given the chance to raise them, as you were with Sithian. However, Sithian will be there to watch over you, make sure you do not make the same mistakes you did with him. King Rahlan plans to come to you soon to get Haydyn on his way," the demon lapsed into silence as he ran the rag over Tlonna's arms.

She watched in weak amazement as her cuts began to stitch up leaving only fine white scars in their place.

"Why are you doing this?" Tlonna asked after a long while.

Kelus looked up from her legs and stared at her from the black cowl. "Like I said, I too am victim of having a conscience."

"That is not it."

The demon sighed and straightened. "You proved to me that my ruined flesh is not permanent, it could be taken away, and my soul is happy about it."

Tlonna stared back at Kelus, shock registering in the back of her hazy mind. She was silent as the Darkwight finished her legs and backed away, tucking everything back into his robes. With a slight bow, he left her cell.

True to his demon's word, Midian returned the next day and forced his seed into her, laughing as she cried. Tlonna was taken from her cell and put in the same room she had raised Sithian in. A large platter of food was given to her, along with a pitcher of water and cooled cider. Ravenous, Tlonna dove into the food, only to find that she could eat only a handful of the fodder. New clothes were brought to her to replace the filthy rags that scarcely covered her body.

Tlonna gratefully accepted the bath that was offered to her, and dressed in the loose black robes, identical to Kelus'. A week passed as the elf grew steadily healthier, her body rejuvenating with the food and water. Midian visited her only to modify the unborn child within her, as he had with Sithian. Every time he muttered about something not being right, too involved with his thoughts to torture Tlonna. Fear embedded itself in her mind at his mutterings. Weeks later, she was taken from her room to the room where she had given birth the first time. Everything happened as it had the first time, but Midian was still confused as the squalling boy Haydyn was handed to him. Then it happened. More contractions hit Tlonna and the nurse knelt between her knees once more.

"Milord, you have twins."

Midian rushed forward in disbelief. "What?"

Tlonna couldn't believe it either, although she pushed again until the second child was taken from her. The maid cleaned the child and cut the umbilical cord, wrapped it in swaddling clothes, and handed it to Midian.

"It's a girl, Lord Rahlan."

Holding both his children, Midian stared at the tiny infant girl. Her dark blue eyes stared back at him. The man smiled at her, then at his son. "Haydyn and Rhiannan, meet your brother, Sithian."

Sithian stepped forward and studied his young siblings. His eyes roved over Haydyn's sleeping face to Rhiannan's curious gaze. "They will grow as I did?"

"Yes, and hopefully your mother will have learned her lesson. Just to make sure, I want you to watch her like a hawk, Sithian. Any elfish foolishness and I want you to beat her as you have been trained. Understand?"

"Yes Father," Sithian took his brother and sister and left the room.

Tlonna was cleaned up and sent back to her room where Sithian sat on the bed reading. The twins lay in the bassinette, sleeping. Tlonna watched them sadly, fearing what they would surely become. "Is there another bassinette coming?"

"Yes."

"Good."

Sithian marked his place in his book and set it down on the table next to him. "Books are being brought as well. Along with parchment, quills, and a few toys. They will be allowed to play for a half hour each day."

Tlonna nodded and turned to the table that held two platters of food. She selected a piece of bread and began to gnaw on it. The twins awoke shortly after that and began crying, begging to be fed. Reluctantly, Tlonna let each of them feed until sated. After that, she read to them from *Nymyños, A History.* Haydyn's gray-blue eyes watched her as keenly as Sithian did, whereas Rhiannan looked about the room, obviously uninterested. The days passed as such until they were near grown. Haydyn was as fair as his mother; shaggy blond hair framed his angled face, his cold blue eyes dancing with mischief.

Rhiannan was as dark as her brother was fair. Waist length black hair hung in tight curls, shiny and lustrous. Her face mirrored Haydyn's but with her father's eyes and tanned skin. She and Sithian were prone to having whispered conversations while Haydyn relentlessly bombarded his mother with questions.

Tlonna held high hopes for her younger son. Rhiannan, she knew, was going to be exactly like Sithian and Midian. Her beautiful face showed disgust whenever her eyes fell on Tlonna, and she was constantly fingering her pointed ears. Haydyn loathed his sister and brother. The lighter half-elf pointedly ignored his twin and was painfully cool to his brother. When Midian would appear, Rhiannan would attempt to favor him, showing her obvious displeasure at being stuck in a room with her mother. Midian would smile and push his daughter out of the way to converse with Sithian. On the last day, when the twins celebrated their sixteenth name day, Midian strode in.

"Elf, you know what day it is?"

Tlonna stood and regarded her captor with cold eyes. "Yes."

"You can stay here in this room, or depending on your behavior, you can go back into your cell. Which would you prefer?"

"You know damn well what my answer is, Midian," the elf snapped, steeling herself.

Midian sniffed disdainfully. "One wrong move and I will have you locked up for the rest of your life. Children, say goodbye to the bitch that bore you."

Sithian and Rhiannan left the room without looking back. Haydyn, too cautious to be stupid, turned and bowed his head slightly to Tlonna. His perfect lips mouthed the words, 'goodbye mum.' Tlonna gave him a small, sad smile and sat down again, hiding her eyes. The door shut softly behind her son and the elf was reduced to sobs. When the maid entered to replace the tray of food, she scuttled away as soon as she had the used platters in her hands. A key clicked the lock into place, and Tlonna was alone.

The days were long and dull. The Magin read books on magic, the history of Nymyños, the races, cultures, and nearly everything in between. Her hope of ever leaving withered to a dry husk inside her; she had no contact with anyone except the maid who replenished her food and drink. Tlonna nibbled at the scraps of food that was brought her, and sipped the stale water. Though she was no longer tortured, the sadness and depression of her situation ate away at her soul just as well. Tlonna had no idea of how long she had been Midian's captive, or how long she had been stuck in her room.

The elf had had no news of Kelus, or her children for what

seemed weeks before her door opened to admit a darkly clad figure. Jumping out of bed, Tlonna started to say Kelus's name before the cowl fell. Haydyn put a finger to her lips and smiled.

"Hello mum."

"Haydyn!" Tlonna whispered excitedly. "What are you doing here?"

"I had to see you. Everyone else is abed so I don't fear being caught. How are you?" the lean youth swung his dark cloak off and sat on the corner of the bed.

"I am well, and you?"

"Good, though I fear Father suspects me. I am not a terrible heathen like him or my siblings. However, I can out-power Rhiannan easily, and Sithian is just a step ahead of me. Even Father fears my power sometimes. I can see it in his eyes. I have you to thank for that."

Tlonna grinned and hugged her son fiercely. "Oh Haydyn! I am so glad. Have you heard any news of Kelus?"

"Father's slave? Not really. He stays in the background most of the time, running Father's army."

"Have you heard anything about his execution?" Tlonna asked anxiously, wringing her hands.

"Execution? Oh...Father cancelled it because he needs Kelus to run his affairs. I guess the demon is pretty smart," Haydyn said absently.

Tlonna snorted. "That is because he used to be an elf. Midian tortured him along with all the other Darkwights until they became that ruined memory of what they used to be. Kelus just retained more of his old self than any of the others. He still cares about life. He is the one responsible for me still being alive right now. If not for him, I would surely be dead."

Haydyn shook his head with a grim look on his flawless face. "How could somebody come out so cruel? I would never torture somebody just because of their race."

"That is because Midian is not right. He is sick and twisted, as is your brother and sister. You have no idea how glad I am that you came out right. You are a good person," Tlonna said fiercely.

Haydyn hesitated before speaking again. "Sithian...Mum he's not right. Even Father gets nervous around him. I can see it. I'm not sure what it is, but there's something about his eyes. It is almost as if they're dead. He is so cruel, and he enjoys making others suffer. He frightens me."

Tlonna felt a shiver go down her spine at the thought. "He was raised by Midian from his fourth week. You and Rhiannan had sixteen weeks with me. Tell me she still has some conscience."

"Aye, a little, but not enough. She gets sick sometimes, afterward, but yet she does things in spite of it."

"You make me proud, Haydyn," Tlonna whispered, brushing her son's hair out of his eyes.

The two talked until the sun began to crest the ocean horizon. Haydyn flicked his cloak back over his shoulders and kissed Tlonna on the cheek. "Goodbye Mum. I'll see you later."

Tlonna pulled her son's cowl up and hugged him. He turned and with a wicked grin, left his mother standing alone in her room once more.

Miazie awoke to the sound of frantic scratching at her tent. Groggily, she untangled herself from Sodo, who was sound asleep and pulled a robe on over her shift. Yanking the tent flap open, Miazie glared at Ardenay, who still had her hand raised to scratch. "What?"

"Miazie, we figured it out! I know it! Come, get dressed and meet me in Elwyn's tent as fast as possible, okay?"

Nodding, Miazie ducked back inside her tent and pulled the robe and shift off. In a flurry of cloth, she dressed and woke Sodo. He coolly readied and did not speak though Miazie gibbered at him.

Within minutes, they were standing in Elwyn's tent along with some of the others who had been working the hardest on the prophecy. Seuq, the arms master, and Caydy, a spryte, sat next to Elwyn, and Ardenay was leaning over the woman's chair, pointing at something with enthusiasm. They all looked up when she and Sodo entered and sat on the two stools in front of the desk.

"Well," Elwyn said, grinning. "We have it."

Impatient, Miazie glowered at her. "So I heard. What do you have?"

"Using the list of names and people that surrounded Tlonna in her life, before and after her disappearance, we know who the people are in the prophecy. The friend is you. You are going to discover something, or help her understand something that will lead to her victory. The guardian is Yayènia er'Tiena. She is going to die in service to Tlonna. The lover is Losolin Grisholm, who will rule in her stead. Tlonna Ewôsdírn is going to die to free the slaves of death."

Miazie's heart was beating fast, though from rage or disbelief she did not know. "I swear to the Gods, if that is all you have, I will tear your throat out, Elwyn. If I just spent three months here for you to tell me that my best friend is going to die to free a bunch of slaves, I will kill you."

"There is more," Elwyn said coolly. "We know who the slaves of death are."

When she did not elaborate, Miazie started to vibrate with fury. "Who are they!" she roared finally.

"They are the missing elves. The elves that started disappearing soon after Midian's assent to his throne. When he became the Head of the House of Rahlan, what group of people started appearing in Nymyños?"

Too fraught with emotion to think, Miazie just stared at her.

"Darkwights," Sodo replied for her. "The Darkwights are not humans and dwarves and elves. They are all elves. That is why they are so deadly."

"Correct, if Tlonna succeeds in freeing the Darkwights of their ...imprisonment, the Elven Race will be, in essence, reborn."

"But how is she supposed to do that? She...she can't die. Don't you understand? Tlonna deserves a full life with Losolin, she deserves to have love and life and happiness. She is the quintessential form of life," Miazie said pleadingly, unaware that she was crying. "You can't take that away. You can't say that Tlonna has to die. Tlonna has to live, if she dies, the world dies. She's like an angel, you can't kill her!"

"Miazie..." Elwyn said, and it was the first time she showed sympathy for the younger woman.

Sodo, Ardenay, and Seuq could feel the agony and despair radiating from the human and they too had tears shining in their eyes because of it.

"Miazie," Elwyn said again, "you must tell this to Tlonna. You need to return to her and let her know. This is information she must have. We will go and wake your three companions, and you should be gone by nightfall. Do you understand that?"

Sodo jerked on his stool, alarmed. "Can we not send a message? She does not have to leave today. It...no."

"Sodo, Miazie came here for a purpose, and we fulfilled it, and now she must return, with her *husband* and their companions, to Kajgenia," Elwyn replied cruelly. "Miazie, we will begin the process of waking the three immediately. They will be blindfolded until you are out of sight of Alchemian. Is that understood?"

Miazie stared at her dumbly before lurching forward, her fingers reaching for the woman's throat. Caydy, the spryte, moved so fast Miazie rebounded into Sodo who held her fast. The human flailed in his grip, sobbing with wrath and anguish. Finally she collapsed into him, her heart seeming to shatter into a billion little pieces. Sodo carefully picked her up as though she were his bride, and carried her back to their tent.

There, they made desperate love until late into the evening when Ardenay tapped on the tent to tell them that Damon, Ryun, and Jacinth were awake and blindfolded.

Miazie pulled the sheet around her and curled up against Sodo, tears dripping slowly from her eyes to land on his chest. His hand was twined in her hair and resting in the small of her back.

"You do not have to go," he said quietly.

"Yes I do. I can't know this and not tell Tlonna. I could never live with myself if I just let her die," Miazie replied, and then tipped her head back to look him in the eye. "You can come with me."

Sodo stared at her before looking away and blinking rapidly. "No, I cannot. My place is here, Miazie. It is not safe for me out there, especially now..." he returned his gaze to hers so that she could see the blackened eye. "And if you were to be with me, you would be in far more danger. I would not bring that upon you."

"Then...this is the last we shall ever see of each other," Miazie sobbed and sat up.

"No, it is not. We are young yet, and one day, when this is all over, we can be together again."

Miazie shook her head and pulled on her pants. "I am human, Sodo. Do you forget that?"

"No. But I know that I love you and we will find a way, my heart," the male replied, watching her.

Miazie pulled a fur-lined tunic over her head and belted it. Feeling miserable, she braided her hair and shoved the last few things into her pack. Stomping into her boots, she turned to Sodo, who was lacing his pants.

"I wish..." she shook her head. "When it is safe, promise me you will come to Blackhaven and find me. Please."

"I promise," he took a deep breath. "Do you have everything?"

Miazie sniffed. "Yes. There isn't really anything else to do," she said quietly and then began to sob.

Sodo's arms came around her and she wept on his shoulder until her tears ran dry. Pulling away, Miazie looked up at him, her lip trembling with sorrow. "I will wait for you, then."

"I will come to you, Miazie. I swear to you I will. Now come, you need to be on your way," Sodo said quietly and walked her out of the tent. Night was falling quickly and a few alchemists were gathered around the entrance to Alchemian to bid her farewell. Seuq and Ardenay hugged her and then stepped aside to subtly flank Sodo. Elwyn was there as well, consoling a seething Damon whose mouth was curled beneath the thick blindfold. Ryun stood rigidly to one side, Jacinth shivering next to him.

"Ryun!" Miazie cried and hugged her sight-impaired friend.

Bound as he was, he could not hug her back, but his chin lowered to the top of her head and he sighed. "Miazie, thank the gods. What is going on?"

"I will explain later, but we must go. I have what we sought. Damon," she said coldly as the assassin general stumbled up to her.

"Miazie, I demand you to tell me what is happening. Why are these heathens treating us this way?"

"You will not demand anything of her, you worthless swine," Sodo snarled and punched him in the face.

Damon hit the ground hard and writhed around, unable to get back on his feet as he could not see nor use his hands. The elf got in another kick before Seuq hauled him back.

"Hold yourself together, Sodo!" the arms master snarled. "What is wrong with you?"

"Sodo, please," Miazie cried, tears threatening to overwhelm her again.

Recklessly, she pulled the elf against her and kissed him thoroughly, trying to memorize everything about him. Finally, they separated and Miazie was yanked against her horse by Elwyn.

"Get on your flaming horse and out of my walls. I don't ever want to see your face here again, understand?"

"May the gods damn you to deepest ninth hell, Elwyn," Miazie spat and mounted Kaia. The mare tossed her head in impatience and Miazie twisted in the saddle to look at Sodo one last time. He held up his hand to acknowledge her, and then she took Damon's reins and led the way out of Alchemian.

Chapter 19
Zaedic

Erdwyf said a tearful goodbye to her parents and the company departed the manor house. They traveled swiftly over the land of Narnen, with the help of Erdwyf's guiding. In a few hours, they reached the bank of a gigantic body of water. Even with their enhanced sight, the elves could not see the shore.

"Welcome to the R'Kunad Sea, a vastness that has never been fully mapped," Erdwyf exclaimed to her awestruck companions.

Yayènia scowled. "The Fãrthyn is bigger, Erd. Besides, why would anyone take joy in living by a vast amount of water? Vile stuff in large quantities. Keep it in a container as far as I am concerned."

"So you say, but I was born with the ocean, Yayènia. Every morning I would come out here and swim. There is much to be learned from the sea."

"You grew up with this?" Kayra asked, her eyes the size of saucers.

"Yes. I used to come here when I was a child and play in the water. I used to pretend I was a corsair captain. I met a corsair crew once, because of the attentions of..." the advisor rubbed her chin, "Seamas Longarm. He was first mate to Captain Joseph Hawk."

"What were they like Lady Erdwyf?" Randi asked, "I've heard stories, about pillage shore towns, rape the women, kill the men, and steal the gold."

Erdwyf laughed. "Well, the ones I met were kind enough, until the last day of their stay, at least. They danced on their ship and sang loud enough for us to hear. They drank too much and swore too fluently, but they were not evil men. They often sail with certain merchant ships as mercenaries. For enough gold, they will protect anything. They were gruff men, but decent enough. Let me come aboard once and see the ship, *Tall Stranger*. It had dark blue sails, with the clan flag of course, a huge wheel, four anchors, and it was so *big*! None of the ships that come into port in Blackhaven are nearly as big."

"What were they like?" Kayra asked excitedly.

"Ah..." the elf sighed with memory. "For a young elf maiden of pure virtue, they were absolutely abhorrent, and therefore completely fascinating. Rough men, Kayra, very rough. They hold no laws but their own, and even those are held loosely. But they had them. They would never harm an innocent that they knew was innocent. But if that innocence was in question, fair game. They once captured a young whore and would not let her off until they had each tasted her. I could hear her cries even in my room. I was so young, it seems an eternity ago. I was curled up on my bed with my pillow over my head so that it would not be so loud.

"I was very frightened of them after that, but it is their way. Very few of them ever fall in love, truly, or marry. They may spawn children, but it is rarely out of love. Seamas found me after that night and asked me what was wrong," Erdwyf said, losing herself in memory.

"Why do ya cower so, Viscountess? Have I not been a friend to you?"

A twenty-year-old Erdwyf whimpered as the corsair moved closer. He was clad in all gray, but it was sea-stained to a darker shade and stiff with salt. His breath reeked of spirits and he was missing two fingers on his left hand. He'd lost them in a bet.

"You hurt that woman," Erdwyf said angrily.

"Nah...she hurt herself, Viscountess. Ya see, she's a whore, she likes it. Unlike ye, my bird, she's unclean and diseased. She likes it when a man slides between her thighs and enjoys himself. Ya don't understand that, though, do ya?"

"My mother says you and your crew raped her. That is wrong, sir. Very, very wrong and I wish your company no more. Please leave my presence."

"Ahh," Seamas replied and took a step closer so that Erdwyf had to lift her chin to look him in the eye. "Yer so proper, so tightly wound, Viscountess. It was intercourse, and ever'one knows it. I know it, me crew knows it, and the whore knows it, but it ain't rape really, if the girl's a whore, see, 'cause that's how she make a livin'. We did pay her, ya know. So really, it's just a real busy business transaction for her. Understand, Viscountess?"

Erdwyf could smell his unwashed body, almost taste the spirits he had been drinking. She grabbed a fistful of her silk skirts and swept them out of the way.

"I understand that you and your men are filthy...pirates."

"Pirates! Ye insult me, Viscountess! I don't take lightly to insults, see."

"I am sorry, Seamas, but I really must protest your presence. I, as you said, am clean and I will not be spoiled by the likes of you," Erdwyf lifted her hand and pointed out toward the sea.

Instead of leaving, Seamas grabbed her hips and pressed them hard against his. Even through her skirts Erdwyf could feel him harden. She stared at him in fear, though she tried to mask it with arrogance.

"Ye are ripe, Viscountess, jus' ready to be popped, but I say that is for some other man. An elf, of course. I will say this, though. What we do on our ship, what we say and how we act is our way of life. Ye will find that out soon enough, I s'pose, but I jus' wan' ya ta know that, see. One day, when yer arching under some elf-man as he rides between yer legs yer gonna think of me, an' yer gonna remember." Erdwyf fell silent as she finished her reminiscence.

"And do you?" Ghealan asked quietly, though no one else heard him as they were all talking about Erdwyf's story.

Erdwyf turned to him in surprise. After a moment's pause, she gathered her courage. "Do you think of Yayènia, sometimes?" she asked, and rode ahead, fearing the answer in her husband's eyes. "Well, it is a long way to the first harbor. We had better get going. We will stay along the beach for the rest of the time. It has always been a safe place," she said when she reached Aidyn and Losolin.

The crew followed her out along the beach for three and a half days before they reached a harbor surrounded by a small village. Six ships were anchored just off the shoreline. People were running along the beach, up and down boarding planks, along the decks, and everywhere in between. A few stopped and stared at the company riding their horses to a sprawling wooden building. They tethered their horses outside and left the soldiers with them. The elves and Kayra walked into the main office and up to a large desk with a scrawny, mouse-like man. His beady eyes stared at them, his cheek twitching.

"Whaddye want?" he asked Losolin in a high, gravelly voice.

"We need a ship to take us out to sea," Losolin replied carefully.

"Where's about are ye goin'? An 'ow many?"

The half-Magin leaned into the desk. "We are going to an island that may not exist, in a place no one really knows. And there are seventeen of us."

"Yer tryin to get to Zaedic, aren't ye? Well I'll tell ye, tain't no such place. An even if there were, no one'd take ye. 'Sides, it costs quite a bit to get seventeen passengers on any ship, lest it's a corsair ship, an ye wouldn't want yer nice ladies here to meet any 'o them. Nasty, vile, and boorish creatures the lot o' them."

"Yeah? Well leave them to us then, man. We have met far worse, I am sure. How much for passage?" Losolin snapped angrily.

"Fer seventeen...three hundred geld, and that's fer supplies and yer beasts out there."

"We are not taking the horses, we need a place to keep them until we return. How much?" Ghealan growled impatiently.

"Without the beasts it's...two hundred gold spikes minimum. That's sleepin' in the cargo hold and eatin' on minimum rations," the small man said haughtily.

He squeaked when Ghealan grabbed him by the lapels and hauled him upwards. "You had better give us the best you can get, for the cheapest amount of gold, or you will lose all your nasty little teeth, understand?"

The man attempted to pull away, "I don' make the prices, that's cap'n's business. I only write up the papers as most sailors don' know how!"

"Well then, you had better find a captain who will acquiesce to our terms, understand?" Ghealan shoved him back into his chair and crossed his arms. "Now, how much for what?"

"One hundred fer four to a room in the passenger hold with small rations, must have food for the sailors as well," the man squeaked hurriedly. "That's the best I'll be able ta do. Ye might wind up on a corsair ship, though."

"Fine," Losolin said as he counted out the money. "Where do we stable the horses safely, and when and where do we board?"

"The stable behind the building. The stable master will ask ye fer a charge, normally about twenty silvers. No available ship 'as come in yet. Two merchants, and one naval ship is s'posed to come in, an' we get about two or three unscheduled ships in a night."

"Good," Losolin said and led the group outside in the afternoon cold.

A breeze came in off the ocean, but the wetness of the air was nearly unbearable. They took the horses to the rear stables and paid the stable master a pricey sum, with a threat of bodily harm if the horses or tack were missing when they came back.

They waited the rest of the day by the shore, sitting on the beach next to a dock. Night rolled in with one merchant ship and the naval soldiers. The crews brought supplies off the ships and into the building behind the companions. Mostly, they ignored the strange group, but a few watched them out the corner of their eyes. By eleven, the second merchant ship was coming in to dock, and another ship was just turning into the harbor. By midnight, it had docked, and one other was coming in. The small mousy man came out and beckoned them into the building office. Two rough looking men stood against the wall, watching them. Losolin felt an immediate unease at their appearance. They both wore dark, sea-stained clothes, ragged with wear and smelling of salt.

The mousy man held his hand out to the taller of the two and looked at Losolin. "This be Captain Alexander Willis, of the Clan Esmoden. He's agreed ta take ye on his ship."

Captain Alexander stepped forward. "Fair meetin' to ye. Me crew and I have naught to do for nigh on two months, so I figured we could take ye on this journey of yourn, as we wouldn't be gettin' no pay nor luck for them two months. What be yer names?"

Losolin stepped forward and introduced everybody to the captain and his first mate. When he finished, he bowed slightly to the man and stuck out his hand. "My friends and I have an urgent task on Zaedic, wherever it lies. Speed is of the utmost importance, or many lives could be lost. We will pay you extra for your help, at the end of our journey."

Alexander took the elf's proffered hand. "We have an accord. Me crew and I need only to replenish our supplies and we will be on our way. If it please you, Troaz here will take ye aboard and get ye settled in. We'll be leavin' port at dawn."

Kayra sighed and turned to Yayènia. "Why is it always dawn with you people?"

The warrior shrugged, "It is a creepy time, and we like to be creepy people."

Kayra snorted loudly in an attempt to stifle a guffaw. The captain turned and began discussing finances with the little man in a clear dismissal. Troaz left the building and they followed him out to the gigantic ship that had come in at midnight. They walked up the steep boarding plank onto a glossy, dark deck. A few sailors were hauling at lines or preparing crates to be taken off. Troaz turned and stood before them. "Welcome aboard *The Silver Crest.*"

Yayènia studied the ships decks with a warrior's gaze, memorizing the placement of obstacles and openings. Her eyes stilled when they fell upon the black flag with a red sickle waving high above on the main mast. She elbowed Suneelo in the ribs and nodded her head toward the flag.

Her husband looked at it and smiled. "I guess Erdwyf lost her right to brag about meeting a corsair once."

Yayènia chuckled and followed her departing friends toward a door in the deck. Soon, they had their packs stored away and their beds claimed. They spent the rest of the night exploring the ship, meeting the crew, and getting used to the swaying rhythm of the craft. Yayènia glowered down at the water with distrust. By dawn, the ship was fully boarded, prepared, and the anchors hoisted. The company stood on deck by the smooth railing watching the shore fade away and endless water replace it. At midmorning, the crew sat down at a long table set up in the center of the deck and made room for the seventeen passengers.

Captain Willis sat at the head of the table next to Losolin and Troaz. The company was spread out among the crew, getting to know the supposed thugs. In spite of rumors, the crew was a jovial one, laughing and making crude jokes. Yayènia and Erdwyf befriended the youngest sailor; a twenty-two year old named Jack Willingsford.

Yayènia constantly nagged the boy about wanting to be the pet on board. "You know Jack," she said one day during his break, "you really should aim higher. I mean, dream about being the captain, or even a commodore! Think about it!"

She made a motion like smoothing the air in front of her. "Commodore Jack, the most fearsome corsair in all of Nymyños, with his crew of base and immoral men. They own the seas and sell the land, taking all the women aboard and killing the stupid men," the elf smacked the human in the shoulder. "Can you just see it?"

Jack smiled wickedly. "Yeh, and I could 'ave pertty elf women as me crew as well. One named Yayana and one named Erwulf. Course they'd all answers to me, wouln't they?"

Erdwyf punched him. "How many times do we have to tell you Jack? It is said *air dwif* and *yuh yee nia.* How would you like it if we called you Juck?"

"Ye could call me anything and I'd like it," the corsair said and grinned, showing his two gold front teeth.

Yayènia stuck her finger in his face. "Hey there boy, I will rip all that greasy blond hair of yours out and make you eat it if you don't watch it."

The human raised his eyebrows and leaned forward. "'Ow much do I 'af to pay ye to play nice?"

"Oh that does it!" the two females leapt up right after the human and began chasing him around the deck.

Ghealan, Suneelo, and the other male elves watched them in high humor. Losolin leaned towards them and snickered. "You had better watch that boy, mates. He may just steal your wives out from under you."

"Shut up, brother. That boy does not have a chance with them. He would lose his cock when either of them is in the mood to play."

They all laughed and resumed watching the females. The days dragged by with the same routine while tainted snow whirled around the masts and scudded across the decks before the sailors could sweep it off. The passengers shared in the work given to them by the sailors, and the corsairs taught them how to run a ship. Slowly, they learned all of the main crew's names. There was Jack, Snickers, Fritz, Tom, Stik, the insane Legless Mo, who actually had legs but refused to acknowledge it, Matt the Dramatic, Boxer, Azerath, Axl, Malcolm, Izzy, Cat, Les the Cook, Angus, Troaz, and Captain Alexander. There were others, sweeps men, a sail mender, and various linemen that Alexander and Troaz picked up at each town they visited. The pike man Shawn became good friends with a sweeps man, Joseph.

All of the corsairs were good humored, albeit crude men, living by their own rules and standards. At night and when they were pulling in lines or doing other such work, they sang rhythmic songs that the companions were quick to memorize.

Losolin wandered over to the captain as he stood at the wheel. "Captain, I heard that corsairs hold no laws, and are rarely honest folk."

The man grinned, his hands steady on the cogs. "We used ta

be, but we lost our dear reputes in the corsair wars, oh...fifteen years gone. Some call 'em the Pirate Wars, but we ain't no filthy pirate scum. We roam free, doing as we please, robbing merchants blind and sleeping with ladies of a less than savory nature, aye, but we have our loyalties. There are nations we don't rob, Blackhaven, Narnen, and Zeynuwn, mainly. Ya see, lad, we freebooters, as such, find it in our best interests to stay on the happy side of the strong nations, savvy?"

Losolin nodded, looking out across the endless water. "I wondered, is all."

Alexander grunted, waving his hand in the air for a reason unknown to the elf, before settling it back on the wheel. "Wind's shiftin'." he said suddenly.

Losolin looked at the corsair. "Ah..." he said, and left to rejoin his friends.

Many days into the voyage, when Yayènia and Losolin were discussing tactics, a fog descended until Alexander snarled and shook his compass, trying to decide on a heading. Everyone was on edge, there was an evil feeling in the air and even the humans could sense it, rubbing their bare arms to rid them of goosebumps. All of a sudden there was a scream from the crow's nest, and out of the mist, Stik came hurdling down toward the deck. His safety line snapped, jerking him upward and then back down. The corsairs scrambled to stretch out a ruined sail and Stik landed with a thump in the center of it. The man lay like a lump in the middle of the canvas, heaped over himself. A black arrow shaft stuck out of his back like a flagstaff.

Captain Alexander began roaring out commands. "*Drop the main sail! Get below and run out the sweeps! Jack! Axl! Light the lanterns! Snickers, Mo, Tom, Fritz ready the castles! Azerath, Matt, load the starboard ballista! Izzy, Cat, port side ballista, get it loaded! Malcolm, Boxer, Angus, prepare the lines for boarding!*"

Troaz and the captain sprinted up the stairs to the captain's deck. Losolin herded Kayra down to her bunker and ordered her to stay put. He grabbed all the bows, quivers, and swords that he could and ran up the ladder to the main deck. The weapons were handed out to their owners and readied. Losolin was suddenly aware of how easily the jovial corsairs slipped into battle mode, their faces hard and full of lethal intent. Stik's body still lay in a heap in the center of the deck, the arrow protruding from his broken body like a standard. The elf looked around him and saw Yayènia and Aidyn to his right, Ghealan and Suneelo to his left, Erdwyf, Randi, and Jairus behind, and Aladorn, Nayn, and Demus in front. The others had spread themselves out with the corsairs, back to back with friendly strangers.

It was the first time he saw the warrior elves in their true element, and it terrified him. Yayènia's face was stone cold, unreadable, and she stood perfectly still, her twin blades resting on her shoulders, crossing behind her head. Aidyn next to her had his bow knocked and drawn, his muscles standing out in the glistening mist as he held the heavy bow with little effort. Ghealan looked a little more stiff, though Losolin saw the wolfish grace that he knew was what the male was famous for, his long elfin blade steady in his hands. Suneelo surprised him the most, however. His friendly, smiling brother had turned completely. He had his bow out, rather than his sword, and it was ready as Aidyn's was. There was a freezing deadliness in his stance, in the way his legs were spread to shoulder width and bent just so at the knees.

None of them was in their armor, so the absence of metal seemed to enhance the elves' natural lethality. Even Erdwyf was ready, a slim bow looking odd with her slightly rounded belly. Losolin saw this all in a matter of seconds as he drew the elfin long blade Demetrius had commissioned for him. Then he saw the spectral shapes of Alexander and Troaz alone on the captain's deck. "I am going up there. I want some of you to stay here."

For once no one argued, but with a silent agreement, the six elves followed Losolin up the stairs and took their stance around the captain and first mate. The humans looked at them in shock. Losolin declined his head and gave a small smile to Alexander.

"You are not alone in this."

"Thank ye," the captain said quietly, his green eyes grateful.

Jack's voice carried on the wind from the fore warned them of the ship coming up on their port side. Everyone on the main deck rushed to the left side of the ship, but those on the captain's deck stayed centered. A white hull loomed out of the thick fog carrying bellowing men. Losolin twitched at the sight of Midian's insignia floating above the mast. Wood crashed as great missiles were launched across the decks to career into the enemy ship. Arrows zipped overhead, most missing widely and falling in the water or on the starboard deck. The corsairs hollered back at the men on Midian's ship. Losolin and his companions loosed a shower of arrows on the enemy, never missing one. At least fifty men crowded the white ship's decks, all of them yelling.

Jack clambered up the short stairway to the captain's deck, out of breath and sporting a wound in his arm. "Captain, there's too many. We 'ave to out-run them! Cat and Tom are dead, and there's gonna be a lot more if we don' run!" his hazel eyes were wild beneath his greasy blond hair.

"We'll hold a bit longer, boy. Get back to yer post!" Alexander yelled over the boom of the ballistae.

Jack fled the captain's deck, nocking an arrow to his bow. Erdwyf shot a shaft through a fat sailors head and was knocking another when a crossbow bolt buried itself in her thigh. Roaring, the elf broke the protruding shaft off, leaving the buried part in. Without stopping, she loosed the arrow at the man who had shot her. He screamed as he fell into the water, the bolt coming out his back. Yayènia dodged a bolt and grabbed it as it *thunk*ed into the floor. With a grunt, she snapped it off at the shattered stone head and tossed the point into the water. With a heave, she sent the splintered shaft spinning back toward its owner. The jagged point sunk into his neck, ripping apart flesh and vein. Alexander stared at the elf in surprise, being narrowly missed by spear. The two ships were close enough now to see the color of eyes.

Ropes and hooks flew across the span of water between them, followed by men. Losolin shoved his sword through a man's body hard enough that it caught another man behind the first. Those who had them now tossed aside their bows and drew swords.

The elves spun into action, their skill far and beyond the humans attacking them. Suneelo took a man's head off, its body still swinging a cutlass. Yayènia was kicked in the chin, forcing her to lose her grip on her long blade. The elf skidded across the deck to land next to a spear. Blood running from her mouth, the warrior leapt up, spear in hand. She spun the shaft like a quarterstaff, making it blur into invisibility. The enemy who had assaulted her went white, his eyes wide. Yayènia stopped the staff in one movement and smiled at the human. Before he could react, she sent it between his eyes. Yanking the bloody spear out, the warrior leaped off the captain's deck onto the main deck. She landed on top of a human attacking

Jack. The young corsair nodded at her and jumped back into the fray. Aladorn appeared at her side, swinging his blade with ease, a bored look on his face.

His opponent died with a gurgle and the wiat smiled at Yayènia. She smiled back and followed Jack into the fight. By nightfall, the corsairs were victorious, unceremoniously dumping their enemies' bodies into the ocean. Seven had died, four sweeps men, Tom, Stik, and Cat. At midnight, the seven bodies were wrapped in old sails, tied with extra lines, and laid by the railing. The corsairs spoke fond words of their companions, and one by one, lifted the bodies and slid them into the ocean with words of luck. The ships both had their anchors down at daybreak and the corsairs boarded the enemy vessel.

The elves went with them, swinging over on ropes to land on the whitewashed deck. Losolin took Aidyn into the captain's cabin and found a map pinned to the table. There lie a large mapped portion of the R'Kunad, and in the center an island with the swerving letters of Zaedic scrawled across it. Losolin unpinned the map and rolled it into his sleeve. He took letters from the table, a large pouch of gold, maps, books, and a finely wrought single edged cutlass from the room. Aidyn grinned and pinned a red cape onto his shoulders.

"How do I look? Corsair-ish?" the assassin said as he admired the floor length garment.

"Very. Help me with the books, will you?" Losolin replied.

Captain Alexander strode into the cabin and roared with laughter. "Ye would make good sailors! But yer not takin' the right things! Here, have some fine clothes, some pretty treasures. Take what ye will, corsairs ain't picky!"

The captain began rummaging through the closet, throwing away things that bored him. When the sun was high in the sky, the corsairs had created a huge pile in the middle of the white ship. Finery glinted in the warm sunlight, sparkling in the beholders' eyes. Yayènia stood draped in what looked like deep purple velvet, a fur-lined, heavily embroidered floor length cloak, with ribbon paneling down the front. Jack was putting a bejeweled crown on her head, to both her and the corsairs' amusement.

Erdwyf sported a beautiful headdress, with lace falling down her back in ripples. Losolin and Aidyn laughed, but the assassin ran to join the females, flashing his red cape about. Losolin pulled

Alexander to one side.

"Do you know why this ship was heading to Zaedic with a bunch of finery?" the elf asked quietly.

"No, but Zaedic is a myth, remember?" the man whispered back, watching his crew.

Losolin pulled the map out of his sleeve with difficulty as he was still holding the things he had found in the cabin. Setting down his newly acquired objects, the elf unrolled the map and showed it to his companion.

"Look, it is mapped out with the coordinates and everything."

The captain took the map and studied it. "Ah...very interesting. Quite unexpected as well, I might say."

"I also took some letters and scrolls; they might explain why all of this," Losolin indicated the pile, "was headed to the island."

"Good plan. Let's get ever'thing back on board. I would take this ship as me own, but as it is riddled with evil, we burn it," Alexander said.

Addressing the crowd he bellowed, "Boys! Get this swag back to the ship! We'll sort it out later. Izzy and Fritz get to the hold and ready this ship for burning!"

The crew burst into action. Great piles of riches were carefully tied to the lines and swung over to the *Crest.* Alexander and Losolin swung over with the rest of the crew and waited until Izzy and Fritz hastily swung on board. The sweeps men below began oaring hurriedly, the anchors already drawn up. Just when the clipper ship reached a safe distance, the white ship burst into flame, the oil spread around the hold by the two men, catching flame. Everyone on board cheered, whooping and hollering at the white ship. A pounding shook the floor near the door in the deck. Losolin, remembering, opened the hatch and was nearly bowled over by Kayra exploding up at him.

"You lock me in there all bloody day and night and you forget me! I thought that once the fighting stopped and it got so quiet, that you were all dead! Next time fighting breaks out, I'm locking *you* in a room for hours on end with nothing to eat! Gah!" the young woman shouted, waving her hands in the air.

Losolin backed away from the livid human, turning red. It wasn't until Jack started laughing that the tense moment was broken. The corsairs started to bellow with glee, their earnings flashing in the sun. Kayra stopped shouting and looked about her, her ears reddening. Jack went and took her into the galley, his long arm around her waist.

The sweeps men stopped rowing and came up to eat. Troaz and Alexander were dolling the treasure out, with piles for the companions as well. The soldiers dived into their loot with fervor. Losolin looked at his pile of a cloak, a cape, a long dagger, a bag of money, three rings of silver, two tunics, one red and one green, a pair of black leather trousers, a pair of knee high black boots, and the load he had taken from the cabin. The ship sailed on, the main sail bellied out and catching the strong wind that had carried away the morning fog. Alexander took the map to Zaedic and pinned it to the desk inside his cabin. Everyone took their loot down into the rooms and hold and walked back to the deck.

The great ship banked as the captain swung the wheel hard to starboard. The crew braced their sea legs against the sudden change in ground, but the passengers found themselves hard put to stay upright. Yayènia stamped her lower foot down hard and glared at the water below her.

Alexander yelled at them from the captain's deck. "Brace yerselves! We're hittin' stormy waters!"

Losolin looked up at the clear blue sky in confusion. Suddenly, a tremendous wave crashed into the side of the pirate ship. The passengers were slammed up against the guardrail, barely had enough time to grab hold before another wave smashed into them from the other side. Jairus was knocked away from his hold and sent sprawling across the deck. As the ship heaved again the archer was sent spinning back into the group. He reached out for the rail but missed, and was nearly sent back again before Suneelo grabbed his ankle and hoisted him toward the guardrail. The man wrapped his arms around the solid wood and gasped his thanks to the elf. A wave crashed over the deck, drenching them all in frigid seawater. Yayènia howled in dismay at being wet.

They were soaked by another wave, and another, and yet another. Water sloshed around on the deck, chilling the crew and passengers even more. Kayra and Jack had not appeared from the galley, but were presumed okay for the swearing that came from inside. The sails and flags snapped in the wind, speeding the ship toward their destination. Troaz walked over to them and grabbed a shroud as the ship lurched, and grinned down at the companions.

"Lovely day for sailing isn't it! This is what *real* sailing is! Not that shoreline shit those merchants do!" the first mate laughed and returned to his captain's side.

"Stupid blighter," Erdwyf growled. "This must be what the fourth level of hell is, I am telling you."

Any remarks to her comment were wiped away by water cascading over them once more. Three days passed as such, giving the corsairs reason to rejoice, and the seventeen reason to grumble. On the fourth day the water calmed down and allowed roiling stomachs to settle. The elves and their guards were sitting out on the deck wishing for a bath when Legless Mo shouted down at them from the crow's nest.

"Land ho! Land ho! Five leagues north!" shouted the mad old man.

Captain Alexander swung the helm over to port and beckoned Losolin up. "What kind of dockin' do ye want? A grand, hidden, quiet, what?"

"We do not want anyone to know we are here. Is that possible?" replied the half-Magin.

"It'll be hard, most likely this Midian fellow'll be on the lookout fer any foreign ships coming near 'is domain. Best we can do is drop anchor off shore near an uninhabited area and proceed on foot from there. It'll take longer, but we'll be less than noticed, if ye catch me meanin'."

"Of course. I do not know how long this will take, so if it takes longer than a week, I want you to get your ship out of here. Understand?" Losolin said fiercely.

"No. I refuse to acquiesce," Alexander stated boldly.

"What?"

"We're going with you boyo. Ye and yer friends saved me crew, me life, and me ship from those bastards. 'Sides, I ain't about to let a whole castle go unlooted. Now what are we here fer?"

Shocked, Losolin stammered for a moment and then said, "My fiancée is being held captive there, and tortured near to death. She is the princess of Blackhaven Forest, and the Magin Queen."

"Ye mean the Lady Tlonna?" Troaz asked from behind Alexander.

"Yes, Tlonna," Losolin replied, confused. "You have heard of her?"

"Aye, we've 'eard of her. It was she who allowed us to make berth at Blackhaven Port. Met her meself, I did," Alexander said in wonder. "She's yer lass?"

"Ah...yes."

"Good fer ye mate, she's a damn good sailor, and a damn good friend," the captain remarked happily.

"Well, she will not remember you. She has memory loss from being tortured a while back. And when has she sailed?" Losolin asked.

"Well, when Princess Tlonna allowed us to drop anchor in her harbor, I asked her if she'd like to come aboard an' learn how to sail. So she did, and I took her on a weeklong sail to Kismath and back. I even let her be captain fer a day, an' a damn good job she did," said Alexander.

Losolin smiled and then ducked his head. "I had better go tell my crew what is happening, then. Thank you, Captain, and you, Troaz. You are good men, good sailors," the elf ran down the steps and relayed the information to his companions. Everyone gave him small smiles, relaying his own emotions.

Now that they were at Zaedic, the task ahead of them seemed impossible. Even Yayènia looked nervous. The soldiers looked decidedly grim and frightened. The Rahlan's had always been frightening bedside stories, threats from irritated mothers, and half-imagined monsters. Losolin left them and went to stand at the bow, watching the island grow larger before him. Fear embedded itself in the elf, gnawing its way into his belly to sit like a cold weight.

Waves of long, brown grass shifted in the high wind, making the island look like a golden ocean. Stunted trees grew in grotesque forms, their tough green boughs adding stark color. No taint whirled around, there was not even a whiff of winter in the air.

The ship lowered anchor just off the desolate shore, wallowing in the shallow water. No living creature obscured the deadness of the land. Izzy, Fritz, Les, and Boxer stayed on the ship to watch it. The sails were lowered and tied down with only the clan flag of Clan Esmoden snapping in the wind. Lines were secured, the boom tightened down, and the ballistae prepared. The dinghies were dropped into the water and the crew departed. Losolin leapt out to haul the boat in and helped its female passengers out. Yayènia grinned at him, flashing her perfect teeth. Losolin grinned back at her, too panicked to do anything else.

The troop hid the boats, gathered their belongings, and started inward. The island was large and sparsely populated. On the third day of hiking, they wandered onto a dilapidated house. Its walls of wooden planks sloped to one side, and the door hung askew from its rusted silver hinges. The company entered the silent building, lighting the webbed torches that hung in brackets by the door. The flickering torchlight revealed a once fine tearoom. Cobwebs covered the white sheets that hung like poltergeists over the furniture. Rats skittered along the dusty floor, squeaking at the intrusion.

Taking a torch from Felton, Yayènia and Erdwyf climbed the wooden spiral staircase in the center of the floor. Losolin and Aidyn followed them, the steps creaking under their combined weight, light as they were. The others began exploring the rest of the house, the silence still ensuing.

Erdwyf opened a door by the stairs and poked her head in. "It is a bedroom. I wonder who owned this place."

Aidyn shrugged and they continued. Other doors revealed more bedrooms, a study, a library full of crumbling books, a nursery, and a drawing room. At the end of the hall was another set of stairs, this one straight. The elves climbed the rotting steps and found themselves in yet another hallway. A doorless entry opened into a large parlor with a glass ceiling, the edges brown and green where moisture had crept in. As in all the rooms, white sheets covered the furniture. Erdwyf yanked a cover off a chaise lounge and they gasped.

A magnificent piece of furniture sat before them. Plush blue cushions decorated with gold spirals sat encased by shining rosewood. The legs ended in claws, curling in a fearsome poise. Yayènia pulled a sheet away from a long table, uncovering a beautiful work of craftsmanship. Also made of rosewood, the unmarred top gleamed in the light coming from the glass ceiling. Legs identical to the lounge supported it, three at each end. Every piece of furniture in the room revealed the same rosewood style, untouched by time and wear. None of the wood was scarred, the material bright as the day it was made. But what was most entrancing were the things sitting on or in the chairs and couches.

Two children sat in a large chair, their young faces full of joy as they played. A young woman sat delicately on the lounge, watching the younglings. Her emerald eyes sparkled, rimmed by long raven eyelashes. A waterfall of auburn hair cascaded down her thin back, twisting in natural curls. Her skin was pale as snow, her face flawless with high cheekbones, rosebud lips, and a delicate nose. A dress of pale pink silk covered her fragile body, clinging to her curves and flowing over her long limbs. A slightly older man lounged in an overstuffed chair. A wicked grin played on his handsome face, curling at the corners. A shock of unruly red hair lay over his amber eyes, coming to rest just below his chin. A black ribbon tied a thick tail of the bright hair to trail down the man's broad back. A coat of dark green velvet lay open to reveal a flowing white tunic. Black breeches lay tight against the long, muscular legs. The man's face was pointed toward the woman; his own high cheekbones flush with color against the freckled skin. White teeth glinted, adding charm to his features.

The elves stared at the still-life forms. Aidyn bent down close to the woman and gently ran his fingers over her cheek. The flesh moved as it would on a real person, but the figure did not move. Losolin studied the gold band on the man's left hand.

"They are married," he said, looking into the man's bright eyes.

"They are elves," Yayènia said, brushing the red hair back away from the long pointed ears. "I have never seen anything like this. They are not dead, and they are warm to the touch, but it is as though they have been frozen in time. Elves dressed like this hundreds of years ago, around when we were all born," the High Commander said, her voice shaking.

Running footsteps alerted the four elves and they turned to see Axl standing in the doorway.

"They're here too? These people are all over the place. Frozen in mid-life. What is it?" the corsair asked, fingering his long red-blond hair.

"I do not know, Axl. What have you found?" Losolin replied, still staring at the man.

"We found a young man and woman in bed together, that was awkward, an old woman in a bed, a cook in the kitchen, two dogs and three kittens and a parrot. Angus found a man repairing a model ship too," Axl said. "Can we leave this place now?"

Aidyn straightened from the female and nodded. "I think we need to cover everything back up first, and then we should leave these poor souls alone."

They nodded and everything was covered up to leave the silent and still family to their fate. The large group left the house and started hiking once more inland. By nightfall, they had found a truly empty house and began preparing it to occupy. Losolin dropped his pack on the floor of a small bedroom. Dust floated up to meet him, making him wrinkle his nose. The elf pulled the covers off the bed and dumped them on the floor as well. A downy mattress in decent shape greeted him, its cover a yellowish white.

Losolin left the room and explored the rest of the house. The soldiers were rolling their bedrolls out in a large parlor, a merry fire dancing in the grill. The corsairs were bedding down in the common room, another fire warming the old walls. Yayènia met him in the hallway, took him by the wrist, and led him into a small room with a tub, table, and washing board.

"We need to prepare a bed for Tlonna. We need clean sheets and whatnot, so, I will wash, and you dry with your magic. Okay?" the female said, filling the tub with water from a pump in the wall.

Losolin touched the water and jerked his hand away. "It is freezing!"

"Yes, so would you warm it?" Yayènia asked irritably.

Losolin sent a stream of heat into the water and soon it was steaming. His female companion dumped a handful of crushed soap root into a bowl and filled it with some of the heated water. Soon the first sheet was handed soaking to Losolin, who squeezed the water out and once again sent a tendril of heat into the cotton. Within the hour, the elves had a bed in the room next to Losolin's prepared for Tlonna. A downy comforter was plumped up and stretched out across the sheets. They spent the rest of the night cleaning the room, sweeping out the dust and wiping down the walls.

The next day the seventeen original companions left the abandoned house with Snickers, Jack, Matt, Axl, Azerath, Troaz, Mo, and Alexander. Malcolm and Angus waved goodbye to them from the house and closed the door. The now twenty-five strong troop walked the rest of the way to a shoddy city shadowed by a bleak gray castle. No pennants snapped in the wind, no trees gave life to the dead community. Dirty people swarmed the streets; whores leaned against buildings flashing their goods, merchants sold their wares, and all around filthy children begged and stole.

Azerath caught the fancy of a bulbous whore. The grimy

woman smiled at him through broken brown teeth and pulled at his wide belt. The corsair sneered at her and shoved the fat woman away from him. However, when a pretty girl came up to flirt with Axl and Azerath, the men smiled and promised her a visit. Losolin grimaced at them, showing his displeasure. Jack grinned at the elf, pinching the bottom of a passing woman. Kayra harrumphed and elbowed the young man in the ribs. Grunting, the corsair begged for mercy from his new beau.

The elves were disguised in long brown woolen cloaks, hiding their flawless faces, pointed ears, and by hunching over, distorted their unmatched height. It also concealed their armor, and their helmets rested in the crook of their arm, hidden with the cloaks. The entire group blended in with the crowd, separating in waves but always keeping an eye out for each other.

Kayra was nearly dragged to the ground by a trio of rowdy men, but was gallantly rescued by Jack, who punched the leader in the face, breaking his nose. The short brawl was not out of place in the streets. All around them were fights, and even a few murders. The people merely walked around them, ignoring everything. Finally, the bunch of companions found themselves at the road to the castle. Two guards stood at the wrought iron gates, watching them. Alexander marched up to them and argued with the two shorter men. At last, the guards allowed Alexander to enter the gates, but stopped the rest. With a flash of steel, the guards flopped to the ground.

The captain withdrew his knives and wiped them on his prey's clothes. No one seemed to notice the murder of royal guards, so the corsairs pulled the bodies behind the wall and stripped them. Mo and Snickers resumed the guards' place, nodding to their companions.

Hurriedly, the party progressed towards the castle, meeting no resistance on the way. Yayènia reminded everyone of their duties and then rallied them all together. With a final good luck, the troop effectively silenced the guards, burst into the castle and found themselves surrounded by mercenaries and Darkwights. The evil men were as surprised as the companions, as they stared for a moment before attacking. Corsair and elf and human swirled into action, going for throats and heads in order to stop a cry from going up.

"Is everyone all right?" Losolin asked as they regrouped.

Everyone nodded.

"Then move," Yayènia said, wiped the blood off her sword,

and nodded to them all, "and good luck."

She and her chosen companions sprinted off down a hall. Losolin nodded to his friends and waved a short goodbye before gathering his companions around him and heading down a different hall. The corsairs split up into pairs and went in all directions, or along with the rest of the group.

Tlonna heard shouts and screams echoing down the hall to her room. Going to her door, the elf bent down and looked under it. She saw booted feet run passed her door, brown cloaks flapping at their ankles. To her shock, a pair of boots came to rest at her door at little while longer. In trepidation, Tlonna scooted away and stood up. Her door unlocked and Midian entered in full armor. Backing away from him, Tlonna bumped into the wall behind her.

"Your friends are here, slut. How did you communicate with them?" Midian screamed, smashing his fists into the elf's jaw.

Sliding down, Tlonna looked up at him. Once more, as she had a thousand times, she attempted to use her magic. The power welled forth in her body, but nothing happened. Midian shoved his boot into her legs. Scrambling, Tlonna tried to crawl away but the human grabbed her by the hair and yanked her up. Excruciating pain bloomed in Tlonna's gut. The pain spread until the elf let out a scream. Midian slapped her so hard her head snapped back, neck cracking. Lights exploded in the Magin's head. Midian slammed the female back into the wall over and over again. When he finally let go, Tlonna dropped like a rag to the floor.

She opened her mouth to breath and blood poured forth. Vomiting, the elf got to her feet shakily and moved toward the human, who had his back to her. Howling savagely, Tlonna wrapped her hands around his neck and squeezed. Midian laughed, and she was thrown off him and slammed to the floor. He crawled on top of her, ripping the black robes off in one mighty yank. Pulling out his member, the man shoved inside her. Tlonna sobbed as he ravaged her once more. His teeth pulled flesh away from muscle and sinew. Blood stained his lips and teeth. His fingers bruised and clawed at her breasts and neck. When Midian pulled out of her, Tlonna curled into a ball on the floor, trembling like a child.

Grabbing one of the large books Tlonna had on her bed, Midian yanked the elf up and forced her to stand. Winding away, he hit his captive across the face, shattering her jaw and cheekbone. Tlonna fell on the bed, blood staining the expensive coverlet.

"You *bitch*! How did you lead them here! *HOW*? I'll kill you! And then I'll tie each of them up and strip the flesh off their bones! Do you like that? Do you like that, slut?" Midian screamed at her, shoving her off the bed.

The man pummeled Tlonna until her entire body was covered in welts, bruises, cuts, lesions, and broken bones. The door slammed open and Sithian ran in, his face full of rage.

"Father! They've killed nearly every one of the guards! We can't touch them!"

Midian cursed and grabbed Tlonna by the wrist. "Are any of them in the hallway?"

Sithian shook his head and stared at his mother. "What have you done to her?" his voice trembled.

"None of your business boy. She deserved it." Midian dragged Tlonna into the hall and down it.

Sithian followed, averting his eyes away from the ruined mess that was his mother. Midian tossed the elf into her old cell and locked the door.

Quivering in agony, Tlonna pulled herself along the floor by the chains that had held her for so long. She scooted around until she was at the door, and began pounding weakly on it. From the bottom, Tlonna let out muffled shouts and pounded with her fists.

Losolin grabbed Nayn's elbow and hauled him backwards. "Do you hear that? That thumping?"

Nayn stared at the elf for a moment before listening hard. "You are right. Where is it coming from?"

Dawson pointed at a door a little farther down the hall. Kayra nodded silently at the scout. The four ran until they were standing in front of a small wooden door. Losolin looked at the door that came up to his chest dubiously. He could hear a faint pounding coming from the other side, accompanied by weak, soft wails. In terror, the elf tried the handle.

When it did not open, Losolin kicked the door. "TLONNA! Tlonna is that you?" he shouted, putting his mouth near the wood.

From behind the door came a quiet '*Lushin*?' In renewed fervor, Losolin slammed his fists against the wood, magic crackling around his knuckles, until it began to splinter under his strength. Dawson hauled him back, shaking his head. Nayn explained.

"My Lord, you can't break down the door. It's too thick and probably reinforced against magic. We've got to try and open it some other way," he said.

Kayra looked around her and down the hall both ways. "Maybe if we can break the handle off, we could pull the lock out and open it."

"Yeah, that would work," Nayn concurred.

Losolin's breath was wheezing out of him. He was so close, but he could not touch her. Desperately, as the others ran around looking for something to break the handle with, Losolin clawed at the door. His fingers were raw and bleeding within seconds, but he didn't stop.

Nayn appeared at his side minutes later and shoved the elf out of the way, carrying a piece of firewood. He hammered at the door handle until the log splintered uselessly. He pulled out his sword and did the same, but the blade merely struck sparks off it, and was marred in the process.

"Stop!"

The four spun around and lifted their weapons toward the young, fair man who hastened toward them, his sword still sheathed.

"Let me help you," he said breathlessly.

"And who in the nine hells are you to help us?" Losolin snapped, still holding his sword up.

"I'm Haydyn, Tlonna's son, one of three children. Please, I want out of here too."

Losolin jerked. "Tlonna does not have any children."

"Yes she does. Sithian and Rhiannan are with him now. Please, let me help. I have a key to this door," Haydyn explained impatiently. He jingled a ring of bloody keys in front of his face and raised his eyebrows. "You are Losolin, aren't you?"

"Yes," Losolin replied uncertainly, shaking with rage.

"Mother told me about you a lot. She really loves you," the young man said as he searched for the right key. Losolin glowered, his terror and wrath warring with curiosity, and horror.

The young half-elf was tall and slim with broad shoulders. His blond hair was thick and shaggy, hanging down in front of his ice blue eyes. A delicate mouth and nose made him pretty with long black eyelashes. His hair, what wasn't too short to be, was tied in a club at the nape of his neck, reaching his shoulders. Finally, he found the right key and he forced it into the lock. The door started to swing open but stopped when it hit something soft. Losolin shoved passed the boy and slipped into the cell. In horror, he took in Tlonna's form.

Slamming to his knees, the half-Magin pulled on his power and the greenish light enveloped his hands. He yanked off his helmet and ran his fingers down her face. The others crowded in behind him and Haydyn shut the door. Tlonna looked at Losolin and managed a weak smile.

"Lushin," she murmured through her broken jaw.

Losolin smiled back and kissed his fingers. He pressed his fingertips to her lips gently and whispered, "Hi."

He tried to heal her, but she was too weak to handle the pain. Writhing on the floor, she screamed and clawed at the air. He only was able to heal her legs before the agony forced him to stop.

"Tlonna," he sobbed, trying to wipe the blood away with his sleeve. "I am so sorry. I cannot...please do not die."

Tlonna stared at him as though he were an angel, tears pouring down her face as she clutched his arm. "*Lushin*," she said again.

Losolin bent over her and gently gathered her into his arms. Haydyn gripped his shoulder and leaned close.

"He has never beaten her this bad. He must have just done this. We must leave now, before Father comes back."

Nodding, Losolin hugged Tlonna's broken body to him and stepped out of the low door. They left the cell and hurried away, trying to steer away from the fighting as much as possible. As they ran down a corridor, something slammed into Losolin's back and he stumbled.

"You don't know when to give up, do you boy?" Midian taunted, rubbing his fingers together.

Tlonna quivered in Losolin's arms, hiding her face in his shoulder. Gently, he set her down and barely blocked Midian's fist from crashing into his face. With a grunt, the elf grabbed the human's wrist and yanked downward, pulling Midian closer.

At the same moment, Rhiannan spat at her twin's feet. "Traitor! Father has given us all that we could ask of him, and yet you still hide behind the elf. I'll kill you!" the young woman lunged forward, outstretched arms wreathed in brown light.

Haydyn tossed his hand upward and black power flickered into his sister who slammed hard into the floor. Sithian stared at his brother in disgust, paying his sister no attention. Rhiannan struggled to her feet glaring. Losolin twisted as Midian stumbled into him from the yank, and grabbed hold of his neck. Rage seethed through the elf and his green magic surged into Midian's spine. The human howled in pain but he spun around and retaliated. Losolin dodged the black light and swung his fist into Midian's face. The king stepped back just in time and took a steadying breath. The hallway stilled as the two males glared at each other. Then, without preamble, their companions lurched into each other, grappling and slicing around the two.

"How in the nine hells did you get here?" Midian demanded, ignoring his children as they fought two to one.

"Your little demesne is not as secret as you would like, Midian."

"There is no reason to keep it secret, boy. Do you not see my power in the very air? Even the sun is weaker than I am. Soon, the world will fail and I will reign over all. Your time is at an end."

"You are weak and worthless human, Midian. The people of Nymyños mock you as you hide, laughing in your face as you pretend to be a king. Look at your people. They would follow a pig they are so brainless."

Apoplexy threatened Midian as he stared at Losolin. "Look at your bitch, elf. She cowers before me. She was too weak to resist me, and now she knows what a real man can do. She'll look at you, and see me."

Fury erupted in Losolin so strongly he roared as he launched himself on Midian, drawing his sword. The human backed away in surprise as the blade whistled before his eyes. It scored a thin line across the bridge of his nose, and he yanked out his own weapon.

Steel rang out as they collided, their armor scraping together. Losolin broke free and kicked the human in the gut. Midian stumbled backward and then regained his balance. His gauntleted fist struck the side of Losolin's helmet, jerking his head to the side, but the elf caught the fist and pivoted. Midian was slammed into the wall hard enough to chip the granite blocks.

Grunting in pain, the king struggled to his feet and ducked Losolin's sword. Knowing the elf would soon best him in the fight, Midian Wove. Losolin roared in searing pain as the magic lashed into his side, ripping through his armor and flesh to leave a bleeding gash. He collapsed as the magic convulsed through his body, grabbing hold of his nerves and taking over his motor skills. The elf was thrown into spasms, unable to get to his feet.

Midian sucked in a breath and pressed his hand to the back of his head, and it came away wet with blood. Seeing Kayra kneeling by Tlonna, the Magin grinned. His hands shot through the air and he snatched handfuls of blonde and cinnamon hair. Both Kayra and Tlonna fell inward to slam against Midian's chest. Tlonna cringed and went to her knees. Kayra, however, clamped her teeth on the left nipple and wrenched away.

Midian howled in pain as blood blossomed on his shirt. He twisted his hands so the females in his grip were forced to expose their pale necks. Suddenly, a blast of black power exploded into the man's body. Midian twitched backward, releasing his captives. Haydyn stood rigid as he watched his father thrash under the very same magic he himself wielded. With a heave, Midian launched himself at Tlonna, attempting to ignore his son. His hands clamped on the elf's ankle and he scrambled up.

Haydyn was beginning to tire, his blasts of power becoming weaker and weaker. Sithian howled in the background, and Kayra screamed as Midian yanked Tlonna down the corridor. Haydyn collapsed, his over exertion taking hold. Rhiannan leapt away from Dawson and grabbed hold of Losolin as he finally regained control of his body. The elf aimed his fist at Rhiannan and clipped her hard on the nose. The girl's head snapped back, her front teeth and nose broken. She went limp and slithered to the floor.

Exhaustion plagued everyone in the hall, but they fought on. Tlonna clawed at the floor, attempting to stop Midian, her fingertips leaving smears of blood in their wake. Kayra stood frozen in a swarm of magic held by the king. Losolin pounded after the two progressing down the hall. In a final burst of energy, the elf slammed into Midian with both body and magic. Losolin's superior strength knocked the human on his back, but not before he twisted Tlonna's leg until it snapped at the knee.

The half-Magin pounded at Midian, his fists shattering bone.

Midian struggled against the elf, unable to summon magic as both pain and weariness throbbed through his body. Both males struck at each other with pure loathing and blind rage. A well-aimed blow from Losolin slammed Midian's head back into the stone floor. Losolin's face contorted as he smashed his fist into Midian's face again. Grabbing handfuls of raven hair, the elf slammed the man's head into the floor until blood pooled beneath him. The human's consciousness slipped away, leaving the elf the victor. With a violent twist, Losolin wrenched Midian's head around, snapping his neck.

But, unknown to everyone other than Midian, the white pendant rested against his chest, and was already at work.

With a groan, Losolin stood and gently gathered Tlonna up in his arms. Dawson was now beneath Sithian, who looked up at the wrong moment. The now free Kayra slammed her boot into the soft area just under his chin. The boy wailed as he bit through his tongue. Seeing his sire and sister lying defeated on the floor, Sithian fled the corridor.

Dawson picked up the unconscious Haydyn, Losolin handed the comatose Tlonna to Kayra and picked up Nayn, and they fled the corridor. Corsairs appeared as they sprinted through the corridors, hands full of silver and gold treasure.

Losolin and his companions burst out of the castle and sped through the filthy city. The Zaedicans watched them pass with dull eyes.

"What about the others?" Kayra gasped, when they finally reached a safe spot outside the city.

Losolin gently put Nayn down and moved to take Tlonna from the young woman. Though the elf weighed less than the average human, Kayra was white-faced with exhaustion, her breath ragged. Jack dropped his booty and comforted her.

"They will be fine, I am sure," Losolin replied, stroking Tlonna's face.

Her head lolled against his shoulder. The elf stared at his love, bloody and dying. "We have to keep going. Come on," he said after Kayra had caught her breath.

They had gone less than a mile when the young woman collapsed, dropping Tlonna in the grass. Losolin situated Nayn on one shoulder and picked Tlonna up to drape her over the other. Kayra struggled to her feet, shamefaced as Jack supported her.

Midian opened his eyes and moved a hand to the back of his head. Suddenly, a fist whacked into his mouth. Midian grunted and rolled to the side. Yayènia wrapped her hands in the human's lapels and hoisted him to his feet.

"Remember me?" she spat, shaking the human like a doll.

Midian, dazed and groggy, stared at his assailant blankly. Finally recognition clicked, and he began to laugh. He watched Yayènia's large blue eyes widen then narrow. Her lips curled into a snarl and she shoved the Magin back. Drawing her longsword, Yayènia advanced slowly. Midian fumbled at his side for his own blade and drew it shakily. His head pounded, his face stung, and the Resurrection Pendant throbbed against his chest.

The elf before him tilted her head to the side, blue eyes darkened with hatred.

"Are you going to kill me?" Midian crooned.

"In a bit," she replied, and twisted the elfish sword in an intricate dance before settling into her stance.

Midian nodded once, and then saw the others behind her. Elves and men stood side by side, with arms folded, watching passively. Rhiannan was held by a huge wavy haired elf that Midian recognized as Ghealan Tomyvon. Midian's eyes slid over the other elf that he had hung from the wall in Blackhaven.

Suneelo met the mad king's gaze unflinchingly, and flexed his hand on the hilt of his sword. Midian turned his attention back to Yayènia.

"You killed my brother," he said simply.

"Yes, I did."

Midian nodded again, and touched his blade to the elf's. Immediately she moved, spinning to the right and slashing out, faster than he thought possible. The human barely scooted back in time to avoid being gutted. His sword clanged against hers, making his arm go numb. Yayènia turned, her arm swinging. Her body twisted backward and then her weapon was whistling through the air. Midian raised his blade and caught hers. The monumental strength behind the blow knocked him off his feet.

The female took a step back, allowing him to stand. Snarling at the insult, Midian got to his feet, glancing at the sniggering audience. Sneering, he lashed, black magic sparking toward Yayènia. She dropped to the floor, rolled, and sprang up, untouched. Fatigue plagued the Magin. He struck out again and caught her on the side. She did not cry out, but ignored the blood now blooming against her shirt.

Rhiannan bared her teeth, trying to twist away from the large elf that held her. His grip was so strong, it was squeezing the circulation out of her wrists. Icy prickles stabbed up and down her fingers. She attempted to blast him with magic, but the elf merely squeezed tighter until she couldn't focus like she had to. A corsair wearing a captain's signet eyed her greedily. Rhiannan snarled at him.

Her head whipped around when she heard another commotion in the hall behind her. A horde of black-garbed men and Darkwights charged at them from down the hallway. The elves and men stiffened to attention, drawing their assorted weapons. The huge elf holding her swiftly hogtied her and threw her against the wall.

Ghealan gripped his sword and smoothly knocked a Darkwight to the ground. Erdwyf slammed the heel of her palm in the throat of a man, crushing his windpipe. Beside her, Suneelo yanked his sword out of the belly of a screaming demon. Blood sprayed across the two elves.

Rhiannan watched in stunned horror as her rescuers were easily torn apart. Her mind was eased slightly when she saw that three of the human guards lay on the floor amidst her rescuers. The elves and corsairs cursed loudly and gathered up the bodies of their fallen comrades.

To Rhiannan's displeasure, she saw that the elves had no cuts or bruises on their fey faces. The corsair sported a razor thin cut along his jaw. She cursed him. The only female, other than the one fighting Midian, was beautiful in such a way that men would die of want for her. The Magin cursed her too. Her own beauty was unmatched on Zaedic, but certainly, this elf surpassed her.

Midian ducked low as Yayènia's sword whistled over his head. He sprang forward, catching her in the midriff so that she lost her grip on her sword. Elf and man slammed to the ground. She twisted, switching the advantage. Midian now had his back to the cold stone floor, his waist between her muscled thighs. The steel of her greaves cut into his ribcage. Yayènia bent over him so that her chest was level with his eyes.

Against his will, Midian felt himself harden, as did she. Yayènia drew one of her twin katans and held it against his wrists. Midian struggled, thinking keenly of how Tlonna had been where he was, just days ago, and he had been in Yayènia's place. Suddenly, a new pain slashed down his arms as Yayènia slowly dragged her katan across his wrists. She moved so that she could look directly into his eyes.

"Is this how you do it, Midian? Is this how you like it?" she hissed, putting her mouth close to his.

He swallowed, feeling blood pumping from his severed arteries.

She stood and kicked his sword toward him. With weak hands, Midian gripped the hilt. His fingers were hard put to stay wrapped around the leather. Yayènia watched him coldly. He charged her, knowing he had only one more chance. She sidestepped him and shoved her blade through his back. Midian, facing the crowd of elves and men, stared at his adversary's husband, remembering the torture he had put them through. Suneelo did not blink. Without turning, Yayènia yanked her sword out of his back.

Rhiannan screamed as her father fell to his knees, blood pouring from his wrists, chest, and back. He did not look at her. The elf turned slowly, planted her boot on his back, and slid her sword across his throat, and vaguely she thought she saw a silver chain become severed and fall from his neck. She did not remember when she finally stopped screaming; only that a large black boot slammed into her forehead, and she went out cold.

Chapter 20
Zaedic's Bane

Everyone met back at the house near midnight. The crew mourned the losses of Nayn, Randi, Merrill, and Felton. The original guards took the loss of their old friends hard, spending the rest of the night huddled together silently by the fire.

Losolin laid Tlonna on the prepared bed and stroked her cheek. He was too weak to fix her leg, so Erdwyf and Yayènia set it properly and splinted it for the time being. Axl held Rhiannan, not knowing what to do with her. Haydyn ignored his senseless sister pointedly. Finally, Suneelo put her in one of the windowless center rooms. He dumped her unceremoniously on a filthy bed littered with spiders and other pleasantries. Her nearly transparent gray tunic fell about her immodestly, but the elf ignored it.

Malcolm and Angus, surprisingly, had spent their time cleaning and cooking. A wholesome meal sat on the table steaming and hissing juices.

"We found the underground larder an' Les has showed us all a thing or two 'bout cookin'." Malcolm boasted as he passed a bowl of potatoes. "We was surprised most of the stuff was good, what with the house being a dump hole."

"Figured it 'ad somat to do wit magic or whatnot," Angus added through a mouthful of chicken.

The group ate ravenously, even though it had been only a day they had been gone. Captain Alexander recommended they exit the island as soon as possible.

"We are not leaving until Tlonna is well enough to walk. Tomorrow I will be strong enough to heal her knee, but I want her to rest, and the pain of the healing will incapacitate us both," Losolin replied.

Alexander dipped his head. "Day after tomorrow it is then. I won't risk me crew anymore than I have to."

Everyone concurred, and Losolin went to feed Tlonna. He was surprised at how healthy she was. Her skin was pallid, the lesions and bruises plentiful and large, but her organs seemed in working order, and she had a healthy appetite.

The next day, Tlonna woke up fully aware for the first time. She gingerly felt all of her wounds, staring at her splinted leg. The door opened, and Aidyn slipped inside.

"Aidyn..." Tlonna whispered. "I thought you dead."

The assassin rushed to her side. "Nay, my friend, Losolin healed me, else I would have been. I...I am so sorry." He laid his head on her arm and wept. "I was not prepared. I should know better."

"No, Aidyn, no. It was not your fault. Please, do not blame yourself. I am safe now, see? Things are good, now."

Aidyn pulled himself together, green eyes shining. "I am sorry it took us so long to get to you. Losolin and I tried again and again to come after you, but Demetrius stopped us, saying that we were not yet fit, and the army not ready. If only we had come sooner."

"And would it have made much difference, Aidyn?" Tlonna asked. "He tortured me day after day, then had me healed so he could do it again. If you had arrived a month sooner, it would have been the same. I do not blame you, or Losolin, or any of the others. I blame only Midian. I hope he suffers."

"Midian is dead, Yayènia killed him, and quite magnificently, I hear. Though... it makes me wonder how she did, when Losolin said he broke his neck. Those with him watched him do it," the assassin said with an attempted laugh.

"It was the second pendant of the Magins. The Resurrection Pendant, as he calls it. I have not seen Yayènia, or the others. I should like to get to know them again."

"And so you shall, but rest, Losolin still slumbers, and so should you be."

Tlonna smiled. "No, I have rested enough. I wish to meet my rescuers. Will you help me out?"

Aidyn stood and gingerly picked up his queen. With his precious burden, the assassin stepped into the common room where the five elves, the corsairs, and the remaining guards were. When they entered, the four Blackhavenites shot to their feet. Aidyn set Tlonna down in a cushioned chair and then took a seat next to her.

"Tlonna," Yayènia and Erdwyf breathed together, sinking to their knees before her.

Tlonna smiled faintly at them. Her eyes took in the multitude of weapons on Yayènia, and the elegant way Erdwyf held herself, even kneeling.

"Yayènia, and Erdwyf," she said, touching their hands briefly.

The females grinned. Ghealan and Suneelo stood behind their wives, grinning as well. Tlonna named them too, the faces in her foggy memories becoming clearer.

"It has been too long since I have seen your face, my friend," Erdwyf said, tears in her eyes.

"And a sight it must be," Tlonna laughed, touching her busted lips.

"Beautiful, as always," Ghealan said.

"Tlonna!" Losolin said from his doorway, staring at her. "Tlonna... my heart."

He rushed to her side, shoving aside the others. Taking her hands, he buried his head in her lap. Everyone in the room fell silent as the half-Magin sobbed in relief. Finally, he lifted his head, and touched her face.

"I love you. I love you. More than life itself, more than anything in the all the world. I love you so much. You are the breath in my lungs, and for the time you were away from me, I could not breathe. I could not see or feel. You are everything to me. Tlonna... I love you."

"I love you too, Losolin," Tlonna replied tearfully, lifting a hand to his.

"Can I heal you? Can you stand it?"

"My leg, but anything else is too much, my heart. Just let me mend naturally, and save both our strength."

Swallowing, he laid his hands on her splinted leg and looked at her to make sure she was ready. Tlonna nodded, biting her lip. Green light swelled from his hands, and they both convulsed. Pain shot through them as one. Tlonna sobbed once, Losolin growling. After a tense minute, the magic subsided, and they fell back, exhausted.

The room was still quiet except for their harsh breathing. Tlonna's hand crawled to Losolin's bowed head, twining her fingers in his hair. "It is all right, Losolin. I am all right. Are you?"

Losolin nodded, brushing his thumb over her swollen bottom lip, tears running down his face. Tlonna let out a gurgling laugh. Losolin grinned slowly until everyone in the room was laughing. They laughed for relief, for joy, and for the sake of laughing.

The house was bustling by midday. Tlonna was introduced to the corsairs and the soldiers. She even joined in a few games of dice, losing miserably.

Erdwyf, Ghealan, Suneelo, and Yayènia watched her from the background. Losolin joined them and conversed quietly. The guards from Kajgenia still were wrapped in mourning, but seemed better. At dinner, during a quiet moment in conversation, they heard a loud thump and curse. Everyone looked up and then hastened to Rhiannan's room. When Troaz yanked open the door, they saw the young woman writhing on the floor.

She looked up at the crowd and glared. "Take these damn bonds off me!"

Tlonna stared at her daughter, her mouth open. "Haydyn, do you know how to seal people?"

"Yes Mother. Do you want me to seal her?"

"Yes."

Haydyn stepped into the room and placed his hand on his twin's forehead. Rhiannan tried to bite him. A flash of black light and Rhiannan howled.

"She is sealed."

Losolin knelt by the twins. He undid the bonds holding the girl and stepped quickly away. She raised her hands and then bit her red lips. "Damn you! Damn you Haydyn!" she screamed as nothing happened. Her delicate hand balled into a fist and she swung at her brother. Haydyn caught it in midair, frustrating Rhiannan further.

"My dear twin, Anna, does not deserve to live," he said coldly to the men around them. "She has raped, murdered, tortured, and debased people mercilessly, finding pleasure in it. I placc her at your disposal, to do with as you will."

Tlonna did not stop him or disallow his statement. She looked her son in the eyes, searching. Finally, she nodded. None of the men went into Rhiannan's room for a long time, but it was plain some had visited her in the night. Her skin was bruised, her hair tangled, and her clothes torn.

Even the guards seemed to enjoy this spectacle, taunting her. They set out at midmorning, retracing their steps back to the ship. Near midnight, they passed the house with the frozen elves. Losolin was minded to bypass it, but the others wanted to make sure they hadn't been hallucinating. Hesitant, Alexander knocked on the front door. He, as well as the rest waited for a long moment before pushing the door open and stepping inside. Their hands flew up as they became face to face with rusty crossbow bolts. Yayènia gasped as she recognized the handsome male from upstairs.

"Who are you and what are you doing in my house?" he asked in a deep, melodic voice.

"My name is Yayènia er'Tiena. We passed by here a short time ago, and we saw you...well...frozen. We came by again to see if we had imagined it."

The crossbow didn't budge. "Your accent is strange. From whence do you come?"

"Blackhaven Forest. We are friends. Please lower your weapons," Yayènia replied gently.

"I am loath to believe you," the elf's finger tightened on the trigger.

With one swift movement, Yayènia grabbed the bolt, upturned the crossbow, and yanked it out of the other's hands. "You have been in a trance for a few hundred years. Aderiaen Rahlan is dead, as is his son, Midian."

The male stared at her in disbelief. "Who do you speak of? How is this true? My family and I just awoke from a nap!"

Suneelo sighed and took the weapon from his wife. "Good sir, look around you! Would your beautiful home be like this if you had merely taken a nap? A house does not decay in a few minutes! I do not know what happened here, but accept the fact that you have been lost in time. Please tell your kin to lay down their weapons."

The elves from the house lowered their spears and crossbows. The male took a step back to allow the rest of the corsairs to enter the house. He placed both hands on the small of his back and bowed low, extending one leg. "My name is Niander Saryth. This is my wife Syntyche er'Saryth. This is my family."

Niander introduced each of the seven elves behind him. Syntyche held the girl child, Seraphia, who was staring at the strangers in amazement, her large gold eyes drinking in their roughness. Lukein, her brother, attempted to repeat his father's bow, but failed miserably, his red hair falling over his small shoulders in a wave of shine.

"Would you like some refreshments?" Syntyche asked quietly, her voice the sound of a soft wind.

Tlonna studied her before replying. "No, we were just passing by."

"You cannot be leaving, you must explain yourselves." Niander's brother snapped, grabbing hold of Erdwyf's arm.

Ghealan slapped the male's hand away and moved to the other side of his wife. "We have a ship to meet, and we have already been here too long. We just wanted to see if anything had changed, now that Midian is dead."

"Is that what happened? Some maniac had a spell on us? Do not joke," Niander said angrily, stepping up so that he was almost nose-to-nose with Ghealan.

"Indeed Niander, I believe that is exactly what happened. Who was the last sovereign you can remember following?"

"King Hadian Rahlan, but we were in the midst of a war at the time," Nasren, the brother, replied.

"The ruler here was named Midian Rahlan, son of Aderiaen Rahlan, who is, I believe, the grandson of Hadian Rahlan, and from there I do not know. Midian is now dead, and this is his daughter, Rhiannan. This is Tlonna Arune Ewôsdírn, Princess of Blackhaven Forest...perhaps you know it by Everwood City," Ghealan pulled the three forward.

Niander and his family stared at the scarcely clothed Rhiannan in distaste.

"We know of Everwood, yes," Niander said slowly.

Syntyche clicked her tongue and disappeared into the dark hallway behind her. "What is wrong with you people? Can you not clothe your own?" Niander exclaimed. His amber eyes regarded Rhiannan and Tlonna's torn appearance with apparent revulsion.

Tlonna had not paid her own apparel any mind. Now she glanced down at the black rags that clung to her body. Even though she was more covered than her daughter, the Magin felt heat rise in her cheeks. She attempted to tug the rags into place, but gave up when they only ripped more. Syntyche hurried back into the room and shoved a pile of pink silk into Tlonna's arms, and a pile of yellow into Rhiannan's.

"There is a bedroom two doors down the hall, you can use it to change if you would like."

"Thank you, Syntyche. I am in your debt," Tlonna replied, and tugged her daughter after her to the room.

Once there, Rhiannan tossed the yellow material onto the dusty floor and crossed her arms. "I'm not going to wear that."

Tlonna, who was already out of her own rags, looked up. "What? Why not?"

"It's yellow."

Tlonna found the bottom of the pink thing and slipped it over her head. "I do not care. If you will not wear it, you can walk around exposed. Just remember we will be on a *corsair* ship with even more *corsairs* than there are now. Get my drift?" she realized the pink thing was a mid-thigh length tunic.

Enfolded in the tunic had been a pair of gray trousers. The Magin pulled them on and tied the leather laces. Rhiannan still stood with her arms crossed, glaring at her mother.

"You let them rape me."

"You stood by and watched as your father and brother raped and tortured me. Besides, we all heard you, do not pretend you did not enjoy some of it."

Rhiannan sniffed. "It's still yellow."

"So."

"I can't wear yellow. It doesn't look good on me," the younger Magin snapped.

"Fine." Tlonna strode over to her and yanked the rest of the skirt off, leaving only the band around the half-elf's waist. "Then you will walk around like that."

Rhiannan swung. In reflex, Tlonna blocked it and sent her fist crashing into her daughter's mouth. The pretty lips exploded with blood, smearing across her face and already ruined teeth.

"Put the bleeding dress on."

Swearing, Rhiannan tugged the dress over her head and twisted until it fell about her ankles. Frilly lace erupted out of the collar, cuffs, and out the bottom. The back had a row of pearl buttons that Tlonna swiftly did up, nearly choking the young female with the tight collar. With another string of curses, Rhiannan ripped the lace off and tossed it on the floor.

"Pick it up, this is a gift, and you will not leave your mess here," Tlonna growled, opening the door.

Huffing, the two females left the room, rags in hand, and walked out to where everyone was still congregated. They all fell silent when they glanced back and saw Rhiannan's bloody face.

Shrugging, Tlonna explained, "She tripped."

They joined their fellows and thanked Syntyche for the apparel. The other female smiled and dipped her head.

"I think it is high time for us to be gone. Thank you for your hospitality," Losolin said before anything else could happen.

Niander bowed again and opened the door. The troop said farewell and wished the family good luck.

Erdwyf sighed, wringing her hands. "I have a feeling we are soon going to find out what happened to our race. I cannot believe that this...freezing...was an isolated event."

Tlonna eyed her warily and nodded. Three days later, they came upon their dinghies and shoved them out into the water. The corsair ship wallowed a ways out, with Boxer waving at them from the prow. Alexander hallooed back to him and began rowing furiously to get to his ship. Chains hauled up the boats after the crew had boarded, climbing rope ladders. The reunion was a joyous one, with plenty of ale and mead passed around. Tlonna was introduced to the corsairs, laughing at their crude jokes. Haydyn was accepted almost as warmly, and Rhiannan was ignored. Her lips had healed, and were now set into a frightened sneer.

Almost immediately, the anchors were hauled up, and the sails were unrolled. Losolin noticed that the ship was incredibly clean. The deck shone in the sun, the rails were washed of dry salt, and the cabins were cleaned to a high shine.

The journey was boring until the fourth day at sea. A warning was shouted down from Axl, who was in the crow's nest.

"There be a ship coming up 'fore us! Looks to be one of them white ships o' Midian's!" the young corsair stepped out of the nest and spidered down the netting to the deck. "It looks to be fully loaded. Cap'n, what do ye suppose we do?"

Alexander scratched his bearded chin. "Lower the anchor on the port side. Clubhaul so we can face 'em. That way we have a chance ta blow holes in their hull before they reach us."

Troaz shouted out the order and the corsairs obeyed. Snickers, Matt, and Malcolm went down to load the ballistae on the starboard side while the rest tied down the lines and readied their weapons. With a jerk, the anchor hit the bottom of the sea and the ship swung around hard. The passengers were thrown off their feet and slammed up against the railing. Yayènia cursed and leaped up, grabbing onto the mast to hold herself up and the ship rocked into position. Tlonna stared down at the expanse of water just below her in trepidation. The *Crest* settled in the water and three ballistae launched their ammunition toward the Zaedic ship. The white ship shuddered as the missiles careened into its pale hull. The ballistae loosed again, and the enemy crew roared.

Tlonna shoved Kayra beneath the deck, along with Rhiannan, and slammed the hatch door shut. She drew the white sword that Losolin had given back to her, and settled into a comfortable stance to wait, though she knew she was not up to a fraction of her skill or stamina.

Just as they had before, the two ships came up next to each other and the enemy swung aboard the *Crest*. They were dispatched easily with the aid of Haydyn and Tlonna. Haydyn easily slew his father's men with a blast of power, and Tlonna became a weapon herself. Even Yayènia stopped for a second to stare in shock. Within a few moments, the attackers were dead, no fatalities on the corsair side. The white ship was boarded and looted. Haydyn stared at the clothes he knew his father had sent for him and his siblings. A pile of fine velvets and silks was dumped in front of him along with a sword he himself had custom designed.

Tlonna gave him a half-smile and took her gift from the corsairs silently. Alexander ordered the ship to be burned with a sorrowful look.

"Captain Alexander," Losolin shouted before Axl and Snickers reached the hatch door. "You deserve another ship. I myself will help repair it and paint it whatever color you wish, on my coin. I am sure I can help find more crew members too."

The corsairs stared at the elf. Their young and wild faces full of disbelief and hope. Alexander halted Axl and Snickers. "Do ye mean it?"

"You have my word."

"You heard him boys! Half o' ye stay aboard. Troaz, you be captain o' this here ship. I now be Commodore Alexander!"

The corsairs roared with pleasure, dancing and singing. Tlonna was swung around and passed from sailor to sailor, laughing and singing with them. Jack swung aboard the *Crest* and pulled Kayra out, pushing Rhiannan back down with his foot. It took less than thirty minutes before the two ships were setting sail, a spare clan flag flying up the mast of the commandeered ship.

Having mapped the route, it took much less time to get back to the port in Narnen. During the trip, they watched in hope as the sun grew brighter with each day, and the air became cleaner.

They docked both ships around dawn, unloading cargo and taking it into the corsairs' private storage hut. Loot from both ships filled the hut to the ceiling. In the new light, the white ship was much worse off than it had looked before. Huge holes had been blown into the hull, only partially covered up with the corsairs' hasty fix job. Three of the sails were torn, which they had known, and the hold was leaking badly. The paint was cracking and falling off, revealing the dark, sea-worn wood beneath. Troaz was still proud, however, to be captain.

As he had promised, Losolin sent Augustine and Dawson to the capital of Narnen, Nestra, with a large purse of gold to buy supplies for the repairs. It took them several days to get the wagon train of wood, nails, and everything else back to the harbor. In the meantime, Tlonna became friends with her old comrades, and slowly began to recover from her captivity. Kayra and Jack often disappeared together, provoking smirks and knowing glances from their companions. Finally, the supplies arrived, and the sailors and elves got to work.

The corsairs expertly repaired the hull while the others replaced the torn canvas with the new. Troaz and Alexander concluded on painting the ship red and silver. It would be named *Zaedic's Bane* in honor of the expedition. It took nearly two full weeks to repair, paint, and ready the ship for corsair occupation. Brand new sails and lines were installed, a new wheel, gleaming with polished wood was hooked up to Troaz's glee. Twelve new recruits arrived; answering to the call Augustine and Dawson had left in Nestra. They were sworn into Troaz and Alexander's service, and appointed main jobs on the ship. Izzy, Fritz, Snickers, and Matt went to be with Troaz, even though the corsairs planned on sailing together most of the time.

Troaz remained Alexander's first mate, but on the ships, Matt became Troaz's, and Axl became Alexander's. On the last day, Alexander and Axl recruited the elves to help reload the some of the swag for trading. It took the better part of the day to go through all of the finery and treasure, sorting it for keeping and trading. Most of the ladies' clothes were boarded, but some of it was gifted to the females in the company. Kayra and Jack were missing once more, so Erdwyf took the human's share as well for safekeeping. Some of the arms were given to the companions as well. By dusk, the corsair hut was half empty, and the two great ships were sitting a bit lower in the water. Others at the harbor stared at the corsair ships in awe, never before having seen the huge red and silver vessel before. Troaz doffed his captain's pendant, the sickle of Clan Esmoden.

The elves went aboard the new ship to look around. The deck had been scrubbed clean of the whitewash, and gleamed pristinely in the evening light. The captain's quarters were cleaned of the bleak and angry colors the captain had obviously been fond of, and replaced with the festive adornments Troaz favored. A large map of Nymyños, with a newly charted Zaedic, was pinned to the tabletop. The ink was still slightly damp, shining in the torchlight. The ship was altogether brighter and more alive than ever before. The new crew danced and sang with the old, their rough voices echoing in the quiet of the oncoming night. The original companions joined in the celebrations, not wanting to leave their new friends. Alexander and Troaz came and fetched Tlonna and Losolin from the clutches of a boisterous Axl. The four disappeared into Troaz's quarters, the elves slightly hesitant of what was to happen.

Alexander poured himself a glass of wine and passed the bottle around. "Troaz and me have decided that we are gonna travel the seas together, but make berth at Blackhaven, if it be good with ye. We plan on buying a good-sized hold there, and mayhap an inn or two. We ha' also decided on asking ye if ye wanted to ride with us back to yer home. T'would be faster than travelin' on those beasts of yers, and twice as much fun."

"That is a generous offer, Commodore, but we have an army to meet. Besides, we cannot leave the horses. They have been with us for a long time, and we elves value our animal companions as much as our bipod companions. As loath as I am to leave your company, we just cannot travel with you fellows," Losolin replied sadly.

"Ah, come on. We can take yer bloody beasts with us. An' as fer yer army, they can march right on to yer home. Tha's what armies are s'posed to do. An' they'll pick up more recruits walkin' across the lan' then if they sailed. They've done a'right so far, what's another three weeks gonna do to 'em?" Troaz protested, downing a swallow of wine.

"That is true. But I would have to send them a messenger, and more money for food and supplies too. I am afraid it is just too much trouble," the male elf said.

Alexander shook his head. "Nay. Send a messenger to yer army tonight, and then have him meet us at the old abandoned harbor in Purheae. We'll sail slowly, take ye around to see what the sea is really like, and then we'll meet him. As fer money, yer a prince and princess of the richest land in Nymyños. What gold ye lose here will be repaid in full once ye get back to Blackhaven. 'Side, if yer with us, ye have no reason fer gold. We take what we want fer how much we want. 'Tis as easy as that."

Tlonna and Losolin looked at each other. Tlonna looked away from him. "It would be easier on me. I am weak Losolin. I do not think I would make it all the way on horseback, even if it is Takîreaes."

"All right." Losolin slapped the table. "We will do it. I will send a runner to the army tonight. Help me write it, will you?"

The corsairs grinned at each other and hastily supplied the elf with, pen, ink, and parchment. Within the hour, the message, and large bag of money, was handed to Dawson who slipped it into his bag, mounted his horse, and with a hasty bow, rode away. When they broke the news to the others, there was even more celebrating. Jack and Kayra kissed and then danced away across the deck of *Zaedic's Bane.* The next morning, the horses were brought out and two large harnesses, kept at harbor for the use of all ships, were mounted on the deck of the corsair ships. Takîreaes and Neñyos were the first to be loaded onto *The Silver Crest.* The horses screamed and kicked as they were hoisted into the air. It took until midday to get the beasts all loaded and taken down to the hold. Their supplies were brought on board and stored away. Finally, the crew boarded and the anchors were hauled up.

Erdwyf looked sadly back at the departing land, her large eyes tear bright.

"What is wrong, Erdwyf?" Tlonna asked, coming to stand next to her.

"I just wonder when I will next see my parents. It had been so long, and the visit was a short one. Maybe someday I will come back and spend a while there. It would be nice, I think. They are good folk," the Advisor replied quietly, wiping her eyes. "This land is so wonderful. I will bring you all back here after the war is over, and you will see. Even though magic is not allowed, it is still a good place to live."

"I am sorry you have to leave it again. I am sure we could ask the corsairs to drop us off. I do not think they would say no."

"Ah no. Even though it would be nice, the sooner I am away from here, the sooner I will feel better. It is odd, though. I am the first in my family to have ever moved away from Narnen. The Rhaeetigans have always held the place of Count and Countess or some such title there. When my grandparents decided it was time for their *Haithen*, my parents took on their role. It was to be the same for me, but then I married Ghealan and moved away. They fear now who will take my place instead."

Tlonna studied her thin hands and then looked at the other elf. "What is Hyathen?"

Erdwyf chuckled. "No, *Haithen*, it is an elven ritual. Because of our long lifespan, it is very difficult for a new generation to take charge. There would be no change. When an elf reaches a certain age, most of the time in the thousand years, sometimes more, they decide to make their *Haithen*. Humans call it suicide, but it is not so grotesque as that. When they decide it is time, an elf, or elf couple, will write their will, take care of all their affairs, and then stab themselves in the heart. It is quick, but honorable. That is how most successions happen, in our race. I suppose the human race should call it euthanasia, but they do not see it our way. My parents had planned on making their *Haithen* a few years back, when my mother turned four thousand years old, but they have not found a proper heir yet."

"Oh. Does every elf do it?" Tlonna asked, intrigued.

"Every elf but one or two that I know of. There are those survivors from the most ancient of civilizations, the High Elves of Serenyi. It is a land now gone, sunk into the ocean thousands of years ago. It is the story of how Nymyños was founded, at least according to legend. Called *Udu Serenyi, nó Mlek Nymyños*. I will have to tell it to you later, for it is lengthy and involved, but it says that those elves were mighty and had great power with earth and magic both. They lived endlessly, never dying unless slain. They were true immortals, like gods. At least until Brandon Stynbek came along and destroyed them.

"There is one elf alive who claims to be one of the Serenyi High Elves, and she looks the part. Her face is odd, feral and angled. I have only met her once, a hundred or so years ago. She claims to be nine thousand years old. Can you imagine? *Nine thousand.* I do not even want to think about living that long. Alloran says she will never perform *Haithen.*"

"Wow." Tlonna was dumbstruck. "And that?" the Magin Queen pointed at the half-healed wound on Erdwyf's forearm.

"Ah... consider it a debt paid, Tlonna. There are things that you will be told later, but you do not need to worry about right now. You need to heal before you learn our story."

"I am ashamed to know that anyone was hurt because of me," Tlonna replied sadly.

Erdwyf shook her head. "We were not hurt because of you. We were hurt because of Midian, you most of all. Do not discount your own injuries just because they are no longer visible. Kayra told us of the condition you were in when they found you. Your mental suffering will take much longer, but we will all be here for you."

"I know, and that is what makes it all bearable," Tlonna replied quietly, smiling at the advisor.

The two females stood in companionable silence before Yayènia joined them.

"Hoi! What are we talking about over here?" the warrior put her arms around her two friends' necks.

"I was just telling Tlonna about *Haithen* and Alloran, the purported Serenyi High Elf. What have you been up to?" Erdwyf replied, laughing.

"I was teasing Jack and Kayra. They want to wed, if you can believe it. Kayra, the little proper lady, marrying a corsair. Ha! Just think of their poor children. Raised on a ship with Kayra's manners. Poor brats," Yayènia laughed.

The trio chuckled at the thought, but found themselves smiling at the prospect. As if summoned, the two lovers appeared on deck from below, Jack's arms wrapped tightly around Kayra. Losolin jumped out of their meandering way and trotted to where the females were standing.

"I was just down to see the horses. They are getting used to the sea, I think. At least their stomachs have settled. It smells much better down there, now that it is all cleaned out. And I checked in on

Rhiannan. She has finally stopped shouting, and is actually sleeping. I think we need to get her out of that dress. Are any of you willing to part with some clothes?" Losolin said, wrapping his arm around Tlonna.

"I think that is a good idea. I will go find something right now. Perhaps we can get it to her before she wakes up," Tlonna replied, kissing his cheek.

She twisted out of Losolin's grip and walked across to the hatch door. She climbed down the ladder and went into her bunker. She found her extra bag beneath Yayènia's, Suneelo's, Aladorn's, and Losolin's.

The Magin pulled out a gray tunic and a pair of black trousers. Rhiannan still had her boots so Tlonna left her other pair in her bag. Walking out of the bunker, the elf strode quietly down to the end of the narrow hall and quietly unlocked to door to the tiny storage room Rhiannan occupied. A small cot was pushed up against one side, and a chamber pot was on the other side. Rhiannan lay sleeping on the cot, her bounteous raven hair tossed over face to hide the savage beauty beneath. One slightly pointed ear poked out of the curls, catching Tlonna's attention. She knelt and placed the pile of clothes beside the cot and watched her daughter sleep.

The thin shoulders rose slightly as Rhiannan breathed, the filthy yellow dress partially ripped open in the back, freeing the half-elf's neck. Smiling grimly, Tlonna stood and walked out of the room, closing the door behind her. Turning down the hall, she went down the short stairway to enter the hold. The horses greeted her with whickers and snorts. She visited them a while before heading back up to be with her friends.

Evening was coming on fast as the ships sailed further away from land. They turned hard to starboard as they sailed out of the main way for the harbor. The sails snapped as the wind caught them, and the ships lurched forward. Great waves crashed against the hulls, spraying seawater on the sea goers. The passengers actually found themselves happy to be back on water, their sea legs having finally grown.

A shout from Mo up in the crow's nest made all on deck look up. The corsair was pointing down at them, towards the boom sweep. The crew swung around as a large crack and a whooshing sound filled their ears. Kayra screamed as the boom swung inward. Alexander attempted to turn the ship around hard enough to slow the boom, but to no avail. Jack careened into Kayra just before the boom, slamming her hard into the deck. They rolled across the deck too fast for anyone to catch them. At the worst possible moment, the ship heaved with the waves, and sent the two overboard.

"Man overboard! Man overboard!" screamed Losolin, along with most of everybody else.

He grabbed onto the loose boom line and swung out over the water. He dropped into the frigid sea. Salt water exploded into his mouth and nostrils, making the elf gasp. He pushed himself upward toward the surface until his head broke, and he gasped in air. Kayra and Jack had disappeared beneath the water. Sucking in a large breath, the elf dove under and opened his eyes. Green ocean filled his sight, stinging his eyes with salt. A glimmer of white caught his attention and he swam after it. Just when he thought he was about to run out of air, Losolin grabbed onto Jack's tunic and Kayra's arm. With elfish strength, he held them with one arm and swam toward the surface with the other.

Water rushed off his head as he broke surface once more. Kayra and Jack floated unconscious on his arm. A rope ladder came hurling at him from atop the tall ship. They had not dropped anchor, so the elf had to lunge for it before it passed him. With a tremendous heave, the corsairs and elves above him hauled the three in, pulling them on board. Hands slapped Losolin on the back, making him spit more seawater up. He stood and watched as the crew slapped Jack on the back, trying to get him to wake up, and they pushed on Kayra's diaphragm. With a cough, Jack vomited up water, and what looked like his lunch. He wiped his mouth and then looked at his lover. Kayra still lay limp in Axl's arms. He grabbed her shoulders and shook her.

"Kayra! Kayra wake up! Come on! It's me Jack! Wake up! Come on!" he shouted at her, shaking the young woman like a doll.

Losolin pulled him off and set Kayra down on the deck. With a few murmured words, he placed his hand on her forehead. When he drew away, Kayra promptly sat up and vomited over the side of the ship. Her brown locks hung limp across her face and back. Jack grabbed her and wrapped his arms around her waist.

"Oh Jack! You saved my life! That wooden pole would've killed me. Oh Jack I love you!" Kayra sobbed, kissing her lover all over.

With the spectacle over, the corsairs and elves left them to themselves. Axl helped Boxer tie down the boom and check the rest of the ship for malfunctioning parts. Night descended over them like a blanket and the ships slowed in the night air. Troaz swung aboard from his own and was greeted with jests all around. He took and gave accordingly, even grabbing Angus in a headlock and giving him a good knuckling. He then disappeared into his commodore's quarters and stayed there for a long while. The corsairs hallooed each other across the water, tossing odds and ends that the others had forgotten on *The Silver Crest* to *Zaedic's Bane*. It was nearing eleven before Alexander and Troaz walked back onto the deck.

They grinned at the corsairs and elves before throwing their arms up in the air and shouting "Dinnertime!"

The crew cheered and jumped in the air, always happy for food. Long trestle tables were pulled out and hastily set up for dinner. The ships dropped anchor, and the crew from *Zaedic's Bane* swung over to join the others. They rejoiced as Les and Corin, the new cook, brought out steaming plates of bread, hearty stew, wine, and corn straight from the cob. There was hardly a wait before they all dug in to their dinner.

Chapter 21
A Breath of Fresh Air

Miazie and her companions reached the city of Derid just as the gate was about to be shut for the night. The guards hailed them cheerfully and then slammed the doors closed. Relieved to be finally back in the city, Miazie grinned and sped Kaia forward with great haste. The city was still bustling, though no more travelers were allowed in. Hawkers and merchants shouted the quality of the goods over the usual dull roar of a city crowd. Lamp boys walked around on stilts holding their torch lighters and brought light to the streets.

The horses were slowed to a walk in the crowd, even stopping now and then. Miazie and Damon shouted at the mass below them, but few even looked up. It was much later when they finally reached the castle. Stable boys took the horses and sighing with relief, Miazie led her companions into the castle and greeted the doorman happily. The old man bowed his head and tipped his hat to her, smiling with crooked teeth.

A maid, lounging on a bench in the hallway started at their appearance when they rounded the corner. She leapt to her feet and curtsied hastily. Long red tresses swept off her shoulders like a waterfall as her face touched her knees. "My lords and ladies. Forgive me, I was just taking a small breather. I will get straight back to my chores," she started to turn when Miazie grabbed her arm.

The maid squeaked in fright and went to her knees. "Oh forgive me, your ladyship. I will go straight to the Head Maid to be punished first hand!"

"Stand up girl. I want only to ask you where King Demetrius is," Miazie said lightly, letting go of her.

The maid bounced to her feet and smiled. "He is in his study my lady. Would you like me to take you there, or would you like to freshen up first?"

"We will go to him now."

The maid curtsied again and then beckoned them to follow her. They went up a flight of stairs and into a large oval office. Demetrius looked up from his desk where a thick pile of parchment lay stacked before him. "Yes?"

The maid fell to her knees and bowed her head. "Your Excellency, this lady asked to see you right away, sir."

The king then looked at Miazie and smiled brightly. "Miazie! How good to see you alive and well. And you've brought friends!" the older man stood and came around his desk, taking no heed of the trembling girl on the carpet.

The four bowed deeply and then looked upon the king. Miazie grinned back at him. "This is Damon Suutson, my...*husband.* You should remember my friend Ryun the hunter who left with me this winter, and his new wife, Jacinth. We have brought news back for Tlonna. Where is she?"

Demetri's face fell. "Tlonna was taken months ago by Midian. Losolin left with most of your companions to go find her. The army marched behind them. I have not heard word of them since they left. I am sorry, but the likeliness of her being alive is scarce. However, this is not the right time to speak of this. You must be weary from your travels, and you smell to the high heavens. My servant here will take you to your rooms. Come speak with me at dinner. We shall have it here in my office. Go now," the king dismissed them and returned to his paperwork.

Stunned, the four departed behind the maid and were soon immersed in warm water and soap. At dinner, they spoke of what had occurred to them over the last few months Miazie had been gone. By the end, the Belau was in tears, desperate over the story of Tlonna.

On their way to bed afterward, a desperate Shireen launched herself at Miazie, sobbing and touching her face as though for reassurance.

"Shireen!" Miazie cried, hugging the other woman fiercely.

"They took her, Miazie! And Losolin left me here to keep watch for you. Oh gods, you're okay! I thought for sure you had perished as well. Months, it has been, Miazie, months that have been years for how terrible the wait has been. I don't know the words to express my relief at your return. Have you any news?"

Miazie found herself clutching the woman's arms in return. "I do not, my friend. I have no answers, for I have just received the story from King Demetrius myself. How was Aidyn when they left? Demetri said he nearly died, and would have were it not for Losolin."

Shireen took a deep breath to steady herself, for she had a soft spot for the assassin. "He was better. It took him over a month to be able to move once we got him to settle down. He killed a Healer by accident, but felt no remorse. Oh, Miazie it has been a horrible time."

"I am sorry Shireen. We are leaving tomorrow for Blackhaven, what will you do? Will you come with us?"

The young woman shook her head. "I think not, though one day I will go. There is a man, here, the royal herald. He is very kind to me, and we may...*may* wed."

Miazie summoned a smile from somewhere deep inside. "That is truly wonderful, Shireen. You must invite me if you do, I would be honored to attend."

Shireen smiled too, and hugged Miazie. "It is good to know you are safe. May the gods speed your journey, and the good spirits protect you. Miazie, you are a true friend, and I will always value all that you taught me. Thank you, and...when you see Tlonna and Losolin, give them my love. Please, for I know they will survive."

"I promise, blessed be, Shireen. Blessed be," the Belau returned and kissed her on the cheek.

Miazie slept badly, unable to keep the image of Tlonna weeping and bloody from her dreams. The next morning, the four washed and ran a list of supplies down to the kitchens and the horses were readied.

Miazie, back in her own comfortable red woolen dress with a split skirt for traveling, knocked on Demetrius' door. The king bade her enter, and the woman curtsied before him.

"King Demetri, I thank you for all of your kindness and hospitality. My friends and I must go to Blackhaven City to see what we can do to help the poor citizens there. Hopefully the rest of the kingdom is in safer hands."

The king rose and walked around his desk. "My child, do not fear for them. They are a strong people, they have survived worse than this. Most fought in the war of Aderiaen, remember. However, go in haste and safety. You will always have my support and aid if you need it. But, I would suggest that you take the route that runs around the border of Kajgenia, across the Liberated Lands on the north end, and straight through Purheae and Schelum. That will be the safest and fastest way. It is a well kept road, but not often used. I believe that it used to be a main road. Even paved with stone in some places. They do call it the Royal Road, but as for its real name, I don't know. I will supply you with a map as well. In fact..." Demetri stood and turned to the large cabinet behind him. He opened the doors and ruffled through some pieces of rolled parchment. "Aha! Here it is. The most recent mapping of the road that I own. I'm afraid it is old and stiff, but it should make its way for you," he handed Miazie the rolled paper.

"Thank you, your majesty. I will not forget you or your benevolence. I am in your debt," Miazie said, curtsying once more. She took his proffered hand in farewell and then hurried to meet her companions in the front hall.

Damon smiled, though it did not reach his eyes, and they walked out of the doors onto the steps, where just below them the horses stood ready. They mounted wearily and were out of city by midmorning and looked out across the farmland that covered the flat land for many miles.

Miazie situated herself, grimacing at her stiff muscles, and opened her book, *Tales of Nymyños, The Complete Works of Idid*, as Kaia plodded onward. Damon rode beside her and pulled out a piece of wood he had been whittling. A small bird was starting to form out of the block of pine. Behind them, Ryun and Jacinth conversed quietly.

It took almost an entire month and a half to get across the continent of Nymyños. The four companions rarely met any other travelers, and those they did would not talk or even look up from the road. As Demetri had said, parts of the road was paved with cobblestones, but most had been grown over and was now just hard packed earth. The month of Kayab was in full tilt and spring was overtaking the land. The taint had disappeared a few days earlier, suddenly. The black snow had melted, and no new snow fell. Brown grass erupted in patches along the border of the province of Blackhaven Forest. That which was normally green was bleak and depressing, silent in its oppressiveness.

"Sweet Spirits," whispered Miazie in shock. "I never dreamed a place of life and beauty could ever look like this. It is terrible."

The riders passed over the border and into the land of the elves. It took them almost a week to cross the kingdom to the walled city of Blackhaven Forest. Huge trees of bark so pale it was silver with black-green leaves shimmered in the dying sunlight of evening. They seemed to be the only thing living. A huge, impossible gate scowled down upon them from its great black wall. Fear gripped the travelers as they looked upon the formidable gate. The silence was oppressive, and rot was beginning to take its hold.

"How do we get in?" Jacinth asked in a hushed tone, her large eyes wide in her fair face.

"I don't know. Maybe we should ride around the wall to see if there is any other door that might be unlocked," Miazie proposed.

Damon moved his horse into a slow trot heading south along the wall. It took almost an hour to get to the back end of the city wall. The Fãrthyn Ocean splashed onto a long beach, crashing against the wall that extended on sand banks until the sea floor dropped away. Miazie cursed loudly and then sat down on the sandy bank. The others joined her, flopping down beside the frustrated Belau.

"Maybe we should ride back to the gate and wait for someone to open them," Ryun contributed to the silence.

"We might as well, for all the good it will do," Damon replied moodily.

Another hour-long ride took them back to the front gate where they hobbled the horses and started a fire. The next morning, Ryun saddled his horse and climbed atop her. His companions looked up at him.

"I am going to ride around the other side and see if there is a door there. I should be back before too long," the hunter turned his mare around and rode off into the evening.

Halfway to the sea, Ryun came upon the door the four elves had escaped from months earlier. He tested his strength against it and found it solid. He tried for many minutes to open it. Finally, he took out his sword and fitted it against the wall and the door. He tugged this way and that until finally he heard a creak. With a heave, Ryun yanked his sword out and the door slowly opened. He tied his horse to one of the trees behind him and entered the city. Silence even greater than outside the wall greeted him. Piles of ashes, mud, and debris filled his sight as he looked around. There was a rotting Darkwight a few feet away. Looking toward the west, he saw the great black castle of the elves, rising from the hill it sat on as though it had merely been formed there as a natural structure. A massive staircase caught his eye, the only seemingly unnatural part of the castle, it rose to the third floor, narrowing slightly. Even from this distance he could see where the wall simply fell away to form the entrance from the stairs. A shiver went down his spine as he stared at the castle. Huge trees rose against its beautifully crafted walls, the veins of pearl, silver, and gold shone in the waning light.

Ryun stood in awe for a moment before ducking back through the door. He carefully shut it and rode hastily back to the camp. His friends looked up at him, startled.

"I've found a way in! It is only halfway down the wall, a small side door. I got it open and stepped inside. I have seen the great castle!" the hunter was ecstatic with his news.

"What else did you see? Is there anyone alive? Was there anything promising?" Miazie asked urgently.

"No. I saw nothing but destruction. There was no one moving, it was so silent. But didn't Aidyn say they were living underground?"

"Indeed. We should go now," Miazie replied, kicking dirt on the fire.

The four packed up and readied the horses. They hurried to the side door, and reached it just as the sun was going down. It was a tight fit for the animals, but they got through and Ryun closed the door behind him. They headed in the direction of the castle, staying on the ruined, grass-woven street to muffle the horses' hooves. It took them nearly twenty minutes to get to the castle gates, another great black wall and another great gate. This one, however, was destroyed. Splinters of wood and metal lay forgotten on the ground, a memory of the siege. A few yards away, an entire section of the wall had been blown away. The companions stepped onto the entrance grounds to the castle and looked upon a large bridge that arched over a wide canal. The water was thick with mud, refuse, the dead, and other terrible things.

The four travelled quickly over the bridge and found themselves in a courtyard. Massive trees whispered above them, creating shadows within darkness. Ahead, the castle loomed great and beautiful, its giant glass-filled openings dark with the night.

"Around back," Miazie whispered to the others, who nodded.

They rode around the castle to the rear courtyard and shook their heads in dismay. In the moonlights, they could see the bleakness of what was once beautiful. A large statue sat in the center, an elf holding a bow knocked and ready for battle. His face was fierce and delicate at the same time. The amount of skill that had gone into the figure was overwhelming to the humans who sat before it. With a sharp breath, Ryun pointed at the base of the statue. A fine crack about the size of a small door had caught shadow in the moonlights.

"This is it! It must be!" Miazie whispered excitedly. She dismounted and began pushing on the door. It inched forward slowly until the others joined her. It finally swung open and revealed a dark passageway leading downward. The four looked at each other and smiled nervously. They entered.

It took them not long to reach a lighted passage that branched off in many directions. A dwarf started at their appearance and stood frozen. The male came up to the four humans' waists. His face was covered in a thick red beard and moustache. His green eyes peered at them in shock for a moment before narrowing.

The dwarf unstrung his hammer and smiled grimly. Before he could act, Miazie went to one knee and placed her hands flat upon the ground. "Sir Dwarf, I am a friend of Princess Tlonna. My name is Belau Miazie Paron Ughtren. Please, lead us to the king and queen. We have urgent news."

The dwarf grunted as he dropped his hammer in disbelief. "Is it true?" he whispered in a coarse voice.

"Yes. Please, take us to King Dietirin and Queen Constancias," Miazie pleaded, still bowing.

"Of course, this way," the dwarf beckoned them to follow and went through the passage ahead of them.

Elves, men, dwarves, sprytes, dryads, nymphs, and others stared at them as they passed. Some retreated back into their dirt rooms, closing doors of bark. Soon, the four stood in a large room in front of two thrones. Two imposing elves sat before them, their hard and wise eyes staring at them.

The four bowed as Miazie had to the dwarf. They felt oddly crude, even though the people around them were living underground and in shabby clothes.

King Dietirin spoke first. "*Leae feaen valõn, aikaid leae hochan shä klamen owne?*[1] "

"I am Miazie Paron Ughtren. This is my husband Damon, and my friends Ryun and Jacinth. We are friends of Tlonna, your daughter. We have urgent news of her, Losolin, and Aidyn," Miazie

---

[1] Who are you, humans who look of the east?

answered, hoping the king understood Hindarün.

"Tlonna? You know her? How does she fare? Why is she not with you?" Dietirin asked, stepping down from his throne and kneeling in front of Miazie. "Please, tell us all you know."

Miazie told the king and queen all of what had happened that she knew from the time she had first met Tlonna. She did not realize what a long story it was until she finished, her mouth dry and tears leaking from her eyes. Tlonna's father wept in grief, his face contorted into the impossible beauty of anguish. Those in the throne room wept as well. Constancias, her mother, did not weep. She gazed on her husband's back with narrowed eyes. Miazie felt for sure she would be killed because of the new she bore.

At last, Dietirin wiped his eyes and took a deep breath. "You said you have horses outside the door? I shall send someone to retrieve them. I am sure you are hungry and tired. Rooms will be prepared for you, as much as they can be. Tell me, have you heard nothing of four elves, Suneelo, Yayènia, Erdwyf, and Ghealan?"

"No, I am sorry. I received a letter months ago from them, addressed to Tlonna and Losolin, and I replied, but that is the last I heard," Miazie replied, shaking her head.

"Yes. We received your letter. What of the city, did you see anyone alive? Anything moving?" Constancias asked, wringing her hands.

"No. There was no life in those streets. No black shrouded guards and no giant birds either. Your kingdom has been abandoned," the Belau said, standing at the king's bidding. Her silent companions remained bowing, shaking with the effort. They rose with the king's finger.

"I do not know whether that is good or bad news. I had hoped that there were at least a few of our people still living. But I suppose most of them did come down here with us. Hiding like cowards, living in squalor and famine. You know, most of the humans and dwarves have died? Us creatures of the land though, we persevere!" Constancias said angrily, shaking her fist at the dirt ceiling.

"I am sorry your highness." Miazie said, backing away a step.

Dietirin interrupted his wife before she could attack the human and said, "Your rooms are ready. Dinner is served in the long hall. Just follow the crowd. It should be coming up here soon. You may have time to take a quick sponge bath and change your clothes. I will have some water sent to your rooms."

The four humans bowed their way out of the room and followed a tall wood nymph down a passage to yet another hall of bark doors. She gestured to two rooms across the hall from each other with a brown finger. The two couples separated and they collapsed onto the small straw pallet beds. Almost too soon, another nymph knocked on the door and entered holding two pales of warm water and clean rags. Miazie and Damon smiled and took the burden from the female, who smiled back. Her green hair looked like grass in the summer time, dark and soft. Soon after the two had washed, a tumultuous clamor was heard in the earthen hallway outside their door.

Pulling aside the bark, Miazie thought at first the underground hideout had been attacked, but then realized a smell of onions wafted through the hall. Children skipped and leaped about, their filthy clothes flapping in the air. A young woman beckoned to the couple standing in their doorway and they followed. Damon and Miazie clung together, as comrades in a city full of strangers, and they were swept down the hall to a large chamber filled with rows of long tables. Lines of people of all different races jostled each other in mostly a good humor, waiting for food. Steam filled the air as tubs of salted beef were opened. Pots of white rice, stored for years and years after being imported from Zeynuwn, were carried from the ovens and placed on the serving tables to be spooned in heaps onto the plates of the hungry mass. Onions spilled out of more pots, and fresh baked bread was lifted out of bread ovens.

Miazie and Damon stared about in awe as impossible masses of people and food poured into the hall. The Belau tapped the shoulder of a woman in front of her. The elderly female turned, revealing a blue tinted face and dark blue eyes.

"Yes?" the water nymph asked in a voice like calm old waters.

"Where does all this food come from? I would expect famine to be part of living underground for nearly nine years," Miazie asked.

"Ah. Well it was. Then the dwarves became restless and began carving tunnels into the city. All the food stores were relocated slowly here. Food is growing sparse though, I fear soon we will be surviving on very small rations."

"Oh. Well fear no longer. There is help coming. And with the city abandoned, it can now be repaired and inhabited once more," the

Belau replied.

"The city is abandoned?" the water nymph asked quietly, excitedly.

"Ah...yes. But do not spread it around. We haven't come up with a plan yet to bring back the life of Blackhaven."

The old female turned away from Miazie then and became silent. It took a long time for the two humans to reach the serving line. While they were eating, a hush fell over the meal hall and an important looking elf walked down the aisles to the front of the room. He was a strange and exotic looking male, with silver hair and amber eyes.

"That's Feorien, the queen's personal protégé," a man said to the couple he was sitting across from.

Miazie nodded understandingly.

The elf cleared his throat to command attention. "The honorable King Dietirin and Queen Constancias have called an audience with you all. It shall be in the public meeting hall tonight before curfew. All are commanded to attend. Continue," Feorien announced haughtily, his chin high.

"He's the queen's bastard," the man said after the elf had left the meal hall.

"The queen had an affair?" Miazie asked, shocked.

"Nay, that's just what we call him. Thinks he's of noble blood, the queen's own son. King Dietirin hates him, and Feorien returns the feeling. The king's tried several times to dispatch him to be a runner, but Queen Constancias continually forbids it. He used to try and get the Lady Yayènia, the High Commander, to split with her husband and marry him. The Lady strung him out a window once by his feet and left him there to hang all night. She was almost discharged for that by the queen, but the king wouldn't allow it. Now he tries to weasel into any relationship with any female he can get."

"I heard he proposed to Lady Aralir, and she accepted!" a dryad two seats away from Damon said quietly.

"Nay Forla, that's all rumor. Lady Aralir would never stoop that low. Even if that dog was of noble blood, she wouldn't say yes to someone that snooty," someone else replied.

"I don't know Arjuna, it is said that lady Aralir is getting lonely and even put out a proclamation saying she would marry the first man to win her heart," Another said.

Soon, nearly the whole section was in an uproar about Feorien and Aralir and some other elf by the name of Waithen and his sister Sharntun. Miazie and Damon slipped out unnoticed and began to explore their surroundings. The underground city was complete with workshops, training rooms for the fighters, thousands of rooms, even some small gardens and pools. Everywhere there were more citizens of Blackhaven. Dwarves repairing the walls with water, chisel, and hammer. A swarm of people ran screaming toward the two humans, waving their hands in the air. A man grabbed Miazie arm and was knocked aside by Damon. A small army of dwarves trotted back to where the people ran from, and they followed.

Wreckage and a few bodies lay in heap, a portion of sky showing above the collapsed tunnel. The dead were pulled out and hastened away. The rest of the dwarves stared up at the sky, their eyes full of longing. A wind full of fresh air filled the tunnel like a refreshing drink of water after a long hike in the desert. For a moment, nothing happened except the breathing in of air. Then, reluctantly, the dwarves began shifting through the rubble to find the supports. Only one was undamaged. The rest was in splinters.

Damon and Miazie bent to the task of shoveling the dirt way. Finally, Damon lifted his hands and beckoned the dwarves away. They hesitantly obeyed, standing back next to Miazie. The human twirled his hands in the air and red light enveloped them. The earth lifted away and plastered itself to the hole and the support embedded itself against it. The splintered wood packed itself back into poles and took their place once more. The dwarves stared uncomprehendingly before cheering the Magin, clapping him on the lower back.

That night, the king and queen told their subjects about Tlonna and her story. The crowd was bittersweet after that. Having learned about their precious city being abandoned, they were cheerful, but they had loved Tlonna and Losolin dearly.

After that, Damon was called upon to help repair this or that, to lift a dwarf up to the ceiling in the meal hall, and many other things. Ryun and Jacinth had gotten separated from them except for at night when they said goodnight across the hall. Ryun had been recruited as a curfew soldier, so he often slept during the day. He wandered the halls at night, making sure everyone was in bed so that the dwarves and others could repair things without being hampered by tons of people. Jacinth was hired as a kitchen maid and helped serve food.

Miazie was called into Dietirin and Constancias' throne room day after day to help fill in the gaps of Tlonna's recent life.

The underground city life continued on as it had for years. The people remained barely conscious of the struggles their leaders fought to keep them fed and cared for. Repairs were needed more and more often as the halls got older and worn. And still the people of Blackhaven City lived on.

Chapter 22
Reclaiming Blackhaven

The two clipper ships turned into the wide harbor of Blackhaven and everyone got their first glance of the city's desolation. Visible above all was the gigantic castle and its wall, shining like a beacon in the morning light. Most of the seaside buildings were destroyed, along with the buildings farther up near the castle wall. Tlonna and Losolin gazed out in awe, their hearts lifting at being home, even if it was destroyed. The others with them looked about in trepidation. The ships waded into the docks and the corsairs tied the lines down. The sails were tied up and the anchors dropped. The gangplank was hauled out and the crew disembarked.

Within the hour, the crew and their friends had unloaded the horses and were riding toward the castle wall. Yayènia and Erdwyf rode ahead to check for Midian's retainers. When everyone met them, they had opened the gate at the back of the wall and were holding it open to the great courtyard. Tlonna was the first to step inside, gazing about her forgotten home in wry joy. Everything was dead. No birds sang in the trees, except scavengers and most of those were silent. The only thing that seemed to be untouched was the great statue of the archer in the center. It was there that Yayènia and Erdwyf led their companions. They opened the door and led them inside.

Dank mustiness greeted them, with the faint smell of onions and rice. The horses whickered in the darkness. Soon they were in the center of the hallways and heading towards the middle one when a spryte saw them. She stared at them, not recognizing them for they were cloaked and hooded. Nothing showed of their faces except the torchlight gleaming in their eyes. The spryte turned and fled back down the hall she had come from.

After that, the company moved faster, still hidden within their cowls. They met lots of people who all turned tail and fled. However, within a few minutes they were standing in the throne room. The king and queen stared at them in shock before standing.

It was the queen who spoke first. "Who are you and how did you find this place? Speak now or never speak again!" she drew a dagger from her sleeve and advanced toward them.

The five elves, Yayènia, Erdwyf, Suneelo, Ghealan, and Aidyn all dropped their hoods quickly and bowed. Dietirin and Constancias stood stock still as they stared down at their old subjects. Yayènia rose first.

"I see you are out of prison. Too bad, that."

Constancias raised her arm, but Dietirin stopped her. The queen shot her husband a filthy look.

Yayènia went on. "King Dietirin, we have crossed Nymyños twice, once by land, and once by sea to bring you a great gift. We have suffered losses great and small, and have made many friends. Do not punish us, for this gift is greater than any you can imagine," the warrior said, not flinching before their hard gaze.

The four others rose and looked straight into Dietirin's kind blue eyes. Constancias backhanded Yayènia, bringing blood to the younger elf's lips. "First you leave without permission, write no letters back to us to tell of where you are, go romping across the land, and think to go unpunished because you bring a trinket? You bitch! I shall have you hung for your treachery. You and these four others."

Yayènia wrapped her fingers around the still raised wrist and bent it backward until the queen was forced to her knees. Dietirin stepped quietly aside and watched. Suneelo's knife was laid against her throat, the edge pricking the snow-white skin. A tiny drop of blood appeared, stark color against pure white.

"Call this gift a mere trinket and I swear to you and all present I will slit your throat from one ear to the other. Understand?" Suneelo growled dangerously.

Constancias nodded almost imperceptibly and was allowed to stand. Dietirin looked from each face to another and his eyes narrowed, but not meanly. "What is this... gift you bring us, my friends?"

Ghealan took Tlonna and Losolin by the hand and led them to the front. With a whispered urge, the two took down their cowls. For a moment, nothing happened. Then the throne room erupted in howls and cheers. The king stared at his daughter for a split second before pulling her into a great embrace. The royal guard and the others in the room careened into the new arrivals with laughs and hoots. When everyone had calmed slightly, Dietirin flopped onto his throne, tears shining on his face. He took Tlonna's hands and pressed them to his lips.

"My daughter... my daughter," he whispered. "I have waited so long, my child, I lost hope, but here you are, you and your wonderful consort. Losolin, my son, I officially grant you the title of Lord Consort of Blackhaven. Tlonna," here the king's voice broke and he sobbed into his daughter's hair.

The next day, they all gathered in the throne room to tell the entire story, though they left out that Haydyn and Rhiannan, standing off to the left, were the offspring of Midian and Tlonna, or that children had even been birthed. People rushing into the room to see if the rumors were true often interrupted it. Finally, near dinnertime, when the whole story was told and the companions were allowed to eat separate from everybody else, a runner was sent to fetch Miazie and her friends. Tlonna stood and embraced her friend as the human rushed in. Losolin and those who had known him before greeted Ryun warmly. When finally Tlonna and Miazie broke apart, with plenty of tears, the Belau was introduced to the corsairs and the other elves. The human was slightly awed by meeting the legendary warriors but smiled and accepted hands readily enough.

It was then that the announcement was made to Tlonna.

"You must go before your people and tell them of your return. You are their beloved Princess Tlonna. They are at dinner now. We have three separate times of dinner so the announcement will have to be made three times. They, as we did, believe you dead. Go now and spread the wonderful news," Dietirin said, hugging his daughter. "And you all as well. Go with her. You all deserve great honor."

So they went to the great hall and traversed the two center aisles, feeling the hundreds of stares upon them. They stood at the front, running their eyes over the disbelieving faces of so many races. No noise could be heard except the hissing of the steam from the kitchen. No child even gurgled. Taking a deep breath Tlonna began.

"People of Blackhaven City,"

Erdwyf joined her in Elvish. *"Muchen shä Kairhotuss Arben,"*

"I, Tlonna Arune Ewôsdírn have returned."

"Inkan Belidona yercht so."

"The city that you so love is now safe to return to."

"Klamen arben hyan valõn est yayena puscheb melas hovan eshoun sa eshoun."

"There is much work to be done and so much to rebuild."

"*Konuae puscheb vena lobar eshoun eaf klamen est vena eshoun kruen.*"

"However, an army is on its way to help us. No home will remain rubble, and no street will remain destroyed. Life will come back to this city if I have to do it all myself!"

"*Udwa, lãn sanf puscheb mün shaeben vwek eshoun adi akod. Noya duned bene suddi slad, klamen noya way suddi nasen. Sen bene yest tauon puscheb taietan arben halo inkan yercht puscheb nyn shaiben xellt sârtyn!*"

The crowd erupted into wild cheers of jubilation and happiness. Many rushed forward to embrace the companions up front. It took a long time for the hall to calm down again and Tlonna left with her friends and a happy farewell.

Early the next morning, Tlonna and Losolin went to the throne room where Dietirin and Constancias were breakfasting. The king beamed up at them and had two more chairs brought in. While bowls of porridge were being poured, the four began to speak.

"I am going to take my companions and go into the city today. Our people deserve to return to the lives they want, and need. We are going to make sure all is safe and then come back and report on what we find," Tlonna said, watching her parents' faces.

Constancias came close to sneering. "And what are you going to do if you run into trouble? You are a princess, Tlonna, you do not know how to fight, and neither does your...Losolin."

Tlonna gave her mother a searching look. "I have taken many lives, and fought back to back with Losolin more times than I can count, and we are the ones left alive. I am sure, Mother, that whatever awaits up there is nothing to what we have endured."

"I agree, but first we must unseal you. Move away from the table," Dietirin replied before Constancias could argue, pushing back his chair.

Tlonna did as she was told, kneeling before father. Red light surrounded her, warming her flesh. She felt it settle in her gut and wrap around the cold ball of nothingness. There was stillness for a long, terrible moment, and then for the first time in months, Tlonna felt her power infuse her body.

The elf felt complete happiness at that moment. With an overwhelming urge, she stood and let a ball of light dance on her palm. Tears ran down her face, exulting in being able to use her magic once more. Letting the ball fade, Tlonna rushed her father and embraced him. After a few seconds went by, the princess stepped back and wiped her eyes.

"Thank you, Father... thank you," she said thickly. "I thought it lost forever."

"Such things are never lost forever, my child, even though in darkness it may seem so," Dietirin replied, smiling.

Tlonna grinned and pulled Losolin up from his chair. "We will take our leave, now, and go into the city. We will be back sooner or later,"

"Make it sooner, daughter, for I have missed you too much."

The princess returned her father's embrace and bowed to her mother, who snorted.

Tlonna, Losolin, Miazie, and their friends left the underground city before the mist of dawn had completely evaporated. Alexander and his crew formed a wide circle around the elves and other humans. Yayènia unsheathed her twin blades and rested them against her shoulders. Tlonna held the white sword at her side, the armor Demetrius had commissioned resting comfortably against her body. Dawson, the scout sent to the army, had been waiting at Purheae Harbor as planned, but he had brought the armor with him. Tlonna had been reduced to tears over the gift.

They bypassed the castle and walked directly into the city. Darkwights and mercenary soldiers were spread throughout the city in small numbers. The group moved first into the Peerage District set between the western wall and the castle wall. It was where Yayènia, Suneelo, Erdwyf, and Ghealan lived. A small patrol of mercenaries had taken over Tiena manor and Yayènia and Suneelo reclaimed it with vengeance.

In a rare display of emotion, Yayènia fell to her knees and cried at the sight of her home, burnt in many places and viciously looted. Her one consolation was the room she had asked Dietirin to ward was untouched. It held her and Suneelo's heirlooms, their money, books, records, and their weapons. Otherwise, the two-story sandstone mansion was empty but for the beds and belongings of the mercenaries.

A few other manors had been occupied as well. Many, those

made of timber, had been burned to the ground, but others had been claimed. Ghealan and Erdwyf found their house unlooted but partially torn down. Erdwyf, too, wept. The entire front was laid out on the ground, exposing the dining hall, kitchen, and upstairs bedrooms to the elements.

All the gardens in the District had been burned or torn up, leaving only large clumps of dried soil and dead foliage. After that, the company moved into the Inner Farm District where farms were nestled against each other within the walls of the city. Most of them had been burned and the entire place seemed abandoned.

They moved from there to the Market District, where most shops were set up, split in twain by the main road of Blackhaven City, Obsidian Way. Here, they found the most wreckage. Shops had been razed to the ground, windows were shattered, inventories thieved, doors ripped off hinges, and bodies strewn everywhere, partially decomposed. Obsidian Way's grass weave was stained rust brown from old blood. Here and there, a wasted dog would snarl at them, or a cat would flee. Darkwights and mercenaries roamed the stores, looking for escapees. They always tried to run when they saw the group, but they died before they made it three steps.

It was late afternoon by the time they made it to the Civilian District, where the city folk dwelled. Homes in every sort of architecture lined the serpentine streets that wound through the trees. Dwarven structures of stone with sharp lines and rough edges, human houses of timber and brick, gabled and pristine, elfin homes that melded into the landscape, beautiful and unobtrusive. There were nymph buildings with clay glazed in bright colors that reflected their personal elements: fire, water, wood, and stone. Faery dwellings were found as well; tiny little huts placed in the spaces between lawns or perched in trees. Spryte buildings with spiraling outside stairways and small towers, made from white or rose colored granite. And more, every race having found their way to Blackhaven City, the city of wonders and monarchical freedom.

All of it, representations of every race, destroyed. Ashes lay soaked into the ground, stone felled by hammers and siege weapons. Trees uprooted and left to rot. Faery huts smashed underfoot, gardens and lawns burnt to leave starving dirt exposed to the unrelenting elements. The devastation was horrible to see, but it was the bodies within the homes that brought most of the companions to their knees in misery and nausea.

Families huddled together for protection, hewn through unmercifully. Children slaughtered, babies dashed against walls, women raped and made to watch their children die. Men made to watch their families slain. It was visible on their decomposing faces, mouths agape in screams of pain and horror. Hands outstretched, fingers bent like claws.

Miazie retched for the third time upon entering yet another scene of destruction. Erdwyf sobbed into Ghealan's shoulder. Yayènia and Tlonna glanced at each other, their features shadowed and grave.

It was there that most of the enemy had taken up residence. On each street, they found at least two occupied houses, the original occupants heaped outside or buried in crude mass graves. The companions slaughtered the Zaedicans with fury, their wrath lending strength to muscles. They were dripping with blood and splattered with offal when they finally reached the Militia District. It sat in the center of the Civilian's District. They had made a wide spiral, closing in on the wooden wall that surrounded the compound.

Yayènia yanked open the door to her realm and howled in dismay. The training yards had been churned by thousands of enemy feet and never flattened out. The barracks had been torn down; the weapon sheds emptied and burned. Ghealan closed his eyes and looked away, his anger barely contained. Yayènia grabbed a plank of wood that lay by her feet and chucked it. It clattered against the barracks a score of yards away.

Tlonna shook her head and patted Yayènia on the shoulder. "We will rebuild it, Nia, do not worry. We will rebuild it even better than it was."

"Of course we will, but stab me thrice and drown me, the bastards destroyed everything! My home, my city, and my compound! I... I should have killed more of them. I should not have given that bastard even a chance to decide his fate; I should have cut his head off the second I found him!"

Suneelo grabbed his wife's shoulders and hugged her against his chest. "You did what was honorable and right, my love, and that is what separates you from the enemy. You do not take heedlessly and you do not destroy that which is beloved to innocents. Tlonna is right, we will rebuild it all, and it will be better. You will see, love. I promise."

Tlonna nodded and Yayènia sniffed, her big blue eyes rising from the ground to assess her beloved training yards. "I suppose we should return to the underground."

"Aye," the group agreed and trudged down the tree-lined path that led directly from the Militia District to the castle's rear courtyard.

It was nearing dark when they opened the door in the fountain. They could hear the clamor of dinner and headed for the throne room.

The next morning, Tlonna and Losolin met with Tlonna's parents again for breakfast. Constancias attempted to hide a glare at Losolin, but they saw it and Losolin met it with a steady gaze. The queen dropped her eyes first.

Tlonna sighed and took a seat beside her mother. Losolin bowed to Dietirin and sat next to the king. When the porridge and cheese arrived, the older male cleared his throat and laced his fingers together behind his bowl.

"You said last night you and your companions wiped out the remaining forces of Midian's army?"

Tlonna blinked. "Yes."

"Would the people be able to handle seeing the city as it is now?"

"It will be hard," she began, "but they are a strong people, Father. Most of their homes have been destroyed, the shops and stands razed or burnt. But, I think seeing it the way it is now will make them work harder and faster to rebuild it. It is their city, Father, and even I, not remembering it, want to get knee deep in sludge rebuilding Blackhaven."

Constancias made a sound akin to choking. "Tlonna, you are their princess! You will not get knee deep in anything! That is a job for," she cast a look at Losolin, "*peasants.*"

"You forget, Mother, that I have spent the last few months of my life in a cell, wearing nothing but rags and my own blood. I reached the lowest of low, and I count peasantry not among that list. Common folk are what make a city. They are the people of a race, culture. They bring in food, merchandise, and money. They build the things we use, the things we need. They are the blood of society, and no amount of poverty can take that away."

Constancias looked saddened. "Oh, Tlonna my daughter, you are yet naïve, for all the things you have seen. What you experienced was not a lowly thing. You survived, and now it does not matter, nothing came of it that has made any change in you. Peasants do not matter, either, and I hope one day you will realize that."

Dietirin placed a hand on Tlonna's before she could reply. "Love, you and I will speak later of some petty issues, but for now, do you think it safe for me to make the announcement that Blackhaven is reclaimable?"

Taking the hint, Tlonna smiled and nodded. "I think our people have been down here eight...no, *nine* years too long, what say you we take them home?"

Dietirin grinned and said, "Aye, let us take them home."

The four elves left the throne room and went to a massive chamber that Tlonna and Losolin had not known existed. Dietirin went to a podium with a red orb floating above it. He bent down so that his mouth was close to it. When he spoke, his voice echoed through the underground city.

"This is your king. People of Blackhaven, there is to be a city meeting now. Please drop all things and come to the city cavern now. This is an order."

Within a half hour, the cavern was jam-packed with milling people of all races. Feorien and a dryad shoved their way to the front and climbed the dais where the four stood. They went to stand behind the king and queen, folding their arms threateningly. As the last few people squeezed into the hall, Dietirin raised his hand and the crowd quieted. The king smiled down upon his people and then stepped to the edge of the raised platform.

"My dear subjects. As most of you are aware, my daughter Tlonna has come home. Along with her, our dear friend, Losolin, and the five elves that risked their lives to find her. In addition, a select number of corsairs and people from all of Nymyños who played a very important role in her rescue and return. We have met new friends and old in this hole that we have lived in for nine years. How many of us have strived for a bit of fresh air, how many have us have yearned for a bit of sunlight? It is time, my children, for us to go home! Our beloved city awaits us! This will be no small task, cleaning up the wreckage of Midian Rahlan. But he and his kith are dead. Our time is nigh! Gather your things now and ready your families to go above. Do not stampede or rush, but please stand in the main hallway as we help you out. After you are out, stay in the yard until we have told you what to do. This night, we sleep beneath the stars!" the elf king shouted, punching the air with his fist.

The crowd below cheered and roared with such vehemence that the cavern shook and clods of dirt fell down. The people left the cavern in a rush and soon the hall was empty.

Tlonna left Losolin in their room and found her father in his. "You wished to speak with me?"

Dietirin smiled at her. "My daughter, I have missed you so. I have prayed to the gods and spirits for you to return. Know that I love you."

"I do, father, I do," Tlonna said tearfully. "Oh!" she gasped suddenly and rooted around in her pocket. "I found one of them," she said, handing her father the black pendant from Kajgenia.

Dietirin took it with shaking hands. "This... how did you ever find it? Tlonna, the pendant! You found one! That is amazing!"

Tlonna shrugged. "A Cleick had it, in Kajgenia. Midian had the other one, and I could not retrieve it."

"You are wonderful, do you know that?" her father laughed, putting the pendant around his neck.

Tlonna laughed. "Mother does not seem to think so."

Dietirin sighed. "Your mother... she is... well... she loves you, but she is not one who displays emotion."

Tlonna let out a small laugh. "I have heard the stories."

"Then you know her feelings about you and Losolin?"

"Aye, and I do not care what she-." Tlonna began, but cut off when her father lifted his hand.

"I know, I know, daughter. I just want you to know that she will not interfere again. You have my permission, as father, as king, as blood descendant to the throne, to love him. To marry him."

For a moment Tlonna merely stared at Dietirin before flinging herself into his arms. "Thank you, *a'da*. Thank you."

"You know the word for father in Parlêthian?"

Tlonna frowned. "I guess I do. Perhaps I will start remembering more."

"That would be wonderful," the king said, laughing. "Now go, prepare for the city."

Tlonna and Losolin had to fight their way to the front of hall. People were crammed into the hall, all of them looking around excitedly. While they were struggling through, the two elves ran across Axl, Jack, and Kayra who were giving some teenage male elves a hard time. Axl grinned at Tlonna and saluted her.

"Good te see yeh, darlin. Thought ye had disapperd on us."

"Nay, Axl, just swept up in the chaos. We have got to get to the front. Talk to you later," Tlonna replied, kissing the corsair on the cheek.

The two young elves were awed and shoved the corsairs around a bit saying, "You know the princess? No way!"

It took a long time for Tlonna and Losolin to get to the front where the king, queen, Feorien, the dryad, and the five companions were standing.

Yayènia plucked at a strand of Losolin's hair and grinned. "You two look harassed. A little drama down in the tunnel?"

"Just a little," Losolin replied.

Constancias snorted in a very un-queenly, un-elfish way. Everyone looked at her for a moment, and then ignored her. Dietirin took a deep breath and said loudly to those in the front, "Ready?" and he pushed the door open.

Sunlight streamed in and fresh air wafted by. The crowd, their freedom at their fingertips, pushed forward. The elves at the front were almost knocked down before Tlonna hollered. "Stop! You will kill us all! Stop! We will get everyone out, just WAIT!"

The people stopped pushing and blinked up at her innocently. The royal elves took a deep breath and then stepped outside. It took them the better part of the day to get everyone out of the tunnel. The old and ill had to be carried out on beds, and then everyone else had to be kept calm. Some went into shock and some became helpless with relief. Finally, when all were taken care of, Tlonna stood on the statue base and called for attention.

"Good people of Blackhaven, there is so much work to be done. Do not be overwhelmed with sadness when you see the city. Homes can be rebuilt, business restored, parks replanted, crops re-sown. It will take a long time, but in the end, it will be our city once more. Now, I want all the previous castle workers to stand by the wall until I am finished giving out orders. Go now."

A crowd of people departed from the hundreds of others and

stood by the wall. Tlonna began again. "All fit and able males, I want you to sweep the city to find anything alive. If it is on our side, save it, if it is evil, kill it."

Once more, a section of the congregation left. "I want this group," she pointed to a slightly separated group, "to find the hospitals and either fix or rebuild them. You all, go find all the salvageable timber from the wrecks and pile them somewhere in a convenient place so that all can reach it. You people, start a bonfire in of the old parks and keep it burning; it will be used to rid us of the trash, refuse, and carcasses of the evil we find. This group will find all the bodies of our own and take them to the graveyards," Tlonna continued to hand out jobs to groups of people until they were all gone.

Finally, she turned to the castle workers who were waiting patiently by the wall. All of her friends had stayed as well. Miazie and Tlonna hugged, still elated at being reunited.

"We must speak later, though I fear it is not joyful news," Miazie said quietly once they had let go of each other.

"I take it you were able to decipher the prophecy." Tlonna said.

"Yes, but not here. Not now."

"Of course," Tlonna turned and smiled at her friends. The corsairs, the elves, and the humans smiled back. "Are we ready for the castle?"

Nervous nods replied.

With a gesture, she sent them toward the great doors where the massive dining hall and ballroom, the High Hall, sat waiting.

Blackhaven Castle was four stories tall, and the ceilings rose to twenty feet in the smallest of rooms. Five towers stood slightly apart from the main building and one more stood fifty yards away, connected by an arcing bridge. The main corridor ran from the front entrance to the back, open-ceilinged at the rear where it split the throne room and the High Hall. Bridges crossed it as well at the third and fourth levels. The outer walls of the main building's first floor were split in twain by elegant pillars. The outer half was open to the elements, the inner shielded.

In the very heart of the castle was the famed Inner Courtyard, formally named the Garden of Tonora. Three bridges crossed it as well, though only at the fourth floor, and a spiraling stair curled from the center of one to surround the middle and largest *kairhotuss* tree.

The front of the castle angled away from the very center of the wall, where the main entrance was. Directly above the door, was another, that could only be reached by climbing the massive staircase called the Stairway of the Moons. At the foot of the stairs, it split to allow carriages or riders to pass beneath it.

It was pitch black inside. The windows were covered with musty black cloth, and no torches were lit. A red ball of light flashed into existence and Dietirin was illuminated. A horrific smell invaded their senses. The king motioned to a servant who ran to the wall, disappearing in the dark. Soon, a flicker of light, and then a torch was lit. The flame ran along an oiled string to another torch, and so on until it reached the end of the hall. The servant was lighting the other side by the time it ended.

When the room was all lit, the small crowd stared around in horror. The bodies of hundreds upon hundreds of the dead lay about in great heaps. It was impossible to tell the identities or even the race of most of the corpses.

"These all should have decayed and become skeletons by now." Alexander stated quietly.

"Probably some devilry of Midian. I saw things like this at his castle. He loved the dead," Tlonna replied.

Erdwyf sighed. "There is no way we can tell who gets burned and who gets buried. What do we do?"

"Burn them all," someone said.

"Yes, burn them all," Yayènia said, looking undisturbed by the amount of dead around her.

It took three full days for the hall to be emptied. The large black coverings were pulled off the windows and small crews were sent to check out the rest of the castle. When the patrols returned, they always had depressing news of destruction and death.

After all the bodies had been cleaned away, buckets of water, soap, and rags were brought in. Everyone pitched in to clean. It took a good, hard day, but at the end, the great feast hall was gleaming once more, and across the corridor, the throne room was progressing as well. Tlonna wiped at the dust that was covering her forehead and smiled at the young man next to her.

"Do you know where the tables are?" the elf asked him.

"I don't, milady. I was a butler. That's the seneschal over

there. Her name is Narda," the man said, pointing to the dryad who was usually with Feorien.

"Thank you, sir," Tlonna said as she dashed away to meet the seneschal.

"Narda, are you Narda, the seneschal?"

"Yes I am your grace. What can I do for you?"

"Do you know where the tables are?"

"Yes I do, your highness. Would you like me to get them out?" the dryad asked politely.

"Yes please. Take however much help you need," Tlonna replied.

The seneschal left, beckoning to a few of the servants. A disturbance of screams had Tlonna running toward the entranceway. A few men were laughing while the women swept their skirts away from a small gray animal. Laughing, Tlonna held out her hands and a small creature leapt into them. One of the maids blushed and held out her hand for the creature.

"I'm sorry, Ma'am. He's my Smallum. I thought it would be all right if I brought him along. I'll take him away," she said.

Tlonna handed her the furless cat-like creature that was the size of a rat. "No, no. It is not a problem." Tlonna turned to Aidyn who was tapping her shoulder. "What?"

"I think we should move on. There are lots of rooms in this castle, Tlonna, and they all need to be cleaned," the assassin said, holding his broom as he did his bow.

"Of course," she turned and clapped her hands. "Everyone! Listen, half of us are going into the next room and the other half in the room after that."

The servants split into two groups and they all moved into the hall beyond the feast hall. Tlonna and her friends went into the auditorium, which was in front of the throne room. The others went into the main kitchen. Massive white cloths covered the different sections of the seats. Dust swirled around their feet as they walked from one end to the other, lighting cobwebby torches. The stage curtains loomed above them like great blue shadows. Tlonna and the others began yanking off the sheets that protected the chairs. Dust and filth from rats blew about as the sheets gusted in the air. The seats themselves were in decent condition. The dark blue satin cushions were a bit stiff and musty. The rosewood frames gleamed in the torchlight.

Aladorn walked onto the stage and pulled open the curtains. The stage was made of rosewood as well. Its planks were dirty and scratched from rat claws, and other beastly things. Some of the servants followed him and began sweeping. The wiat opened a door on the side of the stage and disappeared into it. He stuck his head out and shouted, "This room is good!"

Tlonna stuck her hand in the air to acknowledge him. She was pushing air out of her hands to pile all the dirt in the doorway. People in the hall were on ladders wiping down the walls and shining the pictures and mirrors on the wall. A nymph had a piece of elfish armor in pieces, and was running a rag along the gauntlets. The male looked up with his dark gray eyes and smiled happily. Tlonna smiled back and then went once more into the theater.

Aidyn had Yayènia on his shoulders as she wiped down a shield from years ago. Suneelo and Ghealan were folding the white covers and placing them in a credenza behind the stage. Miazie and Damon were beating the seat cushions, along with many others, to get the dust and stiffness out. Tlonna had briefly met Miazie's new husband, and Ryun's young wife. She had also seen the discontent in her friend's eyes, and knew there was no love in her marriage. The hunter and Jacinth were also beating the seats. It did not take long to finish up the theater with the help of Tlonna's, Damon's, Haydyn's, and Losolin's magic.

When they moved on, the others were still working on the High Hall, putting the tables and benches in place, and cleaning the rooms on the other side of the corridor, the kitchen and storage room. Tlonna's crew walked down the hall and came into a wide, open, dead courtyard. A massive tree rose above the castle turrets, rooted in the middle, two slightly smaller trees were on each side, a little ways down the courtyard. Under the great canopies were benches, statues, dry fountains, smaller trees, bushes, flowers, and many other floras. Nestled against the side walls were two guard towers, their spires hidden in the dead branches of the two smaller trees. The people behind her choked back tears and some failed, for this was the great inner courtyard of Blackhaven Forest, fabled and revered throughout Nymyños.

Tlonna and Losolin stared at the trees way above them. "I have never seen such magnificent trees before. What are they?"

"They are kairhotuss trees. The forest around us is in an infantile stage compared to these. These trees are older than even the oldest elf. I am glad they are still around," Suneelo explained, smiling.

Tlonna's mouth stood agape, her eyes wide with wonder. Their trunks were white as snow, the bark old and thick.

"I want all the gardeners working on this courtyard. I want it blooming again. Do you hear me? Find all the gardeners in the city and fetch them here. Start with those already in the castle. The rest of you, come on," Yayènia said, talking to the seneschal.

"Yes High Commander. Right away," Narda replied, bowing her formal bow. She gestured to two young dwarves that jogged off instantly.

The crew moved through the courtyard and into the front foyer of the castle. Through the gloom, Tlonna could see the massive double doors that would open to the public. It was in decent shape, mainly dusty and spidery. A few rats skittered across the obsidian floor, but Aidyn instantaneously dispatched them. A figure was running towards them from the open doorway, caused them all to stiffen with readiness. Feorien held up his hands and bowed.

"Princess Tlonna, I was sent to tell you that your mother requests you and Losolin's presence immediately. Please follow me," the amber-eyed elf was still bowing when he conveyed the message.

"Of course Feorien, lead on," Tlonna said. She gestured to the servants and her friends behind her to start cleaning.

Losolin, Yayènia, Erdwyf, and Aidyn stepped forward.

"I suppose you all must come then?" Tlonna asked half-heartedly.

"Naturally. We would not want to disappoint the king and queen," Aidyn replied.

"My Lord and Ladies, the royals did only mention the princess and Losolin," Feorien said, turning around.

"Are you going to stop us Feor?" Yayènia asked, idly fondling her sword hilt.

"Nay, of course not, High Commander," the elf turned once more and led them out of the hall.

They moved further into the foyer and then turned abruptly and started up a large curving stairway. It took a few minutes to reach the room where Constancias and Dietirin were. Feorien bowed them into the small study, and then followed, hiding his gaze from the irate queen.

"Feorien, I thought I had summoned my daughter and the other, not my commander, the assassin, and advisor as well," Constancias asked loudly, her golden eyes flashing.

"Yes my queen. I did not intend for them to come as well. I am sorry, my queen," the steward said, falling to one knee and placing both hands on the floor.

The room had already been cleaned. The furniture gleamed and the glass panes sparkled.

Yayènia glided forward and grinned wickedly. "We did not want to disappoint you, Constancias. We thought you would have learned by now that we do not follow your rules very well. You should have realized we are not your subjects, and we will not succumb to your rule."

The queen jumped to her feet and stuck a finger in the warrior's face. "You have been gone for months now, and you think you can just come back and treat me like that? I will have you thrown in the dungeons, along with you other two! You are all stripped of your ranks and demoted to commoners! Get on all fours and beg mercy of your queen to let you live!"

"No. That would not be very comfortable. We are not Feorien, we do not grovel like dogs," Erdwyf growled, folding her hands behind her back.

"Mother, I refuse to let them be demoted at all. I would rather they be here anyway. They saved my life more than once. You are still of your ranks, my friends," Tlonna said, ignoring their amused looks.

"Daughter! After all these years, you still cannot abide by my word? I thought for sure something would have changed. Do not you love me at all? After all, I am your mother."

"Of course I do, but I love my friends too. They deserve their honor, let them have it," the young elf replied.

"Fine, sit down, the lot of you," Constancias commanded, sitting herself.

Dietirin smiled cheerily at them all and passed around a bottle of fruity wine. "What your mother would like to talk to you about, Tlonna my dear, is this young rogue," the king said, nodding to Losolin in a friendly way.

Losolin gave an uncertain smile back, not sure what to think.

"Yes, it is blasphemy for you to marry him, or even court him.

There is a young prince of Seaduens named Isadorr Lostug, Iyaner's younger brother, if you remember. He is also a very nice elf and extremely smart. I spoke with his father, and he has agreed to forget your previous offense and allow your betrothal to Isadorr. Is that not wonderful?" the queen looked as though she actually expected a good comeback.

"You damn whore! You will die!" Tlonna hissed, clutching her sword hilt.

Losolin stood and stared at her while everyone else moved into action. Yayènia pulled Dietirin and Feorien out of the way of Tlonna's sword. Erdwyf yanked Losolin down out of his chair, and Aidyn stopped Narda from leaping to her queen's protection.

Constancias stared dumbstruck at her daughter, and at those who had left her to her fate. Dietirin shook his head and said coolly to his wife, "I told you not to do it. I will not stop her from killing you. Unlike Yayènia, she will not be hung for taking your life."

The queen swallowed audibly and gave a quavering smile to her daughter. "Tlonna, calm down. Calm down. Put the sword away. You do not want to be a kin killer, do you? Come on dear, put your weapon away."

"Damn you! Shut up! You are no kin of mine! How dare you attempt to betroth me again, when one has already died! I am going to marry Losolin, and I do not care what you want! I wear his ring, can you not see it?" she held her hand up to show the band to everyone.

"That is all very well and good, but why do not we see what this Prince Isadorr has to say, hmm? Let us say we give him a chance, all right? Now put the sword away before I have to take it by force," the queen stated simply, twitching her finger at Feorien.

The silver-haired elf leapt up from where Yayènia had pulled him. He reached for the sword hilt, smiling benignly all the while.

White magic smashed into his hand and crawled up his arm. The steward screamed and tried to shake the power off of him. It crackled up his shoulder and then encompassed his entire body. He screamed as the magic took hold of him and slammed him into the wall. Blood spurted out from beneath his fingernails, spraying across the freshly cleaned room. Feorien's eyes swept madly over the occupants of the room. His body convulsed, and his head lolled to one side. Narda gave a small squeak and stared in terror at Tlonna.

"Oh please, madam, don't kill me. Please don't kill me!" the dryad shrieked, drawing herself into a ball.

"He is not dead. Narda, take him to the infirmary. As for you...Losolin has proven himself more times than I can count. He has risked his life over and over for me. You should be glad it is him I have chosen to marry, for he will be a far better ruler than you could ever dream of being."

"You are a *princess*! You have to marry a prince!"

"I am the Magin Queen, and I will marry whomever I choose," Tlonna said, pulled her sword back and then slashed it across her mother's face.

Constancias screamed and fell as blood welled out between her fingers. She tried to stop the bleeding, but it was futile. A terrible gash ran across her face from her right cheek to her left temple. The left eye was sliced in half. Tlonna stepped forward and, grabbing the queen's dress sleeve, wiped her blade clean.

Dietirin swallowed and looked away, his eyes tightly shut. Nobody moved to help the queen. Constancias continued screaming as her daughter turned and left the room with her friends. It was Dietirin who finally picked her up and took her to the hospital wing.

Weeks later, Tlonna was in her new study signing papers when Erdwyf burst into the room, her expression fierce with anger. The High Adviser's armband was straining against the tense bicep, and Tlonna feared the intricate silver band of office would break. She was startled by the apparent fury on Erdwyf's face, for the elf was the most composed of all her friends. It was also odd she was alone. It seemed that someone was always around her, making sure no harm came to her unborn child.

"Tlonna, you will *not* believe this!" Erdwyf shouted, waving a curled piece of vellum about.

"Believe what? And close the door, people are staring," Tlonna replied coolly, taking the paper.

As Erdwyf slammed the door shut, Tlonna read the message.

' Tlonna Ewôsdírn

I have had news from King Athelias of your desire to wage war on peace, and I cannot allow it. You have had too free a reign on the happenings of our great continent, and I mean to put a stop to your reckless tyranny. As soon as I received word from Athelias, I sailed as fast as possible to Purheae Harbor, where I then marched my great

Ivory Army to the northwest border of the Liberated Lands and stopped your own blasphemous renegades from entering more civilized countries. One Tyre, and one Aselios have begged me to let them pass, but I am afraid I cannot. You have committed one too many offenses against me, and I will no longer stand idle. If you want your mercenaries, send word with Queen Constancias' guarantee that they will be disbanded as soon as they reach Blackhaven.

Defender of the Eastern Waters

Son of Air and Fire and

King of Seaduens

Stoffnias Lostug'

"Is he serious?" Tlonna asked when she finished reading, her blood pounding with anger. "Word cannot have yet reached Seaduens of Blackhaven's revolution, so how can he know that it is free? He would have stopped my army were Midian still sitting on the throne or not! He cannot know that Midian is not here!"

Erdwyf's lips curled in disgust. "He knows, because he is in league with the Rahlans. Either that or he *meant* to stop your army from reaching Blackhaven, and in turn keeping Midian's seat secure. He is a flaming traitor, and we need to act quickly. If Stoffnias is anything, he is hasty and impulsive. He would not hesitate at mowing down those people."

"Where is Yayènia?"

Erdwyf shrugged. "Home, most likely."

"Get her here. Is Narda around?"

"Sitting outside your door with that bleeding lap desk of hers. I will send her in."

"Erdwyf, is Stoffnias a traitor, or is he just willing to thwart me at any cost?" Tlonna asked quietly as the advisor began to leave.

Slowly, Erdwyf turned to face her friend, her tilted eyes grave. "We have no proof of the former, but I would stake my life on it that he is," she replied coldly.

Tlonna nodded silently, and the High Advisor left, immediately replaced by the dryad Narda.

"Narda, I need the king and queen, now, and if you see the Lord Consort, bring him as well. Tell them this is urgent, and that I ask as the Magin Queen, Princess of Blackhaven."

The female curtseyed gracefully. "As my lady commands."

Tlonna shook her head as the dryad left, and then looked

down at the letter on top of the pile on her desk. Her heart seemed to be thudding at half time in her chest. She felt weary and unmotivated, so she spun her chair around to look out the openings that allowed a large view of the inner courtyard three stories below. She was staring outward in a daze when the door opened behind her.

"Narda said you required our presence?" Dietirin's voice said.

Tlonna turned her chair back around and wordlessly handed the letter to her father. Constancias read over her husband's shoulder, a small smile on her scarred face. She wore a jeweled eye patch to hide her missing eye.

The king finished reading and set the letter down, his eyes wary. "What are you planning?"

"Nothing. I have neither the energy nor the desire to do anything but seclude myself in a room and cry. That is why I need you. What would you do? You are the king and queen."

"I will write him the letter, but I would guess you do not desire that?" Constancias said airily, her one eye trained on her daughter.

"By all means, send him the letter. I would not follow through on it, but if it releases my men, then it would be worth the smudge on my honor," Tlonna replied.

"Lonna, I agree that getting your men here is top priority, but you cannot lie to any sovereign, even one so corrupt as Stoffnias. It sets a bad precedent. Come, let us plot," Dietirin cut in, dragging a chair over to the desk and sitting down. He even went so far as to prop his booted feet on the corner of Tlonna's desk.

Tlonna could not help but smile at her father's gesture. Constancias also pulled a chair over, but she sat primly, folding her hands in her lap, back straight. The child could not help but stare at the blatant differences between her parents.

"I would like most to ride straight there and take the bastard's head off myself," Tlonna muttered after a moment. "But... I do not think it would be wise to leave the city so soon after my return."

"Quite so," Dietirin acknowledged. "But what if you sent an emissary? Pros and cons, love, what are they?"

Tlonna sighed. Her father seemed to take every event as a chance to test her on diplomacy. "It would be advantageous because it would mean I took his threat seriously. I would be well represented, and it would have more weight than a letter or single messenger. However, from what I hear and remember, Stoffnias is a prickly blighter. He could easily be offended, and that would endanger my men. Also, the more people that go, the longer it will take for them to get there."

"And you do not want to seem nervous. If you send even one too many people, Stoffnias will see that as a weakness," Constancias supplied unexpectedly.

Both king and princess stared at her in shock. "Yes, that is true," Dietirin said slowly, his eyes narrowing suspiciously.

The queen returned her husband's glare flatly. "I have been a queen long enough to know how things work, Dietirin. Tlonna is my daughter too, I do not want her to be made a fool of."

"I cut your eye out. Why would you care about my reputation?" Tlonna asked mildly.

"Because your reputation reflects back on us, on me," the older female snapped. "Now, I will write your letter, we will send an emissary, but we will be vague on our promise to disband them. After all, I understand the necessity of having an army. I do not want to see my kingdom get razed again."

"Then that is what we shall do," Tlonna replied, pulling a new piece of parchment from her desk and handing it to her mother.

Dietirin let his feet fall to the floor and he leaned in as Constancias began to write. "Who will you send?"

Tlonna fingered her chin for a moment. "Aladorn and Aidyn, two bannermen, and... Miazie. She needs to get away, and her and Aladorn have a... history."

The king nodded. "Good idea. I do not like that husband of hers. He was the general of the Shitan-Kulata, and despite the Honor of Assassins, their reputation bothers me. Can you do nothing to annul her marriage?"

Tlonna shook her head. "Nothing. It was sealed, signed, and consummated. Nothing I can do will change that. It was made out of our borders."

"That is too bad. I like that little human, but she seems so unhappy," Dietirin said quietly, watching his own unwanted wife write.

Tlonna smiled sadly. "We will find a way to free her. She is in love with someone else, though. An elf."

The king looked up in surprise, his lips parted slightly. "Aladorn and Miazie?"

"No, an alchemist named Sodo," Tlonna replied absently.

"He was attacked by Darkwights, apparently, and that was when they realized they were in love. Miazie said he was shocked that she did not care one of his eyes was black."

"Love does things to a person that reason does not understand," Dietirin said, smiling.

Tlonna grinned back, thinking of her own scandalous relationship with Losolin.

"If you two are done gossiping, I think I have this," Constancias butted in, sprinkling sand over the vellum.

"Read it," Tlonna commanded lightly, staring at a portrait of her and Losolin the castle painter had presented her the week before. They were standing side by side, gazing serenely out of the painting, hands linked. It was a pretty image, but Tlonna did not think she and her Lord Consort had ever looked that complacent.

Constancias began to read.

"*Stoffinias*

We are happy to inform you that Dietirin, Tlonna, and I have resumed our rightful positions, and Blackhaven is once more on its way to stability. When those men you are keeping company reach the city, they will be set to work rebuilding. We have no need of soldiers right now, and so they will be incorporated into society, in hopes of getting the population back up to reasonable numbers. Lord Aidyn and Lord Aladorn will take them off your hands, and Lady Belau Miazie Paron Suutson will handle any diplomatic issues you may encounter.

High Regards
King Magin Dietirin Ewôsdírn,
Queen Constancias Ewôsdírn,
and Princess Tlonna Arune Ewôsdírn, Magin Queen."

Tlonna smiled. "Well enough for me. Should we all use our seals, or the Great Seal of Blackhaven, or just yours?"

Constancias rolled the letter up and, taking a ribbon from the box on Tlonna's desk, tied it up. "Just mine. He will trust it more. Feorien!"

The queen's assistant appeared in the doorway, his amber eyes terrified when they landed on Tlonna. "Yes, my queen?"

"My seal, if you will."

Feorien dug in his pouch and handed the female her seal,

three stars over a moonflower. Constancias found the purple wax bar in her own pouch, and sealed the letter.

"I will send them now," Tlonna said, taking the letter and standing.

Both royals stood with her, and they left her office all together. "We will see you at lunch?" Dietirin asked as they parted ways.

"Maybe," Tlonna replied as she rushed off, her mind already on other things.

"Aidyn!"

The assassin turned on his heel and started back toward Tlonna. He was wearing a green silk belted tunic and his usual black pants, but he wore no cloak, which was odd. He almost always wore his assassin's cloak, his badge of office if he had one.

"Yes?" he drawled, folding his arms as the princess hurried up to him.

"I have an errand for you and Aladorn and Miazie."

"Oh really? That is an odd grouping, is it not?"

Tlonna shook her head. "It is who was best for this task. Stoffnias is holding the army hostage at the eastern border of Purheae. I need you three and two bannermen to take this to him, and bring me my men," she said, handing him the letter.

Aidyn's face was as expressionless as a stone. "Why us?"

"Because I trust you."

"Ah. Well... I suppose this is an urgent deed?"

"Most urgent. I still have to tell Aladorn and Miazie, and find two bannermen, but as soon as I do, I want you on your way. Please."

"Tlonna, of course. Is there anything else you need me to do? I am oath sworn to you, remember? Although, if I remember correctly, I am supposed to stay by your side."

The Magin shoved the male, laughing. "You are not getting out of this. No, there is nothing else. Do you know where Aladorn is?"

Aidyn shrugged, carefully slipping the rolled vellum into his sleeve. "Probably fornicating with some awe-struck noble. He does that a lot."

Tlonna grinned. "Well... I had best be on my way, then. Thank you, my friend, and I will see you when you are ready to leave."

The assassin said nothing, but he gave her a lazy salute and strolled back to his apartment. Aladorn was not making love to anyone when she found him. Rather, he was stretched out on a bench in the courtyard, a book atop his chest.

"Aladorn?"

"Mm?"

"Are you awake?"

"I am now, Tlonna."

Smiling, the princess sat down next to the wiat's feet, which were not visible, and told him about the new task.

"And why, what possible crime did I commit, would you make me spend weeks in the saddle with Miazie?"

Tlonna grinned toothily. "You fornicate with nobles."

Against his will, Aladorn laughed. "That I do. Now... what if Aidyn and I decide to jump ship and kill the bastard?"

"Well," Tlonna mused, "I suppose I would have to rescue you from the clutches of brassed off Seadueni."

"That you would," Aladorn grunted, sitting up. "All right. I will do it, but damnation, why Miazie?"

"Because she is in a loveless marriage, and she is a Belau. She needs to get away, and she can handle Lostug's games."

"All right," the wiat sighed, dragging his hands through his black hair. "All right."

Miazie threw a dress at her. "I appreciate the chance to get away from Damon, but why, *why* does it have to be Aladorn?"

"Because he and Aidyn can protect you the best, and they are forceful males who will not be cowed by Stoffnias," Tlonna said stiffly, trying not to laugh.

Her friend was looking rather paranoid, her long raven hair slightly mussed by the many times she had run her fingers through it and her eyes wide. Her gray satin dress was wrinkled from her frantic pacing, and she kept smoothing it across her hips.

"I don't like it! I don't like it all!" she cried after a minute.

Tlonna sighed. "Nor do I, but I trust you three implicitly, and I need people I can trust on this one."

"I know. But gods it will be awkward... Tlonna you owe me for this."

"Yes."

"Fine. I suppose I need to get ready then. I hope you know what you're doing. I hope I know what I'm doing."

Tlonna laid a hand on her friend's shoulder. "If anyone knows, you do. Now get ready. We do not have much time."

The two elves and woman, with two armored banner men, were standing in the castle stable yard when Tlonna and Losolin appeared, trailing Erdwyf and Suneelo.

Tlonna hugged them all, and Losolin shook their hands. Erdwyf pulled Miazie into a tight embrace as well.

"Be safe, my friends," Tlonna said as they mounted.

Suneelo gave the banner men some last minute instructions, and then bid the trio farewell. "Give that bastard Stoffnias a whack on the head for me."

Aidyn and Aladorn laughed, both bristling with weapons, while Miazie wore the katan Damon had commissioned for her, and looked sick. They rode out of the stable, the banner men behind them holding the Standard of Blackhaven, the silver Kairhotuss Tree on a field of black, and the emblem of House Ewôsdírn, Tlonna's seal, the eight-point star and sun on pale blue.

Aidyn sighed, pushing his horse between Miazie's and Aladorn's. Whäd nipped at Kaia, and the assassin distractedly pulled her head back in. "Look, we have three days more before we reach Stoffnias, can you please try to find some semblance of maturity?"

Both the wiat and the Belau turned their eyes away in abashment. Aidyn shook his head, looking back at the banner men for help, but they hid smiles behind their hands and avoided looking at Aidyn as well. For the past five days Aladorn and Miazie had incessantly been at each other's throats, arguing over the best way to get Stoffnias to hand over the men, which route to take, and who had forced who into bed. Aidyn usually wound up taking the lead while the other four followed, the banner men chuckling and rolling their eyes, the wiat and the woman too incensed to notice that all their arguing was for naught.

"It is not as though you were all that spectacular anyway," Aladorn finally snapped, when they settled down to camp for the night.

Aidyn barely managed to catch Miazie around the middle

before she drew the katan on the other elf. The woman writhed in his arms, cursing and shouting loud enough to bring an army upon them.

"Let me *go*! Aidyn! Put me down!" Miazie screamed, kicking her heels against the elf's knees and trying to free her arms.

"Not until you calm down!" the assassin yelled over her continued threats.

"Did you hear what he said? Did you *hear* what he *said*? Aidyn! I am *great*, he's the lousy one!"

Aidyn was laughing so hard he nearly dropped her, but Aladorn looked a thunderhead, entirely in focus and tense with it. The banner men were standing quietly off to one side, as though afraid to attract attention.

"Why do you care, anyway?" Aidyn finally managed to get out. "I hear you have an elf waiting for you. An alchemist? What should one night with Aladorn mean if you found love elsewhere?"

Miazie immediately went limp, and then starting shaking so hard Aidyn realized she was crying. Letting her slide down his body, he took his arms from around her, but she simply turned and buried her head in his chest. Sending a surprised look at the now gaping Aladorn, the assassin put his arms around Miazie again. The little human sobbed in his chest for a long time, long enough for the banner men to pitch both theirs, and her tent.

When she finally drew away, she blinked up at him in surprise, her face tear-stained and swollen. Aidyn looked down at her, cautiously drawing away. "Aidyn?"

The assassin swallowed, "Yes?"

"I'm sorry."

Uncomfortable, he shrugged. "Ah...it is all right. You should get your stuff set up for the night. I will start dinner."

"Okay...thank you."

"*Aiya.*" Aidyn muttered as she ducked into her tent. Then he turned on Aladorn, green eyes blazing. "You are as crude as a human sometimes, you know that?"

The wiat grunted as he sat down and began to build a fire. "I just snapped. Who can take that kind of badgering forever? But why would mention of her lover make her cry?"

"She is human. They are sensitive like that. Why do you not ask her?"

"Ask her? And start that all over again? No. I am not insane like you. Besides, you are so much better at the comforting bit of it than I ever was."

Aidyn grabbed a chunk of wood off the ground and threw it at the wiat. It cracked against his blocking fist, but left little trails of blood down his knuckles. The assassin pointed an accusing finger at him. "This is your fault. You need to rectify it."

The two banner men, Bret and Saul took careful seats on either side of Aidyn, wary of the two elves' sudden tempers.

Aladorn glared at his friend, said nothing, and continued to build up the fire. Aidyn sullenly started cooking. After a while, when the thick hasenpfeffer was wafting thick aromas, Miazie appeared, looking as regal and cool as she usually did. The only show of discomfort she displayed was squeezing herself between Bret and Aidyn, forcing the other human to move next to Aladorn.

Once the stew had been served and everyone was eating in uncomfortable silence, Aladorn cleared his throat loudly, startling his companions. "I am sorry, Miazie. I spoke in haste. You are the best human I have ever been with."

Aidyn stared at his friend in shock, bowl forgotten in his hands. Miazie had dropped hers. Saul and Bret began eating with uncalled for fervor.

"Th-thank you...Aladorn. I am sorry I said you were lousy. You're phenomenal."

Bret choked and Saul began to beat him on his back hard. Aidyn bit his lip to keep from laughing hysterically, he could feel the heat coming off Miazie. Looking at her sideways he could see her face was a bright red. Aladorn grunted and resumed eating, then suddenly he was gone. Aidyn shook his head.

It was late afternoon when they found the two armies camped near the border of Purheae. The Seadueni army was arrayed in a thick circle around the mismatched recruits of Nymyños. Green and gold seemed to shine from the elfin army, whereas the recruits were a beacon of silver and blue, their new armor winking against the Seadueni. It created a nauseating affect, when two groups of elf-armor were pitched against one another.

Aidyn and Aladorn shared a long look, then they both turned to Miazie, who was looking pale and ill.

"We should change," she said after a moment.

"What?" the two elves said in unison.

"We should change into the best clothes we have. It would not do if we rode in looking like we were travel worn. We don't want to give them the upper hand straight off."

Both males shook their heads, but rather than argue, they pulled their horses into the shelter of the Purheae Forest. It was the thinnest portion of the forest, farthest away from the destruction caused by the backlash of power when the Tower of Magins fell, and it had escaped most of the damage. Here and there a tree twisted upward in a most grotesque way, its leaves always brown. Miazie, now used to the presence of the four males, had Aidyn undo the buttons down the back of her plain riding dress, and then pulled it over her head.

She turned her back on them, but smiled to herself when she heard the collective moans when she pulled off her chemise, now clad in only a very thin shift. She bent down and found the coppery gown she had commissioned in Arseninis. She stepped into it, and then turned to find all four of her companions staring at her.

"What?"

They all shook their heads and resumed changing. Miazie had to admit that they were all finely shaped males with well-toned muscles and sun-dark skin. Bret had a fine covering of blond hair on his chest, though, and Saul a thick mat of black. Both the elves were hairless, of course, and their skin was flawless. Aidyn pulled his inky black tunic over his head, leaving the laces open to his navel, and walked over to Miazie.

She turned and let him do up the laces that crisscrossed the bodice in the back. He was getting quite good at helping her dress, though he muttered the whole time. With a final jerk that was a little too rough, he tied the knot and let her go.

"You are a beautiful human, Miazie, but that does not mean you should flaunt it at every chance."

Miazie turned gracefully and threaded a lock of Aidyn's raven hair through her fingers. "And you are a beautiful elf, Aidyn."

The male's jaw clenched, but he let her draw him to her. Behind them, Aladorn was instructing the banner men on how to act. Miazie had to stand on her toes even while Aidyn was bent over, but she managed to press her lips to his. Their tongues met briefly, and Miazie was acutely aware of how long it had been since she'd been with an elf.

The elf's hands gripped her waist, and then he was backing away, green eyes slightly clouded. Miazie swallowed, painfully aware of her own body, and then cleared her throat. Turning, she folded her riding dress into her pack and slung it across Kaia's rump. Aidyn was lacing up his tunic when she finished, and Aladorn was slinging his cloak around his shoulders.

The banner men were already mounted, and the males were only seconds behind them. Miazie pulled herself into her saddle, realizing as she did so that her dress was not meant for riding. Her skirts were pushed up to bare her thighs, revealing her knee-high boots and thigh-high stockings. Despite her previous nonchalance, she blushed.

Aidyn sent her a cool look, but none of the others commented on it. They rode down into the camp. Ten minutes later they were standing in a large tent before King Stoffnias Lostug and his heir, Isadorr. The two elves immediately ignored the three humans and turned their attention on the wiat and the assassin.

"Aidyn Sestuns... it has been a while since I last saw you. And Aladorn, Tyular's little pet," Stoffnias crooned. "This is who the Ewôsdírns send to retrieve their mercenaries? An assassin, a wiat, two banner men, and their whore?"

Miazie opened her mouth to protest, but Aladorn beat her to it. "This is Belau Miazie Paron, Advisor to the Magin Queen of Blackhaven, and a princess in her own right, Stoffnias."

"The Magin Queen? Is that what their calling that little chit Tlonna now?"

Aidyn hissed, his hand tightening on his blade, but he did not draw. Instead, he ripped the letter from his belt pouch and shoved it at the other elf. Stoffnias raised his eyebrows, but he took the letter, studying the seal.

"So...Constancias wrote it. Good. I know she will show sense where the rest of her blighted family will not," he murmured, cracking the seal and reading.

When he finished, he passed it to his son, who was studying Miazie with new found interest. Isadorr was handsome, rather than beautiful like the Blackhaven elves. His amber eyes were set in a strong face framed by glossy auburn hair that reached his waist. He visibly tore his gaze from Miazie and took the letter from his father.

"Constancias is a smart queen, but I fear she has been tainted by her husband and daughter. I think I will need more convincing than this letter."

"It is what you asked for, Stoffnias," Aladorn growled.

"Yes... but I doubt the sincerity of it. I think I need payment. My son, Prince Isadorr, is apparently impressed with your little human."

Isadorr gave a slight start, but a sly smile bloomed on his haughty visage. Both Aidyn and Aladorn stiffened, both sets of green eyes tightening with fury. Stoffnias gave a little laugh.

"So... she means something to both of you. Tell me, has she warmed both your beds?"

Miazie was frozen in shock. This was *not* part of the negotiations they had expected. The Seadueni hated humans, were repulsed by humans.

"It does not matter whether she has or not, Stoffnias. She is no bargaining chip. She is a representative of the throne of Blackhaven, not a whore," Aidyn snapped, stepping closer to the king.

Isadorr moved suddenly, grabbing Miazie around the middle and pressing a dagger to her throat. His hand moved up to caress her breasts, and she whimpered.

Stoffnias smiled cruelly. Aidyn and Aladorn both drew their weapons with the air of people readying themselves to die. "Give her back."

"No."

Isadorr began unlacing her dress, and carefully pushed it down to her ankles, carefully so as not to remove the knife from her throat. Miazie was trembling now, staring at the two elves prepared to die for her.

"Stoffnias, I swear, if you do not give her back, you will die," Aidyn said, moving closer.

"No!" Miazie cried, as Seadueni guards began to ring the four Blackhaven males. "No! I will go. Just... do not die for me. I will go. One night, King Stoffnias, and then you release us all. Myself, my four companions, and the army. All of us. Immediately."

"Damn it, Miazie!" Aladorn snapped, swinging his sword at the guards.

Stoffnias began to laugh. "Ready to die for a human! Really? Is she that good? Perhaps I will have to taste her myself. Woman, I agree. You are ours until dawn, and then you are all good to go. Guards!"

The four Blackhavenites were set upon, until finally they were all bound hand and foot. Seven guards lay dead upon the floor, but the king merely had them removed. Turning to his son, he motioned for him to leave. Isadorr grinned, and pulled Miazie further into the tent. Aidyn and Aladorn struggled against their bonds, muscles straining. Aladorn faded from sight, causing alarm, but one of the guards got a lucky swing in, and he reappeared, unconscious.

Aidyn ran his tongue along his lower lip, which was bleeding. He snarled at Stoffnias. "You have lost whatever remnants of honor you may have once had. You are a curse on the name elf, and joke to the title of king. Did you know Midian is dead? Yayènia er'Tiena slit his throat. I bet you remember who she is. Now that your master is gone, what will you do? Your treachery will not be allowed. Tlonna is back, along with Losolin, and together they will rip you apart like nothing more than a bite-me. Long live Tlonna! Long live Blackhaven!"

Bret and Saul joined in with the elf, shouting their allegiance until Stoffnias had them beaten to the ground.

Miazie lay still, refusing to respond to the elf-prince moving inside her. Pain and pleasure warred within her, but she managed to keep herself from crying out. The male had practice with rape, and he did it now with skill. She wondered if it could be considered rape, being as how she had agreed to it to allow her companions their lives. Lives they had been willing to give up for her freedom.

She had heard them shouting, heard the shouts cut off, but she did not think them dead. Suddenly, the elf above her tensed, and she felt her body respond against her will. Such was the power of elves. Miazie cried out, her hands gripping Isadorr's forearms which were like slick steel. The prince laughed as he began to move once more. Miazie felt tears sliding down her face even as her body warmed once more.

Looking out the opening in the top of the tent, she stared at the black sky. They had been here for well over five hours, and the elf showed no signs of fatigue. Suddenly her vision sparked as he slapped her.

"Move, damn you, or I will tell my father to renege on the

agreement so that you will have to stay with us. You can be my whore."

Miazie blinked to clear her vision, but she began to meet his strokes, moving her hips with his rhythm. Hours passed, finally Isadorr stiffened above her, this time for much longer, and he gasped as he exploded within her. Miazie felt a vast relief when he pulled out, but it was shattered when he pulled aside the flap that marked the entrance to the room, and called his father.

Stoffnias entered as Isadorr finished dressing, and left.

"So... you brought him pleasure, but he is young yet, and not quite up to my stamina. We shall see what those boys were ready to die for."

Miazie tried to curl into a ball, but the king pulled her legs apart and plunged in without any warning. When she merely lay there and did not respond, he grabbed her nipple and twisted hard. "Move."

She moved.

Aidyn woke with a pounding head, and then jerked upright. The sun was well above the horizon, and he and his three companions were still tied together in a small tent. Jerking, he woke the three others and then all began shouting. A guard stepped into the tent and silently untied them. Furious, he and Aladorn leapt to their feet. The two humans could barely walk, but walk they did.

They stormed into the main tent, but no one stopped them. Aidyn heard Miazie weeping and Stoffnias' labored breath, and he ripped aside the flap to reveal them. The king pulled out of Miazie and lazily stood, but before he could do anything else, Aidyn's fist smashed into his mouth. The older male crashed to the floor, but Aladorn and Aidyn set upon him in fury.

"You bastard! The agreement ended at dawn! You were supposed to release us all at dawn! It is past noon!" Aidyn bellowed, pummeling the naked king.

Stoffnias yelled for his guards, and they came rushing in to detain the furious Blackhavenites. Aladorn wrenched away from the elf holding him and gathered Miazie up in his arms after wrapping the sheet around her. Saul picked up her discarded clothing, and they marched out of the tent.

Miazie wept against Aladorn's neck, shaking uncontrollably.

His arms held her tight, keeping the sheet wrapped securely around her body. Pain and pleasure seemed to be exploding in her body every few seconds, making her cry out, but the scent of Aladorn, a hint of musky cleanness, helped calm her.

"Princess Miazie!"

Miazie turned her head away from Aladorn's neck to find Tyre staring at her in horror. The other captain, Aselios, glared past her, to whoever was standing behind Aladorn.

"It is time to go," Aidyn said, his voice coming from right next to her head.

"We will not forget this, Assassin," Isadorr's voice said.

Miazie cringed against her will, and Aladorn's arms tightened around her. She buried her face in his neck again.

"Neither will we, Traitor," Aidyn snarled.

Almost an hour later, they were mounted and moving back toward the Purheae Forest. Aladorn still held Miazie, and she did not mind. The movement of his body and the horse beneath them lulled her to sleep.

"Miazie!"

Miazie jerked awake to find herself in a high-ceilinged room. The infirmary at Blackhaven. She looked for the owner of the voice, and found Tlonna standing next to her bed. The princess's face was dark with wrath, but her eyes held only concern.

"Tlonna."

"Aladorn and Aidyn told me what happened. I am so sorry. I never expected this. Miazie, can you ever forgive me?"

Miazie chuckled. "It is not your fault, nor anyone else's but Stoffnias and Isadorr. Did everyone make it?"

"Yes, because of your sacrifice. Miazie, I can never repay you. I do not know what I can do to help you, but know that anything you need, anything you want, is yours. I know material things will not change what happened, but-"

"Tlonna," Miazie cut in quietly. "Tlonna your arm. You performed *El shä Rók* didn't you?"

The Magin Queen hid her torn arm behind her back. "I needed to. Aladorn said you were with the Lostugs for nearly twenty hours. You have strength and endurance beyond your race, and the courage to go with it."

Miazie smiled at the compliment, but it faded quickly. "They were willing to die for me. All of them, but Aidyn and Aladorn...how can I ever let them know how much that means to me?"

"I think they know," Tlonna said, and nodded to the other side of Miazie's bed.

Aidyn and Aladorn were there, sitting side by side, their heads bowed in sleep. Miazie's heart started beating faster, her blood pounding through her veins. They were still in the clothes they had changed into before going into the camp.

"Bret and Saul tried to stay as well, but Yayènia made them go home. They received honors for what they did," Losolin said as he strode up to the bed. "I am glad you are awake."

"Losolin," Miazie managed before she choked up.

After a while more, Tlonna and Losolin left to resume their duties. With the army back, the city had doubled their efforts. Miazie stared at the two elves by her bedside until Aidyn woke with a start. His eyes flashed around the room, the way warriors always did, and then his gaze settled on Miazie. Nudging Aladorn, the wiat flashed in and out of vision for a few seconds before coming to his senses and staring back at Miazie.

Both males stood suddenly, and then they were babbling nonsense as they tried adjusting everything about her. They finally gave up when Miazie started laughing. They flushed in unison, and she realized they were much alike both in appearance and in manner.

"You're related!" she cried without thinking.

Both males stilled immediately, going pale.

"Brothers... actually," Aidyn finally muttered, glaring at Aladorn as though it were his fault.

"But... how? Why did you not tell me? Anyone?"

"We did not know until recently. I grew up with our father, Aladorn grew up with our mother."

"And it would have complicated matters had everyone found out. Aidyn has a title, land, a House. I am older by ninety-three years, though. We did not wish that to change. You must not tell anyone, Miazie, though we do not deserve to ask anything of you."

"Oh for crying out loud," Miazie muttered, sitting up. Then she realized she was naked.

The brothers averted their eyes as she rearranged herself, and then looked back at her face, steadily at her face. "I will not tell anyone, and you owe me nothing. You got me out of there, and you were ready to die for me. That is something I can never repay you for. Now, which of you wants to help me dress?"

Almost four months passed by before Blackhaven was inhabitable again. The castle shone from inside out, the gardens were beginning to show growth, and the waters ran crystalline clear. The businesses began to rebuild and prosper. Trade started moving again, and ships began to come into harbor once more. The corsairs left the day after the army arrived with many sad goodbyes. Alexander and Troaz had both promised to return often.

Before they left, Jack and Kayra married. It was a glorious wedding inside the castle's temple. Kayra, of course, left with the corsairs. Tlonna and her companions had waved until the two ships disappeared on the horizon.

It was the third day of Resen when the castle was finally complete, a full six months since Tlonna and her companions had returned. There was a new statue in one of the city gardens of Andramaky, the Cyree, carved in rose marble and surrounded by a small pond in reference to her sacrifice. Tlonna had shown her father the Staff of Cyree and he had touched it with reverence and no little fear, for its power was beyond anything he had ever held.

Tlonna twirled around in the throne room laughing as Losolin attempted to read a list of songs for the feast. "Tlonna, dear, I love you but would you please stop giggling? I am trying to do all these Lord Consort duties, and I cannot figure out which songs I like best."

"Give it to Narda to take care of. She likes those things. That is what I always do. Besides, our apartment is finished. What say we go up and inspect it eh? We have our own tower! Can you believe it! This time last year we were sleeping on the ground freezing to death in the snow. We are finally home!"

"Why do we not go see the city? We have not actually been down there. Suneelo said that his house is finished. I would like to see it. Let us find Narda and get out of here."

"All right," Tlonna said, taking her cloak off the throne arm rest and following her consort out of the room.

The two elves left the castle and walked across the large front courtyard to the castle gates. The guards gave them a stiff salute and they walked into the city. Trees filled every possible corner and open space, their leaves the vibrant oranges, reds, and greens of late autumn. People milled about carrying boards or pushing carts of stone. Children ran through the streets with bags of nails and other small objects. As they passed into the Civilians District, Tlonna and Losolin saw more families and were greeted more often. Women brought their children to be blessed by the princess and men shook the hands of Losolin.

A she-dwarf was holding up a large block of granite while her husband reached from the roof of their house to grab it. The female began to stagger backward as their short arms strained to reach each other. The two elves hastened to the female's side and took the granite from her. Losolin handed it to the male who smiled gratefully.

"What is your name Madam?" Tlonna asked, steadying the dwarf.

"Krina, my lady. Thank you both kindly. We have been doing this all day and my arms are just about jelly by now," the she-dwarf said, brushing her hands together.

"That granite was just about as big as you are, Krina. I had heard of the strength of the dwarves, but apparently I had underestimated it," Tlonna replied.

The female smiled, showing short silver teeth. Her face was rough and wrinkly. The dwarf had strong thick shoulders and stubby hands, and long, course brown hair sprouted like weeds from her head. There was definitely something feminine and curvy about her, but one had to look properly to see it.

"Aye, and my Krina's just about the strongest female you'll find, as far as Dwarves go," the man said, climbing down a ladder that was about as tall as Losolin. "The name's Garner. I'm a second-degree master mason. I helped build the underground city."

"Pleased to meet you, Garner. I am Tlonna and this is Lord Consort Losolin."

"Aye, we know who ya are. Not many elves would stop by and help a dwarf like you two did. We are much obliged," Garner looked much like his wife, though with a beard.

"Not a problem. Do you have anything else we could help you with?" Tlonna said.

"No. That was the last piece. We've been too busy rebuilding our shop that we hadn't got to our home. We've been sleeping in shop since we got it built. It'll be nice to sleep in our home again," Garner replied.

With a goodbye, Tlonna and Losolin left the dwarves and continued down the street. They often stopped to help families in difficult chores. As they turned a corner, they saw a woman sitting on the steps of a half finished house, her face in her hands.

"What is wrong Miss?" Losolin asked, putting his hand on her back.

The woman looked up and stared at the male in front of her. Freckles danced across her fair skin and large green eyes filled with tears.

"Oh Lord Losolin! Princess Tlonna! Oh, I am so sorry. Excuse me," she stood and fled into the house.

"Miss?" Tlonna shouted, stepping after her. They followed the woman and found her pounding hard at a uselessly bent nail. "What is the problem?"

"Oh! Princess Tlonna. I...I don't know how to do this!" the woman threw the hammer across the building and covered her face in her hands again.

"Do what?" Losolin asked.

"My husband built our house and he died in the siege! I don't know how to build the house again! My children have been sleeping with their aunt and uncle while I've been sleeping here. I've got no money, no home, and no more nails. What am I going to do?" the woman sobbed into her fingers, the tears dripping down onto the dirt floor.

Losolin took the woman by the shoulders and led her outside. Tlonna unbent the nail and sent it into the wood pole. She continued placing the remaining nails into the wall flats and attempted to straighten them up from their sloping positions. She started when Losolin returned a little while later.

"I bought more nails and brought help. Her name is Izabella and her husband was a third rank cavalryman. She didn't work," Losolin explained, handing her the nails. Two men followed him, a dwarf and a human. "This is Badin and Stefan. They weren't doing anything so I got them to help."

The two men bowed and looked around. The dwarf pulled a large hammer out of his belt and grinned. "Whaddya say, Stefan?

Let's build this house eh?"

The human grinned back and then looked at the elves. "So where's the supplies? We can't build without supplies."

"They're out back," a timid voice said.

They all looked at Izabella who was standing inside the doorframe hugging herself. "It's all I could salvage from the wreck."

The two men went outside and came back holding a board loaded with bricks. They began laying them out to form the wall. They looked perfectly able so the elves took Izabella back outside. She thanked them and stared at the purse Losolin placed in her hands.

"My lord, I can't take this."

"Nonsense, use it to buy supplies and food. Take care of yourself and your children," Tlonna said.

The elves left her and continued walking down the street. They wandered through the city to the Peerage District and found themselves in a calmer atmosphere. There was far less people about, and so it was much quieter. Trees lined the grass-weave streets, baring the signs of the siege, but there was growth too, as it was throughout the city. Scorch marks were covered in sap, broken branches had been cleared away to leave room for new foliage. Tlonna had begged the city's elves to work in the gardens, lending their particular gift to hasten the reparations, and it showed.

Losolin touched her arm and pointed to a wide pathway marked with a standard, dark blue and white split diagonally down the center, a badger head in the center with a bloody claw just visible, the standard of House Tiena.

Walking up the pathway, Tlonna and Losolin were delighted to see soft lights among the trees, a special trick Dietirin had discovered. When they reached the clearing where Yayènia and Suneelo's manor sat, they found their breath taken away. The lights were everywhere so that the house itself was bathed in the warm, ambient glow. The manor was made of rose sandstone and simply emerged from ground. Though it was two stories tall, the manor house seemed a natural formation. Most of the walls had large openings in them, covered in filmy netting that hid the inside from view, but allowed nature in. The yard was all garden and trees so that it seemed even the Green Man could live there comfortably.

Tlonna and Losolin approached the door and pulled on the

rope so that a bell rang inside. An exotic young woman opened the door and blinked in surprise.

"Please come in, your highnesses, I will inform the High Commander and the Captain that you are here," she said, beckoning them in.

They entered into a small foyer adorned with old weapons and tapestries of battles. Immediately to the left was the kitchen and dining room, to the right a staircase. Directly beyond were more wide openings curtained with netting.

"Tlonna! Losolin!" Yayènia cried as she descended the stairs, looking slightly odd in a loose tunic and short pants that only went to her knees, for it was the first time she had completely doffed her armor.

"Yayènia, I had heard that it was the most beautiful plot in all of Blackhaven, but... I did not expect this," Tlonna said, waving her hand to indicate the house and yard.

The High Commander beamed. "Ah, well, Neelo and I decided to go all out, and make it the place we always dreamed of. Come, I must show you my favorite part."

Tlonna and Losolin followed the elf up the stairs and looked out the openings onto the front yard. It looked as though a meticulously crafted forest had grown there, rather than a landscaped yard. Yayènia led them across the floor into an empty room, the only item in it a tall fireplace.

"This is the bedroom. We have not yet had the time to get it together, so we have been sleeping in the library, which is through that door," Yayènia pointed behind her. "But this...this is my treasure."

They were now standing in a large, tile-floored space with only two solid walls. The front and left wall were merely sandstone pillars that descended to the ground twelve feet below. Carefully arranged in water-tight barrels were practice weapons, equipment, and tools. The netting whispered across the glossy red tile as Tlonna moved around in awe, lifting a waster here, a repair kit there. Losolin watched her, smiling. Yayènia was nearly vibrating with excitement.

"Is it not wonderful? It is twice as big as our old training room, and so much nicer," she said happily.

"It is quite amazing, Nia," Losolin said as Tlonna studied a set of bars parallel to the ground, but one was a foot taller.

"What are these for?" She asked.

"Ah..." Yayènia grinned and took a step back, motioning Tlonna out of the way.

Then she was sprinting across the tiles, and just as she was about reach the first bar, she sprang upward to catch the second one. Her momentum flipped her around and she grabbed the lower bar, and began a complex, fast-paced routine on the bars. Tlonna and Losolin watched her in awe. After nearly a minute, she dropped to the ground and bowed, her face aglow with adrenaline.

"That was amazing, but what is it for?" Tlonna asked again.

Yayènia drew in a breath. "Mainly for reflexes, arm strength, and control. They are used by acrobats in shows, and I figured they would be a good thing to learn."

"Aye, and one day you are going to misjudge a distance and fly out of the window," Suneelo said, entering.

"Perhaps, you had just better make sure you are there to catch me then, hmm?"

Suneelo grinned and clapped Losolin on the shoulder. "So what do you think, *bruun*?"

"Spectacular," Losolin replied, smiling at Suneelo's habit of calling him brother.

"Glad you like it. This one gave me a hell of a time picking out the tile. The *tile*, for spirit's sake," the captain laughed, gesturing to his wife, who was now showing Tlonna a move on the bars.

It was nearing midnight when Tlonna and Losolin left Tiena manor and found themselves in the middle of a celebration. People danced around to lively music provided by a band of elves. Laughter and talk drifted on the evening breeze as the different races mingled.

As Tlonna and Losolin were noticed, the revelers stopped and stared. The music died down and soon all faces were turned toward the two. Tlonna smiled and raised her hand. "Do not stop. We are here just for fun."

A cheer went up and soon the two were dancing and laughing with their subjects. A flower wreath was placed on Tlonna's head as she stood aside to catch her breath. The night wore on as the jovial creatures sang and celebrated. Colorful lanterns were hung in the trees and lit.

Near dawn, Tlonna and Losolin returned the castle, exhausted and grinning. They walked through the blooming courtyard and met the occasional early morning stroller. The fair people of the castle bowed their heads and walked by them, their silk and velvet robes rustling the petals on the stone walkway. The couple strolled through the bottom foyer of the castle and then out to the courtyard.

They wandered through a corridor created from the bowing branches of willows to a small clearing in the courtyard, which sported a small fountain that spilled crystalline water over a silver bowl into a trough at the bottom. There were wind chimes made of wood placed skillfully in the trees so that there was always a soothing natural music to comfort whatever soul had sought the courtyard. The paths were sunken into the ground, rough cut stones worn smooth by generations of feet, while thousands of different floras whispered to the breezes that passed through. Exhausted but content, Tlonna pulled Losolin through the winding corridors of foliage to the very center, where the grandest and oldest of all trees stood rooted like a beacon. The trunk was silver; the lowest branch a hundred feet from Tlonna's head, where black-green leaves the size of her hand shimmered in the early morning mist.

"This is home, is it not, Losolin?" she asked quietly as they stood beneath the massive tree's shadow.

"Yes," he whispered, "and we have earned our right to call it so."

"We feared so much on our return, *if* we returned, and now it all seems so pale in comparison. I feel that this peace is but a passing cloud, and soon we will be tossed back into the ragged claws of treachery and corruption. Each morning I wake and fear that this is all a dream, and I am back in the violent clutches of Midian. I see Haydyn in the halls of the castle and I see his smile and I love him for it, but he is also the living reminder that I...that such things happened. I go to Rhiannan's room to make sure she is eating, and I see the hate and revulsion in her eyes that are so like Midian's, like Sithian's. I see the pendant around my father's neck and am reminded that the Resurrection Pendant is still in the castle on Zaedic, still within the reach of Sithian. Oh, Losolin, I fear the day it all comes crashing down upon us," Tlonna said, her voice breathy and small as she gave words to her fear.

Losolin's hands were tight on her back as she trembled against him. "Loni, do not despair of things you cannot control. Do not give wing to shadows you cannot see. The day will come, yes, but until then, do not let the apprehension rule you, for it will torment you endlessly. When the day comes, we will be ready, and we will meet it with a ferocity born of love and determination, and the hindsight of what happens when we let evil and cruelty win. You are no longer alone, you must remember that."

Tlonna nodded against his neck, where her face was buried. Silently, Losolin led her away from the tree to climb the curving stairs that rose from the ground to the second floor. Unsure of where to go, he wandered around, pulling a half-sleeping Tlonna after him, until he found the opening to the Moon Tower, the tower dedicated to the heir-apparent and its personal staff. Climbing the spiral staircase up to the fourth floor, where the steps narrowed until they came to a single point in the center, on which stood a large carved door of kairhotuss wood, Losolin took the new silver key Dietirin had handed him earlier, and unlocked it.

They shuffled into their new apartment and gaped. The door was sunken into the center of the room and one must take several steps upward to reach the floor of the room, where it extended in a circle surrounding the door. The obsidian walls were adorned with tapestries of landscapes and paintings of maps, for Tlonna had had the revelation that she was fascinated by them. There were silver and blue drapes that were gathered in the center of the circular ceiling to fall decoratively about the walls where there were no paintings or tapestries. Upon a slightly raised floor was a painted screen that hid a ridiculously large tub and other such hygienic items. Against one wall was a large wardrobe and beside it glass balcony doors that looked out over the harbor, and directly across the room another balcony that overlooked the inner courtyard. At a right angle from the door was a massive canopy bed swathed in dark and pale blue curtains tied back with a silver rope.

The only other furniture in the room was a large desk and two nightstands on each side of the bed. Losolin was overwhelmed while Tlonna had the sudden thought that this room was very like the one that had been trashed by Midian's horde. Without a word to each other, they readied for bed and fell into the deep sleep brought on by a day's work.

Morning came bright and warm, the sun spilling across the large glassless windows and balcony doors, waking Tlonna. She rolled over and covered her eyes against the brightness, cursing the sun. A timid knock on her door roused her enough to answer it. Haydyn smiled at her and stepped into the room.

"Morning Mother. Did you sleep well?" the young man asked, leaning against the doorjamb.

"I had not yet got to sleep, Haydyn."

"Ah... I see," the half-elf replied, looking over at Losolin and raising his eyebrows.

"No! Not that. We were in the city at a celebration all night. We got in at dawn," Tlonna said, pushing her son.

"All right then, no need to push. I'll leave you two alone. Sleep well Mum," he kissed his mother on the forehead and left chuckling.

Shaking her head, Tlonna locked the door and returned to her bed. They did not wake again until midday.

Losolin crawled out of bed and opened the balcony doors toward the harbor. A brisk summer wind greeted him as he stepped onto the warm black stone. The city sprawled before him, partially obscured by the numerous trees. He was staring out at a large mansion a little ways from the castle when someone touched him on the shoulder. Losolin turned to embrace Tlonna and found himself looking at Haydyn.

"How did you... was the door not locked?"

"Yeah, but one of the maids let me in. I actually wanted to talk to you," Haydyn said, shutting the door behind him.

Tlonna still lay on the bed asleep, hidden in the blankets. Losolin glanced at the half-breed and gestured to a pair of chairs. "What is it you want to talk about?"

The boy, for that was what he was in Losolin's view, took a deep breath. "Are you okay with my relationship with Mum? I know it was a big blow for you, but she couldn't do anything about it. My father forced himself on her."

Losolin felt a sharp stab of pain in his heart, but he schooled his face to blankness. "Haydyn, it was hard to realize that Tlonna had a child, much less three children. I had expected to find her tortured and barely alive, if that. I did not want to believe the visions. To find that she had children was not something I was prepared for. To know that at least one of her offspring was kindhearted and virtuous was a relief. Having you around is much easier than it is having Rhiannan around. There is a reason we keep her locked up."

"Yeah, I was wondering, when are you going to tell the queen and king that I'm their grandchild? And Rhiannan, and Sithian?" Haydyn asked, frowning.

"Ah...about that. You see, Tlonna...your mother...is afraid that Constancias will not allow you to live. She is very strict in the law of not allowing enemies or their offspring into her city unless they are in chains. She fears that your and Rhiannan's life will be forfeit as soon as she reveals who you are."

"So what, we're just going to live a lie? Never to be introduced or even known to be a part of this family? Mum wouldn't allow them to exile me, or my sister. My grandparents couldn't possibly do that, could they?"

"Constancias could, and will. She has no qualms about that. Besides, do you really want to deal with being a half-Elven princeling?" Losolin grumbled.

"Losolin, back in Zaedic, I was prince of a dead city. My father and brother ruled above me, ruled with terror and hatred. I don't think being an heir to a great throne of a great city is something I should be afraid of. I may be half an Elf, but I am more Elf than Man. I know that you and Mum would help me become a good and righteous king. I don't fear what I was born to become."

"You were born to be a spawn of evil incarnate, Haydyn. Your life meant nothing to your father. He wanted only to use you in his cruel game against elf-kind, even humanity. You were never to be heir to his throne. That honor and curse was always Sithian's. You were nothing but a pawn in Midian's plans. Sithian was to be king, Rhiannan to bear more children of the line, and you to kill, to be dispensable, but also a safeguard in case Sithian was killed. Do not misinterpret your father's intentions," Losolin replied coldly, leaning back.

"I don't care! I am a prince by right and birth. Mother raised me to be a good person and one day a good king. Nothing you say can stop that. I think it is imperative that the king and queen know who and what I am. Rhiannan maybe not, but I *am your heir*! You know this in your heart, I know you do. You love my mother and I had hoped that one day you might come to love me as your son. My purpose on this earth is to be the best person I can possibly be, and I am to be a king. I know it! I *know* it!" Haydyn was now shaking, his determination coming out in great breaths.

"You are not my son, Haydyn. You are the product of a rape of the female I love. I am not your father. I cannot be. I am not even married to your mother," Losolin returned quietly.

"Don't you understand? You don't have to be my father through blood! Why can't you love me as your son? I have known you now for eight months and yet you still cannot find some emotion for me? I am your lover's son! I will someday be your half-son!"

Fury lashed through Losolin suddenly, replacing the cold pain and remorse he had been feeling. "Well, I guess you are just half of everything, then! How can you expect me to love you as my own when you came from the seed of the man who almost murdered Tlonna? How can you expect me to love you when-"

"Losolin! Enough!" Tlonna's voice cut through the male's irate rant.

Both Haydyn and Losolin cringed as Tlonna stepped onto the balcony. Her movements were stiff and cold, temper seething in her every move.

"Both of you, enough. I have heard enough of this cursed foolery. Haydyn, you are my son and cannot expect Losolin to accept you as his seed, especially so soon. Losolin, how can you say such cruel things to him? It is not like you. As for me, I wish to tell my parents who you are, Haydyn, and your sister, but I must prepare for it first. They will not take to my lie lightly. Now, come inside and let us go down to lunch," the princess took their hands and led them through the hallways to the third floor where the private dining room was.

Both Dietirin and Constancias were there, along with Aidyn and the others. The monarchs looked at Haydyn strangely, frowning.

"Daughter, who is this young man?" Constancias asked, snapping at a servant to bring more food.

"This is Haydyn, Mother, I told you about him and his sister, Rhiannan, the servants from Midian's household. They came with us from Zaedic."

"Ah, right. So why is he here and his twin in the dungeon?" the queen asked, still frowning.

"Because Rhiannan is a whore, Constancias. Do you never listen?" Yayènia explained, sounding irritated.

"Then why did you bring her, *Tlonna*?"

"We could not leave her to help Midian's son, Sithian. They were very close, she and Sithian," Tlonna replied.

"And what about him? Why is he not locked up, if he is the same as she?"

"Because he is good and she is evil. Really, can we eat in peace?" Erdwyf grumbled, sighing.

"You, shut your mouth. I granted you pardon for your treason, and I can easily take that away," Constancias threatened.

"Actually, you had neither right nor reason to pardon us, for we did nothing wrong in the eyes of the king, so you did not do anything, and you cannot do anything. You are nothing but a worthless, gutter-worthy strumpet," Aidyn said casually.

"How dare you!" the queen rose to her feet in fury and pointed her finger in wrath. Purple magic flashed out and struck Aidyn in the chest, throwing him across the room.

Red, black, green, and white power slammed into the queen, forcing her to the ground. Aidyn picked himself up and brushed the ashes off his chest. Constancias stared in horror at her daughter and husband as they held her down with magic many times stronger than she could ever muster.

"Let me up, Dietirin. Tlonna. And you two...let me up."

After a full ten seconds the four released their hold, Losolin and Haydyn the more reluctant, and the queen was able to stand rather shakily. Breakfast passed quickly and silently. As soon as their plates were cleared, the elves left the presence of the monarchs.

Miazie and Yayènia walked on either side Tlonna, the former with her head down, the latter scanning the hallways incessantly, always alert. Behind them trailed their friends, the group that was fast becoming known as the council and the family: Losolin, Suneelo, Ghealan, Erdwyf, Aidyn, and Aladorn, with Haydyn a step behind and not included.

"Tlonna..." Miazie began nervously, immediately catching the attention of the others as well. The Belau fidgeted nervously as she was wont to do, the only human in a group of powerful and nigh-legendary elves. "Tlonna I need to tell you what I learned in Alchemian."

"*Aiya,*" Tlonna murmured absently, knowing that she would not like what she was about to hear.

Yayènia tuned half an ear to Miazie's voice while keeping the rest of her senses on the area around the council. The others did the same.

Miazie swallowed and clutched at her skirts. "The prophecy... *Darkness will mar the land of beauty and evil will wage war. One will hold the power to deliver life from death, but must bow to shadow's caressing touch to find this power. The guardian will fall, the lover will rule, the friend will perceive, and the moon heiress will free the slaves of death.* We know who everyone is, and what it means. It means..." here she took another shuddering breath, glancing at Yayènia in fear, though she had come to have a fledgling friendship with the warrior. "The guardian is Yayènia, and she will fall in her duty to protect you. Losolin, the lover, will rule in your place, and I, the friend, will discover a piece of knowledge that will allow you to find the strength. Do you remember what Andramaky, the Cyree said? You have too much power, but not enough? I will find the way to unlock a dormant power, and it will give you the strength you need to free the slaves of death, and the rest of Nymyños from doom."

"You are speaking in riddles, woman," Yayènia snapped, her attention now fully focused on Miazie.

The council had stopped walking and was standing in the middle of a corridor. Miazie glanced at her and then turned her dark eyes upon Tlonna, willing the elf to understand. "The slaves of death are the Darkwights. They are the Elven race. When you release this power, you will strip from them the ruined flesh and mutilated desires and return to them their elfish life. The Elven race will be reborn, and you will die."

"No. It is just a prophecy from a dying man. It is just gibberish," Losolin countered angrily.

Yayènia was staring at Miazie so hard the human whimpered. Suneelo was so tense as he stared at his wife that he trembled. Then the High Commander was moving so fast no one could stop her. Within the span of a breath, Yayènia had Miazie shoved up against the wall and dangling a foot above the floor, suspended by her hand around her neck. The human gasped for breath, kicking out in desperation.

"You lie!" Yayènia shouted, her teeth bared.

Ghealan and Suneelo yanked the warrior back so that she

released Miazie. "No, I swear, I made them go over it again and again, but it is true," the Belau cried, rubbing her neck and blinking back tears, then gasping when she drew away her hand and saw blood. Yayènia's nails had torn open the tender flesh, short as they were.

Tlonna stood rooted to the spot, the revelations ringing in her ears, Losolin clutching her hand. "Haydyn, will you take Miazie to the infirmary," the princess said quietly.

The young Halfling took Miazie by the arm and led her away from the group of tormented elves.

"I do not believe it," Yayènia snarled. "It is just a worthless and vicious dream written down by a man who died moments later. There is a...the Darkwights are demons and cannot be...Midian did not have that sort of p-power...I will not let you die!"

Tlonna turned and grabbed her friend by the shoulders. "Just because it is Seen that way does not make it solid. We have the ability to choose other paths, Nia. And if I do die, what of it? I am just one life among many others, and my death will echo less than yours, or anyone else in this hall, understand? I am the obscure female in the story that needs rescuing, while you all are the heroes. If I die, then consider it fate fulfilled, and worry about it no longer."

Yayènia nearly bounced in her shock. "How can you speak like this? This city has *hope* because of you! You are the savior of Blackhaven. Understand, sister of war, that if you die, the world dies with you. Tlonna, you are young, and I am three hundred years your senior. You may be my princess, but you are not my elder. In this, *you* will listen to *me*. I will not let you die."

"Yayènia..."

"No! Stab me thrice and drown me, if you so much as allow yourself to get pricked with a pin, I will tear this place down looking for the owner of the pin and strangle them to death. I will not let you give up your life for something as weak as prophecy."

Tlonna froze. Her eyes dilated and her jaw clenched. The others around them felt the air in the hall go cold. Yayènia stared hard into her friend's eyes, never flinching. Ice began to creep along the stone from under Tlonna's feet. Her fingers dug into the commander's shoulders, blood began to drip slowly from under the nails. Still, Yayènia did not move an inch, her face mirrored Tlonna's, hard and cold.

"This life of which you speak *so* grandly of is my exact motive.

What is life when half the world is trying to destroy you, and the other half is consumed with protecting you? What is life when it is all about death? Death, Yayènia, it is greater even than love. I yearn for it. I beg and dream at night of death and its freedom. Life is the feather in my wound. The salt-water baths, the rapes, the needles, the bars, the splinters, the wires, the flames, it is everything I have endured. How can you use life as an argument against death? It will always lose."

"No it will not! Life is all that we may have left! When I thought I would die chained to the same walls I had once adored, I despaired. I treasure life above all, and I *know* how I will die. I do not seek to make that moment come any closer than it is now. How can you say that life is of no importance when it makes all the difference in the world? Why do we fight for good, if life is so horrid? Why? What does it all come down to, Tlonna? Life! In the end that is all we have left! And your life most importantly! Do I mean nothing to you? What about Losolin? And your son? And all those who risked their lives to save yours? Do they not matter to you?" Yayènia screamed.

"Yes, they matter! It is only that that matters! The reason I survived is to make sure you all lived! Now you are safe and I am nothing anymore! I wake every morning in fear of the past becoming real again! Do you understand that? You, who have the emotions of a rock? Do you understand what it is like to live everyday in fear of memory, when you cannot even remember those that made you who you are, only those that destroyed you? If all I must give up is my life to save others, I give it gladly!" Tlonna shoved her friend back and fled the hall.

When the stunned trance lifted, the elves rushed to Yayènia's aid. Her shoulders bled, but they were not deep wounds. The flesh had only been torn open in small portions. Losolin healed them quickly. Suneelo and Ghealan put the High Commander's arms around their necks and held her up. Though not physically harmed, the elf was mentally beaten. Aidyn took Losolin away from the hall and into the apartment he and Tlonna had shared while the tower room was completed. Erdwyf followed Tlonna, running lightly and swiftly up to the floor above, to Tlonna's tower entrance.

The advisor flung open the large door, pushing aside the frightened maid. She ran into the large room and looked about. When realizing the room was empty, Erdwyf walked onto the balcony, but Tlonna was nowhere to be seen. In foreboding, she looked over the edge and sighed with relief. No body hung from the stone pillars, and no corpse lay far below in the courtyard. A black-haired elf looked up and saw Erdwyf hanging over the edge, scanning.

"*Hoy! Quea feaen valõn hochanes ka?*"[1]

"*Inkan sïm hochanes ka eria Tlonna. Yercht valõn ocheanas sääb?*"[2]

"*Noya eria Erdwyf. Inkan sïm klysm.*"[3]

"*Gifte valõn.*"[4]

Erdwyf went back inside and ran to one of the openings that led to the great staircases that wound around the center kairhotuss tree. Taking four steps at a time, the elf reached the inner courtyard quickly. She ran from one end to the other shouting Tlonna's name. It was in the far north corner where she found the Magin. Tlonna sat on a bench staring at the veins in the wall. Her hand lay on one of the silver strands, tears running down her cheeks.

"Tlonna..." Erdwyf began.

"Leave me be, Erdwyf, I do not want to hurt you too."

"Oh, Tlonna," the advisor sat on the bench and put her arms around her friend. "I would never leave you, and you will never hurt me."

The two elves sat together until the sun went down. Losolin appeared once but left before Tlonna noticed him. Erdwyf finally led the Magin back up the stairs, carrying a lantern by a chain. She got Tlonna in bed and then left, closing the door quietly behind her. Near midnight, she returned to the room she and Ghealan shared when they stayed at the castle. She crawled in bed next to Ghealan, comforted by his strong arms.

The next morning, Tlonna slumped in her throne alone. No one was up yet except for the night servants. The men and women smiled sadly at their princess, for whom they held great love.

The sun rose, paled with storm clouds. Rain slashed against

---

[1] Hey! What are you looking for?

[2] I am looking for lady Tlonna. Have you seen her?

[3] No lady Erdwyf. I am sorry.

[4] Thank you.

the glass panes placed in the openings of the walls. On fair days, the glass was removed to allow the earth in. Leaves would cover the floor, the wind would blow through the halls, and the air was thick with freshness. Today however, the castle was blocked up and dreary.

As people began waking, the servants changed shifts and Tlonna was left alone for a few moments. The elf brooded, chin on fist. The new servants appeared, along with most of her friends. Yayènia and Suneelo through one door, Erdwyf and Ghealan right behind them. Losolin stepped down from the last stair in the main hallway and Aidyn and Aladorn appeared in another doorway. The main entrance to the throne room slammed open and a drenched messenger ran to the throne. The boy slammed to his knees in a bow, his soaking black hair falling about his face in thick clumps.

"Milady Princess, I've a message!" the boy gasped, his shoulders heaving.

"Take a moment to catch your breath. Someone bring him a glass of cider!" Tlonna said, standing.

"Please Milady, it's important."

"All right then, go ahead if you must."

"There's a man at the gate. A tall, dark-haired man. His eyes are like death to look upon, so cold and blue they are. He demands an immediate audience with you. He says if you don't acquiesce to his wishes, he'll rip out my entrails with a fish hook and then burn me in an everlasting fire," at this, the messenger choked. Tlonna found and held Losolin's gaze for a mere second before responding.

"What was his name?" she knelt by the boy and grabbed him by the shoulders.

"He refused to tell me milady! He told me to run or die, whichever I chose."

Tlonna released the messenger and stood. She looked eastward, where the gate to the city was. "Was he young, or grown?"

"Y-young!"

"His name is Sithian Rahlan," she paused, dread in her eyes. "Someone take the boy and let him rest. This day, it seems, prophecy begins to unveil itself."

"Tlonna..." Losolin breathed, stepping toward her.

"Do not try to stop me Losolin. I have been waiting for this day for a while, now."

"Tlonna, do not be a fool," Yayènia spat, yanking her

gauntlets out of her belt and onto her hands.

"And how would I be a fool, Yayènia? This is my kingdom, my city, what am I if I do not protect it?"

"Sithian is a boy, and he can be dealt with as such by others."

Tlonna sent the other female such a scornful look the warrior's eyes narrowed. "You know that is not true. Now, get out of my way."

"So you can kill yourself? If he is so dangerous, then it is my duty, and the duty of Captain Suneelo to stop you from getting in harm's way. I will not break my oath."

"Sithian cannot kill me, or cause me any harm," Tlonna lied, trying to hold her impatience in. "You can stay behind, if you wish."

"Tlonna, you know that will not happen," Suneelo put in before his wife could respond. "We will all go with you. A proper escort to retrieve the King of Zaedic, yes?"

Tlonna took a moment to process that. "Yes... he is the king now." Eyeing her irate High Commander, the princess slid by her.

"Tlonna!"

"What?" the Magin spun on her heel as Miazie burst into the throne room.

"I heard Sithian is here. You... you can't go to him. Please, don't go to him!"

Ignoring Yayènia's triumphant grunt, the elf turned to face the Belau full on. "And why not?"

"Because...because he is...he is the one that the graves of good and evil spoke about. Astinus's prophecy. Sithian, not Midian, will be the reason you die. He is the one Astinus spoke about. *Please...*"

"How do you know this?"

"I had a vision. I know this for fact. Sithian will be there when you die," Miazie keened, taking a step toward her friend.

The gathered elves stood frozen, staring between the Belau and the princess. The Magin Queen.

"Does it matter, then? I will die when I die, whether or not it is convenient for all of us. What matters is the *purpose* of my death," Tlonna said quietly and walked out of the throne room to meet her son.

To be continued in Honor of Assassins: Book 2 of The Graves of

Good and Evil

Discover other titles by A.B.B.Olson

<u>Graves of Good and Evil Trilogy</u>
Honor of Assassins
Prophecy's Final Price*

Nkayt'hei

*forthcoming

www.ingramcontent.com/pod-product-compliance
Lightning Source LLC
Chambersburg PA
CBHW030840030726
47495CB00005B/1307